THE

BLIGHTED HEART;

OR,

THE OLD PRIORY RUINS.

A ROMANCE.

BY THOMAS PREST,

AUTHOR OF "GALLANT TOM," "ELA, THE OUTCAST," ETC. ETC.

———

LONDON:

PRINTED BY E. LLOYD, SALISBURY-SQUARE, FLEET-STREET.

———

MDCCCLI.

PREFACE.

——

MANY persons who peruse the present tale may consider that the characters and incidents are extravagant and overdrawn. The author pleads guilty to highly colouring facts (for facts the principal incidents in the narrative certainly are, startling and improbable as such a statement may appear to many), but in all that he has done he has endeavoured to work out a useful moral, and he humbly trusts that in that effort he has not entirely failed.

The character of Bonville is certainly a most revolting one, but it is no exaggerated picture; such a miscreant did exist, and took a prominent part in the atrocities that were perpetrated during the reign of terror.

The author has nothing more to add, than to return his thanks to the public for the very great favour with which they have received his production, and to subscribe himself,

THEIR GRATEFUL SERVANT.

November 1st, 1851.

THE BLIGHTED HEART:

OR,

THE OLD PRIORY RUINS.

A ROMANCE.

BY THE AUTHOR OF "THE GIPSY BOY," "EVELINA," "ALMIRA'S CURSE," &c., &c.

CHAPTER I.

BROTHER AND SISTER.—THE TRIALS OF THE HEART.—THE OLD PRIORY RUINS. —THE FATAL ACCIDENT.—THE INTRODUCTION OF THE LITTLE STRANGER.

It is the season of autumn, and a bright, cheerful, invigorating autumn it is; the heart must bound with ecstasy as the calm breeze fans the cheek; and even the mind oppressed with care must feel some relief in the beauty and tranquil joyousness of all around.

It is a lovely evening in October; see how the trees display the varied tints of autumn, heightened by the golden beams

of the retiring monarch of the day. What a scene is here spread forth for the admiration and glory of the contemplative mind! What painter could do justice to it on canvas—what poet describe it in colours sufficiently glowing and life-like.

Reader, we could pause much longer to linger on the beautiful scene which meets our imaginative eye, did we not fear that we should tire your patience; and yet, oh, how can we leave it, so lovely as it is, especially at this hour, when all around is so soul-absorbing and enchanting?

See, the clouds are tinged with purple and gold, so brightly reflected in the unruffled waters of that noble river, as it gently steals along; beautiful river indeed art thou, and thy fair banks do honour thee in the rich and diversified scenery they display. As far as the eye can stretch, all that meets it is grand and sublime; but if possible, more do we reverence thy banks, oh silvery river, for the numerous remains of noble ruins which meet the gaze at every turn.

Principal among these are the ancient ruins of the Priory of St. Egbert, and well worthy of the attention, the particular attention of those who visit a certain district in the north of England, are they. Most romantic are those gothic ruins, which have not yet crumbled to dust, although they have been left neglected for the last twenty years. There seems to be a Providence watching over their preservation; and all who once contemplate them must feel the deepest regret that such a splendid specimen of gothic architecture was ever suffered to fall into decay.

The principal aisle, though impaired (at the time we commence our story), still retained striking proofs of former grandeur; the noble gothic window, where the luxuriant ivy proudly usurped the place of many a painted pane, appeared now to have regained some of its former brilliant colouring, by the rays of a glorious setting sun, darting its beams betwixt the ivy leaves. It was indeed a noble remnant of antiquity, was the old Priory of St. Egbert, and as this narrative in the incidents which it records is so immediately connected with it, the reader will, we trust, pardon us for making such particular mention of it in this place. We cannot yet withdraw our attention from it; for what melancholy yet chastened meditations arise in our minds as we traverse its mouldering ruins. Most striking emblems are those ancient remains of the mutability of human affairs. They are emblems of the futility of man's designs, and of all earthly grandeur. Here lay, mingling their dust, the high and haughty abbot and the humbler monk, alike forgotten in the lapse of time; here the loud-swelling notes of the full-toned organ, joined to the seraphic strains of the holy choir, raised the desponding soul to peace and happiness.

But turn we now reluctantly away from this scene to one of a different description, it was that of a spacious and elegant mansion, of the Elizabethan era, whose extensive grounds were well laid out, and extended along the banks of the river, while at its back was an open space of country of the most fertile and luxuriant description imaginable. It was known by the name of Sungrove abbey, and had been built upon the site of a religious house which had been levelled with the ground during the reign of Henry VII.

By a sweep round an extensive lawn you were conducted to the principal entrance of the abbey by a broad flight of steps to the great hall, illumined by a dome, and decorated with pillars, statues, busts, and vases from the ruins of Herculaneum, and paved in chequer-work of different-coloured marbles. Everything that the eye rested on bespoke the taste and elegance of the present or former proprietor. There was not a single nook or corner of Sungrove abbey which did not afford a subject for wonder and admiration to the refined and classical mind.

In the eastern wing of this noble edifice was the library, which was furnished with a collection of the best authors in all languages, and every appropriate requisite to such an apartment. A glass door opened upon the pleasure-grounds, which were most admirably laid out, and a small wood led you to the hermitage, formed under an artificial hill, and furnished with a moss bed, altar, and everything appropriate to such a place of sweet retirement. But we fear we are becoming tedious. We must now conduct our reader through a pair of large folding doors, into a vestibule, which led to a suite of apartments fitted up in a style of the most tasteful elegance.

In one of these apartments, seated at an open window which commanded an uninterrupted view of the graceful river, and the adjacent scenery, were two persons. They were male and female, and the extreme likeness which their features displayed, plainly indicated that they stood in the relation of brother and sister.

The gentleman was a handsome man in the prime of life, but some hidden sorrow had given his features the stamp of greater age ; his elbow was bent upon the back of his chair ; his chin rested upon his hand, and although his eyes were steadily fixed upon the objects beyond, it required no very keen penetration to discover that his mind was wandering upon far different objects.

His sister, who was some years his senior, was sitting on the opposite side, and earnestly, but silently contemplating him.

Alas, Albert Coningsby had indeed drank deeply from the cup of sorrow, although his prospects in life had once been of the most brilliant description. He was the last male descendant of an ancient and honourable family, and he had a right to expect that nothing would occur to mar the felicity he at that time experienced. But, oh, how bitterly was he disappointed ; a dreadful storm suddenly burst with overwhelming fury over his head, annihilating all his fond cherished hopes at one fell swoop, and rendering him the most wretched of human beings in existence. The former scenes of pleasure in which he had mingled became hateful to him, and he took the earliest opportunity of seeking relief from the severe, the almost unendurable anguish of his mind, in peaceful seclusion.

It was not long ere Mr. Coningsby had an opportunity of putting his wishes into effect. Sungrove abbey being for sale, and he being well acquainted with its situation, gave his steward the necessary instructions, became the purchaser, and having abandoned his family mansion, took up his residence at the abbey, whither he was accompanied by his sister, who was a maiden lady, and very different to him in disposition.

At the death of their mother, she was consigned to the care of a female relative, who, being brought up almost entirely in the metropolis, had seen her brother but seldom, and not for the last few years, she therefore knew but little of his affairs, and was entirely ignorant of the cause of his sorrow.

On the death of her relation, who bequeathed her all her property, Miss Coningsby once more visited the family mansion, and was astonished and sincerely grieved to find her brother in such a deplorable state of mind, from which it was impossible, it appeared, for anything to arouse him. In vain she endeavoured to elicit the cause ; he evaded her questions with an expression of horror, and implored her, as she loved him, never to press the subject again.

Miss Coningsby was lost in amazement, and her curiosity to become acquainted with all the particulars she felt was far greater than she should be able to conquer ; however, she stifled it for the present ; if it would be any alleviation to his sorrow also, she offered to take up her residence with him, and which he accepted with pleasure ; for Albert was satisfied, that, whatever her disposition might be, and he had had no opportunity of judging of it, it must afford his afflicted spirit some consolation to be constantly blessed with the society of a relative so near and so dear to him.

But to return to the apartment in which Albert Coningsby and his sister were seated. For some time she continued to gaze at him in silence and with commiseration, for, although she possessed all the fastidiousness of the old maid, and had imbibed many bad propensities from the nature of the life in which she had mingled, she also possessed many excellent and amiable qualities, and was most sincerely attached to her brother, whom she knew to possess every intrinsic virtue that ennobles the human race, and who, she was confident was so totally undeserving the poignant affliction of mind under which he laboured.

"Still sad, still a prey to melancholy and corroding care, Albert," she at length said, arousing him from his lethargy ; "will nothing ever arouse you from this state of despondency, and brighten your countenance once more with the smiles of gladness and content."

Her brother shook his head mournfully and sighed.

"Alas! my sister," he replied, "I fear that peace and content must henceforth be strangers to my breast. The poisoned arrow has sunk too deeply in my heart. There is but one circumstance that could possibly restore me to happiness."

"And what is that, my brother ?"

He shuddered and averted his face for a moment.

"Do not urge me, Eugenia, on that point, for never can my lips disclose the dreadful secret," he replied.

"And am not I, your sister, Albert, worthy of your confidence?" she demanded, for she felt vexed and disappointed that her brother should still refuse to gratify that curiosity which her brother's strange conduct had excited.

"Oh, yes, my dear sister," returned Mr. Coningsby, "indeed you are every way worthy of my confidence, and gladly would I make you acquainted with my tronbles, out the horror of the relation deters me. I entreat you then to spare my feelings for the present, and the time may come when you shall know everything."

Miss Coningsby felt still more vexed, and her chagrin for a short time overcame her feelings of sympathy.

"I must confess, Albert," she observed, "that this reserve towards a sister who has made so great a sacrifice, does appear strange, to say the least of it. The dreary, monotonous life I lead here, makes me heartily regret the gay companions I have abandoned, and I only wish that you would seek to banish this enemy by again uniting yourself to some amiable woman, then you would no longer require my presence here.

"God of Heaven !" cried Albert, starting as if he had been struck by a thunderbolt, and his whole frame exhibiting such powerful emotion that his sister was completely terrified; "what cursed power has put it into your mind to torture me thus ? Marry, oh, that word! it conveys ten thousand daggers to my heart. Eugenia you must bitterly reproach yourself for the cruel observations you have made, did

you know all. But—but I must retire; the solitude of my chamber and my own thoughts can alone restore me to composure. Good evening, Eugenia, and I trust for the love of Heaven that the bitter anguish you see you have caused me, will prevent you from ever hinting at such a subject to me again."

Thus saying, with a countenance ghastly pale, and agitated demeanour, Mr. Coningsby abruptly quitted the room, leaving his sister in a state of the utmost confusion, amazement, and regret.

She was vexed o think she had so greatly committed herself, and would gladly have given anything had she been able to recall what she had said, for her brother would henceforth think her selfish, ungenerous, and unfeeling, and that was a character she would not on any account hold in his opinion; but in spite of all, her c riosity and impatience were excited to a more insupportable degree than ever.

"The secret which p esses upon his mind must be of the most dre dful description that he should exhibit such violent emotion whenever the least allusion is made to it;" he observed, "what can it be, that he should even refuse to make me his confidant on the subject ?"

Miss Coningsby did not see her brother again that evening, and at length weary of being alone, and with her own thoughts, she sought her pallet.

When she descended into the breakfast room in the morning, the servant informed her that her master had desired her to say that he had gone out for a walk, and that he should not return to breakfast. This afforded Miss Coningsby fresh cause for vexation and disappointment, and she could not but think that her brother was treating her with undeserved coolness and disrespect.

Mr. Coningsby had passed a restless night, and he was glad to endeavour to chase away the dismal thoughts which tormented him, by a ramble among the luxuriant scenery in the neighbourhood of the abbey. He therefore, left his chamber at an early hour, and after having left a message for his sister, started forth.

It may be imagined by the reader

that because misfortunes of the most trying and melancholy description had caused him to abandon the society of his former friends, and even to disguise his real rank (for he was not what we have at present represented him to be), that Albert Coningsby was a misanthrope; but such an idea would be perfectly erroneous, and doing him a great injustice; never did bosom teem with more noble or social virtues. Humane and generous in every sense of the word, he was ever ready to assist the unfortunate, and he possessed the most enthusiastic sentiments of friendship. The urbanity of his disposition soon became known, and his acquaintance was universally sought. He had a small coterie of friends, who frequently exchanged visits with him, but he was more particularly intimate with Lord Everside, a worthy widower, without family, and with whom resided an only sister who had never ventured upon the perilous ocean of matrimony. Upon this nobleman, Mr. Coningsby resolved to make a call after he had taken his intended walk.

The sun shone forth with the greatest splendour, and the light morning breeze came cool and refreshing to the senses. Mr. Coningsby did feel it somewhat revive and invigorate him, but still he could not banish from his mind the oppressive thoughts which had been excited by the unhappy observations of his sister on the previous evening.

Mr. Coningsby was willing to make every allowance for his sister's discontent, though it naturally grieved him severely. Certainly, the sort of life she now led, so different to that she had been accustomed to, was not likely to soften the natural asperity of her temper, and it frequently broke the bounds prescribed by good manners. He was well aware of the sacrifice she had made to his convenience. She had quitted a circle of gay and agreeable friends, with whom she had passed the early part of her life, to live in comparative solitude, though this last was her own fault, as she refused every advance from the ladies in the vicinity of the abbey.

All these facts Albert made great allowances for, and scarcely ever contradicted her, though she too frequently gave way to fits of ill-humour.

As he proceeded in his walk all these reflections arose on his mind, and he deeply lamented that he could not devise any means to reconcile his sister to her situation, which he felt confidant he might, if she was only to be made acquainted with the unexampled sorrows to which he was the victim, but though he had often made up his mind to do so, he could not find courage sufficient for the painful task.

Except the distant lowing of the cattle, the bark of the shepherd's dog, or the melodious warbling of the birds, an universal stillness reigned around. It was indeed a peaceful hour, and Mr. Coningsby gradually felt its soothing influence, and sought in the contemplation of the scenery, so rich and fertile, which met the gaze on every side, to lose the thoughts to which his mind had for so many hours been a prey.

He was now near the ruins of the old priory, which was a favourite resort of his, for he could there indulge without interruption in his melancholy meditations.

He often paid visits to the honest old couple who now had the care of its humble lodge or portal, which was the only part of the priory which had not suffered from the devastating hand of time, but he did not feel disposed to do so ithis morning, though he stood for a short time to gaze upon the mouldering ruins, upon which the bright sunbeams were now fantastically shining and imparting a transient lustre to what was so solemnly impressive in decay.

"Like thee, venerable pile," said Coningsby, "has ruin fallen upon me, and the withering hand of time will but add to destruction, which was commenced in ingratitude and deceit. These crumbling walls once resounded to the notes of holy happiness. and once I was happy but——"

He checked himself, and then with a half stifled sigh, turned slowly from the spot, and prepared to strike into the path which led to the mansion of Lord Everside.

He had not proceeded far, however, when the pitiful cry of a female for help smote his ears. He paused and listened to ascertain if possible from whence the sound came, and immediately afterwards the mournful cry of a child arrested his attention.

"What can be the meaning of those pitiful cries?" he ejaculated, as he hurried towards a little copse, from whence the sounds evidently proceeded, and at the entrance he was met by an elderly woman, who seemed to be very much alarmed.

"What is the matter, my good woman?" Mr. Coningsby demanded, "and what is the meaning of those mournful cries I just now heard?"

"Oh, sir, pray hurry to the spot," replied the woman; "there has been a dreadful accident. The strange gentleman and his sweet little child, sir."

"The strange gentleman," repeated Mr. Coningsby, with astonishment.

"Yes, sir," returned the woman, "the strange gentleman who has been residing for a short time with his child at the lodge of the old priory. He has met with a sad accident, and he is lying there," pointing in the direction of the copse, "either dead or dying, and the poor dear little innocent weeping over him. Oh, hasten, sir, I pray you."

Mr. Coningsby immediately directed the woman to go to the priory lodge, and desire David to send for surgical assistance, and then to follow him with all possible speed; and having seen the poor woman depart on this errand, he darted through the copse, and there beheld a sight which not only called forth his warmest sympathy, but excited a feeling of horror in his breast.

Upon a slight mound was lying a gentleman, pale and motionless, while a fair child, apparently not more than five years of age, was feebly endeavouring to support his head, while at the same time her plaintive cries for assistance, and the agony and despair which, no doubt, tortured at the moment her own young heart, rendered her an object of the deepest sympathy.

Mr. Coningsby darted forward, and raising the unfortunate gentleman's head, felt his pulse, when he plainly saw that life was all but extinct.

The poor child clung to him, as she looked up in his countenance and sobbed forth—

"Oh, sir! dear, good sir, do not let my poor papa die! He has fallen down —he—he was walking with me, but he fell down, and cannot speak to me. Oh! my poor papa!"

"My poor child," said Mr. Coningsby, in the mildest and most compassionate tone, "do not be alarmed, your papa, please God, will be restored and live many years to bless you with his protection."

At that moment David Ambrook, the person in charge of the lodge of the old priory ruins, accompanied by another man, the old woman who had first given Mr. Coningsby information of the accident having been dispatched by him for surgical aid, arrived at the spot, and the unfortunate gentleman was removed without delay to the priory, the poor child following, as well as her feeble steps and her extreme agitation would permit her, and wringing her little hands at the same time, as though her heart would break, while Mr. Coningsby in vain tried all his efforts to pacify her.

She was, indeed, a lovely girl, with a countenance combining all the innocence and simplicy of infancy, with the intelligence of maturer years. Mr. Coningsby could not but gaze upon her with feelings of the greatest admiration and even love, but at the same time a certain sensation came over his heart for which he could in no way account.

The gentleman was a handsome man, young, and having the appearance of a foreigner, in fact, the accent of the child, who resembled him very much in features, showed that they were not natives of this country.

They arrived at the priory, and Dr. Morris immediately followed, but upon looking at his patient he shook his head, and it was quite evident that he thought there was but little or no chance of his recovery.

Mr. Coningsby immediately pointed out, or rather drew the attention of the doctor to the child, who was now weeping upon the lap of Mrs. Ambrook, and he ordered that she should be carried to bed without delay, and he sent the old woman, who had given the first alarm to Albert, to his surgery for a composing draught. It was not without the utmost difficulty that they could tear the wretched child from her father's side, though she seemed nearly exhausted by her sorrow; but at that critical moment the gentleman opened his eyes, he looked round the apartment wildly, the child was placed in his arms, she clung convulsively to his neck; the doctor tried to interpose, but before he could do so, the unfortunate gentleman, making one or two vain efforts to speak, sunk back upon the pillow of the couch on which he had been laid, and expired with scarcely a sigh.

It was with difficulty that the child was separated from the corpse of her parent.

CHAPTER II.

WHO IS THE DECEASED ?—THE ACCOUNT OF DAVID.—MR. CONINGSBY'S RESOLUTION.

WHEN the interesting little mourner was removed from the room, Mr. Coningsby, who was surprised that a gentleman of the deceased's appearance should have sought refuge in such a place, asked David Ambrook to give him some particulars as to him.

"Well, sir," replied David, "I will do all in my power. About three weeks since sir, as I was standing outside the portal of the old priory, a gentleman on horse-back stopped before me, and said the inn-keeper of the Jolly Farmer had told him that I could accomodate him with a couple of rooms for a short time. I felt rather surprised at this, for I thought the old lodge was not good enough for a gentleman of his appearance, and I told him so, but at the same time I said, that both me and my dame would do all that we possibly could to make him comfortable, if he pleased to become our lodger under such circumstances.

"The gentleman replied that certainly his stay in this part of the country would be for a very short time, but that, having been very ill, he was desirous of a pure air and quiet to recover his health, and that, if I would accommodate him he would be with me the following day; that he had a little girl, who would want some one to attend upon her, as her nurse had died on the voyage. I told him my wife would be proud to do anything in her power for her, with which he expressed himself perfectly satisfied, and

having given his name as Mr. Aunville, took his leave.

"I mentioned the circumstance to my dame on her return from market, and she readily, good soul as she is, entered into my feelings upon the subject. In fact she felt delighted at the idea of having a gentleman residing at the priory, since my noble master, the Duke of Allensford, never visits the neighbourhood, and she immediately with the assistance of myself and Agatha, our daughter, set about putting the place in apple-pie order, and the next morning Mr. Aunville came with little Miss Celestia, his daughter, in a post-chaise, bringing with him two trunks, and an Indian cabinet."

Such was the account given by David Ambrook, and Mr. Coningsby paused and reflected for a few moments upon what he had said, after he had ceased speaking. There was something very extraordinary in the business altogether, and he felt deeply interested in it, but more especially in the beautiful little Celestia, as David had informed him the unfortunate deceased had called her. He was lost in perplexity, but at length inquired of David if any one had called upon him ce he had been at the priory, or whether any letters had been received by him.

David replied in the negative, although, he added, he was often writing.

"And he never informed you from whence he came ?" asked Mr. Coningsby. "As he said the nurse died on the voyage, it must have been from some distant country."

"I can assure you, sir," returned David, "that he never informed me, and of course, sir, it would have been great boldness in me to have put such a question to him."

"Do you think from what you saw of him that he was an Englishman or a foreigner ?"

"Why, sir, he always spoke in the English language to me, but when he conversed with Miss Celestia, I could not comprehend what he said, or what reply she made to it. There could not be a more good natured gentleman than he was, but he was so very melancholy, and he was always wandering in the old priory ruins."

Mr. Coningsby again paused, and

reflected upon what David had told him. He was rather puzzled how to proceed. His interest was deeply excited, more especially as regarded the little Celestia, and a pang shot through his heart at the same moment, the nature of which cannot at the present time be explained. But hoping to hear something from the child in the course of the day, he was preparing to take his leave, when David requested that he would examine the deceased gentleman's pockets, and also take possession of his keys.

"I believe, sir," added the old man, "that you know the character of old David Ambrook too well, to suppose for an instant that he would touch anything belonging to the unfortunate gentleman, of the value of a rush; but the world is fond of scandal, and many a poor fellow like myself has suffered from it."

Mr. Coningsby, of course, could not attempt for a moment to dispute the force and truth of these remarks, and thinking it was most probable that there would be very little difficulty in discovering the relations of the unfortunate Mr. Avunille (as he had represented himself to David to be), he did not at all hesitate in taking charge of his property till that time; he therefore examined his pockets in the presence of Dr. Morris, David, his wife, and his daughter, and an inventory of their contents was made under their observation. They found in them a gold snuff-box, a gold toothpick case, and a purse, containing thirty guineas, and a quantity of silver; a gold watch, chain and seals, with the cypher B. A., the other was an antique.

After they had so far proceeded in their determination, they repaired to his chamber, and put their seals upon the trunk and the Indian cabinet, the key of which was in the pocket of the deceased gentleman, then, giving all but that into the care of David, Doctor Morris and Mr. Coningsby departed from the priory.

On their way home, as they were both going in the same direction, Mr. Coningsby and the doctor conversed upon the singularity of the adventure of the morning, and most anxious was the former once more to behold the little Celestia, whose features had made an impression upon him that he found it difficult to eradicate from his mind. The doctor was of opinion that the gentleman had expired in a fit of apoplexy, a supposition that was fully borne out by all the melancholy circumstances of the case.

Mr. Morris promised to meet Mr. Coningsby on the following morning, that they might go together to the priory and endeavour to ascertain from the papers of Mr. Aunville (if such was indeed his real name), where they might write to his connections to inform them of his death.

Mr. Coningsby was too deeply affected by the melancholy scene he had witnessed, to make his intended visit to Lord Everside, and therefore, on separating from the doctor, he retraced his steps towards Sungrove Abbey, pondering his mind as he proceeded, all the mysterious and dismal events of the morning.

"And should the connections of this unfortunate gentleman not be discovered," he soliloquized, "what is to become of his offspring? Is she to be abandoned to the mercy of the pitiless world uncared for, unwatched over? Oh, no, it would be worse than murder to suffer a little innocent whom Providence has thus miraculously thrown in my way to be sacrificed in such a manner. I will become her protector; and Heaven I am certain will assist me in my benevolent designs. The features of the child too, so expressive, so intellectual, and bearing such an extraordinary likeness to one whom—but away with that thought! It will drive me mad to dwell upon it."

When Mr. Coningsby returned to the Abbey, he felt in no state of mind after the events of the morning, to see any one; he therefore excused himself to his sister, and requested that his dinner might be served to him in his own apartment.

This added to the chagrin and astonishment of Miss Coningsby, and she deeply regretted that the waywardness of her temper had caused her to commit herself in the manner she had done the day before, and feared that she had wounded the feelings of a brother whom she sincerely loved, in a manner which he could never forget or forgive. And yet she knew his character too well to believe that he could entertain anything like a vindictive spirit towards her, and therefore was his conduct on the present occasion the more extraordinary and inexplicable.

At one moment she was half resolved to send an apology to him for the language which she had so indiscreetly made use of towards him on the previous evening, but then directly afterwards a feeling of pride restrained her, and, all her worst passions preponderating, she was induced to form the most ungenerous conclusions, and was determined not to succumb to what she con-

IRRITATION OF MR CONINGSBY AT THE GROUNDLESS TAUNTS OF HIS SISTER.

sidered to be the foolish eccentricities of her brother.

She passed the remainder of the day in the greatest state of misery, and at night retired to her chamber, out of temper with everything and everybody, and ill-at-ease with herself, and all around her.

CHAPTER III.

THE INSPECTION OF THE PROPERTY OF THE DECEASED GENTLEMAN.—INTRODUCTION OF THE LITTLE ORPHAN AT THE ABBEY.—THE RECEPTION.

THE reader may well imagine that the vexation and astonishment of Miss

Coningsby was not at all lessened when the following morning she received another message from her brother, excusing himself for his absence from home as he had business of the most interesting and important nature to attend to, and her curiosity and anxiety were in no less degree excited to know what that particular and important business could be. In vain did she rack her brain, it was a mystery she could not by any possible means fathom, and the more she endeavoured to do so, the deeper she became involved in perplexity. Her vexation increased, and she could find no relief to her irritated feelings. Did her brother mean directly to insult her? He had hitherto declined to confide the mysterious secret which so heavily preyed upon his spirits to her, and what was she to conclude from his present conduct? She considered that he was treating her with the most unbecoming disrespect; her pride felt wounded, and she determined to have a full and satisfactory explanation from him when they again met, or, notwithstanding the affection she bore towards him, and the deep anxiety she felt in all that concerned him, to leave him at once and for ever. She considered Albert's present conduct a cruel return for the sacrifice she had made in quitting the gay scenes and companions to which she had from earliest childhood, been accustomed, and in her present state of mind, determined, unless her brother gave a full explanation of everything, to resent it.

Mr. Coningsby met his friend, the doctor, on the following morning at the appointed hour, and they proceeded at once to the old priory ruins.

The little Celestia was far more composed than they had expected to find her, and the tender caresses of Mr. Coningsby in some measure restored her cheerfulness. He could not but gaze upon her innocent countenance with feelings of the most indescribable emotion, and once or twice he was obliged to hide his face in his handkerchief in order to conceal the tears which started involuntarily to his eyes. There was something in the features and situation of that fair child, which brought the sad, sad past most vividly—most painfully to his memory, and open still wider those wounds which time had been unable entirely to heal.

To the questions of Mr. Coningsby, Celestia lisped out her replies in a voice at once so gentle and harmonious, that it was no wonder she should at once win the heart of her protector. Although her accent was foreign, she spoke English as well as a child of her age could be expected to do, but she replied in French equally correct. She told him her name was Celestia, and her papa's name was Aunville.

"And where, my dear child, is your mamma?" asked Mr. Coningsby.

A sad expression for a moment passed over her beauteous features, and then she answered in a voice of the most melancholy impressiveness, which went to the hearts of those who listened to her.

"Gone to heaven, papa says. Oh, my dear papa! will he never again wake and speak, and call upon the name of his little Celestia? But dame tells me he is gone to heaven, and I will go there too."

Once more the poor child burst into tears, and it was not without the greatest difficulty that they could at all pacify her.

Most deeply affected was Mr. Coningsby at the little orphan's distress, and exerted all the means in his power to comfort her; he told her she should go home with him, and that he would do everything in his power to make her happy, and that she would there find a lady who would love her, and be a mamma to her.

"Oh, no, no, no," she sobbed, clasping her little hands together, and weeping bitterly; "I can't, I will not leave papa—poor, dear, sick papa!"

Mr. Coningsby knew not how to reply; the plaintive eloquence of the little stranger aroused his warmest sympathies; but his gentle reasonings, and tender soothings, at length succeeded in calming her agitation, and a few indifferent questions put to her, directed her thoughts into another channel, and she became once more cheerful.

Happy age of unsuspecting innocence! So easily grieved, and so easily reconciled.

Although so young she was evidently so intelligent and precocious that Mr

Coningsby hoped to elicit much information from her, and he therefore put several questions to her, which she answered with avidity, and to the best of her ability. It was really most extraordinary to hear the fair child talk, the pertinent replies she made to the inquiries put to her, and as Mr. Coningsby listened he became more and more astonished and captivated with her.

"And where, my love," he asked, "did you and your papa come from when you first arrived at the priory?"

"Oh, sir," said the little innocent, "I come a long way off, in a great ship; and papa came there from France, he told me, and that there were bad men there, and I lost dear mamma; papa said she had gone to heaven, and then nurse Janette was very sick, and died while I was in the ship, and now dear papa is gone too."

As the poor child uttered these words her grief returned with more violence than ever. The worthy doctor advised her being taken out with the daughter of Mrs. Ambrook, as little information could be gained from such an infant, but from that little he thought it was most likely they had emigrated from France, and they thought it was quite impossible that they should not gain some information, at least who they were, from the papers of the deceased gentleman, and they now repaired to the chamber in which the corpse lay, attended by Mrs. Ambrook and her husband.

They lost no time in commencing their examination; the cabinet, as being the most likely to contain papers, was the first examined, but afforded them no light whatever, except convincing them the owner was a person of rank and station.

They could find no papers there, but there was a red morocco box containing a great quantity of very valuable jewels; a diamond necklace, ear-rings, and pins, a complete set of the finest pearls that Doctor Morris and Mr. Coningsby had ever seen; several other female ornaments in various precious stones; a gold repeater set with brilliants, with chains, seals, and trinkets, to correspond; a variety of valuable rings, and a locket of a very singular form—it was a heart in the natural shape, upon the point of a

lance. This caused them much surprise and fruitless speculation.

They now turned their attention to a private drawer, and in it they found a box containing Bank of England notes to the amount of five thousand pounds; in another a small gold crucifix, with Emelie engraven on the back; a missal, finely illuminated, also containing the name Emelie on the cover.

Mr. Coningsby replaced everything in the same order in which he had found them, and then opened the trunks; one contained Mr. Aunville's apparel, the other a great quantity of laces, muslins, silks, and various articles of female attire, and a child's wardrobe, very complete.

In all their search no pocket-book, letters, or memorandums, were found; but Mr. Coningsby consoled himself with the hope that a short time would throw a light upon the apparent mystery; for if the deceased were indeed an emigrant, as appeared most probable, he would most likely have some correspondent, who, wondering at his silence, would write to him.

But in the meantime Mr. Coningsby said they would make a correct inventory of the effects, and then seal them up till he should be able to deliver them to the friends of the child who might come forward.

Three inventories were therefore drawn up, one for himself, one for Doctor Morris, and a third for David Ambrook. To each of those they all set their names, and were witnessed by David; the day of the month, and the date of the year in which the unfortunate gentleman died were also put down.

When all this business was settled, Mr. Coningsby requested the doctor to take the trouble of ordering a funeral suitable to the apparent rank of the deceased, undertaking to defray every expense, as he did not think proper to meddle with any of the property, which of right, now belonged to the little Celestia.

He also informed David Ambrook and his wife that he should take the orphan and her property to his own house, where she should remain till claimed by her own family.

This business arranged, the two gentlemen returned to the parlour of the priory lodge, and despatched David Am brook to the abbey to request Miss Coningsby to send the carriage to the priory, in order to convey an interesting young stranger to her protection, and bade him to order a cart to come and fetch away the trunks and cabinet.

We left Miss Coningsby in no very good humour, and certainly it had by no means improved when David Ambrook was announced, and being ushered into the room in which the lady was seated, delivered the message exactly as he had received it.

Miss Coningsby was not a little astonished, and could not fathom the extraordinary conduct of her brother, as it certainly at that time, and not without cause, appeared to her to be.

"An interesting young stranger! What could he mean?" And as she put this question to herself without the least power to solve the problem, a crimson blush mounted in her cheeks, and a feeling near approaching to indignation and offended delicacy swelled her bosom. She put several questions to David, but as he judged it inconsistent with prudence to relate any more of the affair without the special permission of Mr. Coningsby, his replies were so short, and apparently so mysterious, that no one can be surprised that she should be more and more offended with her brother, and she seriously thought that he was engaged in some affair that would not bear the light, or he would not have concealed it from her, and which he had been carrying on ever since she had been with him; and though she confessed that she had no right to expect to control him, yet that he should attempt to impose so shallow a fabrication upon a woman of her understanding, was a crime of such magnitude that it was quite impossible that she should ever pardon it, and by the time her excellent brother had arrived at home, she had worked herself into an absolute rage. Instead of receiving them with the politeness due from the mistress of the house, she turned away with an air of the utmost contempt.

Mr. Coningsby pretended not to take any notice of her behaviour, but led the beautiful little Celestia towards her, saying—

"My dear sister, a very melancholy accident has introduced this young stranger to my knowledge, and I have now the happiness of placing her under your protection, in the hope that by our joint endeavours and kind attention, we shall soon restore her to that ease and cheerfulness so natural to her age."

Miss Coningsby looked at her brother with perfect amazement, astounded at what she considered to be his consummate assurance, and having walked towards the door with eyes flashing fire, and a countenance distorted by passion, she replied :—

"Sir, you have an undoubted right, and it is your duty so to do, to support and to protect your illegitimate offspring, but you have none to impose upon me with a falsehood, so palpable; you must think me an idiot, or a maniac to believe one syllable of it."

With these words the lady was about to quit the room, and the terrified Celestia clung still closer to Mr. Coningsby, who was completely astounded by this violent, ungenerous, and unexpected attack, and turning to his sister with more sternness than she thought him capable of assuming, he said—

"Stay, Eugenia, and hear me. When you made me the offer of residing with me, I considered it as an obligation I could never repay, and for that reason have patiently borne every caprice you have recently practised, well convinced that the spirit of contradiction was with you inherent; but in the present instance it has exceeded the limits of common decency. In the eye of the world, your insinuation would bring no censure upon my moral character even were it just, but as my opinions and actions are regulated by a far different mode of thinking, I feel your charge the grossest indignity you can offer me; nor can I easily forgive it— till I can, I shall avoid the cause, depend upon it."

As he thus spoke, he took the hand of the little Celestia, and then added :—

"Come, my love, I will lead you to one whose mild manners and benevolent countenance will soon banish the unfavourable impression, I fear you have conceived of your present protectors."

It would be impossible to describe the confusion and chagrin of Miss Coningsby, as her brother thus spoke. He immediately led his tender charge from the room, and conducted her to Mrs.

Meredith, the housekeeper, and after having in a few words explained the child's situation, this excellent woman strove, by every attention in her power, to efface the past.

And without much difficulty she succeeded; the affectionate tenderness with which she uniformly treated the young orphan could not fail to win her little heart; and in a few days she displayed so many engaging qualities, that what before she received from compassion to her helpless situation, now became due to her character, and she was very soon an universal favourite.

The utmost malice of a vindictive spirit, could not have planned a greater mortification for Miss Coningsby, than had her brother, by consigning the child to the care of Mrs. Meredith, though he had no other meaning in what he did than to obtain for the poor orphan such treatment as might console her for the irreparable loss she had sustained.

Convinced she had acted wrong, and ashamed of having done so, Miss Coningsby yielded to the natural goodness of her heart, and anxiously sought a reconciliation with her brother, who possessed too much of the milk of human kindness to continue long at enmity with any one, much less one whom nature, as well as inclination, induced him to love. He therefore met the "olive branch" more than half-way, and each endeavoured to efface from the mind of the other, the remembrance of the late disagreement.

This reconciliation having been so happily effected, Mr. Coningsby, detailed to his sister all the melancholy particulars of the manner in which Celestia had been thrown upon his protection, to which she listened with the deepest interest and attention, but when he shewed her the contents of the cabinet and trunks, she could not help giving expression to her astonishment that a gentleman, such as these jewels and the other property seemed to bespeak him, should come unattended, and remain so long at the humble lodge of the old priory ruins; she said that the jewels bespoke the mother of the child to be of high rank, as none but such could wear them; and if any doubts remained, the gentleman's and the child's wardrobe, not to mention the many valuable articles beside, would undoubtedly remove them. It occurred

to her that her mother was a Roman catholic, which was not at all improbable by the missal and crucifix.

When his sister gave utterance to this opinion, Mr. Coningsby sighed deeply, and after pausing some moments in profound thought, he said,—

"My dear sister, I must admit that your observation is perfectly just and reasonable; but as the child is too young to be impressed with any religious principles, I think we may, without a crime, conceal from her that circumstance and till she is claimed by those who have a natural right to direct her faith, bring her up in our own."

"Most cordially, Albert," returned his sister, "will I join in all your designs respecting this little orphan; and when you judge fit to put her in possession of her property, I would retain these two articles till her religious principles be too firmly rooted to be shaken by time or circumstances."

"But you forget, Eugenia, that she most likely will be claimed before that time, and particularly as I mean to employ every possible means to effect it. He most assuredly was a French emigrant nobleman, in which case it will be difficult to discover."

"And if we do not, my dear brother, she shall never feel the loss of her parents."

"Spoken like my sister," replied Mr. Coningsby, warmly pressing her hand, and here the conversation dropped.

The funeral was performed with all due solemnity and ceremony which seemed befitting to the rank of the unfortunate deceased, and then Mr. Coningsby immediately set out upon his inquiries. The innkeeper, who recommended the priory lodge to him, was the first person he applied to, but he could gain little information from him, He said that the gentleman came to him in a post-chaise from Dover, having crossed the passage—that his house being too noisy, he recommended the old priory, as he said he only wanted two rooms, where there were air and quiet, till he should have recovered his health, as he was then going to a distant part of the kingdom, as soon as he was able to undertake another long journey.

From this vague information, Mr. Coningsby could derive no clue, and be resolved to go to Dover; the child said they came a long way in a ship, and as there was reason to suppose he had landed there, he might gain the necessary intelligence respecting him. But all his inquiries proved utterly unsuccessful. He despatched a trusty servant to Liverpool, but with no better result.

Submitting to the only alternatives, time and patience, and the hope of letters arriving at the priory, he prepared to fulfil the duty Providence had allotted him, that of acting by Celestia as if she were his own child; and with all that honour, and generosity which ever characterised his conduct, he made a beneficial disposition of the property which had fallen into his hands, for the use of the orphan.

For this purpose he wrote to his bankers to purchase stock in the three per cents. to the value of the five thousand pounds, in the name of Celestia Aunville, which he ordered should be left to accumulate till her friends claimed her, or she should be of age to take possession of it. Every expense for the child he took upon himself.

And now had Mr. Coningsby an opportunity of realising his theoretic plan of education. In his own person he united both the scholar and the gentleman; by study and application he had stored his mind with all that constitutes the first of these characters, while his leisure hours were devoted to those lighter branches of education that form the latter.

We have before said that the family of Mr. Coningsby was noble, his person was elegant, and though at the period of which we are writing he was fast verging upon fifty, he still appeared young, although the deepest melancholy was imprinted on his countenance, his fine dark eyes and open brow expressed every emotion of his soul; whether animated by pleasure or moved by affection, his actions were all regulated by true Christian charity, and his whole study seemed to be the happiness of all around him. Such was the being whom Heaven had allotted to be the guardian of the little Celestia.

From the moment of her reconciliation with her brother, Miss Coningsby exerted all her powers to gain Celestia's affections, and she found the task by no means a difficult one.

Celestia's disposition was truly amiable; an understanding uncommon for her age, rendered her observant to every desire of her kind friends; and as her grief subsided, she displayed a playful vivacity the most fascinating; and the justness of her ideas were surprising for her age. Her education was to be divided between Mr. and Miss Coningsby, and Mrs. Meredith, who was everyway calculated for the precious charge.

In order to more fully explain the character of our little heroine, as she afterwards progressed under the able tuition of her most excellent friends, it will be necessary to make the reader better acquainted with Mrs. Meredith. She was truly an excellent woman, in the most extensive acceptation of the word.

The husband of Mrs. Meredith was one of those amiable unfortunate men of genius, who possessing education and talents of the most eminent quality, but destitute of family connexions, or aristocratic influence, was obliged to content himself with the holding of a small curacy in the north of England, where, for a trifling stipend, he performed the duty of the rector, who, like too many more Christians(?) of his cloth, while he emptied his well-filled goblet, denied even the dregs to his poor brother.

An accident suddenly deprived Mrs. Meredith of her husband, and well stricken in years, she was left nearly destitute, when Providence introduced her to Mr. Coningsby, who offered her an asylum in his house till he could devise means to render her independent in her own way, as she absolutely refused all pecuniary aid.

It happened very fortunately that, at this period, Miss Coningsby was in want of a housekeeper, and Mrs. Meredith requested to be taken in that capacity; both opposed such an arrangement, as beneath her habits of life, but she most positively declined to accept their kindness on any other terms, and they consequently, with reluctance complied; at the same time, they paid her every respect, and attention her superior qualities merited, her education, and deportment naturally, justly commanded.

Thus, then, it will be seen that our heroine could not possibly have been placed in better hands; as to Mrs. Meredith the principal portion of her education was assigned, that of instililng into her young mind, a proper and reasonable moral instruction, devoid of the cant and humbuggery which unfortunately prevails too much in the present "civilised age," the cant of moral (?) thieves, who, with a sanctimonious visage put their hands in your pockets to see what they may plunder you of, and at the same time their hand in their own, to discover if they happen to possess any deadly weapon to knock you on the head. The monstrous hypocrites of the Plumptree, Spooner, and Agnew school, who, while being only fit subjects for Bedlam themselves, would, in their rabid state bite a piece out of the calf of John Bull to drive all the community as mad, (though perhaps not so villanous) as themselves. Of this descripiton of canting, hypocritical humbugs, we were about to write miscreants, and really we think the title would not be misapplied to a gang of individuals whose whole time is occupied in destroying the happiness of their fellow creatures, and in seeking to reduce them to the same state of barbarism as themselves. It is notorious that Hackney and Islington have the extreme felicity of possessing a far greater number of the animals than any other portions of the United Kingdom combined. We never saw a happy or contented face in "Hackney Old Town," and in the neighbourhood of "Theberton-street, Islington." Mawworms are more plentiful than "Yarmouth Bloaters." But we are digressing from the subject of our narrative, and we feel great pleasure in quitting so unpleasant and so unthankful an office as that of describing the unfortunate fanatics we have been alluding to, to return to our little heroine and her truly amiable friends.

We have said that Mrs. Meridith endeavoured to instill into the ductile mind of her young pupil a moral and useful course of instruction, nor did she forget to impress her with the truth that, flattering even as her prospects were, habits of industry were absolutely necessary.

Mr. Coningsby undertook to instruct her in French, Italian, writing and arithmetic. His sister's province was history, geography, and music. And well did Celestia's docility keep pace with their instructions, and her rapid progress amply repaid their labours. Six years passed away, and in all that time no inquiry or letters had arrived at the priory, a circumstance which gave them no disquiet, as they would all have felt it a severe misfortune to have been deprived of their beloved little Celestia.

Six years had, as we have before stated, elapsed since our little heroine had been under the protection of Mr. Coningsby and his sister, and from what the child could remember, her father had told her the thirteen of May was the anniversary of her birth. This was the thirteenth of May, and as near as they had an opportunity of judging, Celestia was then eleven years of age, and beautiful she was, not only in person, but especially in intelligence; to know her was to love and admire her. And still more lovely, if possible she looked on the memorable morning, as she entered light, playful, and bounding as a little fairy, into Mr. Coningsby's library, and clasping his knees, looked up in his face with an expression of irresistable affection, and requested "her dear papa's blessing."

Mr. Coningsby looked at the sweet little applicant for a moment or two unable to speak, and then conferred the blessing she requested, with all the fervour of true parental affection; he then desired her to go to his sister, and, if she was risen, to request her presence in the library.

Delighted, away tripped Celestia, and in a short time returned with her aunt (an appellation she had lately adopted,) saying,—

"You know, sir, if you allow your Celestia to call you papa, Miss Coningsby must be my aunt, and she permits me to call her so. Now, dear papa, what have you got to tell us? We are both ready to hear it."

"No, my love," replied Mr. Coningsby, "I have not much to tell you, but I have an exhibition to make; what will you give me for the sight, my Celestia?"

"Ah, then," answered the sweet child, "I am afraid I can't see it, for I have given you all my love, and I have nothing else, papa, indeed."

"Then as we have made you bankrupt, I suppose we must exhibit it gratis."

He kissed the cheek of our heroine as he thus kindly expressed himself, and Miss Coningsby then exhibited a very handsome gold chain, which she said she had sent for as a birth-day present.

"And I," said her father, "will increase the value by an appendage which I am sure Celestia will consider the most precious gift I can bestow."

He then unlocked a closet, in which stood the cabinet and trunks.

He looked at her solemnly for a moment or two, and then affectionately taking her hand in his, he said—

"Celestia, my love, these contain all the property belonging to you, except some money which I have disposed of to increase for your future fortune; here is an inventory—read it, and then return it to me, as I think these things safer under my care for the present than your own."

Celestia took the paper in silence, but her countenance betrayed the inward feelings of her mind. Indeed the struggle in her bosom at that moment was almost more than her young strength could bear.

Mr. Coningsby now opened the case of jewels, and presenting them to her, asked if she had ever seen them? To attempt to describe the poor child's emotion at the sight of them would be impossible, in fact, it was so great, that she could not reply till tears had in some measure relieved her; she then told him that her papa had, while at the priory, opened the cabinet, and shewed them to her, telling her, that, when she was old enough to wear them, he would give them to her, bidding her cherish them, as all that remained to her of his adored wife and her dear mamma; the locket he also showed her, and said that a dreadful story was attached to it.

Mr. Coningsby and his sister were completely astonished at the correctness with which their young *protegée* had repeated what had been said to her when a mere infant; but it was a plain proof of the strong impression it had made upon her memory.

However, to give a turn to these melancholy reflections, Mr. Coningsby presented her the locket, wishing her to wear it, as being so remarkable, that if ever seen by those who had known it before, it might lead to a discovery. Celestia received it, and kissing it with emotion, put it in her bosom, while she still gazed upon the jewel.

Miss Coningsby wishing to withdraw her attention from these melancholy mementoes, desired her brother to lock them up, adding;—

"I have ever dreaded this moment, as I foresaw that if she had already seen them, it must remind her of her lost parents."

"Oh, Eugenia, my dear sister," demanded Mr. Coningsby, "and would you have her forget them? It would have evinced a most unfeeling mind if Celestia had beheld them unmoved, and I chose what we believe to be her birthday, as the most likely period for making a lasting impression of events which ought never to be erased from her mind; but she is old enough now, and I hope has prohibited sufficiently by the lessons of the worthy Mrs. Meredith to enable her to correct an excess of unavailing grief; and I trust she will consider it inconsistent with the good she is mistress of, to repine at the decree of Providence, which has thought fit to remove her parents from a world of trouble to a state of perfect happiness."

"Well," said Miss Coningsby, "I see I may twist my gift round Carlo's neck, for Celestia cares nothing about it."

This remark had the effect of awakening the orphan from her melancholy recollections.

"Oh, no, dear madam," she ejaculated, "pardon me for having forgotten everything but my locket; next to that I will consider your gift as my best loved treasure; but I was trying to recollect what my dear papa said when he showed it to me, and have tolerably well succeeded; when I expressed my wonder at its odd shape, he said it was made in commemoration of an event of the most dreadful description, the particulars of which he would inform me of when I was old enough to understand them: that I should then have the locket, which I must never part with; and as you, my now only dear papa and aunt, have thought me old enough to be made acquainted so far with my affairs, I think I may wear it; and its value will be enhanced by its being received from the hands of those who had protected a little helpless orphan."

Mr. Coningsby then put the chain round Celestia's neck, to which the locket was affixed; her kind benefactors embraced her affectionately, and as fer-

vently invoked a blessing upon her head as if she had been their own offspring; and having again locked up the jewel-case, they adjourned to the breakfast-room, although it may be conceived that the interesting conversation that had just taken place occupied their minds so fully that little attention was given to the morning meal.

CHAPTER IV.

SOME EXPLANATIONS OF PARTICULAR IMPORTANCE TO THE READER.

HAVING thus fully introduced Celestia to our readers, we must request them to go back with us to a period many ears prior t the occurrence of the incidents recorded in the foregoing chapters.

There was not a more ancient or distinguished English family than that of Elverton. The earls Elverton had not only been celebrated from time immemorial for the nobility of their rank but for their private virtues.

Coningsby Elverton, was the youngest son of the earl of that title, and as the estates were all entailed, they went with the title, to the eldest son, the youngest ones were disposed of to different professions, but Coningsby, the father of Celestia's protector, being of a domestic turn of mind, preferred the honourable vocation of a British merchant, and he was accordingly placed with a gentleman of the highest respectability in that line.

The lady of this merchant was the daughter of a nobleman, and a most amiable woman. She entered very little into the routine of fashionable life; her circle of friends was the most select, and in this society Coningsby Elverton passed three years, when a mutual affection having taken place between him and the daughter of his excellent friend, with the consent and approbation of all parties their marriage was celebrated, and the following year his father-in-law gave up the whole of the business to him.

There was only one draw-back upon the happiness of the first five years of their union; Heaven had blest them with a daughter, but they both wished for a son, as Coningsby by the death of his elder brothers, had succeeded to the title.

Heaven heard their prayer, but alas! it was productive of greater misery at the time than happiness. The amiable Countess of Elverton, to whom her lord was so devotedly attached, in giving birth to the long wished for heir expired, and left her husband completely distracted at a loss which nothing could repay.

For sometime Lord Elverton was completely deaf to the voice of consolation, and it was more than two years before he could ever find courage to gaze upon the countenance of his innocent offspring, for he continually reproached himself with having been discontented at not having a son, and freely would he have given back that son, if by so doing he could have had his beloved wife restored to his arms. His daughter was sent into the country to her great aunt, the sister of the merchant, her grandfather. But at length parental affection asserted its rights, and assuaged his unavailing grief, and the child Coningsby at last became so necessary to his noble father's existence, that he was wretched when he was out of his sight.

A tutor was engaged to instruct him in all the necessary preliminary branches of education, and at the age of sixteen he was sent to the university of Cambridge, with the most cheerful and brilliant prospects before him. Alas! in after years, how cruelly were those hopes so sanguine, destined to be disappointed. How little did the young nobleman anticipate the many and bitter troubles which time had in store for him. It is a dismal story that we have to relate, and we must solicit the reader's patience while we record the facts connected with our "Romance of Real Life.

It was a lovely evening in the year 17—, that two young men of elegant exterior, and attended by their grooms, might have been seen leisurely riding along an extensive avenue of trees, which led to the ancient and noble edifice known from time immemorial as the parental residence of the Earls Malensbury, Borensforth Hall.

The sun was fast resigning his diurnal course, and his departing rays reflected splendidly upon the noble mansion, bringing forward all its architectural beauties most prominently, as they were chastened down by the sublimity of the season.

" Welcome to thee, good old mansion of my sires; after a long sojourn on foreign shores, how gladly do I hail thee, and Heaven send that all those so dear to me are well and happy as their last communication led me to hope I should find them. It is now three years, my dear friend, since we before had the pleasure of gazing upon this spot, and I only trust that this may be the advent of a return to all the happiness we at that time experienced. You never saw my sister Elvina, Coningsby, and I only hope that she may now be at home, that you may have an opportunity of judging of her sweet perfections."

This speech was addressed by one of the young men before alluded to, to his equally youthful companion. It was Lord Malensbury, the eldest son of the earl of that title, and his friend was Coningsby Elverton, whom we have before introduced to the reader as the protector of our lovely heroine Celestia Aunville.

Lord Arthur Malensbury was one of those sort of individuals whom once to be introduced to was immediately destined to fix himself on your esteem and admiration. His manners were so totally unassuming and so prepossessing, that he at once won respect, and the more intimate it was your good fortune to become with him, the more strongly did his intrinsic qualities impress you with their excellence. His person equally corresponded with the perfections of his mind.

It was at the university of Cambridge that Coningsby had first become acquainted with him, and the similarity of their habits, and the corresponding excellence of their minds, caused a strict, an unchangeable friendship to spring up between them. Lord Arthur was one of the most estimable of characters, as we have before stated, and if any further proof be required of his intrisic virtues, we may mention it as a most extraordinary, and probably unexampled instance, that his lordship passed nearly five years at Cambridge without imbibing a single vice.

When the time arrived that Malensbury was to set out on his travels, although Coningsby, his friend, had not been his allotted time at college, he prevailed on his father to suffer him to accompany him.

This arrangement having been come to, they were placed under the care of a gentleman, whose worth and integrity, joined to sound judgment, and a thorough knowledge of the world, rendered him highly fit for the confidence reposed in him by the fathers of two young men, who attached too much consequence to their situation in life to have been under a restraint with a mentor of inferior talents. Dr. Sinclair was to them indeed on all occasions, the tender, indulgent father, and sincere friend. But to return to the evening to which we have alluded.

"My dear Arthur," returned Coningsby, in answer to his speech, on once more beholding his family mansion, "how truly happy shall I be in being introduced to your sister, Elvina, who notwithstanding the allowances that ought to be made for brotherly affection, I have a right to believe is all, and even more than you have represented her to me."

They now entered the hall, the principal servants having come forth to meet and welcome their young master, and the scene which succeeded we shall not tire the patience of the reader by describing. To the great vexation of Lord Malensbury, his sister Elvina was from home, and he expressed his disappointment at her not being present to welcome him after so long an absence.

Lord Arthur's report procured his friend a warm welcome from the earl, his father, whose affection for his son was as unbounded as his deserts, and each was worthy of the other.

As for the Countess Malensbury, she was as cold and repulsive in her manners as her lord's were warm and encouraging; she seemed to view Coningsby with an eye of suspicion, which, as he was utterly unconscious of the cause, occasioned him no little embarrassment. However, he stayed but two days with the family of his friend, and then hastened to join his own noble and revered parent, after having made a faithful promise to spend some time with Lord Arthur and his parents at the hall.

So anxious was Coningsby to fulfil his engagement, that he suffered only a week to elapse before he rejoined them at the hall. Elvina was still from home, and Coningsby felt as much disappointment as himself at the circumstance.

"I pray you, my dear mother," said Arthur, to Lady Malensbury, "to send your commands to Elvina to return immediately; after so long an absence I could hardly have expected to have been at home more than a week without seeing her."

"Indeed, Lord Arthur," replied his mother, "I cannot comply with your request; my sister would with reason be offended at Elvina's leaving her so soon; I promised, at least, a month's absence."

"But my dear madam," returned Lord Arthur, "I cannot but believe that my aunt is too reasonable to complain of a breach of promise when the cause is explained to her; but I shall think Elvina herself greatly changed, if she can any longer delay her return home, now she knows how anxious I am to behold her once more."

At this part of the altercation the earl entered the room, and to his son's speech added—

"My dear Arthur, I do not wonder you should feel hurt upon this subject; but rest satisfied, Elvina will be here tomorrow, Mrs. Seabroke has resigned her to my request, for a short stay with you."

The countess bit her lip, and with no inconsiderable degree of acrimony, said—

"Your lordship may repent this compliance with Arthur's folly, when it is too late to apply the remedy."

"I am at a perfect loss to understand you, my dear," replied the earl, "and cannot call that a folly which is dictated by affection; for my own part, I should be most unhappy if my children were less affectionate towards each other."

"How easily you are deceived, my lord," said Lady Malensbury, "if that were alone the motive I should be less repugnant at it."

The earl seemed to be perfectly astounded, while his son's countenance fully expressed how much he was hurt at his mother's behaviour, so utterly deficient not only of politeness, but of common decency. Coningsby could not misunderstand that the inuendo was levelled at him, though totally at a loss to divine the cause of it at that time. It was not long, however, before he had ample cause to suspect the truth.

The following morning dawned, and with it arrived the beauteous Lady Elvina, and notwithstanding all that had passed, she was received with equal rapture by both her father and mother, while the transport of her brother and sister at meeting again after so long a separation, we must leave to the imagination of the reader.

How shall we pourtray the charms of Lady Elvina? We must fail in the attempt to give any elaborate description, and we must therefore content ourselves with merely a slight pencil sketch.

At this period Lady Elvina was in all the bloom of youthful beauty. Her figure was most elegantly formed; her height the criterion of female stature; she had a most dazzling complexion, heightened by the blush of modesty; her full blue eyes were shaded by long, dark eye-lashes, and her luxuriant tresses of light auburn hair fell in ringlets on her turned shoulders. A dimpling smile played about a mouth exquisitely beautiful, adorned with teeth of truly pearly whiteness, and in fact the whole contour of her features was commanding, yet gentle and impressive in the extreme.

It may naturally be expected that such a fair being as Lady Elvina, could not fail of exciting admiration wherever she went, and such was the lovely girl at littte more than sixteen years of age.

Coningsby was immediately captivated with her. To him she appeared to be something more than nature, and when he was presented to her by his friend, he felt so awkwardly embarrassed that he could not utter a word. Lord Arthur saw with pleasure the fulfilment of his wishes in the confusion which Coningsby displayed; the earl treated him with the kindest regard, the countess with cold politeness; whilst Lady Elvina behaved towards him as one who was the chosen friend of a brother she so affectionately loved, whenever she could escape the argus eyes of her mother.

When Lord Arthur and Coningsby, for the first time, could snatch an hour alone, he endeavoured to finish the chagrin which the latter had materially imbibed at the behaviour of Lady Malensbury.

"My dear feiend," he remarked, "I am apprehehsive you have beheld Lady Malensbury in a very unfavourable light; and therefore I will, with your permission, make you acquainted with what appears to me her only fault, though it can scarcely be called a fault, since she acts from principle. I need not ask if you admire my sister; I see you do, and am satisfied. Indeed it is impossible to behold her, and not give her your unqualified admiration; for to speak with truth, she is loveliness itself, and her temper equals her personal affections. She is very young, and has not yet seen much of life; I need not tell you, Coningsby, that I love her with the most unbounded affection; it was my love for her made me press your visit, in the hope that the friend of my heart, and the sister of my affections, might receive a mutual impression, I flatter myself that that hope is realised."

"Arthur, my best friend," ejaculated the delighted Coningsby, "need I assure you that you are not mistaken? It only needs the concurrence of Lord and Lady Malensbury to make me one of the happiest of human beings."

"Unfortunately, Coningsby, I must mention to you one obstacle to the gratification of our wishes, but that even, I trust, may not be insurmountable. My mother is a strict Roman Catholic, but as her family were very anxious that she should become Lady Malensbury, they readily consented to every condition made by my grandmother. She was to be allowed the free exercise of her religion, and a confessor to reside in the house, but that it should be restricted to herself alone; that her children, whether male or female should be brought up in the protestant faith. But of what avail are agreements of that sort? Daughters are, and ought to be so entirely under the superintendence of the mother, that it is scarcely possible they should not, in some degree, imbibe the mother's faith; and, as the catholics are taught to believe there is no salvation out of their pale, can it be wondered at that a mother should endeavoured to weaken the contrary profession in the mind of a beloved child? By this means they feel no confidence in either, and can scarcely be said to be of any religion at all. My sister, as I before said, is very young, and if united to a sensible man, whose character and conduct are governed by the just principles of religion and morality, she will escape the errors of her mother, and the artifices of the Jesuit Bonville, who is my mother's confessor, and one of the most crafty and designing of men. What renders him the more dangerous is, that he is one of the best informed and most learned men of the age: he is perfect master of all languages and sciences, and I believe none of the fine arts are unknown to him; to this may be added a most insinuating manner, which scarcely permits you to contradict him upon any subject or opinion he chooses to

adopt. To-day he will return, and you will have an ample opportunity to form your own opinion of him, and are the only man I know fit to counteract him. I already perceive that Elvina beholds you with approbation; my father will be most happy to dispose of his child where her happiness both here and hereafter is likely to be secured. My regard for you, my dear Coningsby, is founded upon a perfect knowledge of your character; and if you find my sister such a woman as I have heard you describe must be the woman you would make your wife, I should feel myself completely happy."

Coningsby could but press the hand of his friend fervently, and briefly expressed to him his thanks for the flattering opinion he entertained of his character, and after a few more observations, the conversation dropped.

Coningsby found Bonville all that Lord Arthur had represented him to be, learned, artful, and insinuating; but a letter from his father pressing him to return, did not give him time sufficiently to investigate his character, though enough to fix Elvina's image on his heart.

When he announced his departure for the following day, it was impossible for him not to observe the melancholy expression which her countenance assumed; her spirits suffered the same depression during the whole of the evening, which her mother remarked, and kept her at the harp or the piano, till the time of retiring; and as Conigsby set out early from the hall, he saw no more of her.

When he announced his departure, Lord Arthur and his father pressed him to renew his visit as soon as possible, and he readily promised to pass the hunting season with them.

Lady Malensbury could not conceal the pleasure which Coningsby's departure gave her, and, of course, did not second their invitation.

The image of the lovely Elvina followed Coningsby to his home, and he felt convinced that she was the only woman on whom he could bestow his heart's affections.

Lord Elverton had ever been too indulgent to all his son's wishes, for the latter to have any reserves wit him; and he therefore seized upon the first opportunity to acquaint him with his passion for Lady Elvina, painting her perfections in the glowing colours of an admiring lover.

The earl heard him to the end with the greatest patience, and when Coningsby called upon him for his permission to pay his addresses to her, he answered him in the following words—

"My dear son, I see that if your visit was short, yet, from the natural ardour of your temper, you have gone a great way in the labyrinth of passion. Lady Elvina may be all you have described; the partiality of a brother has rendered her an object worthy of your admiration; but you cannot, in so short a time be a judge, at least not a competent judge of her disposition, nor can the inclination of a girl of sixteen be decided. But I have one objection to make, which as it not only most materially concerns your future happiness but that of your children; that one weighs more strongly with me than either birth or fortune, both of which Lady Elvina possesses in an eminent degree. As a father and a friend, I would advise, not control you; the prejudices of Lady Malensbury then, appear to me to place an insurmountable barrier to your ever making her daughter your wife."

Coningsby heard his father with patience, but considerable pain, and after a pause, during which he reflected deeply upon all he had said, he replied,—

"Your arguments, my dear father, are in this, as in every other instance which concerns me, replete with wisdom and affection; but I trust your fears are groundless. Elvina's youth is in my favour, her opinions may fluctuate, but not be firmly fixed, and when she becomes my wife, and entirely separate from her mother, I shall be able both by precept and example, firmly to fix her in my own faith. But I shall be better able to judge of her character in my next visit, and shall not determine anything till I have made you acquainted with my opinion.

"Wisely resolved, my son," said the earl, approvingly, and after some further remarks, the conversation dropped.

But, alas! how futile is all advice; when once a headstrong passion takes root in the human breast, reason at once takes flight, and only resumes her empire over us, to show us the vanity of all human happiness.

The time at length arrived when Coningsby Elverton had promised to renew his visit to Berensforth Hall, and sanguine with hope, he set out accordingly.

What scenes of bliss did the young man imagine were in store for him, and certainly to a great extent, Coningsby was not deceived or disappointed; but what afterwards occurred only goes to prove still further the utter futility of all human hopes.

When Coningsby Elverton arrived at the hall, he was most warmly, nay, enthusiastically received by every one but Lady Malensbury. A large party was assembled, and it was with the greatest difficulty he ever obtained any conversation of a private character with her to whom his heart was so fondly attached. But, in his eyes, she appeared far more lovely than she had done on any previous evening.

Mrs. Seabroke, the sister of Lady Malensbury, who was one of the guests, was equally averse to the addresses of Coningsby, and was a continual spy upon the actions of him and the fair being upon whom he had placed his affections, his heart's complete idolatry.

But in spite of all these efforts, as every day added fresh fuel to Coningsby's love, he wrote for, and obtained his father's permission to offer himself as a candidate for Elvina's favour, who appeared so truly worthy of his strongest affections.

He found no difficulty in obtaining the consent of the earl of Malensbury to pay his addresses to the beauteous girl, and though they were received with all the blushing timidity so natural to youth and innocence, the eyes of love could discover that they were not displeasing to the amiable and facinating Elvina.

In spite of all her prejudices, the countess endeavoured to treat Lord Elverton as her future son-in-law; Mrs. Seabroke, on the contrary, comported herself towards him in a manner to create his utter amazement, completely ignorant as he was of any misconduct. Coningsby omitted no opportunity to conciliate her, but his strenuous efforts were all ineffectual—she repulsed all his efforts with silent contumely.

It was not possible that the young man could be otherwise than unexpressibly hurt at such unwarrantable conduct, especially in one so nearly allied to that fair being whom he hoped to make his bride, and he therefore siezed the first opportunity to mention it to Lord Arthur. We need not say that that young noble sincerely sympathised with his valued friend, and in reply to his observations, said,—

"You cannot suppose, my dear friend, that it has escaped my observation, but if that be any consolation to you, (though I don't see how it can) she treats me just the same; however, I think I can readily account for it. You know, Coningsby, my aunt is strongly bigotted to her religion, and anxiously wished to unite her only son with his cousin, and but for this, my father would not have permitted my sister to enter so early into so solemn an engagement, but to ensure her adherence to Protestantism; for if anything should happen to me, Elvina would be exposed to the persuasions of her mother and the open bigotry or her aunt, aided by the wily priest."

Soon after this conversation between the two friends, Lord Arthur was united to an amiable young lady, to whom he had been attached from the earliest days of childhood. The earl wished to secure his daughter's happiness also; the necessary preliminaries were consequently arranged with all possible despatch for her marriage with Lord Elverton; for his father, as we have, we believe, before stated, had succeeded some time previously to the title and estates of Elverton, which were situated in the beautiful county of Sussex.

By the express desire of the Earl of Elverton's father, the former had entirely given up all mercantile pursuits to a worthy man who had been a short time entered a partner in the firm. He wishing to reside entirely at an estate he had recently purchased, gave up his paternal one to Coningsby, together with his town-house, promising to consider the latter as still his own, whenever, after the marriage of his son and daughter-in-law, he might gratify them with his presence.

All these arrangements having been so satisfactorily made, the day was finally fixed for the nuptials to take place. What occurred on that momentous occasion must form the subject of another chapter.

CHAPTER V.

THE UNION.—THE WARNING.—THE ACCIDENT, AND OTHER EVENTS IMMEDIATELY CONNECTED WITH THIS NARRATIVE.

AT the express wish of the Earl of Malensbury the marriage of his lovely daughter with Lord Elverton was appointed to take place in the parish church in which he had himself been baptized, and which was situated in the immediate vicinity of the priory ruins, already described to the reader.

The morning fixed for the auspicious event arrived, and nothing could be more beautiful than the weather; it seemed to rejoice at the union of two individuals so worthy of each other; but there were dark clouds hovering in the atmosphere of fate, that were soon about to burst and discharge their fury upon the heads of the devoted.

Notwithstanding all his efforts to the contrary, Lord Coningsby Elverton could not help feeling a most unaccountable depression of spirits, and an aspect of melancholy clouded the lovely features of Elvina, which nothing seemed to have the power to dissipate. In vain did her friends endeavour to arouse her, and her intended husband; it was all to no purpose, and all parties proceeded to the church with anything but those joyous feelings which had previously animated their bosoms.

Lady Elvina, Conignsby, and the Earl of Elverton and Malensbury occupied the same carriage, whilst Lady Malensbury, her sister, and the bridesmaid, according to the express arrangement of her ladyship, occupied the second. All the principal nobility and gentry in the neighbourhood formed the marriage procession, and it was accompanied by a vast concourse of the humbler classes, all attired in their best, and exhibiting the utmost delight upon the auspicious event.

They had to pass by the old priory ruins on their way to the church, and just as they had approached them, the friends of Lady Elvina were astonished and alarmed, at hearing a cry of terror from her, and at the same time the vehicle was stopped.

Coningsby, and the Earls of Elverton and Malensbury jumped up immediately to inquire into the cause of this extraordinary interruption, and they were still more astonished when they beheld standing by the side of the carriage the tall and emaciated figure of an old man, with long grey hair flowing over his shoulders, miserably clad, and holding an oaken staff menacingly in the air. His gestures were of the most wild and inexplicable description, and his eyes appeared to flash with an expression bordering upon absolute rage. All eyes became fixed upon this singular being in complete astonishment, and Elvina clung to her father and Coningsby in speechless alarm, while the old man came still closer to the carriage, and peering in at the very window, he screamed out in accents scarcely human, the following words—

"A wedding morn, a wedding morn, but oh, what a melancholy one; what trouble it is frought with. She is young, she is beautiful, she is apparently all that man could wish her to be, but mark my words, Coningsby Elverton, it is an alliance that Heaven frowns upon; wed her, and your heart and all your hopes of happiness will become blighted. Thorns will spring up in the path where flowers now blossom, and the present bright sunshine will be converted into worse than the gloomy darkness of midnight. Beware, beware, for you will have reason to repent having mocked the words of the old wandering prophet!"

Elvina heard but a few words of his remarkable speech, before overcome by terror, she fainted, and the persons in the different carriages were so completely astonished that they were quite inactive. Not so, however, the humble persons following in the procession, who hearing the threatening words of the singular old man, rushed towards him, with the intention of seizing him, but the first two that approached him were immediately felled by a heavy blow from the oaken staff he wielded, to the earth, and then with a laugh of derision he bounded with uncommon agility into the old priory ruins and was in an instant lost to the sight, nor could anything more be seen of him, notwithstanding a strict search was made in every part of the ruins after him.

To describe the astonishment of every one present at this unprecedented adventure would be impossible, but no one knew him, or remembered to have seen him before, though all concluded that he must be some unfortunate maniac, who had escaped from confinement, but the manner in which he had eluded them in the old priory ruins was perfectly inexplicable and unaccountable.

Lady Malensbury, who had heard every word that the old man had uttered, and evinced, if possible, far greater emotion than any of the rest, did not fail to throw out certain hints to the effect that the warning ought not to be unheeded, and that it would be only prudent, at any rate, to postpone the marriage to a future day. But her suggestions were steadily combatted with effect by her lord, and Elvina having recovered, and her alarm quieted (for she was kept in ignorance of all that the old man had uttered), they proceeded on their way to the church, all parties interested being determined to make every subsequent inquiry, in order to endeavour to ascertain who the individual who had obstructed them in so bold and extraordinary a manner was. Coningsby could not at the same time help thinking, though he did not express his opinion to any one, that Lady Malensbury knew more about it than she chose to disclose, and he determined to watch her actions narrowly in future, in order that he might be enabled to counteract any sinister designs she might entertain against his peace.

The union was over, and in the joyousness and revelry that prevailed on all sides, the mysterious adventure of the morning seemed to be entirely forgotten.

For several days the festivities were kept up with unabated spirit, and every one joined in wishing the new married couple all the happiness that could befall them.

We will now pass over a period of five

years, during which time Lord and Lady Elverton enjoyed every earthly felicity; never had Coningsby cause to suspect the purity of his lady's conduct, or the strength and sincerity of the affection she bore towards him. But, alas, this happiness was not destined to last for ever.

Heaven had blessed their union with children, a boy and a girl. Lady Elverton was rather retired in her disposition; therefore, though she entered for a time into all the fashionable amusements of a London life, with the greatest spirit, it only gave greater zest to their summer months at Ashbourne Manor.

The first event that occurred to in-

CELESTIA ALARMED AT THE MYSTERIOUS APPEARANCE IN THE OLD PRIORY RUINS.

terrupt their felicity, was the sudden death of the Earl of Elverton, but fortunately for him, he was spared the grief of witnessing the annihilation of all his son's earthly hopes.

Ashbourne Manor was delightfully situated in the centre of a fine park, on the sea-coast. There were a few huts on the shore, inhabited by industrious fishermen and their families; the latter of whom Lady Ivina took under her protection, whilst her lord assisted the others whenever distress of any kind assailed them.

No. 4.

As there was very fine bathing there, Lord Elverton had a machine built, and appointed one of the men the master of it, and his wife the bather.

Lady Elvina doated on her children, and hardly ever permitted them out of her sight; she even attended their bathing. Her lord and her frequently rambled with them and their attendants on the sands and the cliffs for hours, and the delighted children appeared unhappy if anything occurred to prevent them. Lord Elverton was always an early riser, and generally walked two or three hours before breakfast. It was the bathing season, and he walked towards the beach to meet his children (the boy was then three, his sister only two); a violent shriek made his lordship quicken his pace, and he beheld one of the nursery maids wringing her hands in agony, and his little Elvina standing by her.

It would be a fruitless task to endeavour to describe the horror of Lord Elverton's mind at that moment; in an instant his worst fears were aroused, for he saw plainly that something dreadful had happened, but he was for some moments deprived of the power of speech, when she informed him, in accents scarcely intelligible, that his boy, his darling boy, was missing — gone she knew not whither; that Ellen had only turned round to answer Lady Elvina, who was calling to her, and in that moment Lord Coningsby had disappeared; she had called him, but no reply was made; she ran along the shore thinking he might have hid himself behind a rocky projection, the only one between two and three miles along the shore; her cries had brought all the cottagers to her, and they assisted her search, no stranger had been seen that morning, and as the men were all within a few yards of the shore, fishing for shrimps, they were sure he could not have fallen in without their seeing it. Yet where could the poor child be?

How horribly distracted were the feelings of Lord Elverton on receiving this distressing intelligence. However, to satisfy him, each of the men took his boat, and went out to sea and along the coast; but all returned from their fruitless search, and never did his eyes again behold his infant son.

But how could he break the dreadful tidings to his mother? He knew not; her situation rendered it the more dangerous, yet know she must; with a heart ready to burst, therefore, his lordship turned his steps towards home, but first he went round to the stables, that he might without delay, despatch servants over the country; for no one would allow the possibility of his having so suddenly disappeared, if he had fallen down on the shore, and even been washed into the sea by a wave, as the men must have seen him.

Lord Elverton had been absent from home so long, that his lady alarmed, came to seek him. She soon discovered from his agitated countenance, that something extraordinary had happened, and she looked around for the cause; the little Elvina was in the maid's arms, but the boy was not there.

"Where is Adolphus, where is my darling? Dear Coningsby tell me, why does Ellen stay alone with him?" she breathlessly demanded.

"He is coming, my love," faltered out his lordship; "but I am unwell."

This turned all her ladyship's attention upon her husband, but as she continually looked back without seeing the child approach, she implored him to tell her the truth, if any accident had befallen him.

"Oh! I see by your looks it is so!" she ejaculated, clasping her hands with the most indescribable agony; "my boy, my darling is drowned!" and without being able to give utterance to another word, she fell into his arms, deprived of sense or motion.

It was long, ere they could recover her. Edward had conveyed his master's orders to the stables, from which every horse was taken, in order to traverse the country, as all were positive he must have been snatched up by some one on the watch for him. Lord Elverton caught at this forlorn hope, for his own opinion was, that he was drowned. In the meantime, poor Lady Elvina was in a most deplorable condition, going from one fainting fit into another, till, before the physician could arrive, the worst fears were realized, and her life placed in the most imminent danger.

Night came, and with it the tired

and unsuccessful servants. But they brought with them no satisfactory intelligence, no consolation to the mourners.

* * * * *

We must now return to Celestia, who had attained her fifteenth year. We wish to convey to our readers some idea of her personal appearance at this time, for it was surpassingly interesting. She struck every one who beheld her with admiration. The smile of innocence and benevolence, of universal love towards her fellow creatures, ever beamed upon the lips of our heroine. Her cheeks glowed with the pure blossom of health; and her complexion, though not precisely fair, was beautifully transparent; the countenance of the interesting stranger received animation from her dark expressive eyes, in which were pourtrayed every thought of her ingenuous mind before her tongue could give utterance to it, and when she spoke, the harmonious, the silvery tones of her voice fixed itself irresistibly on the attention, and completely fascinated the senses of the delighted listener.

Celestia was remarkably tall, and elegantly formed for her age, and she, therefore, appeared to strangers much older than she really was, particularly as her manners and conversation were so perfectly in unison with her personal appearance; but with exquisite modesty, innocence, and simplicity, she was totally unconscious of her superiority.

To say that Mr. Coningsby and his sister were proud of her, would be but to give a faint and inadequate description of the affection they bore towards her, and amply were they repaid for all their kindness by the love of the gentle Celestia.

Mr. Coningsby had made his sister acquainted with all the particulars of his melancholy and remarkable history; and deeply did that truly amiable woman sympathise with her brother in the misfortunes he had undergone, and regret the annoyance she must have put him to by the remarks she had at different times made when she was in ignorance of the facts.

After Mr. Coningsby had communicated them to her, she was so deeply affected that she remained seriously ill for several days. As we have before said, she most keenly regretted the annoyance her remarks must have put him to, and the agony they must have added to his already deeply lacerated mind. She reflected with shame upon the manner in which she had so frequently teazed him by her petulant humours, and she sought the earliest opportunity, after her recovery, to enter into an explanation with him.

"My dear brother," she said, affectionately pressing his hand, "how sincerely do I grieve at reflecting how often my bad temper must have increased your chagrin, which, notwithstanding I was ignorant of the full extent, was yet sufficient to have checked my unwarrantable behaviour."

"Eugenia," returned her brother, pressing her hand with equal tenderness "if you would not wish me to feel too sensibly for an obligation I can never repay, you will never mention or allude to this subject again. Your society drew me at first from despair; and if we did not know each other sufficiently at that time to appreciate the blessing (at least, for me to do so), believe me, it was owing to that sorrow which absorbed every other feeling. The amiable girl, we have taken under our protection has enlivened us, and, by the interest she inspired for herself, taught my grief worn heart that it was still too warm for a misanthropist. By immuring yourself in this place, so remote from those scenes you were so well qualified to shine in, giving up even your rank in life, you have proved yourself worthy of my warmest gratitude, and I again repeat I never can repay you."

" Say no more, my dear Albert," observed Miss Coningsby, "you have taken an effectual method in order to prevent my renewal of the subject; may you yet experience a renewal of past blessings you know so well how to enjoy."

The conversation then ended between the brother and sister, and from that time it was never again alluded to in any way which could cause anguish to their feelings. But to return to Celestia. We have already given an outline of the amiable character of Mrs. Hardy the lady who supplied the place of her late excellent preceptress; but it will be more fully developed in the course of these pages. Among the various moral duties she inculcated were those of charity and benevolence, and it was impossible for her to find a more ready pupil than Celestia.

The industrious labourer, who maintained an infant family by the sweat of his brow; the widow, whose sole dependance was upon the industry of her children; those who were too old and feeble to contribute to their own maintenance—these were sure to be the objects of the attentive charity of the benevolent Mrs. Hardy.

In these charitable visits, the good woman was always accompanied by our heroine, and she also assisted in making clothes for those who were unable to do it for themselves; nor did her goodness of heart end here—she readily and cheerfully listened to all their real and fancied complaints both of body and mind; to both she administered all the relief in her power, correcting the one by gentle admonition, and relieving the other by consolatory advice; to their bodily complaints she was both physician and apothecary, was the truly noble hearted Mrs. Hardy, and, in short the inhabitants of Sungrove Abbey were followed by the blessings of all who resided in the neighbourhood and for miles around.

Celestia was enthusiastically attached to the romantic and sublime; all that was gently beautiful or majestically grand, both in nature and the works of man, met with her warmest admiration. She was richly cultivated in all the acquirements that could render her fascinating, independently of which, the natural qualities she possessed, were of the first order. She had early shown a taste for poesy, and had at the early age at which we now place her before the reader, composed many sweet pieces of poetry, which would have done honour to genius of the first order. In drawing too, she excelled, and many were the beautiful sketches of scenery she had made, for which the beautiful spots in the neighbourhood of Sungrove Abbey afforded such ample subject for her pencil.

Like her guardian, the old priory ruins were a most favourite haunt of her's. From various points of that venerable mass, a most exquisite and diversified view of the surrounding country could be obtained, and all being

so quiet and tranquil in its precincts, there was nothing whatever to break in upon or disturb the studious and reflective mind.

David and his wife had been dead for about three years; their daughter and son had left that part of the country, and Mr. Coningsby had purchased the right of occupation from the agent of the nobleman to whom the estate belonged, and who for years had resided entirely on the continent. He had made no alterations in the ruins themselves, for that was one of the stipulations in the agreement drawn up between the agent and himself; but he had nevertheless made various additions and improvements to the lodge, furnished it in the most comfortable manner, attached two more apartments to it, and placed in it a worthy and aged couple, old Hannibal Dobson and his wife Dorothy, who had been recommended to his especial attention and sympathy, by his excellent friend, Lord Everside, and whom he supported with every comfort that their age and infirmities required.

Mr. Coningsby still felt a most extraordinary and painful interest in the old priory ruins, whether it was from the warning of the mysterious old man (who had disappeared there in so unaccountable a manner) or not, he could not say, but he still felt a melancholy pleasure in wandering among the ruins of that venerable, holy pile, and in recalling the circumstances of the past to his memory. How painfully had almost every portion of that singular being's prophecy been verified, and although he was no believer in prescience he was at a perfect loss to reconcile these remarkable coincidences. What added not a little to keep the excitement of his feelings upon the subject alive, was the fact that Hannibal and his wife had assured him solemnly that they had once seen a venerable man, of haggard appearance, and in wretched attire, perfectly answering the description of the individual whom Mr. Coningsby had several times pourtrayed to them, in order that he might have every opportunity of arriving at some solution of the mystery,—sitting upon one of the fragments of the ruins. His chin rested on an oaken staff, and although it was dusk, and their sight was not good, they could distinctly perceive that his eyes and his countenance bore a most extraordinary expression, so much so, indeed, that they were almost terrified, and could not approach him nearer, though they were however, at that time, only a few yards distant from him.

While the old couple thus stood, the strange being suddenly raised his head and directed his gaze towards them, and they said they never should forget the gaze he fixed upon them; it was quite frightful to behold, and "froze the very blood in their veins," then shaking his staff menacingly at them, he laughed aloud, arose from his seat, and vanished from their sight so suddenly that they knew not how, though he appeared to sink into the earth, but they had not courage to proceed to the place where they had seen him sitting, but hastened back to the lodge, and were so terrified, that for some time they were half inclined to resign his honour's hospitality, and leave the place altogether.

This story was almost too improbable for Mr. Coningsby to place any particular confidence in it, and he endeavoured to allay the old people's fears, though when he found he could not shake them in the opinion they had formed, he gave up the attempt, and assuring them that they could not have any possible reason for fear, and that he would use every precaution to protect them from danger, he left them.

But notwithstanding all that Mr. Coningsby had said to Hannibal and his wife, he found it impossible to treat the matter so lightly as he had affected to do, and when he was alone he seriously reflected upon it.

The description the old people had given of the extraordinary being, so exactly corresponded with that of the old man who had crossed his path on the morning of his marriage, that he found it almost impossible to persuade himself that it was not the same, and yet the number of years which had elapsed since then, and the great age the man seemed to be at that period, appeared to render it incredible he should be living at the present time.

When he remembered also the extraordinary disappearance of the old prophet (as he called himself), among the old priory ruins, on that occasion, he was still more perplexed than ever.

He strictly examined the spot where Hannibal and his wife said they had seen the old man, and where also he appeared, as far as they could judge, to vanish, but there was nothing whatever to account for his disappearance, unless indeed, taking advantage of the terror the poor old couple had themselves acknowledged they had evinced, he had suddenly concealed himself behind some of the huge fragments of the ruins, until he had watched them return to the lodge, when he could easily depart from the spot.

This conclusion was the most probable Mr. Coningsby could arrive at, and he endeavoured to believe it was a correct one, but he did not fail to make the strictest inquiries respecting the singular being, where he was likely to obtain information, but without meeting with any success, and the circumstance was permitted to drop, though it frequently occupied the mind of Mr. Coningsby.

Celestia was particularly attached to old Hannibal and his wife, and paid them frequent visits, accompanied by Mrs. Hardy. She was also most ardently fond of the lodge and the ancient priory ruins, looking upon them almost as her natural home, and not unreasonably so, for it was in that lodge her unfortunate parent had sought an asylum for himself and her, and it was from thence she had been taken to the protection of her present beloved benefactors.

Young as she was at the time, our heroine could recall most vividly to her memory all the melancholy events recorded at the commencement of our tale, and when alone, many were the tears she shed as these sad retrospections arose to her recollection, and to the memory of her father. But before Mr. Coningsby and his sister she was ever joyous and happy, for she thought she should indeed be ungrateful to appear otherwise before those generous benefactors, who had been so kind to her.

A lovely morning in spring invited our heroine and Mrs. Hardy out at an early hour, and they again, at the request of Celestia, bent their steps towards the old priory ruins, Celestia having resolved to proceed with a drawing of a beautiful landscape of which she had already made a sketch.

It was indeed a fair morning for such a purpose, and our heroine felt animated with the subject, more so, as she had not made known to Mr. Coningsby the task she was engaged upon, and it was intended when completed to be offered by her as an humble present for his acceptance.

Lovely spring! how exhilirating is thine influence, both on the young and the old, the joyous and the careworn. Sad indeed, or insensible must be the heart that does not feel thy gladsome, genial power.

How the sun glistened on the clusters of budding white flowers, and how merrily did his golden beams frisk it over the mirrored surface of rivulet and lake. How fresh and buoyant was the breath of morn, and how soft and plaintive did the song birds begin to chirp their early notes. Lovely spring, sweet emblem of youth, and beauty, and innocence, thou art the most joyous season of the year.

And Celestia had never felt more supremely happy than she did upon that occasion, as she bounded playfully by the side, at some paces in advance of her amiable preceptress. Light, fresh, and happy as the season was she. The roses on her cheeks never bloomed more sweetly; the smiles that glistened like sunlight around her mouth, never beamed more brightly. Sportively her luxuriant tresses floated on the air, and added a finish to a portrait that might be truly said to be perfect. He must have been less than mortal who could have gazed upon that fair and innocent girl, without being enraptured.

It gladdened the he heart of Mrs. Hardy to see her young charge so happy and cheerful on this occassion, and she watched her innocent gambols as they proceeded to the ruins, with the most unfeigned satisfaction.

"Who could contemplate that sweet girl," she said to herself, "in all the rosy hilarity of youth, without admiration? Who could harbour a single thought towards doing her injury, by either word or deed? Oh, may your days, my sweet child, be always as calm and happy as they are at present; may

no clouds appear to darken that which is now so bright and cheering."

Such were the sincere and ardent wishes which animated the bosom of the worthy Mrs. Hardy, but unfortunately they were not doomed to be entirely realized; but where is the mortal who has ever passed through life without experiencing some of the bitters as well as sweets, which form the ingredients of the cup of fate?

"Echo answers—where?"

They were not long in arriving at the old priory ruins, and although it was so early, they beheld old Dorothy standing at the ivy covered porch of the lodge.

Celestia bounded gaily towards her, and the old woman greeted her and Mrs. Hardy with the utmost respect and pleasure, and felt as she always did, highly honoured and gratified by the visit.

They needed no invitation to enter the lodge, where they found old Hannibal seated at the breakfast table, which repast was already prepared, and consisted of some nice light cakes, and milk, of which the dame and her husband warmly pressed Mr. Hardy and her fair companion to partake, and in order that they should not wound the feelings of the good old couple, they did so, Celestia conversing with them all the time in the most affable and affectionate manner. Indeed, pride was as foreign to the mind of Celestia as the least idea of guilt, and she never felt so happy as when she could show her reverence to age or humble worth.

"So, my dear young lady," remarked Dorothy, "you have come to pay another visit to these old ruins?"

"Yes, goody," replied our heroine, "you know that like my kind protector I am very much attached to these venerable remains of antiquity, and I am never so happy as when I am rambling over them. What can be more solemn and impressive than these moss-covered fragments in their decay? Besides, you know I have a much more powerful reason for feeling the deepest and most sacred interest in all that is connected with them; it was here——"

"Very true, miss," deferentially in

terrupted Hannibal, "but I pray you drop that subject, which, I am certain, must make you feel sad and wretched whenever you recur to it."

"No, indeed, my good friends;" replied Celestia, "it does not make me so melancholy as you think. I must ever lament the death of my poor papa, but it was the will of Heaven, and it is my duty to submit to, not to murmur at its wise decrees; besides, I ought to feel more than happy with the blessings I now enjoy. But tell me, have you ever seen anything lately of that singular old gentleman whom, I have heard you say, you once beheld in the ruins, and who disappeared in so mysterious a manner?"

Hannibal and his wife shrugged their shoulders, and looked much more than they chose to speak.

"No, Miss Celestia," said Hannibal, in reply to her question, "nor do we wish, I can assure you. But that he was the same extraordinary being whom your honoured protectors (Heaven prosper them) have stated to me, appeared to Mr. Conignsby many years since, I am satisfied from the description."

"And he appeared to be very aged at that time, I have heard Mr. Conignsby say," observed Mrs. Hardy.

"Yes, madam," replied Hannibal, "as my revered master told me, he seemed to be a man who at that time was fast verging upon ninety;—and as some thirty or perhaps more years have passed since that period, *if he is mortal*, he must be a remarkably old man."

"Ah! bless me," said poor old Dorothy, looking around her, as though she fully expected and dreaded to see the strange object of her terrors close at her elbow, "I shall never forget to my dying day, the time when we saw that very awful being, sitting upon the fragment of the ruins, Hannibal, with his old withered face, and his long pointed chin, with the few straggling grey hairs springing from it, and when he looked up,—oh!—the expression of his little fiery eyes was perfectly awful;—and then his laugh, as he vanished into the earth, I won't be certain whether it was in a flash of lightning, was terrific; oh, miss and madam, saving your presence, I feel convinced, and have ever

since thought so, that that old man could never have been any other than old Beelzebub himself, and——"

"Hush, hush, dame," interrupted her husband, placing his hand before her mouth, "what a strange way you are going on. Mrs. Hardy and Miss Aunville must really begin to think you crazy."

"Ah, Hannibal," retorted the old woman, "and it is not at all times that you are so particularly courageous in speaking on that subject, as you pretend to be at present."

"Well, well, well, dame, we will not argue upon that point. But our young lady and madam have come here' I guess, for amusement, not to be inflicted with the horrors; and very grateful ought we to feel for the honour they pay us."

"And so I do, Hannibal," said the dame, sharply, "and I'm sure that Miss Celestia and Mrs. Hardy will believe me when I say so."

"Yes, yes, goody," said our heroine, smiling, "I am satisfied that it always affords you pleasure to see us, and it cannot be exceeded by that which myself and my kind and beloved Mrs. Hardy feel in return."

"I am sure you are very condescending, my sweet young lady;" was the dame's reply.

"Not at all, my respected Mrs. Dobson," said the fascinating Celestia; "but we will waive that subject, if you please, and return to the one from which we have so far digressed,—the old man, the mysterious man of the priory ruins."

"My dear Celestia," interposed Mrs. Hardy, "why be so importunate upon a subject which cannot but excite the most painful feelings in your breast?"

"Pardon me, my dear madam, but the interest it creates far exceedes anything that you may imagine. I have heard my dear benefactor relate the circumstance of his once meeting, under peculiar circumstances, in this neighbourhood, with a singular being answering the description of the one whom Hannibal and Dorothy state they have seen in these old priory ruins, and the circumstances that transpired (although, of course, he never made me acquainted with them) subsequent to that adventure, have tended to make a powerful and painful, nay, a lasting impression upon his mind; therefore, it is only natural to suppose that I, who have a right, and do feel all that affects him so seriously, with the same solicitude as if he were my own parent, cannot but be anxious to elucidate the mystery. There were, by this remarkable individual, as I have been given to understand, certain warnings and threats held out to Mr. Coningsby which must naturally create alarm, and I'm sure my dear madam, that you will consider it no matter of wonder that I should feel anxious to discover whether this confessed enemy of my revered, my best of earthly friends still exists."

Mrs. Hardy could not deny the truth and force of arguments thus so eloquently advanced and urged, she therefore embraced her fair pupil, and by her looks expressed her approval of all she had said.

"But are you certain," she said, addressing Hannibal and his wife, "that you were not mistaken when you imagined you saw this certainly most extraordinary character, and that it was only some casual wanderer to the ruins?"

"That he might have been only a casual wanderer to the old priory ruins madam," replied Hannibal, "of course, we cannot undertake to say, but that he was there, acted in the manner we have stated, and answered in every respect to the description of the old man who appeared before Mr. Coningsby on the same spot, in so mysterious a manner, many years ago, we are certain."

"Oh, quite positive, Mrs. Hardy," coincided Dorothy.

"It is very strange, to say the least of it," observed Mrs. Hardy.

"So it is, madam," coincided Hannibal and his wife in a breath.

"And you have not seen anything of him since?" asked Celestia.

"Never," was the reply, "although my husband has kept a pretty sharp look out, I can assure you, and you know very well that Mr. Coningsby has done all in his power to unravel the mystery."

"He has," said Mrs. Hardy, "but after all, I cannot help thinking that there must be some mistake. The cir-

cumstances appear so incredible to me, that had I heard them from any other persons, I should have disbelieved them altogether.

"Ah, Mrs. Hardy," said the old woman, again shrugging her shoulders, "depend upon it there is no mistake in all that me and Hannibal have stated. Oh, should the old priory ruins be haunted by some evil spirit, which I have often fancied they were (only Hannibal always laughed at me when I hinted at such a thing), I am sure, notwithstanding all the kindness of my good master, nothing on earth should induce me to abide in the vicinity of them."

"Nonsense, my good dame," said Mrs. Hardy, with a smile, "I am sure you have too much natural good sense to believe in such idle and outrageous superstitions."

"Why, madam," returned Dorothy, "I do not pretend to know much about such matters; I leave that to my betters; but I'm sure any one to have seen that old man as he looked when I and Hannibal saw him, could scarcely have made up their minds to believe him anything human. And then to see how he disappeared. Positively he must have sunk into the earth, for there were no means of his vanishing otherwise, and I am certain, and I told my husband so at the time, that there was a suffocating smell of sulphur when he did so."

Mrs. Hardy and her fair companion could not now help laughing outright, much to the discomfiture and terror of Dorothy Dobson, who once more looked fearfully around her, as if she fully expected to see the old man of the ruins grinning at her elbow, and all the other frightful beings that her timid imagination had conjured up, in attendance.

Her husband, although he was half-inclined to coincide with his simple dame's opinions, seeing the ridicule with which they were viewed by Mrs. Hardy and our heroine, felt ashamed, and hastily observed—

"Come, come, Dorothy, methinks our kind and honoured visitors have heard quite enough upon this subject. That we saw the old man, and that he vanished in a most mysterious manner, is very true, as you say, but to suppose that there are ghosts or hobgoblins, or that these old priory ruins are haunted by them, is perfect nonsense. But, Miss Celestia, and you, madam, I trust will pardon the infirmities of age, especially when you take into consideration that neither my good dame, or myself, are *larned* people.'

Mrs. Hardy and Celestia smiled good humouredly upon the old man's simple speech, and, the repast being over, Celestia took out her drawing implements, and followed by Hannibal, carrying a couple of chairs, quitted the lodge and entered the ruins, where our heroine

MISS CONNINGSBY AND CELESTIA ACCOSTED BY THE GIPSY WOMAN.

having taken her seat on the spot which commanded the most favourable and uninterrupted view of the scene she wished to pourtray, Mrs. Hardy left her to her study, and strolled leisurely among the ruins of the ancient and deeply interesting place.

As we have before said, the morn-

ing was most lovely, and for a short time the attention of Celestia was too deeply engrossed by every contemplation of the various beautiful objects which met her gaze in the direction, to give her undivided attention to the one delightful task she had allotted to herself, but presently she was

No. 5.

completely absorbed in the interest of her subject, and vividly, and it might be almost said magically, her glowing and skilful pencil pursued its office. The pleasure she felt at the thought of the gratification her beloved guardian would experience at the earnest effort to display that talent he had been at such pains to inculcate, urged her on, and quickly each beauty of the landscape was transferred to the paper with the correctness of the most accomplished master. She felt pleased with the success that crowned her efforts, and never had her heart felt more light and happy.

"Oh, how delighted my dear papa," (as the reader is aware she was accustomed to call Mr. Coningsby), "will be to think that his little pupil has so well benefited by his instructions," she said, pursuing her task with increased zeal and spirit; I declare I did not think myself possessed of one quarter of the ability. Yes; there is the pretty old church, with its ivy mantled spire, and its massive gilded vane; there are the green hills which form its back ground, and now I have but to——"

She was interrupted in the midst of this pleasing soliloquy, by hearing a deep sigh near her, and looking up, what was her astonishment at beholding, standing only a short distance from the spot where she was seated, the tall and remarkably fine figure of a gentleman, habited in deep mourning, who was contemplating her with the greatest earnestness, and who from his attitude seemed to be fearful of disturbing her or making her aware of his presence. He appeared to be a man somewhat advanced in life; his countenance was pale, and what rendered it more remarkable was a dreadful scar on his left cheek.

At this unexpected appearance, Celestia in astonishment and alarm started from her seat, and the drawing she had been making, and which had so entirely engrossed her whole thoughts and attention, fell from her hand; but the reader may judge of her terror when no sooner did the stranger catch a distinct view of her features, than he exhibited the most extraordinary emotion and advancing closer towards her, in a voice which thrilled to her very soul, he exclaimed—

"Can it be? Powers of misery, why is this? Girl, girl, thy countenance acts upon my visual organs like a basilisk. God grant I may never more behold thee!"

As the stranger uttered these remarkable words, he clasped his forehead with a frenzied demeanour, and turning away hurried from the spot, and was immediately hidden from the sight by the surrounding ruins.

Celestia completely terrified, uttered a loud scream, and that brought Mrs. Hardy to her, but it was some minutes ere her agitation would permit her to give any explanation as to the cause of her alarm. We need not attempt to depict her astonishment on hearing the account which Celestia had to give. She assisted her into the lodge, where, after a time she became a little more composed, and was enabled to give a more exact account of the behaviour and observations of the stranger, and Hannibal and his wife were not the least amazed or alarmed of the party.

Having somewhat recovered herself, Mrs. Hardy advised that they should return to the abbey without delay, whither Hannibal proposed to accompany them, lest they should be insulted on the road, though, poor old man, he could have rendered but very feeble assistance if they had.

On their arrival at the abbey, and Mr. Coningsby and his sister having been made acquainted with the singular adventure which had taken place, their astonishment and alarm was equal to that of Celestia; but they both expressed an opinion that the stranger was insane.

Various were the conjectures they formed upon the subject, and all were equally unsatisfactory.

"It appears to me to be most probable," said Miss Coningsby, "that Celestia resembles some one who has injured him; for if it was that of a dead friend, he would not have expressed anger."

Mr. Coningsby sighed, and Celestia said, "She was happy to find herself at home, for should she again behold the stranger it would terrify her very much."

When our heroine had retired, Mr. Coningsby and his sister renewed the subject, but it greatly bewildered and agitated them.

"I am determined, if possible, to discover this unaccountable being;" remarked Mr. Coningsby, "for, as we are entirely ignorant of this dear child's connexions, it is not impossible he may have known her mother, or some near relation whom she resembles."

"Ah, my dear brother," replied Miss Coningsby, "that is a most reasonable conjecture of yours, and I would advise that every inquiry should be made in the neighbourhood, for should he have been here for any length of time, his figure, so remarkably fine, as Celestia had described it to be, and that dreadful scar on the cheek, must make him personally known to every person who has seen him once."

"Very true," coincided Mr. Coningsby, "I will set about my task immediately, and I think I cannot do better than to proceed in the first instance to the pricipal inn, the landlord of which may perchance, be able to give me some information respecting the stranger."

Accordingly Mr. Coningsby without delay, ordered his horse, and departed from the abbey on this important errand, pondering in his mind as he rode along, the whole of the remarkable circumstances.

On his arrival at the inn, he had an interview with the landlord, and to him described the person of the stranger as minutely as he could, but the man was unable to afford him any intelligence.

Mr. Coningsby pursued his inquiry, visiting all the different coffee-houses, and the public places in the neighbourhood; he also made inquiries at several of the cottages, thinking that it was not unlikely that some of the humble inmates might have seen such a person, and would be able to give him some clue as to where he might be met with, but he was entirely unsuccessful, and he returned home vexed, disappointed, and plunged into still greater perplexity than before.

Mr. Coningsby was, however, determined not to give up the subject entirely in despair, and he furnished each of his servants with a particular description of the person of the stranger, with instructions to them to keep a constant watch, and if they should happen to recognize any individual that resembled the gentleman, to be particularly cautious whether he went, and to give him prompt notice of the discovery.

He also had an interview with Hannibal Dobson and his wife, and cautioned them as to the manner in which they were to proceed, and to keep a steady look out on the old priory ruins, and closely notice every individual who entered them, and if there should happen to be any one who answered the description of the stranger, not to lose sight of him for a moment, acting with prudence and precaution, and to give him the earliest possible intelligence of the result.

These instructions the old couple promised faithfully to obey, and having made these judicious arrangements, Mr. Coningsby was compelled to wait patiently for what might transpire, and for the unravelment of the mystery. At the same time, the anxiety of himself and his sister continued unabled, and they in vain puzzled their brains to arrive at any fair solution of the singular circumstance.

CHAPTER VI.

FURTHER PARTICULARS.—THE OLD MAN OF THE RUINS.

ALL the plans adopted to discern the stranger proved to be completely ineffectual, and the friends of our young orphan were involved in the same state of mystery as before. Still, they were unremitting in their exertions, and Mr. Coningsby spared neither expense nor trouble to arrive at a satisfactory explanation. He felt confident, from the observations the stranger had made to our heroine, that he was in some way connected with her history, and he was fully determined that there should be no means wanting, on his part, to fathom the facts which were at present involved in so much ambiguity.

He inserted advertisements in the daily journals, giving a brief description of the circumstance, and requesting the individual, should it meet his eye, to come forward and reveal anything he might happen to know appertaining to the fair being whose interests he had so much at heart. But this was attended with no better success than his former efforts; no one answered to the advertisements; no one was seen in the neighbourhood who in the slightest degree answered to the description of the stranger, and all was still involved in the same impenetrable veil of mystery that it had hitherto been. Mr. Coningsby was almost inclined to give up his self-imposed, but welcome task in despair; but the deep affection he bore towards his young *protegé*, and the absorbing interest he felt in all that concerned her, urged him on, and stimulated him to persevere, and he trusted that, notwithstanding he had heretofore been unsuccessful, the time would arrive when fortune would smile more favourably upon him.

He made frequent and early visits, incog, to the old priory ruins, and secreted himself in various parts to watch all who might visit them, but no one did he see who at all resembled the unknown, as described by Celestia.

It was not readily that our heroine could banish the image and the remarkable observations of the stranger from her memory, and the more she reflected upon them, the deeper was the impression they made upon her mind. She had some vague idea of having seen him before, but where she could not imagine, and, if her idea was correct, she felt satisfied that it must have been in her infancy, and before the death of her lamented father. But the fancy was like a broken vision, and as such she was unable to give it form or substance.

The peculiar scar upon his cheek, however, was what impressed her most. Such a scar she was certain she had seen somewhere before, but where she could not now recall to her memory, but it was so coupled with the person of the stranger that she could not by any possible means disconnect them.

She watched the endeavours of her beloved benefactor to discover him with the most intense interest, though from the first moment she never for a moment expected that they would be crowned with success;—for she herself could not but think, as Mr. Coningsby and his sister did, that she either resembled very strongly, or was absolutely related to

some person he knew, and which circumstance, properly developed, might be the means of elucidating such parts of her history and origin as she was too young to be made acquainted with previous to her father's death.

This adventure caused her many painful and melancholy reflections, but the consolation which Mrs. Hardy offered to her was productive of most beneficial effects, and she gradually became more calm and collected.

After a short time she renewed her visits to her favourite haunt, the old priory ruins, but Mr. Coningsby insisted that in addition to Mrs. Hardy, two of the male servants should always accompany her, so, that if any real harm was intended her, she should not be without protection. Sometimes him and his sister attended her themselves, but happy, nay, delighted as she ever was in their society, at present she would rather have dispensed with it, as she had not yet had an opportunity of completing her pet drawing, which she prided herself upon affording an agreeable surprise to them both.

Six weeks had elapsed since the occurrence of the extraordinary event we have recorded, and our heoine and Mrs. Hardy, followed by the two men servants, bent their steps towards the old priory ruins. Poor old Dorothy had but just recovered from a severe attack of illness, and it was more to see her than to complete her drawing, in fact, that Celestia had been so anxious to revisit the ruins.

It was now the " merry month of May," and jocund were the smiles that all bountiful and prolific nature wore. The verdure had its brightest green, the sky its clearest blue; not a cloud to mar its beauty, to detract from the glorious radiance of the sun. The air was rich with sweets, and brought health and cheerfulness to those who inhaled it.

Oh! the bliss of roaming in the green fields, and inhaling the breath, beneath the bright blue canopy of heaven, in " the merry month of May!"

These were the feelings, the sentiments of Celestia, the feelings and sentiments which animated her breast, and imparted elasticity and playfulness to all her actions, as they proceeded on their journey on the afternoon of which we are writing, and Mrs. Hardy could not but fully participate in them, and wish from her heart that such happiness as she then experienced would never fail to attend her young charge.

They found old dame Dobson alone, her husband being called away from home for a short time upon business. She was looking much better than they had expected to find her, and she greeted them with her usual honest cordiality.

"Ah, my dear young lady," she said, addressing our heroine, "it delights me to see you looking so well and happy and Heaven send that you may always continue to be so."

"Thank you, my good dame, for your kind wishes," replied Celestia, "and believe me I am equally glad to see you so far restored to health. You must take care of yourself, goody."

"Yes, child, yes," said the old woman in a half abstracted manner, "and yet——"

She hesitated.

"Yet what, dame?" inquired Mrs. Hardy, eagerly; "a sudden gloom has come over you, and you are not looking so well as you did when we first entered."

"Do not notice me, dear ladies," said the old woman, in a confused manner, "perhaps I am silly for giving way to such feelings, but——"

"Something has happened, dame," interrupted our heroine, "I am certain there has from your looks and your observations. What is it? Do not be afraid to speak."

"Ah, miss," faltered out the old woman, "I am afraid that many of us are destined to experience a great deal more trouble than we have hitherto done, and—and—I am fearful that I and Hannibal will be compelled to leave the old lodge."

"Leave it, dame! what for?"

"I fear that there are some very bad characters lurk about these old priory ruins, and that me and my poor old husband will be murdered in our beds, one of these nights."

"My good woman," said Mrs. Hardy, "what is your reason for entertaining such a fearful idea?"

"Oh, we have had such a fright," said poor old Dorothy.

"A fright!" said Celestia, "when, my good dame?"

"Only last night, miss."

"Last night?"

"Last night as ever was, miss, and I believe that Hannibal has gone to the abbey to make Mr. Coningsby acquainted with the facts."

"Compose yourself, my good woman," said Mrs. Hardy, "and tell us what has happened."

"Yes, yes, I will, madam," replied the old woman, "as well as I can. Lor! I verily believe I have been out of my seven senses ever since. The old man of the ruins has been here again, and —oh dear!"

Celestia's utmost curiosity and anxiety were now excited, but Mrs. Hardy affected to treat the observations of the old woman with incredulity.

"You must have been dreaming, dame," she remarked.

"Oh, no, madam, me and Hannibal were both perfectly awake, I can assure you," answered Dorothy.

"But what was it that so alarmed you?"

"Aye, tell us, good dame," said our heroine.

"Well, I was going to do so, miss, but, bless my heart, I declare I am almost out of my wits. Well then, you must know, that last night as ever was, while me and Hannibal were sitting in this very room, and talking over the events of the past, as we often amuse ourselves by doing, suddenly we heard a tremendous crash, as if all the old ruins were falling about our heads. Oh, it was so awful that I cannot describe it. We both started to our feet, and, as you may be sure, stared about us with amazement, but for a minute or two could perceive nothing, as in our alarm we had upset the candle and extinguished the light, and it was quite dark, dark as pitch, for it was nearly half past ten o'clock."

"Well, well;" said Mrs. Hardy, impatiently.

"Pardon me, madam," returned Dorothy, "but you must give me time, or I cannot proceed. Well, as I was before saying, it was quite dark, and neither I nor Hannibal could see each other, but

I'm certain we were both very much frightened, as any one must be under such circumstances, and were unable to speak to each other. Before we could in any degree recover ourselves, there came another crash, still louder than the first, and then my husband advanced towards the door, saying he was certain that the greater portion of the old priory ruins had fallen down, and that it was necessary to see the extent of the danger to which we were exposed; but bless your souls, my dear ladies, when we both of us looked out, nothing had happened, and the ruins were just the same as you see them now."

"Certainly, so I expected;" observed Mrs. Hardy, with a smile; "you and your husband, Dorothy, suffered your imaginations to lead you astray."

"Indeed we did not, Mrs. Hardy, and so you will say, if you hear me out; but, of course, it is useless for me to say any more, if you do not believe me."

"Pray, proceed, Dorothy," said Celestia, whose interest and curiosity were excited;—"we do not doubt you, but, of couse, you will acknowledge yourself that, as far as you have told us of the story, it is a most remarkable one."

"It is indeed, miss," returned the old woman, "and so you will say when you have heard the whole of it. Well, we returned to the parlour, and relighted the candle, and for a few minutes all was quiet, and I and Hannibal asked each other what could have been the cause of the singular noises we had heard, but without being able to come to any satisfactory conclusion. Hannibal, however, took down the old fowling-piece, which we always keeps loaded over the mantel-piece, in order to defend us in the best manner he were able should any danger threaten, and he had scarcely done so, when, as I am a living woman, there came a third crash still louder than the other two, and which shook us completely out of our seats; I could fairly feel the old lodge totter again."

"Proceed, dame," said our heroine; "what happened afterwards?"

"Why, miss," answered the old woman, "we both of us turned our eyes towards the casement, and sure as I live, there we beheld glaring in upon us, with one of the most hideous and malicious grins it is possible to imagine, the countenance of—but I cannot go on any further."

"Nonsene, Dorothy," returned Mrs. Hardy, "pray finish your extraordinary story; surely you have nothing to fear now."

"Aye, dame," added Celestia, "do not hesitate, after having excited our curiosity to such a degree. What was it you saw?"

"Oh, Miss Celestia, as I hope to be saved, the countenance of that same frightful and mysterious old man whom we had before seen in the old priory ruins."

"Is it possible?"

"It is true, miss, and I'm sure you will not imagine for a moment that I would attempt to impose upon you with a falsehood."

"No—no, my good dame;" returned Celestia; "neither I nor my dear friend here entertain such an idea, for we are well aware that it would be rendering you the greatest injustice. But do satisfy our curiosity."

"Yes, miss," continued Dorothy, "there stood the old wizard (for I feel certain he is nothing else) as plainly as I see you now, gazing full upon me and my husband, with an expression of countenance that was truly awful to behold. I thought I should have sunk through the floor with horror, and Hannibal was so surprised (and I believe alarmed, as well he might be) that he could not speak a word, or move a step; and there the frightful old wretch continued to stand, grinning upon us, and shaking his fist menacingly at us. At length Hannibal having somewhat recovered himself, called aloud upon the old man, and demanded to know his business, at the same time levelling the gun at him, and threatening to fire if he did not answer, though bless you, I do not think he would have done so even in self defence. But the strange being only laughed at him as if in mockery and defiance, and slowly moved away from before the casement. Hannibal's curiosity and anxiety overcame his fears, and although I tried to prevent him, it was all to no purpose; so out he rushed, shouldering the gun, and by the light of the moon beheld the singular being, sitting cross legged upon one of the huge pieces of stone, like a frightful old goblin as he is, and his countenance bearing the came expression as it did when we saw it at the parlour casement. In order to alarm him, Hannibal fired his gun off in the air, but lor love you! there he sat as composedly as possible, and made the place ring again with his wild and derisive laughter. I don't know how my husband could ever muster the courage to do so, but he advanced towards him, and got to within only a few paces of him, when as I live, while Hannibal was still in the act of gazing at him, he was gone—vanished into the earth like lightning, as he did on the occasion when we first saw him, and Hannibal returned into the house completely thunderstruck at the extraordinary and unaccountable adventure."

"Most wonderful," ejaculated Celestia, who had listened most anxiously and attentively to the singular narrative the old woman had been relating.

"It is indeed, so extraordinary and improbable," said Mrs. Hardy, "that had it been told to me by any other person than yourself, Dorothy, I would not have believed it."

"You may depend upon it, madam," returned the dame, "that every word I have uttered is perfectly true, and I'm sure I do not know how in the world I shall ever be able to pass another night in the old place."

"Do not alarm yourself, Dorothy," said Mrs. Hardy, "for I do not think that this strange being intends you or your husband any harm, though certainly his appearing to you in such a suspicious manner is sufficiently alarming. But the whole affair will, no doubt, be strictly investigated by Mr. Coningsby, and every precaution adopted to guard you against any threatened danger. You still think that you have not suffered your fears to exaggerate the facts?"

"Oh, I am quite positive, Mrs. Hardy, why should you doubt me?"

"I do not doubt you, my good woman; but still you must expect that such an extraordinary account must naturally excite considerable surprise, and give cause for much speculation."

"Very true, madam," coincided Dorothy, "but when you see my husband he will fully substantiate all that I have said, and then you will, I dare say, be satisfied. It is quite impossible, under all the circumstances, that we could both of us have been mistaken."

"Right, Dorothy," remarked our heroine, "I perfectly agree with you, and am completely lost in amazement."

"I don't wonder at it, miss, and it has so puzzled and frightened me, that it will be a long time before I shall be myself again."

"What the motives of this remarkable being are for acting in such a manner, I cannot conceive," observed Mrs. Hardy; "but the suddenness of his disappearance is still more wonderful than all."

"Yes, it is that which most astonished both me and Hannibal," said the old woman; "we have not resided here so long but we have taken good care to examine the old ruins, minutely, and there certainly is no place where he could escape from sight so instantaneously. To me it has all the appearance of magic."

Dorothy had scarcely done speaking when her husband returned home, and being requested by Mrs. Hardy and Celestia to do so, gave his version of the singular story, in which he fully corroberated every word that his wife had uttered, and which fully satisfied them that it was perfectly correct.

"Ah," added old Hannibal, "it is a most wonderful adventure, is it not ladies? I declare it has almost frightened my poor dame out of her senses, and I'm sure it is not at all to be wondered at when you come to take everything into consideration."

"Very true, Hannibal," coincided Mrs Hardy, "and I really do not know what to say upon the subject at all. It has so completely taken me by surprise."

"And Mr. Coningsby, I can assure you, madam, is no less astonished and bewildered than yourself," returned the old man.

"Oh, then you have seen my beloved guardian this morning, good Hannibal?" said Celestia.

"Yes, miss," replied Hannibal, "I thought it was best, not to lose any time in making him acquainted with what had happened, lest any danger should threaten him, and he had before told me all about the meeting he had had with the old man of the ruins many years ago, and I well knew that any particulars I might have to communicate to his honour respecting that very singular and unaccountable being, must be of the deepest interest to him. No doubt, he will, as he says, make every possible inquiry he can, in order to elucidate the extraordinary mystery.

"But what is your opinion upon the subject, Hannibal?" asked Mrs. Hardy.

"Why, upon my word, madam," returned Hannibal, "I do not know what to say. The more I reflect upon it, the more I am puzzled. What surprises me most of all, is the manner in which the ancient man could contrive to escape. I am satisfied that I never had my eyes off him for a moment—the moon too, was shining most brightly at the time, and yet he vanished from my gaze like a flash of lightning."

"And you say that you are quite certain there are no means of effecting an escape near the spot where you saw the old man disappear?" said Mrs. Hardy.

"Bless your soul, no, ma'am," answered Hannibal, "but if you please you and miss can judge for yourselves, and as Miss Celestia I see has come prepared to execute her drawing in the ruins, it will not be putting her or you, ma'am, I dare say to any inconvenience.

Our heroine and her preceptress perfectly agreed with this, and Hannibal led the way into the ruins, pointing out the exact spot where the old man had disappeared from his sight, and which, as he had stated, possessed not the least facility of escape.

The whole circumstance was involved in the deepest mystery, and they were neither of them at present enabled to form what they conceived to be a reasonable conjecture upon it.

When Celestia remembered the strange adventure which had also occurred when in the old ruins, her feelings of astonishment were doubly excited, and she could not help thinking that they were in some degree connected. They both made the strongest impression upon her mind, and she fully hoped that a short time would serve to develope the facts.

They having examined this spot and the other part of the ruins without being able to discover any secret place of disappearance, and Hannibal having returned into the lodge, Celestia set herself to her task ; Mrs. Hardy in the meantime taking a stroll over different parts of the old priory ruins, reflecting upon what she had just heard, and being likewise unwilling to interrupt our heroine in that task she was well aware she was so anxious to complete. Some time elapsed without anything worthy of mention occurring, when suddenly Mrs. Hardy was startled by hearing the tread of a hasty footstep behind her, and thinking that it was probably Celestia, she turned round, and her astonishment may be easily imagined on beholding the retreating form of an aged man, whose silvery hair was floating wildly about his shoulders, and who in every respect answered the description given of the old man of the ruins. In a moment, however, he turned an abrupt angle, and he was hidden from Mrs. Hardy's sight in a manner which she could scarcely imagine, and which certainly had about it all the appearance of magic.

She was now quite satisfied (if she had entertained any doubt before), that Hannibal Dobson and his wife had not been mistaken, and her amazement was increased tenfold, for it was impossible for her to form the least conjecture who this old man could be, and what his motives were for the conduct he was pursuing. The most probable idea, at present, however, seemed to be that he was some unfortunate madman, though where he came from and whither he went, no one at present to whom he had been described could tell.

While Mrs. Hardy was still engaged in these reflections, she perceived Celestia hastily approaching towards her, and it was quite clear, from the disorder of her manner, that something had taken place to excite her feelings.

"Oh, madam," she exclaimed, when she had come up to her, "I have seen him."

"Seen him?" repeated Mrs. Hardy, though she had little doubt that she meant the same person whom she had herself just seen, "who do you mean, child?"

"That mysterious being whom old

Hannibal and his wife tells us appeared to them in so singular a manner last night," returned our heroine.

"And so have I Celestia."

"You, my dear madam?"

"Yes, my love; but do not alarm yourself unnecessarily, as I see you are inclined to do."

"When did you see him, my kind friend?"

"Not five minutes ago."

"Ah! and which way did he go?"

THE MYSTERIOUS MAN OF THE RUINS APPEARS TO MR. CONINGSBY.

"He darted swiftly past me, and in a manner most extraordinary and incredible for one of his apparent great age, and disappeared behind yonder angle. But was he near you, Celestia?"

"Oh, yes," replied the latter; "he was as close to me, and gazing as full upon me, as I now do upon you."

"Did he speak to you?"

"Yes; but what the few words he said to me were, in the confusion of the moment, I have forgotten; they were something, however, to the effect that I was marked by Fate to experience many sorrows; and then having fixed upon me such a look at I shall never banish from my memory, he darted from the spot, shaking his hand menacingly at me."

"Well, I am quite bewildered," said Mrs. Hardy," "but let us see about returning to the abbey, as I do not suppose that you feel inclined to pursue your task any further to day."

"Oh, no, this adventure has rendered me perfectly incapable of doing so," said our heroine. "Who this aged man can be, and what can be the motives he has in view, I am at a total loss to form even the slightest conjecture."

"The only conclusion I can yet arrive at, is, that he is deranged in his intellect," remarked Mrs. Hardy.

"It is altogether a mystery, it seems impossible to solve. If this is the same being who appeared to my dear benefactor on the morning of his union, he must indeed be an aged man; but that seems to me to be scarcely possible."

They now returned to the lodge, where they found Hannibal and his wife conversing together; but they arose respectfully on their entrance, and the former said:—

"Ah, ladies, are you going to leave us so soon? But you seem agitated; I hope nothing has occurred to you in the ruins to alarm you."

Mrs. Hardy in a few words related what had taken place, to which Hannibal and his wife listened with much attention and interest.

"Dear me," said Dorothy, "all this is very strange and alarming; I declare, I shall never be able to continue to reside near these old priory ruins."

"Nonsense, my good dame," said Mrs. Hardy, "you would surely never act so imprudently as to resign the kindness of Mr. Coningsby, because forsooth some old wandering maniac has taken a fancy to visit these ruins."

"I am truly grateful to Mr. Coningsby for his kindness, my dear madam," replied Dorothy, "and I should be very much hurt if I thought that he could ever believe to the contrary. He is the best earthly friend myself and my poor old Hannibal here possess in the world; but then you know ma'am it's very annoying to be kept in this perpetual state of alarm."

"Oh, indeed, I do not think that you have any real cause for fear, good dame," said Celestia; "it is not likely that this singular being should intend you or your husband any harm."

"I don't know that, miss," replied Dorothy, "his conduct last night looked very suspicious, to say the least of it. And if he should turn out to be a madman, as Mrs. Hardy imagines him to be, there is no knowing what the extent of his mischief might be, if he had the opportunity."

"Come, come Dorothy," interposed Hannibal, who was afraid that his wife would permit her tongue to run faster than was prudent; "we must not talk in this manner, but leave everything to Mr. Conignsby's superior judgment, and no doubt he will not be long in making some discovery which will lead to the unravelment of this very remarkable and perplexing business."

"Well, I sincerely hope that he may, and that if this old man intends any mischief, he may be thwarted in his designs."

"What possible reason can he have for entertaining any malicious feelings towards Mr. Coningsby, whose benevolence and kindness of heart has rendered him universally beloved?" said Mrs. Hardy.

"None whatever," returned Hannibal, "at any rate he must be a very bad man if he does. But there are yet means of guarding against any evils which may threaten, and this strange unknown may yet be compelled to explain his conduct, and who he is, and what are really his designs. You may depend upon it that I will keep a sharp look out for him, since he has done me the honour to pay me such particular notice; and if he contrives to get the better of old Hannibal Dobson, it is very surprising to me, that's all I can say about the matter."

Dorothy shook her head doubtfully, and she seemed to be far from satisfied. After a few more observations, Celestia and Mr. Hardy took their leave, and returned to the abbey, accompanied by the two attendants.

On their return home they found Mr. Coningsby and his sister in a state of considerable excitement, and conversing upon the subject of the information which Hannibal Dobson had that morning given them.

They soon perceived from the expression of the countenances of Celestia and Mrs. Hardy, that something else had happened more than they were acquainted with, and they eagerly inquired the cause; and when they were furnished with the particulars of what had occurred to Celestia and her preceptress in the old priory ruins, their astonishment and perplexity were even greater than before.

"This must be thoroughly investigated,' said Mr. Coningsby, "there is more in the conduct of this mysterious man than at first appears to the eye. The place of his concealment must be discovered; at least, every pains must be taken to endeavour to do so. You do not recollect the precise words he uttered to you, Celestia?"

"No, papa," she replied, "but at any rate they implied either a threat or a prediction of future trouble to befall me, and he looked quite hideously upon me, while he addressed me."

"Most unaccountable behaviour," said Mr. Coningsby.

"It is indeed," coincided his sister, "why this old man should appear in such a threatening way to you or to our dear Celestia, for it is not possible that either of you could have given him any offence, or cause for malice, I am at a perfect loss to conjecture."

"You cannot be more astonished and bewildered, my dear sister, than I am; but it is a great pity that Celestia did not raise an alarm, so that he might have been secured on the spot."

"His departure was so sudden," replied our heroine, "that before I could recover my surprise and confusion he was gone, and Mrs. Hardy will inform you that he disappeared equally as suddenly from her."

This Mrs. Hardy corroborated, and related the particulars as they have been described to the reader.

"Well, the more I hear of this singular individual the more I am astonished and perplexed," remarked Mr. Coningsby. "His conduct is perfectly impenetrable, but still I trust that the time will come when it will be fully and satisfactorily explained. A sharp look out must be kept for him in the neighbourhood, and every precaution made use of to guard against any evil designs he may have in contemplation, but I do not think it is likely that he will long be able to escape detection."

"But do you actually think it is the same old man who appeared to you, under such peculiar circumstances, many years ago?" asked Miss Coningsby.

Mr. Coningsby sighed as he made answer. "From the description given of him, I can have very little doubt that it is. But I dare say it will not be very long before I shall have an opportunity of gratifying my curiosity upon that subject."

"Why you say that he appeared to be a very aged man at that period," said Miss Coningsby.

"True, and so he most undoubtedly was."

"We'll then, since so many years have elapsed, it is not at all probable that he is still living."

"It is not impossible, sister, have we not had numerous instances of the most extraordinary longevity?"

"Very true. However, it is useless to speculate upon the subject, for it is one upon which we cannot arrive at any satisfactory conclusion. One thing however, I think it would be advisable to do, and that is to to keep your proceedings as secret as possible, so that this strange being may chance to be taken off his guard, and made to render every satisfactory explanation of himself."

"That is a suggestion well worthy of attention," remarked Mr. Coningsby, "and it shall be acted upon exactly; and I should also advise Celestia, for the present, not to visit the priory ruins."

"Your wishes are law, papa," replied our heroine; and yet she could not help experiencing a feeling of poignant regret, seeing that the drawing she had set her mind on, must again be delayed.

CHATTER VI.

DOUBT AND UNCERTAINTY.—A JOUENEY. THE SECOND MEETING WITH THE STRANGER.

THIS adventure afforded them all food for much reflection, but without their being able to arrive at any satisfactory conclusion. Celestia coupled it with the former singular event which had occurred to her in the old ruins, and the remarkable words the stranger had made use of on beholding her, and they made an impression upon her mind which was of the most extraordinary description. That she was destined to undergo some extraordinary trials and vicissitudes, calm and happy as her days had hitherto been, she could not help fervently believing, and it was in vain that Mrs. Hardy did all she could to divest her mind of this apprehension; it was too firmly engrafted there to be easily eradicated.

Mr. Coningsby caused a strict watch to be kept in the neighbourhood, and he paid frequent visits himself to the ruins, but he saw nothing of the unknown, neither did Hannibal or his wife, and when several weeks had elapsed without anything else occurring, they began to think that either the old man was dead, or that he had repented of his extravagant and outrageous conduct, and would not venture to annoy them again.

Celestia again resumed her visits to the ruins, and set about her task with such increased zeal, that in a few days she had completed her drawing, in which she had far surpassed what she had expected to do. When she presented it to her amiable benefactor, he gazed at it with wonder and admiration; and although the heart of our heroine fluttered with delight to find she had so well succeeded, she felt confused at the high encomiuns which both him and his sister bestowed upon it, and which she considered was so much more than it merited.

We have before stated that Sungrove Abbey was visited by a select circle of friends, the urbanity of Mr. Coningsby and his sister having made them the objects of universal esteem—while their extensive benevolence rendered them a blessing to the poor of the neighbourhood in which they lived. No persons could possibly be looked up to with greater admiration and esteem, and certainly no individuals more richly deserved it.

But it will not be wondered that our heroine, now in the full bloom of her innocence and beauty, should, be the chief magnet of attraction at the abbey, and the more admirers did she obtain as the loveliness of her mind as well as the charms of her person and manners more fully expanded themselves.

Among others with whom frequently exchanged visits was the family of Sir Eustace Aubrey, whose lady felt the full dignity of her ancient pedigree, but was in other respects a most amiable and affable woman.

Sir Eustace, though her first cousin, was not so tenacious of his birth, he was a perfect good-tempered bottle companion, and a staunch fox-hunter—he readily acknowledged merit, even without a long pedigree to recommend it, and consequently he and Mr. Coningsby soon became friends, though the latter was adverse to his two favourite enjoyments.

Sir Eustace and his lady, as we before observed, were the only remaining descendants of a most ancient and wealthy family, and the only children of two brothers, who being anxious to preserve their ancient race uncontaminated by any other, determined the union of their two children before they were out of their cradles, and contrary to the usual result of these preconcerted matches, the young people became attached to each other from infancy, and at the age of twenty, Miss Aubrey gave her unreluctant hand to her cousin, it being the day that he completed his twenty-first birthday.

At the period to which our narrative refers, Sir Aubrey and his lady had enjoyed twenty-three years of connubial bliss, and their union had been blessed with two children, one son and a daughter, and the dread of losing the former was the only thing that embittered their enjoyments, as in case of his death their immense estates would go to a very distant branch, known very little more than by name.

Young Collingwood Aubrey, was by his mother indulged in every caprice to which childhood is prone, and let the mischief be ever so fatal, no one dare to offer to correct him in it. He had tired three tutors before he was ten years old, and had gained nothing by their instructions, for they were forbidden to use any coercion, or even to make him take a lesson, unless he liked it.

However, shocked at his lack of knowledge, as of course could only be expected, when almost too late to apply a remedy, a gentleman of high attainments and moral worth, was engaged at a high salary, in order, if possible, to produce a favourable change; and it was remarkable the progress which his pupil made in a short time, for he possessed a good understanding, which only needed cultivation, and being naturally good-natured and affable, he received the instructions of his tutor with avidity.

Miss Aubrey was one year her brother's junior, beautiful and accomplished, and possessed of the most amiable qualifications of disposition; she was no sooner introduced to Celestia, than a mutual friendship sprung up between them, and young Collingwood Aubrey could not gaze upon the lovely girl with any other feelings than those of the most ardent admiration.

Lady Aubrey soon noticed this with alarm, and endeavoured to check it as much as possible, by not allowing her son and our heroine to be in each other's company more frequently than could be avoided.

As has been before intimated, Lady Aubrey possessed the whole stock of family pride; she consided her descent so superior to any other in the country, that she looked forward to uniting her children to the most ancient families in the empire. Oh, the foolish pride of birth! How many evils has it been productive of!

Collingwood Aubrey had now arrived at an age to form an establishment, and his mother had fixed upon a young lady whose high birth and great connexions, she confessed, would not disgrace her own.

The lady to be thus honoured was the only daughter of the Earl Bathurst, one of the oldest titles in the peerage; her person was beautiful, her disposition amiable, she was highly accomplished, and had a very large fortune, independent of that the earl would give her.

The young people had never seen each other, and were entirely ignorant of their friends' good intentions, who hoped a mutual liking would take place, as the earl had determined not to bias his daughter in her choice of a partner for life.

The majority of Collingwood would soon take place, and it was determined to celebrate it with the greatest splendour. All the *elite* of the fashionable world for miles around were to be present, and Mr. Coningsby and his sister, and Celestia were included in the invitations.

Great preparations had for some time been going on for this approaching *fete*, which it was intended should continue a week. The first day a grand ball was to take place, for which several hundred tickets were issued, and this was to introduce the son of one family to the daughter of the other; but the disappointment and chagrin of Lady Aubrey may be imagined, when, on the eve of the approaching ball, a letter arrived to defer their visit for three days. Her vexation was greatly increased by the mirth of the baronet, who ridiculed all premeditated matches, and almost wished that this might never take place.

At length the long anticipated day arrived, and it was ushered in with the greatest spirit. The invitation to the *fete* obliged Mr. Coningsby to defer a visit he intended to his estate in the North of England; he had proposed making it a tour of pleasure for the sake of his sister and Celestia. Indeed this visit caused no small bustle at the abbey.

Celestia had never yet been present at any festival, and this was upon such an extraordinary occasion that Miss Coningsby was uncommonly anxious as to the personal appearance of her young favourite. The finest muslins and laces were taken from the trunks, to be made up for the occasion, and with much entreaty Mr. Coningsby consented to her wearing some of the pearls, thinking them much too fine for so young a girl.

Celestia anticipated the enjoyment of the ball with the most unbounded pleasure; in fact, her head was half turned; in vain her excellent protector urged the observance of her usual lessons; she was incapable of attending to anything except dancing; her harp-strings were continually breaking, the pianoforte out of tune, and her colours and her pencils unfit for use. Her dress had no share in her distractions, she was perfectly indifferent to everything else but the ball, and when the day arrived she had hardly patience with her maid's precision in placing every part of her dress; but when she entered the library where Mr. Coningsby waited to attend them, he could not help agreeing with his sister that Celestia's figure was the most charming he had ever seen.

They quitted the abbey, and when the carriage drove up to the elegant mansion, Celestia was quite lost in wonder, and was almost unconscious of being presented to Lady Aubrey.

And great was the gratification of Mr. Coningsby on this occasion; he felt the pleasure of a fond parent at observing the look of admiration with which Lady Aubrey contemplated our heroine, and the ardent friendship with which she was greeted by Miss Aubrey.

Miss Aubrey introduced her to a party of young ladies about her own age; but as soon as the common place compliments were over, she was again lost in silent admiration of a scene so new to her. And truly a magnificent scene it was, brilliant beyond all description.

Collingwood Aubrey was completely charmed with the appearance and manners of our heroine, and sought every opportunity of being in her company, engaging her to dance, much to the mortification of his mother, who almost regretted that she had invited the young orphan; however, she was prudent enough to conceal her real feelings on that occasion, although she resolved to lecture her son severely upon the subject on the first opportunity.

Celestia was far from being displeased with the attentions of Collingwood Aubrey, who possessed many attractions, both of person and manners. Indeed Collingwood was a young man whom few could gaze upon (especially a young and sensitive girl) with any other feelings but those of admiration. He was tall and well-proportioned, very handsome, if a fine open forehead, piercing black eyes, and a fine set of teeth, may be allowed to constitute manly beauty.

Time fled rapidly on till the supper-rooms were thrown open, a band playing the whole time. Several fashionable dances took place after supper, and the ball was continued with the greatest spirit till daylight in the morning, when those who were not guests for the whole time of the *fete,* departed to their respective homes.

Mr. Coningsby's party had been strongly invited to be of the former number, but as the distance to the abbey was so short, they preferred returning home, particularly as the next day was set apart entirely for rest after the fatigue of the ball.

It was past seven o'clock ere Celestia sought her couch, but the unusual fatigue she had undergone soon closed her eyes, and the pleasures of the day were renewed to her in dreams of the most lively and interesting description.

The next day was one of the greatest enjoyment to the poor people, for whom the most hospitable provision had been made, and for their accommodation, a large temporary building, and a number of tents were erected on the most open part of the park. Men, women, and children were regaled on the best, and no restraint was placed on these innocent and jocund amusements. The day passed away in the most agreeable manner, and our heroine was, if possible more delighted with the rural festivity of the scene, while Collingwood Aubrey was if possible, more marked in his attentions towards her than before.

The third day's entertainments were to consist of a masked ball, and Mr. and Miss Coningsby and Celestia had been prevailed on to take up their abode at the mansion till the day after the ball, requesting then to be excused the remaining amusements, as our heroine was yet too young and unaccustomed to late hours, to be able to continue them without endangering her health.

Collingwood Aubrey could not help evincing his regret and disappointment when he heard this, for such was the impression which Celestia had made upon his mind, that he could not bear the thought of being deprived of her presence, and her amiable society.

Mr. Coningsby also desired that they might be excused assuming a character, or even wearing a domino, and this was also complied with.

How completely astonished was Celestia with the novelty of this scene.

She had never been able to conceive anything at all approaching it. The decorations of the first ball had caused her infinite surprise, but this far surpassed it. The most exquisite taste was displayed throughout the house and pleasure-gardens; every room assumed a character; one in particular was fitted up in the Chinese style, because it opened with large folding doors to a vista terminating by a pagoda.

For this night a Chinese bridge was raised, over which you passed to the pagoda, in which was placed an appropriate band. The room was hung as well as the sides of the avenue with transparencies representing different customs and amusements of the Chinese; this room and avenue had no other light; trees which surrounded the pagoda, were thickly hung with different coloured lamps.

Celestia could not control the pleasure which the surrounding scene excited in her bosom, and the variety of characters which sported around; but her attention was more particularly attracted to one character, which was that of a gipsey, who seemed to regard her with the deepest interest and earnestness, and at length seeing that Celestia was alone (she having strolled from Mr. Coningsby and his sister) she approached her, and laying her hand upon her arm, much to the astonishment of our heroine, the palm of whose hand she had first minutely examined, she commenced singing the following words:—

Damsel, turn thee not away,
  Nor think the words I speak are wrong;
Mark me, there will come a day,
  When thou'lt remember well my song.

Though pleasure now shines on thy path,
  Will it last for ever—no!
All the bliss thou at present hath,
  Shall be changed to bitter woe.

See—the clouds are gathering fast,
  Hark, the voice of destiny cries
"Girl, thy joys will soon be past,
  "Thy laugh of mirth be turned to sighs."

Then damsel, mark well what I say,
  Though thou laughest now in glee;
Not far distant is the day,
  When none shall be more sad than thee."

The gipsey ceased, and releasing her hold of Celestia's arm, hurried away, and was soon lost among the variety of other characters at the further end of the room, leaving our heroine overwhelmed with amazement. There was something so singular in the words and demeanour of the gipsey, that she could not banish them from her memory, but still thinking that it was only one of her friends who had played this little joke off upon her, she laughed at her folly in having for a moment thought seriously on it, and hastened to rejoin Mr. and Miss Coningsby, who were in one of the other apartments.

As she was about to emerge from the folding doors, the tall figure of a man, wearing a black mask and domino suddenly appeared before her, and no sooner beheld her than he uttered an exclamation of surprise, and started back a few paces as is he had encountered something frightful.

Celestia was terrified, and could scarcely repress a scream, but her emotion was increased tenfold when the man suddenly raising his mask, whether by accident or design she could not tell, she beheld the well remembered scar which convinced her that it was the strange unknown whom she had seen twice before.

She now uttered a loud cry, and the stranger replacing his mask, and making use of some words which did not meet her ear, he rushed from the spot, just as Mr. Coningsby who had, accompanied by his sister, came in search of Celestia, entered by an opposite door.

They quickly approached her, and seeing her pale and trembling, they thought perhaps, that the fatigue and excitement of the scene had overcome her, and they therefore eagerly inquired what was the matter with her, and if she was not well. At first Celestia could not return any answer, but at length she briefly informed them what had happened to alarm her, and Mr Coningsby and his sister, having succeeded in tranquilizing her, led her back to the principal ball-room, and having committed her to the care of his sister and some other friends, he proceeded to make a search in the different apartments after the stranger. But this was a fruitless task, for there were many who answered to his description, and he knew not which to address himself to; besides, it was most probable that the unknown had quitted the mansion. He returned to Celestia, whom he was glad to see had quite recovered her composure, and seemed so totally captivated with the gaiety of the scene, as not to bestow another thought upon the incident which had so recently occurred to her.

Mr. Coningsby, however, could not help reflecting upon upon it for some time afterwards, and the longer he did so, the more satisfied he felt that the unknown must have some knowledge of Celestia, or else that she resembled some person who was connected with him, and had done him some injury, and he was therefore the more anxious to meet with him, thinking that it probably might lead to some important discovery.

At length daylight peeped in upon the revellers, and the guests departed to their distant homes, whilst those of the mansion retired to rest.

CHAPTER VII.

THE JOURNEY AND FRESH ADVENTURES.

IT was some days after their return to the abbey, ere Celestia quite recovered from the fatigue she had undergone at the fête, and she thought on the novelty of all she had seen there with most lively sensations of pleasure; still she could not help, at times, reflecting most seriously on the words which had been sung by the gipsey, and her encounter with the remarkable unknown.

Mr. Coningsby had renewed his inquiries in the neighbourhood, in the hope of being enabled to discover whether the stranger resided in it, but without success, and he had also particularly described him, and the circumstances under which they had seen him to Sir Eustace and his lady, for the scar on his cheek must render him easy to be recognised, but they had no knowledge of such a person, and certainly they had not invited any one answering his description to the fête.

Collingwood Aubrey was so fascinated with the intrinsic and personal charms of our heroine, that he could think of nothing else, talk of nothing else, much to the annoyance of his mother, and the displeasure of Sir Eustace. They neither attempted to deny that she was a very lovely girl, and gave promise of future excellence, but that she was yet too young to allow of any decided opinion of her character. They also lectured him severely for what they were pleased to denominate his extravagant folly, in devoting so much of his mind to a young girl who could never be any thing more more to him than a slight acquaintance. Collingwood, however, was not to be so easily restrained, and what increased the vexation of his mother, business still compelled the Earl Bathurst and his daughter to remain in London, and consequently the introduction of the young people to each other was still delayed.

Collingwood was determined to lose no opportunity of seeing Celestia as often as possible, and he was always ready when Sir Eustace rode over to the abbey on a visit to his friend, Mr. Coningsby, to accompany him; and the more he beheld of that beauteous girl, the greater became his admiration, and the more eagerly did he covet her society.

Soon after the *fête* Miss Coningsby and Celestia having gone out together for a morning walk, Mr. Coningsby was left alone, but he had not long been so when Lord Everside was announced.

"Mr. Coningsby," said his lordship, after having taken a seat "I am come a petitioner."

"Indeed, my good friend?" said Mr. Coningsby, "and pray upon what subject."

"The ladies," answered his lordship, "I understood you had business in the north, and only delayed your journey thither on account of the *fête*."

"Very true."

"Then do the ladies accompany you?"

"Oh, most undoubtedly, my lord."

"If that is the case, it is useless my urging my petition, and I may return home the messenger of disappointment to my sister, who has set her heart upon prevailing upon you to entrust the ladies to our care till you can join us in the gay metropolis."

"Alas my dear Lord Everside," replied Mr. Coningsby, " you little know how dreadful a visit to London is to me, and this to the north is little less so. While I feel it a duty incumbent on me to take Celestia to London, as a chance that some accident might there discover to whom she of right belongs, I have not yet been able to name it to my sister. This sweet girl has so wound herself round my heart, that the last few years of my life have passed in comparative happiness, and have made me put off this journey from year to year, till it is become a matter of necessity; my steward is a very aged man, and though he may, and I hope he will live much longer, he feels himself unequal to any exertion; he has

recommended a successor, and I must of necessity go to settle my affairs with both."

"I am extremely sorry," said his lordship, "that I have inadvertently awakened unpleasant reflections; but as the evil is past remedy, may I claim a promise you made me some time since of acquainting me with some of the circumstances of your life? Indeed, it is no idle curiosity, but as you have told me that even your sister, until some two or three years since, was kept in ignorance of by you of the cause of your grief, and, therefore, you have for too long brooded over your sorrows, without a participator; and believe me, my dear friend, evils that are past remedy, may be greatly ameliorated, if they are communicated to a sympathising friend."

Mr. Coningsby readily admitted the truth of these observations, and assuring his lordship that he had not forgotten the promise he had made him, and adding that all the leisure time he could find while away from the abbey should be devoted to the purpose of writing for him the particulars of those melancholy circumstances which had thrown a blight over prospects once so brilliant.

Lord Everside thanked his friend for the confidence he placed in him, and then rising from his seat, he observed,—

"This arrangement completed, Mr. Coningsby, I must bid you adieu for the present, as my sister will be impatient to hear the result of my mission."

"It causes me considerable regret, my lord," said Mr. Coningsby, "to have to occasion her a disappointment, but I know she will not be offended that I decline her friendly offer; one year more, and I shall be most happy to avail myself of it, though even then you know, she will be almost too young to be introduced to the gay and giddy world of fashion, and notwithstanding, I am sure I need not repeat to you, how anxious I am to discover her connexions, I am so selfish as to wish that they may be happy in finding her with those who would rather continue her protectors. If they are emigrants, (and that is not at all unlikely), were it possible to do so with safety, I would go to France, and take her with me, where her resemblance to her parents might be strong enough to lead to a recognition."

"The circumstances under which Mr. Aunville took up his residence at the old priory lodge, certainly gives that supposition the character of probability," remarked Lord Everside; "but what sort of a man was the father of your fair protegee, Mr. Coningsby?"

"I have his person fresh in my memory," answered the latter, "though so many years have elapsed since the melancholy occurrence. He was tall and well made, and, as far as one may judge after death, very handsome. His complexion and hair were very fair. Old David said his eyes were blue. Celestia

is a brunette, but the old people have often told me before their death, that they thought she very much resembled her poor papa."

"Well," said Lord Everside, "my dear friend, I trust that ere long a proclamation of peace will enable you to carry out your laudable wishes, for I do think that it is not at all unlikely a visit to France with your fair charge might be attended with the most favourable results; and now I must once more bid you good morning; my visit has been like a lady's letter, a postcript much longer than the letter itself."

His lordship cordially shook the hand of his friend, and then took his departure.

The suggestion of Lord Everside, had indeed brought many melancholy rereminiscences of the past to the memory of Mr. Coningsby, who sat for some time after he was gone, buried in gloomy meditation. He at length arose, and stalked across the room in a disordered manner.

"How chequered are the ways of fate," he soliloquised; "with what bright prospects did I commence my career of life, and oh, how soon were they obscured by the clouds of unmerited adversity, and annihilated for ever!"

"Aye, it was a joyful wedding; a merry season, but a short one, ha! ha!"

This was spoken in a voice that struck a deadly chill to his heart, and curdled the very blood in his veins. The voice came fresh upon his memory, as if he had heard it only a few hours before the present time. It was the same that had warned him in so extraordinary a manner on the morning of his union with the beauteous and much loved Lady Elvina!

The windows of the apartment in which Mr. Coningsby was, opened immediately upon the lawn in front of the abbey, and turning immediately round as the words met his ears, he beheld standing before one of them, and staring with a malicious grin upon him, the very same remarkable being whom he had encountered on the morning of his marriage, and who had since appeared, not only to old Hannibal and his wife, but to Celestia, in the old priory ruins!

Yes, there was the same old haggard face, and decrepid form, which even the lapse of so many years seemed not to have altered in the least. The same malicious, nay, almost unearthly expression of the eyes, and even the tattered dress appeared to be the very one that he had worn on the occasion when Mr. Coningsby had first seen him.

He could scarcely believe the evidence of his eyes, and for a second or two, stood rivetted to the spot, and lost in amazement and confusion, not unmixed with alarm. The old man still remaining at the window, fixed in the same attitude, and seemed by the expression of his countenance, and his whole demeanour to exult in the sensation his appearance had caused.

Mr. Coningsby, however, soon recovered himself, and advancing to the bell, rung it violently, with the hope of getting the assistance of some of his servants, and securing the person of the mysterious old man, but when he turned round again, he was gone.

At that moment two of the men servants who had been alarmed at the violence of their master's ringing, entered the room and demanded his pleasure.

"Follow me immediately," exclaimed Mr. Coningsby, "I have seen him; not a minute since, he was standing before that window; he spoke to me—quick, he cannot have got far."

The servants stared at each other with amazement, and then at their master, thinking that he had certainly taken leave of his senses.

"Pray what do you mean, sir?" asked one of them, "who are we to go in pursuit of? What have you seen?"

"Ask no questions, but follow me instantly," said Mr. Coningsby, impatiently, and darting from the room accompanied by the two men, who were completely lost in bewilderment to know what all this could mean. They quickly gained the lawn, across which Mr. Coningsby ran with the greatest speed, but when he reached the extremity of it, as far as his eyes could stretch the coast was entirely clear, there was not the least sign of a human being.

Mr. Coningsby stood and struck his forehead in the utmost confusion and astonishment. How so aged a man, and apparently suffering under such decrepitude, could have contrived to escape so suddenly was beyond his comprehension, and had he not been witness of the circumstance he could not have believed it.

He now gave his servants a more particular description of the circumstance, and describing the person of the old man minutely to them, commanded them to go in search of him in the immediate neighbourhood. He then returned to the abbey, meditating deeply on what had taken place, and in vain endeavouring to come to some conclusion, as to what was best to be done.

That the old man should again appear, after the lapse of so many years, was most wonderful, and what business he could possibly have with his affairs, thus to pursue him, was to him still more inexplicable.

The servants returned as might have been expected, without having been able to gain any information whatever, and Mr. Coningsby was left to ponder over the perplexing circumstance without being able to come to any satisfactory conclusion; still he was determined to leave no means untried to unravel this remarkable mystery.

In the meantime, while these events where taking place at the abbey, Miss Coningsby and our heroine pursued their walk to a considerably greater extent than they had at first intended, paying numerous visits to the humble dwellings of the recipients of their bounty, a task which the lovely Celestia felt the most unspeakable pleasure in performing, and which she had every means allowed her by her generous protectors of indulging in to the fullest extent. But as they had now been absent for some considerable time beyond that which they had promised to be, and Mr. Coningsby would be impatiently expecting their return home, they thought it prudent to direct their steps towards the abbey.

They had not proceeded far, when their attention was arrested by hearing the plaintive voice of a female singing a simple ballad, but although they looked around them, they could see nothing of the vocalist.

Celestia listened with mute attention

and deeper interest even than her companion, for it struck her most forcibly that she had heard the voice before, but where she could not imagine.

The air of the song was wild and simple, but they could not distinguish the words. Suddenly the voice ceased, and immediately afterwards there stepped across a low stile which led into an adjoining field, a figure which our heroine no sooner beheld than she recognised it in a minute; it was that of the very gipsey whom she had met at the ball, and who having fixed her eyes for a moment on the astonished damsel and her companion, advanced to within a few paces of them, and then paused and gazed stedfastly upon them.

"You know me, maiden," she said; "I see that you remember me; yes, we have met before, doubtless you remember upon what occasion, and likewise the words, or at least, the subject of the song I then sung to you. Do not scorn the warning, for there is more importance attached to it than you perhaps now imagine. You are going a journey; you will see strange places, and fine dwellings, where the proud and haughty have revelled in pomp and indolence; and you will also again see *him*. Yes; he will once more cross your path; mark my words, and believe them, for you will find them come true."

She said no more, but without waiting for an answer from Miss Coningsby or our heroine, she turned away, and walking rapidly, or rather running, she was soon beyond the reach of hearing.

"It is the same woman whom I saw in the character of a gipsey at the masked ball," said Celestia; "what can be the possible meaning of her strange conduct; and what can be her business with me?"

"It is rather remarkable, my dear, I must admit;" said Miss Coningsby, "but after all I do not think it is worthy of any serious consideration. She is only one of those idle vagrants that infest the country, playing upon the credulity of the simple portion of the community, and extorting the money from their purse."

"At any rate, she has made no such attempt at present with me," returned our heroine.

"She perhaps would have done so, my love, had I not been with you, and have tried to have done so by intimidation. Come, Celestia, let us hasten on our way home, and endeavour to think no more upon this subject."

Celestia returned no answer, and they moved on their way, but she found that she could not easily forget it, or the words of the gipsey, and indeed Miss Coningsby was more deeply interested with it than she chose to make it appear she was, and could have wished that the gipsy had entered into some further explanation.

When they arrived at the abbey they found Mr. Coningsby in a considerable state of excitement, and they were not at all surprised at it, when he made them acquainted with what had taken place during their absence; nor was Mr. Coningsby less astonished when they informed him of their meeting with the gipsy, and the strange words she had made use of.

"These events have so much of the character of romance about them," remarked Mr. Coningsby, "that it is almost impossible to believe them, and as to forming any reasonable conjecture upon them, it is quite out of the question. Of what age does this gipsy woman appear to be?"

"She appears to be a woman in the prime of life," answered Miss Coningsby, "and still retains traces of having once been handsome."

"And are you sure, Celestia, that it is the same woman who accosted you at the ball?"

"Oh, yes, my dear papa," replied our heroine, "there is something so peculiar in her appearance that it would be impossible for any one who had once seen her not to recognise her again."

"I do not wonder at her gaining admission to the fête," observed Miss Coningsby, "for she could easily have done so without exciting any particular notice or suspicion."

"Very true," coincided her brother, "but these events are very annoying and bewildering, here are we pursued, as it were, by three mysteries, in the persons of the stranger, the extraordinary being I have seen this morning, and lastly this gipsy woman, with her ominous predictions. It would seem as if they had all three conspired together to involve us in perplexity, and yet there is nothing to show that they are in any way connected."

The conversation dropped, but it afforded them subject for much reflection, and they all entertained different opinions upon it, though of one thing they were certain, namely, that they could only leave it to time and chance to elucidate the mystery.

The day of their departure for Elverton castle at length arrived, and they bade adieu for a time to their friends in the vicinity of Sungrove Abbey.

The weather was delightful, and our heroine who had never been more than a few miles from Sungrove Abbey, was completely enchanted with all they saw in the course of their tour, which lasted for nearly a fortnight, as they stopped to visit everything worthy of seeing in their route.

Most diversified was the scenery they travelled among, and to Celestia, who had such a keen perception for the sublime and beautiful, it afforded a continual source of the most enthusiastic delight; and most grateful did she feel to her benefactor for the treat he had afforded her.

When they reached Elverton castle, Mr. Coningsby and his sister particularly the former, who had not visited this ancient seat of his ancestors for so many years, were welcomed by the few domestics of the castle with the most unfeigned pleasure, for there was not one of them who had not experienced his humanity and benevolence.

Celestia was very much gratified at this scene, and so she was at everything she saw, but the grey-haired and venerable steward, Mr. Elkins, particularly attracted her attention, and the young stranger appeared no less interesting to him, for as soon as the first compliments were over, he respectfully addressed Mr. Coningsby, in the following words—

"I must crave your pardon, sir, if I appear bold in putting such a question, but I should really like to know who this young lady is, whose extraordinary likeness to——"

The look which Coningsby fixed upon the old gentleman, checked any further explanation, but after a pause he answered—

"This lady, Mr. Elkins, is a ward of mine; I see you are mutually pleased with each other, and, I have no doubt, your regard will increase upon further acquaintance."

This conversation was interrupted by Miss Coningsby requesting to be shown to her apartment, upon which a no less venerable woman made her appearance.

Notwithstanding Celestia intended rising with the sun in order to gratify her eager curiosity to view the beauties of the surrounding scenery, fatigue proved so powerful an opiate, that the summons to breakfast found her but just risen from her couch.

A large hall in the centre of the main body of the castle, lighted by a dome from the top, was the usual breakfast room. It was paved with black and white marble; a railed gallery, running along two sides of this hall, communicated with two of the turrets, and led to all the chambers on that floor. A suite of five grand rooms occupied the ground-floor on one side of the hall; the other contained the library and billiard-room; large folding-doors opened from the hall into a conservatory, through which you passed to the family chapel, which, though small, was neatly elegant. The floor was paved with black and white marble; it was lined with oak, the pews of the same all throughout.

Our heroine hastened Miss Coningsby from the breakfast-table, to view this fine old castle, and hastily ran over the apartments, leaving the minute survey of them till a future period. The chapel detained them some time, as its simple elegance particularly pleased them.

"You will be surprised, Celestia," said Miss Coningsby, "when I inform you that this is the first time I have visited this castle."

"Indeed, madam?" ejaculated Celestia, in evident astonishment.

"It is true, my love. I was taken from home so young—but you shall have a short account of my life when we have nothing better to do."

Our heroine expressed her pleasure at this promise, and they now passed on by an opposite door to that by which they had entered the chapel, to a romantic heath; to the west lay some majestic hills, to the north another range of blue hills, appearing like clouds in the horizon; to the east a vast ocean, which seemed to have enclosed our island in its bosom, in order to defy the attack of any insidious foe.

Celestia was enchanted, and gave full vent to the pleasure she felt.

The castle dated its origin from William the Conqueror, who raised it as a defence to the coast, and it had repelled both time and strength, for it appeared entire and uninjured as the rock on which it stood. One of the turrets seemed to hang over the sea.

"Oh, my dear madam," said Celestia, "If I lived here, how I should wish to have that turret for my apartment."

"You would not be very desirous of it, my love, if you lived here in the winter," replied Miss Coningsby, "when the sea foamed against the rock, and perhaps the waves even reached the foot of the tower—when the wind howled a terrifying tempest, and perhaps, to add to the horror, you might see a distant vessel nearly swallowed up by the tremendous waves."

"Oh, madam! What a terrific picture, and yet how true; — and how doubly horrible it would be if I could not be the means of rendering the poor unfortunate creatures you imagine the aid required in so dreadful an emergency. Is this a dangerous coast, madam ?"

"It is not remarkably so, my dear," replied Miss Coningsby, "but storms drive a vessel so as to baffle the most skilful pilot, and some have been lost not far from hence. But we will now return home, as I am fearful that we shall alarm Mr. Coningsby by the length of our absence."

They bent their steps accordingly towards the castle, Celestia frequently looking back with feelings of the most enthusiastic delight and admiration upon the diversified range of beautiful scenery they had recently been contemplating, and which animated all the most ardent and glowing features of her character.

In the meantime Mr. Coningsby had been so deeply occupied with his steward, Mr. Elkins, that he had not noticed the length of his sister's and her fair companion's absence from the castle.

The steward could not again help expressing his astonishment at the very remarkable and striking likeness which our heroine bore to a portrait at a neighbouring seat. To this Mr. Coningsby answered that the likeness had often also struck him in a most unaccountable manner, as it was quite impossible Celestia should in any way be related to a family whose connexions were all so well-known; besides, he added, his fair ward, from all he had been able to ascertain, was born abroad, and most assuredly there could be no doubt that she was the daughter of Mr. Aunville.

Mr. Elkins's curiosity was more than ever excited, and Mr. Coningsby therefore related to him the principal events, as regarded Celestia's history, which has been recorded in these pages.

The affecting narrative drew tears from the eyes of the venerable auditor.

"Ah, my good sir," he remarked, " in what a multiplicity of ways are we reminded of the instability of all human enjoyments! My time here cannot be long, and it makes me desirous of ending my days in the society of my children."

"Very natural, Mr. Elkins," coincided Mr. Coningsby, "and I am ready to admit that I have detained you longer than I ought; could I have settled our business without coming down here, it would have been done sooner, but I could neither do that or give you up by proxy. Pray is the Earl Malensbury Bathurst come down yet ?"

The reader must here be informed that on the death of a relation, and the acquisition of immense property, the name and title of Baron Bathurst was added to that of Malensbury.

"No sir," said Mr. Elkins, in reply to the question put to him, " the earl is still detained in London by this lawsuit—it is a vexatious business, for his title to the estate is clear to all impartial judges, but the lawyers are loth to give it up."

At this juncture Miss Coningsby and our heroine entered, very much fatigued though they had scarcely seen anything of this beautiful place; however, they remained here nearly a fortnight, and having no inclination to make acquaintance that, if agreeable, they should feel sorry to quit, they had full time to examine everything within and without.

Numerous and capacious were the apartments; but the rich heavy furniture and gilded ceilings gave it a gloomy air of magnificence no ways congenial with modern taste. The grounds were well laid out, a well planted park, inhabited by a numerous herd of deer. The park was bounded by a forest that extended to some majestic hills, and lent its aid to build the safe-guard of our seagirt isle. Orchard, kitchen garden, fruit-garden, withall the *et-ceteras*, were kept in as much order as if the family still resided in it; for none of the old servants were dismissed because not immediately wanted.

The same reasons which occasioned Mr. Coningsby to retire to such a distance from his family residence, prevented him from taking any of his domestics to his retreat, except one faithful man servant.

Some few days before their departure from Elverton castle, Mr. Coningsby proposed to his sister that they should visit Berensforth Hall, the seat of Lord Malensbury Bathurst, in their way.

"It will add only a few miles to the journey," he observed, "it is well worth seeing, and I think it would be a pity not to take the present opportunity."

"Indeed it would afford me much pleasure, my dear brother," replied Miss Coningsby, "if it will not be putting you to any particular inconvenience."

"It will not be in my power to accompany you thither," returned Mr. Coningsby, with a sigh.

"Not accompany us!" repeated his sister, with a look of surprise.

"No; I am obliged to visit a purchase Mr. Elkins has lately made for me. He will attend me to Merton, which place I will appoint for your joining me."

Miss Coningsby and Celestia could not but express their unwillingness to go without him, but he told them they must go, for he wanted them out of his way while going over grounds, &c.

As Mr. Coningsby would not be refused they ordered the carriage for the next morning, when taking a friendly leave of the old domestics, they stepped into the vehicle, and attended by the faithful and trusty Robert, they arrived in the course of a little more than an hour at the hall.

Miss Coningsby well knew the cause of her brother's emotions, when he declined accompanying them; but of course, as Celestia was unacquainted with them, she could not properly appreciate them, and felt considerable disappointment at his not being their companion.

Berensforth Hall was situated in a romantic vale, through which wound a clear and beautiful river, the lofty hills topped with thick woods, which entirely surrounding it, gave it a very gloomy appearance.

Though the hall was very ancient, the inside had been altered and fitted up with great magnificence. The principal apartments were quite modernised, except the great gallery, in which were hung the family portraits.

Miss Coningsby and her companion having been received with every respect, they proceeded to examine the mansion, accompanied by the housekeeper.

The state drawing-room was the first place she conducted them to, the ceiling of which was painted in compartments, describing various important and interesting passages of history. Miss Coningsby and her lovely pupil were competent to judge of the merits and subject of each, they were highly gratified, without attending to the monotonous and hurried account of their venerable guide.

The rest of that suite was nearly as interesting, both as to paintings, and some highly finished statues in marble and alabaster.

One of these rooms, however, was more curious than agreeable; it was completely lined with looking-glass, divided into panels by the most beautiful carved work in wood. Birds, whose feathers seemed in motion, animals whose furry coats were so nicely imitated that Celestia put her hand upon a lion's main before she would believe it to be only a wooden one; he lay supporting a silver branch of twelve lights.

They were lastly conducted to the gallery containing the family portraits. These could only be interesting to the family, or those connected with it, but one of them particularly attracted the notice of both ladies.

CHAPTER IX.

FRESH CAUSE OF SURPRISE.

THE painting to which we have alluded was the whole length portrait of a beautiful girl, apparently about sixteen years of age.

Miss Coningsby was lost in thought, gazing alternately at the picture and our heroine, while the latter was descanting on the beauty of the object before her. Miss Coningsby at length turned to the housekeeper, and asked her who that portrait represented, and if she still lived.

"Ah, no, madam," replied the old woman, "she has been dead a long time, she was the late earl's only daughter, but pardon me if I say that the likeness that young lady bears to it is most extraordinary—may I ask if she is of my lord's family?"

"Indeed she is not," returned Miss Coningsby; "but the resemblance struck me with astonishment—it is the very counterpart of herself."

Again Miss Coningsby gazed at the picture, and now that she understood who it represented, she sighed deeply, and the most melancholy thoughts presented themselves to her mind. She then requested to be shown to her carriage, as she was fearful they would hardly reach the place of their destination before darkness overtook them.

The old housekeeper here said, that if they would just look at the library which was a noble apartment, at the vestibule they would find their carriage and servant.

They accordingly followed her, and were much pleased they had been persuaded to see this really noble library; it was entirely lined with book-cases in divisions, each containing the best authors in the language, marked in large gold letters over the doors of gold wires; busts of every known literary character, both ancient and modern.

The statue of Sir Isaac Newton was placed at the head of the room, where were globes, telescopes, orrery, and every other mathematical instrument, with various other statues and busts of great characters.

They were about to turn away in order to leave the apartment, when they were startled by a low cough, and turning their eyes in the direction from whence the sound proceeded, they were surprised by the sight of a gentleman extended on a sofa, a book lying by him, and who seemed, by the sudden start he gave, to have just awakened, which was really the case.

"I ask your pardon, your honour," faltered out the old woman, "I did not think of finding you here, and indeed you do very wrong in coming down stairs; these ladies——"

But they were gone, however, not out of the room, and the gentleman advancing, leaning on a crutch, and apparently walking with great difficulty, they were obliged to return, apologizing for having disturbed him; he entreated them to be seated, and, the housekeeper having asked him if she should send him his chocolate, added—

"And perhaps the ladies will condescend to take some too; I am sure they must be fatigued."

After some persuasion Miss Coningsby consented, and the old woman left them to provide the refreshment.

A slight pause ensued, when the gentleman noticing the embarrassment of his unexpected companions, addressed Miss Coningsby, in the following words:—

"To that good woman who has just retired I am under the greatest obligations. She has admitted me, an entire stranger, under her lord's roof. It is now three months since I landed in England for the first time, in order to unravel a very intricate and perplexing affair. I was on my way to Scotland, when the post-boys taking a wrong road, found themselves in this valley, when, by a short turn I was overset, the chaise was dragged a considerable distance before the horses set themselves at liberty by breaking the harness; fortunately for me, my servant escaped unhurt, and nearly frantic at seeing me, to all appearance, killed, and no inn or cottage near, the post-boy told him of the hall, so taking one of the horses he soon arrived, and as quickly obtained assistance, and I was conveyed hither with a broken leg and dreadful bruises. When I recovered my senses, I understood that the noble owner was absent. I expressed my fears of having intruded on the servants, but the good housekeeper assured me that her lord would never pardon a neglect of hospitality in his absence, and that instead of incurring blame, as I apprehended, they should receive his highest praise. A skilful surgeon, and an excellent nurse, have nearly restored me ; and as soon as he will permit, I shall pursue my journey, which is of the utmost consequence to me."

The gentleman then apologised to Miss Coningsby and our heroine for his tedious narrative, and inquired if their residence was in that part of the country, to which Miss Coningsby replied

ROBERT IS INFORMED OF HIS MISTRESS'S FLIGHT TOWARDS LONDON.

in the negative, and gave him some trifling explanation.

The old housekeeper now appeared with some chocolate, of which having partaken, they wished the gentleman (who was remarkably interesting) a speedy recovery, and prepared to take their leave.

At parting, he said he hoped this would not be their last meeting, for it would cause him much regret if he thought it would.

Miss Coningsby smilingly said, their acquaintance had been too short to make their never meeting again of such consequence, nevertheless she should feel the greatest pleasure if chance should bring them together once more.

They now repaired to the carriage, into which they were about to step, when they were astonished and somewhat alarmed as they beheld the tall figure of a man, muffled up in a military cloak, and his hat drawn down over his forehead, so as to shade his features from observation, standing at the horses' heads.

Celestia clung close to her companion, and she trembled violently when the man advanced nearer to them, and throwing back his cloak, and raising his head, revealed to her the features of the mysterious stranger who had so frequently crossed her path before.

She shrieked, for she could not suppress the feeling of terror that came over her, and the unknown having fixed upon her one impressive look, fled from the spot, and was soon lost to the view.

Miss Coningsby was little less astonished than Celestia, but she exerted herself to compose her feelings, and having partially succeeded, they entered the carriage and pursued their journey without any more delay.

Celestia could not help feeling the most unbounded amazement at the conduct of the unknown, who seemed to be aware of their movements, and to pursue them wherever they went, but with what design, it was of course, utterly impossible for her to imagine.

Miss Coningsby and her conversed much upon this occurrence as they proceeded, but unable to solve the mystery, they changed the subject to the more pleasing one of their meeting with the gentleman at the hall.

Celestia's eyes sparkled with uncommon vivacity as she spoke of him, and she did not attempt to conceal the very remarkable sensation he had caused in her breast.

"It was a most fortunate thing that the accident occurred where it did," she remarked, "and that they carried him to the hall, where he has received such kind attention. My dear madam," she added, "do you not think him very handsome?"

"Yes, Celestia," replied her companion, "I do think he has been so, and indeed is so still; but such a long confinement must necessarily have greatly changed him."

Celestia paused a moment or two in deep thought, and then said:—

"I wonder, madam, what the business is, that he spoke of; he says it is of the utmost consequence, and this unfortunate accident has now delayed it three months."

"Upon my word, Celestia, you seem wonderfully interested for this stranger."

"I do not deny that I am," replied our heroine, "as I have no doubt I should be for any other under the circumstances."

The day passed away, and as they entered one of the principal towns on their route, the shadows of evening began to fall thickly around, and as they had yet some distance to go before they would be at their journey's end, they put up at an inn for the night, and the next morning set out early, as both were very impatient to rejoin Mr. Coningsby.

By three o'clock they arrived at Merton, and Celestia entirely forgot the handsome stranger who had so deeply interested her, in the pleasure she felt at being once more with her beloved benefactor, and in telling him all she had seen at Baronsforth Hall, and particularly of the interesting picture.

It was quite evident that Mr. Coningsby listened to Celestia's description of the hall with deep emotion, which his sister observed, and knowing well the cause, deeply sympathised with him. But when she described the portrait, and so warmly eulogized it, his anguish was so intense that Celestia was fearful that he was unwell, but he said it was only a slight head-ache, which probably would go off after dinner.

"Yes, Celestia," he said at length, "you as much resemble the original of that picture, as your aunt seems to imagine you do the copy."

"Oh, my dear papa," said our herione, "did you know that lady then?"

"Did I know her!" ejaculated Mr. Coningsby with increased emotion; "alas, alas! I did—too well. But I cannot converse on a subject which is so painful to me."

"Oh, my dear benefactor," said Celestia with a look of unaffected regret, "how deeply do I reproach myself for having said anything that has caused you pain. But you will pardon me, will you not?"

"Pardon you, my sweet girl?" replied Mr. Coningsby, in accents of the fondest affection, "you have done nothing for which you should seek forgiveness."

In order to turn her brother's thoughts from that subject, which she knew was so torturing to him, Miss Coningsby now related to him all that had happened to them at Berensforth Hall, their meeting with the gentleman, and the manner in which the mysterious unknown had again crossed their path.

Mr. Coningsby listened to her with much astonishment.

"I cannot at all comprehend the conduct or character of this strange individual," he remarked; "he seems to follow closely upon our steps, but what his motives can be it is impossible to conceive."

"It is indeed, my dear brother," said Miss Conignsby; and then she returned to their meeting with the gentleman, and so animated was the account she gave, so lively was the picture she drew of him, that Mr. Coningsby's cheerfulness was restored, and he remarked in a most vivacious tone;—

"Well Eugenia, really I am quite struck with the portrait you have drawn of this interesting unknown of Berensforth Hall. I sincerely trust that you have not neglected to ascertain his real name and rank, for he seems to have insinuated himself into your good graces; will you be kind enough to inform me what age he is, and whether I am to have him for a brother or son-in-law?"

"You are perfectly right, Albert," said Miss Coningsby with a smile, "this stranger has indeed prepossessed me in his favour; but it happens most unfortunately that he is too young for me, and too old for Celestia; he seems to be about seven or eight and thirty, tall, finely formed, and but that his complexion is darker, I should think him very like yourself at his age; his eyes are dark and piercing, with very full arched eyebrows; a countenance full of animation, and it was particularly so when looking at our beloved Celestia, who blushed deeply when she saw him gazing at her. And much struck with him she

was, for she talked of nothing else till we reached Merton; and I marvelled much that she said nothing of him when she was describing all that had so much excited her wonder and admiration at the hall."

"And yet it is not so much to be wondered at," remarked Mr. Coningsby; "it is not unlikely that she has forgotten the circumstance, as her own likeness seemed most to engross her thoughts."

"The likeness is certainly a most extraordinary one, my dear brother; but we will say no more upon that subject, for I know it pains you. The strange conduct of the unknown who has so frequently crossed our path, however, completely bewilders me. It is quite evident that he has some sinister design in view, and that by some unaccountable means he has full knowledge of our proceedings and intentions, and that he follows our footsteps like a shadow."

"I confess," observed Mr. Coningsby, "that this man, whoever he may be, causes me considerable uneasiness; his motives for the conduct he has hitherto displayed are perfectly inexplicable to me; could I but obtain an interview with him, some explanation might be elicited from him; but that he sedulously avoids. Then there is that old man of the ruins, as he is now generally termed; his real character and intentions are involved in equal mystery. All these various circumstances have more of the character of romance about them than reality, and would be treated with incredulity by most people."

"Very true," coincided Miss Coningsby, "and Heaven only knows what the result may be. However, I am very glad, and so I am certain our dear Celestia is, that you have completed the business which called you to the north, as we are both very impatient to return to Sungrove Abbey."

"Not more impatient than I am myself, Eugenia, I can assure you;" said Mr. Coningsby, "but really your description of the gentleman whom you met with at Berensforth Hall has deeply interested me, and I should like to have the pleasure of an introduction to him, a wish that I hope will be gratified some time or other."

"And sincerely do I hope so too, Albert, for I should feel the greatest pleasure myself in meeting with him again."

Mr. Coningsby and his sister now separated for the night.

When Celestia sought the chamber allotted to her for the night, various thoughts crowded upon her imagination; but the adventures at the hall held a predominant place in her mind. She could not banish the image of the stranger from her memory; every feature of his countenance was deeply stamped upon her recollection, and she treasured every word that he had uttered during their interview with a vividness and a reverence for which she could not exactly account; but had she thought that they would never meet again she would indeed have been very miserable.

Then the appearance of the unknown at such a time and such a distance from the place where she had first seen him, afforded her much room for perplexing speculation. That he had some knowledge of her she felt convinced, and therefore was she the more anxious that her beloved benefactor should have an opportunity of speaking to him, and eliciting from him an explanation which might be the means of unravelling the mystery in which all the circumstances of her history were so deeply involved.

The mind of Celestia was busy on this occasion, and among the other circumstances which recurred to her memory was her meeting with the gipsy woman at the masked ball, and subsequently, when Miss Coningsby was her companion. The strange predictions that woman uttered on those occasions, had made a strong impression on her mind, and she had often reflected upon them since, and with no little of credulity and painful foreboding.

And was Collingwood Aubrey entirely forgotten? Oh, no, many were the thoughts that Celestia had bestowed upon him, and deep was the anxiety she felt for his welfare. She also felt most solicitous to behold him again, and to enjoy the pleasure of his society, notwithstanding that Mr. Coningsby (for what reason she knew not) had shewn but little encouragement to it, and she had noticed something in the behaviour of Lady Aubrey, when she and her son were speaking together, which was peculiarly repulsive, and excited her astonishment.

The monarch of the day mounted his golden chariot, and Celestia arose from her couch, and having dressed herself, attended the summons of Mr. Coningsby and his sister, who were waiting for her below, already equipped for the journey. They partook of some slight refreshment, and then having entered the chaise, they proceeded on their way without any further delay.

We should mention that Mr. Coningsby had left Mr. Elkins, his venerable steward, at his son's house; and though in such a length of years he might be supposed to have amassed a very handsome fortune, his merits well deserved a handsome gift from his master, who never let the faithful services of any one go unrewarded, and he presented Mr. Elkins with a deed which entitled him to one hundred pounds a year for his life, as a mark of his regard.

Deeply was the old man affected by the kindness of his patron, which he looked upon as a parting gift; for as Mr. Coningsby seemed now as much averse to reside at his family estate as he was twenty years before, and Mr. Elkins's great age prevented the possibility of his making a tour to Sungrove Abbey, therefore, when Mr. Coningsby shook him by the hand at parting, the poor old man was too full for words, and could only say,—

"May the Almighty bless and restore you, *sir*, to peace!"

Mr. Coningsby felt much affected. He pressed the hand of his venerable steward in significant silence, and departed.

Many miles had the chaise proceeded, ere Mr. Coningsby had recovered his cheerfulness. Celestia and Miss Coningsby seemed occupied by their own meditations; however, the stopping of the chaise to change horses brought them out of their deep reverie, and the rattling of the wheels of another chaise behind them, caused them to look up; it passed them with great speed, but not sufficiently so to prevent their observing the head of a gentleman protruding from one of the windows. They all started, for in the countenance of the gentleman they recognized that of the unknown!—His eyes were intently fixed on them, but it was only for an instant, for the chaise was quickly out of sight.

CHAPTER X.

THE MISFORTUNES OF CONINGSBY'S EARLIER LIFE.

In a former chapter we recounted some of the events in Coningsby's career, which had tended to cast a gloom over his future years. We left off our recital at the loss of the child, and we now proceed with the record of what immediately followed.

It is needless to say how painfully Lady Elvina felt this awful deprivation; and it was as much as she could do to submit without repining to the immutable decrees of Providence. Her restoration to convalcesence progressed but slowly, and at times her life was entirely despaired of, which added tenfold to the bitter, the almost insupportable anguish her lord was enduring at the melancholy loss he had sustained.

The search after the lost child was continued with unabated zeal, but entirely without success, and it seemed but too probable that he had certainly perished, but in what manner was involved in the most torturing mystery.

Lord Elverton had sent for his mother-in-law, who evinced almost as much grief at their loss as themselves, and exerted herself to the utmost to impart some degree of consolation to the bosoms of the bereaved parents. To add to their affliction, she had left the Earl of Malensbury confined by a dangerous fit of the gout, and as it continued with unabated violence, she returned to him as soon as her daughter was pronounced out of danger. As soon as she could be moved, they went to the family mansion of her parents, in the hope that the society of her family might tend to alleviate her sorrows.

We will will now pass over a period of two years, during which interval no circumstances of any peculiar moment took place, but the cloud of misfortune was again about to burst upon their devoted heads.

The beauteous little Elvina, who was now their only consolation, was suddenly attacked by a dangerous fever, which baffled all the skill of the medical gentlemen, and on the third day the unfortunate parents found themselves deprived of their only offspring.

To seek to describe the grief they experience, would be a fruitless task; Lady Elverton was again confined to her bed, and this time it seemed really impossible that she could survive such a heavy additional affliction; and Lord Elverton, in the agony of his grief could not help accusing Providence with injustice; but for which impiety he was shortly most severely punished.

Time, however, again restored Lady Elvina to health, and her feelings as well as those of her husband, gradually became somewhat tranquilized.

Ashburne Manor had, however, become hateful to them both, and as the great world had no pleasures for them, now that they were deprived of all they held most dear on earth, they determined to pass the ensuing summer months at the parental estates of Lord Elverton, and as it was only within a short journey of Berensforth Hall, Lady Elvina gave it the decided preference.

They had not visited this estate since the demise of the amiable Earl of Elverton, and as may naturally be supposed, it could not therefore fail to recall melancholy reflections to the memory of Lord Elverton; but he struggled with his emotions, and most sedulously concealed them from Lady Elvina, the more especially as the change of the scene seemed to have so beneficial an effect on her spirits, who gave him the delighful hope of once more becoming a mother, and he at length looked forward to some portion of that happiness of which he had been so cruelly deprived.

Lady Elvina's health being perfectly re-established, they passed their time without alloy; but alas! this fancied happiness was not destined to last long, and little did Lord Elverton imagine the heavy blow which fate was about to inflict upon him.

A strange and unaccountable change suddenly came over her ladyship, which her husband in vain sought to penetrate. She became thoughtful and constrained in her manners towards him, and would for hours remain secluded in her own chamber.

It was with the deepest anguish that Lord Elverton noticed this alteration in the conduct of a wife whom he so fondly loved, and implored her to give him an explanation of it; but she merely tried to persuade him that he was mistaken, and carefully evaded all the questions he put to her on the distressing subject.

She, however, requested her lord, if it was agreeable to him, to allow her to pass some time with her parents, and as he no longer feared the influence of Lady Malensbury over her daughter, he did not hesitate to comply with her wishes, and besides, he considered that he should be acting with injustice by keeping them apart. They departed accordingly, and for one month after their residence at Berensforth Hall, the change that had come over her ladyship was as remarkable as the recent one was painful. The melancholy gloom and reserve entirely disappeared, and since the loss of their children Lord Elverton had never seen her so apparently happy and cheerful.

Lord Elverton was delighted, and hopes once more revived in his bosom, hopes that were soon to be annihilated for ever, and to be succeeded by the deepest misery and despair.

Parliamentary duties called Lord Elverton to London, and thus caused a separation between him and his lady, and a short time after his absence he received a letter from her, informing him that her aunt had lost her only son in a duel with one of his dissolute companions in France.

This news was more terrible than Mrs. Seabroke could support, and she no sooner received it than she sank on the floor apparently lifeless. She remained so long in this state that the physician who was immediately in attendance, expressed the strongest fears that she would never recover; and Lady Malensbury was immediately sent for, but by the time she had arrived, her sister had partially recovered her senses, and Lady Malensbury, little less shocked when made acquainted with the dreadful truth, was obliged to repress her own grief, that she might mitigate that of her sister.

It was not until several weeks had elapsed that Mrs. Seabroke's senses perfectly regained their strength, but it was impossible to persuade her to quit her chamber, or to admit any one but Lady Malensbury, but more particularly Elvina. And at length, it appeared that she had resolved to immure herself for the rest of her days in a convent in France. Not all the arguments of Lady Malensbury could persuade her to abandon this resolution. To her sister she bequeathed a large sum of money in the funds, and to Lady Elvina all her jewels and plate.

The day before her departure, she requested to see Elvina, and having embraced her tenderly she said,—

"Dear child of my affections, alas! I once thought of a still nearer connection; but pardon my selfishness—my son was unworthy of you. Unhappy youth! Early victim of dissipation, what years of bliss might you not have enjoyed with my Elvina. May you my love never know misfortune but by name! let your ever affectionate aunt live in your remembrance, and should trouble overtake you, be assured it is only in the lap of religion you can ever find repose—there only can the child of misery fly for consolation."

Having presented Lady Elvina with the casket of jewels, and once more embraced her and her sister, she bade them farewell, and the following morning she departed to the place of her destination.

We have been thus particular in relating these facts, because they will be found to be most importantly connected with this history.

As soon as business would permit him, Lord Elverton lost no time in hastening from town, and as might be expected he found Lady Elvina in the most melancholy state of mind, but persuaded her to return home in order that she might be in readiness for her confinement. She however, expressed great unwillingness to leave her mother in her present affliction, and requested her husband to allow her to remain at the hall till after her accouchement was over, as it would engage her mother's attention to herself, and make her forget her recent loss.

Lord Elverton had many objections to this arrangement, but still it was so natural that he found it impossible to do otherwise than comply with her request, and Elvina affected so much gratitude for his kindness in granting it, that he felt but too happy in having had it in his power to gratify her wishes.

And now that event so interesting and important to Lord Elverton arrived, and his lady presented him with a lovely daughter. He hoped now her maternal duties would restore her to her natural cheerfulness; but in this he was most unhappily deceived; she became gloomy, peevish, and abstracted, and he not unfrequently surprised her in tears. How torturing was this to him, and in vain he racked his brain to divine the cause, for from Lady Elvina herself he could not obtain the least explanation. The storm that had been so long gathering was about to burst upon the unfortunate nobleman with destructive fury.

He was once more compelled to go to town, and urged her to accompany him, thinking that by entering into the amusements of a London winter, her health and spirits would be restored; but his astonishment may be readily imagined when she refused to leave the country, in the most positive and determined manner.

It should have been mentioned that Lady Elvina had insisted on nursing her infant herself, and her husband could make no objection; indeed, he thought it would engage her thoughts, and turn her from that gloomy despondency which seemed to possess her. Could he conceive that she had so long formed a plan to ruin his peace of mind for ever? Could he suppose for a moment that Elvina, the wife of his soul—the object of his adoration—could so cruelly deceive him?

Finding all his persuasions useless, Lord Elverton took his solitary departure for town, his mind filled with the most strange and melancholy, and at the same time unaccountable, forebodings. Elvina's letters were by no means calculated to enliven him; they were dispirited, and he could not but think, most remarkably cold. He could not leave London, and she still persisted in remaining in the country—a perversity of conduct which much annoyed his lordship, and which he could not have believed his wife capable of.

How often did Lord Elverton recall to his mind the warning words which had been uttered by the old man near the priory ruins on the morning of his marriage, and which seemed about to be so fearfully realized; and taking all the circumstances into consideration, he could not but look forward to the future with feelings of dread.

Thus passed away two tedious months, Lord Arthur Malensbury being his only visitor. The last letter which Lord Elverton received from his wife informed him that she was going to spend a few days with a friend, and would return by the time he left town, which he hoped he should be able to do in little more than a week.

Two days before his departure, his brother-in-law came to him early one morning, and Elverton was astonished to notice the extreme agitation of his countenance and his whole demeanour.

"For Heaven's sake, my dear Arthur," he said, "what is it that moves you thus?"

"Oh, Elverton," answered his lordship, "I tremble to tell you; but you must muster all your fortitude to listen to the dreadful truth."

"I beseech you, keep me not in suspense. You torture me."

Lord Arthur, with a deep sigh, placed an open letter in his hand. It was from Lady Malensbury, and addressed to her son; but Lord Elverton had no sooner glanced over the few first lines, than he uttered a cry of mingled amazement and terror, and sunk overpowered on the floor.

His idolized Elvina, the mother of his child, had fled—abandoned him—eloped —no one knew whither! She was accompanied by the maid and the infant!

As she had stated it was her intention to do, in the last letter she had addressed to her injured husband, she had gone on a visit to her friend, Mrs. Ebsworth, the child, and only her maid, and an old attached male servant attending her, alleging the smallness of her friend's house as an excuse for not taking the child's nurse with her.

Some few days after she had been at the house of her friend, she sent Robert on horseback to some distance with a fictitious message, telling him not to return till the morning, as his horse and himself would require rest after the journey.

When the servant returned the next day, he found Mrs. Ebsworth in a state of the greatest alarm, and when he inquired for her ladyship the poor fellow was completely astounded when he was informed that she was gone.

It seemed that Robert had not departed on his journey more than a couple of hours, when Mrs. Ebsworth was quite astonished at Lady Elvina's asking if the carriage was ready, and was answered, that the post horses were not come. She appeared greatly vexed, and attributed the fault to the neglect of Robert in not ordering them, though this was all a subterfuge, as she had never said a word to him about them. However, they were sent for, and Lady Elvina set off with the child and her maid, and against the persuasions of Mrs. Ebsworth not to leave her so suddenly, and expressing her wonder that Lady Elvina should go without a servant. To this her ladyship answered that she had sent Robert on a message, and that he was to meet her with fresh horses.

Robert immediately hurried to the inn where the horses had come from, and he there learned that they had taken the lady yesterday a stage on the London road, where she changed horses and continued her journey.

Robert immediately set out for the hall, but we need not attempt to pourtray the consternation of the earl and Lady Malensbury on receiving the fearful news. As soon as the earl had somewhat recovered from his emotion he started in pursuit of the fugitive, and Lady Malensbury with much difficulty sat down to write these particulars to her son, so that he might break them to his unfortunate friend.

"Great God of heaven!" cried the distracted Lord Elverton, when he had perused this letter—"little did I ever anticipate such a blow to my hopes as this! Elvina false to me! Fled, deserted me! oh, it is too monstrous to be true! Alas, alas! would that I could persuade myself that it was all a fabrication; but circumstances too strongly corroborate the truth of it.

Now is her conduct fully accounted for, her apparant gloom, her reserve, her coldness towards me, and her positive refusal to accompany me to town, are sufficiently explained. All the time she was planning the disgrace of her family, and how to ruin my peace of the mind. Cruel, fallen Elvina, to make such a return for the love I lavished upon you. But who is it to whom she has thus sacrificed her honour? There is no one whom I can suspect, and—but what am I saying? I shall lose my senses! Oh, Arthur, you can, you must feel for your wretched friend!"

Lord Arthur pressed his hand, and the agitation he evinced was almost equal to his own.

It was some time ere they could so far calm their feelings as to consult what was best to be done in this dreadful emergency. But while they were planning and rejecting, a letter was brought to the distracted Lord Elverton, by his valet, who said that a man had left it, stating that it required no answer. He recognized the hand-writing of Elvina in a moment, and with frenzied haste tearing it open, he read the following words—

"DEAR CONINGSBY, for such I must still call you, though you may in future hate and dispise me. It is the will of Heaven I fear, that on this earth we shall never meet again. Circumstances over which I have no control have driven me to this step, which I know will cause the greatest misery, but do not I beseech you, my husband, condemn me altogether. Do me not the injustice to suspect my honour. I fly from a world (together with my innocent child) with which I am disgusted, to seek in holy seclusion that peace of mind I cannot hope to enjoy elsewhere. To the good Bonville I owe my conversion. My intention is immediately to enter a convent, and though I shall not take the veil, to conform to the rules as strictly as if I were professed; my child I shall myself instruct through the first years of infancy, nor will I afterwards influence her inclinations, whether they lead her to the world's enjoyment or the cloister. And now my dear Coningsby,
"ADIEU FOR EVER!"

With what horrible feelings did Lord Elverton peruse this letter. He could scarce bring himself to believe that it was not all some fearful dream.

"It is false!" he exclaimed, "she would deceive me farther, and hide her guilt under the mask of religion. Oh, Elvina, you will surely repent this cruel, this monstrous, this unnatural conduct!"

It was with the utmost difficulty that Lord Arthur could appease the anguish of the unhappy nobleman, but the rage he was in at his sister's base conduct greatly assisted Lord Elverton; her own flight was sufficient to overwhelm him, but to deprive him of his child was the extreme of cruelty. But it is quite

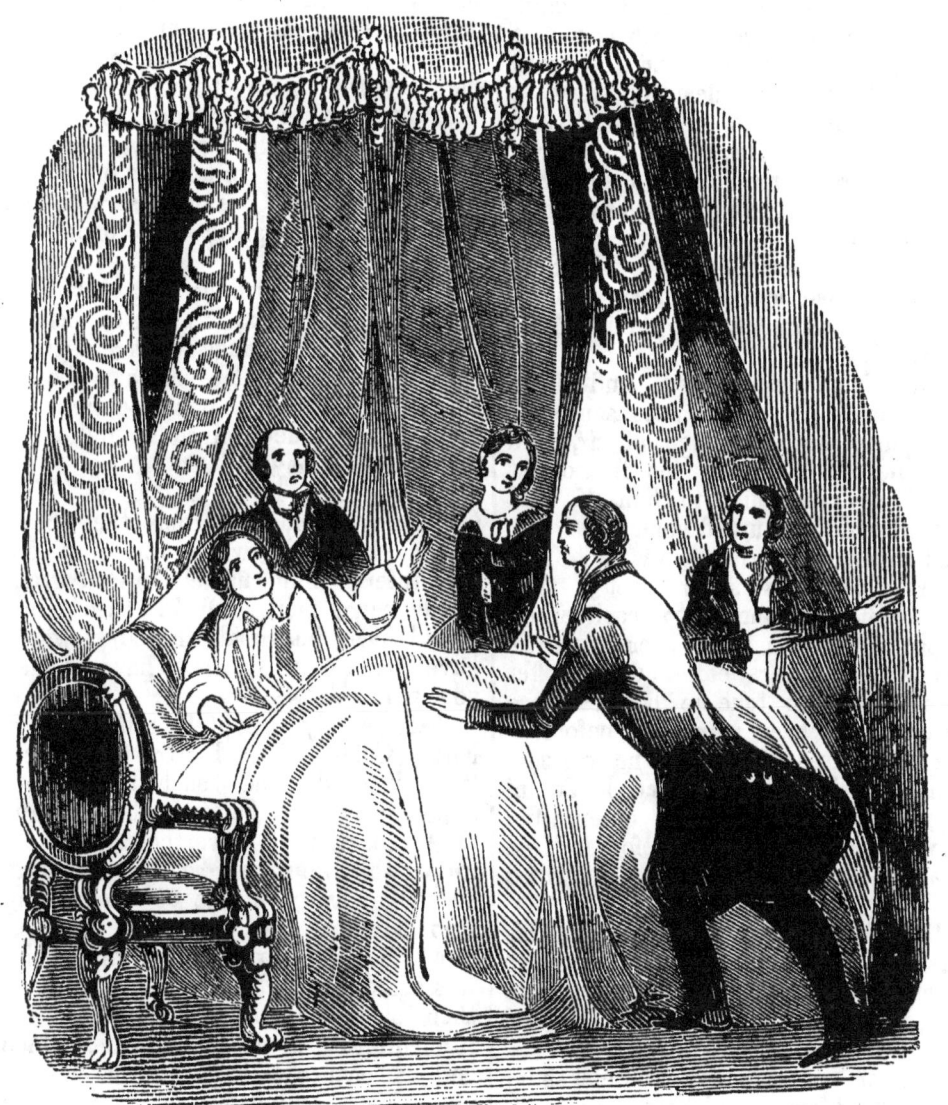

fruitless to seek to depicture the sufferings of Lord Arthur, or the despair of Elverton. However he at last advised his lordship to go to France.

"But, dear Coningsby," he added, "do not think for a moment I wish you to do so to induce your wife to return. Her conduct is unpardonable; she has brought disgrace and misery upon her family and yourself, and she deserves not the noble and generous affection you so ardently bestowed upon her; but should we be able to trace the place of her retreat, we might compel her to restore the child to your arms."

The Earl of Malensbury arrived while

No. 9.

they were discussing this subject, and his indignation was even greater than that of his son. He had traced the fair fugitive all the way to London, but there he lost all clue.

We have little more to add; in vain did Lord Elverton and his brother-in-law make the most rigid inquiries all over the continent, not the least information could be obtained of her and her child, and nothing whatever to throw any light on the dreadful mystery; and filled with disappointment and despair, they at length returned to England, Lord Elverton in a declining state of health, and with a temper ruffled by misfortune. He shunned society; a long and severe fit of illness reduced him to the verge of the grave, and for several months a kind of stupor so overpowered every faculty, that he was entirely lost to himself and the world.

Travelling was advised, and Lord Arthur and his lady kindly consented to accompany him. Change of air, and the kind attentions of his friends at length restored him to himself, and they once more returned home.

At about this period it was that Lord Elverton and his sister met; they were almost strangers to each other, as she had been away ever since he was fourteen years old, and the offer she made him to take up her residence with him has been mentioned before.

The unpleasant remarks he was constantly overhearing from the lovers of scandal, rendered him tired of entering into society, and he therefore retired into the country, as we have described in the previous chapters.

Lord Arthur died suddenly, and his lady took it so much to heart that she never held up her head afterwards, and in less than six months, she followed him to the tomb.

The earl and countess of Malensbury lived a very few years after their son's death, and left the title and estate to their grandson.

Such are the melancholy particulars of the misfortunes of the noble character with whom the reader is already familiar.

CHAPTER XI.

THE UNKNOWN.—THE RETURN HOME.— THE OLD PRIORY RUINS AGAIN.

WE will now return to our travelling friends, Mr. Coningsby, his sister, and Celestia.

"What an unaccountable being is this unknown," remarked Mr. Coningsby, as he conducted his sister and our heroine into the coffee-room, while the horses were being changed; "he pursues us everwhere, is always crossing our path, and yet avoids speaking to us, in order that he might explain what his business is with us. Truly such ambiguity of conduct is very annoying."

"And most alarming too, my dear papa," said Celestia, "I never behold that man, but a strange feeling of dread comes over me. He seems to be as well acquainted with our intentions as ourselves, and determined to follow us wherever we may go."

"True, my love," remarked Miss Coningsby, "and yet from the observation he made when you first encountered him, namely, 'God grant I may never more behold thee!' one would have imagined that he would have taken equal pains to have avoided you in future."

"He surely cannot intend you any harm, Celestia," said Mr. Coningsby, "for if he did, he has had plenty of opportunity for putting his designs into execution. Nevertheless, it is proper that we should be on our guard, and take every means of discovering who and what he is."

All being in readiness, the chaise was again entered, and they resumed their journey, all three of them absorbed in meditation upon the incident which had just occurred, but Celestia started when Mr. Coningsby suddenly asked her if she had forgotten the interesting invalid whom she and his sister had seen at Berensforth Hall.

"Forget him, my dear papa," replied our heroine warmly, "oh, no, I can never do that; he seemed so sensible and so interesting—I—I wish we may meet again."

"That, I am inclined to imagine," said Mr. Coningsby, "is not very probable, for I should think that England is not his native country, and he will most likely leave it, as soon as the business is accomplished which brought him into it."

" Oh,-indeed I hope not," ejaculated Celestia.

Astonished at the uncommon earnestness with which Celestia uttered these words, Mr. Coningsby could not help observing—

" Upon my word, my dear Celestia, you make me quite anxious to see this paragon, who seems to have so entirely gained both your's and my sister's good graces."

Miss Coningsby was so truly happy to see that her brother had recovered his spirits, that she resolved to avoid every subject which might lead to the hall, or the picture.

The journey home was at length accomplished, without anything more material occurring, and it was with feelings of the utmost delight that Celestia once more beheld those scenes to which she had been from the earliest days of childhood accustomed.

Mrs. Hardy greeted her fair charge with the affection of a mother, which was fully equalled by the pleasure which Celestia experienced at again beholding her most excellent preceptress, to whom she related all that had occurred to her since they had last met, and with which Mrs. Hardy was no less astonished than interested, especially in the account which our heroine gave of the gentleman whom they had accidentally met with at Berensforth Hall, and the re-appearance of the unknown. She was also much struck with the description Celestia gave of the picture which had so much attracted her attention and admiration, and, which Miss Coningsby declared she bore so remarkable a resemblance.

Mr. Coningsby was somewhat surprised when he had been at the abbey only a short time, at receiving a visit from Lord Everside, to take leave of them previous to his going to London, for he had imagined he was already there.

" My excellent friend," said his lordship, " visitors, and my wish to see you on your return from the north, have detained me, but to-morrow I depart, and I go alone, for my sister will not accompany me, in revenge, she says, for being such an unsuccessful agent in procuring your consent to Celestia joining us."

" I am sorry, my lord," said Mr. Coningsby, " but indeed I can give you no better reason than that you have already had, and which you yourself allowed to be sufficient."

" True," replied Lord Everside, " and I am still of the same opinion, but we will say no more upon that point. I sincerely thank you for having fulfilled your promise in confiding to me your melancholy history; and I wish that I could have prevailed upon you to do so many years ago. Indeed, my dear friend, your trials have been very severe, but I think the loss of your children is by far the greatest; as for your wife, she deserves not for you to bestow a thought upon her. The woman who could after an union of nine years, an union of happiness, abandon her husband, deprive him of an only child, lay herself open to the suspicion of the light, and censure of the worthy portion of the world, is unworthy of the smallest regret. It is my opinion that your affection rendered you blind to her real character. She loved you because she had every wish of her heart gratified; but as soon as an artful priest talked her into (for his own ends no doubt) a love for herself alone, she sacrificed you and every moral duty to a chimera that I fear she too soon felt the fallacy of. But I am sanguine enough to think there is a possibility of your having both a son and a daughter still living."

" Merciful Heaven !" exclaimed Mr. Coningsby, " what grounds have you for such an idea ?"

" I have none that are certain;" replied his lordship, " but you had no proof of your infant son's death."

" True, my lord," returned Mr. Coningsby. " But what chance have I now ? it is eight and thirty years since I lost him ; therefore, even were he still living, he must be so fixed in his opinion of his being an orphan (and he was too young to retain any knowledge to the contrary), that he never can discover to whom he belonged."

" Even so far as that I will agree with you," remarked Lord Everside, " but as there was no proof that he was drowned, he might be stolen, and you know a thief takes care that no one shall see him steal; however, I have no other reason than possibility for my first suggestion, nor have I much more for your daughter being still living, though, if she was saved from the dangers of the revolution, and her mother has had the grace to tell her who was her father, she will certainly find him out by coming to England when she can procure an opportunity."

Here the conversation on the subject for the present, dropped, and after awhile Lord Everside took his leave of Mr. Coningsby and the ladies, and quitted the abbey.

Mr. Coningsby felt so melancholy after the conversation he had had with Lord Everside, and the many painful recollections it had called up fresh in his mind, that he excused himself to his sister and Celestia, and retired to his study, where he might meditate without interruption.

He traversed the apartment for some time with an air of the greatest agitation, and deep sighs frequently escaped his breast.

"Cruel Elvina," he at length soliloquized, "I have too much reason to fear that the estimate which Lord Everside has formed of your character is correct. That you could never have really loved me is certain, or nothing would have induced you to abandon me in so heartless a manner, and to rob me of my child. Oh, how basely was I deceived, how cruelly were all my hopes blighted; what a monstrous return was it for all the affection and indulgence I had lavished upon her. But should Providence decree that my children are still living, and that I shall again behold them, and clasp them to my bosom before I die, even then I shall be amply repaid for the many years of dreadful anguish I have endured. But whither am I suffering my thoughts to wander? What mad ideas am I giving encouragement to? It is impossible that after the lapse of so many years that I should find my children living or if so, that I should discover them. Away with such thoughts! They do but add to my agony."

He was aroused from this soliloquy by hearing a rattling sound against the window, and, looking immediately towards it, to his utter amazement he beheld once more standing there, and gazing maliciously upon him, the extraordinary old man of the priory ruins.

Quickly Mr. Coningsby advanced towards the window, which he opened. The old man retreated a few paces, and then, leaning on his staff, stood unmoved, and eyeing Mr. Coningsby with perfect indifference and defiance.

"Old man," cried Mr. Coningsby, "who in the name of Heaven are you, and what is your business with me? Why do you so often appear before me? Speak, if you have anything to communicate, either for my good or harm."

"Good falls not to the lot of Lord Elverton," replied the old man, in a croaking voice, "sorrow, sorrow, all sorrow. I told you forty years ago, on that bright, gay morning, when bells were ringing their merriest peals, and all was mirth and hilarity, and the young bride looked so pure and peerless in her beauty, that it would be a *joyful marriage*, did I not? Ha! ha! ha! The words of the old prophet were scorned, derided at then, but they have come true, they have come true, ha! ha! ha!——"

"I will know who you are, and what are your designs, before you leave this place," said Mr. Coningsby, as he stepped from the window on to the lawn, making towards the very singular being, but in an instant the old man turned away, and hurried from the spot with a precipitation that left Mr. Coningsby completely lost in wonder. Had he not witnessed it himself, he could not have believed that one so aged could ever have departed so quickly.

He was transfixed to the spot for several moments in astonishment, and gazed in the direction which the old man had taken, but he could see nothing of him, and agitated and bewildered he returned to the abbey.

The adventure was so remarkable that he was unable to remove it from his memory, and it caused him no little uneasiness. The evidently great age of the man, was not the least extraordinary fact, and why he should take such pains to annoy him, he could not at all conceive, nor did it seem that it was likely he would be able to unravel it. And yet he knew not why he should suffer himself to be alarmed by the actions of one who was evidently a maniac; still there was something in the observations he had given utterance to, which made an indelible impression on his mind, and made him the more anxious for an explanation.

In order that he might dissipate the effects of this meeting from his mind, Mr. Coningsby, after a short time, rejoined his sister and Celestia, who observed his emotion, but did not think it prudent to inquire the cause, as they were fearful that any explanation might be painful to him, and she did not think proper to mention anything about the circumstance to him. By degrees the conversation had its due effect, and Mr. Coningsby became comparatively cheerful.

The second day after their return to the abbey, Celestia proposed to Mrs. Hardy that they should visit the priory ruins, to which the latter assenting, after the morning's repast, they set forth, Mr. Coningsby intending to visit his friend, Sir Eustace Aubrey, whom he had not seen since his return to the abbey.

On their arrival at the priory lodge, old Dorothy expressed the utmost delight at seeing them again, and to see our heroine looking so well. Hannibal was from home.

"Ah, my dear ladies," said the old woman, after they had been seated a few minutes, "I have much to tell you of what has occurred to us since you have been away. Ah me, these are very strange times that we live in."

"Dear me, Dorothy," said Celestia, "what has occurred that should put you so out of temper with the times? You have not been alarmed again by that mysterious old man of the ruins, have you?"

"Yes, indeed, miss," answered Dorothy, "that is just it, and what I was about to relate to you. You may well call him a mysterious old man; really I should feel inclined to think, saving your presence, madam, and Miss Celestia, that he was *the old gentleman* himself!"

Mrs. Hardy and our heroine could not help laughing outright at these superstitious fears of the old woman, but Dorothy shrugged her shoulders, and seemed partly horror-struck at what she probably considered the profanity of her guests. Seeing this, Mrs. Hardy and Celestia changed their tone, and listened seriously to what the old woman had to say, for they really felt interested in the subject.

"Ah, ladies," continued Dorothy after a pause, "you may laugh, and possibly I am a foolish old woman in entertaining the forebodings I do; Heaven send that it may prove to be so, but when I reflect upon all circumstances, I cannot help fearing that some danger threatens my respected master, and those who are connected with him, and therefore do I feel the more anxious for them to be upon their guard."

"But, Dorothy," said Mrs. Hardy, "what has happened to alarm you in this manner, and to cause you to entertain such gloomy presages?"

"I was about to tell you, Madam," replied Dorothy, "when you and my dear young lady here, interrupted me by ridiculing my observations."

The old woman spoke this with some little degree of asperity, and Celestia and her preceptress feeling that they had in some measure committed themselves, apologized and requested Dorothy to proceed with what she had to state.

"Well then, ladies," said Dorothy, "you must know, that ever since the departure of Mr. Coningsby and his sister, and our dear young lady here, from the abbey, me and Hannibal have been frightened half out of our wits, and I really think we shall be compelled to leave the priory lodge, after all."

"Oh, do not say so, dame," observed our heroine; "it would cause me much regret, I can assure you, to lose you and your respected husband, and after all, your apprehensions may turn out to be groundless."

"As I said before, my dear young lady, I hope it may turn out as you wish, though for my own part I have little hopes of it. Well, but to return to the facts I have to relate to you. Ever since, as I said before, you departed from the abbey, myself and my husband have been frightened almost out of our wits.

If we were sitting in this room of an evening, enjoying a little conversation, there was sure to be all of a sudden a noise as astounding as if a thunder-storm had taken place, though no one in the neighbourhood, when we asked them, had heard anything of the kind, and certainly the weather indicated nothing of such a war of the elements. Then the old ruins would seem as if they were about tottering down at one fell swoop, and the very lodge seemed to shake again. Indeed me and my husband have many times felt so con-vinced that an earthquake had taken place, that we have rushed from the house in alarm, but when we got outside, we found all calm, and serene, and the old priory ruins in just the same posi-tion as we had ever known them."

"A satisfactory proof, my good Dorothy," observed Mrs. Hardy, "that you had both allowed some nervous feeling to steal upon you, and that you were labouring under a delusion."

"Oh, no, madam," returned the old woman, "it was not so, as I think you will admit, when you have heard me out."

"Proceed, good dame," said Celestia, "I am most anxious to hear the sequel of your wonderful story."

"Ah, my dear miss, you may well call it wonderful; but if I were upon my dying bed, I would vouch for its truth. Well then, one evening I and Hannibal were seated by the fire-side, conversing upon the events of many years past, and wishing for Mr. Coningsby's re-turn to the abbey (for I assure you, madam, and my dear young lady, that we felt very melancholy during your absence) when, all at once there came a most tremendous knock at the lodge door, enough to shake it from its hinges, and it is strong enough, Heaven knows. Well, as you may imagine, we were very much alarmed, and we sat looking at each other in amazement for several minutes, unable to move. The knock was repeated, if possible, still louder than before, but neither I nor Han-nibal, poor old man (though I believe he is as courageous as here and there a one) could move from our seats, and for my own part, I really thought I should have sunk into the earth. The next moment the door was burst

open with a loud bang, and, oh, gracious me, the old man of the ruins stood before us."

"Are you certain you did not dream all this, my good dame?" asked Mrs. Hardy, looking incredulously at her.

"Well, my dear lady," replied Dorothy evidently picqued, "if that is your idea it is useless for me to proceed."

"You misunderstand Mrs. Hardy, good Dorothy," said our heroine, whose avidity was much excited, and who wished to hear the sequel of the old woman's story; "but pray go on."

"Well, miss," returned the old woman, "as you so particularly request it, I will. We started from our seats in amazement and terror, when we saw the mysterious old man in our presence, but he did not move an inch, and grinned upon us in such a manner as I shall never forget, and as if he enjoyed our consternation. At last Hannibal did muster courage sufficient to demand who he was and what he wanted; upon which the old man laconically replied, 'You!' Oh, dear me, when he said that, I verily thought I should have fainted away. However, Hannibal bore it much better than I could have be-lieved he would have done, and after a slight pause, he demanded what he wanted him for? To this the old man merely replied by commanding my hus-band to follow him. I would have prevented him, for I fully expected that if he did so, I should never behold him again, however, Hannibal seemed to have mustered up all his courage for the occasion, and giving me a signifi-cant look, he told the singular being that he was ready to follow him directly if he intended him no harm."

"And did he follow him?" inquired Mrs. Hardy."

"Yes, madam," replied Dorothy, "and my curiosity overcame my fears, and I followed them also, but at a re-spectful distance. Well, when we got into the ruins, the old man bounded over the different and massive fragments with the agility of youth, until he arrived at one particular spot, which no doubt you have noticed, ladies, in the course of your frequent rambles in the old priory, I mean that part where are the remains of an old stone cross."

"Yes, I have frequently observed that spot," said Celestia, "proceed Dorothy, I beg of you."

"Well, ladies," continued the old woman. "When our mysterious conductor arrived at that very particular spot, he made a full stop, and beckoned to us to approach. We did so. The moon was shining brightly at the time, and everthing was to be seen as clearly as if it had been in the broad daylight. I could but notice the peculiar expression of the old man's countenance at the time. 'Do you observe that blue flag stone?' he said, addressing himself to my husband. 'I do,' answered Hannibal, 'I have observed it many times.' 'It is buried there,' returned the old man. 'What?' demanded both myself and Hannibal, in a breath. 'Search, and you will find,' was the reply, and before we could recover from our surprise, the old man had departed, we knew not in what way."

"Most extraordinary!" exclaimed our heroine.

"It is, indeed, most strange," remarked Mrs. Hardy, "it has all the character of romance about it."

"But did your husband examine the spot pointed out to him by this remarkable individual?" asked Celestia.

"He has not done so yet," replied Dorothy.

"And why not?" demanded Mrs. Hardy.

"Why, madam," answered the old woman, "he thought upon consideration it was better not to do so until Mr. Coningsby's return home, that he might do so in his presence."

"Very prudent," remarked Mrs. Hardy, "the circumstance is one that certainly must not be lightly passed over. But your husband has not yet made Mr. Coningsby acquainted with it."

"He has not, madam, and for this very reason, that he did not like to intrude upon his honour so soon after his return to the abbey, but, perhaps, you will make him acquainted with all the particulars, and then we can enter upon the examination as soon as it suits his convenience."

"We will do so, Dorothy," said Mrs. Hardy, "and no doubt Mr. Coningsby will lose no time in endeavouring to unravel this most extraordinary mystery. I confess that your narrative has excited my utmost curiosity, and I shall be all anxiety until it is gratified."

"It is really most wonderful," remarked our heroine, "but have you seen nothing of this singular old man since?"

"No, miss," replied Dorothy, "neither have we heard anything of the frightful noises that before annoyed us."

"Let us more minutely examine the spot," suggested Mrs. Hardy.

"I was about to propose doing so, my dear madam," returned Celestia, "and perhaps Dorothy will accompany us."

"Most willingly, miss," answered the old woman; "ah, I will never believe but that there is some important secret buried there, but how the old man became acquainted with it, and why he should act in the manner in which he has done, I cannot imagine."

"A short time will probably unravel all," observed Mrs. Hardy; "but perhaps after all it will turn out to be some hoax that this strange old man has practised upon you."

"I do not see what his motives could be for doing so," returned Dorothy; "however, be it as it may, I have told you the plain and simple fact, just as it occurred to us, and if Hannibal was here he could corroborate what I have said."

"We do not doubt you for a moment, my good dame;" said Celestia; " of course, it could do you no good to misrepresent facts."

"Certainly not, miss; neither would I for a moment attempt to do such a thing."

They now left the lodge and entered the ruins, which in every respect bore the same appearance as when Celestia had last seen them. They made their way towards the particular spot about which their interest was so deeply excited, and which Celestia had often noticed in her rambles over the ruins.

It was a plain blue marble slab, one end of which was buried deeply in the earth; and not far from it was the remains of an old stone cross, which was overgrown with moss, and appeared to have stood in its present position for many generations. As for anything else in the immediate vicinity, there was nothing remarkable, and after a few minutes spent in contemplation, they quitted the ruins, and returned to the lodge.

"Well," said Mrs. Hardy, addressing herself to Dorothy, "we will make Mr. Coningsby acquainted with the particulars you have furnished us with, and no doubt he will not lose any time in making an examination of the spot to which your attention has been directed by this mysterious old man."

"Ah!" observed the dame, "and I feel confident that some wonderful discovery will be made, for I have had such dreams—"

"Never mind the dreams, good Dorothy," interrupted Mrs. Hardy, with a smile, "it is the reality we are now looking after. Good day, probably you will hear from Mr. Coningsby between this and to morrow; but perhaps your husband could make it convenient to walk over to the abbey before then, as I have no doubt Mr. Coningsby would like to speak to him upon this subject as soon as possible."

"Very good, madam," replied Dorothy, "Hannibal shall walk over to the abbey as soon as he returns home."

Mrs. Hardy and our heroine now took their departure from the lodge, much surprised at all they had heard, and most anxious for the time to arrive when there should be an examination of the spot which had been so singularly pointed out by the old man of the ruins.

CHAPTER XI.

THE GYPSEY AGAIN. — THE HIDDEN CHEST.—MORE DISCOVERIES.

Mrs. Hardy and Celestia walked on, buried in conversation upon the strange facts which old Dorothy had related, and without noticing surrounding objects, until having got some distance from the priory ruins, they were suddenly startled from their discourse by the voice of a female, who drew their attention towards her. They looked up, and Celestia's astonishment was great, when she beheld standing immediately across their path, the same gipsey woman who had twice before appeared to her.

"For Heaven's sake, my good woman," exclaimed our heroine, much alarmed by the earnestness of the woman's manner, "explain yourself, and if you know of any evil that threatens me, make me acquainted with it, and you shall not go unrewarded."

She nudged the arm of Mrs. Hardy, at the same time that she whispered to her;—

"It is her; it is the same gipsey whom I have twice before seen."

"Aye, 'tis her!" said the woman, who though the words were uttered in so low a tone, seemed to have heard them distinctly. "It is she whom thou hast twice before seen, girl. I told thee that thou wert going a journey, and that thou wouldst see *him*, did I not?—And my words came true, deny if you can."

"Who are you, woman, and what is your business?" demanded Mrs. Hardy.

"I am what I appear to be, *woman*," replied the gipsey, "but my business is not with thee. I would reveal to that fair girl on your arm, her future destiny, dark as it is, and warn her of the dangers by which she is surrounded."

"Begone, begone;" replied Mrs. Hardy with a look of scorn, "we wish not to listen to your nonsense."

"Nonsense, you call it, do you, woman," said the gipsey, with a look of bitter scorn, "'twill be well for the fair Celestia Aunville if it prove to be no more. Girl, beware, beware, for even now danger threatens thee; However, I have nothing more to say to you at present, damsel," continued the gipsy, "than to warn you to prepare yourself, for sorrow is at hand. Probably when we meet again you may know more."

"Stay," cried Mrs. Hardy, as the woman, having given utterance to these words, turned round to depart; "answer me a few questions, I beg of you."

"I have nothing more to say to you," returned the gipsy. "You have treated my words with scorn, and I will not condescend to parley further with you."

Thus saying, she deliberately walked away, leaving Mrs. Hardy and her companion lost in amazement.

"Oh, let not the observations of this woman alarm or agitate you, Celestia," at length said Mrs. Hardy, recovering her usual composure ; "they are totally unworthy of a serious thought. She is only one of those idle vagrants who wander about the country, preying upon people's credulity, and extorting mone from their purses."

"That may be true, my dear madam," replied our heroine, "but the three different times I have met her she has never attempted to extort anything from me, and, consequently, that renders

her motives the more inexplicable. Is it not also singular that she should have prognosticated so truly on the second occasion of my encountering her?"

"Mere chance, Celestia," said Mrs. Hardy, "think no more of it, for I cannot believe you to be so weak as to en-courage any superstitions of the kind. Come, my love, let us hasten home, for I am anxious that Mr. Coningsby should be made acquainted with what we have heard from old Dorothy with as little delay as possible."

Celestia made no reply, and they walked on, but she frequently looked back in the direction which the gipsy had taken, and found it utterly impossible to banish the observations she had made use of from her memory.

When they arrived at the abbey they found that Mr. Coningsby had not yet returned from his visit to Sir Eustace Aubrey, and they therefore sat themselves down, and again conversed upon the events of the morning and the account which old Dorothy had given them. The more excited their interest and curiosity became the longer they reflected upon it, and they longed for the time to come when the spot which the old man pointed out should be examined. His words, "It is buried there;" led them to imagine that some important discovery, would be made, which might serve to unravel many of the mysteries that now perplexed them, but what the nature of that discovery would be, of course they could not form the slightest conjecture.

Mr. Coningsby did not return to the abbey until the day was far advanced, and Mrs. Hardy and our heroine immediately sought his presence, and related to him all the particulars, as they had been given to them by Dorothy,

It may naturally be supposed that Mr. Coningsby was deeply interested, and not less astonished.

"It is a curious story," he remarked, "but do you think it is possible that Dorothy may only have imagined all this?"

"Why, sir," answered Mrs. Hardy, "we put the same question to her, but she was positive; moreover she said that her husband could substantiate every word she had said."

"At any rate, there can be no harm done in examining the spot which they say the old man pointed out," remarked Mr. Coningsby, "and that shall be done without delay. To-morrow morning I will myself go on that errand to the old priory ruins."

"And will you not allow me to accompany you, my dear sir?" asked our heroine anxiously.

"Certainly, my love, if you wish it," replied Mr. Coningsby, "I cannot have the least objection."

Celestia thanked him, and while they were still conversing upon the subject old Hannibal was announced, and was ushered into their presence. To the questions put to him by Mr. Coningsby he answered lucidly and with promptitude, and what he stated went to substantiate everything that his wife had stated to Mrs. Hardy and our heroine.

"And," added the old man, "he pointed, your honour, so particularly to the old blue flag-stone, when he made use of the observations I have stated to you, that I am certain he was serious, and, had your honour been present, I should have immediately examined the spot, for I really think that some great treasure is hidden there."

"I wonder then," suggested Mrs. Hardy, "that he who appears to be so destitute, should not have availed himself of the means of bettering his condition, instead of advertising his secret to strangers. To me, I confess, it appears, that the poor old man is labouring under some delusion; that, in fact, he is an idiot, and so I think it will turn out to be."

"It may be ma'am," returned Hannibal, "but pardon me, if at present, I cannot entertain the same opinion."

"It shall be unravelled to-morrow morning," observed Mr. Coningsby, "and indeed after all that I have experienced from this extraordinary old man, I cannot at present, my dear lady, exactly coincide with your opinion. But, my good Hannibal, have you never been able to trace this singular being to any place of habitation in the locality?"

"Never, sir, although I and many others have exerted ourselves to the utmost to do so. No person that I have spoken to knows anything more of him than from having seen him; but the manner in which he disappeared from them was so sudden and mysterious, that before they could recover from their astonishment, the object of their curiosity was beyond detection. I am not a superstitious man, your honour, although an old one, but from the actions of this strange old fellow, I can scarcely believe him to be a human being."

Mr. Coningsby and his companions smiled at the observations of Hannibal Dobson, although they could not help admitting to themselves that there was some little degree of reason about them.

"My poor old dame," remarked Hannibal, " is almost out of her wits at the strange circumstances which have taken place in the old priory ruins these last few months, and indeed so much so, that I am afraid unless some solution to the mystery is speedily given, we shall be compelled to resign your honour's hospitality,-so far as regards the lodge into other hands."

"Oh, say not so, my good Hannibal," said Mr. Coningsby, kindly, "it would vex me very much to find you leaving that home in which I have ever endeavoured to make you comfortable."

"That you have, sir, and the blessings of Heaven will ever pursue you for it."

"Besides," suggested Miss Coningsby, who had joined the party, "however singular this old man's actions may appear to be, it does not seem that he intends any harm to you or your wife, and consequently you ought to feel satisfied upon that point."

"Certainly," coincided Mr Coningsby.

"Well, ma'am," returned the old man, after a minute or two's reflection, "I have all along endeavoured to think so, and to persuade my dame to think so too. But I hope, as I said before, that a very few hours will reveal everything, and set all doubts at rest. Nothing would grieve me more than to have to quit the old lodge, for I have become as much attached to it as if it had been my birth-place. Your honour, then, will not be able to enter into the investigation till to-morrow morning?"

"I shall not, Hannibal," answered Mr. Coningsby, "but at an early hour you may expect me, for I need not tell you that I am as anxious to penetrate this mystery as you can possibly be yourself."

"Ah, sir," remarked the old man, "depend upon it that some remarkable discovery will be made, like my poor old Dorothy I dreamed that ——"

"Well," interrupted Mr. Coningsby, smiling good humouredly, "we will hear the recital of your and your good dame's dreams after the discovery, no doubt they will be found to bear a wonderful coincidence with the events that may transpire on that occasion. But in the meantime I beg that you will make your minds perfectly comfortable, for, it is quite evident that this strange old man has no sinister designs against you."

"Well, sir, I will," replied Hannibal, "but I shall be all anxiety until to-morrow arrives. Is it not singular if there is really any treasure hidden where the old man of the ruins has pointed out, that he did not avail himself of the opportunity of appropriating it to himself, instead of taking such pains to make it known to others?"

"It is," agreed Mr. Coningsby, "and that induces me to think that there is really no treasure hidden there at all; but there may be a secret, which he has certainly taken a very strange method, if he is in the possession of it, to make known. And after all, it may not concern any of us."

"But your honour will agree that it is necessary we should ascertain that fact."

"Certainly."

After some other trivial observations, old Hannibal Dobson took his leave.

"It appears quite evident," remarked Miss Coningsby, after he was gone, "that so far as the statements of Hannibal and his wife go they are correct. They perfectly correspond."

"They do," replied Mrs. Hardy, "and I begin to think more seriously of this business than I did at first."

"I am completely bewildered," said Mr. Coningsby, "and know not what to think. But to-morrow morning will decide all."

"And you will allow me and Mrs. Hardy to accompany you, my dear papa?" said Celestia."

"As I said before, most certainly, my dear girl."

"And I presume I am not to be excluded from the party on this important and mysterious mission?" said Miss Coningsby.

"Certainly not, my dear sister," replied Mr. Coningsby, "I should wish every one who is interested in the singular business to be present when the investigation takes place. It is utterly impossible to fathom the motives of this old man of the ruins, as he is now called, but probably this may throw some light upon them, though I much fear he is no friend of mine, yet why he should be my enemy I am at a loss to imagine

His predictions on the morning of my marriage are still fresh in my memory as if they had been uttered only yesterday, and the recent interview I have had with him ——"

"Have you then again seen him since our return from the north?" inquired Miss Coningsby.

"I have;" he answered, and he then related what the reader has already been made acquainted with in a previous chapter, which Miss Coningsby and Celestia listened to with much astonishment and interest.

"He is certainly a most remarkable being," remarked Miss Coningsby, "and it is equally extraordinary where he conceals himself; no person seems to be acquainted with the place of his retreat."

"No; and he disappears so suddenly that there is no possibility of tracing him. Certainly, as old Hannibal has observed, there is that mystery about all his actions, which, if we were disposed to be superstitious, might lead us to imagine that he was something superhuman. It is a mystery that must be solved, for it is evident from his conduct towards me, that I am by some means or other deeply connected with it."

"There can be no doubt of it," coincided his sister; "and what with the vagaries of this old man of the ruins; the inexplicable conduct of the stranger, who has so frequently appeared before us, and the predictions of the gipsy woman to our fair charge, we have enough to perplex and annoy us."

"As for the gipsy," observed Mr. Coningsby, "I attach but very little importance to her, and I trust that Celestia will not give a serious thought to anything she has uttered to her. She is only one of that idle class of vagrants who prowl about the country; robbing where they cannot succeed in extorting money from the credulous, depend upon it, and means may soon be adopted of preventing any danger from her."

"But my dear sir," remarked Celestia, "although I would fain endeavour to treat her prognostications with contempt, I must say that she has never directly or indirectly made any demand upon me, and therefore have her conduct and observations made the stronger impression upon me."

"Banish them from your mind, my dear girl," said Mr. Coningsby, "for depend upon it, they are unworthy of serious consideration."

"I will try to do so, sir, replied our heroine, "though I am doubtful whether or not I shall succeed. She predicts to me approaching sorrow, but how I have merited it I know not."

"Certainly not, my dear Celestia," said Mr. Coningsby, "put your trust in Providence, whose will, I am certain you have always endeavoured to obey, and you may bid defiance to all the evil machinations or empty prognostications of your enemies."

The conversation upon that subject, for the present ended, and after a short time Celestia retired to her own apartment, whither she was accompanied by Mrs. Hardy.

They remained together for some time conversing upon the extraordinary events of the day, and Mrs. Hardy exerted herself to the utmost to banish from the mind of Celestia the impression which had been made upon it by the observations of the gipsy. But this was a task not easy of accomplishment, and willing as our heroine was to scout all such superstitions ideas from her mind, she found it utterly impossible to treat the warnings and prognostications of the gipsey woman with the indifference that her friends would have persuaded her to do.

Curiosity, however, superseded every other feeling in her breast, and she awaited with the greatest anxiety the arrival of the following day, when the examination of the hidden secret in the old priory ruins was appointed to take place; for she did not for a moment believe that old Hannibal and his wife could have both been deceived, and she imagined that some discovery of a most extraordinary nature would be made.

She could sleep but little during that night for thinking upon it, and she felt a kind of relief when on the following morning she received a summons to the breakfast-room.

The repast over, Mr. Coningsby, his sister, and our heroine entered the carriage, which had been ordered, and were immediately driven off towards the ruins.

Hannibal and his wife received them with all proper respect and humilty, and after they had been a short time seated in the parlour of the lodge, Mr. Coningsby proposed that they should immediately go upon the business which had brought them there, to which they all very readily assented.

Hannibal had all the necessary implements in readiness, and, leading the way, they soon arrived at the spot which had been so strangely pointed out by the old man of the ruins, and where they expected to make some wonderful discovery.

No one exhibited more curiosity and impatience than poor old Dorothy, and she urged her husband to lose no time in removing the slab, so that the expected secret might be at once revealed. Hannibal, who was as anxious as herself, needed no persuasion, and, setting briskly about his task, the stone was soon removed from a position which it seemed to have occupied for many years, but nothing was revealed but the earth in which it had been embedded.

This, by the orders of Mr. Coningsby, Hannibal set about removing, and he had not dug many inches when his spade came in contact with some hard substance, and to the astonishment of all the anxious lookers on, the lid of a small oak chest was shortly afterwards disclosed.

"The old man of the ruins has not deceived us," said Mr. Coningsby, "and I feel satisfied that some important discovery is about to be made. Proceed with your task, good Hannibal."

The latter obeyed, and, after a little more labour, the chest was removed from the place where it appeared to have been for some years buried.

There was no key in the lock, and the lid was forced open without delay, when the chest was found to contain a boy's vest and tunic, embroidered round the bottom and up the sides with fine knitting; a fine cambric shirt trimmed with Valenciennes lace, a black satin hat and feather, and a purple sash; but, independant of these, there was a coral necklace, with a gold clasp, on which was engraven the cipher E. C.

No sooner did Mr. Coningsby behold the different articles than he exhibited the most indiscribible emotion, and clasping the necklace in his hands he exclaimed—

"Almighty God, how inscrutable are thy ways. This is the very dress, the same necklaue that my poor boy wore on the fatal morning when he was lost."

"Is it possible, my dear brother?" ejaculated Miss Coningsby with the most unfeigned astonishment.

"It is true," replied Mr. Coningsby, "and see, the cipher on the necklace is more than a suffieient proof, besides, the embroidery on the clothes was the work of Lady Elvina's hand! My God, I beseech thee to solve this still impenetrable mystery! By what means came these things here?"

Every one was wrapped in amazement, and gazed at the different articles in the chest in wonder, while the agitation of Mr. Coningsby increased every moment. But in removing the last article from the chest, they discovered a letter without any direction upon it. Mr. Coningsby eagerly seized it, and breaking open the seal, with breathless haste, read the following words—

"Should this ever meet the eyes of the parents of the child to whom these clothes belong, they are informed that at the time this letter is written, he is living and well provided for, though it is more than probable he will never be restored to them. A certain gentleman, while in attendance upon his dying wife, left his child in the care of its nurse (the guilty woman who writes these lines) at ——, and being out one day with a young man in a boat, the child sprang from her arms into the sea. The young man immediately leaped in, but it was impossible to recover him, though he was nearly drowned himself in the attempt. The nurse was nearly distracted, and in order to conceal a fault, committed a crime. We had frequently been out at sea along the coast, and had observed some children with their nurses, one of them about the age of the drowned child, and at the instigation of the young man, they resolved to steal this child; they too well accomplished their purpose, and the father of the drowned boy was so well imposed upon that he had not the least suspicion. He is a gentleman of wealth, and of course the child will be brought up with the same care and affection, as if it were absolutely his own ; however, for reasons which must appear obvious, I forbear to mention the gentleman's name."

"Gracious Heaven !" exclaimed Mr. Coningsby, when he had perused this singular letter, and which had fallen in such an extraordinary manner into his hands, "how truly wonderful are thy ways, the dreadful secret is at length revealed, and my son may still be in existence, but where shall I seek him ? What plan can I adopt to get him restored to me ? This awful suspense is even more torturing than if I had heard of his death. Oh, how can this guilty woman rest with such a crime upon her conscience ?"

The astonishment of Miss Coningsby and our heroine at this most remarkable discovery, was almost equal to that which Mr. Coningsby evinced.

"Then you are certain, my dear brother," said the former, "that these were the clothes worn by your long lost son ?"

"They are the very same that he wore on the morning that he was lost ;" said Mr. Coningsby; "if the circumstances as related by this guilty woman did not satisfactorily prove it, this necklace is more than sufficient. What could have induced her to select these ruins as the place in which to deposit the chest ? Oh, Providence, I humbly beseech thee further to unravel this terrible mystery and if my son be still living to restore him to me, that I may invoke upon his head my parental benediction, ere it shall please Thee to take me to thyself."

Celestia was much affected, and Mr. Coningsby continued to gaze upon the contents of the chest with speechless wonder and emotion; and as the sight of them recalled to his memory in the most vivid colours all the melancholy and torturing circumstances of the past, it was not without the greatest difficulty that he could restrain his tears.

"This certainly is a circumstance," remarked Miss Coningsby, "which excites more astonishment and perplexity the longer we reflect upon it. The woman might for ought she knew, as

well have destroyed these evidences of her guilt, for she must have known that it was almost next to an utter impossibility, that they would ever be discovered ; much less could she expect that they would ever fall into the hands of the relatives of the stolen child. The ways of Providence are wonderful and inscrutable, and I trust that it will yet fully unravel this painful mystery, reveal to us the name of the gentleman on whom the child was imposed, and if he be still living, restore him to your arms, my deeply injured brother."

"God send that it may ;" fervently ejaculated Celestia.

"Alas ! alas !" sighed Mr. Coningsby, "I fear that there is but little hope of such a result. The number of years that have elapsed since the fatal circumstance seems to render it most improbable."

"Nay, my dear brother," said Miss Coningsby, "you must not give yourself up entirely to despair ; Providence has led you to the discovery of these articles in the most miraculous way, and you know that there is nothing impossible to him. But that this singular old man should be aware where the chest was deposited is not the least extraordinary part of the affair, and it goes to show, I think, beyond very little doubt, that he must have been in the guilty woman's secret, and therefore if we can only by persuasion or force, get him to confess, the whole truth may be unravelled, and your son restored to you."

"Would to Heaven that I could discover the place of that old man's concealment," said Mr. Coningsby, "and obtain an interview with him. There must be no means untried to effect that object. Hannibal, I request you most earnestly, not to be daunted by any idle fears, but to watch the motions of this mysterious being narrowly and cautiously, so that you may happily discover the place of his retreat, and give me immediate notice of anything that may transpire which may be at all likely to forward our plans."

"You may depend upon me, sir," replied Hannibal, "God knows there is no one who is more anxious to serve your honour in any way than I am."

"It would be advisable, I think,"

suggested Miss Coningsby, "to keep this discovery secret for the present."

"Very true," coincided her brother, "by prudence and silent precaution, we may effect much. Oh, my son, may it please the Almighty in His unbounded goodness to restore you to me, and I shall feel more than repaid for the many, many years of anguish I have endured."

The various articles were now replaced in the chest, which Mr. Coningsby desired Hannibal to see removed to the abbey in the course of the day, and the whole party then returned to the lodge, where they continued to converse for some time on the singular event of the morning, and the important discovery which it was not at all improbable might result from it.

At length they returned home, and a short time after they had arrived there, the chest was forwarded by Hannibal. Again Mr. Coningsby contemplated the precious contents, with feelings such as we need not attempt to describe, and again and again he perused the letter, and in vain endeavoured to elicit from it some clue to the guilty writer. That the old man of the ruins was acquainted with the whole of the secret seemed quite evident, and he determined that no exertion should be wanting on his part to obtain an interview with him, and to elicit from him the truth; but still he apprehended that that would be a most difficult task, especially as the old man for some unaccountable reason seemed to entertain feelings of malice towards him.

This strange adventure gave food for much conversation and speculation between Mrs. Hardy and Celestia, and sincerely did they both wish that the whole truth might shortly be disclosed, and that the long lost son might shortly be restored to his deeply injured parent, whom it had pleased Providence to visit with misfortunes of such a description, and whose numerous and transcendant virtues were deserving of so very different a fate

CHAPTER XII.
THE LONG LOST FOUND.

NOTWITHSTANDING all the exertions of Mr. Coningsby and his friends, they could not elicit anything more to throw the least light upon this mysterious affair, nor had they seen anything of the old man of the ruins, or been able to gain any clue to the place of his concealment.

Mr. Coningsby was at a perfect loss what further course to adopt, and the anxiety, perplexity, and suspense he experienced was almost beyond endurance.

In this manner a tedious month passed away, when Lord Everside returned to his estate from London, and took the earliest opportunity of paying a visit to his esteemed friend.

Mr. Coningsby immediately confided to his lordship the particulars of the discovery he had made, and Lord Everside listened to him with the most unfeigned astonishment and interest.

"This certainly is one of the most singular circumstances I ever heard of," he remarked, "and I know not how to advise you. What an abominable creature must this woman be to have been guilty of such a heartless crime. But do not resign all hope, my dear friend; I firmly believe that your son is still living, and although so much is involved in so much mystery at present, the time will come when he will be restored to you."

"Would to Heaven that I could think so," said Mr. Coningsby, "but alas! I see but little prospect of such a happy event at present."

"Do not say so; but by some means or other this old man must be discovered, and be made to speak out, for it is my firm belief that he knows all about it."

"I am also strongly of that opinion, my lord, or how should he know where the chest was concealed?"

"Certainly not, and it seems as if he was half inclined to divulge, or he would not have pointed out the spot where it was buried. Endeavour to wait patiently, Mr. Coningsby, and there is no knowing what favourable results a few days may produce."

The ladies now entered the room, and after the usual compliments had been exchanged between them and his lordship, and they were seated at the dinner-table, he turned to them, and said—

"My dear madam and Miss Celestia, I have seen an old acquaintance of yours's while in town, who desired me to present his compliments to you ; but you shall have the particulars at dessert."

"But pray tell us who the gentleman is?" requested Miss Coningsby.

"Indeed I shall leave you to guess," replied Lord Everside, but, if your memory fails you, I'm sure Celestia's will not."

Our heroine blushed, though she knew not why, and she was at a perfect loss to imagine, who it was to whom his lordship alluded. She recollected no old acquaintance that she could have in town, to inquire after her, and she was disposed to think that Lord Everside was only joking. Her suspense and curiosity were, however, soon gratified.

The dessert being placed on the table, and the servants having withdrawn, Lord Everside turned to Mr. Coningsby and said—

"It is not a very usual thing for me to be taken with people at first sight, but I met with a gentleman whilst in town whose countenance and manners so entirely won my heart that I made the first advances towards an intimacy. His name is Augustus Clemments, and he comes from Bengal. He inherited a large property from his father, but what is very remarkable, you will admit, he fears he has no claim to it ; however, it yet remains in doubt."

"Fears he has no claim to it," said Mr. Coningsby "how is that, pray?"

"Listen to me, my friend, while I give you all the particulars which have as yet come to my knowledge. This Mr. Clemments quitted Bengal for England, in order to come at the truth ; unfortunately they were encountered by a French ship of war, captured and conveyed to France, thrown into a French prison, where he lay nearly two years, but made his escape with some of his companions, landed at Dover and set out for the north, as soon as he had repaired his finances at his bankers in London—but as if fortune had resolved to throw continual stumbling blocks in his way, his carriage was overturned and himself severely injured, in fact half killed."

As Lord Everside thus spoke, he looked archly at Miss Coningsby and Celestia, who exclaimed.

"Ah, it must be the gentleman whom we met at Berensforth Hall."

"Yes, your favourite," said Mr. Coningsby, with a smile, "my sister could talk of little else during the whole evening."

"Very true, my dear brother," said Miss Coningsby, "and after what his lordship has said, you must admit that we are not singular in our sudden partiality ; but pray, my lord, proceed, for I presume it is from him you have compliments. How did he find us out?"

"You shall hear, and should have heard before now, if your eagerness to acknowledge your favourite had not delayed it ; but I must preface, that I know not which of you is destined to wear the willow, he was so equal in his admiration. But tell me, sir, where did I leave off? O, most inhumanely, just, where he had nearly been killed ; well, his servants claimed the rights of hospitality at an ancient hall, where he was received by the good housekeeper, who performed every office of kindness for the gentleman, for upwards of four months. About that period two beings of celestial mould made their appearance ; one of Minerva-like appearance, seemed to be the protectress of a young and interesting female, apparently betwixt childhood and adolesence. They were at first shocked at their intrusion, they would have made a precipitate retreat, had he not made use of his most persuasive rhetoric to prevail upon them to stay ; having made himself a strong interest in both their hearts, when, behold, though their stay did not amount to more than a quarter of an hour, they left him minus of his heart, without the smallest information of who they were ; fortunately, their servants were more communicative, and he learned their names afterwards from his attentive nurse, who thinking it might amuse him—but I shall say no more, but leave it to himself to tell the rest, when he pays me the promised visit. At the same time he deputed me to make his respectful compliments to both ladies."

Lord Everside ceased to speak, and

after a very few questions, the ladies withdrew and left the gentlemen to their wine.

But there was one individual who felt annoyed and uneasy at his lordship's tale; and one who neither drank nor conversed, and who seized the first opportunity to quit the room.

This individual was Collingwood Aubrey, who had been invited to the dinner, and whose seat became uneasy from the moment Lord Everside coupled the stranger with the ladies; his arch look at Celestia naturally raised a blush on her cheek, but the evident pleasure with which she heard of his convales-

cence conjured up the demon of jealousy in his breast. His only consolation at present was, that they were nearly strangers to each other; but then the promised visit, and when would it take place? These were questions that greatly tortured him, and he felt truly miserable a he rode on his way home.

"And how soon do you expect your new friend, my lord?" asked Mr. Coningsby, when they were alone.

"It is quite uncertain," replied his lordship, "but it may be some time first, for he seems to have a wild goose chase upon his hands; but I will make you acquainted with what he made known to me of his affairs, and then you will be able to judge of his situation."

There was something in the manner of Lord Everside, and sort of preparation, which gave Mr. Coningsby an idea of being somehow implicated in this story, though he never remembered to have heard the name of Clemments, till it had been mentioned by his lordship.

After a pause, Lord Everside resumed:—

"Mr. Clemments left Bengal," he said, in consequence of a letter he found among the papers of an old steward after his decease; the letter was from a sister of his wife, who had been dead some years. It expressed great sorrow for her affliction, at the same time an action she had related in her last letter was sufficient to render her for ever miserable, as fraud of any kind was unpardonable; at the same time that Mr. Clemments entertained not the slightest suspicion that Augustus was not his own son, and had brought him up as such for upwards of thirty years, he was deceived into happiness, as the death of his only child under such aggravated circumstances might have been fatal to him; but that which must for ever weigh down her spirits, was the misery which the real parents of the child must experience from his loss."

"God of Heaven!" exclaimed Mr. Coningsby, with the greatest agitation, and starting from his seat; "this story corresponds in every respect with the contents of the letter which I found in the chest. Oh, my friend, where is this young man? My heart already tells me that in him I shall discover my long lost son. Merciful Providence, grant that my fond hopes may not be disappointed!"

"I pray you, my dear friend," said Lord Everside, "to compose yourself, and to endeavour to have patience. Mr. Clemments has left England, as I before told you; nothing can be proved till he finds the person he is in search of; but to continue my story; this letter raised a strange tumult in the breast of Mr. Clemments; his supposed father had been dead nearly two years, he had of course succeeded to all his vast possessions; and though having but one relation in the world, and he as rich as himself, and beside very distantly allied, yet honour forbade him retaining possession of a

name and property he could have no right to, if the aforesaid letter was to be depended upon.

"The circumstances were such as to render it highly imprudent in him to make the disclosure till he could arrive at the explanation of the enigma; and if he was not the son of Mr. Clemments, to whom did he then belong? by the tenor of the letter, some diabolical act had been committed."

"Diabolical indeed!" ejaculated Mr. Coningsby; "Mysterious Providence! thy ways are intricate, but always just. Pray proceed, my lord, for I am all impatience to hear the sequel of this strange narrative. Oh, should it indeed prove to be as my hopes suggest."

"The daughter of the steward," continued Lord Everside, "had married an officer in the company's service, and resided at some distance up the country; to her Mr. Clemments immediately went, and told her he had some thoughts of going to England; if therefore she had any friends or relations there to whom she could be of use, or had any wish to write to them, he would with pleasure execute the commission.

"Though surprised at this condescension, she nevertheless expressed the pleasure it would give her, if he would take a letter and a present of some value, (which she had kept in readiness till a safe conveyance offered) to her aunt.

"'Is it your paternal aunt?' asked Mr. Clemments.

"'No,' she answered; 'it is my late mother's only sister, from whom I have received no letters for above two years.'

"At first Mr. Clemments was tempted to question her concerning the letter he had found, but a moment's reflection changed his purpose, naturally judging that a mother would conceal from a child an action such as the letter described. He therefore determined to pursue his intention of going to England to see this woman; and proceed in the affair as circumstances should require.

"With all the expedition they would admit of, he arranged his affairs, and embarked in the first ship that sailed for England, unfortunately they were arrested in their course by a French ship of war, and after an obstinate resistance, were obliged to strike, and were carried prisoners into France, where Mr. Clemments lay in a French prison for two years; fortunately he secured his papers about his person, therefore they were safe; everything else became the prey of the captor.

"At the end of that period he made his escape, and arrived in England, where he arranged his affairs at the bankers, and hastened towards the north, where the letter was addressed; unfortunately the accident he met with on the way again delayed his purpose, and when he was able to go thither, he had the vexation to learn that she had been gone nearly two years to Switzerland, with her husband, to settle there, as he was a native of that country. Mr. Clemments now traced his way back to London, where, as the same banker served both, we met and dined there together, where he mentioned the reason of his leaving Bengal, and his intention of setting out immediately for Switzerland, notwithstanding all the terrors of capture, imprisonment, &c., which I endeavoured to impress him with."

Thus Lord Everside concluded, and Mr. Coningsby's agitation was so great, that he had scarcely power to let him proceed to the end without interruption.

"Gracious Heaven!" he exclaimed, "surely this young man must be my long lost son. There was no positive proof that he was drowned, nay, the clothes and the letter in the chest, sufficiently prove that he was not; the age of the stranger, too, and the period he has passed at Bengal so exactly correspond with the period at which my child was lost."

"Why, my good friend," said his lordship, "I must confess that when I recollected that part of your narrative, I could not avoid making the same remark, and it is not at all unlikely, that in my usual way I might have said something about it to Mr. Clements, which I as hastily should have repented, for till he has seen this woman, no certain conclusion can be drawn, and therefore, I might have done mischief, and certainly no good."

"Oh, my lord! you may judge of my feelings after this account, but I must admit the truth of your observations, at the same time I shall be in a state of cruel suspense until his return from Switzerland; but I must think the hand of Providence directed it throughout to bring that hope to me, the accident he met with introduced him to my sister, who was very much struck with him, and who, when she described him, said she should suppose me to have been like him at that age."

"And by-the-by," said his lordship, "that picture he mentioned as being so like the youngest of the ladies, (meaning Celestia). Whose portrait was that?"

"That of Lady Elvina when at her age," answered Mr. Coningsby with a sigh, "she does resemble her so strongly that I never look at one without being reminded of the other. Heaven alone knows why it is so; but the greater part of my life has been a state of agitation by an accumulation of extraordinary events; whatever happiness Providence may have in store for me, it is my duty to wait in patience."

"And I am sanguine enough," remarked Lord Everside, "to think it will be amply rewarded."

"But he did promise to write to you?"

"He did, and I think it will not be long ere he does so, unless the French have again met with him, which is not likely."

The conversation now ceased, and Lord Everside soon afterwards took his leave. The feelings of suspense, doubt, and hope now distracted the mind of Mr. Coningsby, and it could not escape the observation of Miss Coningsby and Celestia when they returned to the room, and his sister eagerly enquired the cause.

"It related to Lord Everside's young friend, Mr. Clemments," answered Mr. Coningsby.

"Ah!" said his sister, in alarm. "I hope that no fresh accident has befallen him."

"No," said Mr. Coningsby, "such is not the case, I believe—but my mind is too much disturbed to enter into particulars at present. In the morning I will relate to you the whole of the wonderful story, and you will then be convinced that I have good cause for the agitation I at present endure."

With this promise, Miss Coningsby and Celestia were obliged to be satisfied.

Mr. Coningsby passed a restless night, for his thoughts were continually fixed upon the remarkable narrative which he had received from Lord Everside. When Miss Coningsby joined her brother and Celestia the following morning in the breakfast-room, she was distressed to see his countenance display a disquiet he had long been a stranger to, and impatiently awaited the promised explanation, which Mr. Coningsby soon afterwards gave them.

Great was the astonishment of the ladies at the wonderful interposition of Providence, for that it was the long lost Edgar, Miss Coningsby would not admit a doubt of; time and circumstances, as far as the half sentences in the letter might be understood, seemed to agree that the child of Mr. Clemments was killed, and the other put in his place to deceive the father, and that this young man would turn out to be the son of Mr. Coningsby appeared nearly a certainty in the mind of his sister.

"Oh, my dear brother," she ejaculated, "encourage hope, for depend upon it, that the Almighty has yet every happiness in store for you. There can be little or no doubt that the writer of that letter we found in the chest, and the author of the imposition upon the late Mr. Clemments is one and the same person, and if so, the identity of your long lost son is most unquestionably and satisfactorily proved."

"My heart tells me that it is even so," returned Mr. Coningsby, "and if it should unfortunately ultimately turn out that I am mistaken, I know not how I shall ever be able to support such a terrible disappointment. With what anxiety do I await the return of this young man from Switzerland, or the receipt, by Lord Everside of a letter from him."

"I trust, my dear brother, that you will not long be kept in suspense, and the result will be all that we can hope for. But I feel satisfied in my own mind, that it will turn out as I anticipate, and that ere long, you will have the felicity of embracing that dear child whom you had never expected to behold again."

"God grant that your anticipations may be realized my sister, then shall I be repaid for the many years of suffering it has been my lot to endure.

What a fortunate thing it was that Lord Everside became acquainted with him; surely the hand of Providence was in it all."

"It was," said Miss Coningsby, "and the same kind Providence will yet reward you for the patience and resignation with which you have borne the misfortunes it has been pleased to visit you with. Could we meet with this old man of the ruins, and persuade him to become communicative, I am satisfied that we should very soon arrive at the facts that we are so anxious to ascertain."

"Yes," said Mr. Coningsby, "I perfectly agree with you, my dear sister, there, it seems evident to me that that unaccountable being must be immediately connected with the guilty parties in this nefarious transaction, but it seems equally unlikely that he will come forward to divulge what he knows, especially, as from his actions, I have a right to suppose that he entertains some of the most vindictive feelings towards me."

"And yet, why should he do so?" said Miss Coningsby.

"There, my dear sister, you put a problem to me that I have never yet been able to solve. Who that ancient man can be, and what are the motives for his conduct, I am perfectly at a loss to conceive. Certainly I could never have given him any just cause for malice, for never till the morning of my marriage did I behold him."

"Is it not possible that he may be related to the woman who committed this dreadful offence, which has been productive of so much misery."

"That is not at all improbable," replied Mr. Coningsby, "but it is useless to form any idle speculations, we must leave it to the wisdom of the Supreme to unravel all."

"Which I trust, my brother, he will do ere long, and that you will be reinstated in that happiness, you are so justly entitled to, and which you so well know how to enjoy and appreciate."

The was no one who felt more deeply interested in the issue of these events than Celestia, prepossessed as she was in favour of the supposed Augustus Clemments, from the short interview that she had had with him; she was most anxious that one apparently so worthy, so estimable, should prove to be the long lost son of her venerated guardian, a discovery that might restore him to that happiness to which he so long had been a stranger.

When she was alone, she deeply reflected upon this subject, but she was aroused from her cogitations by receiving a message from Mr. Coningsby to attend him and his sister in the library, as they had something of particular importance to communicate. She immediately obeyed the summons, and on her entrance found Mr. Coningsby and his sister engaged in deep conversation in one corner of the apartment. On perceiving her, they received her with much affection, and requested her to be seated; a pause then ensued, which was most embarrassing to our heroine, for she could judge from the countenances of her benefactors, that the subject upon which they to speak desired with her, was indeed a most delicate one.

"My dear Celestia," at length began Mr. Coningsby, "I am satisfied that you duly appreciate the affectionate feelings with which myself and sister have ever regarded you, and how anxious we are for your future welfare and prosperity in life."

Amazed and bewildered at this solemn preface, Celestia for a few moments was at a loss what reply to make, but at length she said,—

"Oh, my dearest papa and aunt, can you for a moment doubt the full sense I entertain of the unparalleled kindness you have ever evinced towards me? Mention one instance in which I may have erred and how readily will I make all the atonement in my power."

"You mistake me, my love," returned Mr. Coningsby, "I have nothing to reproach you with, but all to admire and commend; but you must be aware that all which concerns your future happiness and prospects in life must engage our most paramount solicitude and anxiety. To be brief then, young Mr. Collingwood Aubrey has imbibed a passion for you, which I believe to be sincere and honourable; he has been here this morning, made serious proposals, and asked my permission to endeavour at gaining your love."

Celestia blushed deeply, and hid her face in the bosom of Miss Coningsby, while her heart palpitated violently against her side.

"Be composed, my love," said Mr. Coningsby, "and think not for a moment that I am going to attempt to bias your inclinations. I have the highest opinion of Mr. Collingwood Aubrey, and, as I assured him, I could not form the least objection to his paying his addresses to you, but on the contrary, that I wished him success most sincerely, but that he must promise that neither himself or my sister would make the slightest use of their influence over you in that particular. I feel satisfied that the heart of my dear Celestia is at present disengaged, but, my love, I must add, as I told Collingwood, that I consider you yet too young to enter into so solemn an engagement; therefore, all the authority I or my sister will exert is, not to consent to your union with any one until you have completed your eighteenth year."

"Oh, sir," said the blushing Celestia, "how shall I reply to you upon so delicate a subject. I will not for a moment attempt to deny that Mr. Collingwood has my warmest esteem, but—but his parents would be indignant at his attaching himself to one whom no one knows, and——"

She paused.

"I am not quite sure of that, Celestia," said Miss Coningsby; "admitting that your birth is inferior to his, there is a wide distinction to be drawn; the woman must descend to the level of her husband, whereas, the man being superior, ennobles the woman he weds; but I am of opinion that your birth is superior to his, and noble also."

"And how can I prove that?" said our heroine. "Alas! my dear madam, there is now so little probability, from the miserable state of the continent, that I should ever discover to whom I belong, that I feel no inclination to introduce myself into any family; indeed, my dearest benefactors, I assure you that I have never myself given a thought to the subject, and I should think it highly ridiculous in a girl of little more than sixteen, to form so solemn an engagement, not knowing to whom I belong, and dependent on the bounty of strangers for support."

"I admire your sentiment, my Celestia," remarked Mr. Coningsby, "but still I would wish you not to reject this young man altogether, for I think him worthy of you, and I am much deceived if you do not entertain something of a warmer sentiment than that of mere esteem towards him. At the same time, my dearest child, I am rejoiced that at so early an age you possess a firmness, which, if always tempered by judgment and consideration, will, I trust, preserve you from the many evils precipitancy brings us mortals into. I would wish you, Celestia, not to let the idea of dependence dwell in your mind; believe me, my child, were you my own, I could not love you more sincerely. I have no tie, at present, that I know of upon earth that calls upon me for support; my sister's fortune is nearly equal to mine, and, like me, independent of every tie; let us leave our property to whom we will, they will be little obliged to us, since we cannot take it with us; therefore, Celestia, when you meet with an individual, whom you think qualified to make you happy, remember fortune on his part is unnecessary—provided he is a gentleman in education, manners, and connections—the man of worth and honour, in the most comprehensive sense of the term. When you meet with such an one, and a reciprocal esteem takes place, put confidence in your affectionate aunt, who will ever be a sincere adviser."

Need we attempt to describe the feelings of Celestia, at this truly parental address of Mr. Coningsby? She was so deeply affected that for some moments she was incapable of making any reply; at length, recovering, she threw herself into his arms, as she ejaculated—

"My more than parent, how blessed is your Celestia in two such friends! Never more will I name the word dependence, or once remember I am an orphan—no, from this moment I will never name a subject that must stamp me with the crime of ingratitude; and you, my dearest aunt, shall have my most implicit confidence; no thought of your Celestia's shall ever be concealed from you; then can she never be guilty of any fault of sufficient magnitude to call a blush on your cheek for her."

Mr. Coningsby and his sister embraced her with affectionate tenderness, and the former said—

"I am certain that my dear Celestia can never be guilty of anything that can call for anything like reproach from those who have her happiness so dearly at heart. But Collingwood Aubrey, my love—what answer shall we return to his petition? You will not leave him entirely to despair."

Celestia blushed more deeply than before, and her heart palpitated with still greater violence, but she quickly recovered herself sufficiently to reply—

"No, my dearest, best friends, I will not treat with such unmerited disregard the honour which Mr. Collingwood intends me; I shall ever receive his friendship and attentions with all becoming respect and pleasure."

"Well spoken, my love," said Mr. Coningsby, "I will not fail to deliver your answer to Mr. Collingwood Aubrey, and I am certain that it will make him one of the happiest fellows in existence."

After some further conversation Mr. Coningsby and his sister allowed our heroine to retire, and she was glad of the opportunity, that she might alone give vent to those feelings which the nature of the interview had naturally excited in her bosom.

That she felt a sentiment even stronger than esteem for Mr. Collingwood Aubrey, Celestia did not attempt to deny to herself, and after the observations of Mr. Coningsby, she saw no reason to discourage them in her bosom.

Mr. Coningsby took an early opportunity of informing Collingwood of the result of his interview with our heroine, and the reader will be able to form a pretty just conception of the delight he experienced, when he was assured that the fair Celestia was far from looking upon him with indifference, and that he might hope in time to win her heart's most ardent affections. Had she been the veriest beggar—the most friendless individual in the world, his sentiments must still have been the same towards her, for the treasures of her mind far counterbalanced anything that riches could supply.

Mr. Coningsby and his sister had very much endeared themselves to Sir Eustace

Aubrey and his lady, and they could not but warmly admire the unassuming virtues of the young orphan whom they had under their protection. Mr. Coningsby had informed Sir Eustace of every particular concerning her, and of his having adopted her, and he added,—

"Her fortune shall be equal to any one her birth may entitle her to, which I have not the smallest doubt is noble."

Though Sir Eustace did not quite approve, he yet wished not to oppose his son's choice of an object so truly worthy of affection, and Lady Aubrey's consent being obtained, Collingwood was allowed to pay his addresses to the lovely being who had made an impression on his heart which nothing could eradicate. The favour with which he was received by the amiable girl herself, added to his felicity, and he entertained the most sanguine and brilliant hopes of the happiness that was in store for him. But, alas! Collingwood, you were doomed to the most painful disappointment, however bright the sunshine of your present prospects might appear to be.

It may well be supposed that Mr. Coningsby's mind was in a state of the most painful suspense and anxiety until the return of Mr. Clemments, or that Lord Everside should receive the promised communication from him, but his patience was doomed to be put to a severe trial. Weeks flew away, and still no intelligence was received from the object of his anxiety, and he began to fear that some accident of a serious nature had befallen him, and such was the state of anguish to which he was at last reduced (confident in his own mind, from all the circumstances that the supposed Mr. Clemments would really turn out to be his own son), that it was with difficulty he could be dissuaded from setting out for Switzerland in search of him.

In the meantime all the endeavours of himself and friends, and the persons they had employed, to discover the old man of the ruins, had been completely unsuccessful. Every likely place in the neighbourhood had been examined to no purpose. Most persons had seen at some time or other the mysterious being, but they had never by any possible means been able to find out who he was, or the place of his retreat, in fact, he was looked upon by the humbler classes with a feeling of awe and superstition, they declaring that many of the predictions he had on various occasions given utterance to, had been fearfully realized, and they therefore dreaded to penetrate too closely into his secrets.

Lord Everside was a daily visitor at the abbey, and he exerted himself to the utmost to endeavour to buoy his friend up with hope; but the state of suspense in which the mind of Mr. Coningsby was placed, had the most serious effects upon his health, which his friends were quite alarmed to see.

Three months elapsed in this manner, when one day Lord Everside suddenly entered the dining-parlour just as they had sat down to table. Mr. Coningsby rose to greet him, and he could immediately perceive by the expression of his lordship's countenance that he had something of importance to communicate.

"I am extremely glad to see your lordship," said Mr. Coningsby, "and I am much mistaken if something interesting has not brought you hither."

"Why, in that respect, my dear friend," returned Lord Everside, "you are not mistaken. I come self-invited, but I have not the least doubt that I am not the less welcome."

"Oh, my good lord," replied Mr. Coningsby, "I am certain that I need not assure you that it always affords me the greatest possible pleasure to see you. But pray tell me, have you any news?— Have you received any letters from Switzerland?"

Lord Everside merely contented himself by laconically replying in the negative, and the countenance of Mr. Coningsby turned very pale, and he trembled violently. When the servants had withdrawn, however, Lord Everside turning to his friend, thus addressed him:—

"My dear Mr. Coningsby, as I said before, I have not received any communication from Switzerland, but I have one from Germany, and from my young friend too; and if you will pledge me in a bumper of Madeira to his health, I will perhaps indulge you with a sight of it."

"Oh, pray my lord, keep me not in

suspense. You must be perfectly well aware what my feelings must be; and I know you too well to think for a moment that you can wish to torture me further."

Seeing Mr. Coningsby too much agitated even to fill the glasses, Lord Everside took the decanter, and obliged the ladies to join in the toast. Miss Coningsby was almost as much agitated as her brother, for she imagined she perceived from his lordship's manner, that he had received some elucidation upon the mystery of Mr. Clemments' birth.

After they had honoured the toast, Lord Everside presented a letter to Mr. Coningsby, but scarcely had that gentleman perused a few lines when his senses forsook him, and but for the attentions of his friend, who was prepared for the effect it would have upon him, so deeply concerned as he was in them, he would have fallen from his chair.

Miss Coningsby seized the letter, and thought she had sufficient fortitude to undertake the reading of it; but before she had proceeded half-way she was obliged to resign it to Lord Everside.

The contents were as follows:—

"MY DEAR LORD EVERSIDE.

"To the vanity of a young man, apparently so unconnected in the world as I am, it is no small gratification to have been honoured with the countenance and friendship of a nobleman so distinguished as your lordship; and I must ever rejoice at the happy chance which introduced me to your acquaintance. I am happy in having your permission to draw upon your friendship by laying my difficulties before you, for I am apprehensive that it will be no easy matter to discover to whom I really belong, to whom I owe my being. My mind at this time is in the most dreadful state of agitation, and I cannot write as I would wish. I have already obtained sufficient knowledge of the nefarious transaction, to know that I have no right to the name and property of the late Mr. Clemments, and if I should not be able to find out those to whom I have a claim, my future prospects in life will indeed be wretched.

"I had sat down with the intention of making your lordship acquainted with every particular, but I find that my mind is so bewildered and agitated that I cannot accomplish the task, and must even delay the explanation until I can deliver it verbally to your lordship's ears. I can only inform you, to account for my letter being addressed from this place, that when I arrived at Geneva, the place where I had hoped to end my suspense, I was informed that Mr. and Mrs. Raimbach were gone into Saxony, where a relation, from whom he had great expectations, lay at the point of death. I must acknowledge that I did not like the journey, considering the state of the country; however, as my wonderful adventures I hoped drew near their close, I knew I must proceed now I had come so far, and I therefore continued my journey, and at length was introduced to the object of my search. But I must reserve the particulars of what transpired at the interview until I have the honour of meeting your lordship. God only knows if I shall ever discover my parents, even if they are living. Providence I know is all sufficient; in that I put my trust. If when I arrive in England, your lordship is not in London, I shall apply to our worthy banker for your address, and go down immediately to consult with you on the measures I must pursue, in order to discover my family connections; till when I remain, dear Lord Everside, your obliged and most humble servant—I cannot sign a name I have no right to; even my baptismal one I am unacquainted with; I will therefore only say he who was

"AUGUSTUS CLEMMENTS."

Lord Everside was not permitted to read the whole of this letter without frequent interruptions. The emotions of Mr. Coningsby were of the most painful description that can well be imagined.

"Oh, how dreadful is this suspense;" he exclaimed, striking his forehead; "oh, that Providence had given him strength to enter into a full explanation, then would all my doubts have been at once dispelled. But still I cannot, I dare not think otherwise than that he is my long lost son, and most anxiously do I await the blissful time when I can press him to my heart as such."

"My dear friend," remarked Lord Everside, "I am every way inclined to think that your hopes will be realized.

Indeed, all that has yet transpired serves to sanction such an opinion.   But still let me advise you to compose yourself, and not to be too sanguine, for should a disappointment take place, it will be more I am afraid, if you suffer yourself to be too much excited, than you can find strength to support."

" Support," repeated Mr. Coningsby. " Oh, no, indeed, I could not, the very thought of a disappointment is maddening.   But it must be he, he is proved not to have been the son of the late Mr. Clemments, he was stolen from the same neighbourhood where my poor child was lost; the letter in the chest containing

the clothes which my son had on at the time confirms the same statement.   Can anything be more clear or conclusive? It is impossible ! and doubt as to his identity can no longer enter my mind. But yet this delay, how torturing it is ; some accident may again occur to

him and retard our meeting.   I am sure, my kind friend, that you can and do sympathise with the feelings I must experience in such a situation."

" Indeed I do," replied Lord Everside, " and I sincerely trust that the time will soon arrive when your doubts will be removed entirely, and everything turn out as our most sanguine hopes anticipate."

"Dearest Edgar," ejaculated Mr. Coningsby with much emotion, "would that you were here, that I might press you to my heart by that name! But will not your lordship accompany me to London, in order to give him the meeting?"

"I need not assure you that I would most willingly do so, but I am fearful that we should cross him on the road, you may depend upon it, it would be better, if it meets with your approbation, that I should write to my friend the banker, and inclose a few lines addressed to Mr. Clemments, requesting him to come down here immediately, as I have some idea that I can point out a means of discovery to him that cannot fail. For, indeed, my dear friend, you would be ill able to support the agitation of such a meeting after a long, fatiguing journey. I shall receive him at my house, and hear the important particulars he has to relate, though in my own mind there cannot be a doubt of his identity, in the meantime we must endeavour by amusement to shorten the pain of expectation."

"Ah, Lord Everside, and think you it possible I can be amused, under the circumstances?" said Mr. Coningsby. "To count the hours till I am blessed with the sight of my long-lost Edgar, will be the sole amusement I shall be capable of, and assuredly, if not detained by any misfortune, his arrival may be shortly expected."

"It may," returned Lord Everside; "for it is quite certain that he will not make any more delay than is possible."

"But why was he not more explicit in his note?" said Mr. Coningsby. "Surely he might have persevered to command his feelings sufficiently to explain that which he must feel satisfied, from the friendship you evinced towards him, you would be so anxious to hear."

"Why," said his lordship, "I confess that I feel somewhat surprised and disappointed that he did not do so; but I suppose the explanation was of that nature that it could not properly be given in a letter, and he expected that the time would be so short ere he would meet me, that he considered, as he hints in his communication, that it would be better to deliver it to me verbally."

"Indeed," said Mr. Coningsby, "I cannot see any reasonable excuse for his deferring the explanation. Alas! did he but know the painful, the almost insupportable anxiety of mind that more than one individual is enduring until their doubts are removed, he would certainly have been more eager to communicate the facts."

"Doubtless," remarked Lord Everside, "he is as anxious to disclose to me all the particular circumstances that have attended his journey, as the tenor of his letter expresses; but still the circumstances may be too complicated for him to do justice to them in a letter. He seems to look upon me as the only friend he now has in the world, and it is evident that he is anxious to confide everything to me, and to seek my advice. It was a fortunate chance which introduced me to him, or these particulars might never have come to our knowledge."

"Oh, yes, it was indeed," said Mr. Coningsby; "the hand of an All-wise Almighty was in it all; and should this young man really prove to be my dear Edgar,—and I dare not venture to think that he is not—I shall for ever bless the day your lordship went to London. I regret that I did not accept of your invitation to accompany you, for then the discovery upon which all my hopes are fixed might have been at once made."

"It might so," returned Lord Everside; "however, it is of no use to regret now, and everything is going on much better towards the unravelment of this perplexing and painful mystery than might have been expected. I will lose no time in writing to my friend, the banker, and it is not unlikely that Mr. Clemments (as, for the want of another name, we must still continue to call him) will arrive in London almost as soon as the letter, and you may be sure he will then not lose a moment in coming down here."

"Yes, if no accident should have befallen him on the journey," returned

Mr. Coningsby, "which in these times of trouble is not at all unlikely."

"Now, my dear friend, I must beg of you not to torture your mind with such apprehensions. You may be sure that Mr. Clemments will be on his guard, and avoid that route where he is at all likely to be again captured by the French. Have a little patience, and I trust that everything will turn out in accordance with our most sanguine wishes. It is evident, from the letter of Mr. Clemments, that he has made some important discovery, and the circumstance of his being stolen from the same neighbourhood as that from whence you lost your child, and about the same period, leave but very little doubt on my mind that he is that very identical son."

"Heaven send that it may prove to be so; for should it not, after all these hopes have been raised in my breast, I know not how I shall support the disappointment."

"I trust that you will not be put to any such trial, my dear brother," said Miss Coningsby; "and indeed I am entirely of his lordship's opinion, namely, that there can be but little doubt that this young man is no other than your long lost Edgar. The circumstances so correspond, that it to me seems to be almost as certain as if it was already confirmed."

"Well, I will endeavour to think so too," said Mr. Coningsby; indeed, I should be wretched could I imagine that these new formed hopes were doomed to be disappointed."

Lord Everside passed some time longer at the abbey, when he returned home, resolving to write directly to his banker.

The letter of Mr. Clemments served Mr. Coningsby and his sister to talk upon for the remainder of the day; and when the former retired to his chamber for the night, his mind was in a state of great agitation, which entirely precluded the possibility of sleep. But doubt had no share in his feelings, for there did not appear any question as to the identity of his son, though the whole of the proofs were not yet before him.

The time would appear to him to be an age until he should behold him, or hear something further from him, though he could not suppose that his anxiety would allow him to delay a moment in coming down to Lord Everside on the receipt of his letter. All that he feared was that some accident on the road would retard his journey, and if so, the period at which they would meet might be an indefinite one; and the suspense he would thus be kept in would be almost too torturing for endurance.

"God grant that I may not be put to such a severe trial," he said, "and may he be protected from all harm. Oh! it must, indeed, be my beloved Edgar, who for so many years has been so cruelly torn from me; my heart tells me, assures me, that it is. The clothes in the chest are the same that he wore on the fatal morning that he was lost; and if anything were wanting to prove that this young man is he, the letter in the chest, and the one he had found among the papers of the steward of his late supposed father, so corresponded in the nature of their contents, that all doubt must be at once removed. Guilty woman, what misery has your unpardonable crime been the cause of! And then the likeness which my sister discovered the supposed Augustus Clemments to bear to me, serves more than all to strengthen the supposition, and to increase my hopes. My dear Edgar, and shall I indeed again be permitted, after the lapse of so many years, to press you to my heart, and to lavish upon you all a father's affection? Heaven, in Thine infinite mercy, grant that such may be the happiness in store for me; then will I cease to murmur at the unparalleled misfortunes with which it has been Thy will to visit me, and I may then hope that my future days will be those of serenity and peace."

Thus did Mr. Coningsby continue for some time to reflect, until, at length, worn out with fatigue, he sunk off to sleep.

Lord Everside again visited the abbey the following day, and Mr. Coningsby met him in better spirits than he had been in for some time before, and eagerly inquired whether he had written to London.

"I have," answered his lordship.

"You might be sure, my dear friend, that as I promised, I would not delay a moment in doing so; and I trust that Mr. Clemments will speedily be in town to receive it, and then all our doubts will be set at once at rest, for he will be sure to come down immediately, and the meeting, I need not say, I sincerely hope may be productive of the most happy consequences. The ladies, I dare say, are as anxious as yourself to see their favourite again."

"I can answer for myself," replied Miss Coningsby, with a smile, "that your lordship's imagination is perfectly correct; and as for my dear Celestia, I am much deceived if the meeting will not afford her equal pleasure."

"Indeed it will," said our heroine, fervently, "trusting as I do that it will lead to a discovery so important to the happiness of my dear guardian."

"Well," remarked his lordship, "we are all equally sanguine in our hopes, but we must wait patiently, notwithstanding, and I flatter myself that Providence will not suffer us to be disappointed. The way in which all these remarkable circumstances have been brought to light, is really most miraculous, and we cannot but admire the wisdom of the Almighty in bringing them about."

"It is a pity your lordship did not give the young man your address when you were in town," observed Mr. Coningsby, "he would then no doubt have made his way direct here, and much delay might have been prevented."

"True;" agreed Lord Everside, "I regret that I did not think of doing so, and know not how it came not to suggest itself to me. However, it cannot be helped now, and perhaps after all it may only cause the delay of a few hours."

"I hope it will not," returned Mr. Coningsby, "for I am sure your lordship will make every allowance for the anxiety and uneasiness which I feel until this important mystery is entirely developed."

"Of course, my friend, it is only natural that you should feel so, and I hope that the joyous expectations you have permitted to take possession of your breast will be fully realized, and that in a few days you may have the felicity of once more embracing that son whom you never expected to behold again."

"I feel satisfied myself," said Miss Coningsby, "that such joy is in store for us. But it is strange who this old man of the ruins can be, and where he conceals himself. I wish we could find out and obtain an interview, for it is most probable that he is acquainted with the whole secret."

"I think there can be little doubt of it, after what has transpired," said Lord Everside; "and that he has been in some manner connected with the guilty woman who committed the crime, or otherwise how could he have pointed out the spot where the chest was buried? His conduct is most remarkable and unaccountable, but I dare say that will be explained anon, like everything else that we feel so deep an interest in."

"Since the evening when he pointed out to Hannibal the place where the chest was concealed," said Mr. Coningsby, "he has disappeared altogether, and it would seem as if he had quitted this part of the country entirely."

"Well, after all," remarked his lordship, "I do not know that it can be of much consequence whether he has or no, for probably we shall arrive at all we want to know, without any assistance from him."

"When do you expect to hear from the gentleman to whom you have written."

"I requested him in my letter, to write by the return of post, which I dare say he will not fail to do."

The day passed away in this manner, and as hour after hour elapsed, the impatience of Mr. Coningsby increased, and again the most painful doubts and apprehensions crowded upon his mind, the principal of which was that some fresh accident had befallen Mr. Clemments, and interrupted his return to England.

The following day brought a letter to Lord Everside from his banker, in which he acknowledged the receipt of his communication, and promised to give the most prompt attention to the request it contained, as soon as Mr. Clemments should call upon him.

Lord Everside had related to him the particulars of the discoveries which had been made, and Mr. Harcourt the banker, expressed his firm conviction that the supposed Mr. Clemments would really turn out to be the long lost son of Lord Elverton, which he added he most heartily hoped might be the case.

Mr. Coningsby felt some little more at ease on the receipt of this letter, which breathed that spirit of hope which was so consonant with his feelings.

CHAPTER XII.

THE ACCIDENT AND THE MEETING.

MORE than a week passed away without anything occurring to gratify the feelings and expectations of Mr. Coningsby and his friends, nor had Lord Everside heard any more from Mr. Harcourt. He there despatched another urgent letter to him, and by the return of post he received an answer, in which the worthy banker regretted that they should continue to be kept in such a state of suspense and uncertainty, at the same time stating that up to that time he had not seen or heard anything of Mr. Clemments.

We need not seek to describe the agony of Mr. Coningsby, and they were all at a perfect loss in what manner to act.

Days, weeks elapsed, and still they received no intelligence and Mr. Coningsby gave himself up entirely to despair, and vain were all the efforts of Lord Everside to console him.

Miss Coningsby and Celestia were much afflicted to see the anguish of mind Mr. Coningsby was suffering, and they were also seriously alarmed, for continued anxiety, had made serious inroads upon his health, and they apprehended the most dangerous consequences if something did not shortly occur to banish his suspense.

Nothing could induce him to believe otherwise than that something of a serious nature had happened to Mr. Clemments, or he would certainly have been in England before this, and the idea was such a probable one that his friends found it would be useless to attempt to contravert it.

A heavy gloom settled upon the minds of all the members of Mr. Coningsby's establishment, and even Lord Everside lost much of his accustomed spirits, and became restless and uneasy.

Although every inquiry had continued to be made, nothing whatever had been seen or heard of the old man of the ruins, and it was at length concluded that he was either dead or had quitted that part of the country. This was a source of no inconsiderable annoyance to Mr. Coningsby, for he had hoped to have been able to have elicited much from him, and there was much with which that extraordinary being was immediately connected that needed explanation.

Mr. Harcourt, the banker, exerted himself to the utmost to discover what had become of the object of their anxiety, and corresponded constantly with Lord Everside, but all his efforts were unavailing, and nothing occurred or seemed likely to occur to unravel the painful mystery.

It seemed but too probable that the unfortunate young man had again fallen into the hands of the French, and was probably now incarcerated in a dungeon, and from which it would be quite uncertain when he might be liberated. They felt certain that something serious must have happened to him, or they would have been sure to have seen him before this, and it was in vain that Mr. Coningsby tried to support this torturing suspense and anxiety with any degree of patience. It at length had such an effect upon his health, that it was with difficulty he was enabled to leave his chamber, and his friends became more seriously alarmed for him than ever.

"Oh, what have I done," he would say to himself, when alone, "that Providence should thus frown upon and annihilate all my hopes? Oh, my son, my long lost Edgar, (for such I am certain you are) are we never destined to meet again? Just as I had hoped that that happiness was in store for me, the demon of despair interposed his cruel power, and all is gloom, and darkness, and misery again. Alas! alas! how little was I prepared to bear such a bitter disappointment as this."

Days passed on with little or no change, and all remained wrapped in the same state of impenetrable mystery, which it did not seem likely at presen would ever be unravelled. Mr. Coningsby did become a little more composed, but his grief and disappointment had settled down into a profound melancholy, which nothing seemed to be capable of removing. Even Celestia failed to engage his attention, and to interest him, as she had formerly done, and he seemed anxious to avoid all society as much as possible.

Three months had elapsed since Lord Everside had received the letter from Mr. Clements, when as they were all seated one night in the drawing-room, engaged in conversation upon that important subject which engrossed all their thoughts, they were suddenly aroused by the abbey bell being pulled violently, and immediately afterwards a servant entered the room, and informed them that a travelling chaise had just stopped at the door, in which was a gentleman, perfectly insensible, having been shot in an encounter with highwaymen, who had made their escape after having robbed him of his purse, and that his servant requested that he might be taken in at the abbey, so that his wound might be immediately attended to.

"By all means," said Mr. Coningsby, "let the unfortunate gentleman be conveyed to a chamber immediately, and Dr. Sinclair sent for with as little delay as possible. Perhaps your lordship will have the kindness to see after this wounded stranger, for at present I feel myself too weak."

"Certainly," replied Lord Everside, and he immediately quitted the room. The circumstance created quite a sensation in the breast of Mr Coningsby, his sister, and Celestia, and they awaited most anxiously the return of his lordship, so that they might learn all the particulars. He was absent more than a quarter of an hour, and when he returned to the room, his countenance evinced the utmost agitation.

"Well, my good friend," demanded Mr. Coningsby eagerly, "how is the unfortunate gentleman?"

"He is still insensible," replied Lord Everside, "having fainted through loss of blood. Dr. Sinclair is in attendance upon him and has dressed his wound, which is in the left shoulder, and he does not consider it to be at all dangerous, thank God for it."

"Ah! your lordship appears to be unusually agitated," said Mr. Coningsby, "may I ask what is the cause of it."

"My dear friend, I beg you will prepare yourself for a most extraordinary surprise. The ways of Providence are indeed wonderful! Who could ever have dreamt of such an event as this?"

"Pray do not keep me in suspense," said Mr. Coningsby, "now that you have so deeply excited my curiosity. What fresh surprise have you for me?"

"The wounded gentleman——"

"Yes, yes."

"Is no other than he we have been so long anxious to see; it is Augustus Clemments!"

Mr. Coningsby uttered an exclamation of astonishment and sunk back in his chair, speechless and nearly senseless. Miss Coningsby and Celestia were scarcely in a better condition, and looked eagerly at his lordship for a further explanation, as if they could scarcely believe the evidence of their ears.

"Great God!" at length cried Mr. Coningsby, clasping his hands, "is it possible? Hast thou, indeed, at last heard my prayers? In this house, and too—perhaps dying. Oh let me at once hasten to him, and remove these torturing doubts."

"My dear friend," said his lordship, "I again implore you to subdue these transports, and to endeavour to be calm. You are not at present in a condition to bear the excitement of such a meeting, and it is absolutely necesssary that he should be prepared for an interview of such an extraordinary a nature and so totally unexpected. I once more tell you that the worthy doctor assured me there was not the least danger to be apprehended from the injury he has received, and that in a short time he may be able to converse."

"Gracious heaven!" exclaimed Mr. Coningsby, "who could ever have thought of such an event as this taking place? Oh, my son, should it indeed be you. But where has he been all this time? What can have caused this delay?"

"I questioned his servant," replied Lord Everside, "and from him I learned that just as they were on the eve of returning again to England, his master was taken suddenly and alarmingly ill caused I suppose from the unusua fatigue and anxiety of mind he had lately been undergoing, and that confined him to his chamber for several weeks, and he was in a condition that totally incapacitated him from writing, but that when he was restored to convalescence, he immediately commenced his journey, and was about to make his way to some inn in this neighbourhood, for the night, when they were attacked by the robbers. But there is no time at present for further explanation, I must return to the chamber of the sufferer, and see how he is. How great will be his astonishment when he finds me in his presence. In the meantime, Mr. Coningsby, I must again request that you will conquer your feelings as much as possible, and rest assured that your doubts and anxieties will quickly be removed."

Lord Everside then quitted the room, leaving Mr. Coningsby, his sister, and our heroine in a state of surprise and agitation, which it will be no difficult task for the reader to imagine. Mr. Coningsby clasped his hands together, and for some minutes was unable to express his feelings in words, while Miss Coningsby and Celestia looked at each other in the most unfeigned amazement. They were in no condition to endeavour to tranquilize his feelings, so powerful were their own emotions, but they saw the necessity and policy of Lord Everside's advice, namely, for Mr. Coningsby to defer his interview with the suffering gentlemen, lest the excitement should prove too much for both, and be productive of the most dangerous results.

"Gracious Heaven!" at last cried Mr. Coningsby, while his countenance plainly shewed the intense agony of mind he was enduring, "how wonderful are all these events. Oh, suffer me not, I beseech thee, to be disappointed in my hopes, but let me once more clasp my son to my bosom, and then I am content to die."

"Oh, my dear brother," said Miss Coningsby, "talk not thus, that your hopes will not be disappointed, I feel satisfied, and but a few hours more will your patience have to be tried, ere your doubts will be at rest. It is most extraordinary that the outrage should have been committed in this neighbourhood, and that chance should

have brought him to the very residence of those who were so anxious to behold him."

"Oh, yes," replied Mr. Coningsby, "and God grant that the opinion of Doctor Sinclair may prove to be correct, and that the wound this unfortunate gentleman has received may not prove dangerous."

"Heaven forbid!" exclaimed our heroine, emphatically; "and fervently do I trust, my dear papa, that all may turn out in accordance with our fondest and most sanguine expectations."

Mr. Coningsby pressed her hand vehemently, and made a powerful effort to conquer the emotions to which the sudden and unexpected event had naturally given rise in his breast.

"Oh, how anxious am I to behold him whom I have so much reason to believe to be my long lost son," he ejaculated; "I am sure, my dear sister, and my darling Celestia, that you can fully appreciate the feelings of anxiety I must be enduring on this trying occasion."

"Indeed we do," replied Miss Coningsby, "and I think I need not assure you, that our anxiety is equal to your own. But you must admit the reasonableness of Lord Everside's advice, and we must all endeavour to wait patiently that revelation of facts which only a short time may bring about, and to our mutual satisfaction.

Half an hour had passed away in conversation of this kind, when it was interrupted by Lord Everside once more entering the apartment, and they all three, in a breath, most eagerly inquired the condition of the patient.

"As well, or better, my dear friends," replied his lordship, "than we could have expected."

"Oh, thank Heaven!" cried Mr. Coningsby, clasping his hands vehemently together; "but has he spoken? Did he recognize you, my lord? May I not be permitted to see him?"

"Be calm, be calm, my dear sir, and however trying it may be to you, you must, indeed you must, defer that pleasure for the present. Mr. Clemments, as I have the worthy doctor's instructions to say, must not on any account be disturbed. When he recovered from the fainting fit, into which he had fallen through the excessive loss of blood he had sustained, I deemed it prudent that he should not see me, lest the excitement it would be sure to cause, might be more than his exhausted strength could very well support. He only uttered a few unintelligible words, and then, completely worn out, but apparently suffering little or no pain, he gradually sunk off into a deep sleep, in which he remained, and is likely to remain for some hours, when I left him. Doctor Sinclair will not leave him for a moment, and I am so anxious to watch the course of his injuries that I have dispatched a servant to my house, informing my sister that business of importance will detain me here till to-morrow, and I intend, therefore, to keep the good doctor company in the chamber of the invalid during the night."

"Oh, my lord," said Mr. Coningsby, pressing his hand, "how can I sufficiently thank you for your kindness; but may I not be permitted to attend you in the chamber of this unfortunate young man?"

"My dear friend," replied his lordship, "as I have before endeavoured to impress upon your mind, that would be most imprudent, and you are far from being in a condition to encounter such fatigue and excitement. Wait till to-morrow, and try to fortify your feelings, in the meantime, for what may take place. Leave everything to me, and rest assured that nothing shall be wanting on my part to bring about the most happy results."

It was now now getting late, and the ladies retired to their chambers, their minds deeply interested in the important and remarkable events of the evening, and both of them waiting most impatiently the results which the course of a few hours would in all probability produce.

Mr. Coningsby sought his chamber immediately after his sister and our heroine had retired, but he pressed not his pillow that night. Oh, no, his mind was in too great a state of agitation to suffer him to think for a moment of repose, and he continued to traverse the apartment, at intervals, and so give vent to the various conflicting ideas that perplexed him, until the light of morn entered the windows of his chamber. Frequently his anxiety arose to such a pitch that he was half inclined to break through the promise he had made to Lord Everside, and to make his way to the chamber of the invalid, that he might at least gratify his uncontrollable anxiety and curiosity by the sight of him, but prudence restrained him, and he sought to await patiently the result of the following day.

In the meantime Lord Everside and Doctor Sinclair remained in the chamber of Augustus Clemments, and were happy in perceiving that he seemed to be almost entirely free from pain; indeed the worthy doctor declared that nothing could be more favourable than the present appearance of the wound, and that he considered that there was not the least danger to be apprehended. He continued to sleep calmly throughout the night, only awakening at intervals, and then not to consciousness, otherwise than to receive the medicine which was administered to him, and Doctor Sinclair argued the most favourable results from the symptoms he evinced.

At length when the first beams of the morning sun streamed in at the windows of the chamber, Mr. Clemments awoke to perfect consciousness, and apparently much refreshed, and raising his head from the pillow, and gazing with amazement and curiousity at the doctor (Lord Everside had retired to a corner of the room where he could not be observed, in order to prevent the effect of any sudden surprise) he inquired in a faint voice where he was.

"You are in the mansion of a benevolent gentleman, my dear sir," replied the doctor, "whither you were carried last night after your encounter with the highwaymen, by your servants. I am happy to inform you that the wound you have received is not at all dangerous, and that a few days' quiet and attention will doubtless restore you again to convalescence."

"Oh, sir, how greatly am I indebted to the gentleman who has acted with such humanity towards me;" said Mr. Clemments; "but pray may I not see him, that I may return him my acknowledgements? What is the name of this benevolent gentleman to whom I am under so great an obligation?"

"Coningsby," answered the doctor. Augustus started.

"Coningsby, Coningsby!" he repeated, "that is surely the name given me by one of the amiable ladies whom I accidentally met with at Berensforth Hall. Tell me, sir, is this place called Sungrove Abbey?"

"It is," replied Doctor Sinclair.

"Gracious Heaven, how strange! Surely it was Providence that guided me hither. Then I cannot be far from the mansion of my noble friend, Lord Everside?"

"You are not, sir; but I must beg that you will not excite yourself. Think you that you have strength to support an interview with that nobleman?"

"Oh, yes," replied Mr. Clemments, eagerly, and his eyes sparkling. "Would to Heaven that he were acquainted with my situation, that I might have the pleasure of again beholding the only friend that I now have in the world."

Lord Everside could hold out no longer. He came forward; and no sooner did Mr. Clemments behold him than he uttered an exclamation of astonishment and delight, and seemed at if he could scarcely credit the evidence of his eyes.

The reader may picture to himself the scene which followed. It was some time ere the young man could recover anything like a degree of composure; but at length he said,—

"Oh! my lord, how can I sufficiently express my amazement and delight at the accident which has again brought us together? No doubt you have thought me very neglectful in not writing to you again, or in absenting myself so long from England, especially after the kind interest your lordship was pleased to express in my affairs, but ——"

"Your servant has told me everything respecting your illness," interrupted Lord Everside; "and I need not assure you, my worthy young friend, how much I regret the inconvenience and anxiety to which you have been put, and the present accident which has befallen you; but still I trust that these various annoyances combined will only form the prelude to future happiness. It is most remarkable that chance should have thus conducted you to the very residence of the ladies with whom you were so deeply interested some time ago at Berensforth Hall."

"I am lost in amazement and delight; but oh, my lord, do you know, have you any idea to whom I may lay claim? The hints you gave me before we separated in London, have raised hopes which I trust will prove to have some foundation."

"Pardon me, my dear sir," returned his lordship, "but I cannot answer your questions until you have fully explained all the particulars of your journey, which you failed to do in your letter. But, however, impatient as I am to hear them, I fear that you are at present in too weak a state to satisfy your curiosity."

"Oh, no, my lord," said the impatient Mr. Clemments; "I feel but little, or scarcely any, ill effects from my wound, which fortunately is only slight; and this business is of too vital an importance to me to admit of any delay. I will, therefore, at once, with your permission, relate all that has happened to me, which you will, I am

sure, be ready to admit is most extraordinary."

Doctor Sinclair administered a cordial to him, which greatly relieved him, and he then retired from the room; and Mr. Clemments, after a brief pause, commenced his narrative, in the following words:

"I will take up my narrative, my lord, at the point where I so abruptly left off in my letter. Never did impatient lover, pursuing his adored mistress, torn from him by a cruel guardian, feel more joy in overtaking her, than I did in being introduced to the presence of the aged and infirm Mrs. Raimbach, who, when I inquired if I had the pleasure of addressing Mrs. Raimbach, replied with much politeness in the affirmative. I immediately availed myself of my credentials, by presenting her with her niece's letter, and giving her a short account of the present sent her, and my unfortunately losing it. I entreated her to accept the one I had endeavoured to procure, which was as near in value as the one sent to her. I allowed her to peruse her letter, which having done, she overwhelmed me with thanks, supposing I had taken this long journey into Germany merely for the purpose of bringing them to her.

"When I had so far gained upon her good graces, I began by saying I had a very extraordinary affair upon my hands, but that it was to serve a particular friend (for as they had not asked my name, I thought I might as well not declare it at first) and upon which I knew that she could give me the requisite information. Without giving her time for consideration, I continued,—

"'You had a sister in Bengal?'

"She started, and said,—

"'Yes, sir.'

"'Married to the steward of Mr Clemments?'

"'Yes, sir.'

"'Mr. Clemments is dead, and his heir found among his steward's papers—for he soon followed his master—a most extraordinary letter, relative to a child having been drowned, and another stolen. The letter contained some judicious remarks and admonitions. Now, it rests with you, from whom this letter came, I presume, to give me a clear insight into the whole affair.'

"Whilst this passed, her countenance underwent a variety of changes. I continued speaking without appearing to notice it. 'The present Mr. Clemments supposes from circumstances named in the letter, that he is implicated in this iniquitous business, and that he has no natural right to the inheritance.'

"'Gracious God, sir!' exclaimed the old woman, 'are you that Mr. Clemments? if so I shall be happy to disclose a secret that has long preyed upon my spirits; thank God, I was no otherwise implicated in it, than having it confided to me long after the commission. You, sir, are not indeed the son of Mr. Clemments, his child was drowned, he was confided to his nurse, who was that sister you have named, during her master's attendance upon his dying lady, this was at —— in the North of England; it was accidentally drowned while she was out in a boat with a young man, and to hide her fault, she stole a child about his own age, whom she had frequently seen out on the sands with its nurse, and passed it on her master for his son. You, sir, are that child. The clothes you had on at the time, and some trinkets, together with a letter, she confessed to me some time before her death, she had at the instigation of the young man, and his aged father (an old villain) secured in a chest, and conveyed to a place some miles off, but whither she had occasion to go, and buried them at night beneath a blue marble slab, near a stone cross in some old priory ruins!"

"Good God!" cried the agitated Lord Everside, when the long supposed Augustus Clemments had arrived at this part of the narrative, "but proceed, my dear, sir, proceed."

"I have nothing more to add, than that I determined to visit these ruins, on my way to London, and ascertain whether or not the woman had confessed the truth. But why do you evince so much emotion, my lord? For God's sake, relieve my impatience! say do you know any one who lost a child in the way I have described?"

I do, I do," replied Lord Everside, joyfully, "and I entertain very little, or indeed, no doubt that you are that son, so long lost, and so deeply lamented."

"Father of mercy!" cried the young man, starting up in the bed with more energy than could have been expected, "is it indeed so? Oh, my good lord, tell me I implore you, what is the name of this gentleman, and where shall I find him?"

"Have you strength for a most important meeting?"

"Oh, yes, yes; I feel aroused to all my usual strength and energy, by the power of my hopes, but oh, do not delay."

"I must leave you for a few minutes," said his lordship, " but while I am gone, seek to compose your feelings, and hope for the best."

Lord Everside quitted the chamber, after having given utterance to these words, and made his way with a palpitating heart to the apartment in which he knew he should find Mr. Coningsby.

Doctor Sinclair on leaving the chamber of his patient had hastened to Mr. Coningsby, whom he knew would be most anxious to hear how he was. The favourable account he gave of him somewhat tranquillized his feelings, but still he waited most impatiently the appearance of Lord Everside that he might be made acquainted with what had transpired between him and his friend.

On his entrance he could see in a moment, from the expression of his countenance, that he had something of the deepest interest to impart, and most earnestly he implored him to make him acquainted with it immediately.

"Hope for the happiest results, my dear friend," replied his lordship, " but be firm, while I introduce you to one whom we have hitherto known as Mr. Clemments. The disclosure must be made in his presence suffice it to say that he has made such disclosures to me as leave not the least doubt in my mind."

"Oh, God!" cried Mr. Coningsby, starting up, and grasping his lordship by the arm, " are then my hopes fated at last to be realized? Let me hasten to him, for it would be torture worse than insupportable any longer to delay the interview."

Lord Everside took his arm, and they

hastened from the room, leaving Miss Coningsby and Celestia in a state of the greatest suspense and anxiety.

When they arrived at the chamber door, Mr. Coningsby was compelled to pause, to endeavour to collect himself, but at length Lord Everside opened the door, and leading Mr. Coningsby towards the bed, in which the wounded gentleman was sitting, he said—

"My young friend, I have a twofold pleasure in introducing Mr. Coningsby to you, from his connection with those amiable ladies who hold so high a place in your esteem, and from a most sanguine hope that he may prove a dear connection."

The agitation that both evinced while his lordship was thus speaking, may readily be conceived. Mr. Coningsby no sooner fixed his eyes upon the young man's countenance, than his emotions redoubled, and in a tremulous voice he said :—

"Young man, there is something whispers to my heart, that in you I shall find that long lost son, who was so cruelly torn from me; and the circumstances I have heard of your extraordinary history all but confirm that blissful idea. If then you have made any further discoveries which may further unravel the painful mystery, I pray you at once make me acquainted with them, that I may know at once my happiness or despair."

"Oh, sir," answered the young man, with what fresh hopes have you and his lordship inspired me. I will at once, and as briefly as I can, relate to you that with which I have just made Lord Everside acquainted; and as you have, I understand, seen the contents of my letter, it is only necessary that I should relate the subsequent particulars."

He then proceeded to recapitulate, with as much composure as he could assume, those particulars which he had already detailed to Lord Everside, but he no sooner came to that part which mentioned the burial of the box of clothes in the old priory ruins, than the enraptured Mr. Coningsby exclaimed—

"All bountiful God! thou hast heard my prayers. That chest has been found, it is in my possession, the clothes it contains are the same my child had on, on the morning when he was stolen.

My son, my son! my long-lost Edgar!"

In a moment they were in each others arms, and the scene which followed baffles description, Lord Everside was almost as deeply affected as the father and son, and could not but return his thanks to the Supreme ruler of events who had restored them to each other in such a miraculous manner, after the lapse of so many years.

It was some time ere they could either of them give utterance to their feelings in language sufficient to express their emotion, upon the important discovery which had, after so much labour, and through such various intricate means, been brought about. But when they did, the scene was indeed most interesting, but now, like the painter who finding it impossible to do justice to the countenance, only exhibited the back of the figure, we must draw a veil over the picture.

CHAPTER XIII.

JOYOUS MOMENTS.—THE MEETING OF FRIENDS.

THE wound which Mr. Clemments (or as we must henceforth call him, Lord Coningsby) had received, was so slight, that, in the course of three days he was sufficiently recovered to quit his chamber, and to be introduced by his delighted father to the ladies. Their pleasure at the meeting, may very well be imagined, but Lord Coningsby felt disappointed on learning that Celestia was not connected with him by that tie which he had flattered himself with the fond hope that she was.

When Lord Elverton introduced his son to Lady Eugenia, as his aunt, it was no surprise, but, as we have intimated above, when the same ceremony passed to Celestia (whom he supposed to be the daughter of his father or his aunt) as Miss de Aunville, he could not conceal his astonishment.

"Miss de Aunville;" he said? "I had hoped to have seen in this young lady some near relation."

"Indeed, Edgar," replied his father, "you have not that happiness. I say happiness, for when you are more acquainted with my sweet Celestia, I am satisfied that you will regret that she is not a portion of your family. Heaven sent her to me to be my comfort in an affliction that had for years weighed me down. You shall have my narrative on some future occasion, it will take you some time and patience also to read, but it will make you acquainted with your family; you shall, if my Celestia does not forbid, be also made acquainted with her's, at least, as far as has come to our knowledge; but as she always called me papa, she may call you brother, if she likes you well enough."

Our heroine, at being thus 'called into notice before a stranger for although she had forgotten that he was so, in the first transport of her joy at seeing her beloved guardian restored to happiness, she had regained all her accustomed timidity, and in reply to Lord Elverton (as we must now call him) said—

"My dear lord, you know I was accustomed to call you papa, and my beloved Lady Eugenia, aunt, from my infancy, but Lord Coningsby was a stranger to me till within the last few days."

"But indeed Celestia," said Lord Coningsby, "I shall not let you off so. I am determined not to be cheated out of one of my new relations. You may call me papa, or uncle if you please, for I acknowledge I am too old for your brother."

Celestia smiled, and replied—

"Well then, probably my lord, I may in time bring myself to call you uncle."

Thus ended the conversation, and the faithful old Robert was now called in to partake of the universal joy that prevailed upon the discovery of the long lost son of his venerated master. And various and amusing were the antics that the poor old man displayed on the occasion. He laughed, danced, whistled, and sang by turns, then rubbing his hands together in a fit of ecstacy, he cried—

"Well, who would have thought of it? It is the most wonderful thing I ever heard of. I don't care a button if I die to-morrow, since I have lived to see this 'day, and never shall I forget the grief and consternation of us all, my lord, when you was lost. Oh, I wish poor old Mr. Elkins was near enough to be told the glad tidings."

"I wish he was, Robert," replied his master, "but he shall speedily know it, for I shall write to him immediately, and I am certain that the joy of old Mr. Elkins will not be less than your's, he, I am sure will be glad to announce the happy tidings himself at Elverton, and prepare them in a few weeks to receive their long lost favourite."

"Then you will go like yourself, my lord, and no longer pass for plain Mr. Coningsby."

Lord Elverton smiled at the old man's love of title, but immediately answered—

"Most assuredly, Robert, whilst I thought myself left alone in the world, and that even my name would die with me, I felt all distinction irksome, but now that Providence has restored to me part of that which it thought fit to deprive me of, I should be ungrateful for the blessing, if I did not endeavour to forget the past and to enjoy the present. But I must begin where I have passed so many quiet years. I will have a jubilee for all the parishes round, and I leave it to you to lay out the plan of it, and when done, and I have approved of it, you shall be the conductor."

"Shall I, my lord?" said the delighted Robert, "then it shall be a jubilee indeed."

"You have resolved to make me of some consequence, my dear father," said Lord Coningsby; I trust I shall not disgrace it, for you know I have been bred an East Indian, though I can say with perfect truth, my feelings have been truly British, without knowing that I had any claim to that pre-eminence."

"My dear son," returned the Earl of Elverton, "however you have been educated, your exterior gives me assurance that it has not been a neglected one in that point, and I have a presentiment I shall not be disappointed in the mental part. But at present I have certain reasons for preferring your, my dear Lady Eugenia, with my Celestia's assistance, in sending round invitations to the few friends we have in this part of the country, although I am so anxious to present my Edgar to them."

What those reasons were, were only known to himself, but the news of the strange discovery (although the real title of Lord Elverton was only known to Lord Everside) quickly spread around the country and occasioned no little sensation; all who so well knew the amiable and benevolent character of Mr. Coningsby heartily rejoicing in this addition to his happiness. Sir Eustace Aubrey, his lady and Collingwood were the first to pay their respects to Lord Elverton, and have the pleasure of an introduction to his son, as they knew they could do so without a formal invitation, and the mental qualities and prepossing exterior of Lord Coningsby immediately won upon their favour, and made them now, although they were ignorant of Mr. Coningsby's distinction, most anxious to form an alliance between their son and protogê.

The more that Collingwood saw of our beauteous heroine, the greater became his admiration of her, but although she received his attentions with some degree of favour, there was that in her manner which was far from encouraging his ardent hopes.

Time now seemed too short to answer all the questions which passed between the Earl of Elverton and his son. The latter quickly recovered, and in less than a fortnight he was completely restored to convalescence.

Lord Coningsby's life, while the supposed Augustus Clemments, has little or nothing to do with our narrative. The late Mr. Clemments was a most excellent man, dotingly fond of his supposed son, whom he educated with the utmost care, procuring for him a tutor in England, every way qualified for the task by education and principle. This was a happy circumstance, as the customs of the East are so different to those of Europe, and particularly so to those of Great Britain. Lord Coningsby had a faint recollection of going from England, or from hearing it spoken of at the period of his supposed mother's death, fancied he had, and though he could not feel affection for her he never knew, that which he experienced towards Mr. Clemments was all that a parent could wish.

It may naturally be expected that Edgar most earnestly inquired of his father for his maternal parent, but Lord Elverton's laconic reply ever was—

" Alas! my dear son, she is lost!"

This answer greatly bewildered Lord Coningsby, and the only conclusion he could arrive at was that lost meant dead, and the melancholy which overspread his father's countenance prevented him from making any further inquiries. But when he found by the manuscript which Lord Elverton had given him for perusal, the real meaning of the term, pity, affection, and anger, alternately took place in his breast, how much did he pity his father's sufferings—how much did he honour his fortitude! and while he dwelt on these, he felt only anger at his mother for her inhumanity to her husband, a husband who had ever behaved to her with such devoted fondness. But a second perusal made anger give way to pity at her weakness, and in the fervency of the moment he vowed never to unite himself to any woman whose tenets in the smallest degree differed from his own.

But most ardently did he wish to discoved her retreat, and if alive, endeavour to prevail on her to return to her long forsaken home.

About a week after these events had taken place, Lord Elverton, accompanied by his friend Lord Everside, had paid a casual visit to Sir Eustace Aubrey's, when being prevailed upon to prolong their stay, Lord Elverton was greatly surprised and embarrassed when the sudden and unexpected arrival of the Earl Malensbury Bathwist, his son, Lord Malensbury, and his beauteous daughter, the Lady Eglantine, was announced. He would fain have withdrawn, could he have done so decently, for his mind was too much agitated by recent events to meet the earl as he wished, but as the family of Sir Eustace were unacquainted with his real title, he hoped for the present to preserve his incognito.

More than twenty years had elapsed since they had met, and the change it had wrought in Mr. Coningsby, as he was supposed to be, precluding all remembrance of his person or features, and when he was introduced, the earl little imagined so near a relation stood before him.

Being seated opposite to each other

at the dinner table, Lord Elverton had an opportunity to study his nephew's countenance, where he saw in his fine open brow, all that urbanity and good sense which had marked his father's character, and before dinner was concluded he longed to embrace him as the son of that friend and brother, whom he still so deeply mourned.

The Earl Bathurst, indeed, inherited all the noble qualities of his father, Lord Arthur Malensbury, and though left an orphan at a very early age, and consequently entire master of his fortune at the age of twenty-one, he steered clear of all the rocks and quicksands so sedulously laid in the path of every young man of fortune. He married a most amiable lady, and several children blessed their union, but at the time of which we are writing only the two eldest remained, one son and one daughter now constituted all their affectionate hopes and cares.

The Earl Bathurst saw with the most ardent pleasure the blossoming virtues of his son, whose progress in the several branches of his education gave fair promise of his future excellences, but one unfortunate circumstance in the young nobleman's career (which may afterwards be explained) was near annihilating these hopes for ever.

And a fair and gentle, and fascinating creature was Lady Eglantine. Imagine all that is beautiful and captivating in woman, and her portrait is complete. Collingwood Aubrey saw her, he admired her (he must have been less than man had he not), but he felt that admiration and esteem were all he could award her; he had seen Celestia, and no other woman could possess his heart. Lady Eglantine, on the contrary, no sooner beheld Collingwood Aubrey, than she felt a sensation at her heart which she had never experienced before.

The visit ended, Lord Elverton declining a pressing invitation to go to the mansion of Sir Eustace, accompanied by his son, his sister, and Celestia in a day or two, and the former returned home without the least recognition between the uncle and nephew, though the latter was observed by those who were in the secret, to gaze upon the countenance of Lord Elverton, as if endeavouring to recollect where he had seen it.

A few days after this Lord Elverton gave his sister instructions to send invitations to their friends to dine with them.

"And pray, my dear brother," said Lady Eugenia, "shall I send the cards in our name or title? It is not very likely, I think, that they will know us by the latter."

"Oh, there is no fear of that," returned Lord Elverton, "for depend upon it, old Robert will take good care to spread the good tidings all over the country long before you have written the cards."

"Lord Elverton and Lady Eugenia Coningsby request the honour of, &c. Upon my word, my dear brother, I have been so long out of the habit of writing in that style, that I shall certainly waste my cards by my blunders; however, Celestia, we will do our best to save them as much as possible."

Lord Elverton and his son smiled at the observations of Lady Eugenia, and the remainder of the day was passed in much cheerfulness, every one looking forward to the future with the brightest hopes.

Old Robert, who was delighted with the task which was imposed upon him, lost no time in making out his bill of fare; oxen and sheep were to be roasted whole, plum-pudding, damson, and apple pies, with plenty of strong ale.

Lord Elverton was pleased to express his approval of Robert's arrangements, and added twelve geese to the dinner, and told him there should be as much punch made as would allow two half-pints to each guest, in order to drink their healths; but that it should not be taken out till they were near retiring, lest it should overpower their senses, with the strong ale. The time was fixed for the day month when Lord Coningsby made his appearance at the abbey; their own dinner party was to be two days later.

When the invitation cards of Lady Eugenia arrived at the mansion of Sir Eustace Aubrey, universal surprise prevailed.

"Who can these new comers be?" said Lady Aubrey; "and if really they are people of rank, how can they be so totally ignorant of the etiquette of high life?"

"May I request your ladyship to read the card again?" said Lord Bathurst.

Lady Aubrey did so, when his lordship exclaimed, with no inconsiderable degree of emotion:

"It must be, it can be no other than my uncle and his sister."

Lady Aubrey rung the bell, and ordered them to inquire of the servant where Lord Elverton's residence was?

"Why, where he always lived, at Sungrove Abbey, to be sure," was the answer.

"Why," said the butler, "I thought the only Sungrove Abbey in this part of the country was Mr. Coningsby's."

"Why, and so it is," answered Lord Elverton's servant, "but you see my lord's son is found—lost sin' he was three years old—and so we are now all happy as we can wish, and our dear master too—and so he will not be nobody no longer."

Here the bell rung, the butler repeated what Caleb had said, received an acceptance card, and Caleb rode off, well pleased to think he had been the first herald at the mansion of Sir Eustace Aubrey.

The Earl Bathurst had but a confused recollection of his uncle's domestic misfortunes; the last time they had met was a few months after his marriage; Lord Elverton being obliged to visit his estates in the north, congratulated his nephew on his marriage, he being then with his lady at Berensforth Hall; he therefore could not give them much information.

Though Sir Eustace and Lady Aubrey were upon too intimate a footing with the family at Sungrove Abbey to pay visits of ceremony, yet a morning visit was now necessary to congratulate them upon this wonderful discovery; and Lord and Lady Bathurst were too happy to find themselves related to the Mr. Coningsby who had so much pleased them in the short period of the dinner party, not to take this opportunity of paying their duty to him. The carriages were immediately ordered, and the party set out for the abbey.

When they arrived there, the most sincere congratulations took place, and Lord Malensbury was particularly struck with the captivating graces of Celestia, while he made an equal impression upon her. Lady Eglantine also immediately won upon her friendship, nor was her ladyship less delighted at being introduced to one whom she was at first sight prepared to love as a sister.

The uncle and nephew, already mutually pleased with each other, embraced cordially, and Lord Bathurst entreated him to transfer all the friendship his father had possessed to him, and to look on him as a second son.

"And you, Lord Coningsby," continued the earl, "I hope, will promise to give me yours; I feel a pleasure in presenting my son to you, and I trust you will find him every way worthy of your esteem."

"Oh, my lord," replied Lord Coningsby, "I know not how to express my feelings as I ought. Such a tide of happiness has flown in upon me at once, that it will be well for me if I do not become intoxicated with pleasure. I have hitherto passed my life in indolence, more suited to the manners of the East than my own inclinations, but I shall soon shake it off, if my father's friends will lend me their assistance."

"I hope," answered Lord Bathurst, "that my uncle will revisit Elverton Castle, I will then give you sport enough to drive the Goddess of Indolence from her throne."

"It is my intention," said Lord Elverton, "to go to the castle early in the next month, in order to show my son his paternal estate, and to celebrate Christmas. I mean to go town early in the spring, where I must provide myself with a town residence, that my sister may once more live in that society from which she has been so long secluded, and my Celestia too—could I discover to whom she belongs, I think my happiness would be complete."

But the sigh which escaped his bosom, while he made it, denied the asseveration. Lord Malensbury fixed his eyes upon the lovely countenance of our heroine, and he felt a sensation at his heart which was quite new to him.

"I see," said Lord Bathurst, drawing his uncle aside, and speaking in an under tone, "that already your lordship's fair *protege* possesses no small interest in the bosom of my Eglantine; if they have the opportunity of meeting often, which I hope they will, it may turn to a friendship perhaps advantageous to both."

"And most happy shall I be to promote it," said Lord Elverton; "Celestia is a most amiable girl, and has hitherto felt herself perfectly happy; but a friend of her own age would soon inform her that her happiness will bear improvement."

And the opinions of Lord Elverton and his nephew were correct. Celestia and Lady Eglantine had each found a congenial spirit. The latter was just seventeen, possessed of excellent sense and much vivacity; neither levity nor

coquetry had any share in her composition; and they were as well acquainted in this their first meeting as if they had been known to each other all their lives.

When the interview was over, Lord Malensbury felt that the fair unknown had made an impression on his heart which nothing could eradicate, and belonged for the opportunity of being in her society as much as possible. He could think of nothing, dream of nothing else but the beauteous Celestia, and having no suspicion of the sentiments which Collingwood Aubrey entertained towards her, he saw no reason why he should attempt to stifle a passion which he was compelled to acknowledge to himself had already taken deep root in his breast.

The jealous eyes of Collingwood Aubrey had noticed the admiration with which Lord Malensbury had beheld Celestia, and he also imagined that she viewed the young nobleman with anything but feelings of indifference. Nothing could exceed his chagrin and disappointment, and he was glad when the interview was over, and he had an opportunity of retiring to his own apartment that he might give free vent to his feelings. The charms of Lady Eglantine (although she beheld him with interest and esteem) had failed to make any impression upon his heart, and therefore the wishes which his mother had in the first instance formed, were completely foiled, and she herself, who could not but perceive the indifference with which Collingwood regarded Lady Eglantine (although she was aware of and had given her sanction to his paying his addresses to her) could not help feeling both vexed, and disappointed.

And had Lord Malensbury really made a favourable impression upon the heart of our heroine? Oh, yes, even at that, their first interview, her heart acknowledged his transcendent merits, and when alone, she recalled his imagina- to her mind with feelings of the most exquisite pleasure, and felt the greatest anxiety to behold him again. The striking contrast presented between him and Collingwood Aubrey came most vividly home to her imagination, and she now for the first time felt convinced that she could never regard the latter with any other feelings than those of esteem and friendship. But there were other thoughts that more especially occupied the mind of our heroine.

No one than her more sincerely rejoiced in the change the discovery of his son had made in the spirits of her revered guardian, but at the same time, it occasioned many a bitter tear, and many a sigh agitated her bosom, it cost her some pains to conceal it from her friends, for, she reflected to herself, should she not be the most ungrateful of human beings to appear before them with a sad countenance, when their's had

been all cheerful towards her, when their hearts were torn with anguish.

The wonderful discovery of Lord Coningsby at such a distant period from that of his loss, caused her to reflect upon her own strange destiny, cast upon the protection of, though the best of human beings, yet strangers, and in a foreign land, not even certain what land gave her birth.

These thoughts caused her the most bitter anguish, and many and painful were the sensations it gave rise to.

"Alas!" she would exclaim when left alone, "would that my dear papa did not die till I was old enough to be told his misfortunes, great they must have been from what I can recollect of his sad countenance, and the frequent tears he shed over me."

These melancholy thoughts frequently deprived our heroine of sleep, but when she more seriously reflected upon the unexampled kindness of her protectors, she would implore the forgiveness of the Almighty for her ingratitude, breathe a pious wish for their health and happiness, and sink into repose.

Notwithstanding the carefulness with which Celestia imagined she concealed what passed in her mind, her friends ever watchful over their beloved protegée saw the change and guessed the cause, but Lady Mary thought it would sooner pass over if unnoticed, and, as her time would be pretty much taken up betwixt the visits she had to make, and the preparations for going into the north, she trusted that the change of scene would make her regain her former cheerfulness. But as Lady Eugenia observed to her brother, Celestia was of a reflective, serious turn of mind, and it was very natural for such a one to be affected with the wonderful discovery of Lord Coningsby, and from that to revert to her own mysterious situation.

"I believe you are right," replied Lord Elverton, "it is best to take no notice of it, the change of scene will have, I hope, a good effect, and I have prepared a surprise for her at Elverton Castle."

"Oh, I remember now," said Lady Eugenia, "and she has such a grateful heart that she will endeavour to conceal, till at length she can overcome, the gloomy ideas that have taken possession of her mind."

"Most fervently do I hope, my dear sister, that you may be right in your conjectures," said Lord Elverton, and the entrance of the object of their solicitude put an end to the conversation.

The day set apart for the festivity at length arrived, and as there were not rooms large enough to accommodate the guests at the Abbey, a large barn, with a temporary building annexed, was appropriated for the dinner-room, the oxen and sheep were roasted in an adjoining meadow, near enough for the guests to see them cut up and brought to table. About two hundred and fifty respectable farmers and cottagers with their wives and families sat down to table, and a rare jubilee it was, well worthy of the donor and the guests. All seemed to be determined to enjoy themselves in a rational way, and to do full justice to the good fare provided for them.

The day was a remarkably fine one for the season, and care had been taken to make the rooms warm. When dinner was over, and Robert had the punch brought in, Lord Elverton entered with his son, and followed by his sister and Celestia.

"My friends," he said, taking Lord Coningsby by the hand, "I have the happiness of presenting to you my son, whom from three years old I have mourned as lost to me for ever, till this day month, when he was restored to me."

The loudest acclamations followed this speech, acclamations that came from the heart, and the meeting did not break up until a late hour.

Nor had the earl forgotten his humble friends in the north; he wrote to his steward to give all his tenants a dinner of the best the country afforded, and to the poor inhabitants for three miles round, a plentiful supply of good meat, ale, and every ingredient to make a large plum-pudding, and stated that he should be there himself, with his family, in a month at the furthest. Thus all that hospitality could supply was enlisted on that joyous occasion, and blessings from many a grateful heart were heaped upon the heads of Lord Elverton and his son, and every wish expressed for their future welfare.

CHAPTER XIV.

STARTLING EVENTS.—THE RING.—DEATH OF THE OLD MAN OF THE PRIORY RUINS.

LORD BATHURST and his family were daily visitors to the abbey, after this joyous discovery, and Lord Malensbury was delighted at the opportunity that was thus afforded him of being in the society of our heroine, and, the more he saw of that charming girl, the warmer became the sentiments in his breast towards her; and Celestia could not deny the deep admiration and esteem she felt for the manly graces and many intrinsic qualities of the young nobleman.

Lady Eglantine perceived with much pleasure how strongly they were prepossessed in each other's favour; Celestia and her were already on the same terms of affection as if they had been allied by blood, and she had not yet seen the female whom she would sooner select for the wife of her brother. That her virtues and accomplishments were of the first order of excellence, it required only a very brief period of time to be in her company to become convinced of, and that her birth would prove to be noble, Lady Eglantine entertained not the least doubt.

Lady Eglantine frequently rallied her brother upon the sudden attachment he had formed for the fair young orphan, to which he replied, with the utmost good humour, but in a manner which quite convinced her that she was by no means mistaken in the conjectures she had formed.

The weather had hitherto been very mild and fine for the season, and Celestia frequently took long walks, accompanied by her friends, but there were times when she preferred indulging in these healthful rambles alone.

It was on one of these occasions, about a week prior to the time which Lord Elverton had fixed for their departure from the abbey, that Celestia felt inclined to visit the various cottages of the humble individuals who had been recipients of her bounty, and in bidding adieu to them, she did not forget to leave them very solid marks of her friendship. The poor people showered upon her head their blessings, and wished her all the happiness that heaven could bestow.

Our heroine was much affected by the simple, but unfeigned gratitude the poor people evinced, and then took her departure, having yet her most important call to make, namely, at the old priory ruins.

Old Hannibal and his wife received her at the lodge, with every demonstration of respect and pleasure; and after some time passed in conversation upon the wonderful events that had recently taken place, and the worthy old couple again and again expressing their delight at their lord's discovery of his long lost son, Celestia requested Hannibal to open the gate, and she walked into the ruins.

As she wandered over the dilapidated place, the most melancholy thoughts presented themselves to her imagination. She revolved all the melancholy circumstances of her father's death, she thought of the uncertainty of her ever discovering with whom she was connected, and what had led to the misfortunes which her father had evidently experienced.

At length, tired with her ramble among the ancient ruins, she seated herself upon a fragment, and once more became completely absorbed in the variety of conflicting reflections which crowded upon her brain.

So deeply was our heroine's mind occupied in this manner, that she quite forgot she was so far from home, till the last rays of the setting sun warned her of the approach of night, and she immediately arose to depart, and as she did so, happening to cast her eyes towards the ground, something glittering very brightly met her gaze.

She was at first inclined to think that it was merely a bit of glass reflected on by the sun's rays, and was about to retire without taking any further notice of it, but led by a secret impulse, she returned to the spot.

The golden orb of day had now sunk behind the western hills, and she looked in vain for the supposed treasure; and hastening to the lodge, she requested Hannibal to attend her with a lantern, telling him and his wife what she had seen.

Hannibal immediately complied with her request, and old Dorothy, whose curiosity was as much excited as that of her husband, also accompanied them to the ruins.

On arriving at the spot, what was the astonishment of our heroine and her companions, when the former picked up a ring, containing a miniature, set round with brilliants. It was the portrait of a lady, young and beautiful. She gazed on it with fixed attention and admiration, and while she did so, she could not help fancying that the features were familiar to her, but where she could have seen the original, if indeed she had done so, she was completely at a loss to imagine.

The more Celestia gazed at the miniature the deeper became the interest she felt in it; but she left the ruins, and entered the lodge, in order that she might examine it more minutely.

There was a pensive cast about the countenance, which represented that of a female. The eyes were blue, shaded by long dark lashes, a profusion of bright auburn hair fell gracefully over her shoulders in ringlets; a veil of fine lace was thrown gracefully over the head, and partially concealed one side of her face. The ring was large, and evidently had been fitted to a man's finger.

The increasing lateness of the hour now warned Celestia to depart, and Hannibal requested to be permitted to attend her, as it might not be safe for her to go alone.

To this our heroine readily assented, and the old man having provided himself with a stout walking-stick, they issued from the lodge, and made their way towards the abbey, Hannibal unable to resist expressing his wonder at the discovery of the ring.

Celestia's stay had been protracted so far beyond her usual hour when alone, that a universal alarm seized every person at the abbey, so that when our heroine and her aged companion entered the first gate of the avenue, she encountered several servants, who were going in quest of her.

Lord Elverton and his sister were with difficulty prevented from joining in the general search by Lord Coningsby. He, however, had preceded the servants, who now hastened after him, in order that they might save him unnecessary trouble.

Lord Elverton and his sister gently chided Celestia for having remained so long from the abbey, but she excused herself by relating the cause, and immediately placed the ring in the hands of her beloved guardian, who no sooner fixed his gaze upon the portrait than he trembled and turned pale, which did not escape the observation of Lady Eugenia, and she anxiously inquired the reason.

"My dear sister," answered the earl, "you will not wonder at my emotion when I have pointed out to you the cause. Examine that miniature, and tell me if it does not strongly resemble one you have seen before."

"Yes, yes," replied Lady Eugenia, gazing most eagerly at it, "the resemblance is very great to the one I think you mean, but it appears to me to be that of another person. The cast of countenance has a particular air of melancholy, which the other has not; and yet each gives you an idea of the same age, but the costume plainly bespeaks it of more recent date."

While his sister was speaking, Lord Elverton had been attentively examining the ring, when suddenly, with much emotion in his manner and tone, he exclaimed,—

"By Heaven! I cannot persuade myself that it is otherwise. No—no—it must be so."

"What do you mean, my brother?" asked his sister with a look of astonishment.

"Why, that this is certainly the miniature likeness of your mother, Celestia, though your complexion is not so fair, your features are very like those."

"Oh, my dear lord," ejaculated our agitated heroine, "do you really think it is the portrait of my mother?"

"Indeed my love, I do; and see here in the inside of the ring is engraven, 'my beloved wife.' To me it appears most likely that it had dropped from your father's finger, when in the old priory ruins, where he spent much of his time."

"Not at all improbable," remarked Lady Eugenia; "if old David or his wife had been living they might have set our doubts all at rest, by informing us whether they had seen M. de Aunville wear such a ring."

We need not seek to pourtray to the reader the various emotions which agitated their bosoms; that of Lord Elverton was fully equal to that our heroine was enduring. Again he steadfastly fixed his eyes upon the miniature, and as he did so the deepest sighs escaped his bosom, at which neither his sister or Celestia were at all surprised, as the likeness bore so striking a resemblance to the portrait which had so particularly attracted their attention at Berensforth hall. It was some moments ere they could at all compose their feelings.

"My dear Celestia," said Lord Elverton, "this is a most important circumstance; this ring may be the means of unravelling the mystery by which you are surrounded. It is too large for your finger, but I would not advise you to have it altered yet, for I still hope that we shall make some discovery of your family, and that, together with the jewels, will be very strong proofs of your identity."

Celestia could not speak; she received the ring from Lord Elverton, and pressing it to her lips, retired from the room to give freer vent to the feelings which struggled in her breast.

"Oh, my beloved parent," she sighed, "of what avail is it to discover my family when those who cherished my infancy now lie mouldering in the tomb! Oh, my mother! if thy blessed spirit is permitted to hover over thy child, guard her future days from evil! May her future conduct be ever such as you would have approved, had she been blessed with your instructions. While I look at your resemblance, my mother, for I feel satisfied that such this portrait represents, I will fancy myself still under your guardian care."

The expression of these feelings much relieved the beauteous girl's bosom; she then fastened a bit of ribbon to the rings, and once more kissing the por-

concealed it in her bosom, and returned to the drawing room.

- When Celestia retired for the night, she had recovered her spirits sufficiently to look on her treasure with dry eyes, She recollected the exclamations of Lord Elverton with no small degree of surprise, and she sat endeavouring to assign a reason for the emotion he evinced.

This brought to our heroine's remembrance what the old housekeeper at Berensforth Hall had said of her resemblance to the picture in the gallery, and which she had since learned, was the Countess of Elverton.

"Ah!" she suddenly exclaimed, "it is not at all impossible that I may be related to my beloved guardian; oh, that it were indeed so, and that I could know it. But no, why should I entertain such a wild and extravagant thought? Had it been so, it is not likely that my poor father would not have taken the earliest opportunity of making himself known to him. Ah! no! I am the child of some unfortunate beings, most probably victims to the horrid cruelties which have been perpetrated in France."

Such were the thoughts which agitated the bosom of Celestia, and it was long ere sleep closed her eyes, and she awoke pale and unrefreshed, but composed herself tolerably before she went down to breakfast.

Lord Elverton had passed an equally restless night, for the circumstance of the discovery had raised the most conflicting feelings of hope and melancholy in his bosom; but in the course of the day they all recovered in a great measure their composure. But there were still more extraordinary events about to take place, with which we will as speedily as possible make the reader acquainted.

We must now return to the old priory ruins. Although the weather had hitherto been so particularly fine for the time of year, two days after the discovery of the ring, a sudden change ensued; a sharp frost set in, with boisterous winds, and the snow descended incessantly for many hours, so that it lay upon the ground several feet deep, and rendered every road in that part of the country quite impassable.

Lord Elverton fearing that this weather was likely to continue for some time, and that it would be impossible to travel, was compelled to postpone his journey to Elverton Castle for some weeks.

The fire blazed cheerfully in the lodge attached to the old priory ruins, and Hannibal and his wife drew their chairs closer to it, and endeavoured to divert their attention from the noise of the inclement season by conversation. The late events; the restoration of Lord Coningsby to his father, after the lapse of so many years, and the recent discovery of the ring in the ruins by our heroine, afforded good topics for them, and they gave various opinions upon them, not one of which was very remarkable for its wisdom or probability. However, they served to amuse the old people, and consequently that answered every purpose.

Suddenly when the wind abated for a short interval, the old man started from his seat, and first gazed towards the door and then at his wife.

"What's the matter, old man?" said Dorothy, "what is it that alarms you?"

"There's nothing alarms me, dame," replied her husband; "but I thought I heard a noise."

"It would be very strange indeed if you didn't on such a tempestuous afternoon as this. Why it is all noise."

"Ay, ay, Dorothy; but the noise I thought I heard, seemed to me to proceed from a human voice. It sounded like groaning. There it is again."

"I heard it then, sure enough," said the old woman; "it must proceed from the ruins. I hope no poor creature has come to any harm there among the snow, and the fragments of stone that are so thickly strewn about."

"I trust not," said Hannibal, "but at any rate we will go and see; for we must never suffer any person to want our aid, when we have the means to assist."

The sounds were repeated, and they were now fully satisfied that they came from the ruins, and that some unfortunate individual was there suffering great pain. It was not without great difficulty that the old people could make their way through the snow, and over the broken fragments, but at length they were guided to the spot where the sufferer lay, and their astonishment may be imagined when they found stretched upon his back, and half covered with snow, while the blood was flowing freely from a wound he had received in his head, by its coming in contact with a stone, the old man of the ruins.

They, however, saw that there was no time to be lost, and they therefore conquered their feelings of surprise sufficiently to raise the aged man, and to carry him with as little delay as possible to the lodge, where the dame immediately bound up his head in the best manner she was able.

The old man was perfectly insensible, and Hannibal and his wife were afraid that the injuries he had received were so extensive that he would not again be restored to consciousness. The first thing they did, after having placed the unfortunate old man upon a bed, was to call in the assistance of their nearest neighbour, one of whom they requested to go for surgical aid, while another was despatched to the abbey to make Lord Elverton acquainted with what had happened, and to receive his instructions as to how they should act.

Lord Elverton and the others were not a little amazed when the messenger arrived and brought the news.

"This strange old man, I feel satisfied," said the earl, "is acquainted with some important secrets, which he may be prevailed upon to disclose, if he is in a fit condition to do so. I will immediately hasten to the priory lodge."

"And with your permission, my dear father," said Lord Coningsby, "I will accompany you.

As not a moment was to be lost, Lord Elverton rang the bell, and ordered the horses, although they scarcely knew how they should be able to make their way throught the snow. They were soon on their way accompanied by two attendants.

They proceeded much better than they had expected, and in the course of about half an hour they arrived at the priory lodge, where they found old Hannibal in the parlour, and eagerly inquired after the sufferer.

"He is still alive, my lord," answered Hannibal, "but the worthy doctor says that from his great age and the nature of the injuries he has received, it is impossible for him to live long."

"Is he sensible?"

"Yes, my lord, he seems to be conscious of what is passing around him, and to suffer great pain; but he is unable to speak."

"Show me into the chamber where you have placed him, immediately," said the earl.

Hannibal opened the door of the back parlour, and Lord Elverton and his son entered. The old man was groaning heavily. They approached his bedside, and plainly saw from his ghastly features, and glassy eyes that he could not possibly survive long.

The sound of their entrance met the old man's ear, and he fixed his eyes upon them, but no sooner did he behold them than his emotion was plainly visible. He made several efforts to speak, but to no purpose, and his agony of mind seemed to increase with every ineffectual attempt.

Lord Elverton looked into the dying man's face with compassion, and then in a mild voice said,—

"Unfortunate old man, think not we come here to reproach you, for all the evil you may have practised towards me or mine, or whatever further harm you may have intended us; I freely forgive you, but if you have any secrets to reveal that concern me, I beg of you, as you hope for mercy from above, to endeavour to find strength to disclose them to me."

Again the old man exerted himself to speak, and at length he was enabled to articulate faintly—

"Too late—too late, I have much to say, but the hand of death is on me. Lord Elverton I was always your enemy, though you never did me wrong, but your father injured me by accusing me of a crime I did not commit, and getting me dismissed from a service in which I had been for more than a quarter of a century. I swore revenge against all his family. But my breath grows short—it was at my instigation that your son was stolen. I could have murdered him, but thought that was a more glorious revenge. It was I who aided the priest De Bouville in carrying out the projects which deprived you of your wife and daughter, and—but— I ——"

His tongue refused its office, and it

was evident that death was approaching fast.

The agony of Lord Elverton and his son at that moment needs no description. That which the poor dying old wretch had already disclosed convinced him that he was thoroughly acquainted with those secrets he was so anxious to have explained, and upon which, in all probability, his future happiness, in a great measure, depended; and both Lord Elverton and his son were fearful that the power of speech would not be again allowed him, and that they would thus again be left in the same state of painful doubt, suspense, and mystery.

Still, although the old man could not speak, his senses did not appear to forsake him, while at the same time he appeared to suffer as much from his being unable to divulge to them all he knew, as he did from the agonies of death.

"Wretched old man," said the earl, "what dreadful agonies of suspense have you created in my breast by what you have already had the power to state. Oh, why did you not before repent of your crimes, and by an ample confession, make at least some atonement to your innocent victims? What years of misery would you thus have saved me. Can you not yet speak?"

The dying man shook his head and groaned.

"The dew of death is gathering fast upon your brow, wretched sinner," said the earl. "I see plainly that your mortal career is near its close, and that in a few minutes you will be in eternity. May the Almighty pardon you the many crimes you have committed, and be more merciful to you than you have been to others."

The poor guilty creature fixed upon him a look, in which horror, gratitude, and despair were blended, but the doctor moistened his parched lips with some soothing liquid, and he appeared to rally again for a few minutes, and once more he made an effort to speak, but could not.

"This is, indeed, most torturing," said the earl, striking his forehead. "Old man, you can, perhaps, answer by signs to my questions. Is my unfortunate wife still living?"

The dying man nodded his head affirmatively.

"Gracious heaven!" cried the agitated Lord Elverton, "gracious heaven, I thank Thee for this. Oh, my poor misguided Elvina! But my daughter, does she, too, still survive?"

The poor struggling wretch shook his head, and the earl gave utterance to an exclamation of intense grief and despair.

"But know you where my unfortunate mother is concealed?" eagerly demanded Lord Coningsby.

The dying man again exerted himself to the utmost, his lips moved, but no sound, save a pitiful moan, escaped them. He, however, managed to raise his head slightly from the pillow, and glaring eagerly around the chamber, motioned with his shrivelled hand towards an ink-stand, which, with some paper, was placed upon a side-board in one corner of the room. The earl and his son immediately understood him.

"Ah," said the former, "if we can but guide his hand to paper, it may not yet be too late for him to make known to us the name of the place so much required. Quick, quick, the writing materials."

They were brought—the unfortunate sinner was raised gently from his recumbent posture—the pen was placed in his feeble hold, and his hand was guided to the paper; but before he could form a single letter, his limbs stiffened, the pen dropped from his hold, his eyes became fixed, one awful groan escaped him, and the guilty old man was called before the awful tribunal of the Almighty, to answer for the many crimes he had committed.

For a few minutes the earl and his son stood and gazed upon the corpse with feelings of horror and despair, and then slowly retired from the room.

"How agonising is this," said the earl, "and must I still remain in ignorance of the place where my unfortunate Elvina is concealed? But she lives, oh, thank God! and there is still some hope left that we may meet again. Oh, that compunction had before seized this guilty man's heart, then might we all now have been restored to complete happiness. But my poor daughter, of whom I was so cruelly deprived of in infancy, she then is no more."

"We must submit to the will of heaven, my dear father," said Lord Coningsby. "Providence will, I trust, yet restore my beloved mother to our arms; but I regret that we forgot to question the dying man whether my sister died in childhood, or lived to the age of womanhood."

"Ah," said Lord Elverton, "I am sorry that we did not do so; but I feel satisfied that she did not die until she reached the years of maturity, though what induces me to think so I cannot exactly imagine."

"Pardon me, my lord," said Hannibal, now venturing to speak, "but what is to be done with the corpse of this old man?"

"I will see that he is decently interred," answered his lordship, "but let his clothes be first minutely examined, to see whether we can discover any clue to his connections."

This was done accordingly, without any delay, but nothing whatever was discovered to show to whom the old man belonged, or whether he had any relations living, and after leaving some further instructions with old Hannibal, and his wife, (who were not very well pleased with the charge which had devolved upon them) Lord Elverton and his son took their departure from the priory lodge, deeply impressed with the solemn events of the evening.

CHAPTER XV.

MORE REMARKABLE DISCLOSURES.—WHO IS THE STRANGER?

GREAT was the excitement which the death of the old man of the ruins, and the facts which Lord Elverton and his son had elicited from him, created amongst all the inhabitants of the abbey and their friends, and fervently they congratulated him on the existence of his wife, and expressed a hope that she would yet be restored to his arms, and that they would pass many years of happiness together.

Lady Eugenia and our heroine were much affected, and deeply felt for the state of agonizing suspense in which the earl was kept. Lord Everside and the Earl of Bathurst were not the least interested of the party, and most heartily did the latter rejoice that his aunt was living, and that there was a probability of her yet being restored to the friends she had so long been estranged from.

"How mysterious are the ways of Providence," remarked Lord Everside, "but a few months since you were the victim of utter despair, my dear friend, but now by the most miraculous chain of events you have discovered your long lost son, and learned that your wife is still living, nay more the resemblance of the miniature on the ring which Celestia found in so singular a manner in the old priory ruins, bears to the portrait of Lady Elvina in Berensforth Hall, is more than sufficient to lead us to hope that you will in that dear girl find a close connection, if that likeness should indeed prove to be that of her mother."

At the mention of that dear name, our heroine could not refrain from tears.

"Oh," she ejaculated, "should it be the will of Almighty God to realize that hope, how shall I ever be able to support so much happiness?"

The earl and his sister embraced her tenderly, and all were much affected.

"But what an old villain that man of the ruins, as he was called, must have been," said Lord Everside, "to act in such a base and revengeful manner towards those who had never injured him."

"He must, indeed," coincided Lord Elverton; "but had repentance seized upon him before his dying hour, I have no doubt that he had it in his power to clear up the whole of the mystery, and thus to make some atonement for the heinous crimes he had committed. It is most strange that no one seems to know to whom he belongs, where he resided, or whether he has any relations living."

"It is," said Lord Everside, "but all conjecture is completely thrown away upon the subject, and it is, probably, a secret that will never be properly explained."

    *   *   *   *

In the course of another month, beautiful, clear, frosty weather set in, and Lord Elverton resolved at once to depart to his castle in the north.

The day before their departure, Sir Eustace Aubrey, Lady Aubrey, and their son, came to Sungrove Abbey to bid them farewell.

Collingwood Aubrey was particularly low-spirited, and the feelings of jealousy he had suffered to take possession of his bosom, prompted him to imagine that Celestia viewed him with utter indifference, and that she bestowed all her attentions upon Lord Malensbury; and as these thoughts arose to his mind, he could scarcely conceal his chagrin and disappointment.

When the hour of separation arrived, it was with difficulty that he could go through the necessary ceremony, and Celestia was scarcely less embarrassed, for she imagined that she could read the thoughts that were passing in his mind, and she was now more than ever convinced that she could never feel for Collingwood Aubrey any warmer sentiment than that of friendship.

The parting between Collingwood and the lovely Lady Eglantine was of the most cold and formal description. He felt that, however great her attractions, she could never be the woman of his choice ; and she, feeling her pride mortified by the total indifference with which he viewed her, although she at first felt a partiality towards him which might, and probably would, have ultimately ripened into a tenderer passion, parted from him without the least pang of regret.

Nothing, for the time of year, could be more lovely than the morning on which our travellers set out on their journey.

Our heroine, by endeavouring to appear cheerful, gradually became so in reality, and they arrived at the castle the third day, very little fatigued by their journey.

So very anxious was the late steward of the Earl of Elverton, the venerable Mr. Elkins, to congratulate the earl, and to see his son, that when they arrived at Merton, he was ready to receive them.

Lord Elverton was very much gratified at this, and taking the worthy old man by the hand, he said,—

"My dear Edgar, here is one who feels sincere joy at your restoration to your family."

"Indeed, Lord Coningsby," replied Mr. Elkins, " when your revered father's letter arrived, informing me of the joyful event, I could hardly wait the period of your arrival, so anxious was I to behold one so long lost to us, but I felt my strength unequal to so long a journey. But as I knew Mr. Edwards intended to meet you at the head of the tenantry, I was resolved to have the happiness of paying my congratulations beforehand."

Lord Coningsby was greatly affected at the manner in which the worthy old man had expressed himself, and said,—

"My good Mr. Elkins, it is a great addition to my present felicity to see one whom my father so highly values among the first to welcome me home. To say that I was not happy under the protection of my supposed father, the late Mr. Clemments, would be the height of ingratitude; but to compare my past with my present happiness is impossible. Who shall scoff at the power of nature over our feelings ? I respected Mr. Clemments because I supposed him to be my father, and felt it my duty to obey him implicitly, but I never felt for him that extreme affection that I do for Lord Elverton, though only known for so few weeks."

"You may believe me, my lord," remarked Mr. Elkins, "that I fully appreciate and commend your sentiments. From the first hour of your loss I never believed you to be drowned; but so many years elapsed without bringing any tidings of you, that I despaired of ever seeing this day, and I bless God that I am permitted so to do. May the earl, and your lordship, and Lady Eugenia live long to enjoy that happiness so long debarred you· and you, too, my dear young. lady," addressing himself to Celestia, "I see, participate most truly in the happiness of your protectors."

These observations deeply affected our heroine—tears started to her eyes, and her heart was too full to speak. Death had for ever deprived her of participating in the feelings of the earl and his son, but that did not prevent her from sympathizing in the joy of her beloved protectors, and she would have replied to the speech of Mr. Elkins, but her emotions overpowered her, and she was unable to give utterance to a syllable.

They now came to the last stage, where the tenants, headed by Mr. Edwards, were waiting to receive them. Their shouts of gladness rent the air, but the earl expressing a wish to go on at once to the castle, the cavalcade preceded the carriage, which was soon followed by a multitude of the peasantry shouting aloud their simple, but earnest expressions of welcome, the bells from every village church sending forth merry peals, so that it might almost be called a triumphal entry.

And oh, how different were the feelings which now agitated the bosom of the earl, when he entered the noble seat of his ancestors, to those which had oppressed him on the last year's visit. No sooner had he alighted from the carriage than affectionately embracing his son, he ejaculated :—

"Oh, may you, my beloved Edgar, though so long estranged from your paternal home, enjoy a long life of uninterrupted happiness! for myself, though far advanced in life, the principal part of which has been passed in sorrow, I feel a greater desire for length of days, than I could ever have supposed I should."

"God grant that far distant may be the period of its termination, my dear father," said Lord Coningsby.

The servants and peasantry having for some time continued to give vent to their feelings of gladness, money was distributed amongst them, and they were dismissed, Mr. Edwards having informed them that a day would be appointed for a general jubilee, to celebrate the restoration of Lord Coningsby to his family.

The Earl Bathurst and his family had parted with them at the last stage, and made their way to Berensforth Hall, and when the dinner was over, Lord Coningsby requested his father's permission for Celestia to conduct him over the castle, as she had promised to do, particularly to the old turret, which he understood she had taken such a fancy to on her last visit.

Celestia led the way, smiling, to the east turret, but when she threw open the door of the upper room, she started back in amazement to observe the alteration which had been made in it, since she had last seen it, and the elegance and comfort with which it was fitted up.

"Oh, my dear benefactor! how can I behold such repeated marks of your affection and indulgence," she said, "without feeling how impossible it is for me ever to be sufficiently grateful?"

"Say not so, Celestia," said Lord Coningsby, "your actions hourly prove far more than words could do, the heartfelt gratitude you feel for all the kindness that is bestowed upon you."

Having examined this little apartment, Celestia, impatient to thank the earl for this fresh instance of his kindness, begged Lord Coningsby to excuse her further attendance; but he followed her, and when she had entered the drawing-room, she poured forth her gratitude to the earl in the most ardent and sincere terms.

Although not much fatigued, they retired early to repose, but Celestia arose with the early dawn, in order to repair to her turret, and there she remained, enjoying the beauty of the marine views, and indulging in the varied feelings to which the contemplation gave rise, until she was summoned to breakfast, and before the meal was over, the Earl Bathurst and his family were announced.

Since the restoration of his son, Lord Elverton appeared to have forgotten that he had ever had any other cause of sorrow; but it was in appeaeance only, for thoughts would too frequently obtrude, and the scene in the priory lodge with the old man of the ruins, would often rush most vividly on his memory.

Lady Elvina still reigned supreme in his heart; the loss of her son had nearly cost her her life, and to one of her turn of mind, illness often raises gloomy ideas; had not that misfortune taken place, she might have borne the deprivation of her other child with more fortitude, and still have been his loved companion.

"Ah, my Elvina," he would often soliloquize, "and are you indeed still living? Could I but discover her retreat, she might be prevailed upon to return to me, and we might pass the rest of our days in peace; but alas! I now see no means of discovering the place where she is concealed, and I am compelled in my despair to give her up as lost to me for ever."

Such were the dismal reflections which would occasionally occupy the earl's mind, till gratitude for the unexpected blessing bestowed upon him, in the restoration of that son he had so long deplored as dead, would calm his perturbed mind, and he would then seek the society of those who shared his love, particularly of that son whom he hoped would prove the pride and the comfort of his declining years, certain as he was from all that he had yet seen of him that he was possessed of every noble and honourable feeling.

A few days after they had been at the castle, the earl arranged everything with his steward for the jubilee. The tenantry were to be entertained the two first days, the first a dinner, the second a ball and supper, for the entertainment of their wives and daughters; the two following days for the peasantry, and their families; and the fifth and sixth for the poor of every parish round the estate.

The week after the jubilee, a grand dinner was to be given for the nobility and gentry; and a ball and supper on the succeeding day; and, as soon as the servants should be recovered from the fatigue of these several entertainments, they were to have two days for themselves, the first day a dinner; the second a ball and supper; to both of which they were to invite all their friends and relations, and that they might all partake equally of the pleasure, people were to be paid for dressing their dinner and supper, and a sufficient number also to wait upon them.

Universal joy prevailed among all classes in the neighbourhood, and they looked forward to the days of festivity with the most eager anticipation.

In the meantime, Lady Eugenia and our heroine were most benevolently employed. They visited all the villages round, and took an account of the number and wants of all the poorer labourers and their families; this filled up the first day's leisure. The next took them to the nearest market-town, where they purchased different materials for new clothing them all; and the next fortnight was occupied in cutting out, and assisting to make two complete changes for men, women, and children; so that the guests of the last two days made as good an appearance as any of those of the preceding ones.

The time set apart for the entertainments, at length arrived, much to the delight of every one, and admirable, indeed, were all the arrangements, and excellently was everything conducted. Nothing could exceed the universal hilarity which reigned around, and it would have been strange indeed, if it had not, after the pains which had been taken to ensure every one happiness. Plenty crowned the festive board; the healths of their noble host, Lord Coningsby, Lady Eugenia, and our heroine, were drunk with the greatest enthusiasm, and the week concluded the festivities, with every one grateful for the attention that had been paid them by the whole family; each returned to their respective homes, contented and happy, and in talking it all over their frugal meals, kept up an amusement for many weeks.

The grand banquet, given for the nobility and gentry, passed off with the greatest *eclat*, and nothing could exceed the magnificence of the ball which succeeded it. All the fashionable families, for miles around, hastened to do honour to the occasion, in fact the castle doors were open to every respectable person who liked to come, whether invited or not, and perhaps such a splendid assemblage had seldom been seen on any similar occasion. It was, indeed, a most gorgeous display, and all seemed determed to do full justice to the treat which their noble host had provided for them.

Most brilliantly illuminated and decorated was that noble ball-room; it was, indeed, one glitter of splendour—a concentration of all that was beautiful in tasteful arrangements, in the elegance of the dresses, and the loveliness of the fair portion of the guests who were assembled on that most joyous occasion.

Lord Malensbury engaged our heroine in the dance the whole of the evening, and many were the young noblemen present who envied him his graceful partner.

Celestia was in unusual spirits on that occasion, and certainly never did she appear more captivating or beautiful. She was dressed in the most elegant, yet simple manner, which set off the graces of her person to the greatest advantage.

Many of the richest jewels which had been found in the Indian cabinet, particularly that singular locket, mentioned in the early part of our tale, namely, the heart upon the point of a spear, she had been permitted by her beloved guardian to wear, and the uncommon splendour of these ornaments, attracted universal attention.

It was with that object that Lord Elverton always wished her to wear them upon all public occasions, in the hope that they might accidentally lead to some discovery.

The Earl of Elverton's fair protegeé was, in fact, the greatest attraction of the evening—the admired of all. And fully deserving was she of the admiration she excited. Perhaps never had she so well acquitted herself on any former occasion.

Her friends were in raptures with her, and flattering compliments poured in upon Lord Elverton and his sister from every side, for the extreme care they must have taken to bring the lovely orphan to such a state of perfection in every elegant accomplishment.

Never had Lord Malensbury felt so extremely happy, and the looks and observations of Celestia convinced him that he had the felicity to have made something more than a favourable impression upon her heart. Indeed, Celestia could not but acknowledge to herself the pleasure she felt in his lordship's society, and the extreme delicacy and unassuming character of his demeanour divested her of a great deal of that timidity and reserve which was so natural to her, and inspired her with the same confidence towards him as if they had been acquainted for many years.

During one of the intervals of the dance, the company retired to an elegant saloon, attached to the ball-room, to partake of refreshments, but Lord Elverton his son, the Earl Bathurst, and Lord Malensbury, being for a few minutes engaged in some particular conversation, did not notice the retirement of the company, and consequently our heroine, Lady Eugenia, Lady Bathurst, and her daughter followed the other guests to the saloon, Lady Eugenia playfully remarking that "those ungallant gentlemen would, no doubt, soon be aroused to a full sense of the heinous offence they had committed, and would quickly follow them, to offer up every apology for their misconduct."

The ladies had only been seated a few minutes, and were so deeply engaged in conversation that their attention was wholly diverted from the objects around them, when they were aroused by an exclamation of agony, followed by the words,—

"Great God! that locket!—that heart!" and looking up, Celestia beheld standing on the opposite side of the table, and gazing intently at her and the locket suspended from her neck, with a countenance in which the expression of the most poignant anguish was dis-

played, the unknown, who had so frequently appeared to her before. But it was only for a moment; covering his face with his hands, he turned hastily away, and was immediately lost among the number of persons that were assembled together in the saloon.

Our heroine was so much alarmed by this incident that she could not repress a scream, and her companions were no less astonished, at a circumstance for which no one but Lady Eugenia could account.

At this moment the gentlemen joined them, and Lord Elverton perceiving the extreme agitation of Celestia, and the excitement which prevailed among all parties, he eagerly inquired the cause, which was quickly explained to him by his sister.

"Most astonishing!" exclaimed the earl, "which way did he go?"

It was pointed out to him, and while Lord Malensbury and his father remained with the ladies, Lord Elverton and Lord Coningsby went in pursuit of the stranger, but although they searched every part of the castle in which the guests were assembled; they could see nothing of him, nor gain any information respecting him. According to the description given of him, none of the servants had observed him enter, and Lord Elverton and his son returned to the ladies, lost in amazement, which was much increased when they were told the observations the stranger had made use of respecting the locket, and the extraordinary emotions he evinced.

"The behaviour of this individual is most remarkable and unaccountable," said Lord Elverton, "I confess I am at a perfect loss to fathom it. However, there is one thing appears quite certain to me, namely, that he is acquainted with some of the connexions of our Celestia, and his emotion on beholding the locket convinces me of it, and renders me the more anxious to have an opportunity of speaking to him, that I may obtain some explanation from him."

"If he has anything to inquire into or to disclose," remarked Lord Coningsby; "is it not singular that he should thus shun every opportunity of doing so?"

"It is," coincided Lord Elverton, "but let us drop this subject for the present, and return to the ball room, for see, most of our friends have retired there, and our absence will be accounted extraordinary. I trust that chance will yet give us an opportunity of having an interview with this mysterious stranger, when everything may be explained to our mutual satisfaction."

Celestia endeavoured to regain her spirits, but the event was one of such a peculiar nature that she found the greatest difficulty in doing so; she however, accompanied her friends, and in the mazes of the dance, soon regained her former gaiety.

Lord Malensbury was again the partner of our heroine, and though obliged to change partners in the two next dances, he took good care to engage her afterwards. It was plain to every one that the young nobleman had no eyes for any other female, nor did Celestia appear to dislike his attention; though perfectly unconscious of it herself. Lord and Lady Bathurst saw the increasing admiration of their son for the unknown orphan, and though they would have preferred one whose family was known to them, they were convinced that he could not make choice of one more amiable, in every sense of the word; but they still were determined to take no notice of it, nor for the present, give him the smallest reason to think they would approve of it.

The ball was over, and the guests having departed, the castle resumed its usual quiet.

Celestia passed a sleepless night; the words of the stranger seemed continually to ring in her ears, and by the agitation he betrayed when he exclaimed: "Oh, God!—that locket! that heart!" she felt convinced that he must have known it before it came into her possession.

"Mysterious Providence!" she ejaculated, "what will be the result of all these extraordinary perplexing events? Oh, that my dear father had at least told me to whom this locket belonged!—or, if my mother's, I should have remembered it!"

She arose in the morning, pale and unrefreshed, and when she joined her friends in the breakfast-room, the conversation naturally turned upon the event of the previous night, and various were the conjectures which were formed upon the subject.

The meal was scarcely over, when a note was delivered into the hands of the Earl of Elverton, the superscription to which was written in an unknown hand; he opened it, and to his amazement read the following words:

"Sir Roderick Ainslie, requests the Earl of Elverton to grant him an interview to morrow morning.

"No doubt Lord Elverton will feel much surprised that a stranger should make such a request, but it may be productive of more important results than can be explained in this note. It is of particular moment to Sir Roderick, or he would not have taken this liberty with the earl.

"*Flemmington Hall.*"

"This is most remarkable," said Lord Elverton, when he had perused the note, "I do not remember to have heard the name of Sir Roderick Ainslie before, but Sir William Flemmington, from whose seat he directs his letter, I was on intimate terms with many years ago, at least his father, for he was only a boy at the time. What business can Sir Roderick possibly have with me?"

"But you will grant the interview to Sir Roderick?" said Lady Eugenia.

"Most assuredly," replied the earl, and he immediately despatched a note to Sir Roderick, saying he would be happy to see him at eleven the next morning, to breakfast with him alone.

The more they reflected upon this event, the more perplexed and astonished they became, and when Lady Eugenia and her brother were alone, the former said,—

"It strikes me that this Sir Roderick Ainslie has some connection with the stranger we saw at the ball, if it is not he himself; if so, I hope from his exclamation regarding the locket, it is some one who knew it again, and in that case will be able to inform us who Celestia is."

"You are very sanguine, my dear sister," said the earl; "God grant your conjecture may be right."

CHAPTER XVI.

THE MEETING.—THE NARRATIVE.—THE DISCOVERY.

THE day passed tediously away, and they all regretted that Sir Roderick had not requested the interview to take place at an earlier period, for most anxious and impatient were they to know what he had to communicate.

Celestia again slept little that night, but when she did, dreams of the most extraordinary and impressive character occurred to her imagination.

At one time she imagined herself folded to the bosoms of her father and mother, she felt the affectionate throbbings of their hearts, and the warm glow of their fond kisses upon her cheeks; suddenly several fierce-looking ruffians tore them asunder, and the next moment, she beheld the bleeding, mangled, lifeless form of her mother stretched at her feet. With the horror of the sight she awoke.

She found it impossible to compose herself to sleep again, and as daylight was fast beginning to dawn, she arose and gave herself up to the torturing reflections which this frightful dream had naturally engendered in her breast.

"Oh, my poor mother," she ejaculated, "I fear indeed, that you met with some terrible and untimely fate. Cruel destiny that should thus separate you at so early a period from your husband and child."

Her tears flowed fast as these melancholy thoughts occurred to her, and it was some time ere she could in the least regain her composure. She most anxiously wished for Sir Roderick's arrival, and the result of his visit.

At eleven o'clock precisely, a carriage stopped at the castle gate, from which the tall and graceful figure of a gentleman alighted, and was instantly conducted to the library, where the earl awaited him; but who can describe the astonishment of Lord Elverton, when he recognised the man who had created such a sensation on the night of the ball, and who had so frequently appeared to Celestia in so extraordinary a manner.

"I see your surprise, my lord," said Sir Roderick, "and I do not wonder at it; I have to apologize to you for my singular behaviour on several occasions, and for the alarm I probably created on the night of the ball, but after you have heard what I have to state, I trust that you will accept my apology, as my conduct sprang from no unnatural cause; the extraordinary likeness which that young lady whom I have so frequently seen, bears to one whom I loved, was the first thing that induced me to watch and follow your footsteps, but still I had not the courage to seek an interview with you till now."

"Your observations, Sir Roderick," said the earl, "interest me greatly; pray proceed."

"For some months past till now," replied Sir Roderick, "I have been confined on account of a malady I have laboured under at intervals for some years."

It instantly occurred to Lord Elverton, from the circumstance of his strange behaviour at different times, that the malady he spoke of was mental derangement, and he therefore endeavoured to turn him from so melancholy a retrospect, by bringing him back to the present occasion of his visit, and which he was himself most anxious to become acquainted with.

"In your note, Sir Roderick," he observed, "you said that you requested this interview upon an affair of moment to yourself, will you favour me with the communication while we take our breakfast?"

Sir Roderick no longer delayed, but said,—

"The business which brings me here, my lord, is respecting the young lady whom I saw at the ball the other night."

"Ah!" exclaimed the earl, much agitated, "what of her? Proceed, Sir Roderick."

"Then may I ask if that young lady is in anywise related to your lordship?"

"She is not related to me, Sir Roderick, but I love her as my own child, she having been with me from infancy."

"And her age, my lord?"

"About seventeen," answered the earl.

"Such a likeness," inwardly muttered Sir Roderick, "and the same age too; it is strange; then, my lord," he said aloud, "her name is not Coningsby?"

"No, it is not; her name is Celestia de Aunville!"

"Gracious Heaven, 'tis she!" cried Sir Roderick, starting from his seat, and clasping h s hands together with the greatest emotion, "'tis the child of her I so fondly adored."

"Is she then your child?" eagerly demanded the earl.

"Oh, no!" answered Sir Roderick, "but her mother was beloved, idolised by me, but never knew it—never was mine."

"Thank Providence!" cried Lord Elverton, "then you knew my Celestia's parents and connections, Sir Roderick, and the secret we have been so anxious to penetrate will at length be revealed."

"As far as my means extend, my lord, it shall. The lovely mother of Celestia was married to the young Marquis de Aunville, who was my friend. But I must endeavour to overcome feelings, which, at this distance of time, bring back fresh horrors that almost overpower me."

He took a glass of water, which revived him, and he then observed—

"The tale is long and melancholy, and I fear that I may intrude upon time o'herwise appropriated, my lord."

"Oh, no," replied Lord Elverton,

"what can be of such importance to me as anything connected with my Celestia. I pray you do not delay, Sir Roderick."

"I will not, my lord," said Sir Roderick; "but first, has not Celestia a locket of singular construction, with the miniature likeness of a lovely female?"

"She has a locket, and, from its singularity, I have often wished to know its history; and I desired her to wear it when she went into public, in the hope of its leading to the discovery of her connexions; but I know of no picture."

"Could I behold it?" asked Sir Roderick, "at the same time, I would not wish her to know of my request, till I have made your lordship acquainted with every particular, which I think, concerns her and her father and mother, though I cannot doubt her being the child of those loved friends."

The earl rung for Robert, whom he sent to Celestia, desiring her to send the locket she wore at the ball. Robert quickly returned with the locket, which was presented to Sir Roderick, and no sooner did he behold it, than he exclaimed, with a burst of indescribable emotion,—

"Oh, God! my beloved Elvina!"

"Elvina!" repeated the earl, starting and trembling in every limb, "tell me, for Heaven's sake, was that the name of Celestia's mother?"

"It was," answered Sir Roderick.

"And had she parents living?"

"A mother."

"Her name?"

"Mrs. Hargrave."

"She was an English lady, then?"

"She was," replied Sir Roderick.

"Could it be?" muttered the earl to himself with much emotion. "That name so dear to me; what am I about to hear?"

Sir Roderick now touched a secret spring in the locket, when it instantly flew open, and discovered the likeness of a beautiful female on one half the heart, and on the other was engraved, C. H. de Salvois."

"It is the same, my lord," said Sir Roderick, "and belonged to Elvina, Marchioness De Aunville. The lady whom this portrait represents, was the unfortunate Duchess de Salvois, who was barbarously murdered. She was the particular friend of Elvina, and equally cruel was the fate which befell them."

Lord Elverton could not but feel deeply affected, but he requested Sir Roderick to give him a further explanation, but requested that Celestia should remain in ignorance till he knew the whole, lest it should be necessary to make any reservation; for much he feared that there was some tragical event attached to it.

"My lord," commenced Sir Roderick, "I will endeavour to be as brief as I possibly can in my melancholy recital, but it will be necessary that I should give some account of myself, as I was, unfortunately for my own peace, deeply concerned in the fate of that lovely woman."

"When I had arrived at age, I found myself possessed of a large fortune, and master of my own actions. On making the tour of Europe, I became acquainted with a young French nobleman, nearly allied to some of the most distinguished families of that country, and our dispositions being assimilated, and being also about the same age, a warm friendship quickly sprung up between us, and as he was summoned home by his father, I resolved to accompany him.

"Nothing particular occurred to us on the journey, and in a few days we arrived safe in Paris. The seeds of dissension were already disseminated in the capital, and that bloody revolution which was destined to fill all Europe with horror, was on the very eve of breaking out. Suspicion, doubts, and horror filled the breast of every noble family.

"The family of my friend was high in the esteem of the king and queen, whom they adored; but to be brief, I accompanied my friend on a visit to his near relation, the Duke de Montalvert. The religious houses had just then been dissolved; the Duchess de Salvois, in visiting the lady abbess of St. Genevive, became acquainted with an English lady of the name of Hargrave, who with her daughter had long been boarders in that convent; and so amiable were their qualities, that in a short time a most ardent friendship took place between them; and when they were driven from their late peaceful habitation, the Duchess de Salvois offered them an asylum in the house of her father-in-law. On our arrival we were introduced to them, and the charms of Elvina immediately captivated both our hearts. Oh, she was most lovely; heaven ne'er formed a finer creature. Elvina! while the tide of life continues to flow within my veins, I must ever worship thy sainted spirit."

Sir Roderick was obliged to pause to give vent to his emotions, and then the agitation of the earl was not less than his own. The name of Elvina recalled innumerable painful, almost torturing recollections, and he covered his face with his hands and sobbed deeply. At length Sir Roderick resumed.

"On retiring from their presence, my friend was lavish in his praises of her, declared that he could never love any other woman after beholding her, and stated his determination to use every honourable effort in his power to make a favourable impression upon her heart. Alas! with what agony did I listen to him, for Elvina was the very idol of my soul, as well as that of De Aunville, but I could not think of endeavouring to supplant him, and a short time convinced me that he was the supreme master of her warmest affections. Having obtained the consent of his father, in a short time he led her to the altar, and left me to misery and despair.

"Fearful of betraying my real feelings, I quitted France a short time after their union, but I could not make up my mind to return to England. Shortly after, the revolution raged in all its bloody horror. I heard of the king's flight and recapture, but when the news of the barbarous and inhuman murder of the lovely Duchess de Salvois reached me, I determined at all hazards to hasten to the chateau of the Duke Montalvert.

"Terrible was the scene that there awaited me; my friend De Aunville was in a state bordering upon madness; his lovely wife was given over by her physician, and the duke lay at the point of death.

"My unfortunate friend De Aunville embraced me with transport; thanked me in the most moving terms for my kind attentions, and led me to the nursery of his little daughter; the cherub smiled upon me, unconscious of the misery of her relations.

"Mrs. Hargrave appeared to be the only collected person in the house; she attended to the sick, and spoke consolation to the afflicted."

Here Lord Elverton again betrayed the greatest emotion; the character and description of the person of Mrs Hargrave so well answered to that of his wife, that he could not divest his mind of the idea that she was his long estranged Elvina, and he listened with redoubled interest to Sir Roderick's narrative.

"I was anxious," continued the baronet, "to learn some of the particulars of the melancholy situation in which I found the family, and my friend saw my anxiety, and informed me, that when the Duchess de Salvois was seized, and conveyed to the tribunal to be examined, Madame de Aunville could not be persuaded from accompanying her; her friends attempted to dissuade her from such a course, which was most imprudent, but it was all to no purpose, she still persisted in going, till De Aunville, taking the infant Celestia in his arms, declared his intention of following her, and at the same time turning to the Duke and Madame Hargrave, he solemnly bade them farewell, saying—

"My dear friends, I can never hope to see either of you again."

"Oh, my friend, my benefactress," exclaimed Elvina, "whichever way I decide, I must be miserable—my mother— my child—my husband——"

"The torturing intensity of her emotions here overpowered her, and she fainted, in which state she was conveyed to her bed.

"The savage, the cowardly murder of the Duchess Clarisse, I have before alluded to, and I cannot trust my feelings to enter into a more lengthy description of it. When the fatal intelligence reached the chateau, Elvina was in the height of a fever, and insensible to all that passed. At this juncture I arrived; it was long before she was pronounced out of danger.

"When her anxious inquiries after the duchess obliged them to break the fatal truth to her, a relapse, as might naturally be expected, was the consequence ; but her youth surmounted all, and in a short time she was once more convalescent.

"Elvina had a miniature of the Duchess de Salvois in a ring; this she dared not now be seen to wear, yet she was determined not to part with it. She requested, nay entreated me to get it done for her after her own design, in Switzerland; she had heard the fatal particulars related when supposed not present. It was not long ere I procured this treasure for her, in the form you now see, which was an exact representation of one of the atrocities committed, and held up before the windows of the Queen of France."

Sir Roderick's feelings were here so powerful that he could not proceed for some minutes with his painfully interesting narrative; and not less powerful were the emotions which Lord Elverton experienced, There was something which told him he was more intimately connected with the facts recorded by the narrator than might at first appear, and the strange coincidence which the character of Mrs. Hargrave and her daughter, Elvina, presented to that of his wife and daughter was so very striking, that it was not at all wonderful that he should be deeply affected.

A pause of some minutes ensued, daring which interval Sir Roderick and Lord Elverton exchanged no observations but at length the former resumed as follows—

"As my unfortunate friends appeared to derive consolation from my society, I remained with them. I was master, as I have before remarked, of my actions and fortunes. The Duke Montalvert was fast verging to the grave, with the insupportable weight of grief that for some time had pressed upon him; in him, I knew, they would lose their only friend in France, for De Aunville's father had already paid the debt of nature, and Mrs. Hargrave wanted consolation herself. She seemed to have some secret grief which preyed upon her spirits, and undermined her constitution, for when she thought herself unobserved, she would clasp her hands and say—

"Oh, God! Thy judgments are just, though terrible, all this have I

brought upon myself—and not myself alone; my child suffers with me."

Here the emotions of Lord Elverton became insupportable ; he suspected, he hoped, he feared the sequel of the tale ; it might be productive of joy, it might sink him into absolute despair, and he groaned in the agony of his feelings.

"Tell me, Sir Roderick," he said, "I beseech you, is Mrs. Hargrave living ?"

"As far as I have the means of knowing, she is," replied Sir Roderick.

"Thank Heaven !" ejaculated the earl, "then my hopes may not yet be doomed to disappointment. But know you, Sir Roderick, where she at present is ?"

"In England, I believe," answered Sir Roderick, "from the last advices I received, "but in what part, I have, unfortunately, not been able to ascertain."

"Truly unfortunate," sighed the earl, "but if there is a possibility of finding the place of her retreat, she must be discovered."

"I am determined to lose no pains or exertion to achieve so desirable an end, my friend," returned Sir Roderick, "but you seem to take an uncommon interest in the fate of this lady, my lord."

"Ah, Sir Roderick," replied Lord Elverton, "if you were acquainted with the peculiarly melancholy circumstances of my history, you would not marvel at it ; but she is the grandmother of my dear Celesta, and that of itself is sufficient to make me feel no common interest in her fate."

"Certainly," coincided Sir Roderick, "but to proceed with my narrative. The death of the king gave the death blow to the Duke Montalvert, he only survived him a few weeks. After his demise I endeavoured to prevail upon my friends to quit Paris, knowing that as an Englishman, I might obtain passports for myself and suite, but I found it much more difficult than I had anticipated. However, we packed up all that was moveable and most valuable, and conveyed them, at the risk of our lives, to Monsieur Le Sage, our banker, and a man of most excellent and amiable qualities. We resolved that they should remain there till an opportunity should present itself of conveying them on board a vessel bound for a safe port: We were then determined to make our escape if possible, either by passport or a bribe, the latter of which expedients, we thought was not likely to fail.

"But the situation of the queen and Madame Elizabeth, called forth the sympathies of Elvina, and she expressed a wish to remain until their fate was decided, apprehending the worst. She had often accompanied the unfortunate Duchess de Salvois to the queen, who soon became very much attached to her, alas! most fatally it proved for her. She had determined, if possible, to attempt seeing the queen before she quitted Paris. We entreated, remonstrated, did all but use force, but all in vain. She left the Chateau de Aunville, and I followed, but we were hardly in sight of the Tuilleries, when a ferocious band of ruffians surrounded us, and seized the unfortunate Elvina as one of the queen's favourites. What a moment of excruciating torture was that; never, never can it be erased from my memory! Oh, Elvina, what scalding tears of agony have I since shed to thy memory, what a bitter curse have I invoked upon the heads of thy brutal, thy cowardly assassins."

"Good God!" exclaimed Lord Elverton, with feelings which it would be vain to seek to describe, "they murdered her then?"

"Alas! alas!" groaned Sir Roderick, "but hear the termination of the frightful tragedy, my lord. In vain I offered any sum they would demand, they bade me quit her, or take the consequence.

"I remonstrated, and fought desperately. I had lost sight of my friend De Aunville. I no longer heard the shrieks of the lovely, the unfortunate Elvina, but I received a thrust from some broad instrument in the face, (the scar of which you see) and I felt, I heard no more than a piercing shriek as they bore their innocent victim along. Oh, God! the ill-fated Elvina was the second innocent female sacrificed for her love to the queen."

"Monsters! barbarians!" groaned Lord Elverton. "Oh, my Celestia, what an awful fate was that of thy mother. And the name too, should it indeed prove to be my child."

"Covered with blood," continued Sir Roderick, "I lay, and should in all probability, have been thrown into the lime-pits, if my faithful valet had not recognised me by a ring on my finger. By his outcries in English of 'Oh, my master!' one of the officers permitted him to convey me home. My wounds were dressed, and I lay composed some time.

"The following day when my wounds were again dressed, I so far recovered my reason, as to inquire after my friend and his wife.

"'Sir,' replied my servant, 'the Marquis de Aunville has been conveyed to prison, in spite of the greatest resistance.'

This information overcame me, and I fainted, but no sooner had I recovered my reason than I resumed my interrogatories. My valet evaded all my questions with his utmost skill; and though I knew how little chance there was for my friend's, or his loved Elvina's escape, I still waited the confirmation, and peremptorily refused to have my wounds dressed, declaring if Elvina was no more, I had nothing worth living for. He then conditioned with me, that, if I would be composed and submit to the surgeon's orders, I should know the whole. I promised, and he revealed the whole truth; Elvina had been guillotined when he found me, but he knew nothing more of my friend.

"Good God! what horrible intelligence was this!—I heard no more. Insanity followed. I was conveyed to England, where I was placed under proper hands for my recovery. At intervals I regained my reason sufficiently to converse with tolerable composure; but an accidental reference by any person present to the affairs of France, would again banish reason from her throne. Need I then offer any further explanation for my excitement on first beholding your fair protégée, Celestia, the very counterpart of her unfortunate murdered mother, and whose strong resemblance threw me again into a state of derangement."

"Ah!" ejaculated Lord Elverton, "and is it possible you did not know our Celestia for that child?"

"I scarcely thought it possible," answered Sir Roderick, "although the likeness struck me so forcibly, but when I saw the locket on the night of the ball, it engrossed my whole attention, and it now remains for you to satisfy me how that locket came into her possession."

Lord Elverton immediately complied, and told Sir Roderick all the particulars from the moment that our heroine first came under his protection."

"What you have related, my lord," said Sir Roderick, when the earl had concluded, "is quite sufficient to convince me that Celestia is undoubtedly the daughter of my friend De Aunville, and his ill-fated Elvina; but I have a letter that places the matter beyond dispute. My servant gave it to me in one of my lucid intervals; I placed it in my pocket-book when I came here, thinking I might have occasion for it."

Sir Roderick unfolded the mentioned letter, and read the following words:

"To SIR RODERICK AINSLIE,

"My dear friend: broken, crushed in spirit, every hope annihilated, my health destroyed, and broken-hearted, I am just landed at Dover. I feel that I am trembling on the verge of eternity, and could I but discover the connexions of my Elvina, that I might place my child under their protection, I should joyfully resign my life into the hands of Him who gave it, in the sure hope of meeting, of joining my Elvina in those realms where her pure spirit, relieved from mortal persecution, enjoys the bliss of angels.

"Oh, my dear friend, how shall I describe my feelings? But I am certain that I need not attempt to do so to you. That dreadful moment that tore me from my Elvina bereaved me of my senses; I recovered them but to be witness of her murder. Wretches! murderers! could nothing satiate your thirst for blood, but the murder of an innocent woman? As soon as they learned she was my wife, they bade me be content—I should bear her company—they scorned to part us.

"At this moment our mutual friend Le Sage seized me, demanded the assistance of those nearest me, to convey me to a place of confinement, where I should remain till interrogated, declaring that I was a traitor to the cause

of liberty, and unworthy so easy a death as the guillotine.

"I could scarcely believe the evidence of my senses, was it possible that such language could proceed from the lips of the man who had hitherto appeared to be my sincere friend? My reason was completely overpowered by such an unexpected shock, and for several days, as I afterwards learned, my life was despaired of.

"By degrees I received both health and reason, and the first objects I beheld were my child, my Celestia, and her nurse. The latter gave me a note from Le Sage, containing these few word—

"' My stratagem has succeeded. Thank God you are safe! Live for the sake of your Elvina's child, your Celestia, your Elvina is no more. Her mother I will guard as though she were my own. I must conclude, for I am suspected. Adieu! God preserve you!'

"I need not say, my friend, what effect this note had upon me. I found on being in a condition to make inquiries, that I had been conveyed on board an American vessel, with my child, and her nurse, and the trunks which now contained all my worldly possessions. I also learned that we had advanced seven days on our voyage. Gracious heavens! can I ever forget my feelings at that moment, when I reverted to the past! I implored the Almighty to take me to himself. Then the gentle voice of my child would recal me to reason.

"Oh, my dear friend, are you in England? and where shall I find you. I have much to reveal, but can scarcely find strength to do it; however, it is necessary, that probably the connections of my child may be discovered. These then are the brief but important particulars.

"My murdered Elvina, was born in England of noble parents, but her mother would neither reveal to me her real name (for she acknowledged that Hargrave was an assumed one), nor other reasons for her concealment than a mistaken notion, or rather zeal for religion, which had deprived her of peace and happiness, 'Extremes,' she would say, 'in every case are most dangerous, had I possessed a right sense of religion, I should not have violated its most sacred ties.'

"I started at the idea the words naturally excited in my mind, which she observing said :—

"'Do not mistake me, De Aunville, calumny itself cannot throw a stain upon my character in the way you imagine; no, your wife, my spotless child, is not more innocent than is her mother, and the child of my still and ever adored husband.'

"Great God!" interrupted Lord Elverton, with a burst of emotion which may easily be imagined, "You say, Sir Roderick, that she still exists? Oh, where can I find her?—her from whom I have been so long cruelly separated? It is, it must be my beloved wife, my Elvina."

"That she still lives, my lord," said Sir Roderick, "I have every reason to hope, and that she is in England, but where I cannot say. If she is indeed your wife, may you meet and be happy, as each, I am certain, deserves to be."

"Alas! alas! how torturing is this suspense," ejaculated Lord Elverton; "My unfortunate Elvina, shall I indeed, ever again behold you?—And will it be found that the darling object of my care and anxiety for so many years, is indeed so dearly and nearly related to me. But pray proceed, Sir Roderick, with the letter."

Sir Roderick complied in the following words :—

"After stating what I have read, my friend De Aunville continues in the following manner : "We had a most prosperous voyage, and at length our vessel reached its destined port. Letters of recommendation from the kind, good Le Sage, procured me a comfortable asylum, but I wanted to go to England, the only safe refuge for a miserable emigrant. Besides, though I had no other clue than what my mother-in-law had said, I thought I might obtain some knowledge of my child's family. After staying there nearly three years, I took my passage in an English vessel, and bid adieu to the good merchant, who did all he could to prevail upon me to remain. On the voyage the poor nurse died, worn out with grief for the death of her loved mistress. I lamented her death, both for her own worth and the affection she bore for my child.

"We landed at Dover. I shall seek some healthy, retired spot in the beautiful county of Kent, which the captain told me would, he was sure, re-establish my health; there I will remain at least till I have recovered from the fatigue of the voyage, and am able to go to London. I shall inclose this to your banker at Brussels. Oh, Sir Roderick, if still abroad, hasten to England, your presence alone can give consolation to your poor friend, DE AUNVILLE."

The feelings of Lord Elverton while listening to the perusal of this letter, we need not seek to pourtray.

"Oh, Sir Roderick, how grateful am I to that Providence which has introduced you to me I cannot any longer doubt that Celestia is the child of that Elvina whom I think was my child. Dear, ill-fated child! Why did her mother flee her country to bring destruction upon your head? But my good Sir Roderick, continue your narrative, that when concluded, I may embrace my Celestia as my grandchild, and as soon as possible, my still beloved Elvina."

"I have little more to add," said Sir Roderick; "and I regret to say that I am in total ignorance of Mrs. Hargrave's present place of abode. Upon perusing this letter, I hastened to Dover; but all my inquiries were vain. Indeed too many years had elapsed since it was written, and I find from your lordship's account, he died a very short time after his arrival in Kent. I was disappointed at not being able to hear from him, or to ascertain where he was; my temper was so irritable, that my servant must have led a most uncomfortable life of it. He followed my footsteps, unknown to me, wherever I went; and fortunate for me it was that he did so, for it saved me from getting into many a *fracas*. The first time I beheld your Celestia, the remarkable, the striking likeness she bore to Elvina, once more drove reason from her throne. But still I had sufficient sense left to render me anxious and curious to behold her again; and that it was which induced me to appear so frequently before her, and to watch your lordship's footsteps wherever you went. Until a few months since, when my unfortunate malady assumed such a dangerous and alarming state, that it was found necessary to place me under restraint; what passed during that interval until I beheld the locket suspended from Celestia's neck on the night of the ball, I know not.

"But Mrs. Hargrave," with painful impatience inquired Lord Elverton, 'know you not where she is?'"

"Unfortunately I do not," answered Sir Roderick, "although I have every reason to believe that, if living, she is in England; as soon as I recovered from my unfortunate affliction, (and I have reason to hope that I am now entirely cured) I endeavoured to find my friend Le Sage if still alive, but, unfortunately, I have not been able to do so, and I am fearful that some calamity has befallen him, otherwise he would have been certain to have employed every means of discovering me."

"And my poor Elvina," exclaimed Lord Elverton, "where are you? Shall I never more behold you? Oh, why did you not at once seek that being, who while the purple current of life continues to circulate throughout his veins can never cease to love you. I crave your pardon, Sir Roderick, for many frequent interruptions during your narrative, but when you have heard the history of the early part of my life, you will not feel surprised if my recollection of the past should make me forget what was due to you, whose life has not been less tinctured with grief than my own."

"Make no apology, my lord, I beg," said Sir Roderick, "most wonderful have been the ways of Providence in the facts of so much importance to us. What but the wisdom of the Supreme Being could have ordered it so, that my poor friend De Aunville should accidentally bring his child to the very spot where her grandfather resided, in order that he should, when death seized him, leave her under the protection of the only being on whom she had any claim, and that I should, through the recognition of a trinket, have the felicity of possibly reuniting two people who have been sundered so many years."

"Ah! should my Elvina be again restored to me," ejaculated the earl, "I shall be the happiest of human beings. But I cannot but feel most grateful to the Almighty for the many blessings which have been conferred upon me. My dear Celestia was sent to be my comforter, when I considered myself to be bereft of all that rendered life desirable. I was deprived of an only son, by means, at the time, no way to be acounted for, deserted by my wife, who, not content with leaving me to deplore her loss, took with her our only remaining child; I became indifferent to the world, and all that were in it, till the unfortunate De Aunville came to the old priory lodge, and left me that dear child. She roused my dormant faculties; I had something to live for. Her truly filial affection repaid me for years of suffering, and I again endeavoured to return a little to society for the sake of those who contributed to my comfort. An only sister has lived with me almost ever since my Elvina deserted me, but when I tell you that within these ten months, that son so long deplored, has been restored to me in a most miraculous way, and that from what you have stated, I do no despair of a reunion with my ever-loved, though mistaken wife, and to sum up all, that the child I have fostered and loved as mine own should indeed prove to be my grandchild—are altogether such marvellous events, that I think it would bring even the atheist to acknowledge, that they must be the works of some supreme power."

"Oh, yes," coincided Sir Roderick, "depraved indeed, must be the mind, and ignorant as depraved, that would not admit the incontestible truth of those observations."

"And now, Sir Roderick," remarked the earl, "with your leave, I think it is necessary that I should send for my sister, acquaint her in a few words of the most material parts of your narrative, and then desire her to prepare Celestia for our reception; and I hope, Sir Roderick, you will allow me to claim your time for the whole of this day, unless a prior engagement should render it impossible; for I have so much to do and say that I shall scarcely think the day long enough."

Sir Roderick assured his lordship that he was at perfect liberty, and then enquired if Lord Coningsby was with him at that time. Lord Elverton replied in the affirmative, but added that he probably was not in the castle at the present time. At this juncture Lady

Eugenia entered the room, and no sooner did she behold Sir Roderick, than she recognised in him the unknown whom she and Celestia had encountered some months since, on their leaving Berensforth Hall. Naturally enough she started with amazement, but she quickly recovered herse'f, and when the mutual compliments were exchanged they resumed their seats.

Lord Elverton inquired of his sister where Celestia was, and she replied that she had gone into the park with Lady Eglantine Malensbury; but that she was certain she would not be long absent, for though she gave herself up to despair

CELESTIA IN HER CHAMBER.

upon their returning the locket with so indifferent a message, she (Lady Eugenia) was prepared for some material information concerning her.

"And my dear sister," returned Lord Elverton, "I am happy to inform you that in that respect you will not be disappointed. Oh, Eugenia, how shall I be able to repeat to you the heads of the melancholy story? but suffice that I must request you to prepare her to receive *me*, as her maternal grandfather."

"Good God!" exclaimed the astonished Lady Eugenia, "is it possible?"

"It is true," replied the Earl, "and

what is more, from what Sir Roderick Ainsley has stated to me, I have every reason to believe that my Elvina is living, and in England, but where to find her at present I know not. But I will without keeping you in further suspense, relate to you how these wonderful events have been brought about."

Sir Roderick now asked permission to walk into Lord Everside's study, in order to write letters, but in fact, to avoid hearing a repetition of that mournful tale which was so harrowing to his feelings.

Lord Elverton related it in as few words as possible, and we need not say with what intense interest his sister listened to him, and when he had concluded, she congratulated him most affectionately on his partial restoration to happiness, and trusted that ere long he would have the felicity of once more embracing his long estranged Elvina.

"God grant that your wishes may be realized, my dear sister," said Lord Elverton, "and something seems to whisper to me that they will. But I must desire you to caution Celestia to guard herself as much as possible against saying anything that may remind Sir Roderick of the scar in his face, for as it proceeded from the dreadful event that so long deprived him of his reason, it might be productive of the most fatal consequences."

Lady Eugenia promised that she would do all that her brother required, and at that moment Lord Coningsby entered the room, and informed his aunt that he had brought back Celestia. Lord Elverton introduced him to Sir Roderick, and Lady Eugenia retired, leaving her brother to relate to his son the wonderful facts we have just recorded, while she went to inform Celestia of the happy change that was in store for her.

Celestia, when Lady Eugenia entered the room in which she was sitting, eagerly inquired whether the stranger was gone.

"No, my dear," answered Lady Eugenia, "he dines here."

"Dear me," said our heroine, "who can he possibly be?"

"One whom you have frequently seen, Celestia," answered Lady Eugenia, "and that, too, only recently."

"Oh, madam," said Celestia, "how you excite my curiosity. Is he old or young?"

"Why, not absolutely either; he appears not much older than Lord Coningsby."

"You have seen him then, madam."

"Indeed I have, but suppose I tell you he is the one who has so much alarmed you on different occasions? The last time at the ball."

"Ah!" ejaculated Celestia, surely you must mean the horrid man with the scar?"

"True, that is the individual I mean; but, my dear Celestia, you must not notice that, or by the least look remind him of it; that does him honour, he obtained it in defending the innocent, and was from that period, for a great number of years in a state of mental derangement from the same cause. The likeness you bore to the lady he defended, and whom he in secret loved, occasioned him a return of his malady, and accounts for the singularity of his behaviour towards you."

"Oh, madam," eagerly, and with much emotion demanded our heroine, "tell me, I beg of you, and do not keep me in suspense, does he know to whom I belong? is he acquainted with my parents? His exclamation when he beheld the locket, his coming here this morning, and what you have just stated, convince me that you know more. Do, dear madam, relieve my anxiety! I can bear anything."

Lady Eugenia fondly embraced her.

"Be composed, my dearest child," she said, "while you agitate yourself thus, I dare not give you the particulars, but I will give you some drops and water to recover your spirits, for I have a long, melancholy tale to unfold, though there is great consolation in store for you."

"Oh, tell me then, have I a mother living?"

"You have not, my love, but you have a grandfather and grandmother, besides other relations to love and protect you."

"For Heaven's sake, my dearest madam," said the agitated girl, "keep me no longer in suspense, I am prepared, fully prepared, to hear all that you have to reveal to me."

"Say you so, Celestia? Well, then, let me remind you of Lord Elverton's narrative. Do you recollect that Lady Elverton, when she left England, took with her their daughter Elvina."

"Yes—yes, but——"

"Hear me out, Celestia. Lady Elverton retired with her daughter into a convent." Lady Eugenia then went on to relate all the particulars with which the reader has already been made acquainted, and which it is consequently unnecessary to repeat; and the emotion of Celestia may very well be imagined, especially when she was informed that she was the daughter of the Marquis de Aunville and the daughter of her benefactor.

"Gracious Heaven! is it possible?" she exclaimed, "but my mother!"

Poor Celestia could say no more, but sunk senseless into the arms of Lady Eugenia, who thought it best to send for Lord Elverton and defer the remainder of the melancholy tale for the present.

CHAPTER XVII.

THE MEETING OF JOY.

So anxious was Lord Elverton to embrace Celestia as his grandchild, that, thinking there had been sufficient time for Lady Eugenia to make her acquainted with the particulars, before the servant could answer the bell, he was in the room.

Proper restoratives being administered, Celestia opened her eyes, and found herself enfolded in the arms of Lord Elverton. How shall we attempt to describe her emotion?

"Oh, my dear, my ever-honoured grandpapa! have I indeed a right to call you so?" she ejaculated. "But my mother!"

Tears came to her relief, which Lord Elverton and his sister did not attempt to check, and she then said,—

"I beseech you, my lord, to tell me what remains to know."

The earl immediately saw from the question Celestia thus put to him, that she was uninformed of the fatal truth, and he therefore thought it most pru-

dent to conceal it from her, and informed her that her mother's attachment to the Duchess de Salvois, and her frequent visits with that unfortunate lady to the queen, while a prisoner, had induced her to continue her attentions towards her after the death of the duchess, for the queen became very fond of her. In one of these visits, attended by her husband and Sir Roderick, the populace enraged at every attention shown the unfortunate queen, insulted the Marquis and Marchioness de Aunville; Sir Roderick in their defence was wounded in the face and fell; that Celestia's father was seized, and the danger he was in occasioned the death of her mother. That her father was ultimately saved by a friend, who under the pretence of taking him before the authorities as a traitor to liberty, conveyed him on board a ship bound for America. He then added all the particulars which have been recorded in the previous chapter.

With what powerful feelings of emotion did Celestia listen to his melancholy and important narrative; she paid the most breathless attention to him, and had not the least power to interrupt him. Fast flowed her tears, and when she perceived that her noble relative had ceased speaking, she pressed his hand, and as soon as the power of speech was restored to her, she ejaculated:—

"Oh, my dear lord, I beseech you to pardon me those tears; for though I knew that my mother was dead, the manner of it has revived her loss to my mind with double force, and I am convinced I never could have any remembrance of her which I sometimes fancied I had; but is the ring I have her picture?"

"I dare say it is, my love;" replied Lord Elverton, "but Sir Roderick will prove it beyond a doubt if you will let him see it."

"Gracious Heaven!" ejaculated our heroine, clasping her hands together, and scarcely able to persuade herself that she was not dreaming, "and am I indeed the child of your daughter, and my grandmamma living?"

"Oh, yes, my dear Celestia," replied Lord Elverton, "I trust that she is, and moreover that we shall soon have the happiness of seeing her, though at present, unfortunately, I know not where to find her, although Sir Roderick believes her to be in England."

Celestia could not controul her emotions; she could not but admire the wonderful works of Providence, who had thus so miraculously made her acquainted with so many kind and dear relations.

"Oh, my dear grandpapa, and my beloved aunt," she said, "I have loved and honoured you so long for your goodness to me, as my protectors, my benefactors, that though I am such a gainer by the wonderful discovery, I cannot increase my love, my reverence, my gratitude."

Lord Elverton and his sister embraced her affectionately, and at that moment Lord Coningsby entered with Sir Roderick.

Tenderly embracing her, Lord Coningsby said :—

"My dear niece, how shall I give utterance to the joy I feel at being able in reality to call you so? Allow me the pleasure of introducing to you the earliest of your friends, Sir Roderick Ainslie."

Celestia bowed to him, but found herself utterly incapable of speaking to him, and Lady Eugenia seeing her agitation, asked if she should send her maid for her locket and ring? She replied in the negative, saying she must go for them herself, and quitted the room for that purpose, but quickly returned, and presented both to Sir Roderick.

No sooner did the baronet's eye rest upon the ring than he started and turned ghastly pale, at the same time uttering a suppressed groan, while his bosom heaved with the agony of his feelings, he exclaimed :—

"Oh God! this likeness; it is that of the unfortunate Elvina."

It was some time ere he could recover from the emotion into which the contemplation of the miniature had thrown him, but when his presence of mind was restored to him, he turned to Celestia, and remarked :—

"I trust, my dear young lady, and you my friends, that there is no necessity for my making any apology for the feelings I have displayed, when I inform you that I well remember my lamented friend, wearing this ring; the

picture is the exact resemblance of the sainted Elvina, though not a stronger one inscription than you, Celestia, yourself are to her, at the same time that your eyes and complexion give you a striking look of your father."

Our heroine was much moved by these observations, and she pressed the ring again and again to her lips with the deepest reverence, Sir Roderick next took the locket, and showing her the secret spring, touched it, it opened, and showed the portrait of the beautiful Duchess de Salvois. He next shewed her the inscription engraven on the spear, and lastly opening that part whereon the initals were engraven, she found it concealed a beautiful lock of the hair of the ill-fated duchess.

Celestia, doubly affected by her own feelings and those of Sir Roderick, requested permission to withdraw for a short time, in order that she might endeavour to regain her tranquillity, and when alone she gave free vent to the powerful emotions which agitated her breast.

It was indeed a joyful day for all interested, and the Earl Bathurst, and his family, came in time to offer their congratulations. No one was more sincerely delighted than Lord Malensbury. The discovery of the noble origin of Celestia, he thought, would remove any objections which his parents might have had to his paying his addresses to that lovely girl, and his heart was buoyed up with hope, and he flattered himself with the idea, that the thoughts and feelings of our heroine were in unison with his own. And could he have penetrated to the deepest recesses of that lovely maiden's heart, he would have had the felicity of discovering that the hopes he had suffered to form themselves within his bosom were not without foundation. The more that our herione had an opportunity of being in the society of the young nobleman, the greater did her admiration of his superier talents and amiable disposition become; and she never parted from him without the deepest regret, and looking forward with feelings of impatience to the time when they should meet again.

Yes, it was a day of happiness and mutual congratulation to them all, and never did Celestia appear more lovely or deeply interesting than she did on that occasion. Seated between her noble grandfather and Lady Eugenia; on every side gladdened with the smiles of friends so dear to her, she felt herself at that moment to be one of the most favoured and blest of human beings. All the troubles of the past were forgotten, and she looked forward to a brilliant future with the most sanguine anticipations. But alas! how limited is the foresight of human nature, and perhaps it is as well that it is so, or what miserable beings we should be; never suffering a gleam of the bright sunshine of hope to steal in upon us, we should be entirely incapable of encountering and combatting those heavy trials to which it may be the will of Providence for its own wise ends, for a time to subject us.

The troubles of Celestia had not yet began; she was doomed in the midst of her fancied happiness to experience them with double severity.

And what of Lord Elverton?—Great indeed was his bliss at discovering that the fair girl who had been so miraculously thrown under his protection was so nearly related to him, but the dreadful and untimely fate of his daughter; the uncertainty of the place where his wife was concealed, or whether he should ever behold her again, cast a gloom over his mind which he struggled in vain to dissipate. The blighted heart was not yet entirely at peace, and unfortunately, many more troubles were yet weaving in the web of fate to try its fortitude.

The day passed swiftly away in conversing upon these important and extraordinary events, and it was not until a late hour, that the friends thought of separating for the night.

Lord Malensbury parted from our heroine with regret, although he knew the time would be so short before they would meet again, and Celestia could scarcely conceal the favourable impression which the manly accomplishments and amiable qualities of the young nobleman had made upon her heart.

———

CHAPTER XVIII.

AN ALARMING ADVENTURE.—FRESH TROUBLES THREATEN.

It may naturally be expected that the important and extraordinary events of the day, busily occupied the mind of Celestia after she had retired to her chamber, and prevented her for some time from thinking about seeking repose.

It was a beautiful, clear, frosty moonlight night; myriads of twinkling stars bespangled the heavens, stillness reigned around, and the scene was altogether one of the most pleasing and soothing description. Celestia seated herself at the casement, which commanded an extensive view of the ocean, and her thoughts gradually, but naturally wandered to the incidents of her earliest childhood, when she and her poor father were crossing the broad waters of the Atlantic, and before she had arrived at sufficient knowledge to have any idea of the sorrows which had already befallen them, or those that were in store for them. Many were the tears the poor girl shed to the memory of that beloved father, and sincere and devout were the prayers she offered up to heaven for the repose of his soul.

And then the dreadful fate which had attended her mother arose to her recollection in all its terror, and froze the very blood in her veins. What heartless miscreants, what inhuman monsters must those have been who could have consigned so much beauty and innocence and virtue to so untimely and end. The reflection was maddening, and yet Celestia in vain endeavoured to banish it from her brain. It haunted her like some hideous spectre, and became still more frightful the longer she suffered her mind to dwell upon it.

At one time she had suffered her thoughts to rise to such a pitch of terror, that she was almost inclined to hasten to the chamber of Lady Eugenia, who slept near her, fearing to be alone, but a feeling of shame withheld her, and she remained where she was.

The silence that now reigned throughout the castle convinced her that all the inmates had retired to rest, and the solemnity of her thoughts increased; notwithstanding the wonderful and im-

Portant discoveries which had been made that day, and the change in her future prospects which they had consequently wrought, she felt an unaccountable depression of spirits; a dismal foreboding of some approaching calamity which she could not comprehend, but which at the same time she was convinced it would be impossible for her to avert. She continued to sit at the casement, with her eyes fixed upon vacancy, and she felt as if she had no power to move, or to cast her eyes around her, lest they should encounter some dreadful vision. What could be the meaning of these fears? There seemed to be no cause for them, and yet she could not, with all her exertion, dismiss them from her mind. The brightness of the moon, the glittering of the stars, had no light for her, she gazed at them, but she saw them not; her whole thoughts were, as it might be said, wrapped in a dream of nameless and incomprehensible horror. All before her and about her bore the gloom of her own sickly thoughts, and undefined apprehensions.

These are no imaginary creations of the writer's brain; there are times when such thoughts, such painful and overwhelming sensations occur to every human being.

At length worn out with thinking, and these accumulated terrors, Celestia withdrew herself from the casement, and having committed herself to the care and protection of the Almighty, and invoked blessings upon her beloved relatives, she threw herself, without undressing upon the bed, and closing her eyes sought to compose herself to sleep. For some time she tried in vain; the same tears continued to crowd upon her imagination, and drove repose from her pillow. She chided herself for giving way to such apprehensions. What had she to fear? she reflected; was she not safe under the protection of her noble relative? And who could have a wish to harm her? She had never injured any one by word or deed, then surely she could have no enemies. She would be firm, and dismiss all such childish thoughts from her mind. They were unworthy of her.

By dint of great perseverence she succeeded much better than might have been expected, and at length worn out with fatigue of mind, she did fall asleep. But far from bringing to her any relief, the most painful visions flitted before her imagination. The whole of the horrors of her mother's dreadful fate; the melancholy death of her father, and every other sorrowful circumstance connected with her history, was repeated to her, and that in far more vivid and appalling characters than she had hitherto heard them or could imagine them.

But suddenly the scene changed, and she beheld herself once more moving in the joyous scenes which had taken place at the memorable festivities given at the mansion of Sir Eustace Aubrey, as related in the early part of this history. Every incident was re-enacted as distinctly as if it were reality, and Celestia imagined in her dream that she felt all that exhuberance of mirth and enjoyment with which the novelty of everything around her had inspired and animated her on that occasion. Once more the mysterious gipsey sybil seemed to eye her with the most extraordinary interest, and approaching her, laid her hand upon her arm in the same manner that she had done on that occasion, and once more the prophetic words of the ballad saluted her ears:

"Damsel turn thee not away,
  Nor think the words I speak are wrong;
Mark me, *there will come a day,*
  When thou'lt remember well my song.

Though pleasure now shines on thy path,
  Will it last for ever—no!
All the bliss thou at present hath,
  Shall be changed to bitter woe.

See—the clouds are gath'ring fast,
  Hark, the voice of destiny cries,
'Girl, thy joys will soon be past,
  Thy laugh of mirth be turned to sighs.'

Then damsel mark well what I say,
  Though thou laughest now in glee;
Not far distant is the day,
  When none shall be more sad than thee."

As the last words of this ballad died away on the ears of Celestia, she awoke in great alarm and agitation, and for some time was so much confused that she feared to look around her.

The lamp was burning very dimly, and one half of the chamber was buried in darkness, but at length Celestia had a slight conception that some shadowy form was moving in the room, which gradually became more palpable as it moved from the obscurity into the more immediate light, and then she heard her name pronounced in a low but distinct and solemn voice, and plainly beheld a female form exactly corresponding with that of the gipsey sybil standing at the foot of the bed. Good god! was she awake, or still dreaming?—No!—there she stood, with her eyes fixed on her with the same degree of interest as they had always been whenever they had met.

Celestia could not repress an exclamation of terror, but the woman raised her hand to enjoin her to silence, and approaching nearer, said:—

"Hush! hush, Celestia; do not raise any cry which might alarm the inmates of the castle, or the worst consequences will follow. Do not fear me, I will not harm thee. I came but to warn thee of danger, and to caution thee not to busy thyself up too much with hope. We have met several times before, fair maiden; dost then remember the words I formerly sung to thee?—They will be fulfilled; they will be fulfilled. Fate wills it so; oh, there is woe, there is much of woe for Celestia de Annville yet, before she can hope to experience uninterupted happiness.

"For the love of Heaven, my good woman," gasped forth the terrified damsel, "who and what are you? For what purpose do you obtrude upon me at this solemn hour of the night, and how have you obtained admittance to the castle?"

"Some of these are questions that I do not deem it prudent to answer," returned the sybil, "I have constantly followed your footsteps, and know all that concerns you, all that has happened to you. At any time, in any place, at any hour, I can gain admittance to your presence, and no one can detect me. Again I warn you not to buoy yourself too much up with hope, for great are the troubles that are in store for you and those connected with you."

"Mysterious woman," ejaculated our heroine, "how know you this?"

"How do I know it, I?" repeated the woman; "oh, damsel, there is little that is hidden from my knowledge, however much mortals may affect to despise my words. Again I tell thee I come to warn thee of danger which threatens thee and thy aged relative!"

"Oh, God! can this be true?"

"Can it be true, girl; I tell thee it is; dost doubt my word?"

"Whom should we fear?" eagerly demanded Celestia.

"One who seeks revenge, and will stick at no means of gratifying it."

"And who is that?—Oh, tell me, I beseech you?"

"Bonville!"

"Bonville," repeated Celestia, passing her fair hand across her brow, to recall her recollection. "I have heard that name before, surely."

"The jesuit Bonville," said the woman, emphatically, "he who was the means of separating Lady Elverton from her husband, under the mask of religion, but in reality because he had conceived a base passion for her himself. Lady Elverton scornfully and indignantly resisted his infamous importunities, and he swore a deadly revenge against her and all related to her. He it was, the villain, who was the principal cause of your mother's inhuman butchery."

"Horror! horror!" groaned our heroine, at the same time covering her face with her hands. "But he is dead!"

"He lives, and still cherishes the same brutal spirit of revenge. For years he was confined in prison, but he escaped, and is even now in this country, and only awaiting a fitting opportunity to put his designs into execution."

"Where, oh, where is this cruel, guilty man concealed?" asked the trembling girl.

"At present that I know not, but I will discover him," answered the gipsey.

"But why have you sought this secret and extraordinary method of communicating this important intelligence to me. Why not have presented yourself to Lord Elverton, since your object seems to be to render him service, and to warn him of danger?"

"My reasons are cogent, damsel, but I do not think proper to disclose them. Again I tell thee that a tempest is fast gathering that will overwhelm thee and those connected with thee in trouble. But my time is up, I must be gone. Watch not the manner in which I depart, or raise any alarm, for there would be danger to thyself in so doing. Remember, my words; repeat them to Lord Elverton, and tell him to beware, for the bloodhound is abroad who seeks to hunt him to destruction."

"Oh, stay, stay, I beg of you," said Celestia, " will you not tell me more?"

"No more, no more, at present," answered the woman; " be satisfied with what I have already told you, and do not despise my words, for they will be fulfilled to the very letter."

Thus speaking, she drew the curtains round the bed of Celestia, to prevent her from seeing her depart, and the astonished and terrified damsel heard her cautiously retire from the room. She sunk back on her pillow, and for a few moments she was so overcome by this remarkable and alarming adventure, that she was unable to move.

At length, however, she ventured to withdraw the curtains and look into the chamber;—the sybil, as she had expected was gone, and the door was fast, though she had not heard it closed.

Every word that this extraordinary woman had uttered was indelibly impressed upon her memory, and she shuddered with horror at the dreadful import of her observations. But how had she contrived to enter the castle at that hour of the night, and reached her chamber? That was a mystery which was altogether inexplicable. But there was no time to be lost. She feared to be alone, and taking up her lamp, she determined to make her way immediately to the chamber of Lady Eugenia and make her acquainted with what had happened.

She opened her chamber door, and stepped out cautiously into the gallery. All was still in the castle, and she had no doubt that the woman had left it; but still she felt somewhat timid and reluctant to disturb Lady Eugenia, who would naturally feel surprised and alarmed at her appearance at such an hour of the night, and to find that she was still undressed. However, she knew that she would blame her if she

did not immediately make her acquainted with what had taken place, and she therefore proceeded.

On arriving at the door of Lady Eugenia's chamber, she gently laid her hand on the handle, and finding it was unlocked, she silently opened it and stepped into the apartment.

Lady Eugenia was wrapped in a calm and sound sleep, and Celestia hesitated to disturb her, fearing that her unexpected appearance at such a time might cause her some alarm. However, she could not endure her suspense any longer, and she therefore ventured to shake her aunt gently, and to repeat her name. The old lady started up confused and amazed, and at first had no conception who it was.

"Who's there?" she demanded, in a faltering voice.

"Be not alarmed, my dear aunt," said our heroine; " it is only me, Celestia."

"Good gracious, Celestia," exclaimed Lady Eugenia, staring at her with astonishment, "what brings you from your own chamber at such an hour? Not undressed too; what is the matter, child? You look pale and frightened, has anything particular happened? Do not, pray do not keep me in suspense."

Celestia tried to speak, but for a few moments her emotion overpowered her.

"Oh, my dear aunt," she ejaculated, " how shall I relate to you the strange and alarming event which has happened to me since I retired to my chamber for the night?"

"A strange and alarming event, Celestia?" said Lady Eugenia, with a look of surprise and incredulity, "what can you mean, child? You have been dreaming. Compose yourself."

"Yes, aunt," replied the damsel, " it is true that I had been dreaming, but it is no dream that I have to relate to you. Not long since, the very same gipsey sybil who crossed my path on two or three former occasions was in my chamber."

"In your chamber, and at this time of the night; it is impossible!"

"I solemnly declare, my dear madam," replied Celestia, "that what I state is a fact. I awoke after dreaming of her, and to my alarm and unspeakable amazement, beheld her standing at the foot of my bed."

"My dear girl remarked Lady Eugenia, "you must certainly be labouring under some singular delusion."

"Indeed, I am not aunt," replied our heroine, "I not only beheld her but she held me] in conversation for more than a qnarter of an hour."

"Amazement! How could she obtain admittance into this castle, and what was her purpose? Tell me everything."

Celestia obeyed as well as she could, and Lady Eugenia listened to her with the most indescribable astonishment, but was frequently obliged to give free vent to her emotions.

"Good God!" she exclaimed when Celestia had concluded, "what an extraordinary and alarming adventure is this indeed. Were it any one but you my dear Celestia, who stated it, I could not believe it. Who cau this woman be, and by what means has she contrived to gain entrance to the castle at such an hour? She must have concealed herself in some of the rooms in the course of the day."

"I think that is the most probable, my dear aunt," said our heroine, "but oh, how terrible and alarming are the observations she made use of."

"Do not think seriously of them, my love, depend upon it she is only some poor wandering maniac, and her prognostications and assertions are only the offspring of a disordered brain."

"Ah, no," said Celestia "I cannot think so, indeed, I can't. There was nothing to denote madness in her demeanour; besides, how can she have become so well acquainted with all the circumstances of our history? Remember what she said about the jesuit Bonville, the bitter enemy of my beloved grandfather, the indirect murderer of my unfortunate mother. Alas, alas! should that guilty man be still living, and cherishing the deadly feelings of revenge which this extraordinary woman attributes to him, have we not good reason to fear him? I fear indeed that the predictions of the sybil will be fulfilled, and that our troubles are not at an end."

Lady Eugenia paused and reflected, and it was evident that her mind was deeply impressed with the force of Celestia's observations.

"It is a strange and torturing affair," she said at length, "can this Bonville have been the miscreant this woman represents him to be? And should he be still living! Oh, what will be my poor brother's anguish when he is made acquainted with these melancholy particulars. But a searching inquiry must be made into all the particulars, and no means must be left untried to avert the evils that may threaten us. Poor Lady Elvina, would to Heaven that we could discover the place of her concealment, for my brother can never know complete happiness unless she is restored to him."

Lady Eugenia and our heroine were both too much agitated to think of going to sleep again, and the former arose, and in conversation with her fair niece on the remarkable and almost incredible events of the night awaited the arrival of the morning with much anxiety.

Daylight came at last, and Lady Eugenia and Celestia in order that they might collect themselves before they met Lord Elverton, and communicated to him the singular and painful facts, left the castle, and as the morning was particularly fine for the time of year resolved to take a walk. Their minds, however, were both wholly engrossed by the circumstances of the night, and various were the unsatisfactory conjectures they founded upon them; but in one thing they both agreed, namely, that it was necessary to use every precaution to guard against any danger that might threaten them, and also to endeavour to find out the gipsey, and to induce her to become more explicit, and make them acquainted with all she might know. Surely if she entertained the friendly feeling towards them she professed to do, she would not hesitate to do so, and she could have no reason for further concealment since she had divulged so much.

"As for her predictions," remarked Lady Eugenia, "they are only worthy of exciting contempt; you are not superstitious, my love, I know, and will therefore take no notice of them."

"I do not wish to do so, my dear aunt," replied our heroine, "but I must confess that I cannot readily dismiss from my breast the alarm with which this woman's observations have inspired me. I had hoped that my dear grandmamma would soon have been restored to us, and that our happiness would then have been complete, but now alas! I fear that fresh clouds are gathering above our heads, and that the tempest will soon burst upon us, perhaps with greater violence even than it has previously done."

"Do not encourage such dismal thoughts, my dear Celestia," said her aunt; "there is a just Providence above, who will protect us from the evil designs of our enemies, while we continue to put our trust in Him."

They now returned to the castle, and shortly afterwards they were summoned to breakfast. They entered the apartment where Lord Elverton and the rest of the family were awaiting them, with sad hearts, and the agitation of their looks instantly attracted the attention of the earl and his son.

"Why, my dear sister, and Celestia," said the former, "what in the name of goodness is the matter with you?—You are both pale and agitated, and any one to look at you would think that you had neither of you been to bed all night. Tell me, what is the meaning of this?"

"I am sorry to say, my dear brother," replied Lady Eugenia, "that I and Celestia have something of a very important and unpleasant nature to communicate to you, and which we are afraid will cause you some anxiety and alarm. But I trust that you will hear it with firmness, and endeavour calmly to consider what is best to be done under the circumstances."

Lord Elverton and all present looked surprised at this preface, and the earl eagerly demanded :—

"What am I to judge from your observations, Eugenia?—What is the extraordinary and disagreeable intelligence you have to impart? Do not keep me in suspense."

"Perhaps Celestia had better relate it herself," said Lady Eugenia, "since it was to her the extraordinary adventure occurred."

Our heroine would fain have been excused, for she well knew the agitation it would cause her beloved grandfather, but being so urged she was compelled to comply, though she did so in a trembling and hesitating voice. The earl was frequently compelled to give vent to his feelings of emotion, indignation, and astonishment, and when she had concluded, he hastily arose from his seat, and traversed the room in a state of the most indescribable emotion, unable to give utterance to anything but broken exclamations.

"For Heaven's sake, my dear father, compose yourself;" said Lord Coningsby.

"Compose myself!" repeated the earl, "can you expect me to be calm after what I have heard? The villain Bonville living; he dare to raise his impure thoughts to my unfortunate Elvina,—to become the cold-blooded assassin of my child,—God! God! it seems scarcely possible that such a monster should be suffered to exist and to wear the human form. Alas! alas! I see that my days of sorrow in this world are not ended;—there are more cares, more tortures for this seared heart!"

He threw himself into a chair, in an agony of extreme grief, and covering his face with his hands, sobbed convulsively. Celestia and her aunt flew towards him, and sought to console him; but he was for some time deaf to their expostulations.

"But are you sure, my dear Celestia," said Lord Coningsby, "that you were not deceived?"

"Oh, no," replied our heroine, "alas it was impossible for me to be so. Every word that I have related to you is exactly the same as this remarkable woman spoke it to me."

"Most torturing!" groaned Lord Elverton; "oh, what a dreadful fate has mine been!—When will my troubles be at an end?—Never, never, till I rest in the silent tomb. But where is this woman? Who is she who is acquainted with all my secrets, and who seeks so singular a method of warning me of the danger which she says threatens me?— Why does she not come boldly forward, if she is sincere in what she professes, and divulge all she knows?—Why act with all this mystery if her intentions are honest? She is some base imposter! She only acts as she has done to add to my agony. I will not believe her. No, no. But she must be discovered and made to give an explanation of her conduct."

After having thus given vent to his feelings, he became more calm, and none of the persons present offered to interrupt him in his reflections, which, however, only lasted a very short time.

"It is most extraordinary," he said, "too; how could this woman gain access to the castle at such a time of the night?"

Of that no one could form any idea, unless indeed that she got into the castle in the course of the day, unseen by any of the servants, and concealed herself in one of the rooms which was not inhabited, which seemed, in fact, the most reasonable conclusion to come to.

While they were still conversing upon the subject, Sir Roderick Ainslie was announced, and Celestia and her aunt having retired together, Lord Elverton immediately made the baronet acquainted with the whole particulars. During the whole time the earl was relating them, Sir Roderick evinced much agitation and sighed deeply, and when he had finished he said,—

"My God! can this be true? But Bonville was miscreant enough for anything, and therefore am I the more inclined to believe this statement. The terrible retribution of offended Heaven will surely overtake him, if he still lives, for his atrocious crimes."

"It will! it must!" ejaculated Lord Elverton, "but how would you advise me to act, my dear friend, under these circumstances?"

"Do not give yourself up to any unnecessary alarm, my lord;" answered Sir Roderick, "and we may be shortly enabled to discover the truth, and to counteract the designs of your enemies; every effort must be made to induce this singular woman to come forward and to divulge all that she knows, though how she has come by her knowledge, I cannot form the least idea."

"But my wife! my unfortunate Elvina," said the earl, "where shall I seek her? How snatch her from the jaws of danger? Shall I never behold her again?"

"Oh, yes, my lord," said Sir Roderick, "I feel convinced that you will. If I have your permission, I myself will go in search of her, and I have every confidence in the success of my undertaking."

The earl pressed his hand fervently, and expressed in the most eloquent terms his gratitude for his kindness. After some further conversation the earl became more tranquil, and inquiries were immediately instituted about the neighbourhood of the castle to ascertain whether any person was known, or had been latterly seen, to answer the description of the gipsey woman, but they could obtain no information of a satisfactory description; but the servants were ordered to keep a sharp look out, and to detain any suspicious looking individual whom they might perceive lurking near the castle.

The day passed away without anything more particularly occurring, and when night arrived, Lord Elverton and his friends went all over the castle, and examined every room and passage, to see that no one was concealed in any part of the building, and having seen all the doors properly secured, and giving strict injunctions to the servants, they became satisfied that there was no danger to apprehend, and retired for the night.

Celestia slept in the same chamber as Lady Eugenia, but the night passed off without anything particular, taking place, and they arose in the morning more composed, though the prediction of the gipsey, and the other observations she had made use of, still continued to hold their painful impression on the mind of Celestia.

During the whole of the following day, Lord Elverton was sad and thoughtful, from which nothing could arouse him, and he frequently retired from the company to indulge in the gloomy thoughts which beset his imagination alone.

The evening approached, and every one seemed to partake, more or less of the melancholy of the earl, when they were suddenly aroused from their lethargy by the entrance of a servant with a letter addressed to Lord Elverton, which he said had been brought by a man on horseback, who immediately on its delivery rode of, without waiting for an answer.

The earl looked at the superscription, but he did not know the hand-writing, and wondering from whom it could be, he excused himself to the company; he retired to one of the window recesses, and breaking the seal, he read to his astonishment the following words:—

"MY LORD,—You may flatter yourself that your troubles are now over, and that Lady Elvina, who you are aware still lives, will shortly be restored to you. But you will be deceived, you shall never meet again. There is also another who still lives, and who now addresses you, who burns for revenge against both her and you, and all connected with you, who works his secret plot in darkness, and sets detection at defiance. Years ago he partially satiated his vengeance in the blood of your fair daughter. But his thirst is not yet appeased, nor will it be until he has bathed his hands in the blood of all he hates. Think not to escape me, for no one knows my power and the resources I have to put my designs into execution. Mock not this, as a mere idle threat to frighten you. Every word it contains shall be fulfilled, as true as you now draw that breath of life which it has been my wish to extinguish. Again I say tremble, for I, your bitterest enemy will pursue you to destruction."

The unhappy earl had no sooner perused this diabolical epistle than he uttered a loud groan, and the letter dropped from his hand. His friends flew towards him in alarm and amazement, and eagerly inquired what was the matter.

"Read! read!" he ejaculated, pointing to the letter, "and judge for yourselves."

Lord Coningsby snatched up the letter, and having thus received his father's consent, read the contents aloud. Various were the comments passed upon it; but all agreed that they were of the most atrocious description, and deeply sympathised with the earl in the fresh troubles which seemed likely to attend him. No one evinced greater emotion than Celestia, and Lord Malensbury viewed her agitation with the deepest concern, but thought that she never appeared more lovely than when sympathizing with the unmerited persecutions of her noble relative.

"This is a most torturing circumstance," observed Lord Coningsby, "have you no knowledge of the handwriting of this infamous epistle, my dear father?"

"None whatever," replied the latter, "but there can be little doubt that it proceeds from the villain Bonville. How —how am I to protect myself from his insidious designs? I see at once a fresh tempest of trouble arising before me, but if its fury were permitted to exhaust itself against myself alone I might bear it with fortitude and resignation, but it involves all that is dearer to me than my own existence. Would to Heaven that I were dead!"

"Oh, my dear, my revered grandpapa;" sobbed the agitated Celestia, throwing her fair arms affectionately around Lord Elverton's neck; "do not talk thus;—courage, courage; heed not the threats of the miscreant who has written this letter, however terrible and alarming they may appear to be. The all merciful God will not suffer you to fall a victim to the guilty, the diabolical machinations of your enemies; He will assuredly frustrate their designs, and restore you to that peace of mind, your spotless virtues merit."

The earl embraced her with the utmost tenderness, and by his looks expressed far more than he could give utterance to. It was some time before he could be restored to any degree of composure, but at length the remonstrances and arguments of Earl Bathurst, Lady Eugenia, Sir Roderick, and Lord Coningsby prevailed, and he did become more tranquil.

"If only ordinary precaution is used," remarked Sir Roderick, "however deep laid and artfully contrived the designs of your lordship's enemies may be, depend upon it they will be foiled, and recoil upon themselves. As for the wretch Bonville, secure as he may consider himself to be, I do not despair that he will yet be detected when he little expects it, and brought to that condign punishment which his guilt so richly merits. We must be cautious, and a light may soon be thrown upon this painful mystery."

"But my Elvina," sighed the earl, "from the confident tone of his letter, may she not be in his power, and at the heartless, the diabolical villain's mercy?"

"Heaven forbid that it should be so," returned the baronet, "but I do firmly believe that it is only an empty boast of the miscreant for the purpose of alarming you, and weakening your endeavours to discover her."

"And my poor child, my ill-fated daughter," groaned Lord Elverton, "it was then by his fiendish means that her blameless life was sacrificed. God of Heaven! have you no thunder bolts to crush such a monster, in the midst of his iniquity?"

At this allusion to the dreadful fate of her unfortunate mother, our beauteous heroine burst into a convulsive flood of tears, and it took some time for the combined efforts of her affectionate friends and relations to soothe her. But at length by degrees they all became more calm, and then the servant to whom the letter had been delivered was called in and questioned more narrowly, but they elicited nothing further of any importance. The man, he said appeared to have travelled fast, he uttered not a word when he presented the letter, and immediately rode off at the greatest speed. His features were also so muffled up in a large shawl or cravat, that they were almost entirely concealed, and it would therefore be impossible to recognize them again. It was evident that every precaution had been used by the writer of the infamous letter, and all chance of detection was consequently at present hopeless.

The friends sat consulting upon this painful and alarming event for some time, and it was not until a late hour of the night, that they could make up their minds to separate.

CHAPTER XIX.

THE FIRST PORTION OF THE THREAT FULFILLED.—THE DEED OF BLOOD.— THE HORROR AND DESPAIR OF LORD ELVERTON AND HIS FAMILY.

NOTWITHSTANDING the firmness and calmness he had evinced, there was no one of all the individuals so deeply interested, who retired with a more sad heart and dismal presentiments than Lord Coningsby. A weight of lead seemed to press upon his heart, and to enchain every faculty; his faculties for the time seemed to be enervated, and sickly and harrasing thoughts crowded upon and tortured his brain. The sorrows of his parents, the dreadful fate of his sister, and the dangers which still threatened them all had the most agonizing influence upon his senses; vague fears of some approaching calamity which it would be almost impossible to avert or to avoid, beset his imagination, and in vain he endeavoured to shake them off, the more he did so, the more powerful they became. When he entered his chamber, he found himself trembling in every limb, and large drops of perspiration stood upon his temples; his brain was giddy, a mist seemed to float before his eyes, strange shapes and visions danced before his fancy, and he sunk in a complete state of lassitude and exhaustion in a chair.

The silence that now reigned around appeared to his perturbed imagination, particularly awful. It was only interrupted at intervals by the distant murmuring of the waves, or the solemn voice of the wind. Lord Coningsby felt his agitation increase, and he shook as if he were suffering from a sudden attack of the palsy.

"What can this mean?" he said, "have I become a child again? Why these cowardly fears? I never wilfully injured human being, by word, by deed, or thought, then what shall I dread? Let me be firm, for I am ashamed of my own feelings."

He tried to arouse himself, and to retire to his bed, but on endeavouring to rise from his chair, he found himself so weak that he sank back again completely powerless. And now his brain became more distracted, the mist increased before his eyes, and he became insensible.

He was suddenly aroused from this state of lethargy by feeling himself roughly seized, and opening his eyes, what was his alarm and astonishment at finding himself in the hands of several men, whose features were concealed from observation by black masks.

He struggled violently, and was about to call for aid, but the wretches presented their weapons at his breast, and threatened him with instant death if he raised his voice beyond a whisper. He gave himself up for lost, for what could he do, unarmed as he was, and in the hands of at least a dozen ruffians, at that solemn hour of the night? He had no alternative but to submit in silence; but he felt assured that some dreadful fate awaited him, and which appeared to be inevitable.

The villains now bound his arms behind him, and throwing a cloak over his head, which they drew so tight about him that he was almost suffocated, and he was unable to give utterance to the slightest sound, they hurried him out of the room, and after traversing the gallery with noiseless steps, and descending the stairs at the end, they issued from the castle by a private door, which was standing open, and by which they had in all probability entered.

They hurried him on at a rapid rate, and Lord Coningsby felt it was useless to attempt to resist, and gave himself up to despair. Now was his anguish of mind, and the dark presentiment that had haunted it, fully explained.

The wretches no doubt intended bloodshed, and he considered his doom sealed. Mentally he invoked the mercy and the protection of the Supreme, and he then resigned himself to that fate from which he saw no possibility of escaping.

The night was stormy, the wind howled terrifically, and the rain poured down in torrents. From the neighbouring forest the dreary screech owl sent forth its dismal and ominous cry, and kept wild accompaniment with the voice of the tempest. Fit night it was for the perpetration of a deed of blood such as the wretches; who hurried the unfortunate Lord Coningsby along, evidently contemplated.

How shall we endeavour to pourtray the feelings of the hapless nobleman in that dreadful moment? Must his life be sacrificed in that inhuman manner? Was there no hope, no help at hand? What would be the anguish of his relations and friends should they ever ascertain the melancholy, the horrible fate that had befallen him? The thought was maddening, the heart of the wretched Lord Coningsby was full to bursting, Where were now all those bright visions of future happiness his sanguine imagination had formed? They were doomed to be annihilated at one fell blow. And must he be thus cruelly sacrificed in the prime of life, never having committed any offence against his fellow-creatures? How agonizing was the thought, surely the Almighty would never permit the perpetration of so hideous a crime.

By the murmuring of the waves, Lord Coningsby could perceive that the ruffians were conveying him towards the ocean, and in a short time they arrived upon the beach, where they halted, and were saluted by a coarse and malicious voice in the following words,—

"So you have secured our victim. Well done, well done, my brave lads, you have performed your task to admiration, and the first step in my career of vengeance will speedily be accomplished. Uncover the noble lord and let me gloat my anxious eyes upon his features."

The cloak was immediately removed from the head of the unfortunate Lord Coningsby, and he beheld standing before him the tall and robust form of a man, whose features were expressive of every fiendish passion.

He seemed to be upwards of sixty years of age; his hair was of an iron grey, and combed straight over his low and receding forehead. His eyebrows were thick and shaggy, and his eyes though small seemed to flash with more than human fire. His countenance was ghastly and livid like that of a corpse, and his whole appearance was frightful, disgusting, and revolting in the extreme. His form displayed great muscular strength, notwithstanding his years; his shoulders were broad, and he was far above the ordinary stature. He was attired in a suit of black, of ancient cut, and a dark cloak depended from his shoulders. In spite of all his efforts to the contrary, Lord Coningsby could not help trembling in the presence of this frightful being, who seemed to exult in his emotion, but at last he recovered himself sufficiently to demand in a firm voice,—

"For what purpose am I brought hither by these ruffians, and who are you that seem to triumph at my helpless situation?"

"Triumph!" repeated the man, in a harsh voice, "aye, you have judged my feelings well, son of the detested husband of that Elvina who many years ago rejected my proposals with scorn. Look at me, and know me for the bitterest, the most deadly enemy, of thee and thine. Hast heard of the Jesuit Bonville; he who persuaded thy mother to abandon her husband, and would afterwards have sacrificed her to his lust, but she escaped him? Hast heard of that Bonville who was the means of bringing thy fair sister's head to the block, and of sacrificing her dearest friends? Doubtless thou hast. Know then that I am he; aye, the wily priest Bonville stands before thee, and tells thee that he will not rest until he has bathed his hands in the blood of thee and all thy race!"

Monster!" exclaimed the unhappy man, "can you thus boldly assert your fiendish deeds? What have I or my unfortunate relatives done, that you should thus pursue us with your deadly vengeance? For what guilty purposes am I dragged hither?"

"That thou wilt quickly know," answered Bonville, "thou art my first victim, in the tragedy of blood I mean to enact. Prepare thyself, for thy minutes in this world are numbered."

"Great God!" cried the agonized Lord Coningsby, "you cannot, do not mean to murder an unoffending man thus in cold blood! Beware, for the vengeance of Heaven will most assuredly overtake you."

"I defy the power of both Heaven and hell!" cried the wretch; "I hold thee now in my power, and never more shall thou return alive to the castle of thy parent. It was thought that the priest Bonville was dead, but it will be found he still lives to work revenge against those whom he so thoroughly hates and despises. Hark, how the night winds howl; it is thy death knell; see how the white foam gurgles upon the surging waves, it is thy funeral shroud! Where are now all thy blissful visions? thy ambitious hopes? They are crushed, annihilated, and even the veriest worm that crawls the earth would not exchange places with thee."

"All Merciful Father! must I perish thus?" exclaimed the distracted Lord Coningsby, looking around him, and large drops of mental agony standing upon his temples; "is there no help?"

"None, none!" replied Bonville, with a demoniacal look of triumph; "you call in vain; no assistance can reach you here, and in such an hour. Bid farewell to the world, for it will shortly close upon you for ever."

"Mercy—mercy!" cried the wretched man, in the frenzy of his despair.

"Mercy!" repeated the Jesuit, "you appeal in vain, I know it not. I feel this one of the greatest moments of my triumph. Know too, that your mother, father, and all your relations are destined to become my victims. My plot is so well, so deeply laid, that it will be impossible for them to escape me. The fair Celestia, young as she is I have marked out for my embraces, and—"

"Monster! fiend of hell!" cried the enfuriated Lord Coningsby, "for human being you cannot be;—you will not, dare not attempt to fulfil your threats. Oh, God! if it be thy will that I should perish by the hands of this inhuman wretch, watch over and protect my un-

fortunate parents and Celestia from his deadly malice."

"Into the boat with him!" cried Bonville, addressing the ruffians; "his time is come; a few moments and yon raging waves will have closed over him for ever."

"For the love of God, spare me!" exclaimed the distracted Lord Coningsby, as the ruffians seized him and dragged him toward a shattered and crazy boat which was moored off at a short distance.

"Away with him!" shouted Bonville, in a voice of thunder; "he will have rather a rough ride of it, I think, and I wish him much pleasure of his excursion."

Lord Coningsby fixed upon him an appalling look, it was one which was enough to make the stoutest heart tremble, but Bonville marked it with perfect indifference and scorn, and motioned to the ruffians to proceed. Their unhappy victim raised his eyes towards Heaven, with a look of agony and despair;—and breathed a brief but fervent prayer for mercy. The next instant he was hurried to the boat, into which he was violently thrust. It was then unmoored, and was dashed with furious speed over the foaming and mountainously swelling waves.

Fiercer raged the tempest!—Louder roared the wind, whilst the rain poured down with overwhelming violence. Bonville and his villanous companions stood upon the lofty summit of a rock and watched the progress of the frail boat with looks of malicious triumph and delight.

"Ha! ha! ha!" laughed the murderer, "the boat of death rides merrily. See how it is dashed upon the surface of the billows, and anon overwhelmed by their waters. It cannot live many minutes, and yet the poor wretch clings to it with the madness of despair, and fears to precipitate that fate which is inevitable. Earl Elverton where is now that son who was so lately restored to thee, and in whom was centered all thy hopes?—What now would be thy anguish did'st thou but know his present situation, and that no human help could save him?—Oh, revenge, revenge thon art sweet. See, the boat is being driven towards the rocks; she

will be dashed to pieces against them, and still the wretched victim remains in her! And now he rises in her! He raises his head towards Heaven! It is his last appeal for mercy! Ah! he leaps from the boat; he has not the power to swim, for his arms are pinnioned; he sinks, he sinks! Lord Coningsby's earthly career is at an end!"

Yes, the fate of the unfortunate nobleman was sealed; he had sunk to rise no more, and another innocent victim was sacrificed to the insatiate vengeance of the fiendish Bonville. Black were the clouds that lowered upon the hideous deed; and the fierce voice c the tempest howled a funeral dirge.

"Triumph! Triumph!" cried Bonville; "follow me, my lads, and let us see to the accomplishment of our other designs. Not one of my intended victims must escape me."

Thus saying, the guilty man drew his cloak closer around him, and descended the rock, followed by the other ruffians and making their way towards the wood, were soon out of sight.

The storm continued to rage with unabated violence throughout the night, and what with that, and the agitation of their minds at the stirring events of the day, none of the inmates of the castle were able to sleep. Strange apprehensions tortured the mind of Lord Elverton, but what would have been the horror and agony of his feelings had he known the dreadful deed which had that night been perpetrated, and the awful fate which that beloved and amiable son, who had so lately been restored to him, had met with! Alas! what agony was in store for him.

Unable to compose himself at all to sleep, he at length quitted his couch, and paced his chamber in a disordered manner, listening to the voice of the storm, with feelings of the most melancholy intensity, and imagining all sorts of horrors. Again he perused the threatening letter he had received, and the more he did so, the greater his emotion became, and the more his fears increased.

"No doubt this letter is written by the miscreant, Bonville;" he said, "and if it is, have I not everything to fear? He will not fail to attempt to put all his diabolical threats into execution, and how can I guard myself against so desperate and determined a man? I plainly see that fresh troubles are in store for me, and I fear to contemplate them. Oh, God! I beseech thee to protect me and mine from any evils that may threaten us, and to counteract the guilty designs of this terrible enemy."

Still the most gloomy forebodings continued to crowd upon him, and he longed for the arrival of morning, when he should meet his family again, for he had some misgivings that some fresh calamity awaited them; yet what the nature of it would be, he could not form the least conjecture.

"My unfortunate Elvina," he sighed, "has cruel fate ordained that we shall never meet again? If you are indeed still living, why do you not hasten to return to me? Oh, if you could form the slightest conception of what my sufferings are, or the happiness that awaits you in your restoration to our son, and the lovely Celestia, surely you would no longer delay. And one would think that if you are in England, the joyful intelligence must have reached you. I can scarcely believe that you are still in existence, and this state of painful suspense is most intolerable and insupportable. But the villain Bonville declares that you are living, and he threatens to pursue you with his vengeance; should you be in his power, how terrible will be the sufferings that brutal man would inflict upon you. Better, far better would it be if you were dead. But what peace of mind can I hope to experience whilst I remain in this dreadful state of uncertainty as to the fate which has befallen you?"

A loud gust of wind now rattled through the castle, and gradually died away in hollow murmurs, which, to the disordered imagination of the earl sounded like the sullen mutterings of evil spirits, or moans of some poor wretches in their dying agony. At one time he became so excited with nameless terrors, that he almost feared to remain in his chamber; but he chided himself for giving way to such weakness, and endeavoured to become more calm and collected, in which effort he partly succeeded.

More than once, between the pauses of the blast, he fancied he heard footsteps upon the stairs, and one time so strong was that impression upon his mind, that he cautiously opened his chamber door, and listened, but all was silent.

"How weak and nervous I am to-night," he said, "it must be from the effects of the events of the day, or the storm. I must not give way to it, for it is useless to alarm myself thus unnecessarily. Hark!—Surely I heard a door close."

It certainly sounded like one, and probably it was at that very time that the ill-fated Lord Coningsby was being forced from the castle by the ruffian emissaries of the murderous Bonville; but Lord Elverton concluded that it was only one of the doors blown to by the violence of the wind, and he soon became more confident.

He sat himself down and meditated upon all the painful circumstances and vicissitudes of his eventful life, and as he did so, heavy sighs escaped his bosom, and the prospect of the future appeared more gloomy than before.

"There was but one thing more I wanted to render my happiness complete, and suffer my declining years to close in peace," he soliloquized, "and that was the restoration of my unfortunate Elvina to my arms. I might then indeed, have learnt to bury all my past troubles in oblivion, and to look forward to the future with hope and joy. But that seems to be denied me, and how can I be otherwise than miserable? And then the threats of Bonville torture me, and bewilder my brain, leaving me uncertain how to act; and those beloved and innocent beings who are so dear to me, I would care little what happened to myself, could I only see them secure."

He now reflected upon the singular adventure that had occurred to Celestia, and the observations of the gipsey sybil, and although he had at first been disposed to treat them with indifference, after what had since occurred he could not do so; and he was only the more anxious to see her, that he might elicit such particulars from her as might put him upon his guard against the designs of Bonville. It was evident that she was acquainted with all the circumstances of his melancholy history, and after the warning she had given to Celestia that she was fully aware of all the schemes which the Jesuit Bonville had in contemplation; and if she was indeed the friend she pretended to be, why did she hesitate to come boldly forward and reveal all she knew?

The whole circumstances were shrouded in the deepest mystery, and the longer the earl reflected upon it, the greater became his perplexity. Thus the night passed away—the night of horror and of bloodshed, and the fatal moment was approaching when the wretched earl would become acquainted with the full extent of the dreadful calamity which had befallen him, and his feelings were destined to receive a shock, from which it would be difficult for them to recover.

The earl left his chamber at an earlier hour than usual, and soon afterwards Celestia, Lady Eugenia, and his other friends joined him in the breakfast-room.

"How is it that Edgar is not here yet?" said the earl, after waiting his appearance for some minutes with some impatience; "he is not wont to be the last in his chamber, and perhaps he is ill. Let his valet go and summon him to breakfast."

The valet was despatched accordingly, and in a few minutes returned, and with a look of alarm informed them that Lord Coningsby was not in his chamber, and that the bed had evidently not been slept in the previous night.

"This is extraordinary!" exclaimed the earl, "is not his lordship in any part of the castle?"

"He is not, my lord," answered the valet.

"It is not likely that he would walk out on such a morning as this," remarked Lady Eugenia, "are you sure you are not mistaken, Simmonds?"

"Oh, I am quite positive, my lady," replied Simmonds.

"And have none of the other servants seen him leave the castle?" asked Lord Elverton.

Simmonds answered in the negative, and the surprise and uneasiness of the earl and all present increased.

"I do not know what to think of this," said the earl. "You say that his lordship's bed does not appear to have been slept in, Simmonds?"

"It does not, my lord," answered the valet.

"That is more remarkable and unaccountable than all," said Lord Elverton.

"I must go to Edgar's chamber myself; I do not know how it is, but strange misgivings came over me and continued to harrass me all the night."

"Oh, do not alarm yourself, my dear brother," said Lady Eugenia, "probably Lord Coningsby did not feel inclined to sleep last night, which was the case with myself and Celestia, and may only have walked a little way from the castle in order to refresh himself."

"It is not usual for him to be absent from the breakfast-table at the regular hour," observed the earl, "and it does not seem very likely that he would choose such a gloomy and disagreeable morning as this for a walk. But I will go and see whether I can make anything out."

He quitted the room accordingly, and repaired to the chamber of his son, accompanied by Lady Eugenia, who also had her fears that something had happened, though she endeavoured to conceal them from her brother.

On entering the room they beheld everything as the valet had described it; the bed had evidently never been disturbed since it had been made, nor was there anything to denote that Lord Coningsby had been in the chamber at all, except the lamp which stood upon the table, and which had apparently been burnt out several hours.

"This is really most extraordinary and perplexing," remarked the earl, " where can he be?"

"He must have left the castle for some purpose or other," replied Lady Eugenia, "do not alarm yourself——"

She was interrupted by an exclamation of surprise and emotion from the earl, and she beheld him gazing steadfastly upon some object on the carpet.

"Oh, see here!" he cried, "here are the marks of several muddy feet upon the carpet, some persons have been in the chamber as well as Edgar. My fears increase.

With trembling impatience they followed the footmarks from the chamber, and traced them all the way along the gallery and down the stairs to the private door, out at which the unfortunate and ill-fated Lord Coningsby had been conveyed by the ruffians. In the ground beyond, also, there was the print of feet which corresponded in shape and size with the marks in the chamber and on the stairs. They traced them to some distance from the castle, when they were entirely lost sight of.

The earl and his sister now looked at each other with amazement and alarm, and for a moment or two both of them were too much agitated and bewildered to speak.

"Good God!" at length ejaculated the earl, "what can we make of this? My worst fears are fulfilled, something terrible, I feel confident, has happened to my son."

"Be calm, my dear brother," said Lady Eugenia, "and notwithstanding it looks very strange and alarming at present, I admit, our apprehensions after all may turn out groundless. There is no time to be lost, we must dispatch persons in every direction immediately in search of him."

But it was in vain that Lord Elverton sought to compose himself; what could look more suspicious or ominous? There had evidently been several persons in the chamber of Lord Coningsby, and if so, it appeared but too probable that he had been forced away, and had perhaps met with some violent death. The bare idea of this smote the heart of Lord Elverton with horror, and he could scarce support himself while he and his sister returned to the castle.

The reader may easily imagine the surprise and alarm of Celestia and the others when they were made acquainted with what they had seen, and they could not but feel convinced that there was now good ground for serious apprehension.

The Earl Bathurst and his son, and Sir Roderick, immediately started in different directions in search of him, and most of the servants were dispatched upon the same errand; but Lord Elverton's agitation increased every moment, and it was not without the greatest difficulty he could be persuaded to remain at the castle, and to await with patience and fortitude the result.

Celestia and her aunt exerted themselves to the utmost to soothe the anguish of the earl, although their fears were almost equal to his own; but his uneasiness became greater every minute and he paced the room to and fro in a state of the most feverish excitement.

"My worst surmises are about to be realized," he said, "I feel certain of it; the footmarks in the chamber, the unentered bed, tell a fearful tale, something must have happened to my unfortunate Edgar; something seems to tell me that he has fallen into the hands of our enemies, and has met with an untimely fate."

"Oh, Heaven forbid!" cried Lady Eugenia, fervently; "do not encourage such dreadful ideas, my dear brother, for I trust that they will turn out to be erroneous."

"Where can he have gone?" demanded the earl, "it is not likely that he would voluntarily have alarmed me thus; besides, it seems evident to me that some ruffians or other have entered his chamber, and forced him away."

"But how could they have entered the castle?" asked his sister.

"By the private door, from which we tracked the footprints, the lock of which they might contrive to pick. Alas! alas! am I never doomed to experience a moment's peace."

In this manner the unhappy earl continued to bewail his hard fate, and turned a deaf ear to all the expostulations of Lady Eugenia and Celestia; in fact they were at a loss what arguments to make use of to soothe him, and as the time passed away, and still nothing was seen or heard of Lord Coningsby, their agitation became almost insupportable, and they really began to think that something serious had befallen him.

At length Lord Bathurst, his son, and Sir Roderick returned to the castle, and their looks fully shewed that their search had been entirely unsuccessful. They had not, in fact, been able to gain the least information respecting him, and in the course of the morning, the servants also returned to the castle, their efforts having likewise been equally fruitless.

Lord Elverton clasped his forehead in an agony of despair, and sinking into a chair, groaned aloud with the intense anguish of his mind. The persons present did not attempt to interrupt his grief, for they wisely thought that the indulgence of it might serve to relieve him.

Celestia and her aunt were scarcely in a better condition than their noble relative, and as Lord Malensbury watched the pale and agitated countenance of her he so fondly loved, his uneasiness became so great that he could not conceal it from the persons present, but they were so much occupied with other important matters and speculations that they took no particular notice of it.

"Some fiend has been at work," at length sighed Lord Elverton, "to work me deadly mischief; that crafty and malicious miscreant, Bonville, is at the bottom of all this. Desperately has he commenced the operation of his threats, conveyed to me in the letter which was doubtless written by him, and how—oh, Heaven!—how can I defend myself and those who are far dearer to me than mine own life's blood, from his secret and bloody machinations? My son, my noble boy, where art thou?

what has become of thee? Thou art torn from me—thou art murdered! I shall never behold thee again!"

"Oh, God forbid!" simultaneously uttered all the deeply agitated persons present; but the same fears possessed their breasts.

"I shall go mad!" exclaimed the earl, vehemently striking his chest, and staring around him with a wild and wandering look. "All Merciful Father, what have I done to deserve this additional and horrible calamity?"

He started from his chair, and traversed the room with the wild air of a maniac. No one was in a position to attempt to offer him any consolation, for their apprehensions were almost as great as his own. They could see no reason for Lord Coningsby having voluntarily absented himself from the castle, and placing them in such a dreadful state of suspense, and what conclusions could they come to, but the most terrible?—The footmarks in his chamber, plainly shewed that there had been several individuals there, and therefore the only conclusion they could reasonably arrive at was, that he had fallen a victim to some dark and insidious plot; that he had been seized by villains employed by the wretch who had sent the threatening letter, and who had gained admission to the castle by the private door, as their footsteps were traced to that, and far beyond it, and if so, might not the worst conjectures of his unhappy father have been realized, and he have met with some horrible and untimely end? The idea, even dreadful as it was, was too probable for them easily to reject it, and they were therefore all at a loss to offer the least consolation to each other.

Again were the servants despatched in every direction on their hopeless errand, and the melancholy news being now spread over the country, for miles around, every individual sympathised with the fresh troubles of the benevolent and amiable Lord Elverton, and set themselves heartily to work to discover some clue to the torturing and apparently unfathomable mystery.

Hour after hour, however, elapsed, and still no intelligence was received, nothing to throw the least gleam of hope upon the hearts of the distracted inmates of the castle. And now when night came on, and the same uncertainty prevailed, the agony of them all became almost insupportable. Lord Elverton was conveyed to his chamber in a state bordering upon madness, and was obliged to have several persons in constant attendance upon him; and Celestia and Lady Eugenia were scarcely in a better condition.

The sybil's words were already fulfilled; the dark clouds that had been louring over their destiny, had burst, and the tempest had commenced its fury against them. There was yet no peace for the blighted heart; there was yet no peace for the blighted heart!—The voyage of life is dark and chequered, and who can expect to pass in calm and peace to "that bourne from whence no traveller returns?"

CHAPTER XX.

THE BODY OF THE MURDERED DISCO-
VERED. — THE FUNERAL. — THE RED
MASK.—THE BLOOD WARNING.

ANOTHER day, and another day, have passed since the horrible murder described in the last chapter; inquiries had been instituted in every direction, immense rewards held out to any person that could give any information, every exertion that wisdom could suggest had been made use of, but still not the least clue could be obtained to the mysterious disappearance of the unfortunate and ill-fated Lord Coningsby. The servants and all the tenants and residents on the estate had been rigidly examined with the hope to throw some light upon the dreadful affair, but, of course, with no better success; no person could give the slightest information, and they all sympathised with the earl and his relations on the fresh calamity that had befallen them, and that in the midst of their anticipated happiness.

There was something peculiarly awful in the circumstance of Lord Coningsby having so suddenly disappeared after his recent restoration to his noble father, and so soon after the festivities given on the occasion of his introduction to the proud estates of his ancestors, and many were the expressions of regret and hor-ror which sprung from the warm and honest hearts of the humble beings who had the happiness of being the dependents of the unfortunate earl. Bitter were the execrations that were lavished upon the heads of the miscreants who had worked this unexpected and unmerited misery. It was generally believed that Lord Coningsby had been seized in his chamber by a gang of ruffians who had contrived to get secret access to the castle, and that, if he were not murdered, he was placed in such a position that he could not have any opportunity of escaping from his terrible enemies, and that his friends and relations would never behold him again.

Every person who knew the amiable character of the earl, and all those connected with him, considered it to be their duty to exert themselves to the very utmost to try to unravel the mystery, and they did so accordingly, nor were Earl Bathurst, his son, and Sir Roderick Ainslie, as may be imagined idle on the occasion; all their energies were at work, but, unfortunately, with little or no prospect of success.

Lord Everside, who had received the melancholy and alarming intelligence of what had happened, repaired to the castle without delay in order to render any assistance that might be in his power, and a letter of commiseration was received from Sir Eustace Aubrey, expressing his heartfelt sorrow at what had happened, and regretting that a sudden attack of illness prevented him from hastening to the castle, in order that he might render such aid as might be in his power.

The castle, which so lately had been the scene of rejoicing, was now the abode of sorrow and despair. Lord Elverton was unable to leave his room, and was little better than a maniac, and Celestia and her aunt were so much distracted that they were unable to attend upon him, or to offer that consolation they so fervently wished.

The third morning came after the murder, and all was misery and the most poignant anguish at the castle, Lord Elverton had sunk into a state of complete imbecility, which it was quite melancholy to behold, and seemed to entertain but a vague comprehension of the observations that were addressed to him by his friends and sorrowing relations, and poor Celestia was reduced to such a state of weakness by the horrible anxiety of her mind that she was scarcely able to leave her chamber.

"My God!" she would utter to herself when she was alone, "what have we done to offend thee, that we should be visited by these terrible calamities? My poor grandfather must sink under this dreadful trial, and then what will become of me; where, oh where can I look for happiness? I had hoped that peace was permanently restored to us, that nothing would again occur to interrupt our happiness, that the future path opened before me and my dear relations was one of pleasure and contentment; weak sighted mortals as we all are, how soon has this blissful spell been broken by the stern reality of evil destiny! My poor uncle, amiable Edgar, who never wronged one of thy fellow creatures by word or thought, where art thou now? What has become of thee? All merciful Parent of every good, throw I humbly beseech thee some light upon this dreadful mystery, and restore him to us."

The agony of Lord Malensbury at seeing the melancholy and deplorable situation of that fair being to whom he was so fondly, so devotedly, so enthusiastically attached, was extreme, and he seized every opportunity to endeavour by the most delicate and persuasive means in his power to console her, and inspire her with hope, but with little or no effect. Alas! what were the arguments he could offer under the painful circumstances? They admitted of none.

In the midst of all these troubles every effort had been made to discover the gipsy sybil who had appeared to our heroine on several occasions, and a handsome reward offered to her it she would come forward, and state all she knew, but it was all to no purpose, she still remained concealed, and that rendered the mystery still more torturing and inexplicable. Every one was at a perfect loss to fathom her real character. That she was thoroughly acquainted with all the melancholy circumstances of the earl's history was quite evident, that she was also aware of the secret machinations of the Jesuit Bonville and his other enemies, was equally apparent, she professed likewise to be favourably disposed towards Lord Elverton, and all this rendered her neglect to come forward on this occasion, when her services and information were so much required the more unaccountable. How true had been her predictions; the ridicule and indifference which before had been attached to them could not know be awarded to them, and she wss looked upon by all persons interested as a most important actor in this tragic drama, and one whose confidence might be the means of unravelling the mystery, and resolving the painful, the torturing doubts which naturally now prevailed.

But might she not also have fallen into the power of the dreadful and implacable foe whom they all had so much cause to fear, and thus prevented from coming forward to aid them, and put them on their guard against the dangers which threatened them? was a question which reasonably suggested itself to them and they were unable to answer it in the negative. Thus they were kept in a continual state of anxiety, which nothing could ameliorate.

The third morning came; it was dark, cheerless, and boisterous. It had been raining all the night, and now the bellowing of the thunder, coupled with the fierce voice of Boreas, and the flashing lightning, rendered the scene perfectly terrific.

It was more than six o'clock, but several of the poor fishermen who resided on the coast, about a mile and a half distant from the castle, were assembled on the beach, as near as they could approach the raging waters, looking with anxious eyes at their little craft, and expecting every moment to be deprived of their only means of existence.

The ocean was swelled in an awful manner, wave battled against wave, and the surge dashed over the highest rocks. It was a grand but a fearful sight. Good God! how many thousands of human beings were probably at that moment being swallowed up in the boundless deep, with all their sins upon their heads, and without having time to say "Heaven have mercy on me, a wretched sinner!"

In this way two hours elapsed, wher

suddenly the dense black clouds that had obscured the horizon dispersed; the voice of the thunder was hushed; the lightning no longer darted its forked flashings; the waves lowered and receded from the shore on which they had recently made such rapid inroads, threatening to overwhelm everything in their destructive course, and everything betokened a coming calm, as beautiful as the tempest had previously been horrible. The poor fishermen raised their eyes with fervent gratitude towards Heaven, and murmured their thanks with the best eloquence that it had pleased Nature to bestow upon them.

A cluster of about half-a-dozen of these simple, but honest and laborious fellows had gathered together on a shelving rock, and were busy discussing the horrors of the late storm, and expressing their happiness that it had subsided without doing any material injury to their craft.

"Ah, Ned;" observed one of the group, a sturdy, grey-headed old man, who had evidently cruised his share on the rough ocean of life, and weathered its tempests with patience, fortitude, and resignation; "we may indeed, be thankful to the Great Commander for His mercy towards us and our poor families during this storm; but how many poor fellows have doubtless met with a watery grave; how many hundreds of wives are made widows, how many children left fatherless! It is a sad reflection, but one that always occupies my mind on occasions of this sort."

"You say true, Jem Ansley," replied the man to whom these observations had been addressed;—"it is a sad reflection, but let us hope that God has extended the blessings of His mercy to the majority of His humble creatures during this rough season: see, what is that floating on the top of yonder wave?"

"It is a human form, or I am much mistaken;" observed one of the men, "It is being washed towards the shore, and from its inanimate appearance it seems to be that of a corpse. Some poor fellow has been summoned to his last account, I fear. Yes, it is a human form and that of a man too."

He had scarcely spoken these words, when another wave dashed the body to a considerable distance on the beach, and they all rushed towards the spot, to secure it, and to see if life was yet remaining.

"Poor fellow," said one of the fishermen, "he is dead enough, and has clearly been so for some days; by what strange circumstance has his body been washed ashore here? Oh! there has been some foul work here; see, his arms are bound behind him with a strong rope; he has been murdered."

"He has," said the old man who had been called Jem Ansley, "there can be no doubt of it, poor fellow, and from his dress he is evidently no common seaman."

They now searched the pockets of the corpse, with the hope of discovering some clue to his identity, but without success. Whilst they were thus occupied, they were aroused by hearing a loud and malicious laugh of exultation, and raising their eyes towards the part from whence it seemed to proceed, they beheld standing on the rock they had so recently quitted, a figure which immediately rivetted their whole attention.

It was that of a tall, and powerfully framed man, attired in black, and with a long cloak of the same colour flowing from his shoulders. He wore a slouched hat of the most ancient fashion, but his features were fully revealed, and they were of the most repulsive description, while his small and sparkling eyes were fixed with a fiendish expression of triumph, upon the ghastly corpse of the unfortunate man, which was stretched at the feet of the fishermen on the beach. But we need not describe this revolting looking being any further, when we say it was the murderer Bonville.

No sooner did he behold that the fishermen's eyes were directed towards him, than he gave utterance to another laugh of diabolical exultation, and folding his cloak around him, descended the rock by the opposite side, and when some of the men rushed round to observe him and impede his progress, he was lost to the sight. They returned to their companions.

"Who can that fellow be?" said Ansley.

"He is a black looking customer," observed Ned; "and what could he mean by laughing at such an awful sight as this?"

"Oh, he is some madman, you may depend," said another of the men; "never mind him, I'm anxious to know who this man is."

"From the richness of his dress, I should say that he was a gentleman," replied Ansley; "assist me to convey the body into my hut, and then we can give notice in the proper quarter, and perhaps his friends and connections may be discovered."

They did so, and the lifeless form of

the unfortunate man was conveyed to the hut of Ansley, which was the handiest to the spot.

"Who can this unfortunate man be?" said Ansley, again looking earnestly at the swollen and disfigured features of the corpse.

"Ah!" ejaculated Ned, "an idea suddenly strikes me."

"What is it, Ned?" asked two or three of the men together.

"Why," answered Ned, "of course you have all heard of the sudden and mysterious disappearance of the good Lord Elverton's son from the castle?"

"Certainly," replied every one present.

"Might this not be him?"

"God forbid!" exclaimed Ansley, "and yet it is not at all unlikely. Have any of you ever seen Lord Coningsby, as I think he was called?"

They all replied in the negative.

"And if we had," remarked Ned, "he is so disfigured that it would be almost impossible for us to recognise him."

"I will instantly repair to the castle," said Ansley, "and make them acquainted with the facts, and if it should prove to be that unfortunate nobleman, doubtless some one of his family will be able to identify him."

They all approved of this course, and the honest fisherman immediately departed on his melancholy errand.

He was not long in arriving at the castle, and requested to see Lord Elverton, but this could not be granted, as the earl was too ill to leave his bed. He was, however, ushered into the presence of the Earl Bathurst and his son, who were at the castle, and to whom he related the dismal particulars, describing as minutely as he could the dress which the deceased had on.

"Good God!" exclaimed Lord Bathurst, "this description corresponds exactly with the unfortunate Lord Coningsby, and fills my mind with the most dreadful apprehensions. Can it be? Oh, Heaven avert such calamity! for should it prove to be correct, it will be the death of my noble relative."

"And Celestia, too," said Lord Malensbury, "how will her gentle bosom be enabled to endure so horrible a shock? But this stranger that you say you observed on the rock, my good man, while you were examining the lifeless body, have you described him minutely?"

"I have to the best of my ability, my lord," answered Ansley.

"Who could he be?" said Lord Malensbury."

"It might be the miscreant, Bonville," remarked the earl; "but come, let us accompany this good man to his hut, and see whether we can identify the deceased; it will be better that Lord Elverton, his sister, and Celestia should know nothing of this business till our return, and should it indeed prove to be the body of Lord Coningsby, we must then devise the best means of breaking the intelligence to them."

To this Lord Malensbury perfectly agreed, and starting Ansley before them, they followed him on horseback, and arrived at the hut a short time before him. They were immediately shown into the room in which the body was lying, and no sooner did they behold it than they recognized it as that of the unfortunate and ill-fated Lord Coningsby. Their anguish may readily be imagined, and after having given instructions to Ansley, and left him in charge of the corpse of the murdered nobleman, they retraced their way with sad hearts to the castle, and endeavouring to devise on the road the best means of imparting the horrible discovery to Lord Elverton and his relations. That Lord Coningsby had been murdered, and that the wretch, Bonville, was his assassin, they could now have no doubt, and many were the curses they invoked upon his head.

"My God!" ejaculated Lord Malensbury, as they proceeded; "what a dreadful occurrence in this. The good and amiable Coningsby, so soon after his restoration to his afflicted father, to meet with so horrible a fate. It will certainly prove a death blow to the earl; and poor Celestia, too, how will she be able to support so awful a shock? Oh, may the most horrible retribution of Heaven overtake the bloody and inhuman perpetrators of this hideous deed!"

"It will, it will, of that we may rest assured," returned the earl; "but endeavour to compose yourself, my son, for we have got a most difficult and painful task to perform, and it needs all our firmness and prudence to accomplish it. I know not how we can break the dreadful intelligence to my noble relative in his present precarious situation. But we must consult Lord Everside and Sir Roderick, and take their advice upon the subject. There is no time to be lost, for the remains of the ill-fated Coningsby must be removed to the castle, and then it will be impossible to keep the fearful truth any longer a secret."

Lord Malensbury was completely bewildered, and was unable to throw out any suggestion, and in this manner, with the most melancholy hearts when they reflected on the horrible and untimely fate of Lord Coningsby, they arrived at the castle.

Celestia and Lady Eugenia had not been aware of their absence, and were still in the chamber of their suffering relative, contributing all they could to his relief and consolation, though it was what they so much needed themselves.

Lord Bathurst and his son immediately made their way to the apartment in which they were informed Lord Everside and Sir Roderick were seated, and they immediately saw by their looks that they had something of a melancholy nature to communicate.

"Your lordships have been absent from the castle," observed Lord Everside, "and to judge by your looks, your ride does not appear to have much recruited your spirits."

"My lord," said Earl Bathurst, I have something of a most melancholy and dreadful nature to impart to you, upon which I must request the prompt and serious advice of yourself and Sir Roderick."

Lord Everside and the baronet looked amazed and very much agitated, and requested the earl to make them acquainted with everything without delay.

"We have discovered the unfortunate Lord Coningsby," said Lord Bathurst.

Lord Everside and Sir Roderick started with amazement, and the former impatiently said—

"Discovered him, my lord? Is it possible? I hope that nothing serious has happened to him; but where is he?"

"Alas!" replied the earl, in the most melancholy accents, "he is no more."

"No more!" repeated Lord Everside and Sir Roderick in a breath; "for Heaven's sake do not keep us in suspense—tell us the whole particulars."

"There can be no doubt, from what we have seen," said Lord Bathurst, "that my unfortunate relative has come by his death by unfair means—that he has been murdered."

"Oh, horrible!" exclaimed Lord Everside, "it surely cannot be."

"Alas!" returned the earl, "I fear it is too true. There can be little or no reason to doubt it. His body was washed on to the shore this morning. His arms were pinioned, which shows at once that he was barbarously assassinated, and his cold and lifeless remains now lie at the hut of one of the fishermen who found him. He came to us and we have just

been and identified the body of the ill-fated young nobleman."

"Gracious Heaven!" ejaculated Sir Roderick, "what a dreadful discovery in this; and what will be the anguish of Lord Elverton when he is made acquainted with it, which he must be? Who can have committed this hideous, this atrocious deed?"

"I think there can be very little doubt that it has been perpetrated at the instigation of the heartless and hardened miscreant, Bonville," replied Lord Bathurst.

"It is indeed most probable," coincided the baronet; "especially after the threatening letter which Lord Elverton received from him. Unfortunate Coningsby! little did we expect that so horrible and untimely a fate awaited you so soon after your restoration to that parent from whom you had been so long separated. Better would it have been had you indeed perished in your childhood; for your father might long ere this have become resigned to your fate. Unhappy family, what a strange and awful fatality attends you! What will be the sufferings of Lady Elvina, should she ever be discovered, when she comes to hear of the fearful death of her son? Oh, monster, monster! if it is indeed you that have done this, may the most terrible retribution overtake you. Inhuman Bonville, could you not be satisfied by separating the wife from her husband, and afterwards destroying their lovely and innocent daughter, but that you must also bathe your hands in the blood of the unoffending son? How can we act? What must be done under these dreadful circumstances?"

"I know not," answered Lord Bathurst; "but certain it is, that we must not venture to communicate the awful intelligence to the earl at present, or it would be sudden death to him. But I have not told you all the particulars of this melancholy catastrophe; listen, therefore, and then we must come to some speedy decision as to what course it will be most advisable to adopt."

Lord Everside and Sir Roderick did indeed listen with the most profound attention and the deepest emotion while Lord Bathurst detailed to them all the melancholy facts, just as they had been related to him and his son by Ansley the fisherman.

"The man seen by the fishermen on the rock," and Sir Roderick, when the earl had concluded, "was doubtless one of the murderers, and his description exactly corresponds with what I remember the features and person of the Jesuit Bonville to be."

"Indeed?" said Lord Bathurst.

"Yes," answered the baronet, "and that all but confirms our suspicions that he is the inhuman wretch who has committed this fiendish crime. How unfortunate it was that he could not have been secured, and brought to that punishment which his frightful deeds so richly merit; but he seems to be concealed somewhere in this neighbourhood, doubtless with the intention of watching an opportunity of putting the whole of his monstrous threats into execution. No time must be lost; every exertion must be made to discover and secure him."

"There must," said Lord Everside; "but, alas! I fear it will be to little purpose. The blood-stained miscreant no doubt has well matured his diabolical plans, and has taken every precaution to avoid detection. I am completely bewildered, and know not what to advise. It is impossible that we can long keep the dreadful facts concealed from the unfortunate earl, for the remains of his murdered son must be conveyed without delay to the castle for interment. Ill-fated Coningsby, that you should thus perish in the prime of life, and with the bright prospect of every earthly happiness before you. When will the misfortunes of this ill-fated family terminate? Alas! how fearfully are the predictions of that mysterious woman, who appeared to Celestia, being fulfilled. Lady Elvina, too, should this monster in human form really know the place of her retreat, as he declares in his infamous letter, to what a dreadful fate may he not also consign her? He will suffer no limit to his vengeance while he remains undetected."

"He will not," coincided Sir Roderick; "he has already given us the most terrible proofs of that; and how to thwart his infernal plans I know not."

"Poor Celestia, too," said Lord Malensbury, "how will she be enabled to endure the terrible shock? I shudder to think of it."

A dismal pause ensued, during which the four friends meditated deeply, and with feelings of the most poignant anguish. They then consulted together, but it was some time before they could come to any satisfactory conclusion.

They were, indeed, placed in a most awkward position, and plan after plan was rejected almost as soon as it had suggested itself to their minds. But at length, as there was no time to be lost, and as there was no possibility of keeping the dreadful facts secret long, they came to the resolution of breaking them in the gentlest manner they could to Lady Eugenia, and through her to Lady Celestia, and for that purpose they dispatched a servant to her, requesting her attendance.

Lady Eugenia frankly obeyed the summons, and on entering the room in which the four gentlemen were seated, she immediately perceived by the extreme anxiety depicted in their countenances, that they had something of a melancholy nature to impart.

Having requested her to be seated, Lord Bathurst then undertook the painful task of communicating the dreadful intelligence to her in the most gentle and cautious manner he could, but no sooner did Lady Eugenia hear of the violent death of her nephew than she uttered an exclamation of horror, and immediately fainted.

It was some time before she recovered, and when she did, her agony of mind may be imagined.

"Great Heaven!" she exclaimed, "when will our troubles cease? This horrible catastrophe will certainly prove a death-blow to my unfortunate brother. Ill-fated Coningsby, little did I expect that such would be your untimely end, and so soon after your restoration to us."

She wrung her hands, and remained for some time in a state of agitation, that would admit of no consolation; but at length she became more calm, and then Lord Bathurst continued his melancholy narrative, and related to her all those melancholy particulars with which the reader has been already made acquainted. The details increased her horror. It was some time before her friends could bring her to a sufficient state of composure to converse with any degree of reasonableness.

"It must be the work of that monster, Bonville," said Lady Eugenia.

"No doubt of it," replied Lord Bathurst, "and some immediate steps must be taken to apprehend the inhuman miscreant, and to bring him to that punishment which his frigtful crimes have merited. But how had the intelligence better be communicated to the earl? It would not be safe to make him acquainted with it at present, and whenever it is done, it must be in the most delicate and cautious manner."

"It is a most dreadful task," said Lady Eugenia, "but I will endeavour to accomplish it. Alas!—alas!—What troubles are still in store for our wretched family. My beloved Celestia, too, how will her tender heart be able to receive this awful intelligence?"

Some further time was occupied in conversation, and it was finally arranged that Lady Eugenia should at first only by degrees impart to the earl the death of his son, without relating the dreadful circumstances under which there was every reason to believe he had come by it; and she left the gentlemen for the purpose of first breaking it to Celestia.

The four friends then departed for the cottage of Ansley, the fisherman, accompanied by several servants, in order to convey the body of the unfortunate murdered nobleman to the castle.

With a heavy heart, and a bosom filled with horror at what she had heard, Lady Eugenia made her way to the chamber of her brother, but met Celestia on the staircase, just returning from the garden.

"My dear grandpapa has just sunk into a calm sleep," said our heroine, "so as the nurse and the doctor are in attendance, I thought I would take the opportunity of retiring for a short time in order to refresh myself. But dear me, my dear aunt, how pale and agitated you look. You tremble too. I hope that you have heard nothing more to alarm you?"

"Follow me, Celestia," said Lady Eugenia, "I have indeed something of a most agonizing and awful nature to impart to you, which will require all your fortitude to listen to."

Celestia looked amazed and terrified, but followed her aunt in silence into an apartment, where, being seated, she eagerly demanded what she had to communicate.

"Have you heard anything of my uncle?" she asked, "has any clue been obtained as to what has become of him?"

Lady Eugenia sighed deeply, and tears gushed to her eyes, and this more than all increased the alarm of Celestia.

"Oh, what has occurred?" she ejaculated, "for Heaven's sake, my dear madam, do not keep me in suspense."

"Celestia," replied Lady Eugenia, in a voice of the greatest agony, "your unfortunate uncle has indeed been discovered."

"Oh! thank Heaven! but how? Where?—Where is he?"

"Compose yourself, my love, for you will need all your fortitude to hear that I have to inform you of."

"These preliminaries fill my mind with dread," said Celestia. "I implore you to let me know the worst at once. Something dreadful has happened; I see it by your looks."

"Alas!" sighed Lady Eugenia, "your forebodings are too true, my dear girl; Lord Coningsby is no more."

"No more! Dead!" shrieked our heroine, and her countenance became as pale as that of a corpse, and it was not without the greatest difficulty she could preserve herself from fainting. "Oh, God!—what a terrible affliction is this! —My noble-minded relative no more; oh, how will his father be able to support this terrible shock?"

"Alas, I know not, and it is for that reason I implore you to exert all your energies on this trying, this dreadful occasion, and to listen with calmness and fortitude to what I have to tell you."

"Oh, my dear aunt, how has this awful catastrophe occurred?—By what fatal means has Lord Coningsby met with his death?"

"There is too much reason to fear, in fact, there is every reason to believe, by violence."

"Murdered!" gasped forth our heroine, and her blood seemed to freeze in her veins at the horrible thought. Lady Eugenia's feelings were too much overpowered to suffer her to reply in any other way than by a groan. Celestia covered her face with her hands, and her anguish of mind became more intense and insupportable.

"The wretch who sent the threatening letter to my poor brother," at length observed Lady Eugenia, "the blood-stained villain Bonville, no doubt, has been the author of this atrocity. Oh, God!—how shall I ever be able to communicate the fearful intelligence to that unfortunate man who is already worn down with unmerited troubles?"

"Heaven help us!" ejaculated Celestia, "we are indeed an unfortunate family. But tell me the whole of the dismal particulars; dreadful though they may be, I am better prepared to hear them than to endure this suspense."

With much difficulty Lady Eugenia complied, and no language can describe the agony of our heroine, as she proceeded. A flood of tears, however, came to her relief, and she gradually became more calm.

"Unfortunate Coningsby," she ejaculated, "in whom was combined every noble, virtuous, and generous feeling, what a shocking and unmerited fate is this for you to meet with. Surely Heaven has visited us too severely. Oh, what a cruel wretch must the miscreant be who has committed this monstrous, this bloody deed."

It was some time before Celestia or her aunt could at all tranquillise these feelings, and then they were unable to come to any conclusion as to what was best to be done under the melancholy circumstances. That the fatal truth could long be witheld from the knowledge of Lord Elverton, was impossible, and they could not but anticipate the most fearful results.

The remains of the ill-fated Coningsby were removed to the castle, and many were the tears that were shed over them, and bitter were the curses and execrations that were heaped upon his brutal assassin or assassins.

The melancholy news quickly spread around the neighbourhood, and caused the most painful sensation in the bosoms of all to whom the noble and generous character of the deceased was so well known and so highly appreciated, and means were immediately set on foot to discover the murderer.

The day passed away, and Lord Elverton continued to get better, but still his friends shrunk with horror from the task of communicating the dreadful truth to him, although they knew it could not be much longer withheld from him. The following morning, however, he felt so much better that he persisted in leaving his bed, and was about to go down stairs, when Lady Eugenia, mustering up all the firmness she could, sought to dissuade him, and the vehemence of her manner convinced him that she had some very particular reasons for so doing.

"Why, my dear sister," he demanded, "do you wish to dissuade me from so reasonable a course?—You ought to feel happy to think that I am enable to become calm and resigned under this dreadful trial, the mysterious disappearance of my beloved son, and the uncertainty of the fate which has befallen him."

"And so I am," returned Lady Eugenia, "Heaven knows how grateful I am, and how sincerely I pray that you may have fortitude to sustain the still more terrible shock that is in store for you."

"Ah!" ejaculated Lord Elverton, grasping his sister's arm, and staring wildly upon her;—"what mean those ominous and ambiguous words?—What fresh trial is in store for me?—Speak, speak!—if you sincerely love me, you will not keep me in suspense. Have you heard anything of Edgar? Is he—"

"Alas! alas!" sighed Lady Eugenia.

"Something dreadful has happened; I read it in your looks and words; for the love of God tell me all."

"How shall I give utterance to it? Would that the task had devolved upon somebody else."

"You torture me, Eugenia," cried the earl; "tell me all, I beseech you. To be kept this way in doubt is worse than death. Where is my son?—What has happened to him?"

"My dear brother," gasped forth Lady Eugenia, "our worst apprehensions are fulfilled. Edgar is no more; his cold remains are at present in the castle."

The wretched earl heard no more, but with one long groan of agony sunk insensible upon the floor. Lady Eugenia immediately summoned assistance, and the unfortunate Lord Elverton was placed upon the bed, and everything done that humanity could suggest to restore him to animation. But it was some time ere that could be accomplished, and then the agony and horror of his feelings may be far better imagined than described. He clasped his burning temples in a state of perfect frenzy; prayed to Heaven to terminate his earthly troubles by taking him to itself, and invoked the bitterest curses upon the murderer of that son who after being separated from him so many years, had so lately been restored to him. His friends were fearful that the dreadful shock would destroy his reason, and it was some time ere they could calm his feelings in the slightest degree. But at lenght it pleased Heaven to abate the intense agony of his sufferings, and he become more tranquil and resigned than could have been expected.

He persisted in going to the room where the ghastly remains of his son were lying, and having given vent to his feelings in a flood of grief which no one offered to interrupt, he sunk on his knees and breathed a solemn vow to Heaven never to rest until he had discovered the atrocious assassin, and brought him to that punishment which his fiendish crime so richly deserved.

"Oh, my poor Edgar," he sighed, "what had you done that you should meet with so horrible a fate as this!—Where is now all the happiness that I had flattered myself was in store for me? My noble boy! My noble boy! better would it have been for you had you never been restored to me; then might you not have met with this untimely end. It is the work of the arch-fiend, Bonville; terribly has he commenced putting his diabolical threats into execution. And it was him, no doubt, who came to exult over the ghastly corpse of his unfortunate and unoffending victim. Oh, why was he not secured?"

"It is unfortunate that he was not," said Lord Bathurst, "but it could not be helped. Oh course the attention of the men was too much occupied with the corpse of the ill-fated Coningsby to allow them to try to secure him, and he was immediately gone. But I still hope that it will not be long before the villain is apprehended."

"Alas! alas!" groaned the earl, "while he is still at large what fresh horrors may he not perpetrate. We are none of us safe for a moment. And my Elvina, may she not be in his power, and suffering under all the barbarity that his demon mind can suggest and inflict!—Oh, God! give me fortitude! Do not try me beyond my strength, for surely these accumulated horrors are almost too much for human nature to endure."

With difficulty they persuaded him to retire from the chamber of death, and then they all exerted themselves to the utmost to pour the balm of consolation into his distracted bosom; but it was almost a fruitless task, and indeed they wondered and were grateful that he was not in even a more deplorable state than he was, under all the dreadful circumstances, which were sufficient to unnerve the stoutest heart.

Universal gloom and despondency reigned throughout the castle and the neighbourhood around, and deep was the sympathy which was expressed for the unparalleled misfortunes of the earl, and loud were the execrations that were uttered against the perpetrator of the frightful crime. The excitement increased every day, and every one exerted themselves to discover the murderer of the unfortunate nobleman, and to bring him to punishment, but with little prospect of success.

The time wore gloomily away, and at length the day arrived for the funeral to take place. It was a day of sorrow for miles around the castle, and numerous were the persons who assembled to pay their last respects to the memory of the departed, who had been known to them so short a time, but during that brief period had gained the good will and esteem of every one.

The friends of Lord Elverton would fain have persuaded him not to attend the melancholy ceremony, for they apprehended that it would be more than his strength could endure, but he persisted, and they could find no further arguments to alter his determination.

It was a mournful sight, and many were the tears shed when the remains of the ill-fated nobleman were deposited in their final resting place.

The funeral obsequies were at an end, the spectators had gradually dispersed, and the sad procession was about to move from the tomb, and to retrace its way to the castle, when their attention was suddenly arrested by hearing a hollow laugh, and looking towards the spot from whence it seemed to proceed, they beheld, standing at a short distance from them, the tall figure of a man enveloped in a large black cloak, and his features concealed by a red mask.

For a moment they were all transfixed with astonishment, and unable to act, but at length Lord Elverton exclaimed with much emotion—

"Ah! 'tis he! the monster! the murderer! who comes here to exult at the tomb of his unfortunate and unoffending victim. For Heaven's sake seize him! do not suffer him to escape!"

Several persons immediately rushed forward to secure the stranger, but in a moment he drew a couple of pistols from beneath his cloak, and levelling them at their heads, stretched two of the attendants bleeding on the earth.

Appalled at this unexpected act, the others drew back, and the stranger having given utterance to another loud laugh of triumph and defiance, darted from the spot, and was out of sight almost with the rapidity of thought.

It would be impossible to do ample justice to the feelings of horror and amazement of the earl, and all the persons present, and it was some minutes ere either of them could move or speak, so great was their confusion and dismay, but at length the earl exclaimed—

"Good God! surely you will not suffer this fiend in human form thus to set us all at defiance, and to triumph in his atrocious crimes!—Let him be pursued, and he may yet be overtaken and secured."

Several persons hurried away immediately in the direction which the red mask had taken, and the two wounded men were raised from the earth, and conveyed to a place where they might receive prompt assistance, while the distressed Lord Elverton was led from the spot followed by his friends, and in a few minutes arrived at the castle. Here those feeling of intense anguish so long pent up burst forth, and he was obliged to retire to bed, where for the remainder of the day and during the night he remained in a most wretched and alarming condition, and the situation of Celestia and Lady Eugenia was scarcely less deplorable.

The efforts of those who had gone in pursuit of the unknown were fruitless, they could not discover the least traces of him, and they returned to the castle to inform the inmates of the ill success which had attended them.

The wounds which the two men had received were fortunately not dangerous, and every attention being paid them, they were soon in a fair way of recovery.

Sad, indeed, were now all in the castle, and nothing seemed likely to dissipate the univeral gloom that prevailed. For several days after the funeral of Lord Coningsby the earl continued in the same deplorable state, and his friends began to fear that he would never recover from the terrible shock his feelings had received. At times his mind wandered, and he would rave in the most piteous terms of the cruel and fatal destiny that attended him and all connected with him; and fervently beseech the Almighty to end his earthly troubles by terminating his existence at once. In vain did Celestia, Lady Eugenia, and his other friends and relations seek to impart consolation to his distracted mind. He turned a deaf ear to them, and his melancholy seemed rather to increase than abate.

Lord Malensbury was not the least affected among them; while he deeply felt for the misfortunes of his noble relative, the effect which all that had happened had had upon the sensitive mind of our heroine grieved him still more. In the most gentle and unobtrusive manner possible, he tried to comfort her; and her looks sufficiently expressed how grateful she felt to him for his kindness and solicitude; but powerful as was the impression which the engaging young lord had made upon her heart, her mind was too much occupied with the dreadful events which had lately followed each other in such rapid succession to suffer her to think of anything else.

At length a favourable change took place in the earl; the intensity of his grief subsided into a deep melancholy, and he appeared to resign himself to the will of the Almighty, and no longer to murmur at his stern decrees. He was enabled to leave his chamber, and once more to mingle in the society of those so dear to him, who sought by every means in their power to divert his thoughts from the melancholy subject that at present engrossed them ; but this was a task which it was impossible for them to accomplish.

At times he remained for hours secluded in his own chamber, and would not see any one or permit any interruption, and it was then that he gave himself up to all the horrors of racking thought, cursed his cruel destiny, and bewailed the dreadful and untimely fate of his son, and invoked the vengeance of Heaven upon the head of his murderer. As for Lady Elvina, he no longer encouraged

the hope that he had suffered to take possession of his mind, that she would be restored to his arms. He gave her up as lost to him for ever, if she had not indeed already fallen a victim to the diabolical vengeance of the terrible Bonville, which was, alas, more than probable.

No. 21.

Every effort was made to discover and apprehend the murderer of Lord Coningsby, but without any favourable results; all remained wrapped in the same profound state of mystery as before, a mystery which all interested in it began to fear would never be unravelled, although they entertained no doubt that

Bonville was the miscreant who was the base and inhuman author of all.

They had also endeavoured to discover the gipsey sybil and induce her to come forward and to state all that she knew, with no better effect, and at length they gave up the task in despair, and were forced to leave it to Providence to bring about the discovery in its own wise time, applying all their energies to guard against and avert any fresh dangers that might threaten them.

A fortnight had elapsed since the funeral of the late Lord Coningsby; and his friends and relations by dint of great perseverance and philosophy began to feel some little degree of tranquillity, when a circumstance occurred which again created their alarms, and convinced them that their troubles were not yet at an end.

Lord Elverton had retired early to his chamber one evening, when they were alarmed by hearing him give utterance to an exclamation of horror the very minute after he had entered it, and hastening to the room, beheld him seated in a chair ghastly pale, and his eyes fixed wildly on an open letter which he held in his hand.

"For Heaven's sake, my dear brother," said Lady Eugenia, "what is the matter? —From whom is that letter, and how did it come into your possession?"

"The demon is at work again," said the earl; "again he holds out his diabolical threats. I found this letter on my bed on entering the chamber, and know not by what means it came there. Read, read, and wonder not at my agitation and alarm."

Lady Eugenia took the letter, which was written in characters of blood, and read the contents aloud as follows:

"The first portion of my threat has been accomplished; your darling son perished by my hands; I glory in the deed, and again set your attempts to detect me and to thwart my deep laid plans at defiance. All that I have promised shall be fulfilled. I now hasten to the imprisoned Elvina to add fresh tortures to her soul.

"Your deadly and implacable foe,

"BONVILLE."

"The wretch!" exclaimed Lord Bathurst; "then there can no longer be any doubt that he is the author of all the horrors that have taken place. But by what means could he have contrived to place the latter where you found it, my lord?"

"Alas! alas!" sighed the earl, "I cannot form even the slightest conjecture."

"The servants must be examined," said lord Bathurst, "to see whether they know anything about it, or have observed any one enter the castle, though I do not think it likely that they have, or they would have been sure to have detained them, and created an alarm."

"My unfortunate Elvina," groaned lord Elverton, clasping his forehead in agony; "art thou then indeed in the power of this terrible man? Oh, God! if thou art, how dreadful is the fate which threatens thee."

"Let us hope that it is only an empty boast, my dear brother," remarked lady Eugenia, "for the purpose of adding to our agony."

"Oh, no," said the earl, "this inhuman villain is not the man to make idle boasts; have we not had proofs of that already. My poor son! My noble boy! Oh, may just Heaven avenge your cruel death, and visit your murderer with every earthly and future torment."

It was some time before Lord Elverton would receive the least consolation, and Lord Bathurst and his son, who were apprehensive that some danger might threaten him, armed themselves, and insisted upon keeping watch by him in his chamber during the night.

The contents of the letter was a fresh source of astonishment and uneasiness to Celestia and her aunt, and they sat for some time discoursing upon it in the most melancholy manner, and in vain endeavouring to devise some means by which the atrocious designs of Bonville might be frustrated, and himself brought to justice.

"What a dreadful miscreant is that man," said our heroine; "the very thought of him makes me shudder with horror. But surely avenging Heaven will not suffer him to continue in his guilty career; a terrible retribution must before long overtake the barbarous murderer of my innocent mother, and the unfortunate Lord Coningsby."

"It will, my dear Celestia, depend

upon it," said lady Eugenia; "such foul, such hideous crimes will never be suffered to go unpunished. God grant that lady Elvina may not be in his power, for if she is, how terrible will be the sufferings this monster in human form will inflict on her. Better would it be for her if she were dead, than to be subjected to so horrible a fate."

"Unfortunate lady," sighed Celestia, whilst tears of compassion started to her eyes, "I fear, alas! that what the murderer Bonville has stated is too true. Heaven protect her, for I shudder to think what otherwise will become of her."

Lady Eugenia had nothing to offer in reply, and they soon afterwards retired in a most melancholy state of mind to their chambers. The night passed away without anything more occurring to disturb them, and by the morning lord Bathurst and his son had succeeded in somewhat quieting the apprehensions, and appeasing the anguish of the earl. The servants were questioned minutely, but nothing was elicited from them, and all remained enshrouded in the same state of torturing mystery.

CHAPTER XXI.

THE PRISONER OF THE DUNGEON—THE MURDERER AND HIS VICTIM.

WE must now, in order to elucidate our narrative, shift the scene, and bring even more startling events upon the stage. In a lonely and little frequented part of the country stood a square stone building of ancient date, and there was not another human habitation near it for several miles. For what purpose it had been originally erected it was difficult to imagine, and certainly it was possessed of no architectural beauty to recommend it. A few months before it had been for sale, but it did not seem at all likely to find a purchaser, until one appeared in the person of a foreigner, apparently a Frenchman, and having come to terms with the proprietor entered, upon it immediately, and no further notice was taken of the matter, though every one agreed that whoever the individual might be he must be a person of rather singular taste. The reader will not need to be informed that this man was no other

than the villain Bonville, and that he had taken the house in order the better to enable him to carry out his infamous designs; and never was a place better adapted for deeds of darkness. Its lonely situation was every way favourable to secrecy, and Bonville thought that here he might safely put in force the nefarious schemes he contemplated without the least fear of interruption.

The house contained many dark and gloomy rooms, and underground was a range of vaults or dungeons, as they might more appropriately be called, which Bonville discovered with the most infinite satisfaction.

It is to one of those dungeons that we must now direct the attention of the reader. It was a frightful and gloomy place, and no one could possibly imagine that anything human could live in it an hour. Noisome damps hung upon the blackened walls, and the broken stone pavement was covered with the accumulated dust and filth of years. A faint light glimmered in a lamp depending from an iron chain in the roof, rendering the horrors of the place, if possible, still more fearful.

There is a heap of straw in one corner of this frightful dungeon, and something living moves upon it, while as it does so the clanking of a chain may be heard. Heavens! can it be possible that it is a human being? Can there be so great a monster in existence as to consign a fellow creature to such a horrible living tomb? There is, and that monster is Bonville the murderer.

But who is this wretched and unfortunate being? It is the form of a woman, an aged woman, with hair of silvery whiteness, features haggard and careworn, body emaciated and worn to a perfect skeleton, and scarcely covered with an old ragged garment of the most dirty and filthy appearance. Her flesh has evidently not been washed for many weeks, her hands are long and hooked like the talons of a bird of prey. She seems scarcely able to rise from her filthy heap of straw, and when she does so, can only proceed to a very short distance, for she is chained to the wall. Who is this poor unfortunate being? Doubtless the reader has already guessed, that it is her of whom they have been told so much, the much wronged and suffering Lady Elvina Elverton.

But who could recognize in that revolting and miserable figure, that scarcely human countenance, the once peerless beauty, who inspired all persons with love and admiration the moment they beheld her. Alas! what a fearful change had years of trouble and persecution wrought in her! Who but a demon in mind, could behold her without pity and commiseration? How the hapless lady had fallen into the power of Bonville will be explained anon.

She attempted to rise and with great difficulty and excruciating pain she at last succeeded, and eagerly reached a stone pitcher, which was standing near her and looked into it; but pushed it away from her again with a look of despair, and with a heavy sigh exclaimed—

"All gone, all gone! not even a sup of water left, and my poor burning throat is parched with thirst. God of Heaven, what will become of me? Bonville, Bonville, the retribution of an Almighty God will assuredly overtake thee for this. Three days he has been away, and my food and water are now exhausted. Surely, monster as he is, he cannot intend to consign me to a horrible death of starvation. And yet to what other conclusion can I come? Oh, that I were dead, then would my earthly troubles be at an end. Oh, how severely have I been punished for the errors of my youth, but still my deeply injured husband I know that you must pity and forgive me did you but know my present horrible and miserable situation.

She sunk back on her wretched pallet of straw, and groaned aloud in the anguish of her despair and suffering.

She was suddenly aroused by hearing the sound of a footfall approaching her dungeon, and she immediately started to her feet with more vigour than might have been expected in her exhausted condition, but which was only natural under the circumstances, and instantly after, the bolts of her dismal and wretched cell were withdrawn, and a fellow bringing with him some coarse food, and a pitcher of water entered.

He was a ferocious, fearful-looking man, but had he been an angel in appearance, he could not have been more welcome to the unfortunate and cruelly persecuted lady at that time. She would have put some questions to the man, but evidently anxious to evade them, he retired, before she could do so, and immediately she seized upon the pitcher, and quenched the burning thirst that was upon her.

"Thank God! thank God!" she gasped forth, "for this relief; and now let me die as soon as it is thine Almighty will. For what should I wish to live? Oh! my husband, my much wronged husband," she added after a pause, "for thee I wish to live, though I tremble to meet thee. And yet Heaven knows, I acted from the best of motives; mistaken they were, but not criminal; and that insidious fiend, Bonville, has all to answer for."

Again she threw herself on her pallet of straw, and became completely absorbed in the misery of her own reflections.

Thus with the wretched sufferer wore on two more hours, during which time she was almost inanimate, and offered not to partake of any of the food which had been brought her. Oh, the suffering of that poor victim of persecution, during that brief interval only, language could not do adequate justice to it, imagination could not sufficiently depicture it.

Night came on; night! it was all night in that wretched cell. There was no means by which even the most transient gleam of sunshine could be admitted to it. All gloom, all gloom, and sorrow, and hopelessness.

Night came, and the unfortunate prisoner was in a state of stupor, sleep, we were about to say, but sleep was not the relief that could ever come to the wretched inmate of that awful dungeon. But from this state of torpor Lady Elvina was suddenly aroused by once more hearing the bolts of the door withdrawn, and the next moment the miscreant Bonville stood before her.

She shrunk from him with a shudder of horror, but he contemplated her with a look of fiendish malice and triumph.

"So," he said at length, "you are still alive. I am glad of it; I rejoice to see you live to enjoy the pleasures of your *apartment*, and the luxuries which are so amply afforded you. Certainly they may not be quite equal to those you experienced with your husband, the favoured Elverton, but still they must be very comfortable to a lady of your delicate taste and peculiar notions in your declining days. See how joyfully the rat snorts about you, and participates in your happiness; in what happy indolence the slimy slug crawls its slow length down the damp and blackened walls. Oh, it is a splendid place, a fit abode for the fastidious and refined Countess Elverton."

"Taunting devil, hold!" exclaimed the persecuted and distracted lady, "kill me with your dagger; if you will, it would be a mercy, but torture me not with your malignant and cowardly words. Wretch, is not your bloody revenge already sufficiently gratified? Is it not enough that you have sacrificed the life of my innocent daughter; that you have separated me from the best of husbands, rendered his fond and generous heart desolate, and incarcerated me in this loathsome dungeon, but that you must now endeavour to add to my anguish by these demon observations? Oh, slay me, kill me at once, I again implore you, but do not murder me by the worst of means."

She covered her face with her hands and groaned in the anguish of her feelings, but Bonville evidently exulted in her sufferings, and laughed aloud in derision.

"Well, this is better yet, even better yet," he said. "I did not expect such a pleasant reception on my return. I bring you good news, Lady Elverton. Your son, Lord Coningsby, he whom you thought dead many years ago, has been discovered."

"Great Heaven!" exclaimed the unhappy lady, suddenly starting to her her feet, and fixing upon the villain a look of such intense anxiety that ought to have penetrated to his very soul. "You do not mock me! My Edgar! Do you speak the truth?"

"Indeed I do," replied the murderer, "and moreover your daughter's child is found, the fair Celestia, and is at present, and has been for several years, residing with her grandfather."

"God of Heaven!" cried Lady Elvina, "can this be tru?—And shall I ever be permitted to behold these beloved beings again?"

'One," cooly replied Bonville, "Celestia, I mean your granddaughter, you undoubtedly will, for before many weeks are over she will be in my power, and forced to yield that indulgence to my will which you in your youth refused."

"Monster! you dare not, will not attempt to put such a fiendish project into execution."

"Ha, ha, ha! what dare I not do? But you will see, you will see!—As for your son——"

"Oh, what of him?" gasped forth Lady Elverton.

"He is no more."

"No more! torturing fiend, for man I will not call you; just now you told me that he was discovered, that he lived!"

"True, he did, but his body is now food for worms, and I exult in the thought. Oh, it was a brave accomplishment. Ha, ha, ha?"

"Wretch! what mean you?"

"That he perished by my means; that I was his executioner!—Oh, how the wind rattled, the thunder bellowed, the rain poured, and the lighting flashed on the glorious night when I consigned him to the dark waters of the deep. Methinks I now again see his looks of agony and despair, hear his cries for help and mercy when there was none to be had. I murdered him, sweet Lady Elvina, I murdered your son; his father knows it, and I exult in the deed. Lady Elvina, you scorned my words, after, under the mask of religion, I had seduced you from your allegiance to your husband, and I swore to be revenged; I have left my promise hitherto. It was I that consigned your daughter to the guillotine; I that would have murdered De Aunville, her husband, but he escaped me to die in a foreign land;—it is I who have assassinated in his prime of manhood, that darling son whom you thought had perished in his childhood;—it is I who have you cooped up in this spacious and splendid apartment;—it is I who hold the life of your husband in my hands; and it is I who will make the beauteous Celestia the victim of my passions, and no earthly power can save her. My plans are all so well laid that I defy any power to frustrate them. Is not this revenge ?　Ha, ha, ha !—is not this revenge ?"

Lady Elvina looked at him with an expression of the most unutterable horror ; she endeavoured to make some reply, but her tongue refused its office, and she sunk back on her seat of straw, completely exhausted, and filled with the most indescribable horror and despair. The hardened villain, Bonville, continued to view her for some minutes with feelings of malignant satisfaction and triumph, and he then said,—

"Is not this cheerful intelligence, sweet Lady Elvina ?—How extremely rejoiced you must be to hear it. Oh, your pleasure will be greatly enhanced when you behold your grand-daughter, the sweet, the lovely, and innocent Celestia, and know that she is destined to become the victim of that man whose overtures you dared to reject. Is not this a triumph, sweet Lady Elvina ? Does not this indeed look like revenge ?"

"Monster !" exclaimed the unfortunate lady, "if there is a just God in Heaven, which I firmly believe there is, he will not suffer you to triumph in your iniquity. His vengeance will overtake you, and rescue the innocent from your power. Tremble miscreant, and forbear ere it is too late."

"Ha, ha, ha !" laughed Bonville, "how mighty fine and swelling are your words, respected lady Elvina, but ; I set all power, human and divine at defiance. I laugh them all to scorn. Bonville never yet has failed in anything upon which he has fixed his mind, and he will not do so now. I wish you much happiness in your present residence, and beg to inform you that I intend to increase its luxuries for you."

"Oh, for the love of Heaven kill me at once, but do not torture me thus."

"Kill you ! no, no, that would not answer my purpose just yet ; it would not half gratify my vengeance. You shall live to endure unmentionable miseries. What you are at present enduring is perfect bliss in comparison with that which is in store for you. You shall see Celestia degraded, broken-hearted ; all her hopes blasted, all her young joys crushed, annihilated ; you shall hear of the shame and ruin of all your relations ; you shall see the life blood of your husband, and still you shall live to endure

the agony of the thought. This, the monster Bonville, as you are pleased to call him, tells you, and you must know him by this time to be a man of his word."

Lady Elvina could not speak ; her soul was filled with horror, and she could only sway her body to and fro, and groan with the intense, the insupportable agony of her feelings.

"Oh, it pleases me marvellously," resumed the ruffian, "to see you suffer thus. I thought I should learn the way, in time, to subdue that proud spirit of yours, and it seems I was not mistaken. Think of your murdered son and daughter, the devoted Celestia, your brokenhearted husband, and the rest of your doomed relations, and be happy if you can. Celestia is a beauteous creature, fair young thing, so like her mother when she was about her age, and will fully compensate me for the disappointment I experienced in my designs against you. A strange change has come over you, sweet lady Elvina, you are not the same fair and peerless woman that you were when I tempted you to abandon him whom you had plighted your faith to at the altar. You are now old and shrivelled, and frightful to look upon—a very hag, sweet lady Elvina. And what a sweet pleasant residence you have got too ;—oh, how particularly grateful you ought to be to me for these happy changes."

"Heartless miscreant !" cried the distracted prisoner, "taunt me no longer, but leave me to myself ; inflict upon me the worst of tortures that your demoniacal mind can invent ; you canot punish me more than you have done already."

"Indeed ?" sneered the brutal man ; "we shall see, we shall see ; for my own part, I think I have such tortures in store for you, in comparison with which, all that I have hitherto inflicted upon you is trifling. But I will leave you to reflect upon the death of your son, the noble Edgar ! who had been so lately restored to his father's arms, and all his family honours, and to anticipate the future happiness which is destined to overtake you. Good night, sweet Lady Elvina, and may pleasant dreams attend your slumbers."

Thus saying, and fixing upon his

unhappy victim a look expressive of every diabolical feeling, Bonville withdrew from the dungeon, and closed and secured the door after him.

For some time Lady Elvina remained in a state bordering upon insensibility, whilst the agony of her mind was of that intense and excruciating description which may readily be imagined by the reader. But at length she raised herself on her knees, and with clasped hands, and eyes raised towards Heaven, looked the very image of despair, misery, and horror.

"Good God!" she cried, "can all that this villain has told me be true?—can he have been permitted to carry his atrocity to such a horrible extent? My son, whom I had thought perished by accident or by some foul means in his childhood, discovered, restored to his father's arms, but to be snatched from them again, and to be barbarously murdered by this fiend in human form. The thought is too dreadful, too revolting to be encouraged; yet why should I doubt anything that Bonville asserts? Do I not know him for a wretch capable of perpetrating any crime, however monstrous? I do; and therefore feel assured that he has done this hellish deed. Oh, what must be the dreadful sufferings that my much wronged Albert must now be enduring. He whom I so cruelly deserted; Heaven! Heaven! thou hast severely punished me for my blind infatuation and injustice. Had I solemnly adhered to those vows I plighted to him at the altar, these misfortunes, these horrors would never have taken place, but myself and all those so dear to me might now have been happy. Celestia, too, the child of my daughter, she is found and is under the protection of my husband; but this miscreant threatens her with his vengeance, and unless an All Merciful God interposes she will be unable to escape him, so subtle are the means with which Bonville concerts his nefarious plans. Oh, what would I give to be at liberty, that I might return to my husband, implore his forgiveness, clasp that beloved child to my heart, and then if the Almighty so willed it, die in peace. But no, I have so grossly offended that there is no such mercy for me. Oh, God! oh, God! try me not, sinner as I am, too severely, or I shall go mad."

She threw herself back on her wretched pallet, and sobs and moans completely choked her utterance. Happily for the wretched sufferer, unconsciousness shortly afterwards stole over her senses, in which state she remained for several hours. The night, that dreary night passed away, and the morning dawned to bring no ray of comfort to the afflicted and deeply persecuted lady's heart.

Bonville on leaving the miserable cell in which his hapless victim was confined, retired to his own apartment, and there gave himself up entirely to the malignity of his thoughts.

"What a triumph is this;" he ejaculated; "how admirably have I played my cards, and what tortures have I inflicted upon those whom I so thoroughly detest. Lord Coningsby sleeps in the silent tomb, to which he has been consigned by my hands. His father is now reduced to a state of the most abject despair; Lady Elvina is my prisoner and at my mercy, and the lovely Celestia will shortly be in my power. Nothing can prevent her being so, with such consummate ability are all my plans laid. Oh, how sweet is this revenge to my soul. Elvina, I told thee that thee and thine should pay dearly for the scorn with which thou thoughtst proper to repulse my advances, and have I not kept my word?—Ha, ha, I triumph, I triumph!—Oh, they are indeed doomed, who incur the hatred of the Jesuit Bonville. They thought me dead!—They little imagined that I was cognizant of all their actions, and only awaited the opportunity to put my designs into execution. That opportunity has at last presented itself, and I will not fail to take every advantage of it."

Thus the villain continued to exult, at the same time he matured in his mind his diabolical plans against those unfortunate individuals whom he had marked out for his victims. He had accomplished his atrocious plans against the ill-fated Lord Coningsby; he had seen his remains consigned to the tomb;—he had made Lord Elverton acquainted with the truth of his deplorable death, and he laughed aloud in the excess of his triumph. He was determined that Celestia should be his next victim, and for that purpose, he had already arranged his plans for getting her in his power, and with every prospect of success, though he did not think it prudent to attempt to put them into execution at present.

"She is a fine, a lovely, and a dainty prize," soliloquized the guilty and inhuman ruffian, "one well worth running some considerable risk to gain possession of, and she must, she shall be mine; I will suffer no earthly object to annihilate my hopes. Oh, what an additional triumph it will be when I have that beauteous girl at my mercy. How it will wring the hearts of Lords Elverton and Lady Elvina. I will not take her life; no, that would render my deadly vengeance only half complete. I will effect that which shall afford me a far greater triumph. They shall see her a poor degraded, ruined, broken hearted thing, and then will they know the extent to which the hatred and malice of Bonville can go. Lady Elvina first excited my passions, but Lord Elverton stepped in to supplant me in my wishes, and it was that which has stimulated me to all that I have done. It was that which induced me to lure her from the arms of her husband, and though I failed in accomplishing all my designs against her, her lovely granddaughter, the tender and innocent Celestia, the admired of every one, shall share a very different fate. Yes, she shall be my helpless victim; what power can rescue her from my clutches? My plans are so deeply laid that I set every attempt to defeat them at defiance. Oh what visions of delight appear to my ravished senses. It were worth an age of care and anxiety to have them realized, and realized they will, they must be, or I will perish in the attempt. She has her lover too, I know, and one whom she regards in return. Lord Malensbury, loves her to distraction; few as have been my opportunities, I have nevertheless been able to penetrate to his innermost thoughts. Poor fool!—let him love on, it will only render his despair and anguish the more severe; she shall never be his, unless he likes to take her when she is a poor degraded being, and one whom the world would look upon with scorn, in place of its former love and admiration. Ha, ha, ha!—the thought is food to my revengeful soul.

Lord Coningsby and his sister murdered by my means; Lady Elvina, the proud, the scornful Lady Elvina, my abject prisoner, and Celestia my victim, what triumph can surpass that?"

He paused, and a dark thought seemed suddenly to cross his mind, which threw a transient blight upon his hopes.

"But if all is true that I have heard," he said, "and I have no reason to doubt the authority from which I received the information, Mabel Handerson, the former servant and confidant of Lady Elvina is still living. I must find her out, if possible, and secure her. She bears me no good will; she has no reason to do so, for I effected her ruin, and should she by any means become acquainted with my designs, she will try to frustrate them. The witch, if I had acted wisely, and as the thought first suggested itself to me, she would have been rotting in the grave long ago. But it may not yet be too late; and why should I fear her? She is but a woman, and I should despise myself as a very fool if I suffered one of her sex to frustrate my deep laid plans, which all the ingenuity of man has hitherto been unable to do. I am told that she assumes the disguise of a gipsey sybil, and that she has had some communication with Celestia, and some of the other members of her family. I must ascertain the truth of this, and if I do not speedily stop her in her career, my name is not Bonville. I will set my trusty emissaries to work, and I have no doubt that they will meet with their usual success."

Thus the villain argued with himself, and chuckled in the sanguine anticipation of the success of his nefarious schemes. Fortune had so far favoured him in all that he had undertook, that he could not for a moment contemplate a defeat, and he looked forward to the accomplishment of all his wishes with a perfect certainty. Unfortunately these hopes were doomed, too fatally, in a great measure, to be realized. Ill-fated Lord Elverton, hapless Celestia, what bitter troubles were in store for you

CHAPTER XXII.

THE RETURN TO SUNGROVE ABBEY.—
THE OLD PRIORY RUINS.—BONVILLE
AND CELESTIA.—THE ALARM.—THE
THREAT.

SEVERAL weeks had now elapsed since the untimely death of the lamented Lord Coningsby, and all endeavours to detect his inhuman assassin, or to discover the gipsy sybil had been ineffectual, and they all began to despair of any light being ever thrown on the painful mystery.

Lord Elverton by dint of great personal exertion and the advice of his friends, had become more tranquil and

resigned to his fate, but a deep melancholy settled upon his heart, which it was feared nothing would be able to eradicate.

At length hoping that change of scene might tend to ameliorate his grief, Lord Elverton by the advice of his friends, resolved to quit the castle and to return to Sungrove Abbey, and Lord Bathurst his son, and Lord Everside agreed to accompany him, they being anxious to be in his society as much as possible, in order that they might render all the aid in their power to recuit his depressed spirts. Sir Roderick Ainslie had quitted the castle a few days previously, to fulfil his promise of endeavouring to find the long lost Lady Elvina, though, after the letter which had been received from the villain, Bonville, they feared it would be with little chance of success.

The day before he quitted the castle, Lord Elverton visited the tomb of his unfortunate son, accompanied by Lady Eugenia and our heroine, and many were the tears they shed to his memory, and many and fervent were the prayers they offered up to the Almighty for repose to his soul. It was with difficulty that Lord Elverton could be persuaded to leave the sad spot, and when he returned home, he immediately retired to his chamber, and remained there secluded during the rest of the day.

Nothing worthy of particular notice occurred on the journey, and in due course they arrived at Sungrove Abbey, which had been properly prepared for their reception. Several more weeks elapsed, and the earl improved in health and spirits; and his friends began to hope that he would in time be restored to some degree of happiness. Alas! it was a hope that was not fated to be realised.

He had received two or three communications from Sir Roderick, in which he informed him that he had hitherto been unsuccessful in all his efforts to discover the retreat of Lady Elvina, and that, of course, tended to renew his melancholy and anguish, and he began to fear that she was, indeed, in the power of Bonville, and if so her fate was certain. Many were the hours of agony he endured on this sad subject, and his friends were completely at a loss how to offer him any consolation, for their apprehensions were equally as great as his own, and unfortunately there seemed to be but too much reason for them.

"I shall never behold her again," he would say; "she is lost to me for ever, and how can I look forward to anything but the greatest misery? Unfortunate Elvina, should you be in the power of that inhuman wretch, Bonville, how dreadful must be the sufferings you are enduring. Perhaps, like my illfated Edgar, you have already met with a violent and untimely death at the monster's hands. Oh, God! how terrible and insupportable is this suspense; have mercy upon me, I humbly but devoutly beseech thee, for this is more than I can bear."

What answer could his friends return to these melancholy observations? Could they deny their truth?—It was impossible, and they were compelled to leave it to time and patience to abate the violence of his grief.

One thing, however, that somewhat calmed their fears was the circumstance of their not receiving any further annoyance from Bonville, and they began to hope that he had either abandoned his brutal designs, or that something serious had happened to him, which would rid them of so dangerous and implacable an enemy. Lord Elverton, however, could not participate in those hopes, and he could not divest his mind of the impression that Bonville was only remaining quiet for a time in order to mature his plans, and make them tell with a more thrilling and certain effect. He remembered every word contained in the two letters he had received from him, and he had too much reason to apprehend that Bonville was not the man to abandon any designs he had formed, and goaded on as he was by a deadly feeling of revenge, he would not fail to take the earliest and most fitting opportunity of putting his diabolical threats into execution.

These reasonable fears kept the afflicted earl in a continual state of uneasiness, from which all the efforts of his friends failed to arouse him.

The passion of Lord Malensbury for the lovely Celestia daily increased in strength, and he was sad and miserable when not in her society. Ever hour he discovered in her some fresh charm, something more to admire and esteem, and he felt convinced that if it were not his fate to possess her, he could never be happy with any other woman.

And if such were the sentiments of Lord Malensbury, the heart of our heroine fervently responded to them. She saw in him every amiable quality, the noblest conception she could form of man, and therefore was it wonderful that her young and beautifully susceptible heart—that heart so alive to every generous and virtuous feeling—should love him, should become his entirely?

The deep solicitude and sympathy he had also manifested in the misfortunes which had attended her unfortunate family, greatly enhanced the powerfully favourable impression he had made upon her uncle, and therefore it was not to be wondered at that when he ventured, in the most delicate, but at the same time, the most eloquent terms to whisper the sentiments of his heart and in time to become "a thrifty wooer," she modesty but candidly acknowledged that her sentiments were perfectly reciprocal with his own.

What bliss was this to the worthy and estimable young nobleman. He had in that awowal gained the very summit of his wishes, his brightest hopes.

After the mutual confessions that had taken place between them, they felt less restraint and diffidence in each other's society; in fact, they were seldom apart but when circumstances that must be necessarily attended to prevented them. Together they should ramble amid the most beautiful scenery which surrounded that noble and gothic edifice, Sungrove Abbey, imbibing fresh pleasures and virtues at the luxuriant fount of nature's gifts, and in these blissful rambles the beauties of each other's mind became more distinctly revealed to them.

Lord Elverton and Lord Bathurst beheld the affection that existed between them with the greatest satisfaction; they were convinced that nature had never formed two individuals who were more worthy of coming together and of rendering each other happy, and consequently when Lord Malensbury acknowledged his passion to them, and Celestia admitted that her sentiments were in unison with his own, they readily, and with the greatest feelings of hope and pleasure, gave there consent to their paying their addresses to each other, although their nuptials were providently deferred to some future period, and when happily the dismal clouds which now obscured the horizon of their complete bliss might be dispersed, and the storms of misfortune that had hitherto beset them might have subsided into calm and peace.

The lovers were happy, how could they be otherwise in the security of their love? But sad were their hearts when they reflected upon the dreadful fate of the noble-minded Lord Coningsby, the unmerited affliction of the earl, his father, and the uncertainty of the fate which had befallen Lady Elvina?

There appeared to be too much reason to apprehend that she was in the power of the inhuman wretch, Bonville, and if such was indeed the case, their very worst fears were too likely to be realized.

There was one individual to whom the evident affection which existed between Lord Malensbury and our heroine, and the satisfaction with which it was viewed by their parents and other relations, imparted the greatest mortification, disappointment, and anguish. That individual, need the reader be informed, was Collingwood Aubrey. During the absence of Celestia he had been unable to obtain the least tranquillity of mind, and had turned a deaf ear to all the remonstrances of his relations. But now that it was discovered that she was the granddaughter of Lord Elverton, and more than equal to him in birth and other pretensions, and consequently all the prejudices and objections of his mother on the score of family pedigree were done away with, and to behold her and Lord Malensbury as acknowledged lovers, and sanctioned by their friends as such, betrothed to each other, it was more than his patience could endure. His worst passions were excited, and he viewed the young lord with the jaundiced eyes of jealousy, while in addition his coolness and almost repugnance to the fair and amiable Lady Eglantine increased. To deny the transcendent qualities of her mind, the captivating character of her charms, the extreme fascination of her manners, would have been impossible; and more, he was compelled to admit that if he had never beheld our beauteous heroine, there was no other woman he might see whom he could love and admire like the Lady Eglantine. And precisely the same were the sentiments which Lady Eglantine entertained towards Collingwood, and therefore the greater was her mortification at the indifference with which he treated her. She affected to resent it; she had left him on a former occasion without a pang, as we have before stated, but notwithstanding that, love, in spite of herself, had taken deep root in her heart, and now that she beheld him again, the passion was renewed with tenfold and irresistible power.

But did the lovely damsel experience one jealous feeling towards her beloved friend and companion, Celestia, because she had innocently supplanted her in the affections of Collingwood ? No, her generous mind would not permit her to do that, and she only looked forward with hope to the happy moment when he might be able to conquer his passion for Celestia, and respond to the feelings which animated her own bosom.

Thus stood matters on the return of the friends to Sungrove Abbey, and they experienced very little change for some time afterwards. The family of the Aubreys, of course, frequently visited them, but Collingwood excused himself as often as he could, for he could not bear to contemplate the increasing passion of Lord Malensbury and Celestia, and he had no wish, at the same time, to betray his real feelings to either of them. His respect and esteem for Lord Malensbury were equal to his love and admiration for Celestia ; he could not but duly appreciate the noble qualities of his mind, and to feel the disadvantage under which he laboured if he attempted to institute a comparison between himself and him ; but at the same time he was most anxious to maintain his friendship and his good opinion, and would have been the first to have resented as it deserved to be any imputation that might have been attempted to be cast upon his character.

The reader may be certain that Celestia did not forget or neglect her favourite haunt, the old priory ruins, and the good old Hannibal and his wife, but she paid almost daily visits to them, in which she was sometimes accompanied by Lord Elverton and Lady Eugenia, and almost always by Lord Malensbury.

The season of the year was now most lovely, and the ancient ruins exhibited all their romantic beauty. It was truly refreshing and delightful to ramble amongst them, and to contemplate the varied expanse of picturesque scenery which was commanded from them. One day, however, business of a pressing nature had called her lover from the abbey, and Lord Elverton and his sister were also engaged in other matters, so that they could not attend, and, as they apprehended no danger, and they wished not to deprive her of her favourite enjoyment, they permitted her to wander there alone.

The afternoon was particularly fine ; the air was beautifully serene, the sun shed forth his most congenial rays ; the verdure and the foliage of the trees were clad in their richest mantle of green ; never was there a more light, clear, and cheerful sky ; all nature was sparkling, and bounding, and smiling with peace and pleasure, everything was fresh and buoyant, and how could Celestia be otherwise than happy and enjoy her walk ?—In fact, it was some time since she had felt so elate of heart; bright hope dawned upon her mind, and her soul rose in gratitude to Heaven.

She lingered on her way, for everything was so lovely and cheerful around her, that she hesitated to leave it. On her way to the ruins, she had occasion to pass a large lane overarched on either side by tall and noble trees, and she had reached about the centre of it when her footsteps were arrested by the voice of a female singing in the most impressive and plaintive tones.

The voice of the singer was perfectly familiar to her; she was convinced that she had frequently heard it before, and she gazed anxiously towards the spot from whence the sounds issued, with the hope of seeing the singer, but no person met her gaze. She was afraid to approach the spot more closely to scrutinize the singer, but she paused and listened with the most breathless attention, and was immediately convinced that her conjectures were quite correct.

Yes ; it was the gipsy sybil who had so frequently crossed her path, and at that moment she changed her song to the well know ballad, the warning ballad, with which she had on more than one occasion saluted the ears of our heroine :

‘ Damsel, turn thee not away,
    Nor think the words I speak are wrong;
Mark me, there will come a day,
    When thou'lt remember well my song.

Though pleasure now shines on thy path,
    Will it last for ever—no !
All the bliss thou at present hath,
    Shall be changed to bitter woe.

See—the clouds are gathering fast,
  Hark—the voice of destiny cries,
‘ Girl, thy joys will soon be past,
  Thy laugh of mir h be turned to sighs.’

Then, damsel, mark well what I say,
  Though thou smilest now in glee,
Not far distant is the day
  When none shall be more sad than thee.”

After a brief pause, during which interval our heroine remained transfixed to the spot on which she was standing in amazement and confusion, the sybil added in the same melancholy, plaintive, and impressive tones, which thrilled with the most powerful and irresistible effect to the maiden’s heart.

“ They’ve burst, they’ve burst, the storm’s began’
  Villany deep, dark laid schemes
Awhile will scorn the power of man,
  And prove my words are not mere dreams.

The fiend’s at work—the train is laid,
  Blood and murder rule the hour,
Alas! poor ill-starred guiltless maid,
  May Heaven shield thee from their power.

He comes in triumph, see the wretch
  Stalks to seize his destined prey;
God ! Thy mighty arm outstretch,
  And terminate the monster’s day !”

More astonished and appalled than ever, our heroine stood, and was unable to move an inch from the spot, notwithstanding her anxiety to see and converse with the mysterious woman who had so excited her feelings; but she was not long kept in suspense, for there was a slight rustling among the foliage from whence the sounds had proceeded, and the sybil stood before her.

She gazed upon Celestia with a mingled expression of pity and sorrow, and then advancing slowly towards her, she said :—

“Did’st hear me, maiden ? Did’st hear my words ? Scorn them not; treat them not with indifference, as the mere emanations of a disordered brain; for, alas ! I see too clearly that they will be fulfilled Already have my promises come true. Heaven defend thee, for it alone can, against the evils which threaten thee, and those so dear to thee.”

“ Mysterious woman,” ejaculated Celestia, in reply, “you profess yourself to be my friend, and that of my beloved but unfortunate relations, and your words should induce me to believe that you really are so. Why, then, not reveal to me who you really are ; what are the dangers we have to apprehend ; and how we may best avoid them, and defeat the plans of our bitter and implacable enemy, whom we now too well know ? Oh, why will you not seek the presence of Lord Elverton, and candidly disclose to him all you know ?”

“ I dare not do so for the present, maiden,” answered the sybil, “ for it might cost me my own life, and thwart all my plans. But rest assured that my constant study is to serve you, and to avert the dangers with which you are surrounded. Oh, Celestia, I have reason to hate your inhuman persecutor, but at present I have not the power to revenge myself upon him ; though the time will come—yes, it must come. In the mean time, I caution you that he has followed your footseps from the castle ; that there in not a single movement of you or any of your family that he is unacquainted with ; and that he is, moreover, at the present moment lurking in this very neighbourhood, ready to pounce, at the first opportunity, upon his next unfortunate and innocent victim—yourself, beauteous Celestia.”

“Oh, gracious Heaven,” ejaculated the terrified damsel, “ can this be true ?”

“ It is,” replied the woman, “ unfortunately too true ; I never speak that which is false.”

“ But where, where is the cruel man concealed ?”

“ I know not, or I would immediately apprize you, but, believe me, I will exert myself to the utmost to defeat the monster, and to save you from his power. Maiden, let me not call the blush of shame upon thy cheek, while I inform thee, that the wretched being who now tands before thee, fell the victim to his diabolical arts, and that he seeks thee for the same base purpose.”

“ Good God !” gasped forth Celestia, with a look of horror and disgust, “ can he indeed be so heartless a miscreant ? Can he—but surely Heaven will not permit him to triumph in his monstrous designs ?”

“ I trust not, Celestia, but, at present, the best fortune seems to attend his infernal projects. Beware, beware girl, for what I utter is not erroneous, and if thou and thy friends are not on your guard, you may too soon fall into his snares."

"But who are you, my good woman?" eagerly demanded our heroine, "surely you can have no objection to inform me that."

"No, no," answered the sybil, after a pause, "I can—I have no objection to that, and you may also inform Lord Elverton and your other friends. The earl will well remember the name of the ill-starred creature now before you, and will, perhaps, then place more confidence in what I utter, and in my professions of friendship. Tell him that the gipsy sybil is no other than Mabel Henderson, the once favourite and confidential attendant of his misled and persecuted wife, Lady Elvina."

"Is it possible?" said Celestia, looking at her with increased astonishment and interest.

"It is true," replied Mabel, i melancholy tones, and then she added with a deep sigh, "but, alas! how changed from the happy Mabel Henderson she once used to be. Oh, maiden, look upon this wreck of what was once almost as fair and lovely, and certainly as pure and innocent as yourself, and then imagine what I must have suffered. But let me not dwell upon my own sorrows, for regret cannot remove them or better my condition, for I must begone. Remember well my words, I solemnly enjoin you, and be upon your guard, so that you may be able to counteract the diabolical designs of your implacable and heartless enemy. Farewell, farewell, till we meet again."

"But will you not tell me where you may be found, that we may see you, in case we should require your advice and services?"

"I have before told you, Celestia, that it would not be safe for me to do so at present. But mark me, I will communicate immediately with you and your friends should anything more come to my knowledge which may threaten you with danger."

"Oh, thanks, thanks; but you have mentioned Lady Elvina, and by the respect which you say you bear towards that unfortunate lady, I implore you to inform me whether you know where she at present is?"

"Alas, I do not," answered Mabel, "but of one thing I am certain, namely, that she is in the power of the villain, Bonville, but where he has concealed her I am ignorant of."

"Alas, alas!" sighed our heroine, "is my unfortunate relative indeed in that monster's power? But how know you this?"

"I know it too well," returned Mabel, "but it would not be prudent in me to reveal to you the means by which it has come to my knowledge. Be certain that I will exert myself to the utmost to find out the place of the unhappy and deeply injured lady's confinement, and should I find it out, I will immediately communicate it to Lord Elverton, in order that the plans of the wretch Bonville may be defeated, and she may again, after the lapse of so many years of suffering, be restored to her husband's arms. Farewell, Celestia, and may Heaven watch over and protect you from the evils which now threaten you. We shall meet again; we shall meet again, and in the meantime you will remember Mabel Henderson, and believe that she is your friend, and of all connected with you."

Celestia would have made some reply, but she could not find words to give utterance to the strange and torturing thoughts which crowded so rapidly upon her mind, and while she was still hesitating, wrapped in amazement and anxiety, Mabel waved her hand to her, and hurrying from the spot, abruptly turned an angle in the lane, and was immediately hidden from her view.

"Good God!" at length Celestia ejaculated, "what have I heard? Can it all be true? Is it the intention of the wretch Bonville to carry his inhuman designs to such a monstrous extent? But why should I longer doubt Mabel Henderson, as she calls herself, since what she has hitherto stated has already been so fatally realized? Oh, Heaven protect me and my beloved relations from his deadly malice and revenge! Lady Elvina, too, it is true then that she is in the villain's power. Oh, what will be the agony of her already broken-hearted husband, when he comes to hear of it? Monster, monster! can nothing stay you in your hideous course?"

She wrung her hands, and could not restrain her tears, as these torturing reflections came upon her. At first she was half resolved to return to the abbey, and immediately inform the earl and her other friends of all that Mabel had said, but she could not entrust herself to do so in the present state of her mind, and with the hope of being able to collect herself, she proceeded on her way, and in a short time arrived at the ruins.

Old Hannibal and his wife met her with their usual welcome, and she walked into the lodge, in order to refresh herself, and collect her thoughts.

"But dear me, Miss Celestia, Lady Celestia, I mean," said the good old woman, "how very pale and agitated you do look this afternoon. I hope that nothing serious has happened?"

"No, no," replied Celestia, anxious to evade the question, for, of course, she considered that it would not be prudent to make her honest and humble friends acquainted with the adventure she had met with. "I am a little fatigued with walking, that is all."

"And how is my noble master, the earl, Lady Celestia, to-day?" interrogated Hannibal.

"He is better, good Hannibal," replied our heroine.

"Oh, thank Heaven for that!" said the old man, fervently; "may he continue to mend, and to bear up with fortitude against the heavy and dreadful calamities with which he has been so severely afflicted. Ah, my sweet young lady, I can assure you that no person could more deeply commiserate with his lordship than myself and my poor old dame have done, and still do; but I hope that brighter and happier days are in store for him and you all, and that you will be able to look back upon the dismal past with calmness and resignation."

Celestia thanked him in her blandest and most gracious manner, and endeavoured to change the topic of conversation, which created many sad and dismal thoughts in her breast, but with little or no success.

"Ah, Lady Celestia," observed Dorothy, "it is a sad thing to reflect upon the terrible misfortunes with which it has pleased the Almighty to visit your noble family. To think that Lord Coningsby should meet with so dreadful and untimely a death, so soon after his re-

storation to his noble parent. Oh, surely a just but severe retribution will, before long, overtake his barbarous and unnatural murderer. And Lady Elvina, too, to think that the place of her retreat should still remain undiscovered. Alas! I begin to fear that she is no longer living."

"But I know sufficient," returned our heroine, with a sigh, "to be convinced that she is, but that her situation is the most delorable and dangerous."

"Dear me, Lady Celestia," observed the old man, "how it grieves me to hear you say so. May Heaven in its mercy watch over her safety, and frustrate the designs of your bitter enemies."

"Again I thank you fervently for your kind wishes, my good Hannibal," returned Celestia, "for I know they are sincere; but let us change the subject, I beg of you, for I know that I need not tell you, that it is one that I cannot converse upon without the deepest anguish."

"Oh, Heaven forbid, my lady," remarked the old man, "that we should say any thing that may wound your feelings for a moment. I am afraid we have been too bold; but indeed, Lady Celestia, we meant no harm."

"I know you did not, my kind friends," said our heroine, with a faint smile.

"And I am sure it is very good and condescending of your ladyship to honour us with your visits, and so we always say when we are conversing to ourselves. But will not your ladyship partake of some refreshment? Our fare is humble to be sure and not such as your ladyship is in the habit of partaking of, but it is clean and wholesome, nevertheless. Now do, my lady, do us the honour."

Celestia earnestly returned her acknowledgments for the consideration and attention of the old people, but her mind was in too great a state of agitation to permit her to eat, and she therefore begged to decline.

"I will walk into the ruins for awhile," she observed, "for you know, my good friends, how greatly I am attached to them, and I wish to pass a short time in the contemplation of them."

Hannibal and his wife bowed, and

Celestia left the lodge, and entered the old Priory ruins. She took her seat upon a chair which the old people always provided for her accommodation, and gave herself up entirely to the busy thoughts which crowded upon her mind, the principal subject of which was the adventure she had so recently met with, and the remarkable and important observations which Mabel Henderson had addressed too her. Nothing could banish the impression they had made upon her, and every word was stamped upon her memory in the most vivid and indelible characters.

At the bare thought of the miscreant Bonville, and the atrocities of which he had been guilty, she shuddered with horror, and when she reflected upon what Mabel had said respecting his future diabolical designs, her fears increased. There seemed to be no means of guarding themselves against the effects of his furious malice, or frustrating his designs, so craftily were they laid, and with such secrecy and consummate skill did he put them into execution; and if he was, as Mabel stated, at present lurking in the neighbourhood, and only waiting a fitting opportunity, they had good reason to apprehend the worst. How shocked she was when she recollected that the sybil had told her that he had resolved that she should be his next victim, and how fervently she prayed to Heaven to avert a fate which would be ten times more dreadful, if it was what Mabel had hinted at, than the most horrible and agonizing death. To be convinced too that the unfortunate Lady Elvina was really in the villain's power was a source of the greatest anguish to her. How terrible would be the sufferings that he would delight to inflict upon her, and what little hope there was that Lord Elverton would ever behold her again. She trembled at the idea of making him acquainted with the fatal and torturing truth, for she knew full well that it would plunge him into the deepest misery and despair; yet it was absolutely necessary that she should do so without the least delay in order that he might be upon his guard, to thwart the designs of his awful and implacable enemy. Still she endeavoured to hope that Mabel would be able to render them that assistance which she seemed so ready to grant, and that in spite of his present success the brutal murderer Bonville would not be permitted completely to triumph. She placed too much reliance on the goodness of the Almighty to believe that he would, and with that hope she sought in some measure to compose her feelings and to banish her fears.

These thoughts completely absorbed her whole mind, and diverted her attention from all around her, so that she at last became unconscious of where she was. Hannibal and his wife always left her to herself upon the occasion of her visits to the ruins, therefore she had no reason to fear any interruption to her painful meditations, and never did she feel less disposed to be intruded upon.

She was not half satisfied with the answer which Mabel had given to her eager questions; she could see no reason for her secrecy as regarded the place where she resided, but no doubt she had one, and of course they could do no other than submit to it. The revelation of her name, and the assertion that she had been the favourite and confidential attendant of Lady Elvina, inspired her with more confidence, and she was fain to hope that something favourable would result from that circumstance.

Tired of thinking, and she having been longer absent from the castle than she had at first intended, she at last arose from her seat with the design of retiring from the ruins, when she was suddenly startled and alarmed by hearing her name repeated in the unknown voice of a man behind her, and the next instant her arm was roughly grasped by some individual who seemed determined to detain her. She turned round and beheld the same form which had alarmed them all so much at the funeral of the lamented Lord Coningsby, the red mask, but at this time his features were fully revealed, and from the description Celestia had had of him, the miscreant, the murderer Bonville stood confessed before her.

Yes, it was Bonville; there he stood in all his fiendish malignity, and gazed with eyes of triumph upon the poor trembling maiden in his grasp, and who uttered an exclamation of terror, but he immediately produced a poignard from beneath his cloak, and pointing it at her breast, exclaimed :—

"Girl! hold!—You see that your life is in my hands, at my mercy, dare to raise a cry once more, even beyond a whisper, and this reaches your heart."

"Oh, sir," gasped forth our heroine, "what is your purpose with a poor, inoffensive girl, who cannot by any possible means have given you cause of hatred or vengeance?"

"But you have," replied the ruffian, "you have; because you are one of the scions of that family whom I detest, and am determined to exterminate. Look at me, girl, and know me for the Jesuit

Bonville, the murderer of your mother and uncle, your future master, he to whose passions you must become the slave. But not now; not now; no, I could in a moment bring such force to bear as would place you at once in my power and at my mercy, but it does not answer my purpose! I leave you to in- form your noble relative that you have seen me, and that I defy all his endea- vours to thwart my well-laid schemes. Tell him from me that his much loved and deeply regretted Elvina is in my power, that she lingers in a most miser- able dungeon, where the slimy slug, the loathsome toad, and the venemous rat, are her only companions. Tell him that her once fine form is wasted, emaciated that that face he used so much to admire for its gentle and irresistible beauty, is now frightful to look upon; that it bears all the hideous aspect of the veriest hag. That those bright and expressive eyes that shot the lightning of their intellect into every soul, are wild, blood-shot, and glaring with suffering and despair, tell him that she is dying by the most lingering and torturing process; that I daily, hourly, witness and exult over her sufferings; that he will never behold her again; and that when the breath shall have departed from her body, that body will be left to rot and be devoured by the vermin in the dungeon where it is my triumph to have her confined, and which I defy him and all his emissaries to discover. Nay, shriek not, girl, for it is useless; all that you might call to your assistance must fall victims to my vengeance, and I would bear you off in triumph before their eyes. Tell him that you, his darling grandchild, are destined to supply the place which now his beloved Elvina is too old and ugly to fill. Tell him this, and rest assured that as certain as you now respire, what I have threatened will be performed to the very letter."

"Monster!" ejaculated the maiden, but she could say no more, wound up to a pitch of the most indescribable horror at this inhuman speech, she fixed one look upon the wretch who had given utterance to it, and then sunk down upon the earth in a state of insensibility.

Bonville suffered her to fall from his grasp, and then stood and contemplated her with feelings of the most demoniacal exultation.

"Thou art a beauteous, a delicate being," he said, as he gazed; "it would seem as though it were a most hideous crime to attempt to taint thee; and so it is; but such is my determination; I have the power, and I defy Heaven or earth to defeat my plans. Oh, how I glory in that thought!—Beauteous, all captivating Celestia, what a rich prize art thou, and what a recompense thou wilt be for the scorn I have endured from your relatives. Ha! ha! ha! I never felt my triumph more complete than at the present moment. What a luxuriant form is there; what a heavenly mould;

—what transcendent beauty of countenance!—And all this is mine! Yes mine!—I could seize it this moment, and convey it to where it could never be discovered, but it does not answer my purpose. No; let it remain a little longer at liberty, that it may feed on the torture of anticipation. Oh, Elvina, what agony will it be for thee when thou beholdest the daughter of that loved child whom I was the means of placing beneath the knife of the guillotine, in my power, and to know that she is my destined victim. Ha! ha!—It is a triumph;—but I must let you live long enough to witness it."

The hardened miscreant stooped down as he thus spoke, and polluted the fair cheeks of the unconscious Celestia with a kiss, and once more exulting in the contemplation of her charms, he retired from the ruins by the way he had entered.

He had not long done so, when old Hannibal and his wife, who had felt somewhat surprised at the prolonged stay of our heroine in the ruins, arrived at the spot which he had just quitted, and their surprise at beholding the situation of Celestia may be readily imagined. They at first thought her dead, and uttered an exclamation of horror, but stooping down, and finding that she breathed, they felt themselves relieved, and raising her from the earth they conveyed her into the lodge.

Here they applied themselves with all their energies to her restoration, but it was some time ere they succeeded, or she showed the least signs of returning life; but at length she so far recovered as to open her eyes, and to stare wildly about her, evidently unconscious as to where she was.

"My dear young lady," said poor old Dorothy, "do you not know us?—you are in the Priory lodge; for goodness sake what has happened, what has alarmed you thus?"

Celestia looked vacantly around her for a few seconds, and then said in a voice of horror, "Where is he?"

"He, my lady," replied Hannibal, "whom do you mean?"

"The wretch, the inhuman monster, who has been the cause of all the misfortunes which have attended my unfortunate family," replied our heroine.

"Goodness me!" ejaculated Dorothy, "what does your ladyship mean?"

"That the miscreant Bonville appeared to me in the ruins," answered Celestia, "held out the most diabolical threats, and that was the cause of your finding me in the situation you did."

"Can it be possible?" ejaculated Hannibal and his wife in a breath.

"Alas!" sighed our heroine, "it is too true. Oh, my good friends, can you wonder at my emotion after the horrors which have already been effected by that dreadful and barbarous man, and the threats which he still holds out to me and my unfortunate relations?—"But did you not see him?"

Both the old people replied in the negative, and they endeavoured, as much as lay in their power, to tranquillize the feelings of the poor girl.

And not a little terrified were the honest old couple themselves. To think how near they had such a dangerous enemy as the much talked of desperate ruffian Bonville was much more alarming than the visitations of the late old man of the ruins had been, and they could not disguise their apprehensions upon the subject from our heroine.

"Oh, Lady Celestia," observed Dorothy, "much as I respect your noble family and love these old ruins, still it is a fearful place to live in. These are awful times, very awful times, my dear young lady, when bad men like this Bonville can carry on their evil practices with impunity. God help us!—who are safe?—and although, of course, we have lived long enough, me and my poor old man may be murdered some of these nights. Dear, dear, it makes my very blood run cold to think of it."

"Heaven forbid that such a circumstance should take place, my good dame," said Celestia; "but indeed I believe that there is no occasion for any such apprehensions. The hatred and revenge of this demon in human form cannot be directed against you."

"Very true, miss," coincided Hannibal, "I do not see how it can or should; but what, may I inquire, are the particulars of this alarm you have received."

Celestia informed them of all that had taken place, as briefly and as mildly as the agitation of her feelings would permit her to do, and the old people listened to her with the deepest interest, astonishment, and attention.

"Good God!" exclaimed Hannibal, "what a horrible miscreant is this; mayest thou frustrate his fiendish designs. I cannot wonder, my dear young lady, at the alarm and emotion you evince after such an unexpected and fearful encounter, but I still trust that the abominable wretch will be detected and brought to that punishment which the atrocious crimes he has already perpetrated so justly entitle him to."

"God grant that your wishes may be fulfilled, my good friends," said our heroine, who had now, by dint of great exertion, partly recovered her composure; "but I have been long away from home, and my beloved friends will become alarmed. I must be gone."

"Very good, miss," said Hannibal, "I will, with your permission, conduct you to the abbey, but do you feel yourself competent for the task after the fright you have so recently received?"

"Oh, yes," replied our heroine, "it is all over now; all that I fear is the shock and the terror the intelligence I have to communicate will have upon my noble relations."

She had scarcely given utterance to the words when a carriage drove up to the gates of the lodge, from which alighted Lord Malensbury and his father, and who on entering the house and beholding Celestia, felt greatly relieved from the burthen of anxiety and alarm which had before pressed upon their minds; but the paleness and agitation of her looks once more aroused their fears, and they eagerly inquired what had happened.

"Something of the most alarming description," she answered; "but I will tell you all as we proceed to the abbey. Did you see any one of a suspicious demeanour as you came hither?'

Lord Bathurst and his son replied in the negative, and then again requested to be informed what had taken place to alarm and agitate her so seriously.

"I have seen him," she replied, "he has confronted me in the ruins, and held out his terrible threats. Oh, my dear grandpapa, how will you receive the news? How will you be able to sustain with becoming fortitude the fresh calamities which I feel convinced are in store for you?"

"For Heaven's sake, my dear Celestia," ejaculated Lord Malensbury, "keep us not in suspense; explain yourself. Him!—Whom do you, can you mean?"

"The assassin Bonville."

"Bonville!" repeated Lord Bathurst and his son in a breath.

"Yes," replied our heroine; "it is he who has created these fears in my bosom; but a short time since he suddenly appeared before me in the ruins, and held out the most horrible threats as to his future intentions. But let us be gone; I will tell you all as we proceed to the abbey."

Lord Malensbury and his father, naturally deeply excited, complied with her request, and she having bid adieu to honest old Hannibal and his wife, they handed her into the vehicle and drove away from the lodge towards Sungrove Abbey.

On the way, Celestia having somewhat composed her feelings, related to them all those extraordinary and alarming particulars with which the reader has already been made acquainted, and it may well be conjectured with what astonishment and mingled feelings of alarm and disgust they listened to it.

"The brutal villain," exclaimed Lord Malensbury, "he must, he shall, be detected and brought to justice. Heaven surely will aid us in our praiseworthy designs; it will not suffer a blood-stained monster to triumph altogether."

"It will not, depend upon it," remarked Lord Bathurst, "and we ought to feel grateful that our sweet Celestia has escaped from him this time."

"We ought, indeed," coincided Lord Malensbury, "but still the threats he has so daringly thrown out must not be lost sight of."

"They must not," said the earl, "but should all that he has stated be true we have much to dread. That he was the murderer, the bloody murderer of Lord Coningsby and his ill-fated sister, we cannot entertain the slightest doubt, and we therefore know the extent to which he will suffer his villany to go if he is not stopped in his career of crime. How to do so is the first thing to which we

must direct all our utmost energies, acting with coolness, promptitude, and precaution, and I trust to Heaven that we may then be successful. How to break this melancholy and dreadful intelligence to Lord Elverton I scarcely know. Should Lady Elvina be really in his power, we have much to dread."

"We have," sighed Celestia, "and that she is so I cannot doubt; I have heard it from another source this day, on which I firmly believe we may depend."

"Ah!" ejaculated Lord Malensbury, eagerly, and with evident alarm depicted in his looks, "to whom do you allude, Celestia?"

"To the gipsy sybil," replied our heroine. "I encountered her on my way to the ruins, and she informed me that Bonville was lurking in the neighbourhood; that he had followed our footsteps from the castle, and that at the present moment he held the hapless Lady Elvina in his power, but she was unacquainted with the place of her confinement."

"And think you, seriously, my dear Celestia," inquired Lord Bathurst, "that that mysterious woman may be depended upon?"

"I do, my lord."

"May she not be a colleague of Bonville's?" suggested Lord Malensbury.

"Oh, no," answered our heroine, "I am convinced she is not, from circumstances she stated to me to-day."

"And what where they?"

Celestia informed them, and their astonishment and bewilderment increased.

"But why," said Lord Malensbury, "if she is really the individual she represents herself to be, and she can substantiate what she has stated, does she not come forward and prove to demonstration the correctness of her assertions? Tell us where she may be found if her presence should be required, and thus remove at once all doubts upon the subject?"

"Those are questions," returned Celestia, "of course I am unable to answer, but that she is the bitter enemy of Bonville, I have not the slightest reason to doubt."

By this time they had arrived at the abbey, and Celestia having been excused, and retired to the apartment in which Lady Eugenia was sitting, Lord

Bathurst and his son sought the presence of the earl, and imparted to him the melancholy and startling intelligence as mildly as they could. The reader may imagine with what emotion he listened to it, and when they had concluded, he traversed the apartment for a few moments in a state of the greatest anguish and anxiety of mind.

"The fiend!" he cried, "when will he allow his deadly malice to be satisfied?—Oh, a just God cannot, will not allow him to triumph in all his infernal designs. Already has he been permitted to proceed to too terrible lengths. My poor children murdered by his accursed hands, and my Elvina in his power! —God! God! this is more than human fortitude can patiently endure."

They endeavoured to tranquillise his feelings, and at last succeeded much better than might have been expected ; they then made him further acquainted with the adventure Celestia had met with, with the gipsy sybil. This amazed him even more than all.

"Mabel Henderson," he ejaculated, "can it be possible?—Oh, well do I remember her, and she became the victim of the monster Bonville!—Can we then wonder at the deadly hatred she bears him?—But why should she hesitate to meet me and tell me all she knows? Would that I could see her, then we might defeat the plans of the diabolical, the inhuman miscreant. Oh, my beloved, my unfortunate Elvina, if thou art indeed in the power of Bonville, which I can no longer doubt, better would it be for thee and me if thou wert dead!"

He gave way to a violent burst of grief, which Lord Bathurst and his son did not attempt to interrupt, and he then became more calm. Celestia was then introduced to him, and from her lips he heard a repetition of the alarming and important facts which they had just communicated to him. They mingled their tears together, and it was some time before they could sit down and discuss the matter rationally. Arrangements were at last made to be upon their guard to protect themselves from the artifices of Bonville, and to find out the place of his concealment if possible; and it was also resolved that Celestia should not again venture from the abbey unless she was duly protected, and then only at such periods when no danger might be reasonably apprehended. These matters adjusted, they separated for the night, though there was little portion of rest allowed to either of them.

Celestia for some time tossed about on a sleepless pillow, and when at last the drowsy god did close her eyelids, the most torturing dreams flitted before her busy imagination, and rendered sleep a curse, instead of a relief. All the terrible observations that the villain Bonville had made to her, and the awful and disgusting threats he had held out, rushed vividly to her recollection, and frequently she started terrified from her sleep, imagining that he still stood in her presence. It was a great relief to her when morning dawned, and she could leave her couch. She arose with a sad—sad heart, and seated herself by the window of her chamber. Lady Eugenia still slept, and although she was most anxious for her society, in order in some measure to relieve the agony of her mind, she did not attempt to disturb her.

It was a beautiful serene morning, but our heroine gazed listlessly upon the wide expanse of diversified scenery, a view of which was commanded from her chamber window. Her mind was entirely engrossed by other objects and thoughts.

"My God!" she ejaculated, " should Bonville be really able to put his dreadful, his revolting threats into execution, what will become of me and all so dear to me? But no, I will not, cannot believe that a merciful and just Almighty will permit him to do so. I will yet trust that his nefarious designs will be frustrated, and that he will be brought to that punishment which his hideous crimes so justly merit. Unfortunate Lady Elvina, if you are indeed in the miscreant's power, which I have too much reason to fear you are, oh, may Heaven watch over and protect you from his brutal malice, and restore you ultimately to the arms of that fond and deeply afflicted husband, from whom you have been so long separated."

Thus she continued to reflect, but suddenly as she was about to rise and leave her chamber, her attention was arrested by a noise outside the abbey, and turning her eyes in the direction from whence it proceeded, she beheld standing on the lawn immediately beneath her chamber window, and gazing up at her with the most diabolical and fiendish expression of countenance, the wretch Bonville. He was habited the same as she had seen him the day before, and his whole attitude and gestures bespoke menace and defiance. Celestia could also perceive when the wind blew aside his cloak, that he was well armed, she had not the least doubt that he had his myrmidons at hand to fly to his assistance, if any danger should threaten him, but there was not a person to be seen at that early hour of the morning, and therefore the daring scoundrel was completely safe.

The first impulse of our heroine was to raise an alarm, but Bonville, who seemed to read her thoughts, waved his hand in an authoritative and threatening manner, and continued fixed in the same attitude for several minutes, and appeared to glory in the alarm which the beauteous damsel evinced by her pale looks, but with no other motive than to exult over her terror in his mind.

Celestia wished to move away from the casement, and to seek the presence of her friends, that she might put them on their guard against any danger which might threaten, but she could not; an irresistible power seemed to prevent her; and she continued to gaze at the villain with such sensations as the reader will be better able to imagine than we to describe them.

Again he waved his hand menacingly, and then uttering a loud laugh which sounded hollowly upon the air, he strode hastily from the spot, and his tall and athletic form gradually faded away in the distance.

What a relief it was to Celestia when he was gone; she sunk on her knees, and solemnly and earnestly invoked the protection of Heaven from any evils which might threaten her or her loved friends from the villain's malice, and then feeling somewhat more composed and confident, she quitted her chamber, and sought the apartment of Lady Eugenia, who slept in the adjoining room to her. She found her awake, but not yet risen, and Lady Eugenia observing the paleness of her looks and the general agitation of her manner, hastily demanded what had occurred to alarm her. Celestia informed her as well as she was able, and Lady Eugenia heard her with astonishment and consternation which were almost equal to her own.

"What a horried being is this man," she said, "and how are we to protect ourselves against him and his villanous artifices?"

"Alas, I know not," replied our heroine, "and I shudder with horror at the bare contemplation of the horrors with which he seems so safely to threaten us. No doubt he has his creatures close at hand, to be ready when he shall require their services, and it is quite evident that as he has said, he sets all detection at defiance."

"Heaven watch over us," said Lady Eugenia, "and frustrate the inhuman miscreant's designs, for, alas! it appears too evident to me that some fresh troubles are in store for us. Alas! what an unfortunate family, and yet how little have we merited the calamities, the severe trials, which it has pleased the Almighty to visit us. Heaven only knows what will be the end of it, but after all these alarming events, I cannot but anticipate the worst."

"The predictions of Mabel Henderson are being fulfilled in the most fearful manner," sighed Celestia, "and alas, I fear they will be realized to the very letter."

"Let us hope to Heaven, that they will not, my love," returned her aunt; "but at present it is impossible to help admitting that our prospects are the most dismal that can be conceived. But compose your feelings, Celestia, which I do not wonder should be excited at this constant succession of alarming adventures. Some means may yet be devised to frustrate the monster's plans, and to bring him to punishment. Courage, my dear girl, and hope for the best."

Celestia shook her head with a melancholy and despairing look, but returned no answer to her aunt's observations, for it was utterly impossible that she could bring her mind to think as she enjoined her.

Lady Eugenia arose from her bed, for she heard some of the family stirring below, and Celestia, as well as the agitation of her feelings would permit her, assisted her to dress. When this task was accomplished, they descended below, and on entering the apartment which was always appropriated to the morning meal, they found the earl already there and looking extremely pale and ill. It was quite evident that the agony of his mind had not permitted him to sleep much, if any, and Celestia and her aunt hesitated to impart to him that intelligence which could not fail to add to his mournful anguish, and strengthen the apprehensions and forebodings which already distracted his bosom. But his quick eye saw in a moment that they had something unpleasant and painful to communicate, and he anxiously inquired what it was.

"Do not keep me in suspense, I beg of you," he said; "I am fully prepared to hear anything, however sad it is, for after all that has lately occurred, I cannot be more wretched or hopeless than I am at present."

Lady Eugenia informed him as cautiously and gently as she could, and he listened to her with far more composure than they could have anticipated. But still those frequent and alarming events were calculated to make a deep and lasting impression upon his mind, and to overcloud what small ray of hope and comfort he had suffered to dawn upon his mind. The utter daring and effrontery of Bonville astonished the earl and his friends more than all, and they were at a perfect loss to protect themselves from the malice of a man who seemed to set all human laws and human power at perfect defiance. They consulted long upon this subject but without being able to come to any satisfactory conclusion. Inquiries were made in the neighbourhood, and a strict watch kept without any better success, and at length they were compelled to abandon the task, and leave it to Providence to unravel the truth and to frustrate the designs of their cruel and relentless enemy in its own wise time.

Several days elapsed, and nothing more was seen or heard of Bonville or Mabel Henderson, and the suspense and alarm of Lord Elverton increased every day, especially after the assertion which Mabel had made to the effect that the hapless Lady Elvina was in the villain's power, and after the dreadful threats he had held out, and which they could not have the least doubt that he would put into execution if ever an opportunity should present itself for his doing so.

But how had Mabel come by the knowledge she boasted she possessed, and why should she hesitate to come forward and fully explain everything, if her intentions were so friendly towards them? That was what perplexed them more than all, and the longer they reflected upon all the torturing circumstances, the more bewildered and tortured they became.

In the midst of all this agony and suspense the earl received another letter from Sir Roderick Ainslie, in which he communicated the melancholy intelligence that all his endeavours to find any clue to the place of Lady Elverton's retreat had been hitherto unavailing, and he began to fear that if the unfortunate lady was not in the power of the miscreant Bonville, she was not in England, and that she had been induced by the strength of her despair and the sorrow of her feelings to enter into some religious house on the continent.

As soon as the earl could sufficiently compose his feelings to do so, he sent an answer to Sir Roderick to the place where he was staying, in which he informed him of all that had recently taken place, and that there could be very little doubt of the sad and terrible fact, that his ill-fated Elvina was actually in the power of Bonville, and that if such was the case, there was not the least hope of his ever beholding her again. It would, he thought, be madness for him to flatter himself with such an idea, and that there was therefore nothing left but for him to make up his mind to the worst, and to resign himself as well as he could to his dismal and unmerited fate.

This letter was a source of great anguish to the worthy baronet; especially as he could not but admit the truth and reason of it; and many and fervent were the prayers he offered up to the Supreme to watch over and protect Lady Elvina from the implacable malice of her dreadful persecutor, and to bring him to that punishment which was not only justly due to the monstrous crimes he had perpetrated against her and the members of her unfortunate family. Still, however, he determined not to abandon his exertions to discover the place where she was confined, and to rescue her from the fate with which she was threatened, and for that purpose he returned to Sungrove Abbey, in order that he might consult with the earl and his friends, as to the future course which it would be most advisable to adopt.

Lord Elverton greeted the return of Sir Roberick with feelings of melancholy pleasure, and many were the consultations they held together, and many without being able to come to a satisfactory conclusion. Nor did the baronet know how to advise, so deeply involved in mystery were all the circumstances ; he remembered Mabel Henderson very well, and was not a little surprised to learn that she was the gipsy sybil who had so often appeared to Celestia, and at the alarming and extraordinary statements she had made, but the truth of which he could not for a moment doubt. Still he thought that if she could be persuaded to come forward something more might probably be elicited which would lead to the most favourable results.

"I cannot imagine why she should hesitate," he remarked, "unless it be indeed a fact that she fears by too hastily doing so she might frustrate her plans against the villain, without being able to render your lordship the service she had wished. But I do not entirely despair of her doing so yet, and of being able to accomplish her designs."

"I sincerely trust that your wishes may be realized," said Lord Elverton, "but, alas, I fear that there is no hope of happiness in this world again for me. My poor Elvina, if thou art indeed in the power of Bonville, how terrible will be thy sufferings, how awful are the tortures that he will delight to inflict on you ; better, far better would it be for you that you were dead than to be subjected to so dreadful a fate."

Sir Roderick and the others tried to console him, and after much exertion the extreme violence of his grief was in some measure abated, and he was enabled to converse more calmly on the melancholy circumstances by which they were all so deeply afflicted.

CHAPTER XXV.

THE PRISONER IN THE DUNGEON AGAIN —THE BITTER TAUNTS OF THE VILLAIN BONVILLE.—FRESH DESPAIR AND MISERY.

RETRACE we now our steps to the unfortunate prisoner, in that awful place which we have described in a former chapter.

Hapless, deeply wronged and persecuted Lady Elvina, what a miserable destiny is thine ! What a blessing would it have been for thee had it pleased the Supreme to have taken thee to himself long, long since ; but, alas ! great is the misery that is yet in store for thee, and which it would almost appear there is no human power to arrest.

Again it is night in that fearful den. Night ! when is it day in the living tomb of that ill doomed lady ?—But the smallest crevice placed high in the blackened wall of that loathsome dungeon admits the least particle of light and air, and that only serves, if possible, to render horror still more horrible. But it is night !—and a fearful night it is. How terrific is the voice of the ethereal lion ; how frightful is the lightning as it glares in at the aperture before mentioned, ever and anon rendering the terrors of the place still more hideous, and imparting a ghastly, a still more ghastly hue to the haggard countenance of the wretched and unoffending victim of the most inhuman, the most diabolical and fiend-like persecutor !— Even the rats and other vermin seem terrified at the war of the elements, and crouch and crawl closer into the rotten straw on which the poor prisoner is reclining, now too weak to make the slightest effort to rise. God ! they will surely fix themselves upon the wasted and worn out form of the once beauteous woman, preying upon her in life, and she has no strength to struggle against them. Death would have been a mercy to her, but oh, not such a horrible, such a revolting death as that.

With difficulty she raised her aching and burning head, and with hollow and blood-shot eyes raised above, sought to utter a prayer to Heaven for mercy, but her tongue refused its office. Oh ! the unutterable agony of her feelings at that moment!—The most eloquent pen could not describe it, the most vivid imagination could not conceive it. She sunk back again on her loathsome pallet, and piteous were the moans which escaped her bosom.

Another week had elapsed since she had seen her persecutor, and during that interval the ruffian whom he employed and who resided in the old house, had brought her her coarse food, but she was too weak to partake of it, at least only sparingly; the savage, the ferocious appearance of the fellow so alarmed her that she never ventured to address a word to him, and she always felt a

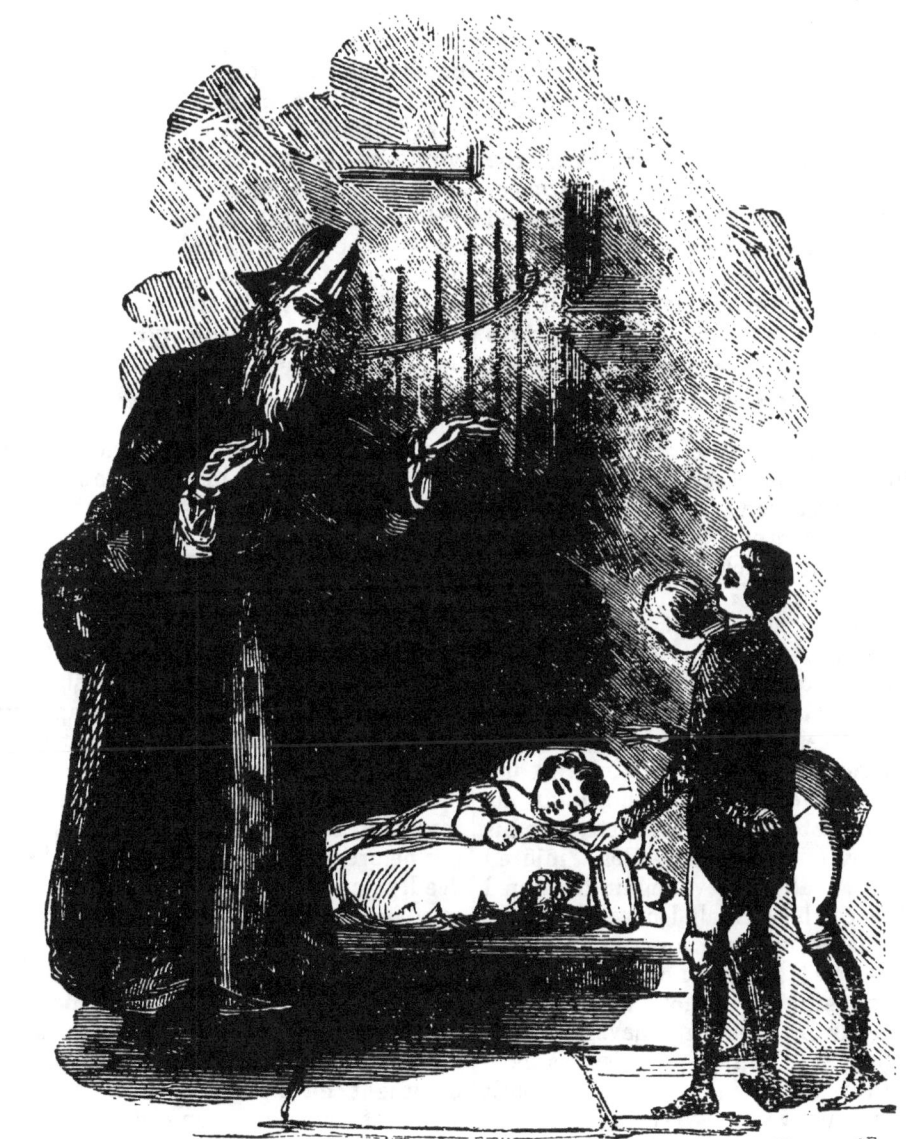

THE FOOTMARKS DISCOVERED IN LORD CONINGSBY'S BED-CHAMBER.

relief when he had departed from her dungeon.

At length, however, the food he brought her was of a more delicate nature than that he had hitherto supplied her with, and he even provided her with a little wine and water at intervals, doubtless having received instructions not to allow her to sink entirely from exhaustion, for then there would have been a termination to the vengeance of the monster who held her in his power.

At first the unfortunate Elvina refused

to partake of this altered food, for could it be possible that she should be otherwise that tired of her existence? But still even under circumstances of the greatest possible misery it is astonishing, but no less true than remarkable, the tenacity with which we yet cling to life, and even surrounded as she was by every horror, amidst all her sufferings, a faint beam of hope would at times steal in upon the wretched bosom of the victim of brutality, that the Almighty would not suffer her always to remain in her present dreadful situation, that she might be permitted to die in the arms of her much wronged and deeply afflicted husband, and therefore did she resolve to cling to the last, to that worst state than living death, surrounded even by all the horrors that it was, and to bear up to the last as well as she could. She partook of the refreshments, and became a little more revived. Once more the power of speech was restored to her, and by dint of great exertion rising on her knees, she clasped her thin and shrivelled hands together vehemently, and in the most melancholy and plaintive accents exclaimed:—

"Almighty Parent of all good, look down with an eye of pity on thine erring creature, and have mercy on me. Or, if it be thy will that I should never in life be released from this horrible doom, oh, in mercy take me to thyself, and suffer not the miscreant who holds me in his power to triumph altogether in his barbarity. Husband!—dear injured husband, shall we never again be united on this earth?—Shall I never hear the words of forgiveness pronounced by thy lips?—Alas! I dare not hope that I shall, but still may I hope that we may meet again in Heaven,—never more to be separated. Oh, what miseries have the errors and weakness of my youth been productive of. Wretched woman that I was, to listen to the voice of the insidious arch-fiend who lured me from my duty to one of the best of men. What horrors has it not entailed upon all my unfortunate family. My daughter met with a dreadful, and untimely death; her husband and infant child disappeared no one knew whither, and I dare not even to cast a thought upon the heart-rending sorrows which my Albert must for so many years have been enduring.

And this is all caused by my own imprudence and the atrocious villany of Bonville. Great God! how terrible, but how just is the punishment I am enduring. But can it be true what the demon Bonville has told me, that my son, my long lost son was discovered again only to fall a victim to his bloody revenge?—Can it be true that my poor grandchild, Celestia, is also found and under the protection of her noble relative, but that he has destined her for his next victim? Great Heaven, Thou wilt surely not permit him to triumph thus in his deadly malice."

It was long ere many tears had been shed by the unhappy lady, but they now flowed abundantly, and she again sunk back on her bed of straw, in a state of almost utter insensibility. It would have been a mercy to her had she been permitted to remain in that state of unconsciousness.

Still raged the tempest without. The horrors of the night increased, and under even the most ordinary circumstances, they were calculated to excite terror in the stoutest heart. But Lady Elvina heard them not. She was too deeply engrossed by the agony of her own thoughts to be conscious of anything else. Not long, however, was she suffered to remain in this state of apathy. She was aroused by the difficult turning of the rusty key in the lock, and once more raising her aching and distracted head, she beheld Bonville standing before her, with his usual looks of deadly malice and triumph. The wretched lady could scarcely suppress a cry of horror, but she covered her eyes with her hands, to shut out his revolting image from her sight. In the attitude he then stood, and with his fearful and hideous expression of countenance, he might have been taken for the evil spirit of the storm, and was sufficient to strike feelings of terror and disgust into the stoutest heart.

For some minutes the cold blooded villain stood and contemplated his unfortunate victim with the same deadly feelings of malice and exultation. Then he laughed aloud, and the sound of his harsh and almost unearthly voice in that frightful place, between the pauses of the thunder, aroused Lady Elvina, and she looked up with an expression of horror and supplication, which was enough to move even the most cruel and insensible heart to pity—pity, that had ever been unknown to the monster Bonville.

"Mercy, mercy!" groaned forth the wretched prisoner, and she could utter no more, but stared at him aghast, with all the wild frenzy of a maniac.

"Mercy!" repeated the ruffian, in his most frightful tones; "yes, such mercy as the wolf shows to the lamb; as the ferocious tiger shows his victim. Mercy!—ha! ha! ha!—I know it not; I despise the word; it may do for canting fools to make use of, but my favourite theme is vengeance, bloody and deliberate vengeance. It is the food I feast upon. It forms the principal ingredient of my revelry. Hast thou not experienced enough, sweet Lady Elvina, to know that in this, at any rate, I speak the truth? Mercy! was it that feeling, thinkest thou, which prompted me to consign thine innocent and beauteous daughter to the hands, the reeking hands of the executioner? Was it mercy that urged me to plunge your son into the raging deep? Will it be mercy that will lead me to tear the young Celestia from the arms of your husband, but to degrade, ruin, and destroy her? Oh, if this indeed be mercy, then am I one of the most merciful beings in existence!"

"Oh, God! oh, God! oh, God!" groaned the horror-struck Lady Elvina, wringing her hands, "Thou wilt surely stay this monster in his inhuman, his unparalleled career of atrocity! Thou wilt not suffer another innocent victim to fall into his power."

"But," cried Bonville, "I defy, I scorn the power you invoke. The fair Celestia,—she, the admired, the envied of all, must and shall be mine, and that before many days have elapsed. But yesterday I saw her, I conversed with her; I feasted my eyes on her beauty, and exulted at the thought of what a rich prize was in store for me, and how powerless were all her friends to frustrate my designs. Or, I shall be amply repaid for all the scorn I have received. Reflect on this, noble Lady Elvina, and comfort yourself in your agreeable apartments at the thought."

Lady Elvina fixed upon the wretch a look of the utmost horror and disgust, but she could not speak.

"Did I not tell you," he continued after a pause, "that one day my triumph would be complete? That day is rapidly approaching;—it will soon be here, and then you will see, if you are not convinced already, how well Bonville can keep his word. Oh, you little thought that he, whom you had flattered yourself had been for so many years mouldering in his grave, still lived for a horrible revenge;—that his eye was upon all your actions, that he watched your footsteps wherever you went, and that he only awaited the opportunity to put his deep-laid schemes into execution. Little did you dream that I was pursuing you to England, and had prepared this beautiful place for your reception. Ha! ha! ha!—How it glads my soul to think of all these things."

Lady Elvina clasped her hands and raised her eyes towards heaven, but still was utterance denied her. Bonville's exultation increased every moment, and he traversed the dungeon, muttering the most diabolical expressions to himself.

"I thought I would inform you that I had again seen Celestia," at length he said aloud, "for I was unwilling to deprive you of any pleasure it might afford you. But I tell you again, that you shall also see her. Yes, I will bring her here, to show her that noble relative whom she never yet knew but by name, and I have no doubt that the meeting will be a most happy one."

It must seem scarcely possible to the reader that such an inhuman villain could ever have been in existence; but, alas! it is too true, and the circumstances we are here narrating are not at all exaggerated.

Lady Elvina at last found power to reply to her tormentor; and again raising herself upon her knees she ejaculated—

"Brutal man, if man indeed you are, whom no feeling of pity can touch; whose deeds are of darkness and bloodshed; terrible as are your words, and hideous as have been your crimes, I will not yet despair. There is a just power above who watches all our actions, knows our every thought, and in a moment can frustrate your monstrous designs, and bring about a terrible retribution upon your head. To that power I now humbly but earnestly appeal, and

I feel confident that the prayer of the sinner will not be heard in vain; but that, whatever may be my fate, and it cannot be more dreadful than it is at present, those innocent and unfortunate beings whom you have threatened will escape your vengeance."

"Idiot!" replied Bonville, "I scorn your appeal. Know you not I defy all the power you can invoke?—But I can allow you to give full vent to your anguish. It does but serve me to laugh at. A few days, a few days only, and you shall see whether or not my threats shall be fulfilled. Oh how I triumph at the thought. I would not have lost this opportunity of gratifying my vengeance for all the wealth that the world can produce. Sweet Celestia, the tender, the transcendently lovely, the gentle, the virtuous, her who has so lately been discovered to be so closely related to you; whom your husband adores, whom your nephew the young Lord Malensbury loves to distraction, and whom she loves in return with equal ardour, is destined to be my mistress."

"Never! never!" gasped forth Lady Elvina, "I will not believe in your fiendish boasting. That God whom you affect to despise will protect the poor innocent girl from your base designs, and crush you, monster, in the midst of your iniquity, when you least expect it."

Again Bonville laughed bitterly in the contempt and triumph of his feelings, and then fixing upon Lady Elvina one of his most awful looks, he said:—

"So sure as you hear the thunder's reverberating peal now rattling on high; so sure as the forked lightning darts its ghastly fires through the sky, so sure I tell you once for all that Celestia shall not escape me!—So deeply have I laid my plans; so well are they at present working, that nothing can save her. In less than another week I will present her to your eyes, and then perhaps you will be convinced that I speak the truth. Do you not think it kind and considerate of me that I should thus restore to your eyes that long-lost girl whom you never expected to behold again?"

"Oh, Bonville, Bonville," gasped the distracted prisoner; "forbear, forbear, and reflect;—is not your cruel revenge satiated by the awful crimes you have already committed, but that you must doom that innocent maiden, who can never have offended you by word or deed, to a fate that is far more fearful than the most torturing and lingering death?—But you cannot, you dare not attempt to put your monstrous threats into execution; monster as you have proved yourself to be, I cannot believe you to be monster enough for that."

"Ha, ha, ha! sweet Lady Elvina," laughed the heartless ruffian, "you judge too mildly of me; but I have no wish to indulge in the flattery. As I have said before, you will have the opportunity, in the course of a few days, of judging whether I will keep my word."

"Then God help her, for from you I see plainly enough she can expect no mercy," sighed Lady Elvina; "alas! alas!—why have I lived to see this dreadful day?—Bonville, I beseech you to keep me no longer in this state of insupportable misery, but to complete your cruelty by immediately piercing your dagger to my heart."

"Yes, that would indeed be mercy!" he returned, "but think not to receive it from me; it would not answer my purpose at present. I have yet much more suffering in store for you, and believe me you shall receive the full benefit of it. I now leave you to the enjoyment of your own reflections, most noble lady, and I wish you pleasant dreams."

Lady Elvina again sunk back on her wretched pallet, and covering her face with her hands, became absorbed in an agony of grief, despair, and horror which no language could properly portray.

Bonville quitted the dungeon, and stalked triumphantly to his own apartments, where he gave himself up to the diabolical, the demon thoughts which crowded upon him. Although it was now very late, he thought not of seeking his pillow, but sat at the casement watching the terrors of the storm with the most horrible feelings of satisfaction. The louder the thunder bellowed, the more fierce the lightning flashed, the greater became the unnatural pleasure which triumphed in his brutal and hardened breast, and ever and anon he waved his hand and laughed aloud as if in defiance of the battling elemens, and then the expression of his countenance became more awful than before.

"Rage on, rage on!" he cried, "such sounds as these are music to my ears. Bonville is not the man to be frightened by the howling storm. No, its utmost fury is in strict unison with the fierce passions which predominate in my breast. Blaze away, ye vivid lightnings, ye have no terrors for me. Such is the storm that I will kindle against all those I so hate and despise. Already my revenge has been in part gratified, but my triumph is not yet half complete, nor will it be, until I have exterminated them all from the face of the earth!—Celestia, prepare thyself, for thy doom is sealed; and oh, what a doom! Thou mayest supplicate for mercy, thou mayest heap thy reproaches and thine execrations on my head, but they will be all in vain; nothing shall move me from my purpose, and in thy misery and despair will be my greatest triumph. Thou and all connected with thee shall be made most terribly to feel the mighty power I possess. What can prevent the accomplishment of all my wishes?—Nothing!—Who shall dare interpose to save thee?—No one; woe to those who should be mad or bold enough to do so! My plans are all laid with such consummate skill, that I defy all human ingenuity to defeat them. Celestia! Celestia! thou art as securely mine as if thou wert even at this moment in my power."

He paused, and still continued to gaze upon the horrors of the night; then he suddenly arose, and walking to a small ebony chest, he took from it a miniature set in gold, and richly studded with diamonds and brilliants. As he gazed upon the lovely features that were there portrayed, a ghastly smile of delight overspread his repulsive countenance, and he resumed his seat at the casement with his eyes still fixed with the most intense earnestness and satisfaction upon the miniature.

"Such was Lady Elvina when she was about the age of Celestia," he said; "how like her, and how lovely. Just the same mild expression of the eyes, just the same sweet innocent smile that plays around the maiden's lips. The same luxuriant silken tresses;—the skin of snowy whiteness, the delicate flush upon her cheeks. Oh, it would warm the heart of a stoic to gaze upon her; it would light up the passions of love in the breast of a savage. And this paragon of beauty, of perfection, is destined to become mine; the mistress of the aged, the despised, the assassin Bonville!—Yes, yes; mine and mine only. Nothing can save her! Transporting thought!—Oh, it were worth an age of torture and disappointment, ultimately to obtain as a reward such a prize as this! And what will be the agony of the Lady Elvina, when I present to her her fair relation, and to know that they must soon part, never for her ladyship to behold her again, only as a degraded, broken-hearted creature?—I triumph every way, and am sufficiently repaid for all the years of trouble, anxiety, and scorn I have experienced."

Thus soliloquizing, the hoary headed villain pressed the miniature to his lips, and then replaced it in the repository from which he had taken it, and after a short time sought his chamber in moody silence.

Poor Lady Elvina remained in the same state of acute mental anguish for some minutes after her persecutor had left her, and it was indeed wonderful that she could survive at all after the dreadful scene which had passed between them. The horrible threats he had held out, and which no one who knew his real character, and the unparalleled atrocities of which he had been guilty, could doubt that he would exert all his power to put into execution, seemed stamped upon her brain in characters of fire. It was a wonder how her senses could withstand such an accumulation of horrors.

At length she somewhat aroused herself, and looking around her, began to have some recollection as to where she was. She raised herself into a sitting posture, and clasped her burning temples. Although the tempest still continued in all its fearful height, she now heard it not, so entirely were her thoughts engrossed by what had just taken place, and the terror and despair of her feelings.

"Still in this horrible place," she sighed. "Oh, Heaven! shall I never be released but by death?—No, no, there is no hope for me. No hope, no hope! But to perish thus!—The thought is frightful. But my poor Celestia, whom I have never seen since childhood ;—and must she too fall into this miscreant's power?—Will he be allowed to carry his revolting threats into effect?—Oh, no ; that omnipotent and all merciful Being who reigns above will not permit it. It were a libel on His holy name to believe it. And yet do I not know from terrible experience how great is the power of Bonville, and that he has never yet failed in the accomplishment of any designs upon which he has fixed his mind?—Alas! too well I do. Oh, Celestia, innocent, unoffending maiden, how I tremble for thee!—Almighty God, watch over and save her and my unfortunate husband from the malice of this inhuman wretch, and then may I still learn to submit to my dreadful fate with fortitude and resignation."

As she uttered these words she clasped her hands vehemently together, and then once more gave herself up to the misery of her own silent thoughts.

The night passed away, another dreadful night in that awful dungeon : —still the storm continued to triumph in its utmost wrath, and the most excruciating anguish and abject despair held their empire in the breast of the wretched prisoner.

CHAPTER XXVI.

THE THREAT FULFILLED.—THE DISAPPEARANCE OF CELESTIA.

DAYS rolled on, and still matters remained in the same state of torturing suspense at Sungrove Abbey. The fate of Lady Elvina still continued to be a profound and impenetrable mystery, and the earl gave himself up to despair, from which it was impossible for any of his friends to arouse him ; and he now indeed firmly believed that Mabel Henderson had spoken the truth, and that his unfortunate Elvina was in the power of Bonville.

But where was Mabel? why did she still persist in keeping out of the way, after she had aroused their anxiety to such an insufferable degree?—It was a mystery which none of them could penetrate, and reflection only served to add to their perplexity.

But the threats which Bonville had held out to Celestia, if possible, cost them more anguish and alarm than all. They looked forward to every day with terror, expecting that something fearful would happen. Our heroine was never permitted to venture from the abbey unless she was under the protection of her friends, and Lady Eugenia and her slept in the same chamber together.

The abbey was also well watched and guarded day and night; officers were on the alert to apprehend any suspicious-looking persons whom they might observe lurking in the vicinity, and in fact every precaution was used to guard against the threatened danger; but Fate ordained that all efforts to protect themselves should prove futile; they had to contend against a most daring and powerful enemy, whom no fear of detection could daunt, and for awhile he was permitted to triumph in his diabolical schemes, and the unfortunate and deeply persecuted family were shortly once more plunged into the most indescribable misery.

There was no one who felt greater uneasiness on account of Celestia than her lover, Lord Malensbury, and he was perfectly wretched whenever she was out of his sight. He would have given the world had it been in his possession, to have been able to trace out the secret retreat of Bonville, and to bring him to punishment ; but there appeared to be very little hope of being able to do that at present, at any rate, and many were the maledictions he invoked upon his head for the barbarities he had already been guilty of.

Sir Eustace Aubrey and his son Collingwood felt the deepest sympathy for the misfortunes of the earl and his family, and alarm for the safety of Celestia, and Collingwood, in his anxiety to thwart the designs of Bonville, forgot the feeling of jealousy he entertained towards Lord Malensbury, and zealously co-operated with him and his friends in devising every possible means to avert the fresh calamities and dangers with which they were so daringly threatened. In fact there was no person in the neighbourhood of the abbey, from the highest to the lowest, who did not exert themselves to the utmost to prevent the occurrence of any fresh disasters to those individuals who were so highly and deservedly esteemed by all who knew them. But it was all of no avail; a fresh storm was gathering in the horizon of their destiny, which was soon about to burst upon them with the most overwhelming violence.

Lady Eglantine was almost the constant companion of our heroine, and in the society of that amiable and lovely girl Celestia felt a great relief from those cares, anxieties, and sorrows which ever oppressed her mind. Two more kindred spirits could not possibly have met together, and it would have been a most difficult task to decide which was the most gentle minded or captivating of the two. It was Eglantine's task to endeavour to console her amiable friend, and to inspire her with hope, and she sometimes succeeded far beyond her most sanguine expectations. It was a beautiful, a refreshing thing, this union between two young and healthful hearts. How it refreshed them, and made them bear up with the heavy afflictions that it had pleased Providence to visit them with.

But the day of sorrow, of deep mourning was coming, and they were all about to experience its most melancholy effects.

Seven days had elapsed from the time that Celestia had encountered Bonville in the old priory ruins, when, as the earl and all his family were occupied in conversation, a servant suddenly entered and presented his worship with a letter.

"Who delivered this letter?" inquired the earl, perceiving that the superscription was written in an unknown hand.

"An old woman in a red cloak," replied the servant.

"And did you ask her no questions?"

"No, my lord, for old and feeble as she appeared to be, she hurried away before I had an opportunity of doing so."

"You observed the direction she went in?"

"Yes, my lord, she took the narrow road that leads to Langstown, but turning up an avenue she was immediately lost to my sight. I called to John and Richard, and—"

"Let me advise, my lord," interrupted Earl Bathurst, "that some trustworthy persons should be dispatched immediately to Langstown and its neighbourhood to see whether they can discover any individual who answers the description that is given by your servant."

That advice was acted upon, and then his lordship opened the letter which had caused them so much excitement, and read aloud as follows, in an agitated voice:

"MY LORD—It is with sincere grief, commiserating as she does in the unmerited misfortunes which have attended your lordship and your respected family, that Mabel Henderson has to address to you this warning, (Heaven send it may be of avail to thwart the diabolical plans of the heartless miscreant, Bonville, your bitterest foe.) My lord, I was honoured by the confidence of your amiable lady, and though I am now a poor fallen creature, fallen through the base artifices of that miscreant from whom you can trace the origin of all your misfortunes, I trust, I sincerely hope, you will not treat my warnings with indifference, because certain circumstances over which I have no control prevent me at present from seeking a personal interview with you.

"The monster Bonville is on the alert. He is thoroughly acquainted with all your plans, and, I am afraid, is prepared to defeat them; the innocent Celestia is his doomed victim; in a few nights I apprehend she will be in his power, unless I can find some means to frustrate his designs. At present I can only inform you that such is his intention, but I have been unable to discover his retreat, but wherever that is, depend upon it, it is likewise the prison of my much respected and deeply lamented mistress, Lady Elvina.

"Believe me to be continually watching after the welfare of your lordship and your amiable family, it is not only a feeling of sincere regard towards your lordship and all connected with you, but a spirit of just revenge against the monster, Bonville, which thus stimulates the miserable outcast,

"MABEL HENDERSON."

" P.S.—I am endeavouring to discover the night when he intends to attempt to put his abominable plans into effect, but hitherto I have been unsuccessful; should Providence aid me in my just exertions, you shall be immediately apprized. M. H."

The sensation which this letter caused in the breasts of all present may well be imagined. Celestia, after the dreadful warning which it conveyed to her, sustained herself with much more fortitude than could have been expected, but Lord Elverton was completely distracted.

"How can we protect ourselves against this insidious, this determined villain?" he ejaculated; "if what Mabel Henderson here states be true, and there is too much reason to fear it is, it seems he makes sure of the success of his nefarious plans, and sets detection at defiance. What is to be done? What is to be done?"

"Oh, my dear grandpapa," said our heroine, "do not agitate yourself thus on my account. Notwithstanding the cruel threats of this bad man, I do not fear. I sincerely and devoutly trust in the goodness of Providence for protection."

Although the damsel said this, it was plain to be seen, from the paleness of her countenance and the general agitation of her demeanour, that she was far from being so confident as she appeared to be, and that her greatest anxiety was to tranquillise the feelings of her noble relative.

"It is impossible that the miscreant can succeed," remarked Sir Frederick, "now we are warned of his designs, and are consequently so well prepared to defeat them. Let us act with firmness, calmness, and deliberation, and the diabolical stratagem of the miscreant Bonville will be of no avail. After all, Mabel may be mistaken."

Lord Elverton shook his head mournfully and incredulously.

"Alas!" he sighed, "I have too much reason to fear that Mabel Henderson is correct to the very letter. There is a tone of sincerity throughout her letter which leaves not a doubt upon my mind."

"But he cannot succeed," said Lord Bathurst; "now we are apprized of his plans, we have every means of defending ourselves from him, and he will not have the boldness to make an attack upon the abbey."

"He has daring and determination enough for anything. I have too fatally experienced the truth of that already. Is he not the murderer of my children? Was he not the wretch who tempted my wife to abandon me and to leave me to the greatest misery, and does he not at present hold her in his power?"

"Heaven forbid!" cried Lady Eugenia.

"I cannot doubt it," returned the earl; "has he not himself boasted exultingly of it?—and now Mabel Henderson declares her conviction of it. Oh, God! how severe have been my trials hitherto, and it is too evident that fresh troubles are in store for me. For myself I would not care, for I am tired of my life, and would to Heaven that my earthly pilgrimage were at an end; but it is those who are so dear to me that are the objects of my deepest solicitude, and anxiety, and apprehension. Could I be certain that they would be protected from the machinations of the guilty, I might be contented, and even dreadful as my fate is, learn to submit with fortitude and resignation."

Again all present tried to comfort him, and Celestia struggled with her feelings as much as possible in order to tranquillize him, and she succeeded much better than might have been expected under the circumstances, but when she and her aunt retired to their chamber for the night, her anguish found vent in a copious flood of tears, which Lady Eugenia was very glad to see, for she was certain it would afford her relief.

"Oh, my dear aunt," she ejaculated, "what a cruel, heartless man, this Bonville must be; the very mention of his name freezes my blood with horror."

"Banish him from your thoughts, my love," said Lady Eugenia.

"Oh, how is that possible?" said the poor girl, "after the dreadful crimes he has committed against my unfortunate family, and the threats he now holds out?—Gracious Heaven! should he indeed get me in his power, what will become of me?"

"Heaven will protect you, my dear Celestia," replied Lady Eugenia; "put your trust in that and fear not."

"I will do so," remarked our heroine,

with more confidence; and she then knelt down and invoked the protection of the Most High, after which, both she and her aunt being somewhat more composed, they retired to rest. It was some time, however, before sleep descended upon the eyelids of Celestia, and then the most frightful dreams flitted before her imagination, the reflection on which disturbed her mind on waking.

The night, however, passed away without anything occurring to alarm them, and Celestia and her aunt left their couch at an earlier hour than usual, and

descending to the breakfast-room, were glad to find the earl and their other friends already assembled, and that the former was looking far less agitated than he had done the day before. He greeted Celestia with the utmost affection, and then the conversation naturally turned upon the threats of Bonville, but the earl either did not, or affected not to place so much confidence in their being put into execution, and talked calmly and rationally upon the subject, which was a source of great satisfaction to all his friends, and they exerted themselves to the utmost to keep him in the same state of mind.

Several days passed away, and nothing whatever took place to cause them the least apprehension, and they began to hope that Bonville had abandoned his designs, or that something had happened to him which might rid them of so dangerous an enemy altogether. They received no further communication from Mabel, and they therefore began to come to the conclusion that she had either not been able to obtain any more intelligence, or that she had discovered she was wrong in what she had already stated.

Though he tried to do so, Lord Elverton could not bring his mind entirely to these conclusions; for he well knew that Bonville was not the man to abandon anything upon which he had formed a determination, especially when it was to gratify his deadly feelings of malice and revenge. He could not help looking with dread to the future, and was in a constant state of apprehension that something dreadful was about to happen. Every precaution was made use of in the abbey to prevent the possibility of any sudden surprise, and our heroine was never suffered out of their sight for a moment.

Time wore on in this manner, and still they heard nothing more of Bonville, nor did they receive any further intelligence from Mabel; but notwithstanding this afforded them the greatest satisfaction, the earl was unable to dismiss his fears, and the uncertainty of the fate of his wife was a constant source of the most insupportable misery to him. He had no doubt in his own mind, and his friends could not persuade him to the contrary, that she was really in the power of Bonville, and if so, the torture he would be sure to inflict upon her would be terrible to think upon. Surely she must sink under such a dreadful accumulation of misery, and death would indeed, under such circumstances, be a mercy to her.

At length, thinking that change of scene might be better for all, and that there, at any rate, they would be safe from the machinations of their bitter enemy, Lord Elverton determined after so many years to go to London. The gaieties of the metropolis ill accorded with his lordship's state of mind, but he hoped they might in some measure serve to recruit the spirits of Celestia, and there, at any rate, she would be secure from the power of Bonville.

Celestia and her aunt received this proposition with satisfaction, and Lord Bathurst, and his son and daughter, and Sir Frederick, determined to accompany them, Lord Everside remaining behind, and promising to communicate with them constantly, and to forward them all the intelligence that should come to his knowledge.

Preparations were immediately made for the journey, and the day was fixed on which they were to depart, and their numerous friends in that part of the country paid them farewell visits; but it was not destined to take place; their implacable enemy was at work when they least expected it, and the dreadful threats he had made he was about to put into execution.

The evening before the day of their intended departure, they separated at an early hour, with the hope of obtaining a good night's rest previous to the commencement of their journey, and Celestia and her aunt retired to their chamber.

The night passed away, but the mind of Lord Elverton was disturbed by fearful and alarming dreams, and he frequently started from his sleep and stared around him, almost expecting to find them realized. Then he would listen attentively to catch the slightest sound, but all remained silent as the grave, and he would then again compose himself to sleep.

He was glad when the morning came, and he arose from his couch, but still he found it impossible to divest his mind of the melancholy forebodings that beset it. He went down stairs expecting to find Celestia and Lady Eugenia and their friends already there, for it had been arranged on the previous evening that they should meet early, but he was disappointed. Lord Bathurst and his son, and Sir Roderick were there, but Celestia and her aunt were absent.

"They have overslept themselves probably," said Lord Bathurst; "had not a servant better go to their chamber and arouse them?"

Lord Elverton coincided with this, but still he trembled in every limb with unaccountable and unconquerable dread. The maid was despatched, and they awaited her return with no inconsiderable anxiety and impatience.

She had not been gone many minutes, however, when they were alarmed by hearing a loud scream, and directly afterwards the girl staggered into the room pale and trembling, and sunk in a chair, being entirely unable to support herself.

"For Heaven's sake," cried all the gentlemen in a breath, "what is the matter? what has alarmed you thus, girl?"

At first she could not speak, but at length she gasped forth in a faint voice:

"Oh dear, my poor young Lady Celestia is gone, and Lady Eugenia is extended on the floor, either dead or insensible."

"My God! my God!" cried Lord Elverton striking his forehead, and he then rushed from the room followed by the three gentlemen.

They hastened to the chamber, the door of which they found open, and darting in, they beheld everything indeed as the servant had described it. Celestia was gone, and Lady Eugenia was extended on the floor apparently dead, but on raising her it was found that she was insensible from the effects of a blow she had received on the temple. They had evidently not retired to rest, for the bed was not disturbed, and Lady Eugenia was not undressed.

"Gracious powers!" exclaimed the distracted earl, in tones of the most indescribable agony, "this is one of the most dreadful blows of all. My poor Celestia has then indeed fallen into the power of the wretch, the inhuman wretch, from whom I have to date all the troubles that have befallen me."

His eye now rested on a slip of paper which was lying on the table, and taking it up, he found written in the hand-writing of Bonville, the following words:—

"All your precautions have been of no avail; the beauteous Celestia is in my power, and by the time you receive this, she will be far away from hence, and where it will be impossible for you to discover her. It is my intention to introduce her to Lady Elvina, who is my prisoner. Tremble, for my vengeance is not yet complete.   BONVILLE."

"God help me!—God help me!" groaned Lord Elverton, "for this shock will surely prove my death."

He could say no more, but sunk insensible on a chair. The agony of the three friends was almost equal to that of the unfortunate earl, and Lord Malensbury was perfectly distracted. He struck his forehead, called upon the name of his beloved Celestia, invoked the bitterest curses upon the head of the atrocious villain, Bonville, and nothing could pacify him.

It was necessary, however, to see to the recovery of Lady Eugenia and the earl, and summoning some of the servants they then had them conveyed below, and the medical attendant of the family soon came to their assistance.

They now strictly examined all the servants, but they solemnly declared that they had not seen nor heard anything to alarm or disturb them in the night, and they were as much surprised and grieved at what had taken place as their lordships themselves.

The greatest consternation prevailed; Lord Bathurst, his son, and Sir Roderick briefly consulted together what was best to be done, and then they all left the abbey, accompanied by serval servants, determined to scour the country round, in pursuit of the unfortunate Celestia and the daring miscreant in whose power she was, and who had doomed her to so dreadful a fate. But, alas! they saw too plainly there was little hope of their efforts being crowned with any success, and the agony of their feelings, especially that of Lord Malensbury, increased until it became almost insupportable.

Lord Elverton was the first who was restored to sensibility, and the agony of his feelings needs no description from us. All the horrors of what had happened rushed upon his recollection, and filled his bosom with despair. He called upon the name of Celestia, and then declared in the frenzy of his emotion that all the fiends of hell were conspired against him, and that death would be a blessing to him. It was some time ere he would receive the least consolation, and he then eagerly inquired after his sister. He was informed that she had just been restored to sensibility, and had requested to see him; he therefore hastened to her chamber, and without for a few minutes being able to speak, he sunk on a chair by the side of the bed, in a state of mind bordering upon distraction. Lady Eugenia groaned, but a flood of tears having come to her relief, she said in the most melancholy accents—

"Oh, my dear brother, what a terrible calamity is this; Heaven help us, for we need all the fortitude we can gather together to bear up against this awful blow. Alas! my poor Celestia, where art thou now? God! God! little did I think that she was so soon to be snatched away from us."

"These accumulated horrors will drive me mad," said the earl, striking his breast with the most heartrending emotion; "but to think that she should be in the power of the monster Bonville, she, my gentle, virtuous Celestia! Horror! horror! But for God's sake, my sister, tell me all, how it happened?"

"Alas!" replied Lady Eugenia, "the melancholy, the horrible truth is soon told. Myself and poor Celestia were sitting up for some time after we had retired to our chamber, for we wished to prepare some few trifling articles of dress for our intended journey; and we were so deeply engaged in conversation, that we paid no attention to anything else.

"From the profound silence that reigned throughout the abbey we had no doubt that you and all the family had retired to rest; but presently we thought we heard footsteps stealing cautiously along the gallery; but all was in a moment silence, and thinking that we might have been mistaken, we resumed our task, and took no further notice of it.

"We were both seated with our backs towards the door, but suddenly raising my eyes, judge of my horror and amazement when I beheld the dark shadows of two or three human forms on the wainscot opposite. Poor Celestia saw them at the same instant; we dropped our work, both of us uttered a scream, and turning round, to our horror beheld several armed and masked ruffians in the room. We were surrounded in an instant, and before I had time to utter another cry I was knocked down by a heavy blow from one of the villains,

and became insensible. This of course is all I know; but how the miscreants obtained an entrance into the abbey, and succeeded in bearing away their unfortunate and innocent victim without creating any alarm, is more than I can comprehend."

Again the earl groaned, and swayed his body to and fro in his chair in a state of anguish which it would be a difficult task to depicture.

"The mystery is torturing," he said at last. "I fear there is no hope, and that sweet girl whom we have so recently discovered to be so nearly related to us, is lost to us for ever. There has not been a single lock or bolt disturbed, and the servants have solemnly declared that they heard no cry or other sound in the night. How is this to be explained?"

"God only knows," replied Lady Eugenia; "but He surely will yet defeat the monster's plans; He will not suffer him to triumph in his atrocity."

"Alas! alas!" sighed Lord Elverton, "the poor girl will die with terror, or if she does not, to what a dreadful, a revolting fate has the murderer Bonville doomed her. May the most terrible vengeance of offended Heaven overtake him. Barbarous man, was it not enough to murder her unfortunate mother, and that mother's brother, but you must now seek the ruin of the innocent daughter? Oh, my Celestia, my kind, my gentle, my loving Celestia, at the thought of your horrible situation my heart will surely break, or madness seize upon my brain."

He threw himself back in his chair, in a paroxysm of unutterable grief, and sobbed like a child, and Lady Eugenia was in no better a condition, and of course was unable to attempt to offer him the least consolation.

Several hours passed away in this wretched manner, and it was not until the approach of night that Lord Bathurst, his son, Sir Roderick, and Lord Everside returned to the abbey. Sir Eustace Aubrey and Collingwood, who were distracted at this awful event, together with a number of their servants, had also gone in search of the unfortunate girl, but with despairing hearts, for where could they direct their search?

Lord Elverton immediately sought the

presence of his friends, but the anguish and despair of their looks convinced him that he had nothing to hope. Lord Malensbury in particular was in a state bordering upon madness.

They had travelled for miles during the time they had been away from the abbey, but all their inquiries had been unsuccessful; they could discover not the least traces of the villains or the ill-fated Celestia; and they now gave themselves up to the most agonizing despair, for it was clear, too painfully clear, that she was lost to them for ever, or that if she were by some miraculous interposition of Providence restored to them, it would not be until the miscreant Bonville had accomplished his barbarous and diabolical designs.

To describe the agony of them all, would be impossible. Lord Elverton raved and tore his hair like a maniac, and the others were all in such a state of mind, that they were totally unable to consult together what was best to be done under the dreadful circumstances. Lord Malensbury was in a most pitiable condition; he shut himself up in his room, and there gave himself up entirely to the violent agony of his grief.

"Celestia, my beloved Celestia," he sighed. "Where are you now?—Shall I never behold you more?—Oh, what a shocking destiny is yours. Could not your innocence protect you?—Oh, may the heaviest curses of Heaven descend upon the head of the monster who holds you in his power. Good God! how I shudder to think of this when I remember the threats which he has held out. And he will not fail to put his threats into execution, unless the Almighty interposes to save you from him. What mercy can you expect from him? None, none; nothing can move his hard heart to pity. Your prayers, your tears, your supplications will all be lost upon him, and they will but serve him to mock at. Horror! horror!—this is a calamity which I cannot find fortitude to support. Almighty Father, on my knees I beseech thee to avert the dreadful evils we have too much reason to apprehend, to restore the poor innocent girl uninjured to her sorrowing friends, and to bring the villain Bonville to that punishment he has so long escaped. Oh, do not permit him to triumph. Too long

has he carried on his hideous career with impunity, but this last crime, if possible, surpasses all the others he has committed in atrocity."

He paced the room in the greatest anguish of mind, and could find no abatement to his grief. Whichever way he looked all was horror and black despair.

The greatest and most painful sensation was caused in the neighbourhood, by the cruel abduction of our heroine, and every one joined in sympathy for the earl and the afflicted members of his family, and in execrating the abominable wretch who had been guilty of such a series of frightful crimes, crimes which only a fiend at heart could be capable of perpetrating.

Lady Eglantine could do nothing but weep and wring her hands for the loss of her amiable young friend, and they were all, in fact, in too distracted a state of mind to attempt to impart consolation to each other.

Collingwood Aubrey and his father did not return from their fruitless search until a late hour of the night, and the agony of the former was as intense as it was sincere. That he really loved the innocent Celestia with a most ardent and unconquerable passion, there was no denying, and even if he had not, the terror of her fate would have been sufficient to have excited the most powerful emotion of grief in his breast, and horror and disgust for Bonville.

The night wore away, but the earl and his friends could not think of separating. It would have been impossible for them to have rested, with such a dreadful weight of care upon their minds, and the morning found them in the same wretched state.

Lord Elverton could not be persuaded to retire to his chamber, and his melancholy bewailings of anguish and despair were quite piteous to hear; to have sought to impart consolation to him, would have been folly, and there was no alternative but to suffer him to indulge his grief without interruption. They began to fear for his senses, and, indeed, under all the dreadful circumstances, there was too much reason to do so.

Numerous persons were despatched in all directions, to endeavour to obtain some clue to the unfortunate Celestia, and a fortune was offered to any one who would come forward to give any information which might be the means of restoring her to her distracted friends. They hoped it might be the means of inducing one of the villains who had been concerned in the rascally plot to betray his employer; but that hope was not destined to be realized, and the unhappy family was doomed to experience increased misery, anxiety, and suspense. Lady Eugenia was still too ill to leave her chamber, and the intense suffering of mind which she endured was almost equal to that of her brother.

CHAPTER XXVII.

CELESTIA IN THE POWER OF BONVILLE.
—HER SUFFERING.—THE INTERVIEW
BETWEEN HER AND LADY ELVINA IN
THE DUNGEON.

IMMEDIATELY after having given utterance to the cry of terror on beholding the ruffians in the chamber, Celestia had fainted; and Bonville, for it was he who led them on, raising her in his powerful and herculean arms with as much ease as if she had been an infant, darted from the chamber in triumph, beckoning his associates to follow in silence.

On reaching about the centre of the gallery, a secret trap in the flooring was standing open, which had never been known to the earl, or any of his family, and beneath it was a winding flight of steps, on one of which a dark lantern was standing, which one of the men took up, and led the way, and then they all descended, treading carefully, and noiselessly closing the trap-door after them.

On reaching the bottom of these steps, they were in a spacious stone vault, and here Bonville paused a minute or two to take breath, and to exult over the insensible form of his innocent and lovely victim. He gazed at her with looks of the most fiendish exultation, and then he thus soliloquised in his usual harsh and disgusting tones—

"So, my dainty fair one, I have thee safely now; in spite of all the precautions of thy noble relatives thou art mine, and nothing can save thee from the fate to which I have destined thee. Oh, this is indeed a triumph. What will be the agony of the earl and all connected with thee, when they shall discover that thou art gone, and learn into whose power thou art fallen? Fools! did they think to intimidate Bonville from his purpose? Did they imagine that I would fail to keep my word? Oh, but methinks that they will scoff at my power no longer. Beauteous Celestia, what triumph it is for me, what feelings of transport does it impart to me, to hold thee thus in my arms. Sweet maiden, thou art mine, the prize of the murderer Bonville, and it will be useless for thee to attempt to resist my wishes. Follow me, my bold associates in villany, for we have no time to lose."

He once more raised the insensible form of our heroine in his arms, and they left the vault and entered a long subterraneous passage, which seemed to wind its way far beneath the walls of the abbey. This passage had many windings and turnings, and seemed to have been constructed with great art; but at length they reached the end of it, and descending a few steps, found themselves in a spacious and lofty cavern. At the farther end of this curious place was an opening sufficiently large to enable a person to pass through it, and beneath it was a flight of rude steps, cut out of the solid earth. These Bonville, with his senseless burthen, ascended, followed by the other ruffians, and passing out at the aperture, they were in the open air. The entrance to the cavern was cut in the side of a lofty hill, and it was remarkable, that it had never been discovered by the earl or any of the inhabitants in the vicinity of the abbey.

Close by the hill, a carriage was standing, to which Bonville conveyed our heroine, and having lifted her into it, and followed himself, accompanied by one of the ruffians, the vehicle was driven off with great speed, and the remainder of the villains followed on horseback.

The motion of the vehicle did not arouse our heroine from her state of insensibility, and Bonville was glad of it, for he was anxious that they should reach some distance from the abbey before she should be aware of where she was. With what mingled feelings of triumph and admiration did he gaze upon her pale but lovely countenance, and then he dared to pollute her lips with his odious kisses, but still she remained unconscious and inanimate.

"Oh, what captivating charms are concentrated in that one fair being," he said; "and she is now the slave of my will, and has no power to save herself. This will fully repay me for the scorn with which my overtures were treated by Lady Elvina when she was about her age, and is a rich gratification to my revenge. Oh, what exquisite torture will it be to my aged prisoner, when she beholds her, and how will I exult over their mutual misery. Oh, it will be a most delicious triumph!"

He placed his arm around the slender waist of the damsel, and again he contaminated her lips with his disgusting kisses. Still she remained fixed and inanimate as a corpse.

The vehicle continued its rapid speed, and soon they were several miles from Sungrove Abbey. They passed through a wild and unfrequented part of the country, such of course being the arrangements of Bonville, and at length arrived at a low and miserable looking inn, or rather a pot-house, on the borders of a dreary waste which they had been traversing for some time.

It was just at this moment that Celestia revived, and looking around her for a short time, was perfectly unconscious of where she was. But the revolting countenance of Bonville, whose malignant eyes were fixed exultingly upon her, and the other ferocious looking villain who was in the vehicle with her, quickly aroused her to recollection, and she uttered a shriek of terror.

"Silence, girl," exclaimed Bonville, levelling a pistol at her head; "all resistance is now useless, you are far away from your *dear* friends. No assistance is at hand, and even if it were, this, I think, would sufficiently quiet you."

"Oh, God!—oh, God!" ejaculated our heroine, shuddering with terror, and staring at the monster aghast, "what do you intend to do with me? Why have you thus dragged me from my friends? Oh, in pity spare me; restore me to them, and I will pardon you the dreadful outrage you have committed on me."

"My sweet petitioner," returned Bonville, with one of his most sardonic and repulsive grins, "I am sorry that I cannot comply with a request coming from such ruby lips as yours. It has cost me some trouble to obtain possession of you, and indeed I cannot now resign you at so cheap a rate. But to make some amends for the 'dreadful outrage' you say I have committed upon you, I promise in a few hours to introduce you to one whom you have never before seen, your beloved relative, the once lovely Lady Elvina Elverton."

Celestia endeavoured to speak, but the horror of her feelings prevented her, and fixing upon the wretch a look which ought to have penetrated to his very soul, she uttered a faint cry, and again became insensible.

The vehicle now stopped at the house before mentioned, and Bonville lifted the poor girl out, and with the assistance of his companions conveyed her into a low dark room, the landlord and his wife, with whom the ruffian was well acquainted, being ready to receive them.

They were two as repulsive-looking individuals as could be well imagined, and, therefore, poor Celestia, if she had been conscious of anything, could have expected very little tenderness of treatment from them.

"Ha, ha!" grinned the worthy host of this respectable hostelrie, "she is a lovely wench, a beautiful wench, just like my sweet Araminta, who is dead and gone, with the exception that my dear Araminta had a club foot, a slight hump on her back, a few holes in her face, and was minus one of her eyes. Yet, take her for all in all, this young lady is the very picter of her."

"Well, well, Sniggers," said Bonville, impatiently, "after you have done enumerating the charms of that beautiful defunct offspring of yours, I would thank you to attend to me."

"Certainly, certainly," said Mr. Sniggers,—"I beg pardon. But—but what an extraordinary resemblance. What a happy man you must be, Mr. Richards, (the name by which Bonville had thought it prudent to be known to the worthy who then addressed him,) but what can I do for you, sir?"

"Change the horses as quick as possible—bring in some refreshment—and take yourself off."

"Oh, very good, sir; but the young lady?"

"Why let Mrs. Sniggers attend to her recovery, if she thinks proper to recover, though I do not wish her to do so at present; it will be time enough when we are a little farther on our journey. And mind me, if she should happen to revive too soon, you have some gentle, wholesome cordial that can *calm* her spirits, have you not?"

Sniggers winked his left eye significantly, and vanished.

The refreshments made their appearance, and with them Mrs. Sniggers and her worst half.

"Give my fellows what they require," said the villain Bonville, "and then depart as soon as you please. Mrs. Sniggers here is a most excellent woman, and can do the amiable for this damsel; can't you, Mrs. Sniggers?"

They sweet lady, made a most profound curtsey, and her beloved partner again vanished to execute the order which had been communicated to him by Bonville.

"What a sweet creature she is," said Mrs. Sniggers, as she approached our heroine, "just like what people used to say I was when I was about her age."

"Hold your clack, you confounded old hag!" cried Bonville, "and attend to your charge."

Some persons are fond of flattery; probably Mrs. Sniggers was; however, be that as it might, when Bonville made the latter compliment she indulged him with another profound curtsey in acknowledgment, and then turned her attention to Celestia, who, reclining on a sofa, was still wrapt in the same state of insensibility as when she was first brought into the house.

Mrs. Sniggers was certainly not one of the most handsome women in the world, though possibly she might have been, but then to admit that must likewise have been to admit that she was a remarkably aged woman, and must have existed when connoisseurs of beauty were not very prevalent. She stood about three feet two, and as her amiable spouse had described his lovely Araminta, she had remarkable indentions in her physiognomy; a fat nose, something

resembling a slug crawling down a pumpkin; a mouth to which a moderate sized horse shoe would form no bad simile; a couple of lips that could have rivalled the finest "small Germans," a few teeth that would have taken the shine out of the best specimens of tusks; a squint in her two grey eyes, that would justly have made all other eyes look cross; and hair of that peculiar hue at which you might very conveniently light your cigar.

In addition to all these charms, Mrs. Sniggers had a natural hump upon her back, which, if it had been capable of being devoted to that purpose, would have made a very excellent travelling trunk or small portmanteau; one leg was considerably shorter than the other, and to sum up all Mrs. Sniggers had a disposition that perfectly corresponded with all her other personal graces. Sweet, amiable woman was Mrs. Sniggers, and we have only been thus particular in enumerating her various qualities, personal and intrinsic, to show the gentle hands in which it had been the fortune of poor Celestia to be placed. It is a well known fact that ugly and deformed creatures, in proportion to the preponderance of the fair proportions with which it has pleased an All-wise Power to bless their fellow creatures, hate them, and seize every opportunity of venting their malice upon them; and such was the case with the most amiable Mrs. Sniggers. As she gazed upon the helpless and lovely maiden before her, all that devil's feeling rose predominant in her breast, and there was no tortures which she would not have become the willing agent to inflict upon her.

"Ah!" said the old hag, as Bonville had very justly and characteristically denominated her, after she had contemplated Celestia for a few moments with evident feelings of a most satisfactory character, but most peculiar nature, "she is indeed a nice girl; and you intend her——"

"Never mind what I intend, old harridan," fiercely interrupted Bonville, "but do as I have bid you."

"Very good, sir, very good," replied Mrs. Sniggers, with another low curtsey in acknowledgment of the compliment. "You wish her to be recovered?"

"Yes; and then placed in a state of stupefaction again ; you understand me ?"

"Oh, certainly, certainly," answered Mrs. Sniggers with a most hideous grin.

"Have you brought the cordial, the composing draught?" asked Bonville.

"Oh, yes," replied Mrs. Sniggers, with a chuckle, and at the same time producing a small phial from her bosom, containing a reddish sort of mixture ;—"I think this will have all the effect you wish it."

"Is it not poison?"

"Good gracious, how could I be guilty of such a thing?"

"Taste it yourself, first, to try its quality," said Bonville sarcastically.

"Dear me, how particular you are, Mr. Richards," returned the old woman, taking a sip of the liquid.

"Oh, that will do," remarked Bonville. "Now mix a portion of it, as much as you think will last for about thirty miles, in that glass of negus, and then you may recover her as soon as you please."

Mrs. Sniggers obeyed, and then by the dint of overlays of vinegared rag to her temples, and singed brown paper to her nostrils, restored poor Celestia to a state of consciousness.

Bonville had concealed himself in that part of the room where he could not be observed by his unfortunate victim, and, therefore, when she opened her eyes and gazed around her, for the moment she was perfectly unconscious where she was, but meeting the repulsive features of Mrs. Sniggers, she shuddered with horror, and in a tremulous voice ejaculated :—

"For the love of heaven, where are we? who are you? and why am I detained in this manner?"

"You are with friends, my good young lady," replied Mrs. Sniggers, "friends who have rescued you from the power of a villain, and will quickly restore you to your home."

"Good God!" said our heroine, "is it possible? Have I indeed been so fortunate? Oh, tell me, to whom am I indebted for this inestimable kindness?"

"Do not thank me, my dear young lady," said Mrs. Sniggers, in her most insinuating tones; "the consciousness of having performed a worthy action is more than a sufficient reward. Poor thing, poor thing! you must be terribly frightened; but never mind, you will soon be better, by and by. Take a drop of this wine, my dear, it will revive you."

"No, no, but tell me where I am, and what has become of the miscreant who has torn me from my home?"

"I will tell you every thing, my sweet young lady, if you will only just partake of this nice wine."

Celestia, scarcely knowing what she did, did suffer the glass to be conveyed to her lips, and slightly partook of the contents. Bonville watched her anxiously from the place of his concealment, but his impatience increased almost beyond endurance.

"Drink heartily, my good young lady," importuned Mrs. Sniggers; "it is very nice, and will do you good. Now, do not be afraid, it will not harm you, my love."

The good Mrs. Sniggers placed the tumbler to the lips of the almost unconscious Celestia, and forced the greater part of the contents down her throat.

"Now, my love," said the wicked old woman, inwardly chuckling at her own mischief. "I know you must feel better after that nice draught. A little more, love; oh, it's most refreshing."

Our heroine placed her hands upon her burning and throbbing temples, and fixed upon her a vacant and stupefied stare. Her head seemed to swim round, a mist gathered before her eyes; her limbs trembled, objects became indistinct to her vision, and with a faint sigh she once more sank on the sofa in a state of the most profound stupor.

Mrs. Sniggers stood contemplating her with a look of satisfaction, and being satisfied that she was perfectly insensible, Bonville came from the place of his concealment.

"Well managed, capitally managed, Mother Sniggers," he said, in a complimentary tone.

"Ah, well," returned the old woman, showing her tusks to the best advantage, and twisting her ugly visage into still more frightful distortion, "I *am* glad I have pleased you for once, Mr. Richards. She is a nice girl, though, a very nice girl."

"Cease your prating, and take your reward," said Bonville, throwing her a purse. "Now send the man, your husband, to me."

Mrs. Sniggers thrust the purse with high glee into her bosom, and vanished, and immediately afterwards her lord and should-be master appeared.

"Are the horses put to the carriage?" demanded Bonville.

"Yes, Mr. Richards," replied Sniggers.

"And have the fellows had their refreshment?"

"Yes, Mr. Richards."

"Then take your charge out of that."

"Thank you, Mr. Richards. When shall you be calling this way again?"

"I don't know, never again; you have never seen me in your life, do you hear?"

"I never knew such an individual, Mr. Richards."

"Nor any person at all corresponding with the description of my person?"

"Certainly not, Mr. Richards."

"You never saw this young lady?"

"Blind as a bat, Mr. Richards," said Sniggers with a sly leer.

"And if you are not dumb as a post too, I will burn your house about your ears, and hang you up to your own sign post."

"Much obliged to you for all favours Mr. Richards. Good-night. I shall be happy to see you again on such another occasion."

"Good-night," gruffly replied Bonville, "and mind what I have told you."

"Oh, I shall never forget you, Mr. Richards," said Sniggers, drily, and shaking the purse which Bonville had given him. "I shall never forget you, depend upon it, while you leave me such good testimonials of your friendship."

"Begone!" commanded Bonville, "but stay, what is the time?"

"Just half-past twelve."

"'Tis well; I can reach the place of my destination before daylight, I think. You know pretty well the road I am about to travel, is there any danger?"

"None that I am aware of, Mr. Richards. But if there should be, you are pretty well protected, I think."

Bonville scowled at him, and the very worthy Mr. Sniggers bowed himself out of the room. Bonville then raised the insensible form of Celestia in his arms and hurried out of the house. He found his villanous associates all ready mounted and prepared to depart, and placing Celestia in the vehicle, and following himself, accompanied by the same ruffian who had attended him before, the carriage was driven off with even increased speed.

Over moor and wild it bounded, through intricate forest it wended its way, but not all the jolting of the vehicle could arose the hapless Celestia from the deep torpor in which her senses were steeped by the powerful opiate which had been infused into the wine she had drunk, by the wicked old woman, Sniggers.

"It acts well, it acts well!" said Bonville, as with satisfaction he gazed upon his insensible and innocent victim; "it was an excellent contrivance, and will save me a great deal of trouble that I might otherwise have incurred. In a few hours we shall arrive at the place of our destination, and at any rate we are now far out of the reach of pursuit. The blow you gave the old woman, Dick, I think would quiet her for some time."

"No doubt of it, master," replied the ruffian, "if it has not silenced her altogether."

"Why, that would be better still," remarkd Bonville, "however, it is of very little consequence, for as they are all unacquainted with the secret entrance to the abbey, they will be in the most profound ignorance of the means by which we effected the capture of my fair prize. It has been excellently managed throughout, and I look upon this as one of my greatest triumphs."

"You may well do that, master," said the villain, whom Bonville had called Dick; "she is indeed a prize that it were well worth running any risk to obtain possession of."

"How beautiful she looks," soliloquized Bonville, feasting his eyes on the inanimate form before him; "how beautiful even in her insensibility. By every power, I would not relinquish this prize for the proudest kingdom in Europe. Oh, what will be the tortures her loss will inflict upon those whom I hate. How will they now shudder at the mention of my name, if they have never done so before. Elvina, haughty Elvina, I told thee I would have a sanguinary, a wholesale revenge for the scorn you dared to heap upon me, and have I not kept my word? Ha, ha, ha! What will be your agony when I introduce this fair thing, the daughter of your murdered offspring to you, and you know that she is mine, my destined victim, my future victim, poor, helpless creature, at my mercy, as thou thyself art? Mercy! ha, ha, ha! when could mercy and the name of Bonville be coupled together? I live but for vengeance, and that I will obtain at any cost. Fools talk of perdition, of future punishment. Pshaw! I mock, I laugh all their drivelling cant to scorn. Bonville has been the despised, the hated of mankind, and he will pay the debt of gratitude in full."

It was horrible to hear the miscreant thus give vent to his deadly and malicious feelings, and even the hardened ruffian who was seated by his side could not help shuddering. Urged on by the commands of Bonville, the vehicle was driven at a still greater speed, until the horse seemed to fly; and yet there could be no possible fear of pursuit, as they were already many miles from

Sungrove Abbey; and from the circumstances under which Celestia had been seized, it was not likely her loss would be discovered for several hours, and even then they could have no idea what route those who held her in their power had taken. But the villain Bonville was impatient to arrive at the place of his destination, that he might gratify his inhuman vengeance to the fullest extent, and every moment appeared to him, in a manner of speaking, to be an age.

Wild and cheerless was that part of the country they were travelling through, but the moon shone brightly, myriads of twinkling stars gemmed the sky, and made all around lively and picturesque which would otherwise have been sad and desolate.

So strong was the opiate which Mrs. Sniggers had administered to her, that our heroine did not seem likely soon to recover from its effects, and thus everything favoured the designs of the heartless scoundrel who had so mercilessly torn her from her home. He threw himself back in the vehicle, and contemplated her with feelings of the most diabolical satisfaction.

"She scorned my threats, no doubt," he said, "but what will they say now? Oh, how I have wrung their hearts, and I glory in it. Bonville was never defeated yet in any project he had formed, and he will not be. 'Tis many, many years since first I commenced my plot, and I shall live to triumph in its completion. Who talks to me of retribution?—I defy every power, human and divine. I affected to be a saint when I was a very devil, and I deceived them all. Oh, it was glorious sport. But my cards are not all played yet, oh, no, they are not all played yet."

In this manner two hours more elapsed, and still our heroine remained in the same state of torpor. The darkness of night had now given way to the grey dawn of morn, and Bonville became still more anxious to arrive at the end of the journey, for persons now began to leave their dwellings, and he was fearful that the manner in which they were travelling might excite suspicion, and cause some obstruction, which might not be attended with very agreeable results. But they were now only a few miles from the place to which they were going, and the hopes of Bonville revived the nearer they approached it.

They had come in sight of the gloomy edifice which was destined to be her future prison, when Celestia suddenly recovered her senses, and filled with horror, endeavoured to rise from her seat, but Bonville held her down.

"Is this all a frightful dream?" she exclaimed;—"no—no—the dreadful truth flashes upon my brain. I remember all now! Oh, God! oh, God!—save me, save me, I beseech you!"

"Sweetest Celestia," said Bonville, trying to assume a tone of tenderness; "pray compose yourself. You are now many, many miles from that dear romantic edifice, Sungrove Abbey, but you are with one who loves you fondly for your beauty only, and who has taken upon himself the responsibility of your future guardianship. Nay, do not shrink from me, or view me with such eyes of scorn, for I assure you it is all useless. We have met before, damsel, in the old priory ruins; do you remember? I told you then that you were my destined mistress, that you should shortly be in my power, and have I not kept my word?—Ay, look at me; I am no phantom, but that same Bonville, whose name no doubt you have been taught to hear mentioned only with feelings of horror. You are mine, sweet Celestia, and nothing can rescue you from my power."

"Monster!" gasped forth the horror-stricken maiden, "release me, return me to my friends, whom you have already so dreadfully persecuted, or the vengeance of God and man will overtake you."

"I am sorry, lovely Celestia, that I cannot comply with your request," returned the wretch with one of his most repulsive and sardonic grins; "that really would be too great a sacrifice after all the trouble I have been at to obtain possession of you."

"Heaven spare me!" shrieked the affrighted and disgusted girl; "oh, help, help!"

"Your cries are useless," said Bonville, "there is no one near who can render you any aid; and see, we have now arrived at the place of our destination. I triumph, I triumph! the prize is securely mine."

At that very moment the carriage stopped at the door of the old house, Celestia caught but one glimpse of the gloomy building, and then, completely overwhelmed with horror, she gave utterance to a frantic cry, and once more became insensible.

"All right," said the villain Bonville, as he alighted from the vehicle, "we have arrived at the end of our journey, and without any obstruction. What ho, there! Are you all asleep?"

He knocked lustily at the door as he gave utterance to these words, and it was immediately opened by one of the ruffians who were in his employ. He then lifted our heroine from the carriage, and conveyed her to an apartment which he had prepared for her reception, and left her in charge of a woman who for some years had been attached to his service, and who from baseness of disposition was every way qualified to serve so villanous a master.

Having imprinted a kiss upon the insensible maiden's pale cheeks, he quitted the room, and retired to his own apartment to exult over the success of his diabolical plot.

He traversed the apartment with hasty strides, and laughed aloud in the fiendish triumph of his feelings.

"So young, so gentle, so lovely, and so innocent," he muttered to himself; "the envied, the admired of all, and she is mine. Oh, how exquisitely transporting is the thought. I could go mad with very joy. And oh, how great is the agony that her friends and relations are now enduring; how I do delight to wring their hearts. But I have a greater source of exultation and triumph yet, in the misery which the certainty of Celestia being in my power will cause Lady Elvina. And what will be the maddening anguish of them both when I introduce them to each other!—I must immediately to the dungeon of my prisoner to apprise her of the happiness which is in store for her."

Thus saying, the villain stalked from the room, and immediately made his way to the dungeon in which the unfortunate Lady Elvina was confined.

On his entrance she was crouched down on a miserable bed of straw, and worn out with anguish of mind and bodily suffering, had fallen into a feverish slumber. He stood and gazed at her a few minutes with such feelings as no other but such a heartless ruffian as himself could experience.

"Her dreams must be very pleasant," he muttered to himself; "this is a delightful place to repose in; not quite so elegant or commodious perhaps as the apartments she formerly occupied, but a very fit place for haughty pride to humble itself in. Ha, ha! it glads mine eyes to gaze upon her. What ho! sweet Lady Elvina, thy lord and—gaoler is here!"

The wretched lady started from her sleep at the sound of his well known voice, and gazed with horror upon him.

"What want you now, inhuman man?" she demanded in a tremulous voice, "will you not suffer me to snatch a few moments of sleep from the dreadful sufferings your demoniacal spirit of hatred and revenge has inflicted upon me?"

"Dear Lady Elvina," said the taunting ruffian, sarcastically, "on this occasion, at any rate, you should hail my presence with joy, for I come to bring you good news."

"Brutal man," she replied, "do not mock me."

"Mock you, indeed I do not; this is ungrateful."

"Wretch, begone, for the very sight of you fills me with horror, and your looks and words convince me you have some fresh torture in store for me. What would you have? what will you say? Let me know at once, but do not taunt me with those cruel observations which are worse than so many daggers piercing my heart."

Bonville folded his arms across his broad chest, and fixed upon her a look of the most diabolical triumph, and then he laughed aloud. Lady Elvina averted her looks in horror and disgust.

"You are impatient, sweet Lady Elvina," he said, after a pause, "but not to keep you any longer in suspense, I have to inform you that she has arrived."

"Arrived! who? You torture me!"

"Your grand-daughter, the fair and innocent Celestia de Aunville."

The hapless woman started to her feet with a suddenness that astonished Bonville, as she ejaculated:—

"Celestia! the child of my sainted Elvina? God of Heaven! it cannot be. You only seek to distract my brain, and add to the agony you have already inflicted upon me ; oh, assure me that you speak not the truth, and that at any rate that poor innocent girl is not in your power."

"But she is," replied Bonville, "and to remove all doubts from your ladyship's mind, I will introduce her to you, probably to-morrow, if she is sufficiently recovered from her fright to see you. She is a beautiful creature, a sweet, dainty girl, just such another as you were when I lured you from your husband's arms, and you presumed to reject with scorn the overtures I made to you. Dear Lady Elvina, do I not triumph now?"

The unhappy victim of the villain's cruelty clasped her hands in agony, and for a few minutes was so absorbed in horror, that she was unable to give utterance to a word. Bonville continued to watch her emotions with delight, and did not offer to interrupt her by any further observations, but at length she exclaimed in a voice rendered awful by the intensity of her feelings—

"Demon in human form, cold blooded heartless miscreant, whom no feeling of pity can touch, beware, for great as your triumph may now appear to be, the vengeance of insulted and outraged Heaven will most assuredly overtake you. Think you that the just God who reigns above us will permit you to continue to commit your acts of atrocity with impunity?— No, the thunderbolt of His wrath will quickly descend upon your head and crush you in the midst of your iniquity. Poor crawling worm, dare you defy that Supreme and All-merciful Power to which we all must bow, however we may affect to despise it ?—Have you no dread of a terrible futurity—think you that crimes hideous as those you have committed, although they may escape punishment in this world, will fail to do so in the next ? I know I talk to a miscreant, but the time will come, when even you will be made to feel. Dare not, I warn you, to attempt, if that innocent girl is indeed in your power, to put your monstrous designs into execution—for assuredly if you do, the retribution of Heaven in its most awful shape will overtake you."

"A very pretty exordium, sweet Lady Elvina," said Bonville, in his most sarcastic and disgusting tones, "but I regret to say that it is not at all likely to have the effect you wish it to have upon me. I tell you, I scorn and laugh at all such idle cant. What care I for the present or the future ?—Ha, ha, ha ! sweet Lady Elvina, your noble relative is a lovely girl, a very lovely girl, which you will acknowledge when you see her, and she will make me a most excellent mistress. You talk of retribution, you warn me to look for some dreadful punishment, but again I tell you that I laugh at it. I brought your daughter to the guillotine ; I murdered your son ; I hold you now a wretched prisoner ; I have your fair relation in my power ; I can crush and exterminate you all ; and has retribution overtaken me yet ? Has the Supreme Power of which you speak, been able, if willing, to stay me in my career of crime, as you are pleased to designate my proceedings ? No, it has not, and I laugh its power to scorn. In spite of every power, human or divine, my revenge, my deep implacable revenge, shall be gratified to the fullest extent. Celestia, the beauteous Celestia, the delicate, virtuous girl, whom every one admires, the loved one of young Lord Malensbury, at whom the world will scoff, and to whom few will tender the voice of pity. I thought I would apprize you of these my intentions, dear Lady Elvina, knowing that it would afford you some means of pleasurable reflection in your present enviable situation."

Lady Elvina could not reply ; she had listened to this brutal speech with feelings of the most indescribable horror ; and when Bonville had concluded, she threw herself back, and covering her face with her hands, to shut out the form of her tormentor, she groaned aloud in the agony of her feelings.

Bonville had accomplished what he wished ; he had driven the unfortunate lady to a state of the utmost anguish and despair, and after glaring at her again for a few moments, with feelings of the most diabolical exultation, he quitted the dungeon while she was still in a state of unconsciousness, and hurried to his own apartment. He then sent a messenger to the woman in whose charge he had left the unfortunate Celestia, to inquire how she was, and he speedily returned and informed him that she was still in a state of insensibility, nor was there much probability of her reviving for some time.

"It is well," soliloquized the ruffian, "she will revive soon enough for me to have an interview with her, and in the meantime I will ripen my plans for mischief. Oh, what a triumph is this!—Elvina and her brother both murdered, and Celestia and Lady Elvina both in my power; the one my destined victim to the passions her charms have excited, the other a miserable wretch, whose existence is by far more horrible than the most torturing death could possibly be. I have kept my word, and I glory in the act."

He laughed outright in the exultation of his feelings, and then coolly sat himself down to partake of the provisions which by his orders had been supplied to him, and drank himself into a state of excitement and inebriation—having arrived at which, he threw himself upon his bed, and sunk to sleep.

But what were the feelings of Lady Elvina, after the miscreant had left her? It would indeed be a difficult task to describe them, and therefore we must leave them to the imagination of the reader. For some time she remained in a state of stupefaction. Only an indistinct vision of what had taken place, at her recent interview with the savage Bonville, floated before her imagination; but at length all the horrors of the dread reality rushed upon her brain, and she started from her bed of straw, and sinking upon her knees raised her bloodshot eyes towards Heaven with an expression of intense anguish which must have excited commiseration in the breast of the most insensible observer. She clasped her hands at the same time together with such a vehemence that her finger-nails perforated the palms of her hands, and in a voice of the most impressive solemnity and agony, she ejaculated:—

"Oh, God! oh, God! why hast thou permitted me to see this day?—Why has the wretch in whose power I am been suffered so far to triumph in his brutal, his hideous designs? What have I and my unfortunate family done to merit these accumulated horrors? My poor Celestia, you whom I have not seen since infancy, and whom I never ex-

pected to behold again; child of my murdered daughter, are you indeed in the power of this inhuman villain, and at his mercy?—Merciful Heaven forbid, and yet, how can I doubt it after what he has said? And must you too fall a victim to his bloody and monstrous feelings of revenge? Will no power interfere to rescue you from the dreadful fate with which you are threatened? Must your innocence be sacrificed at the shrine of his lust?—The thought drives me to madness. Almighty parent of all good, I the most humble and abject of thy creatures earnestly beseech thee not to permit the frightful crime. Let me be assured of her restitution to liberty, to the arms of her afflicted, her deeply persecuted relations, and then what further troubles it may be thy will to inflict upon me, I will submit to without a murmur. Alas! alas! I have lived too long. It would have been a mercy to me to have died years ago. Oh, how severely have I been punished for my youthful indiscretion. How weak and credulous I must have been ever to have been led astray by this cruel man. What manifold sorrows have I not brought upon myself and all who are connected with me. Should the difference of religious opinion ever have induced me to abandon the best of husbands and of men?—Oh no, no, I have greatly erred, but All-merciful God accept the terrible punishment I have already received as a sufficient atonement, and do not visit any further my sins upon the heads of my innocent family."

The heart of the suffering lady was full almost to bursting as she gave utterance to these plaintive words, and she continued on her knees, with her eyes raised in supplication towards Heaven, and her brain burning with the madness of despair and agony.

"Alas, alas," she sighed, "what must now be the insupportable anguish my unfortunate husband and my other relations must be enduring at the loss of her who doubtless formed the principal source of their joy. I shudder to reflect upon it. And am I not the indirect cause of all the horrors which have taken place?—Yes, I am; had I performed my duty to my husband, these dreadful events would never have happened. Bonville would have been rendered powerless; my Elvina, and Edgar, would now have been living; I should have been at liberty, and surrounded by the happy and smiling faces of my family. Yes, it is I who have been the author of it all, and therefore I alone should suffer; but Almighty God, I again implore thee not to punish my innocent family for my transgressions. Look down with an eye of pity and commiseration upon them, and restore them to all that happiness which they can now only hope to enjoy in this world. Above all I beseech thee to protect this innocent girl from the contamination of this fiend in human form, and for ever, whilst life remains in my body, will I offer up my gratitude to thee."

Could any one have seen the wretched prisoner as she gave utterance to these words, let their hearts have been ever so callous, they must have been moved to pity. Her appearance was ghastly in the extreme; she looked like nothing earthly; and the agony of her feelings as she reflected upon the situation of Celestia, and the revolting fate with which she was threatened by the monster, Bonville, added to the misery of her looks. At length completely worn out with the frenzy of thought, she sunk back, and was reduced to the same state of torpor to which she was so often in mercy to herself subjected.

More than an hour passed away in this manner, when she was again aroused to a recollection of all that Bonville had said, and the promise he had made to prove the truth of his statement by introducing Celestia. Although she shuddered at the idea of a confirmation of her worst fears, she was yet anxious to behold that poor girl, the offspring of her daughter, whom she had never expected to see again in this world, and she looked forward to the important and trying moment with the most trembling impatience.

"And yet," she ejaculated, "how terrible will the meeting be under the circumstances. Even under far different circumstances I should have shuddered to encounter the child of that daughter whom I was the indirect cause of bringing to so untimely and fearful a fate; but now to see her, and know that she is in the power of one of the most atrocious villains on earth, and that she is destined by him in all her purity, youth and innocence, to become the victim of his brutal passions and deadly spirit of revenge, will be torture the most exquisite, the most maddening. Oh, Bonville, Bonville, no one but you could have devised such a diabolical scheme to gratify their malice. May God visit you with the retribution you merit. But this poor persecuted, unoffending girl, how will she be able to endure the terrible shock?—What will be her feelings of agony when she beholds the emaciated form of her wretched relative, and knows that she has no power to aid her but by her prayers?—Surely the trial will be more than her fortitude can endure. God! I could have been content to suffer, for now I am inured to misery, did not my suffering involve the happiness of all that is dear to me. Oh, that I were dead! oh, that I were dead!—I have lived too long, and for many, many years of misery and compunction existence has been a curse to me. Would to Heaven that I could at once lay down my head and die in peace. But it will not be!—I am still doomed to linger on in this frightful dungeon the most miserable of all God's erring creatures. How terrible is the punishment that one act of crime never fails to' entail upon the misguided delinquent.'-

She wrung her hands, sobbed convulsively, and then a violent flood of tear came to her relief. Once more she sunk upon her knees, and silently but devoutly prayed to Heaven for mercy.

The day passed away and she saw nothing more of Bonville, and she would fain have persuaded herself that all which had taken place was only a frightful dream, some delusion of her disordered imagination; that Bonville was still absent from the house, that Celestia was still at liberty, and safe under the protection of her noble relatives, but those efforts were useless; the fearful truth would make itself apparent to her, and become the more vivid and torturing the more she endeavoured to dismiss it from her thoughts.

She listened with breathless attention and impatience to catch the slightest sound, expecting every moment to see her dungeon door opened, and Celestia stand before her, but all remained silent, and night now having set in, she gave up the thought of beholding the poor girl at present, and sought to tranquillize her feelings. This, however was a task not easily to be accomplished, and she remained in the same state of anguish and suspense until tired nature could endure no more, and she sunk off to sleep.

But did sleep bring any relief to the mind of the unfortunate prisoner?—Oh, no; there was no rest for her. The most frightful dreams tortured her imagination, and rendered sleep, if possible, more agonizing to her than her waking moments. She again beheld the inhuman Bonville; he stood grinning in demonia-

cal triumph before her; she heard his bitter taunts, his diabolical threats, and she felt powerless to reply to, or resent them. A girdle of fire seemed to encircle her form; ghastly phantoms flitted before her and mocked at her sufferings. Great Heaven! now she struggled to release herself from the heavy chain by which she was secured to the wall of her dungeon, for she felt that if she could have done so she would have had the power and the determination to wreak a terrible retribution upon the head of her brutal persecutor, but she had no more strength than an infant, and the more she struggled the more the villain laughed and taunted her. Oh, it was very sport to him.

And now the scene changed, although she felt herself to be still in the dungeon, and chained to the wall; she beheld before her a chamber fitted up with a degree of comfort; and on the couch reclined a damsel of exquisite beauty, wrapped in deep sleep. She had a distinct view of her features, and in them recognised an exact resemblance of that daughter who had perished in so awful a manner so many years before. It could be no other but Celestia, she felt satisfied that it was her, and she tried to speak to her, to call her by her name, and to arouse her, but, she had not the power to utter a single syllable. How terrible was her anguish at that moment; the perspiration seemed to issue from her every pore, her blood ran boiling hot through her veins, her eyes were ready to burst from their sockets; but still the power of speech was denied her, reality could not have been more horrible than the delusion of that fearful vision; and she seemed to possess a consciousness that some terrible danger threatened Celestia at that moment. Hollow and sepulchral voices murmured all kinds of fearful predictions in her ears, and bade her despair. And there were no means of warning the lovely sleeper, and of rescuing her from the dreadful fate which was impending over her; she felt that she was completly powerless, and that the doom of the poor girl was sealed; while she strained her eyes, and endeavoured to call to Celestia, Lady Elvina imagined in her dream, that she saw a door opened, and the miscreant Bonville entered the apartment. His countenance was flushed a if with drink, and his eyes flashed forth a disgusting expression, which was enough to make the most courageous tremble to gaze upon. He pointed triumphantly towards the sleeping maiden, and then approached her, he polluted her lips with his odious kisses, and then she awoke but to find herself in his embrace. Frantically the poor girl shrieked for help and mercy, but there was none for her, the wretch Bonville laughed in scorn and exultation, and Celestia struggled to release herself from him in vain. Horrified at the scene which her bewildered imagination had kindled up, Lady Elvina awoke, and for a few moments so confused and bewildered was her brain that she could not recollect where she was, or persuade herself that what she had witnessed was merely a dream, but that it had actually taken place.

"Oh, God of Heaven!" she cried at last, "I beseech thee in thine infinite mercy not to suffer this frightful vision to be realised: but thou wilt not, in spite of all that the villain Bonville has threatened, I feel convinced that thou wilt defeat his monstrous designs, and restore his intended victim to liberty unscathed and innocent as when he bore her from her home, I care not what I may be doomed to suffer, but oh, let not my unoffending relations become the victims of this fearful man."

She now heard the hour of midnight strike from an old clock which was fixe in some part of the building; but her mind was too distracted to suffer her to compose herself again to sleep, and she looked forward to the approach of morning with mingled feelings of dread, anxiety, and suspense. With the deepest emotion she recalled to her memory all the circumstances of the remarkable and alarming dream, and the longer she reflected on them the more powerful became her apprehensions. When the morning came, she looked forward every moment to see Bonville enter her dungeon, accompanied by Celestia, but hour after hour passed away, and no one offered to interrupt her. A faint ray of hope dawned upon her mind, but it was only transient.

"After all," she ejaculated, "it may be false; Bonville may only have boasted of having the poor girl in his power for the purpose of adding to my torture. She may still be at liberty and I will not yet despair. God grant that these conjectures may be realized, and I will be for ever grateful."

But in spite of all these efforts to encourage hope, again despair beset the ill-fated lady's mind, and in that state she continued throughout the whole of the morning, but Bonville did not visit her, and she was thus left to the uninterrupted indulgence of her gloomy and painful reflections; the nature of which the reader will be well able to conceive. Notwithstanding all her endeavours she could not dismiss the circumstances of her dream from her recollection. She still had the features of Celestia before her mind's eye, and she shuddered with horror when she thought of the danger to which that innocent maiden might at that moment be exposed, and the sufferings she was enduring, and which might be still in store for her. If she was, indeed, in the power of Bonville, the very worst was to be apprehended, for from him she could expect no mercy, and well she knew that nothing whatever would move him from anything upon which he had fixed his mind. The prayers, the tears, the supplications of Celestia, could have no effect upon such a heartless scoundrel, and her agony and despair would serve only to increase his exultation.

"Alas," she sighed, "too severely have I experienced his stern implacibility, the dreadful extent to which his deadly malice will urge him to go. If Celestia is indeed in h s power, he will not fail to put into execution all his diabolical threats, and her ruin is certain. Oh, how I shudder at the thought; but surely the Almighty will not permit such a revolting, such a horrible outrage to be committed. His vengeance will certainly overtake the wretch who has so fearfully sinned against His laws, and rescue the innocent victim whom he has doomed to so horrible a fate."

Thus the hapless prisoner continued to alternate between hope and fear throughout another wretched day, but Bonville did not come, and towards night her feelings became considerably more tranquil. She began to believe that it was all a scheme of her persecutor to torture her, and that Celestia was in reality still safe under the protection of Lord Elverton. But if she was not, what must be the agony that the earl and all her relations must be at that time enduring. It was almost too agonizing for reflection, and the brain of Lady Elvina became completely distracted with thought. But the reader will doubtless now be anxious that we should return to our heroine.

It was not until two or three hours had elapsed after her arrival at the house, that Celestia was restored to consciousness, and then she looked bewildered around her, and at the old woman who was sitting at the foot of the bed, not knowing for the time where she was, or under what circumstance she had been brought thither. But all at once the dreadful truth flashed upon her, and starting up in the bed she uttered an exclamation of terror.

"You may as well be quiet, young lady," said the woman, in none of the most agreeable tones, "you may as well be quiet and endeavour to make your mind easy, for there is no one near this place who could render you the least assistance, if they were ever so inclined. This is a nice, quiet, secluded place, and there is not another human habitation near it for several miles; so you will see the perfect uselessness of creating any alarm. You may as well endeavour to snatch an hour or two's repose, for you have had a long journey, not under the most pleasant circumstances, and I dare say you are fatigued."

Celestia gazed at the old woman with feelings of disgust and terror, and for a few moments she was unable to make any reply to this cruel speech.

"Would you like to partake of any refreshments," inquired the woman in the same disagreeable accents; "it might serve to revive you, and would prepare you for the interview which Mr. Bonville will no doubt seek with you by and by."

At the mention of that fearful name our heroine again uttered a cry of horror, and then clasping her hands, and tears rushing to her eyes, she was enabled to gasp forth :—

"My God! am I then indeed in the power of that heartless villain? Oh, yes, I remember all now. He tore me from my home, my beloved relations, and I am now his prisoner."

"Very true, young lady," remarked the woman, "Mr. Bonville has you secure enough, and he deserves great credit for the consummate ability with which he has managed the whole affair. I must inform him of your recovery, for he will be most anxious to hear of it."

"Great Heaven help me !" exclaimed Celestia, wringing her hands and sobbing bitterly ; "for what horrible fate am I reserved?—Oh, would that I had died in childhood rather than to have to endure so dreadful a trial as this. Cruel woman, have you no pity for a poor helpless girl placed in the awful situation that I am ?"

"Mr. Bonville did not hire me to deal out pity;" sneered the woman, "and if he had I am afraid that I should have made but a sorry servant to him, for I do not know that I ever possessed any considerable share of that commodity. However, that is my business, and we will therefore, talk no more about it, and as you doubtless can dispense with my society, which does not seem to be very agreeable to you, I will leave you to your own meditations."

Having thus delivered herself, and fixed a spiteful look upon the unhappy girl, the old woman vanished from the room, and Celestia heard her lock and bolt the door after her. What were her feelings at that moment? Her bosom heaved with agony, her brain seemed to swim round ; a mist gathered before her eyes, and she sat with her hands clasped together in a state of torpor, if not utter insensibility. And when she was again aroused to all the horrors of her situation, how terrible were her feelings. She sunk on her knees, and clasping her hands vehemently together, whilst the scalding tears streamed copiously from her eyes, she earnestly implored the Almighty either to interpose to rescue her from the wretch in whose power she was, and from whom she could expect no mercy, or to suffer her not to live to experience the awful and revolting fate to which Bonville had doomed her.

But if possible she felt more severely for those beloved friends from whom she had been so cruelly torn. How terrible would be the agony of Lord Elverton and Lady Eugenia. Such a severe trial so soon after the savage murder of his son, would she feared, either prove a death blow to the earl or drive him to madness.

Nor was her lover, Lord Malensbury, last in her thoughts, and poignant indeed was her grief as he arose to her memory. She dwelt with sincere affection upon all his amiable qualities, and as she did so her agony increased. She had never felt the real ardour of her affection till that moment.

"Dear Arthur," she sighed, " what must be your anguish at the loss of her whom I am convinced you so sincerely love ; methinks I see your looks of despair, that I hear your exclamations of bitter grief and anguish. And shall I never behold you again? Are all the fond hopes we had cherished doomed to be thus cruelly blighted? Oh, why did we ever meet if such is the gloomy fate to which we are destined?"

Her tears flowed afresh as she gave utterance to those words, and so great was the distraction of her mind that her fortitude almost sunk beneath it. She listened to the slightest sound that stirred in the house with trembling alarm lest it should be the murderer, Bonville, approaching the room in which she was confined, and she shuddered at the very idea of meeting him. What could she expect from him after the taunts and threats he had held out, but the most brutal treatment ? But still she determined to exert herself to the utmost to assume all the fortitude she could, as on that chiefly depended the defeat of her inhuman persecutor.

"And was Lady Elvina really a prisoner in this very house?" she reflected. "And should she behold her?" She scarcely believed it possible, and yet she had now too much reason to know that Bonville was not the man to make idle boasts, and the conviction that the unfortunate Lady Elvina, therefore, was in his power became stronger on her mind. She wrung her hands in despair, and for some minutes her bosom was the receptacle of every feeling of anguish. All however, remained quiet in the house, and she began to hope that the dreaded Bonville would not obtrude himself upon her for the present, and that in the meantime she might so far collect her thoughts and strengthen her mind as to be enabled to meet him with firmness and resolution.

How Bonville and his ruffian colleagues had effected an entrance, to the abbey, and succeeded in bearing her away without alarming the inmates was a circumstance which greatly amazed her, and she reflected for some time upon it without being able to come to any satisfactory conclusion.

She now walked to the window, which was so secured that it was impossible for any one to open it ; but the prospect commanded from it was cheerless in the extreme, and struck a melancholy chill to the fair prisoner's heart. It seemed to shut out every hope, and to frown despair and misery upon her. The house stood in the middle of a dreadful moor, and as we have before stated there was not another human habitation for miles. Bonville could not have chosen a better place for the execution of his diabolical designs ; and contemplating the dreary scene for some time, she threw herself again in her chair and gave herself up to all the agony of thought.

Oh, why had not the earl thought of going to London before—then this misfortune might never have befallen them, for it was not likely that Bonville would have ventured to attempt to put his villanous designs into execution in the midst of a crowded city. But now he had her secure in his power many miles away from the abbey, in a most lonely and unfrequented part of the country, and might set detection at defiance. As these terrible thoughts arose to her mind her agony increased, and in vain she endeavoured to pacify her feelings. How could she acquire fortitude and resignation, surrounded as she was by every danger ? It was impossible, and the more she endeavoured to do so, the more bewildered and distracted she became, until at length her feelings became almost too torturing for endurance.

"Heaven ?" she sighed, " again I implore thy aid ; I humbly, but earnestly supplicate thee to come to 'my relief, and do not permit me to become the helpless victim of this brutal man. What have I done that I should meet with such a fate ? But you will not, surely—you will not suffer the villain to triumph in his iniquity. Oh, no, I am convinced thou wilt not, and I will not therefore yet despair."

As these thoughts occurred to her mind she became somewhat more calm, and did partake slightly of the refreshment which the old woman had brought her, She felt completely worn out with fatigue, but her fears would not suffer her to venture to go to sleep, lest the villain Bonville should obtrude himself upon her, and she remained in the same state of mind, awaiting the issue of this dreadful adventure with the most trembling suspense. She remained, however, uninterrupted, and as the day wore away, and still Bonville did not make his appearance, she became more firm and collected. He had promised that he would introduce her to her aged relative, and should he keep his word how great would be the anguish of that unfortunate and deeply injured lady when she beheld her and knew that she was in the power and at the mercy of that guilty and heartless man. Although she was most anxious to see her, she almost shrunk with terror from the idea of the meeting ; for what could she say to console her under the heavy misfortunes which she had for so many years been enduring ?

Night came, and then the old woman once more entered the room, bringing with her a light, and the evening repast, and having placed them on the table, she was about to retire again, without speaking a word, when Celestia called her back.

"Oh tell me," she said, " I implore you, tell me, is the villain Bonville at present in the house ?"

"Certainly," replied the old woman, in a harsh and disagreeable voice, " where else should he be ?"

"But he will not obtrude himself upon my presence to-night, will he ? Tell me, I implore you," said our heroine.

"Oh, no, not to night, but to morrow you may expect to meet him ; it is not likely that he will wait any longer."

Celestia clasped her hands in agony, but she could not for a moment or two give utterance to a word, and the woman was again about to leave the room when she ejaculated,—

"Answer me but one word and I have done ?"

"Well, name it ?" returned the woman.

"Tell me is it true what Bonville has stated to me, namely, that Lady Elverton is his prisoner, and in this very house ?"

"She is," replied the woman, " and of that you will be convinced before long if you entertain any doubts.

"God help her then, unfortunate lady," sighed our heroine, " for in the power of such a wretch as Bonville, how terrible must have been her sufferings, and, perhaps, even greater are in store for her."

The old woman fixed upon her a malignant look of triumph, and then without saying another word, she hobbled out of the room and left Celestia to her own reflections. These, as may be imagined, were of the most dismal description, nor could she admit of the least ray of comfort to compose her mind. How was it possible she could do so, surrounded as she was by so many dangers, and with no one at hand to fly to her rescue and to defeat the monstrous designs of Bonville. She gave herself up for lost, and wept and sobbed bitterly. She wished the night over, and yet she dreaded the approach of the following day, for then Bonville would appear before her, he would shock her ears with his odious importunities, and what would the resistance of a poor weak girl like herself avail? She shuddered at the idea of the interview, and heartily wished it was over; but unless Providence should interpose to save her, she saw no possibility of escaping from Bonville's power.

She examined the door to see whether or not there was any fastening by which she might secure it in the inside, but there was none, and she was thus entirely at the mercy of any intruder. This increased her alarm and agitation. Hour after hour passed away, and yet she was afraid to retire to rest, but sat and listened attentively to catch the slightest sound. But all remained profoundly still, and at length her fears became somewhat abated, and after committing herself to the care of the Almighty, being completely worn out with fatigue, both of body and mind, she threw herself, without undressing on the bed, and in a very short time sleep overpowered her.

Bonville's exultation at the success, so far of his nefarious schemes knew no bounds, and he was determined that nothing should prevent him from carrying them out to their fullest extent.

"I am fully prepared to meet with her scorn, to have her bitterest reproaches lavished upon my head," he ejaculated; "but what care I for them? I have her in my power, and of what use will be her feeble resistance?—None, none, she must be mine, and I glory in the thought. What a lovely and gentle being she is, and what sweet revenge it will be to me to know that I have triumphed over her innocence, and rendered what is now so pure and beautiful, degraded and loathsome. All her prayers, her tears, and supplications shall not move me from my purpose. I should be a weak fool to be induced to abandon my designs now I have proceeded thus far. But there is no fear of that; Bonville is not the man to be melted to forbearance by a woman's tears and entreaties."

Such were the thoughts that occupied his mind when the old woman made her appearance before him.

"Well Baldwin," he demanded eagerly, "how is your patient?"

"Oh, better, better," replied Mrs. Baldwin. "She has recovered from her lethargy now, and will soon be right enough."

"That is well," said Bonville, with a triumphant smile, "what did she say on recovering?"

"Oh, a good deal you may be sure. She wept bitterly, and did not fail to compliment you with some very powerful epithets."

"Ha! ha! ha! very good;" returned Bonville, "I expected that; poor girl, it is all that she can do, but I am determined not to be daunted from my purpose."

"I shouldn't think you would after all the trouble you have been at to get her in your power," returned Mrs. Baldwin; "but do you not intend to see her to-day?"

"No, I think not. It will be as well to let her have this day to herself, to-morrow, however, I will visit her; and in the meantime I have apprized my other prisoner of her arrival and that it is my intention to introduce them to each other without delay."

"No doubt the interview will be a very affecting one;" said Mrs Baldwin, with a sarcastic grin.

"Oh, yes, I dare say it will. But I say, Baldwin, do you not think this Celestia is a most lovely girl?"

"I cannot say," returned Baldwin, "I am no judge of beauty; but I dare say she is well enough. What is beauty but a bauble?"

"And a very pretty bauble too;" laughed Bonville. The old woman having made him acquainted with all that Celestia had said, left the room.

Throughout the day the miscreant Bonville occupied his guilty mind by concocting fresh schemes to gratify his vengeance, and in exulting over the triumph he had already achieved. He was determined that our unfortunate heroine should become his victim, and he looked forward to the time when he should have brought the poor girl to shame and degration with fiendish delight and impatience.

He did not retire to his chamber until a late hour, and then his guilty thoughts kept him for some time waking, and when at last he did fall asleep, dreams such as only haunt such guilty wretches as him, arose to his imagination, and rendered the hours of sleep those of the most exquisite horror.

Celestia did not awake until the sun came pouring in at the casement of the room in which she was confined, and she then immediately arose, and kneeling down, returned her heartfelt thanks to the Supreme who had protected her throughout the night; and earnestly implored Him to continue His mercy towards her, and then she might safely set all the nefarious designs of her inhuman enemy at defiance.

"Yes;" she cried, "I will put my ust in the Almighty, who never yet deserted the innocent. He will not suffer this guilty man to triumph altogether in his iniquity, and I will yet hope to be restored to liberty and to the arms of my beloved and deeply afflicted relatives."

These thoughts revived her spirits, and she began to feel more confidence; but she again felt a sensation of dread when she heard footsteps ascending the stairs, for she thought it might be Bonville, and she trembled at the bare thought of beholding him. Her terror and suspense, however, were not of long duration, and the next moment the door opening, Mrs. Baldwin entered, bringing in the morning meal. Having placed it before our heroine, she was again about to retire from the room without speaking, when Celestia requested her to stop a minute.

"What do you want now, young lady?" demanded the old woman.

"Tell me," said our heroine, "does Bonville intend to visit me to day?"

"Why did I not tell you last night that such was his intention? In about an hour you may expect to see him."

Celestia clasped her hands together and raising her eyes devoutly towards heaven, ejaculated,—

"Then God I implore you to give me courage to meet the villain as he deserves, and thwart him in his atrocious designs."

"You are secure enough in his power," sneered the woman, "you may depend upon that, and therefore any resistance to his wishes will be as useless as it would be ridiculous. What is to save you when Bonville is determined?"

"I am only a poor weak, defenceless girl I know," sighed our heroine, in answer to this cruel speech; "but surely base and hard hearted even as Bonville is, he will not suffer his barbarity to go so far as that."

The old woman grinned frightfully, as she replied,—

"Well, we shall see, but if you are sanguine enough to expect any forbearance from Bonville, I can only tell you that such hopes are doomed to be most woefully disappointed."

"And you appear to exult at that terrible, that disgusting thought."

"Indeed, I do not trouble my head at all about it," growled forth the disagreeable Mrs. Baldwin. "It is no business of mine, and what matters it to me, whether you become the mistress of Bonville or not?"

"Oh, God!" cried the blushing and horror-stricken maiden; "can this be a woman, and thus express herself to one of her own sex; and who has never done her or any of her fellow-creatures any wilful injury? Have you no sense of pity, that you can talk thus unfeelingly, when your utmost sympathy ought to be aroused for a poor defenceless, persecuted girl, who is threatened with so terrible a fate?"

"No," replied the old woman, coolly "I again tell you that I am not hired by Mr. Bonville to dispense pity. As for my sex, I disown them, I hate them all, and therefore you cannot expect any sympathy from me. But enough of this nonsense; I have got other business to attend to, so I wish you a very good morning, and a pleasant *tete a tete* with your youthful lover."

Thus saying the wicked old woman made her exit, fixing upon the unhappy Celestia a frightful look as she went out.

"Gracious Heaven!" ejaculated our heroine when she was gone, "what an unfeeling wretch is this, and with such an instrument to pander to his guilty wishes, what hope is there for me? none, none whatever. I tremble to think of it. God have mercy upon me, o r my ruin is seald for ever. And the monster who has thus inhumanly torn me from my friends, for the purpose of gratifying his deadly vengeance, will so soon be here. My ears will be insulted by his bold and omious words! Oh, how, can I support the interview? And there is no escaping from it. God help me, better would it have been for me had I expired in my infancy than to have lived to see this day, and to be threatened with a fate the bare thought of which fills my breast with horror and curdles the blood in my veins."

She wrung her hands in the agony of emotion and despair, and tears quickly chased each other down her cheeks. She tried to calm her feelings so that she might meet her tyrant with becoming fortitude, but that was indeed a most difficult task, and she only partially succeeded.

Two hours elapsed and still Bonville did not come, and Celestia began to hope that he had abandoned his intention of visiting her that day, but would give her further time to compose herself, and as the morning was suffered to pass away, and afternoon to approach without bringing Bonville, these hopes strengthened, and she became more firm and tranquil.

"It is no use repining," she said, "for will that do me any good or relieve me from my present fearful situation? It will not; I will therefore put my trust in an all wise and all merciful Providence, and endeavour to meet the villain with all that firmness which only virtue and innocence can inspire."

She was aroused from this soliloquy by hearing footsteps decending the stairs, and this time felt satisfied that it was not Mrs. Baldwin, and her heart again sunk within her. She was not long kept in suspense; she heard the key turn in the lock of the door, the bolts were withdrawn, the door was thrown open, and the miscreant Bonville stood before her.

The poor girl could scarcely repress a scream when she beheld her brutal persecutor, but she sunk into her chair, covered her face with her hands, and

her gentle and heaving bosom was convulsed with sobs.

Bonville folded his arms, and stood gazing at her for a few minutes in silence, but with feelings of the greatest triumph. But at last he ventured to approach her, and even presumed to take her fair hand to attempt to raise it to his lips; but she succeeded in withdrawing it from his hold, and gazed upon him with an expression of the utmost horror, disgust, and indignation.

"Cruel man!" she cried, "is it not enough that you have torn me from my home, my friends, and all that is dear to me, but you must now add insult to the dreadful outrage? Beware! for great as your power may at present be, there is one above who can immediately level you with the dust, and who will not suffer you to triumph over the weakest of his creatures."

"Sweet Celestia," said Bonville, endeavouring to impart to his repulsive features something like an agreeable smile, "I came not here to listen to a sermon (though even that has charms when coming from such lovely lips as yours), but to offer you the homage of my heart. True, there is some sligh t disparity in our ages I confess, but that will be more than amply made up for by the ardour of my love."

"Monster! assassin! cowardly ruffian!" cried our heroine with more firmness than she had hitherto been able to assume; "I call upon the spirits of your murdered victims to look down upon me with pity, and to supplicate at the throne of that Almighty whose power you pretend to scorn, to bring a terrible retribution on your head."

"Beauteous Celestia," said Bonville, "you may e'en save yourself that trouble, for any such invocation would only meet with my most supreme contempt. To be plain and candid with you I have chosen you to be my future mistress, not only for the sake of your transcendent charms, but in order to gratify the implacable spirit of revenge which inhabits my breast against the whole of your family. I presume I need not remind you that all resistance to my wishes would be sheer madness on your part; for have I not got you securely in my power, far away from your friends, who will find it impossible to discover the place of your confinement, and with no one at hand who can render you the least assistance.   Of what use, then, is your obduracy?—of what avail is your scorn, your reproaches ? You had better yield calmly to a fate it is impossible to avoid, for mine you shall be, and no earthly or other power can save you.''

"Oh, villain !'' gasped the wretched girl, "have you no fears ? Have you no sense of shame or spark of humanity inhabiting your sterile bosom ? But why do

I ask? Have not your crimes already stamped you as one of the most atrocious of miscreants ?   And can I then expect any mercy or pity at your hands ?   No, no, no. You know it not; you are insensible to it.   God of Heaven, help me then, for if Thou forsakest me in this terrible hour of peril, I am indeed lost.''

"Did I not tell thee, damsel, in the Old Priory ruins, that thou should'st be mine, and that no power whatever should prevent it ?'' demanded the exulting ruffian, "and have I not kept my word ? Oh, Bonville never forfeits his word, depend on it ; and therefore thou mayest as well prepare for the worst that your imagination can picture. But on the present occasion I have other views, and I am about to lead you to an interview that cannot but fill your heart with the most pleasurable sensations."

Seizing the unhappy girl by the hand, he drew her into the passage, and led her rapidly through several dreary avenues, with doors on each side which evidently opened upon dungeons. Once our heroine paused, and fixing upon her fierce conductor a penetrating look, a trembling sensation of horror, which she could not resist, came over her.

"Cruel man," she ejaculated, in faltering accents, "you have some diabolical design in contemplation. Beware what you do, for there is a just God above who at present watches all our actions, and whatever may be your intentions towards me, rest assured that He will overwhelm you in the very midst of your anticipated triumph, and bring a fearful, but just retribution upon your head. Let me return to the apartment which I recently occupied, for the very aspect of this dreadful place strikes a deadly feeling of horror to my soul."

Bonville fixed upon the poor girl a malicious look of triumph, but returned no immediate answer, he, however, grasped her by the wrist with such ferocity that she could not help shrieking with the pain, and she was so overcome with horror that it was not without the greatest difficulty she could save herself from fainting.

"Girl," said the ruffian, after a pause, "what is the use of your attempting to resist me? I tell you I intend you no harm on this occasion. No, it is not for that I have taken all this trouble to obtain possession of you; I hold you for another purpose, and nothing can save you from my will. Hark! do you not hear?"

At that moment the clanking of chains, followed by a low, dismal moaning sound, smote the ears of Celestia, and she trembled more violently than before, and with the utmost difficulty gasped out—

"Good God! what can be the meaning of this? Can it be possible that any human being is confined in one of those frightful dungeons? My blood runs chill with horror. Surely there cannot be any one in the world inhuman enough

to be guilty of such an unparalleled atrocity as this."

"You shall see," replied Bonville, with another of his frightful grins; "prepare yourself for the joyous meeting I have promised you."

As he thus spoke he approached the door of the dungeon in which the wretched and heart-broken Lady Elvina was incarcerated, forcing the terrified damsel with him. He withdrew the bolts, and applying a rusty key to the lock, the door flew back upon its hinges, and they stood in the dungeon.

At first her brain was so giddy, and the place was so dark and dismal, that Celestia was unable to behold anything distinctly, but the noxious exhalations which arose from the fetid earth and the damp and clammy walls came with a sickening influence to her senses, and had it not been that Bonville still held her arm, she must have sunk overpowered.

At length she again heard the rattling of the chain, and by the faint light emitted by the lamp suspended from the roof, imagined she beheld a human form moving about. Immediately afterwards a faint and hollow voice ejaculated—

"Who's there? Is it my inhuman tyrant again come to torture the unfortunate Elvina? Or has he in mercy come to rid me of a life which has long been intolerable to me?"

"Sweet Lady Elvina," sneered the heartless miscreant, forcing forward Celestia, "I come to fulfil the promise I made you. Allow me to introduce to you your noble grand-daughter, Lady Celestia De Aunville!"

A cry of agony simultaneously escaped the bosoms of the unhappy prisoner and our heroine on these observations, and Celestia gazed at the ghastly and emaciated form of her noble relative completely appalled, and shuddered in every limb. Bonville folded his arms, and standing close by, contemplated the scene with the most demoniacal feelings of delight.

At length Celestia, unable any longer to contain herself, rushed into Lady Elvina's arms, and they embraced frantically, and the poor girl then beheld for the first time, to her increased horror and dismay, that her deeply injured relative was chained to the wall.

"Child of my murdered Elvina," cried Lady Elverton at length, "murdered by yon savage monster! do I indeed hold you to my careworn, broken heart? Oh, God! oh, God! to meet thus, and to know that you are in the power of one to whom pity is unknown. Let me gaze closer into your features! Ah! by Heaven, there is the countenance of my fair and innocent girl! Even as she looked when she was torn from me to a hideous death. Shade of my Elvina, look down upon us, and supplicate the Supreme for retribution on the head of thine and thy brother's atrocious assassin."

"My revered, my noble, my much wronged relative," sobbed the distracted Celestia, "that we should meet thus!—Wretch!" she added, looking with the greatest horror and disgust at Bonville, "and this is all your fiendish work. Oh, Heaven, my venerable relative, how terrible must have been the sufferings that you have been doomed to undergo. Oh, Bonville, Bonville, man of flinty heart, can you expect to escape a dreadful punishment for these hideous crimes? Repent, repent, ere it is too late, and at least endeavour to make some little attonement by restoring this deeply persecuted lady and myself to liberty."

"Lovely Celestia," replied Bonville, with a sardonic grin, which made him look perfectly frightful and appalling in that horrible place; "I am truly sorry that I cannot comply with your request. This is one of the greatest moments of my triumph. Did I not tell you that I would introduce you and Lady Elvina to each other, and have I not kept my word? Oh, it is a most joyous meeting! A truly joyous meeting."

"Taunting wretch!" groaned Lady Elverton, "is it not enough that you have doomed me and all my unfortunate family to such unparalleled misery, but that you must come here to exult over your fiendish crimes?"

"No, it is not enough," he replied, "and I have still more exquisite tortures in store for you."

"Oh, mercy, mercy!" supplicated Celestia, "on me wreak the whole of your horrible vengeance, inflict upon me all the sufferings you may think fit, but spare, oh, spare my aged relative, whom you have so long and so dreadfully persecuted."

"Alas, alas! my poor girl," sighed Lady Elvina, "it is useless to appeal to him; his black heart knows no pity. Let us on our knees, my Celestia, child of the murdered, and invoke the protection of the Almighty, who alone can interpose to save us."

Solemnly our heroine obeyed, and clasping their hands together, they raised their eyes and devoutly and earnestly supplicated the interposition of the Father of all good in their behalf, while Bonville stood by and gazed at them with all those ironical expressions of exultation and diabolical satisfaction, of which alone his guilty soul could be capable. It was a melancholy, a heart-rending sight to behold the poor haggard and suffering prisoner and her youthful relative kneeling and breathing their prayers in that horrible place, and to notice the look of hatred and revenge with which the miscreant Bonville gazed at them. At length they arose, and once more embracing, sobbed convulsively, as if their hearts would burst, whilst the scalding tears chased each other down their cheeks. It was too much for the exhausted state of Lady Elvina to support; she endeavoured to speak, but her tongue refused its office; her brain seemed to be on fire, the form of her grand-daughter became indistinct, and gradually faded from her view, and with one appalling cry she sunk from her embrace, and became insensible. Celestia threw herself by her side, and in a state of mind bordering upon frenzy, she parted the hair from her pale forehead and gazed with feelings of the most indescribable agony in her care-worn haggard face.

"Great Heaven!" she exclaimed, "she is dead! Monster, you have murdered her! Oh, can you gaze upon this scene unmoved?"

"She has but fainted, and no doubt will soon recover," retured Bonville; "come, this interview must be terminated. You must return to your apartment, while I will leave you to reflect upon all that has taken place."

"Nay!" shrieked the distracted damsel, clinging still more closely to the insensible Lady Elverton, "by Heaven, you shall not tear me from her. I will share her sufferings in this dreadful place; I will endure anything to be near her, but we will not again be separated. Oh, mercy, mercy! You cannot be so monstrous! You——" She could say no more, nature was completely exhausted, and she also fainted.

Bonville raised the poor girl in his arms, and leaving the wretched Lady Elvina to recover as best she could, he bore his beauteous burthen from the dungeon, and conveyed her to the apartment in which he confined her. He placed her upon the sofa, and having contemplated her for a few moments with secret satisfaction, he summoned the old woman into the room.

"Well, the interwiew is over, Baldwin," he observed, "see to her recovery. Oh, it has been glorious food for my revenge."

"I dare say it has," returned Mrs. Baldwin, with one of her most disgusting looks, "and pray, how did Lady Elverton take it?"

"Why, exactly as I might have expected," answered the villain; "her tortures were most exquisite, and I left her in a state of insensibility; but I will now return to see whether she has recovered yet."

Thus saying, he quitted the room, and the old woman applied herself to the recovery of Celestia.

———

CHAPTER XXIX.

THE HORRIBLE SUFFERINGS OF CELESTIA AND LADY ELVINA.—BONVILLE PERSISTS IN HIS INHUMAN DESIGNS.

It was some considerable time, however, before our heroine was restored to her senses, and then she looked around her in bewildered amazement, having only a dreamy recollection of what had happened, and not at first recognising the old woman, so distracted were her thoughts.

"Where am I?" she cried, "what place is this? How came I hither? And where are Lord Elverton and my aunt? Have I had a frightful dream? Methought I was being dragged by a monster in human shape through dark and dismal passages into loathsome dungeons, where the light of heaven had never entered, and that I beheld in one of them a poor emaciated creature, whom I was told was my poor persecuted, long lost relative, Lady Elvina. Ah, no! it was no dream! The whole dreadful truth now flashes upon my recollection. Again I see the poor sufferer, as she was introduced to me; once more I hear her piteous groans of anguish. Again I see her pale and ghastly countenance, her sunken eyes, her wasted form. I hear the clanking of the chain by which she is secured to the wall of that awful dungeon. Monsters! Murderers! Will nothing satiate your deadly vengeance? Oh, why was I ever born to endure such agony as this? But you shall not separate me from her! At least I will be allowed to share her loathsome dungeon; to endeavour to pour the balm of consolation into her distracted bosom, to die with her if such be the will of Providence. Nay, hold me not; I am resolute; I will go to her; you shall not keep me from her!"

In the frenzy of her feelings, the poor girl made a desperate effort to rise, but Mrs. Baldwin held her down, and that in no very tender or gentle manner.

"This is all useless," said the unfeeling old woman, "and will do you no good. You cannot leave this room, and you had better therefore try to rest your mind contented. It is quite true that you have seen Lady Elvina to-day, and precisely under the circumstances which you have described, but you are powerless to help her or yourself."

Celestia gazed at her for a moment or two, with feelings of unbounded horror and disgust, and then she tried to speak, but her tongue cleave to the roof of her mouth, and her brain was distracted; her strength failed her; frightful objects seemed to dance before her eyes, and to mock her sufferings, and once more she became unconscious of everything around her.

"Well," growled the old woman, as she gazed upon her. "I have got into a very pleasant office here with this girl, and I ought to be very much obliged to Bonville for the confidence he has placed in me; however, I will revenge myself for the trouble I am put to, by torturing her all I can. Poor thing," uttered the frightful and malicious old crone, sneeringly, "what a pity it is that one so young, and lovely, and so innocent should be doomed to such a fate. Well, there is one consolation in ugliness, that we hold out no temptations to the libertine, and can see others who are handsome and miserable."

As the hateful old wretch thus gave vent to her unnatural feelings, she sat herself down on one end of the sofa on which the insensible form of Celestia was stretched, and gazed at her with an expression of countenance, which we will not disgust the redear by attempting to describe, but leave it to his imagination.

On leaving Celestia in charge of Mrs. Baldwin, Bonville once more made his way to the dungeon of Lady Elverton. He found her still in a state of insensibility, and at first thought that our heroine had been correct in her apprehensions; that the shock had proved too great for his wretched victim, and that death had at last put an end to her earthly suffering; but stooping and putting his ear to her pale lips, he discovered that she still breathed.

"'Tis well," he said, "my triumph would not be half complete if she were to die yet. Oh, no; I have many tortures yet in store for her; and yet I marvel how she could ever find strength to endure those I have already inflicted on her. What an interesting scene to me was this interview between my helpless victims. Lord Elverton, you shall know it all, and likewise that you have no power to thwart my plans, or to help those who are so dear to you. Bonville has not lived for nothing, and he has proved to the world how terrible are the consequences of those who shall dare to offend him or treat him with scorn. The world looks upon me as a monster, a demon in human form; be it so; I glory in the titles; I was sent into the world to hate and prey upon mankind, and I have well performed my office."

As he uttered these words his countenance bore an expression that was still more horrible and revolting to look upon, and even the stoutest heart must have shuddered to contemplate it. There

was nothing at all human about it, and had he lived in the days of superstition he would have been looked upon as some supernatural being.

"And this is the once lovely and scornful Lady Elvina," he resumed, after a pause; "this is that proud beauty who presumed to reject my vows and to heap upon my head all her bitterest reproaches. Alas! poor lady, how fallen and degraded from your high estate. The veriest worm that crawls the earth is better off than you. As I gaze upon your ghastly corpse-like visage, your sheleton form, and I know it is all the work of my hands, I do indeed feel she glorious extent of my triumph. May such be the fate of all those who mock the power of Bonville."

A deep sigh from Lady Elvina interrupted the brutal man in his soliloquy, and he watched her recovery with eager eyes, for he was anxious again to add to the tortures of her mind by his savage taunts. She moved slightly on her wretched pallet, and then muttering some incoherent words, she made a faint effort to rise, but she could not, and once more sinking back with a heavy sigh, she seemed to relapse into insensibility. The patience of her persecutor was, however, exhausted, and shaking her roughly, he cried—

"What ho! sweet Lady Elvina, arouse thee, this state of unconsciousness is too much happiness for thee."

The hapless woman started at the sound of his voice, as if from some fearful dream, and gazed as well as the dim light in the dungeon would permit her upon the dark and revolting figure before her.

"Ah! inhuman wretch!" she cried, in tones of mingled disgust and horror, "you here again; oh, begone! leave me to my own agony of mind; to die and shake off this dreadful, this insupportable weight of misery."

"Yes, Lady Elvina," replied Bonville; "it is I, your gaoler, Bonville; I come because I am anxious to inquire after the state of your mind since the delightful and unexpected interview you have had."

"All-merciful Father!" ejaculated the unhappy lady, "look down I beseech Thee with pity on me, and do not suffer this cruel man to proceed to such enormous lengths in the gratification of his ferocious revenge. Hide me from his sight ; let me sink into the bowels of the earth; die a death of the most excruciating torture ; any fate would be far less horrible than that to which I am now subjected. My sins have been great, I know and admit, but surely they do not, they cannot merit so dreadful a punishment as this."

"Ha ! ha ! ha !" laughed Bonville, "how it glads me to see you suffer, and know you cannot help yourself. This place shall be your future habitation and your tomb; no costly monument shall be raised by a loving husband over the spot where your ashes repose."

Shocked, horrified to hear the dreadful language of Bonville, Lady Elvina placed her hands before her eyes that she might shut out his disgusting image, and mentally but fervently she prayed that that very moment might be the last of her existence. Again the voice of her tormentor aroused her.

"What think you, Lady Elvina, of your young and innocent relation ?" he said ; "is she not a beauteous creature ? Fair as opening day; more transcendently lovely than one of the Graces. So like her late mother, when she was about the same age. And this captivating maiden is mine ; she is the future slave of the venerable Bonville."

"Oh, God ! oh ! God !" groaned the wretched woman; "must I listen to such horrible language as this ? I shall go mad ! My heart will break ! Bonville, as you fear the torments of perdition, do not attempt to put your atrocious threats into execution. What has that poor girl done that she should seek her ruin ? Do what you please with me; inflict upon me all the tortures that your deadliest malice can suggest, but spare, oh, spare the innocent, the unoffending Celestia."

"Such mercy as I have shown to all the rest of her hated family will I award to her. I have allowed her a week, at the expiration of which time no power can save her from the fate to which I have destined her. Think of that, Lady Elvina, and let it console you in your present happy situation."

"Heartless miscreant ! I will not yet despair ; that Supreme Power whose holy laws you have so monstrously outraged,

will interpose to save her and to bring down His heaviest wrath upon you. Tremble, cold-blooded man, for the time is at hand when your career of guilt will be brought to a termination."

"You are a prophetess, then, Lady Elverton," sneered Bonville, "but, unfortunately for you, I laugh all such predictions to scorn, and again promise you that all my threats shall be fulfilled to the very letter. You know full well that I am not the sort of man to make empty boasts, and what is to prevent the accomplishment of my present design, since the fair Celestia is in my power ? But I leave you to your own thoughts, and go to inquire after the condition of my future mistress."

Lady Elvina endeavoured to speak, but she could not, and before she could in the slightest degree recover, Bonville had quitted the dungeon, and she was again left alone to her misery.

For some moments she continued to rock her body to and fro in a state of the greatest emotion, whilst her bosom heaved with convulsive sobs.

"All hope is at an end," she sighed at last; "the villain triumphs to the fullest extent, and I see no means by which the innocent Celestia can escape him. Oh, Heaven ! that thought is more agonizing than all the sufferings it has been my hard fate to experience. Unfortunate Celestia, and must your innocence indeed fall a sacrifice to this terrible man ? Will no power, human or divine, interpose to rescue you ? God is just, and it were blasphemy to believe that He will permit such a fate to befall one of the most innocent and lovely of his creatures. But what must now be the agony of my unfortunate, my deeply wronged husband ? He will never be able to survive this additional shock, and perhaps death would be a mercy to him. What can existence be to him but a curse ?—And it is I, wretch that I am, who have been the primary cause of all these accumulated horrors. Had I never listened to the voice of the hypocrite and the deceiver, we might now have all been happy ; and my Elvina and Edgar would not have met with such an untimely and horrible fate. Heaven have mercy on me, for I fear that I have much to answer for."

Thus did the unhappy lady continue to reproach herself for the past for some time, until at length, completely worn out, she once more sank into a stupor, from which it would have been fortunate for her had she never recovered.

Bonville, on leaving Lady Elvina, proceeded to the room in which our heroine was confined, in order to ascertain how she was, and he began to be somewhat alarmed when he found that she was again in a state of insensibility, especially as he had not the means, of course, of calling in medical aid.

"I begin to think that I have proceeded too far," he remarked ; "and I must be cautious, or I may still lose the prize it has cost me so much trouble and risk to secure."

"Well, I must say," returned the old woman, "that if you wish to carry out your designs to the fullest extent, I think you have been rather too hasty. You might have let the girl rest for a day or two longer."

"Well, it can't be helped now," said Bonville, "and we must make the best of it. You must pay every attention to her, Baldwin, and if you happen to possess such an ingredient in your nature, which I do not think you do, when she recovers her senses behave to her with a little kindness and indulgence."

"Well, I will endeavour to do so," replied the old woman, "though it is a rather difficult task for me to perform."

"How beautiful she looks even in her present state," remarked Bonville, as he approached nearer to the sofa on which the poor girl was reclining, and hung over her with mingled feelings of revenge and admiration ; "oh, it would be a disappointment which I could not well endure were I to be deprived of her now. I must act with more prudence, or I might yet be thwarted in the accomplishment of the whole of my designs. Remember what I have told you, Baldwin, and let me know the minute she recovers."

"I will do so," said Baldwin, "but I do not think that is likely to take place for some time."

"Do you think not ?" demanded Bonville.

"No," answered the old woman ; "and there is another thing, I do not understand much how to attend upon these squeamish and delicate young ladies ; I never have had any experience amongst sick people, and as for myself, I never was ill in my life."

"But you do not know what you can do till you try, and I place every reliance on you," said her worthy master. "It is only excitement after all ; nervous excitement, and a few gentle stimulants will serve to revive her."

"Then I would advise you not to venture into her presence again just yet," said Mrs. Baldwin ; "or she will be almost certain to suffer a relapse."

To this Bonville returned no answer, but stooping down, he impressed a kiss upon the pale lips of the unconscious damsel, and then departed from the room.

The whole of that night poor Celestia was in a state of delirium, and it was melancholy to listen to the wild observations to which she gave utterance. She called incessantly upon the names of the earl and his lady, and then, in the most pathetic and touching manner, she would talk of her lover, and sometimes fancy he was standing before her, and had rescued her from the power of the miscreant Bonville.

Bonville was now, indeed, most seriously alarmed, and cursed himself for his folly in being so precipitate in introducing her to Lady Elvina, and in permitting his brutal vengeance to carry him so far. He saw that there was still a possibility of his nefarious designs against the innocent girl being frustrated, and again and again he blamed himself for his want of prudence, and the cruel language he had been led into the expression of by the diabolical malignity of his feelings. And what added to his uneasiness and bewilderment more than all, was his being unable to treat Celestia under her present malady, and its being also impossible that he could call in medical advice, as that would immediately betray him, and probably bring him to that tribunal of justice which he had so long escaped.

"And should the shock she has sustained have such an effect upon her that she may never be restored to reason, all my hopes will be annihilated," he reflected. "Cursed fool that I have been, for the first time I have suffered my thirst for revenge to overreach me, and know not how to extricate myself from the difficulty in which I have placed myself. However, I must devise some plan, and leave the rest to chance."

He was in such a state of suspense and anxiety, that he could not go to bed the whole night, but was continually going to the chamber of the suffering girl to inquire how she was; but, as we have before stated, our heroine continued quite delirious, and when the morning arrived, there was very little, if any, change for the better. It was true that she did not rave in the same frantic manner, but that was owing to her strength being exhausted, for she lay in the most deplorable condition, and Bonville and Mrs. Baldwin were totally at a loss what remedy to apply that was likely to restore her. Again and again the villain cursed his folly and brutal conduct, and would have given anything could he but have recalled it.

Lady Elvina had also passed a most awful night, but towards morning she was considerably better. She had summoned religion to her aid, and by its all-powerful influence had become more calm and resigned.

"Alarming and terrible as my present prospects and those of that unfortunate girl are," she said, "I will endeavour not to give way entirely to despair, for I cannot, I will not, believe that the Almighty, who ever watches over virtue and innocence, will suffer Bonville to triumph in this his brutal determination. Something will yet occur to rescue her from his power, and then it matters not what becomes of me. I have long been weary of life. I have proved the curse of all those dear beings connected with me, and the sooner I lay down my heavy burthen of cares and sorrows the better. I have greatly sinned, but it has been more from error of judgment than wilfulness of heart, and Heaven, I trust, will have mercy upon me. And yet, my beloved husband, I should like to be permitted to behold you once more in this world, that, on my knees, I might supplicate your forgiveness for the manifold sorrows I have caused you; then, methinks, I could lie me down and die in peace. But, alas! that will not be, and I can never hope to leave this awful place. Stubborn heart! why hast thou not broken long ere this?"

Tears came to her relief, and for a short time she remained in a state of comparative tranquillity, though terrible were the thoughts that tortured her mind. All the melancholy events of the past crowded vividly upon her imagination, and again she was driven to a state bordering upon madness. And now she imagined all kinds of terrible things to have happened to Celestia since they had seen each other the day before, and she groaned aloud in the poignant and insupportable anguish of her mind.

She was interrupted in the course of these dismal meditations by the entrance of one of the fellows in the pay of Bonville, who came to bring her her coarse food, and eagerly she was about to put some questions to him regarding Celestia, but he turned from her with a repulsive look, and immediately quitted the dungeon. She wrung her hands, and again wept bitterly; the absence of Bonville increased her fears, and once more she imagined that the worst had befallen our heroine, and that she would never be permitted to behold her again, or if she was, it would be as a poor degraded being.

Still, in the midst of all this anguish and suspense of mind, notwithstanding the horror of her situation, and the utter misery she had endured for so many years—misery under which few persons could have survived so long, but must have perished from the exhaustion of the constitution, independent of broken spirits and annihilated prospects—even in the midst of all this accumulation of suffering, we repeat, now that she had seen her beauteous and youthful relative, Lady Elvina could not entirely banish the hope from her bosom, that something would yet occur to defeat the plans of Bonville, and to restore them both to liberty, and the arms of those so dear to them; and it was this impression, coupled with the idea of her again beholding her lord, and being reconciled to him, which inspired the unfortunate lady with fresh fortitude, and made her still cling to life.

"Yes," she said, "I will still endeavour to bear up against the cruel sufferings which I am daily and hourly experiencing from my brutal persecutor, with the hope that kind Providence will yet look down with an eye of pity upon me and my afflicted family, and interpose in our behalf. Already I feel renewed strength at the thought, and the horrors of my dungeon, and all the cruelties practised upon me, fade into comparative insignificance before my eyes. Henceforth I will treat all the bitter taunts and threats of Bonville with silent contempt, and utter not a murmur to one whom I know is perfectly callous to every sense of feeling. Something whispers to me that fortune will yet

turn in our favour, and that we shall all meet again, never more to be separated but by death. Oh, how blissful is the thought, to be once more clasped to my beloved husband's heart, to hear my forgiveness pronounced by his own lips, and to die in the midst of those dear members of my family whom fate has left me. It perfectly resuscitates me. I will still hope, I will still hope, and, All-merciful Father, who has enabled me to live through so many and such trials, put my every trust in Thee!"

A smile of hope and confidence irradiated her pale and haggard countenance as she thus spoke, and she clasped her hands vehemently together. It was many, many months, nay years since she had felt so composed and resigned under the horrors of her situation, and the dreadful threats of Bonville had, for the time being, lost one half their influence upon her. She knelt down and fervently prayed to Heaven that her happy forebodings might be realised, and that the earl her husband might be able to bear up against his numerous and severe afflictions until it should please the Supreme Being that they should meet again. And yet she could not help but have her misgivings that the additional loss of Celestia, who had been for so many years under his protection, and the uncertainty of the fate which had befallen her, would have a most dangerous effect upon him.

"Alas! alas!" she sighed, "how terrible must now be his agony; and after the many and unparalleled calamities with which he has been visited, how will he have strength to encounter this additional blow? Oh, my much wronged husband, should you sink under this misfortune, then indeed shall I have little or nothing to wish to live for. But, no; I will not give way to these sad thoughts; God is too good and merciful to frustrate all our hopes of happiness."

Again her countenance brightened up, and she awaited calmly and patiently the issue of events. Notwithstanding the desperate and savage character of Bonville, she could not exactly make up her mind to believe that he could ever be so monstrous as to carry his inhuman and revolting threats into effect against one so young, so lovely, and so innocent as Celestia. Alas! she was too sanguine, and had she dared to reflect upon his base conduct to her when she was about the age of our heroine, and the awful fate to which he had in the gratification of his malice consigned Celestia's mother, she would again have been plunged in horror, dismay, and despair.

Most anxious was she to know the situation of the poor girl since their meeting; though of course she could not but imagine it to be one of the most deplorable description. And the miscreant Bonville had declared that he had only given her a week's respite, and if nothing in the interim occurred to rescue her, what might not be the fate, the awful fate which would befall her? Lady Elvina shuddered with horror as this thought occurred to her, and thus did she alternate between hope and fear.

CHAPTER XXX.

THE FRESH APPEAL.—THE ACQUIESCENCE.—THE RELEASE FROM THE DUNGEON.—LADY ELVINA AND CELESTIA.—THE APPEARANCE OF MABEL HENDERSON.

Two days elapsed, and our heroine remained in much the same pitiable condition, greatly to the annoyance and alarm of Bonville, who was perfectly at a loss what course to adopt, in order to bring about her recovery.

The old woman grumbled sorely at the duty imposed upon her, but she secretly dreaded her brutal master too much to venture to disobey him; however, she did so with a very bad grace, and when she was left to herself, she gave vent to her vexation and impatience, in no very measured terms. Notwithstanding, we must, in justice to her, candidly state that, as far as her knowledge extended, and that knowledge in most cases was very limited, she did all that she could to administer to the poor girl's relief, though, most likely, that was more on account of Bonville than from any respect or solicitude she bore towards Celestia; and, probably, with the hope that she might the sooner be released from her tedious and unwelcome duties.

As we have stated in the previous chapter, our heroine no longer suffered from that violent delirium which had at first distracted her brain, but still she was quite unconscious of what was passing around her, or where she was, and she might be said to be in a state fast bordering upon idiotcy. She was not so bad but that she was able to leave her bed, and Bonville thought it advisable to grant her the use of another apartment, which was much more cheerful than the one in which she had been confined; and here at the window she would sit for hours gazing upon the blue and tranquil sky without speaking a word; sometimes, however, sighing deeply, and at others laughing gaily, as if in high glee at some thought which had suddenly struck her fancy.

What would have been the anguish of her fond friends had they seen her in that sad and alarming condition? How would their hearts have been wrung, and how bitter must have been the curses they would have invoked upon the head of the heartless wretch who had been the cause of it all!

Bonville began to despair of her ever recovering, and his rage and disappointment knew no bounds, especially as he was precluded from all opportunity of seeking any advice upon the subject; and was obliged to leave the poor girl's recovery entirely to chance. His temper, before morose and stern to every one about him, was now perfectly ferocious, and they feared to approach or address him. He would not suffer any of the fellows who were engaged by him to leave the house for a minute, for his suspicions were constantly excited that they were going to betray him, and probably to concoct some scheme not only to liberate Celestia and Lady Elvina, but also to consign him to that punishment which his numerous and atrocious crimes so richly merited.

"After all the success that I have met with," he would mutter to himself when alone, "am I now to be cheated, disappointed, and that too at the very moment I thought my triumph most certain?—By all the powers of darkness this is not to be borne. But it is all through my own confounded folly; if I had not been so precipitate, the girl might now be in the possession of her senses, and in a fair way to become my victim. But I will not be defeated yet. No, some plan must be devised to effect her recovery, and then no earthly power shall prevent me putting my designs into effect without delay."

It was in one of these moods that he visited the dungeon in which Lady Elvina was incarcerated, though with no settled purpose. Lady Elvina had not seen him for several days, and she now beheld him with less terror than she was accustomed to do; for she was in hopes that she should be enabled to elicit from him the real situation of Celestia, and she could not help entertaining an idea, (but why she should do so she knew not), that it was not of that deplorable nature which might have been anticipated; and the looks of Bonville on his entrance into the dungeon were fully calculated to give encouragement to that idea, for instead of triumph they only expressed rage and disappointment.

He stood with folded arms, and contemplated her in silence for a few moments, and Lady Elvina met his gaze with perfect composure. He was at a loss to imagine to what cause to attribute it; in fact, after his interview with Celestia, he had fully expected to find her overwhelmed with grief and despair.

"I come to bring you news of Celestia," he said at length.

"Ah!" ejaculated Lady Elvina, eagerly; "tell me, I pray you, what is it. Have you suffered pity for her youth and innocence to enter your breast, and set her at liberty?"

"Set her at liberty!" repeated Bonville, with one of his most sardonic grins; "think you I am such a consummate idiot, after all the trouble she has cost me! No; she is still in my power."

"Heaven help her then. But, oh, tell me, surely you have not been base enough to attempt to carry your diabolical threats into execution?"

"No; for one very good reason, she has escaped me for the present."

"What mean you?"

"That she has been a raving maniac, and is now in a state of idiotcy," replied Bonville, abruptly.

Lady Elvina clasped her hands together with emotion, and all the fortitude she had before assumed vanished in a moment.

"Great God!" she exclaimed, "is this true?—Unfortunate, innocent girl, to what a miserable condition has villany brought you. But tell me, Bonville, can you have the inhumanity any longer to detain her?"

"I certainly shall. Fool! of what use is it preaching humanity to me?"

"Celestia an idiot?" sighed Lady Elvina, and the tears started to her eyes, "and not a friend at hand, to assist her, or see to her recovery. Oh, this is indeed cruel. But tell me Bonville, has she no medical aid?"

"Yes," replied the ruffian, sarcastically, "she has that of Mrs. Baldwin."

"Of that unfeeling woman! Oh, again I say, God help her. Oh, that I might be permitted to see her, to be with her, to converse with her; she would know me, and my presence and affectionate offices might recall her scattered senses."

A sudden idea seemed to flash upon Bonville's brain when Lady Elvina gave utterance to these observations, and he paused and reflected for a few moments. Lady Elvina watched the expression of his countenance narrowly, and she could not help thinking that it was all in favour of her most anxious wishes; determined, therefore, to take advantage of the favourable opportunity to press her suit vehemently, she resumed in the following words :—

"Oh, Bonville, I have suffered, Heaven knows, severely by your cruelty, but much I can pardon even you, if you will but listen to my earnest appeal on this melancholy occasion."

"What would you have?" asked Bonville.

"Suffer me to leave this dungeon for awhile, and to attend to the recovery of the unfortunate Celestia; to be her nurse, her fond and attentive nurse, and to endeavour to rekindle her soul to reason. I request no more; I ask not for liberty, for that I know you would not grant me; and should I happily succeed in my efforts, if it be your will that I should do so, I will return to this fearful place without a murmur. I implore you on my knees not to refuse me this reasonable and humane request; no harm can result to you by granting it, for, alas! you have me too securely in your power."

Bonville again paused and reflected, and Lady Elvina urged her suit with even more vehemence and eloquence than before.

"Humph!" he muttered at last; "I will think of it."

"Oh, for Heaven's sake, decide at once!" she supplicated; "there is no time to be lost. Do not, oh, do not turn a deaf ear to my appeal."

"But," remarked Bonville, with a half sarcastic smile upon his countenance, "you are weak from long confinement in this underground apartment, and not very fit to perform the arduous offices of a nurse."

"God will give me the strength of a giant in such an affectionate cause," returned the unhappy prisoner, fervently; "there is no fatigue that I shall not be able to endure. God knows I am inured to hardships. I beseech you rlease me from this galling chain, and let me fly to the aid of my poor suffering grandchild."

"Stop, stop," replied Bonville, "you must not be in such a violent hurry; I must have some little time to consider of it."

"Indeed it requires no consideration; common humanity shows the necessity of it."

"Bah! humanity again."

"Again on my knees I implore you to consent to what I so reasonably ask!" said Lady Elvina, her heart throbbing with anxiety and impatience.

"Not now," answered Bonville, "but probably I may not refuse after mature deliberation.

"Oh, I pray you to be as prompt as possible. My beloved, but ill-fated Celestia, how horrible, how melancholy is the situation in which you are placed. Bonville, do you wish to destroy that fair and innocent young creature altogether? You surely cannot be cruel enough for that, frightful even as your crimes have been, and if you do not, you will not hesitate a moment in suffering me to fly to her, that by my presence I may recal her to reason, if not to happiness."

"You will see me again anon," remarked Bonville; and without waiting to give Lady Elvina an opportunity to make any further observations, he went from the dungeon.

Lady Elvina sank on her knees; her tears fell fast for the melancholy situation of Celestia, but at the same time she fervently prayed to Heaven that her persecutor might yield to her request; and from his manner and the observations he had made use of, she felt almost confident that he would.

Bonville, on leaving the dungeon, retired to his own apartment, and throwing himself on a seat, he reflected seriously upon what his unfortunate prisoner had proposed.

"An excellent suggestion," he said at last; "I will avail myself of it. There is every probability that the tender attentions of Lady Elvina will have the best effect upon Celestia, while the presence of that old hag, mother Baldwin, is sure to act contrarily. It does not matter my giving her ladyship a short holiday from her old quarters, for after she has accomplished what I require of her, she can be returned to them again. She cannot escape from me, that's very certain. Oh, I shall triumph yet; Celestia will most assuredly be mine. Lady Elvina, I ought to feel extremely obliged to you for the hint you have thrown out."

He now sent for Baldwin, who soon made her appearance, and he communicated to her what had passed between him and Lady Elvina, and the old woman was very well pleased to observe by his manner that he approved of the proposition, for then she would be once more at liberty, and get rid of what was to her a most disagreeable task.

"Well, what do you think of the suggestion, Baldwin?" demanded Bonville, when he had concluded.

"Why, that there could not possibly be a better one," replied that amiable old woman.

"Ah, I thought you would approve of it," observed Bonville.

"Certainly; and do not you?"

"Yes," answered Bonville.

"I don't see how you can do otherwise," said Mrs. Baldwin; "it is the most likely way of restoring the girl to her senses, and then you will be at full liberty to execute your plans."

"Exactly so," coincided Bonville; "and I look forward to the time with impatience."

"But I would advise you to use every precaution," suggested Baldwin; "you see the trouble that your recent impatience has cost you."

"Very true, but I will be more prudent for the future. How is your patient this afternoon?"

"Much the same."

"No change for the better, eh?" eagerly demanded Bonville.

"None that I can see," answered the old woman. "She felt sleepy, and so has retired to her bed, and when I left her was in a sound and tranquil repose."

"Very good," said Bonville; "then now is the very best time to introduce Lady Elvina to her chamber."

"Yes," coincided Baldwin. "but

you would not have her go there in her present wretched state, for that would certainly frighten the girl, instead of working any beneficial result."

"Very true, Baldwin; she must change her apparel, and you, of course, can accommodate her. I will bring her to you."

Baldwin now retired, and Bonville having placed a light in a lantern, once more made his way to the dungeon of Lady Elvina. He found her on her knees when he entered, engaged in prayer, but she eagerly sprang to her feet when she saw him, and awaited impatiently to know what was the result of his deliberation.

"Well," he said, "I have come to the determination to accede to your request."

"Oh, thank Heaven!" exclaimed the unfortunate lady; "then I shall be permitted to be the constant companion of my beloved Celestia, and to administer to all her wants?"

"You will," returned Bonville, "but mark me, there must be no nonsense in this affair. I shall watch you narrowly, and should I detect the least thing that I do not approve of, that moment will I convey you back to your dungeon, and punish you with even greater severity than I have hitherto done."

"Oh, indeed, indeed, you may trust me," said Lady Elvina, eagerly; "but let me be gone. Oh, do no let us delay a moment."

Bonville now set about removing the heavy chain by which Lady Elvina was secured to the wall, which having been done, she sunk on her knees, and returned her thanks to Providence for this, its goodness to her.

"Come, enough of this foolery," said Bonville, impatiently. "Follow me."

Lady Elvina obeyed. She staggered at first from the effects of long confinement and the cruel treatment she had received; but after a few moments, inspired by the thoughts of what business she was going upon, she recovered remarkable strength, and moved with a firm and agile step. For the first time for many months the ill-fated lady was out of that frightful dungeon, which was enough to strike terror in the breast of the beholder, and she felt as if she were already at full liberty; but poor Celestia occupied her whole thoughts, and she followed Bonville along the long dark passages with a throbbing heart, and every moment did indeed seem an age until she had arrived at the room in which her beloved grand-daughter was confined.

At length they reached the room in which Mrs. Baldwin was awaiting them, and there Bonville left them, after giving instructions to the old woman to conduct Lady Elvina to the chamber of our heroine as soon as she was dressed, and then to let him know the result.

Lady Elvina soon completed her toilette with the assistance of Baldwin, and the latter led the way, followed by her ladyship, with a palpitating heart.

When they arrived at the door of the room, such a trembling and sickly sensation came over Lady Elvina, that she could scarcely prevent herself from falling; but she soon recovered, and Baldwin having unlocked the door cautiously, they entered the room on tiptoe for fear of arousing the unfortunate patient.

Lady Elvina immediately stole towards the bed, on which Celestia was reclining, wrapped in a calm and beautiful sleep, and looking as lovely as ever. Lady Elvina, in spite of all her efforts, could not restrain her feelings, she pressed two or thee gentle kisses on the fair girl's lips; wept over her, and then kneeling down by the side of the bed, she devoutly prayed to Heaven for her recovery, and calledd own blessings upon her head.

Mrs. Baldwin having pointed to some medicines on a sideboard, and also to some refreshments that were in the room, left her, and went to acquaint her master with all that had taken place.

It would be impossible to describe the emotion of Lady Elvina as she stood over the couch of her youthful relative. It would be impossible to say whether love or grief most preponderated. How tranquil was that sleep. Who could imagine that the lovely being who slumbered there was the victim of sorrow, or illness? Frequently a smile played around her lips, such as angels might have envied in their blessed abode of everlasting peace.

"Beauteous child of sorrow and cruel oppression," murmured Lady Elvina to herself; "may thy dreams be those of happiness, and when thou wakest may it be to reason and the bright anticipations of future peace. Offspring of my murdered daughter, and do I again behold thee? Alas! but under what painful circumstances! The prisoner of one of the greatest monsters who are permitted for a time to contaminate the very air they breathe. Oh, dreadful thought!—And will just Heaven permit the destruction of so much beauty and innocence as this?—Oh, no, I will not, cannot believe so; it would be blasphemy against the Almighty to do so."

Again she pressed a gentle kiss upon the sleeping maiden's lips, and fast the scalding tears chased each other down her aged cheeks.

"And must we again be separated, my darling child?" she resumed, after a brief pause; "must I once more become an inmate of that loathsome dungeon, and never again behold thee?—Oh, forbid it All-merciful God!—My blood freezes with horror at the thought, not so much for mine own sake as for thine, my darling Celestia; for what will become of thee if thou art not speedily rescued from the power of this brutal man!—Oh, God! that thy young days should thus be overcast by the dense black clouds of sorrow."

Still Lady Elvina continued to watch with feelings of anxious emotion it would be a futile task to seek to portray, and still poor Celestia slept calmly, soundly, and undisturbed. Night came, and her slumbers remained the same. Lady Elvina again and again prayed to Heaven that this lengthened sleep might have the most beneficial effect, still did she await most impatiently till she should awake, to see whether she happily recognised her, and to learn what effect her presence might have upon Celestia's disordered brain.

Whilst Lady Elvina was thus seated by the couch of her grandchild, her busy memory recalled every circumstance of her eventual and melancholy life, and dismal and heart-rending indeed were the feelings that those sad reminiscences engendered.

"Ah! just like you, my beloved Celestia," she sighed, "just as lovely and guileless as you, was your unfortunate mother when she met with her savage and untimely fate, and from the same blood-stained wretch who murdered your noble uncle, and who now holds us both in his power. Oh, when will his hideous career be ended? When will retribution overtake him for the frightful crimes he has perpetrated? Shall he much longer be permitted to wallow in the blood of his unoffending fellow-creatures with impunity? Oh no; there is a just God above, who one day will call him to a terrible account. And can he hope to find mercy in the next world when he has so cruelly denied it to others in this?"

At this moment she was interrupted in her soliloquy by the entrance of Mrs. Baldwin, who had been sent by Bonville to inquire whether Celestia had yet awoke, and if she had, what effect the sight of Lady Elvina had had upon her. But finding that the poor girl still slept, she again departed, after exchanging a few words of no importance with her ladyship, and left her to her own silent and gloomy meditations. Sad, indeed, they were, but still she felt a melancholy pleasure in being the unwearied guardian of Celestia's slumbers, which no language can describe. Several times during the night, Mrs. Baldwin called to make inquiries, but our heroine had not awoke, and so sound was her sleep and prolonged, that any one might have supposed that she was labouring under the effects of some powerful opiate.

Bonville was so anxious to know what would be the effects produced on Celestia by the presence of Lady Elvina, that he could not make up his mind to retire to his chamber.

"It is most extraordinary," he observed, the last time that Mrs. Baldwin returned from the room of Celestia, "and I must confess I do not understand it. And yet you say that she seems to sleep calmly?"

"She does," answered Mrs Baldwin, "and I think that is a very good sign, and that when she awakes we may expect the best results."

"I hope your predictions may prove correct," said Bonville. "I think we may depend upon Lady Elvina doing what she has promised?"

"There is no fear of that. She would not dare to deceive you, knowing that she would be visited by your vengeance. Besides, is she not your prisoner?"

"Very true."

"Then what have you to fear?" asked Baldwin. "But do you mean to consign her again to the dungeon after Celestia has recovered?"

"Not immediately," answered Bonville, "I have a plan in my head which I think will forward my views."

"And pray what may that be?"

"I do not think proper to disclose it at present," said Bonville.

"Oh, very well," retorted Mrs. Baldwin, snappishly. "I don't wish to be inquisitive. Good night."

"Good night," repeated Bonville, and the old woman retired from the room.

Bonville traversed the apartment for some time with disordered steps, and wrapped in deep meditation.

"This is very strange," he remarked, "and in spite of what old Baldwin has said, I can neither understand it, nor am I half satisfied with it. That old she-devil has not been playing me any tricks, has she, for the purpose of getting rid of the trouble of her charge? I know she mortally hates her own sex, particularly that portion of it which is young and handsome, and that she would not hesitate to do anything to revenge herself against them. But no, this is ridiculous, and I have suffered my impatience to overcome my reason. She would not venture to play her pranks with me, for she ought to know my character pretty well by this time. Perhaps the malady under which Celestia is suffering is taking a favourable turn, and the sight of Lady Elvina, I think, cannot fail to be productive of the most satisfactory results. I will endeavour to wait patiently till the morning, and trust that I shall not be disappointed."

He threw himself listlessly in a chair, but still he could not make up his mind to retire to bed. It was now one o'clock, and all was profoundly silent in the house, and he resolved to go himself to the chamber of his fair prisoner, in order to make one more inquiry. He knocked softly at the door, and it was opened by Lady Elvina, who looked confused on beholding him.

"How now?" he demanded, in a peremptory tone, "is she yet awake?"

"She is not," replied Lady Elvina, "she sleeps as soundly as ever. There must have been something in the medicine she has taken, I think, to have so powerful an effect upon her."

"What do you mean?" he demanded; "that the symptoms she evinces are dangerous?"

"God forbid!" fervently ejaculated Lady Elvina; "on the contrary, I hope that this protracted sleep will be productive of the most happy results, and that it will please Heaven to recall the poor girl's scattered senses; but, alas! of what utility will it be her awaking to reason if you still persist in your cruel designs? Better, much better would it be that she should never wake again, than to be subjected to such a horrible, such a disgusting fate. Oh, Bonville, reflect now, and be merciful, if you have never been so before, and—"

"Cease, croaking idiot," fiercely interrupted Bonville; "do not exasperate me; you know the conditions on which I yielded to your supplications; break them, and immediately will I convey you to your dungeon again, where I will inflict upon you tenfold more horrors than those you have yet experinced."

Lady Elvina clasped her hands with agony, and looked at her brutal persecutor with an expression of the most unspeakable horror.

"Spare me, Bonville," she at last articulated; "God knows I meant not to exasperate you, but merely to excite some little feeling of pity in your breast towards yon unfortunate girl."

"Enough of this nonsense," returned the villain; "you know it can have no other effect upon me than to urge me on to that which I should probably not otherwise have thought of. I must see her, and judge for myself."

"Oh, forbear, forbear," implored Lady Elvina; "should she awake and behold you in her present state of mind, Heaven only knows what the consequences might be."

"Pshaw!" impatiently remarked Bonville; "am I not master here? I tell you again I must and will see her, but I mean not to disturb her."

Lady Elvina saw plainly that it was worse than useless to expostulate with this heartless and determined man, and with a deep sigh she, therefore, walked silently into the room, whither she was followed by Bonville, who approached the bed on which his innocent and unconscious victim was reposing, and gazed earnestly upon her. Even his insensible heart could not help glowing with feelings of admiration at the beautiful object before him, who was still wrapped in the same calm and profound slumber which had wrapped her senses for so many hours. A heavenly smile continued to play around her lips, and added, if possible, an extra charm to her lovely and captivating countenance.

Lady Elvina watched the expression of the villain's eyes with the greatest anxiety and trepidation, and trembled lest Celestia should awake while he was present, confident as she was that the shock to her feelings wou'd be too much for her strength to endure.

"It is all right," he said at length, "there is no danger to apprehend; it is evident she sleeps tranquilly, and when she awakes, if you only obey my injunctions, there will be a great change for the better."

"God grant that there may!" fervently ejaculated Lady Elvina, "and that all the troubles and dangers which at present surround her, may be removed."

Bonville frowned, but again directed his gaze towards the sleeping girl, and his admiration increased every moment. He could scarcely refrain from polluting her lips with his odious kisses, and it was only the fear of disturbing her that prevented him. Never did he feel his triumph greater than at that moment, and the most guilty passions predominated in his breast, and gave a still more repulsive aspect to his features.

"Is she not very lovely, sweet Lady Elvina?" he said in his most disagreeable tones; "what grace, what simplicity and innocence of features; what a sunny smile plays around those ruby lips even in sleep. What glossy tresses, what delicately pencilled eyebrows, what long and silken lashes. Oh, she is a beautiful creature, is she not, Lady Elvina? Is she not a prize worth contending for, and of keeping at any risk when once obtained possession of?"

How the bosom of Lady Elvina heaved with shame and indignation, as Bonville thus expressed himself. For a few moments her feelings were too painful for her to give utterance to them, but at length she said in a voice of gentle remonstrance and reproach—

"Oh, Bonville, are you so lost to every feeling of shame and humanity as to talk thus?—Can you look on yon helpless and unoffending girl, and feel no sense of pity? Shame, shame, I blush for you. But pray leave the room, and if you must taunt and torture me, I pray you take a more fitting time to do so."

Bonville fixed upon her a look of scorn and derision as he replied:—

"Well, this time, sweet Lady Elvina,

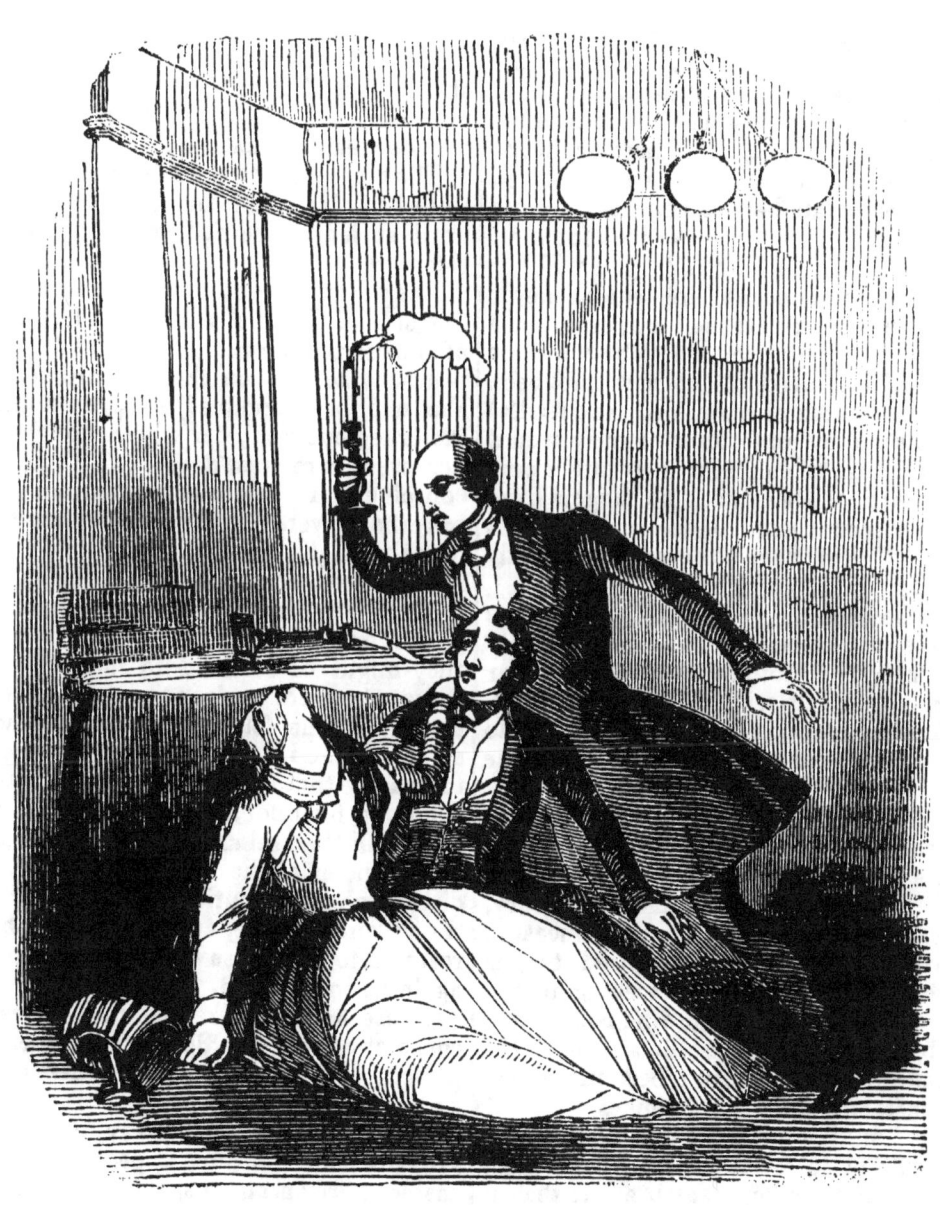

I will obey you, as I have satisfied my curiosity; but remember my injunctions, and as you hope to remain with your darling child, obey them."

Lady Elvina returned no answer, and the villain stalked from the room, and left her with her tender and unconscious charge to her own gloomy and torturing meditations.

She once more seated herself by the side of the bed, and gave herself up to the most racking thoughts, while she gazed with all the agony of intense grief upon the hapless girl. It was quite evident that there was no hope unless Providence interposed to rescue Celestia from Bonville's power; he was determined in his monstrous purposes, and she well knew from woeful experience that he was not the man to relent or to be moved to pity.

"Pity!" she sighed to herself, "it has ever been a stranger to his callous and guilty breast. His fiendish delight has been to torture and oppress his fallen creatures. And must this poor child of misfortune fall a victim to his diabolical passions? Are there no means by which she can be saved from so horrible a fate?—God help her; for it is only to You that she can look for aid!—But I will not despair; you will not desert that innocent being who has never broken your righteous laws, or injured any of her fellow-creatures by word, or thought, or deed. Alas! had it not been for my first fatal error, all these dreadful trials to my unfortunate family would never have taken place; they might now all have been happy and no dangers have threatened them. I feel myself most guilty, and never, never can I sufficiently make amendment."

She beat her distracted breast as she gave utterance to these melancholy words, and nothing could exceed her agony and self-reproach at that moment. A violent flood of tears came at last to her relief, and by degrees she did become somewhat more composed.

The villain Bonville having now satisfied himself that all was safe, and that the long sleep of Celestia was not fraught with any danger, but, on the contrary, was likely to tend in a great measure towards her recovery, retired to his chamber; but even after seeking his bed it was some time before he could go to sleep—and he gave himself up to the same train of guilty reflections which constantly occupied his mind.

"Oh, how impatiently I wait the result of to-morrow," he said; "but my sanguine hopes assure me that it will be everything I could wish—that the beauteous Celestia will awake to reason and to new life; then let me wait patiently but a few days, until she has entirely recovered, and I will see to the full gratification of my revenge. This plan that has suggested itself to me is one that must and shall succeed.

Celestia will yield sooner than see Lady Elvina consigned to the dreadful fate with which I will threaten her, and if she does not, force shall make her. Of what use will it be for her, poor weak girl, to offer any resistance to my will? It would be like the lamb opposing the wolf. She is doomed, she is doomed, and nothing can save her. No earthly power shall stay me in my determined purpose. And what a lovely creature she is. Her charms have quite inflamed my soul, and I would not resign her for the wealth of nations."

Thus the heartless miscreant continued to give vent to his guilty feelings, until at length he fell into a restless sleep.

Lady Elvina continued to watch by the side of Celestia's bed with feelings of the utmost anxiety, doubt, and suspense. She felt no fatigue, although she had been occupied so many hours in her tedious task; her whole thoughts, her every care was devoted to the unconscious girl before her, and frequent were the prayers she offered up to heaven that she might awake to reason and to health, and that the atrocious designs of the wretch who held them within his power, might yet be defeated, and that they might be restored to liberty and those who were so dear to them. Ever and anon she felt renewed hope, and some instinctive power prompted her to imagine that if they only waited with calmness, fortitude, and resignation, and placed all their reliance on the goodness of Providence, the time was not far distant when retribution would overtake the villain Bonville, and they would be restored to happiness which would never again he interrupted.

Those thoughts were a source of sweet consolation to the afflicted and cruelly persecuted lady, and rendered her firm and confident.

Thus passed the time away, until the grey dawn of morning appeared in the eastern horizon, and just at that moment Lady Elvina was startled by hearing Celestia give utterance to a deep sigh. Her bosom throbbed with expectation, and eagerly she watched the countenance of the poor girl, thinking that now the important moment had arrived.

Celestia partially opened her eyes, and raised her head from the pillow on which it rested, but it immediately sunk back again and she seemed to sleep as sound as ever.

"It is strange," thought Lady Elvina, "some powerful opiate must certainly have been administered to her; but for what purpose?"

And Lady Elvina was right in her conjectures; the old woman, Baldwin, had mixed a strong drug in the medicine she had given to her, in order to save herself the trouble of watching her throughout the night, and the effects of which, even after the lapse of so many hours, had not yet exhausted themselves. Lady Elvina, however, could perceive that she now appeared to breathe even more freely than she had done before, and the expression of her countenance was more serene and happy. She impressed kisses of the most unbounded affection upon her beauteous cheeks, and resumed her weary watching with increased zeal and confidence.

"God be with you, my sweet child," she said, "and render your slumbers happy and refreshing. May no painful visions haunt your imagination, but hope and peace and joy shed their bright halo around you."

Again a sweet smile irradiated the features of the beauteous sleeper, as if to assure her unfortunate relative that her prayers had been heard, and to inspire her with the hope that her wishes would all be realized. Lady Elvina felt a ray of happiness steal into her bosom, such as she had not experienced for many years before, and she offered up a prayer of gratitude to the supreme.

Another hour elapsed, during which time Lady Elvina had never for an instant removed her eyes from the countenance of Celestia, so anxious was she to see her awake, and to behold what would be the result of her presence. She was not much longer to be kept in suspense. While she still gazed, she observed a slight movement in the frame of Celestia, she muttered some incoherent words, and then opening her eyes, she raised herself up in the bed, and gazed vacantly around her, but did not seem to observe Lady Elvina.

"It was a sweet dream," she said, in mingled tones of melancholy and joy; "a most delicious dream; but yet I do not see them—where are they all? Alas! they have deserted poor Celestia; they despise the unfortunate girl they once pretended to love, since she has fallen a victim to that bad man. But I am not in his power now! No, no, Celestia is at liberty,—she is as free as the free air. How brightly the sun shines; it is a lovely morning, and here am I like the sluggard, wasting my time in bed. I will arise and take a walk in the green fields."

What language can describe the anguish of Lady Elvina as she listened to these wild observations and saw that all the hopes she had formed were ready to burst; the scalding tears chased each other down her cheeks, and she was unable to speak, but on seeing that Celestia was about to get out of bed, she threw her arms around her neck, and, in a voice of the deepest emotion she ejaculated—

"Celestia! dear, dear Celestia, oh, look at me; speak to me, or I shall break my heart!"

"Woman!" said the poor girl, "release me! Why do you seek to detain me? I am no longer a prisoner, and why am I not permitted to wander in the green fields, and inhale the pure and fragrant breath of Heaven?"

"Celestia, beloved child," cried the distracted Lady Elvina, "oh, look at me; do you not know me? Why do you shrink from my fond embrace? I am your unhappy relative, Lady Elvina Elverton."

"Ha, ha, ha!" wildly and hysterically laughed the afflicted maiden; "do you think to deceive me? The noble lady of whom you speak died years ago in a wretched dungeon, far, far in the bowels of the earth. I was present at her death. What say you to that, now?"

"My God! my God!" groaned the lady, "what a dreadful scene in this. Her senses have evidently fled, and I fear for ever. Guilty Bonville, this is all your hideous work."

During the time that Lady Elvina was thus speaking, Celestia had sunk back again in the bed, and was laughing and muttering some incoherent words to herself; but suddenly she again started up and looked wildly and vacantly around her.

Once more Lady Elvina threw her arms around her fair neck, and in a voice almost choked by sobs, she said :—

"My poor Celestia, Lady Elvina, your unfortunate grandmother, did not die; it is she who now embraces you and calls upon your name. She is here to comfort you and—"

"Ah !" interrupted Celestia, " I know you now; you are that savage old woman who used to attend upon me once when I was ill; Mrs. Baldwin, I think they called her. What do you here ?—Am I not free ?—This is Sungrove Abbey, and if you do not immediately depart, I will call my friends to you."

"Oh, Celestia, Celestia, daughter of my murdered child !" sobbed Lady Elvina, "to see you thus ; it will break my heart."

"Release me, woman !" exclaimed Celestia, suddenly and forcibly disengaging herself from the embrace of Lady Elvina ; "I must apply myself to my studies, or my dear papa, Mr. Conigsby, and his sister Eugenia, will chide me. I must get this task off by heart, ere I can venture to take my accustomed walk to the old Priory Ruins. Do you know the old Priory Ruins ? They are such beautiful ruins, though my poor papa— I mean my first papa—died near them. Ah, me ! I was a very little child then !"

She sighed deeply as she uttered these words, and then closing her eyes, she seemed to be buried in thought. Lady Elvina's agony knew no bounds : it was almost insupportable. She wrung her hands in despair, and the tears rushed in torrents to her eyes.

"Alas !" she sighed, "it is all no use ; she knows me not ; the blow is struck, the doom of our unfortunate family is sealed past recal ; but this trial is one of the severest I have ever experienced. Would that I had been in my grave years ago."

She clasped her hands vehemently together in the intense anguish of her feelings, and it was several moments ere she could speak again.

"Father of Mercy," she at length ejaculated, "I humbly, but earnestly beseech Thee to look down with an eye of pity upon this poor afflicted girl, and restore to her the light of reason, which

has been extinguished by Bonville ; and again I beseech thee to restore her to liberty and the arms of her sorrowing relations, and do not—oh I do not suffer her inhuman oppressor to triumph in his diabolical designs. Oh, God! grant me but this prayer, and then shall I be ready to submit to any fate which may be in store for me !"

Having given utterance to this prayer, she once more turned her attention towards the beauteous sufferer. She was still in the same condition that she had been a few minutes before, and appeared to be totally regardless or unconscious of what was passing around her. Lady Elvina watched her with the most anxious care, but did not think it prudent to disturb her.

She was aroused from her dismal meditations by the entrance of Mrs. Baldwin, who, with a sinister grin upon her repulsive countenance, inquired in a whisper whether Celestia had awoke yet.

"Alas—alas !" sighed Lady Elvina.

"Why, what's the matter now ?" demanded the old woman, in the same disagreeable tones.

"My poor child is a raving maniac !"

"Well, I knew that before," returned Mrs Baldwin : "she is no better, then ?"

"God help her, no !" replied Lady Elvina, in the most melancholy accents, and the tears chasing each other down her cheeks, "and I fear she never will be—at any rate, while she remains in this dreadful place."

"Ah !" said the old woman, with an inward chuckle, " then hers is, indeed, a hopeless case. But come, Mr. Bonville wants to see you : I will conduct you to him."

"Oh, how can I leave her in that deplorable state ?" said Lady Elvina.

"The girl will take no harm during the short time you will be absent," said Mrs. Baldwin. "She cannot jump out of either of the windows, for they are barred ; and she cannot cut her throat, if she were so disposed, for the knives, I perceive, are all put out of the way."

How the Lady Elvina shuddered with horror and disgust at this unfeeling speech !

"Come, come," said the old woman, "this is a waste of time. Bonville will become impatient; and I believe you know that it is rather dangerous to incur his anger."

"But what does he want with me?" tremulously asked the afflicted lady.

"How should I know?" replied the brutal woman. "You will soon ascertain that when you see him. But I suppose he wants to question you about the girl: come."

Lady Elvina saw that it would be useless to contend with the old woman any longer, and she, therefore, with a deep sigh, walked towards the bed, and once more gazed with the most intense emotion and feelings of unutterable despair upon the suffering Celestia.

She appeared to be again sleeping, for her eyes were closed, and there was not the slightest movement in her frame, except the gentle heaving of her bosom as she drew her breath. It was some consolation to see her so calm, after the wild and piteous manner in which her mind had wandered a short time before. The unhappy lady pressed an affectionate kiss upon her lips, and then tore herself away, and passed out of the room with the old woman, Baldwin, who secured the door after her.

They found Bonville seated in one of the lower rooms, and he instantly arose on their entrance. Lady Elvina shuddered with horror in his presence.

"You can quit the room, Baldwin," he said. The old woman obeyed, and he then hastily approached the trembling Lady Elvina, and fixed his flashing and disagreeable eyes full on her pale face.

"Why, how now, Lady Elvina?" he demanded sternly, "you have been weeping. Come, come, no more of this nonsense, for you know very well it is all lost upon me. You may be seated;" Lady Elvina did sink upon a chair, for her trembling limbs would no longer support her. Bonville looked at her for a moment or two with scorn and hatred, and he then said—

"Now then, answer the questions I am about to put to you, explicitly and as briefly as possible. How about Celestia?"

"Alas! poor unfortunate girl," sighed Lady Elvina.

"Beware, woman," said Bonville, sternly; "that is not an answer to my question. I tell you again you had better not attempt to trifle with me. Is she recovered from the state of torpor she was in?"

"She has," faintly replied Lady Elvina.

"How long since?"

"About two hours."

"And she recognised you?" eagerly demanded Bonville.

"Alas! no," sighed Lady Elvina. "Oh, Bonville, if you had any humanity in your breast, surely you would be stung with remorse had you but heard her piteous ravings; she is a wretched maniac, and this is all the dreadful work of your hands."

"D—n!" cried Bonville, stamping with rage, "do you dare to lecture me, woman? Have you no fear of my vengeance?"

"Your vengeance cannot go further," replied Lady Elvina, "unless you take my life, and that is now a burthen to me. Think of the poor girl whose intellect you have made a terrible wreck, and tremble, if you are not insensible to every feeling of compunction."

Bonville bit his lips; but he stifled his rage, and said coolly—

"Well, Lady Elvina, I will allow you even at present to rate me, since it is all you can do; but remember I am not to be deceived, and I begin to think that this insanity is all assumed on the part of Celestia, for the purpose of delaying the execution of my purpose, and with the forlorn hope of something occurring to rescue her from my power; but if that is her idea, I am sorry to say that she is doomed to be woefully disappointed.

"Oh, monstrous and ungenerous thought," said the unhappy lady; "Celestia, my sweet, my innocent Celestia, act the part of the hypocrite? Such a thought could only have entered one of the blackest of minds."

"Well," remarked Bonville, "we will waive that part of the subject at present. I must know all the particulars of what has occurred since I saw you last night. Relate them, and that as briefly as you can."

"Oh, spare my feelings, Bonville."

"Your feelings! Bah! Proceed, proceed, and do not tire out my patience, or it will be the worse for you."

Lady Elvina sighed deeply, and then, as well as her emotion would permit her, related to the ruffian all the melancholy facts, and the wild observations which poor Celestia had made use of. Bonville frequently interrupted her to give vent to his feelings of rage and disappointment, and when she had concluded, he said—

"So then it seems, Lady Elvina, that your presence is not likely to work any beneficial influence upon the disordered mind of Celestia, and that you might as well have remained in your dungeon."

"Oh, no, no, no!" ejaculated the alarmed lady, fearful that the heartless ruffian would again separate her from the poor girl; "there has been no time to prove that yet. Do not let me leave her for the love of Heaven! she must, she will know me ere long; my kind attentions will make her do so, and probably restore her to reason; but if I am taken from her and she is left to the tender mercies of that woman, Baldwin, then indeed is her recovery hopeless. But you will not separate us, Bonville, oh, say you will not?"

Bonville hesitated for a few moments and reflected, then turning to the wretched Lady Elvina, he said—

"Well, be it so. I will try you a few days longer, and should you fail, you return to your dungeon, and therefore you know how it will be most prudent for you to act."

"God knows what anxious pains I will take to recal the wandering senses of that beloved girl," replied Lady Elvina, "and if it please All-merciful Heaven that I shall succeed, I shall be more than amply repaid for all the misery it has been my hard lot to undergo."

"Enough," said Bonville, "I shall see you again by and by, when I hope to hear better news than that you have just now given me."

"God grant that I may be able to do so," fervently ejaculated his afflicted companion.

Bonville now rang the bell, and Baldwin having appeared, he said—

"Conduct Lady Elvina back to the chamber of Celestia, and," he added,

whispering in the old woman's ear, "keep a strict eye upon her and the girl—do you understand me?"

The old woman nodded in the affirmative, and then she and Lady Elvina quitted the apartment to return to that in which the hapless Celestia was confined.

"Curses light upon this misfortune," he said, "which thus retards the accomplishment of my wishes. Had I not acted with such foolish impetuosity it would not have been. But can the girl really be mad, or is it only a *ruse* to foil me? I will watch both her and Lady Elvina narrowly, and should I discover that they are really deceiving me, I will have ample vengeance. That very hour shall Celestia become my victim, and Lady Elvina shall be consigned to all the horrors that my malice can suggest. They are worse than fools who think to tamper with or to deceive me, and Lady Elvina must have known that many years ago, and therefore am I more inclined to think that she will not venture to do so now. However, there is nothing like being on your guard. If the girl is really insane, I have reason to place every confidence in Lady Elvina, for from the affection which she naturally bears her, she will be sure to exert herself to the utmost to restore her to reason."

At this moment there was a knock at the room-door, and the old woman entered on being permitted to do so.

"Well, Baldwin," said Bonville, "what do you think of this business?"

"I scarcely know what to think of it," replied Baldwin.

"Do you believe that the girl is insane?" asked Bonville.

"There is little doubt of it," she returned, "and she is now as bad as she was at first."

"Have you seen her?"

"Certainly, not many minutes ago, and she raved in the most wild and incoherent manner."

"D——n!" exclaimed Bonville, "I had hoped that the long and tranquil sleep she had would have tended towards her recovery. This is a bad job, a most vexatious job. What is to be done?"

"Nothing but to wait patiently,"

replied the old woman, secretly chuckling at the disappointment of her worthy master, whom, the same as all the rest of mankind, she heartily hated.

"Wait patiently!" replied Bonville, furiously. "Baldwin, you are a fool."

"I know it, but I think it will require even greater wisdom than you possess to bring the girl to her senses. I say again there is nothing to be done but to wait patiently."

"Well, well," replied Bonville, more calmly, "it is no use to quarrel upon the subject, and I dare say there is a great deal of truth in what you say. Do you think that Lady Elvina is likely to make any favourable impression upon her?"

"Why I should say if she can't nobody can; but if you make your appearance before the girl, until she is sufficiently recovered, you will upset everything."

"Well, I will not do so," said Bonville, "but you remember the caution I gave you to keep a strict eye on them both?"

"Certainly I do," replied the old woman, Baldwin, "but there was no occasion for you to do that."

"If you should observe anything which excites your suspicion, do not let them perceive that you do so, but immediately communicate it to me, and then I shall know how to act."

"Very well, I will do so," answered Baldwin.

"And mind me, Baldwin," added Bonville, "I think it advisable that Lady Elvina should receive every indulgence during her attendance upon Celestia; for I think that might operate greatly in favour of the recovery of the girl, supposing that her insanity is not assumed."

"That is your business, not mine," surlily replied Mrs. Baldwin; "all that I have to do is to follow your instructions."

"That is all I require you to do," returned Bonville, "and mark me," he added, fixing a look upon her which it was impossible she could misunderstand; "that I expect you will do, or you know the consequences."

"Oh, yes, I know them very well," said the old woman, with one of her most frightful looks;—"I know them

very well, I tell you; but there was a time when you would not have ventured to threaten old Mother Baldwin, recollect that, Mr. Bonville."

"Get out of the room," said Bonville, fiercely, "you are becoming old and crazy."

"Perhaps I am," retorted the old woman, "but," she added in an under tone as she hobbled out of the room, "you may find that the crazy old hag is too cunning for you."

"What are you muttering about Baldwin?" demanded Bonville hastily, as she departed.

"Nothing particular, Mr. Bonville," replied the old woman drily, and chuckling within herself, "I was only saying that I would obey your orders."

"Oh, indeed?" said Bonville, fixing upon her a suspicious and penetrating look.

"That was all," said Baldwin, and she immediately disappeared from the room.

"I must look sharply after that old crone," said Bonville, after she had departed, "or she will work me some mischief. She is crafty and revengeful, and although at present she is in my power, she might find the means of thwarting my plans."

He paused and ruminated. The situation of Celestia annoyed him greatly, but yet he saw that there was no other alternative left to him than to await patiently the result of her malady; for he was satisfied that it was his own imprudence and impetuosity in the first instance which had subjected him to his present vexation.

CHAPTER XXXII.

THE LITTLE GREY MAN.—THE RECOVERY OF CELESTIA FROM HER INSANITY.—THE RENEWAL OF HOPE, AND FRESH DISAPPOINTMENT.

IN order to endeavour to calm his feelings and collect his thoughts, Bonville left the house, and walked towards one of the wildest and most unfrequented spots in that cheerless neighbourhood. The morning was dull, wet, and miserable. The rain descended in a hazy mist, which imparted a shivering influence to the senses; the horizon was obscured by murky clouds, and the wind murmured in sullen gusts as if to grumble at the tempest for being so tardy in its fury.

But the state of the weather had no effect upon Bonville, who was totally absorbed in his own dark thoughts, and he walked on ruminating, and perfectly unconscious and reckless whither he went.

Thus he had wandered on until he had crossed the wild moor on which his house was situated, and had entered a lane, known by the dismal title of "The Dead Man's Walk," from an old superstition which existed in that part of the country, that several centuries previously a number of travellers had been there waylaid and barbarously murdered by a desperate gang of robbers, who at that time infested the neighbourhood, and whose ghastly shades were said to have wandered through the lane ever since, at midnight, on the anniversary of their slaughter. And, indeed, the place was well worthy of such a wild superstition. The light of day seldom or only partially entered it, for tall trees grew on either side, and their branches meeting, formed a complete canopy overhead, which buried it in profound shade, and rendered it always a scene of darkness and gloom.

Still deeply wrapped in meditation, Bonville wandered on, until he was aroused by hearing a low, chuckling sort of laugh, which seemed to proceed from a spot not far from him.

He looked up, but at first he could not perceive anything, but a renewal of the laugh directed his attention more immediately to the place from whence it issued, and he then beheld, seated on the stump of a tree, one of the most singular and grotesque figures which could well be imagined.

It was that of a little old man, of very spare figure, with a sallow and old parchment-like complexion, bright, twinkling grey eyes, and long silvery hair and beard, who was performing some very curious antics with his arms, and, in fact, he appeared to be in high glee altogether.

His attire was no less curious than his physiognomy. He wore upon his head a three-cornered cocked hat, with a peacock's feather stuck in the front of it, and on his shoulders an old grey jacket, patched in various parts with cloth of different colours—his small clothes were of bright flaming red, his stockings yellow, and his feet were encased in great clumsy wooden shoes.

At the sight of such a singular apparition Bonville was somewhat startled, and the latter now perceiving that he observed him, nodded his head three times in a familiar manner, and laughed again. Bonville advanced close up to him and looked narrowly in his countenance, but the extraordinary little being did not in the least alter his position, and maintained precisely the same imperturbable expression of countenance, winking both his eyes, and nodding at the same time.

"You appear to be merry, old gentleman," said Bonville.

"Ha, ha, ha! he, he, he! ho, ho! yes—yes—very merry, very merry; always am, ha, ha!" laughed the little old man; "light consciences make light hearts, eh, Monsieur Bonville?"

Bonville started and looked at him more narrowly than before, but the old man remained in the same position, and his face underwent not the slightest change in expression.

"How know you my name!" demanded Bonville.

"Ha, ha, ha!" laughed the extraordinary being: "how do I know it? Come, that is good—he, he, he!"

"You are an idiot," said Bonville angrily.

"I know it," answered the old man, more seriously; "and so was Lady Elverton when she listened to your hypocritical cant and deserted her noble lord; and so was the more humble Mabel Henderson, when she fell beneath your insidious arts. I am an idiot, I am an idiot, oh, yes, I know I am an idiot; ha, ha, ha!"

The astonishment and confusion of the villain Bonville increased beyond all bounds, and for a moment or two he was completely dumb-founded, during which brief interval the mysterious little old man laughed and chuckled, as if in high glee.

"Who the devil and what are you?" demanded Bonville impatiently

"You have told me; I am an idiot; he, he, he!" was the answer;

"If you are acquainted with me," observed Bonville, with difficulty suppressing that rage which the coolness of the old man excited, "you must know that I am no man to be trifled with."

"Oh, no, oh, no, not to be trifled with; ha, ha, he, he!"

"What if I were to twist that scraggy little neck of yours," fiercely remarked Bonville, "and stop your giggling for ever?"

"Ha, ha," again laughed the old man, provokingly, "I know you are an adept at murder, Monsieur Bonville, but you dare not do that."

"I dare not?" repeated Bonville.

"No, you dare not. Will you make the trial?"

"Pshaw! this is trifling; will you tell me who you are, and what is your business with me?"

"Oh, no, no, ha, ha!" replied the old man; "at least," he added, "not at your bidding."

"What are you here for?" asked Bonville.

"Merely to catch sparrows," was the somewhat ambiguous reply, and again the little old man laughed more heartily than before.

"Bah!" said Bonville contemptuously, and turning away; "the man is mad."

"Stay, Monsieur Bonville," exclaimed the extraordinary being, " I have something to say to you."

Bonville turned back.

"Now," he demanded. " What is it you would say? Be brief, for my time is precious."

"Oh, fear not," said the old man, " I will not detain you long. I merely want to give you a few words of caution. You remember Mabel Henderson do you not?"

"D——n!" furiously returned Bonville, "why do you remind me of that name?"

" Because it was one that you used to pretend to esteem, to love; is not that the truth?"

"Mysterious little wretch," said Bonville, " again I ask who and what are you?"

"Only an old idiot, but one who knows you well. You remember Mabel Henderson, do you not?"

" And what if I do?" demanded Bonville.

"She was the favourite attendant and confident of Lady Elvina Elverton, was she not?" said the old man.

Bonville returned to answer, but looked at his singular interrogator with amazement.

" She was a fair girl at that time, was she not, Monsieur Bonville?" continued the old man, " and good and virtuous withal, and you admired her too, professed to love her, and poured the honey of your flattering and deceptive tongue into her too confiding ears, until in a moment of weakness she fell and brought disgrace upon herself and all her family. Is not that the truth, Monsieur Bonville, and can you deny it?"

" By all the infernal host this is too much," exclaimed Bonville, passionately, " old man, I will know who and what you are."

"And so you shall anon," answered the latter, " but not at present. Mabel Henderson became the unhappy victim to your base and insidious arts; you dare not deny that. What if she still lives; lives for vengeance, which she will assuredly at some time or other obtain?—What if she has been the constant spy upon your actions, has tracked your footsteps wherever you went, and knows of all your atrocious deeds?—

What if she is now at work to discover the place where you have the fair Celestia and Lady Elvina confined, and that I, knowing it, am about to find her out and reveal it to her?"

" Provoking little imp, at least you shall not live to accomplish your design!" exclaimed Bonville, as he rushed towards the old man with the intention of seizing him, but before he could do so, he heard the report of a pistol, and found that he was wounded in the arm, and when the smoke had dispersed, he looked eagerly around, but the mysterious little old man was nowhere to be seen.

No language could do adequate justice to his rage, astonishment, and disappointment. He hastily took a handkerchief from his pocket and bound it round the wound he had received, and then he staggered to the seat which the mysterious unknown had lately occupied, rather faint from the loss of blood he had sustained, and for a few minutes was unable to move or collect his ideas.

At length he partly recovered himself, and stretched his eyes as far as they could go along the lane, but not the least sign of the singular little old man could he perceive.

" By all the infernal host," he ejaculated, " this is one of the most extraordinary, bewildering, and alarming adventures that ever I met with. Who can this old man be, who is so well acquainted with all my affairs, and who has held out such threats to me? I do not remember to have seen him before. My retreat then is known, and he has escaped me; oh, I am not near so safe as I imagined myself to be. Mabel Henderson then it is true still lives, and I may be certain that she will pursue me with all the vengeance in her power. What is to be done? I know not. And am I to be thus shamefully foiled, after having triumphed thus far? The thought is madness; and I see no course open to me to avoid the threatened danger. I cannot think of resigning Celestia and setting the Lady Elvina at liberty; no, I will run any risk sooner than do that. This old wretch must be discovered by some mean or other, and should I only be fortunate enough to get him in my power, I will take good care to stop his babbling for ever."

The pain of his wound now became

intense, and he arose from his seat, and muttering curses long and deep as he went, proceeded to the house. On arriving there he immediately summoned the old woman Baldwin, whose astonishment on beholding the condition he was in may readily be conceived.

"Why, Bonville, how is this?" she asked; "how did you receive this wound?"

"From a little devil in human form," replied Bonville, biting his lips, "but before you ask any further questions, see what remedy you can apply to this wound; it is but slight, I believe, though very painful."

The old woman left the room, and shortly returned with such remedies as her limited knowledge suggested, and some dressing, which having applied, she bandaged it up, and Bonville carefully observed that "he should do."

The old woman, whose curiosity, of course, was greatly excited, then repeated her questions, and Bonville related to her the singular adventure he had met with, which Mrs. Baldwin heard with the utmost amazement, frequently shaking her head, and looking ominously at her worthy master.

"And now, Baldwin," he said, "what do you think of all this?"

"Why, that it is very alarming to say the least of it," replied the old woman.

"Have you any recollection of ever having seen such an individual as the one I have described to you?" asked Bonville.

"None whatever. Who can he be?"

"Oh course, that is what I want to know."

"He is evidently well acquainted with you and all your affairs."

"Yes, that is certain," replied Bonville, "and what is worse than all, the old wretch is aware that Celestia and the Lady Elvina are confined here, and he will not fail, as he threatened, to take every advantage of his knowledge."

"What a pity it is that you did not secure him," remarked Baldwin.

"Why, I endeavoured to do so, as I told you before, when I received this wound, and when I recovered from the shock, the old devil had vanished like a ghost."

"It is a mysterious affair altogether."

"Ah, you may say that, and a confounded alarming one too," said Bonville. "I had flattered myself that here no one knew me, and that consequently I was perfectly safe from detection. I begin to suspect that one of those in my pay has betrayed me."

"That may be the case, certainly," said the old woman, "but I do not think so."

"But does it not look very suspicious, Baldwin?" demanded Bonville impatiently.

"Why, it certainly does; but you have known all the fellows for many years, and you have always found them faithful."

"That is true, but gold may have tempted them."

"If that had been the case you would have been detected long ere this, considering the large reward which Lord Elverton has offered for the discovery of Lady Elvina and your apprehension. I think you would have acted prudently in leaving them in a state of mystery and not to have acknowledged you were the author of all the calamities that have taken place."

"Well, perhaps I should," returned Bonville; "however, it is too late to repent now. Can you not suggest to me any plan by which I may avert the danger with which I am now threatened?"

"None," replied the old woman, "unless it is to quit this place without delay, and seek some other retreat."

"Pshaw! that is impossible; where could we go? and how could I remove Celestia and Lady Elvina in safety? No, let the consequences be whatever they may, I must brave them."

"Well, you know best," said Mrs. Baldwin, "but I must say that your prospects are not very cheerful at present. This old man, whoever he is, I have no doubt, will not fail to put his threats into execution, and then our destruction will be inevitable."

"Curses light upon him!" cried the enraged Bonville; "would that I could discover him and get him in my power, I would then silence him for ever."

"Of that I do not see much chance," remarked Mrs. Baldwin, "and doubtless he will lose no time in putting his plans into operation. And he said that Mabel Henderson still lives, did he not?"

"He did so," answered Bonville, "but

that does not surprise me, for I was convinced that she did before."

"She will not rest, depend upon it, until she has gratified her revenge against you."

"I defy her."

"Nay, Bonville," said the old woman; "it is sheer nonsense to talk thus; she may prove to you a far more powerful enemy that you now seem to imagine."

"A murrain seize them all!" cried Bonville, "but I will yet defeat them or perish in the attempt. Bonville is not the man to be daunted at trifles. Should an attack be made upon this place, I will defend it to the last, and sooner than Celestia and Lady Elvina shall be taken from me and restored to their friends, I will sacrifice them before their sight. I will instantly put this place in a proper state of defence, and should they be bold enough to make any attempt to apprehend me, and rescue Celestia and Lady Elvina, they will find it a much more difficult task than they probably bargained for."

"Well, I hope you may not be disappointed," said Baldwin, "though I have my doubts upon the subject."

"I will discover this old wretch, if possible," said Bonville, "and put a stop to any designs he may have in contemplation. But enough of this; I will not vex and torture my mind by dwelling on it. How is Celestia by this time?"

"There is no change in her for the better!" replied the old woman.

"And has she not yet recognised Lady Elvina?" asked Bonville.

"She has not," answered Mrs. Baldwin.

"How torturing is this!" said Bonville. "Fortune frowns upon me, and everything seems to conspire to vex me."

"A day or two may work a favourable change in her," said the old woman.

"A day or two!" repeated her worthy master, and biting his lips: "that will seem an age to me."

"But you must wait patiently."

"Bah! you are always preaching patience to me."

"Why, you know that it is your impatience which has brought all this trouble upon you."

"Why remind me of that now, when I am not in the mood to listen to it? Leave me. I do not require your attendance any longer. Should I do so, I will summon you; but remember, not a word of what I have told you must you impart to any one."

"You have no occasion to caution me," said Mrs. Baldwin, "for I do not intend to do so. I believe you never yet found me betray any of your secrets."

"No, no," replied Bonville, impatiently; "but leave me, I am in no mood for further conversation."

The old woman obeyed, and Bonville was left to himself. What the nature of his reflections were may be easily imagined. To say that he was not alarmed at the threats of the singular and mysterious old man would be to state that which was wrong; the longer he reflected upon him, the more he became involved in perplexity; and he racked his brain in vain to devise some means by which he might discover him and get him into his power. Sometimes he would fain have persuaded himself that he was merely some wretched maniac to whose assertions none would pay any serious attention; but the observations the old man had made use of, and the facts he had spoken to, convinced him that such an idea was erroneous, and filled him with still greater alarm. It was quite evident that he was well acquainted with all his guilty history, and that he was not the man to be trifled with, but one whose enmity was to be dreaded; and how to frustrate his intentions Bonville knew not. For some time Bonville continued to reflect upon this remarkable circumstance, and the more he did so, the greater his apprehensions became. At length he called the ruffians whom he had in his pay together, and without communicating to them the particulars, for he did not think it prudent to do so, he informed them that he had some slight apprehensions of danger; as he had been fired at and slightly wounded in the morning; and cautioned them to be on their guard, and to be prepared for any attack that might be made upon them. He also described to them the person of the mysterious old man whom he had encountered in so singular a manner, and instructed them if they should accidentally meet with him, not to lay violent hands upon him, as that might be fraught with danger, but to watch whither he went, and then they might devise a plan by which they could immediately get him in their power.

These commands the men promised to obey, and the house having been put into even better security than before, Bonville became more easy, and endeavoured to wait with calmness the issue of events.

Thus the day passed away without anything more worth recording taking place. Bonville felt little or no ill-effects from his wound, which fortunately for him was very slight, and he had not the least doubt but that in the course of a few days it would be quite well.

His principal anxiety now was for the recovery of Celestia, and he sent frequently to inquire after her condition, but although calm, she still remained in the same state of insanity, and the villain began to fear that the shock she had sustained had worked such an effect upon her system that she would never recover her senses, and thus all his guilty hopes be nothing more than a useless burthen to him; but still, let the consequences be whatever they might, he was fully determined not to restore her to liberty. No, the idea of detaining her even as a prisoner, and the agony her loss would occasion to Lord Elverton and her other relations, would be a sufficient gratification to his revenge, and he determined to indulge it to the fullest extent.

"I should be worse than an idiot," he said, "to resign her now, after all the trouble I have been at to get her in my power. To restore her to the arms of Lord Elverton, and see her become the bride of that boy, Lord Malensbury. Oh, it gladdens me much when I reflect on his anguish and despair at the loss of that fair being to whom his heart is so fondly devoted. She shall never be his, if she cannot be mine, and sooner than she shall be rescued from my power, and restored to those friends so dear to her, I will sacrifice my life."

Such were the terrible designs and determinations of Bonville, and there could be no doubt that, unless Providence interposed to save the poor inno-cent girl, he would not fail to put them into execution.

Three days elapsed, and Celestia remained in the same melancholy state, and there seemed to be but little hope of her ultimate recovery.

As nothing more had occurred to alarm the villain Bonville, he began to look upon the threats of the singular old man with indifference, and to imagine that he should hear no more from him; but still he would have been more satisfied could he have discovered who he was, and been able to get him in his power that he might prevent him from doing any mischief that he might really intend. He was still inclined at times to think, from the eccentricity of his manner, and the peculiarity of his dress, that he was insane; but the statements he had made, the truths he had uttered, and that so rationally, gave the lie to this, and Bonville was, therefore, compelled, much against his will, to abandon the idea.

With unremitting care and anxiety, Lady Elvina continued her weary watchings in the chamber of the afflicted Celestia, and constant were her endeavours to make the poor girl recognise her, but she could not. There was one great consolation to Lady Elvina, however, and that was, that Celestia no longer viewed her with repugnance, but, on the contrary, seemed to derive pleasure from her presence, and was perfectly submissive to everything she said, calling her "her good friend, her kind companion," but still whenever she endeavoured to impress upon her disordered memory who she really was, the poor girl would laugh wildly and shake her head, in utter disbelief of all she stated.

She had been for some days enabled to leave her bed, and she and Lady Elvina would sit themselves by the window, and Celestia would amuse herself for hours in talking to the various flowers she imagined she saw before her, or in singing wild snatches of simple ballads, in tones so plaintive, that it was enough to move the most insensible heart to pity to hear her.

What anguish was it to the mind of Lady Elvina to behold the deplorable and almost hopeless condition of her beauteous relative, and how constant and fervent were her prayers to Heaven for her recovery.

"Oh, that I could but make her remember me, to call me by my name, and willingly to receive my fond embrace!" she would sigh, "but, alas! I fear that happiness is never fated to be mine; that my beloved and unfortunate Celestia will never more experience the blessings of reason; and if such it is decreed shall be her melancholy fate, hard as it would be to lose her, dreadful as the trial would be to may afflicted and much wronged husband, it would be much better if it would please Almighty God to take her to Himself; and oh, if such should be His holy will, may the same moment that closes her earthly and innocent career also be my last."

From such melancholy reflections as these she would be aroused by a wild laugh from the poor suffering girl, and she would wring her heart by the utterance of some simple and wandering observations.

Lady Elvina was in a constant dread lest the villain Bonville, thinking that her services were useless in endeavouring to restore Celestia to her senses, should again separate her from her, and once more confine her in that horrible dungeon in which she had passed so many months of misery; and she pictured to herself what the horrors of the poor girl's situation would be if left to the tender mercies of that unfeeling woman, Mrs. Baldwin, and the miscreant Bonville. She had frequent interviews with him, and he questioned her narrowly, and it was evident to her that his patience was almost exhausted, but still she endeavoured to inspire him with the hope that time and attention would bring about Celestia's recovery, and tried to impress upon his mind the danger there would be in depriving her of her attentions, since, although she had not yet recognised her, she evinced the utmost affection for her, and was uneasy whenever she was out of her sight; and that, at least, was a favourable sign.

Bonville could not deny the force of these arguments, and only with the hope of bringing about the restoration of Celestia, and not from any feeling of pity towards the unfortunate Lady Elvina, towards whom he entertained the same vindictive and revengeful spirit,

he suffered her to remain with the poor girl.

And now another week passed away in much the same manner, and the patience of Bonville was now completely exhausted.

"It is all hopeless," he would say, "the girl will remain an idiot for ever, and those bright hopes which I had formed I see are not doomed to be realised. What is to be done? I know not; the presence of Lady Elvina seems to have little or no effect upon her, and I dare not call in medical aid, for that would reveal everything, and probably be the means of effecting my destruction. Curses light on this misfortune, for it has baulked one of the most glorious triumphs I ever achieved."

He bit his lips and traversed the room in the utmost state of disorder, muttering curses to himself, and in this state of mind he continued for some time, and would not suffer any one to approach him.

Lady Elvina felt greatly alarmed when she heard from Mrs. Baldwin the enraged state of Bonville's mind, for she feared that he would now indeed, placing no confidence in the effect which her attendance upon Celestia might have upon her, tear her from her, and remove her once more to that dismal dungeon in which she had passed so many wretched months.

These thoughts were, of themselves, sufficient to distract the mind of Lady Elvina, independent of the melancholy and almost hopeless situation of our heroine, and, after all the suffering she had experienced, it was marvellous how she could find strength to sustain it with the fortitude she did. Thinking, however, that her earnest eloquence might happily have the effect of appeasing the excitement of Bonville, she determined to make another appeal to him, and for that purpose, through the old woman, Mrs. Baldwin, she requested another interview with him, which was granted.

On her being ushered into the apartment of Bonville, she found him pacing the room in the most disordered manner, and muttering curses and imprecations to himself. For a few moments he was not aware of her presence, and she noticed the agitated and violent expression of his countenance with the greatest apprehension, and almost shrunk from the task she had undertaken, and dreaded the moment when she should have to address him.

At length he turned round and beheld her, and a frown lowered upon his brow as he said—

"So you are here, Lady Elvina. You sought an interview with me?"

"I did, Mr. Bonville," she replied, in a trembling voice. "I beseech your dispassionate attention for a few minutes only."

"Well, what would you now?" demanded Bonville, in his usual harsh and disagreeable tones.

"The unfortunate Celestia," began Lady Elvina.

"Ay," interrupted Bonville, "is still in the same deplorable state, as you would call it. Your kind offices have been of little or no avail, and I was a fool to imagine that ever they would."

"Oh, Bonville," returned Lady Elvina, "I entreat you not to judge too hastily. Indeed I have exerted myself to the utmost, Heaven knows I have, and my exertions have not been without good effect. Celestia is better, indeed she is, and I have no doubt but that with proper care and attention such as only one who loves her as fondly as I do can know how to bestow upon her, in a short time she will be completely restored to reason."

"Ay, so you said days ago; but hark ye, Lady Elvina, my patience is now completely exhausted, and, as I am determined that the gratification of my wishes shall not be disappointed, I must try some other means of bringing about the furtherance of my desires."

"Oh, reflect seriously upon what you would do, Bonville."

"Bah! I have reflected long enough."

"Remember," said Lady Elvina in a tremulous voice, "that any act of violence on your part might cost Celestia her life. You would not separate us? Oh, no, you cannot be so cruel as to think of that."

"Of what use is it your remaining with her?" demanded Bonville; "she knows you not, and therefore the attendance of Mrs. Baldwin upon her will do just as well. You may as well prepare yourself to go back to your dungeon;

you have now had sufficient indulgence to recruit your strength, and will therefore be the better prepared to ..... your former agreeable situation."

"Oh, mercy! mercy!" exclaimed the distracted lady, sinking on her knees before her brutal and heartless oppressor and with clasped hands looking in his face with an expression of the most agonizing supplication; "you cannot be so cruel, so monstrous!—It is not for myself that I now appeal to you, but for the sake of that poor, afflicted, and helpless girl, who is dearer to me than my very existence, and who, if deprived of my attendance, and left to the mercy of that unfeeling woman, Mrs. Baldwin, in whose breast not one spark of humanity exists, must fall a sacrifice. Reflect, Bonville, I implore you, upon all these circumstances, and do not, oh, do not separate me from Celestia. Grant me but a few days, another week, and then if I fail in my anxious endeavours, although it will assuredly break my heart, let me no longer remain with her. What good can it do you to tear me from her? You may gratify your hatred and revenge against me it is true, but will it not retard, if not totally prevent the recovery of Celestia?—Oh, I beg of you, humbly on my knees, I beg of you, not to close your heart entirely to pity, but to suffer me still to remain with the unfortunate girl, and then if it should please Providence that I should fail in my anxious efforts, do with me as you please, and I will not utter a murmer of complaint."

Bonville, who during this appeal had averted his face from her, now turned and looked upon her seriously for a few moments; he then walked to the other side of the room, and folding his arms upon his chest, he appeared to be consulting with himself.

During this brief interval, the unfortunate Lady Elvina, as may well be imagined, was in a state of the most violent agitation and suspense, for the fate of herself and Celestia seemed to hang upon a thread; but at length Bonville turned round, and advancing towards her, said:—

"And if I should accede to your request, what guarantee have I that you will exert yourself in the manner which you have promised?"

"Oh, what stronger guarantee would

you have than the natural affection which I bear the unfortunate and innocent sufferer?" earnestly demanded Lady Elvina. "But you will comply with my request; say that you will, and remove the terrible weight of suspense which now almost weighs me down. I repeat that Celestia is better, much better, and although she does not recognise me as her relative, she takes pleasure in my society, she is unhappy when I am absent from her, and should you separate me from her, mark my words, Bonville, it would certainly be attended with the most serious, if not fatal consequences. Besides, what harm can I do by being with her? You do not wish her to be treated with harshness or severity; you have said so; but such she undoubtedly would be if she were left to the mercy of the woman Baldwin, who has no sense of feeling or humanity inhabiting her breast."

Bonville again hesitated and paused; he could not help but acknowledge to himself the truth and reasonableness of Lady Elvina's arguments, and at length he made up his mind.

"Well," he observed, turning to the anxious Lady Elvina, "once more I yield to your request; but mark me, it is only upon certain conditions, namely, that you use no means untried to recall Celestia to reason, and that you never mention my name in a manner to prejudice her against me. On these conditions I will allow you to remain with her another fortnight, and if at the expiration of that time no favourable change shall have taken place in Celestia, you must prepare yourself to return to your dungeon."

"And if she should recover," eagerly demanded Lady Elvina, "what then?"

"Upon that I have not yet decided," replied Bonville, "be contented with the indulgence I have already granted you, and seek to know no more at present. Return to your charge, and remember my words."

Lady Elvina arose from her knees; she tried to speak, but could not; Bonville turned away from her, and ringing the bell, Mrs. Baldwin made her appearance.

"Conduct Lady Elvina back to the apartment of the patient," said Bonville.

Mrs. Baldwin motioned the unfortunate lady to follow her and she obeyed with mingled feelings of joy and sadness. When they had arrived in the room in which our heroine was confined, Mrs. Baldwin left her without saying a word, and Lady Elvina advanced towards Celestia, who was seated as usual at the window, and apparently lost in the contemplation of the certainly anything but cheering scenery before her. The poor girl greeted her with a smile of pleasure, and suffered her to throw her arms around her neck, and to kiss her cheeks and forehead.

"Why do you weep?" said Celestia, looking earnestly in her aged relative's face. "I never cry, for it is useless; see how brightly the sun shines;—how the lambkins frolic and gamble in yonder green meadow;—hark how melodiously the birds sing in the branches of that venerable oak; all is joy and gladness, and yet you weep:—oh, foolish, foolish woman! God made us all to be creatures of gladness and content, and yet you murmur. Oh, it is very wicked."

"My dear Celestia," said the afflicted Lady Elvina, "if I weep it is because I would have you know me and call me by my proper name."

"And do I not know you?" said the poor girl, "oh, yes; are you not my kind nurse, my constant companion? and I do love you for that, indeed I do."

"Heaven bless you, my darling child," sobbed Lady Elvina, as she again pressed her to her bosom; "and restore you to full health and happiness."

"Oh, I am very happy," said Celestia, laughing in her wild manner, "very happy while you are with me, because you speak so kindly to me and remind me so much of——"

"Of whom, my sweet child?" eagerly asked Lady Elvina.

"No, no," replied Celestia, passing her hand across her fair forehead, "it's all gone from my memory now."

"You would say your poor grandmamma, the unfortunate Lady Elvina Elverton. Oh, Celestia, look at me; charge your wandering memory to the utmost, and you must discover that I—I am that unhappy individual."

"You! you! ha! ha!" laughed the poor girl;—"now, now, good'nurse, you must take me to be mad or silly; you Lady Elvina! oh, no! alas! she is dead, dead!—Oh, her fate was a most awful one, and I was present at it in that frightful dungeon, where the light of day has never entered. Did you ever see it?—But no, how should you? How should you?"

Then she relapsed into silence, and the broken-hearted Lady Elvina did not think it prudent to interrupt her. She sunk on her knees and devoutly prayed

to Heaven to extend its mercy to the afflicted Celestia, and not only to restore her to her senses, but to rescue her also from the power of the atrocious villain, Bonville.

But the time was fast approaching when the prayers of Lady Elvina were destined to be heard, and when the unfortunate Celestia was once more to be restored to reason.

Three more days had passed away without any great improvement in the condition of Celestia, and as time seemed to fly with redoubled speed, the melancholy and despair of Lady Elvina increased, when she remembered how brief was the time which Bonville had allowed her to remain with her youthful and afflicted relation, unless some favourable change should take place in her, and of that, alas! she saw very little or no prospect at present. The horrors of her dungeon arose not so vividly to her mind as the cruelty and sufferings to which Celestia would be exposed when left entirely to the mercy of the wretch, Bonville, and that savage woman, Baldwin; and the bare idea of this made her shudder.

Oh, how earnestly she prayed to Heaven to interpose, and not to suffer the innocent girl to fall a victim to such a miscreant; as after all the threats which Bonville had thrown out, she could have little or no doubt that whether our heroine recovered or not, he was monster enough to be determined to go any lengths; and what, therefore, but the hand of the Almighty could save the ill-fated girl from destruction?

On the morning of the fourth day after Lady Elvina's interview with Bonville, she had arisen some hours before Celestia, who was wrapped in a tranquil sleep, and sat watching by her bedside with the most painful anxiety.

Lady Elvina could not help remarking, and she did so with great satisfaction and renewed hope, that the poor girl looked much better than she had done for some time. The roseate flush of health had resumed its place in her cheeks, and the wild expression of her countenance had almost totally disappeared.

"God grant," said the hapless lady fervently, "that this may be the harbinger of approaching health and reason. Oh, my beloved Celestia, what a relief would it be to my lacerated heart to see thee once more well and happy, and released from the power of the villain who has been the author of all the unparalleled misfortunes that have attended our ill-fated family. Could I but be assured that you were restored to the arms of my sorrowing husband and your other relatives, I should care not what became of me. Life has no longer any charms for me, and the sooner I lay down the heavy weight of care it has so long been my hard lot to endure, the better. But to see this innocent and lovely girl suffer thus unmercifully, is more torturing, far more torturing than all."

She was aroused from this soliloquy by beholding Celestia move in the bed, and immediately afterwards she opened her eyes, stared eagerly around her, and starting up exclaimed:—

"Where am I?—Where have I been? What a long, long sleep I have had;—was it then all a dream?—And yet methought the unfortunate Lady Elvina had been permitted to leave her loathsome dungeon, and was my constant companion. But no, that is too great a joy to be real!"

"I am here, my child, my Celestia, my own beloved Celestia," cried the delighted Lady Elvina, snatching the poor girl frantically to her bosom; "look at your unfortunate relative, Lady Elvina; I have been your constant companion for days, for weeks, during your unhappy malady, and nothing shall ever again separate us!"

"Ah!" exclaimed Celestia, as she fixed her beauteous eyes full upon the countenance of her aged relative; "it is now then no dream!—My beloved grandmamma! unfortunate, deeply wronged Lady Elvina!"

"She knows me! She knows me! Reason has resumed its empire!" ejaculated Lady Elvina, while tears of gratitude chased each other down her venerable cheeks; "God, All-merciful God of Heaven! for this receive my fervent thanks!"

To describe the scene which followed would be a task by far too arduous for our pen to accomplish. They continued for some time locked in each other's arms, totally unably to speak, and mingled their tears together; then they mutually raised their eyes towards Heaven, and breathed a silent prayer of gratitude for its mercy.

It was some time before either of them was sufficiently recovered to speak, but at last Celestia said:—

"But I pray you, my dear grandmamma, explain to me;—what is the meaning of all this? It all appears but as a dream to me. What has been the matter with me?—What have I been doing? And how is it that I have the happiness of your sweet society?"

"My darling Celestia," replied Lady

Elvina, "I beseech you to compose yourself, whilst I explain. For more than a fortnight your senses have wandered, and you knew not where you were, or those around you. I made an appeal to Bonville to be permitted to attend you, and he yielded to my earnest request, allowed me to leave my dungeon, and I have been your constant and anxious companion ever since."

"Alas! alas! then," sighed our heroine, "we are both still in the power of that cruel man, Bonville?"

"'Tis too true, my love," answered Lady Elvina, with a deep sigh; "but I beg of you not to give way to despair, for depend upon it that Providence will yet interpose to save us and to defeat the plans of our inhuman persecutor."

"Would to Heaven that I could think so," said Celestia; "but, alas! what mercy or forbearance can we expect from such a man as the cruel Bonville?"

"From him I expect none," said Lady Elvina, "but to the All-merciful God I look with confidence. Come, my beloved Celestia, let us dismiss all these dismal thoughts from our minds, and endeavour to meet with fortitude any future trials which may be in store for us. Rest assured that we shall ultimately triumph, and that we shall yet be happy."

"But he will tear you from me," said Celestia, "he will remove you once more to that frightful dungeon, the very thought of which fills my mind with horror; and then, oh, then what will become of me, when I am left entirely at the mercy of that inhuman man?—And you too, my venerable, my revered relative, what will be your sufferings in that dreadful place? You will never be able to endure them. By Heaven, the monster shall not again separate us! If he is determined that you shall again be incarcerated in that living tomb, I will be your companion; he may murder me, but he shall not part us."

Again Lady Elvina pressed the poor girl to her bosom, and powerful indeed were the feelings that then agitated both their bosoms.

"My beloved Celestia!" at length said Lady Elvina, "we must both endeavour to tranquillize our feelings, and to hope for the best, for Providence, depend upon it, will not desert us while we put our trust in it. Oh, how grateful ought we to be to Heaven for your restoration to health. Alas! I began to despair that you would never recover, and had you not, life would indeed have been a curse to me."

"But Bonville," said our heroine, with a shudder, "will he not persist in his disgusting, his diabolical designs? I remember now that he told me he would only allow me a week to consider, and to make up my mind. Oh, how I tremble to meet him again."

"Be firm, my Celestia, be firm, and you will yet triumph over the villain, who has been the author of all our misfortunes. Villain even as he is, I cannot believe that he will ever dare to attempt to put his odious designs into execution."

"Ah! what is there that such a miscreant as he is will not dare to do?" sighed Celestia. "And my beloved friends! oh, what must be their dreadful sufferings all this time, at the uncertainty of my fate? My dear, dear grandpapa, my kind and indulgent protector from childhood, when I was left without a friend in the world, how will he be able to support this additional calamity? He must sink under the dreadful shock, and I shall never behold him again."

She clasped her hands together, and wept bitterly.

"Alas! my deeply injured husband," sighed the afflicted Lady Elvina, "had it not been for my first fatal error, those dreadful calamities might never have befallen our unfortunate family. Alas! what misery does a single crime entail upon the wretched delinquent. But let us not give way to these sad thoughts, my beloved Celestia. We ought to be too thankful to Heaven for your recovery to give way to present sorrow. Let us hope, my child, let us hope, and in that find sweet consolation under all our afflictions."

They remained silent for a time, and mingled their tears together, and Celestia, by degrees becoming more calm, and inspired with confidence, arose, and Lady Elvina having assisted her to dress, they both sank on their knees, and pouring forth their gratitude to the Supreme for Celestia's recovery, earnestly supplicated His future protection, and that He would save them from the dangers by which they were at present surrounded.

After this they felt more tranquil and confident, and Lady Elvina having prepared the morning repast, they sat down, and were enabled to converse with more freedom. Lady Elvina briefly recounted all the troubles she had undergone, and our heroine listened to her melancholy narrative with feelings which we need not attempt to describe.

Celestia then related to her unfortunate relation all the circumstances that had occurred since the time of her being taken under the protection of the earl, and many were the tears which the unhappy lady shed during the recital.

"Oh, my unfortunate husband," she ejaculated, when our heroine had concluded, "how little did you deserve so cruel a fate. I wonder that yould could find strength sufficient to bear up against such unprecedented misfortunes. But, my dear Celestia, how wonderful have been the ways of Providence in all ; to think that you and your noble-minded father should be led to the very neighbourhood in which your unfortunate relative resided, and that you should subsequently be placed under his protection and adopted as his own, before he knew that you were so closely allied by blood. Had it not been for the mercy of God you might have fallen amongst strangers, who would perhaps have exposed you to every misery, and treated your helpless condition with cruelty and indifference."

"True, dear grandmamma," said Celesti, "and I can never be sufficiently grateful to the Almighty for his goodness. Were we but at liberty, and reunited to those so dear to us, all the sorrows of the past might be buried in oblivion, and we should be the happiest of human beings. But, alas! are we ever destined to experience that felicity?"

"I trust to Heaven we are, my child," returned Lady Elvina, "gloomy even as our prospects now appear."

"But should the wretch Bonville again tear you from me," ejaculated Celestia, with a shudder of horror, "should he once more consign you to that dreadful dungeon—Oh, God! the thought is too horrible to dwell upon."

"Then dismiss it from your mind Celestia," said Lady Elvina ; "I cannot, I will not believe that he will ever be guilty of such barbarity."

"Oh, if he has not a heart of stone, he will not do so," ejaculated our heroine ; "on my knees I will implore him to forbear, and if he can resist my prayers, my tears, and supplications in so virtuous a cause, he must be a monster indeed."

Their conversation was interrupted by approaching footsteps, and the next moment the room door was unlocked, and Mrs. Baldwin entered.

Celestia shuddered at the sight of that repulsive old woman, and shrunk closer to Lady Elvina, and Mrs. Baldwin eyed them both with a look of scrutiny, and noticed at once the remarkable change in our heroine. Lady Elvina in a tremulous voice inquired her business.

"I merely came to inquire after the health of your patient," said Mrs. Baldwin.

"If it be the villain, Bonville, who has sent you," said Celestia, in a firm voice, and fixing her expressive eyes full upon the countenance of the old woman, "you may tell him that—"

Lady Elvina checked her by a significant look, and addressing herself to Mrs. Baldwin, said :—

"You can inform your master that I am happy to say that my anxious exertions have been crowned with success, and that the malady which lately afflicted Lady Celestia has now disappeared, but that she requires a few days' rest and quiet, in order to recruit her exhausted strength, which I trust he will not refuse her."

"You mean to say that the young lady is not prepared to receive a visit from him just yet?" said the unfeeling old woman.

"Oh, Heaven forbid that I should be disgusted with his hideous presence!" ejaculated Celestia, with a shudder of horror.

"I hope," remarked Lady Elvina, "that Mr. Bonville will at least have the good sense, if not the humanity, not to obtrude himself upon my poor Celestia for the present. I will not be answerable for the consequences if he does."

"Oh, very well," returned Mrs. Baldwin. "I will deliver your message, and of course Mr. Bonville can use his own pleasure and discretion."

Thus saying, the old woman hobbled out of the room, much to the relief of Celestia and Lady Elvina.

"Good God!" exclaimed our heroine, "he surely will not attempt to obtrude himself upon me; the shock, the terror of the appearance of that guilty, blood-stained man, would be too much for me. My blood freezes with horror in my veins even at the mention of his name."

"Do not alarm yourself, my love," said Lady Elvina, "for depend upon it Bonville will not venture before you for the present, for fear that you should suffer a relapse. Come, my dear girl, tranquillize your feelings, and with the blessing of God all will yet be well."

"I will endeavour to be calm," replied Celestia, "but, alas! you must acknowledge that it is a difficult task, surrounded as I am by so many terrors."

"True, my Celestia, but there is no task, however difficult, which we may not accomplish if we exert our energies, and put our trust in Providence."

We will now leave Celestia and Lady Elvina for awhile, and follow the old woman, Baldwin, to the apartment in which Bonville was anxiously and impatiently awaiting her return. He saw immediately on her entrance that she had something particular to communicate, and he eagerly inquired what it was."

"I suppose you will be satisfied now, Mr. Bonville," said the old woman, with one of her most disagreeable grins.

"What do you mean?" he demanded impatiently, "do not keep me in suspense. How is the girl?"

"Perfectly recovered," answered Baldwin, "and engaged in comfortable conversation with Lady Elvina when I entered the room."

"Ah!" exclaimed Bonville, with a look of astonishment and satisfaction; "can it be possible? But you are not attempting to deceive me, are you?"

"What should I gain by that I should like to know?" croaked forth the old woman.

"Recovered her senses?" said Bonville, still incredulously.

"Ah," replied his worthy domestic, "she is as sensible as you are, if I am to believe my own eyes and ears, and the statement of Lady Elvina herself."

"Now by all my hopes this is most fortunate," said Bonville exultingly, "and more than I expected. I must immediately see her, and satisfy myself."

He was moving towards the door, when the old woman detained him.

"What are you about to do?" she demanded; "would you again act the fool? Should the girl again behold you in her present delicate state of health, she would suffer a relapse, depend upon it, and that would in all probability prove fatal."

"Right, right," said Banville, "I thank you for the hint, Baldwin. I suppose I must let her rest for a day or two."

"Why, if you act wisely you will," said the old woman; "you know what were the consequences of your former precipitation."

"True, true; but let her only entirely recover and I will not delay a day in putting my designs into execution."

"And what of Lady Elvina?" asked Baldwin;—"do you intend to consign her again to her old lodging?"

"Not at present," replied Bonville; "she must be the means of working out my designs against her fair relation, and thus shall I doubly gratify my vengeance."

"And how can she do that?"

"Hark ye, Baldwin. Celestia will of course be terrified at the idea of being separated from Lady Elvina, and I will, therefore, make her compliance with my wishes the condition of her grandmother's liberty. Is not that a famous idea, Baldwin?"

"Yes," chuckled the hateful old woman, "and, after all, I suppose, you intend that she shall return to the dungeon?"

"Certainly," replied the villain; "do you think that I could find it in my heart to show her so much mercy as to allow her to remain where she is? But leave me, Baldwin, and keep a sharp eye upon Celestia and Lady Elvina, and make me acquainted with anything you observe."

The old woman promised to do so, and

then took her departure, and left the miscreant Bonville to his own meditations.

He had not been left long to himself before he resolved to take a walk through the adjacent neighbourhood, where he encountered the old man who seemed to know more of Bonville and his affairs than was at all in keeping with his safety, and who threatened the villain with vengeance for his outrageous acts. In spite of his earnest desire, and strenuous exertions, he could not come close enough to the old man to do him any injury, otherwise he would have been glad to have taken his life, and destroyed the possessor of so much that he thought was locked in his own bosom alone. He returned full of melancholy forebodings, and sought his closet, which overlooked the walls of his retreat. He stood petrified, as he looked in the direction in which he had seen the old man, to see Mabel Henderson close to the walls, apparently examining the building. He fainted.

CHAPTER XXXIII.

THE CONTINUED PERSECUTION OF CELESTIA AND ELVINA.

BONVILLE cautiously made every inquiry in the neighbourhood, with the hope of discovering the old man or Mabel Henderson; but his efforts were not attended with any success, and when three days had elapsed without his hearing anything more of them, or anything occurring to alarm him, he became more confident, endeavoured to treat the circumstance with indifference, and devoted his whole thoughts to Celestia, and to the completion of his diabolical plans. His patience was now quite exhausted, and as his devoted victim continued to get better, he determined that only two or three days should elapse before he would have another interview with her, and at once convince her that it was useless her offering any longer an obstinate resistance to his desires. The villain made repeated inquiries of his diabolical partner in crime, Baldwin, as to the health of his victim, and from her report he determined upon his purpose,

after giving notice to her of his intention. He took the precaution of securing Lady Elvina in a cell a considerable distance from the room of Celestia.

"Now all-merciful Heaven, direct me how to act; to his heart or mine this must go, should he persist in his villanous designs," said Celestia as she concealed a knife which she had been using at her morning meal.

She had scarcely given utterance to these words, when Bonville entered the room. She met him with a look of firmness for which he appeared to be totally unprepared, for he shrunk back abashed, and said not a word, while at the same time he contemplated her with the utmost astonishment.

He, however, soon recovered himself, and approaching her, said, at the same time assuming a smile that was meant to be insinuating :—

"Beauteous, most adorable Lady Celestia, how it rejoices me to see you recovered from your late illness, and to behold you looking so lovely. Respect, sweet maiden, has hitherto restrained my ardent wishes and prevented me from presenting myself before you; but blame me not for that apparent neglect, nor think that the ardour of the passion I entertain for you is in the least diminished; on the contrary, it has increased, so much so, that I could no longer deprive myself of the felicity of throwing myself at your feet, and once more acknowledging myself your sincere and devoted slave for ever."

The villain knelt as he spoke; a supercilious smile overspread his revolting features, and the coolness and effrontery with which he gave utterance to those observations, took our heroine so much by surprise, that her fortitude almost forsook her; but she quickly recovered herself, and retreating from him a few paces, she thus replied, in a firm voice, which was enough to strike shame and awe into any less insensible breast than that of the hardened miscreant whom she addressed—

"Brutal man, I warn you to forbear; I call upon High Heaven to protect me, and I am convinced that my voice will no be unheard; I invoke the sainted spirit of my murdered mother

—murdered, monster, by your inhuman arts, to watch over me in this hour of danger, and you will not, you dare not, hardened and reckless even as you are, scorn and defy those sacred powers."

"Dare I not, lovely prattler?" said the brutal man, rising from his knee, and approaching still nearer to Celestia, who retreated as he advanced; "but you behold I do;—oh, most incomparable Lady Celestia; sweet, retiring maiden, your superlative charms would tempt me, embolden me to anything. Chosen of my soul, my thoughts have long fixed upon you : but now thou art in my power, there is no one here to dispute my claim upon thee ; thy drivelling swain, the stripling Lord Malensbury, is far from hence, and I am determined to possess thee, though the forfeiture of my life should be the certain consequence. Nay, frown not, for such expressions of anger ill become thy beauteous face. There should be sunny smiles and serenity; but even the indignation which flashes from thine eye enchants me, and goads me on to desperation. Oh, what a fortunate man am I to possess so fair a prize, and," added the taunting wretch, with one of his most sardonic and malignant smiles, "am I not a fair, and promising, and a youthful suitor, most noble and fascinating Lady Celestia?—Surely you cannot put forward the least plea of objection to me; do I not far outrival Lord Malensbury in personal attractions and intrinsic qualities? Certainly you must be insensible indeed, if I do not supplant him in your affections. Oh, yes, I read my conquest even in the scorn of your eyes. We need not the idle mockery of marriage to blend our hearts together; they are already united, and thus, after having allowed you full time to deliberate, I come to claim my soul's idol."

What language could properly describe the disgust, the horror, and indignation of Celestia, while the villain Bonville was giving utterance to this inhuman speech? She felt as if her heart would burst from its tenement, and the crimson blushes of shame mantled in her fair cheeks. For a few moments her tongue refused its office, but her looks sufficiently expressed what her swelling and indignant bosom wished to give utterance to. Bonville, however, marked it all with the utmost indifference and effrontery ; he fully felt the power he possessed, and was determined to take every advantage of it. His fiendish soul exulted at his brutal triumph, and as Celestia marked the strong development of his feelings in his countenance, she could not but feel her own weakness and the hopelessness of her condition, and her heart sunk within her. She recoiled a few faces, and covering her face with her hands, mentally invoked the protection of the Supreme, but at the same time gave herself up almost entirely to despair. Bonville again approached nearer towards her, and again kneeling with all the air of the most impassioned and youthful lover, exclaimed, while he audaciously attempted to seize her hand—

"What, not a word, lovely Celestia, to your adoring swain ? Nay now, but this is cruel, after all the trouble I have taken to obtain possession of you, and the attentions which I have shown you. But, since you will e'en provoke me to it, I find I must be more bold, and at once let you understand me. Know, then, that I have fully made up my mind, in spite of every power, that you shall be mine; that I alone shall be the emperor of your superlative charms, though I be not the happy man of your choice. You may frown, you may supplicate, it will all be entirely lost upon me. Resistance is useless, and, therefore, I advise you at once to abandon all fallacious hopes you may have entertained, and to yield passively to your future lord and master."

"Monster !" cried the unfortunate damsel, aroused to sudden energy, and fixing upon him a look in which womanly and virtuous indignation and shame, reproach and scorn were blended. "Monster ! for man you cannot be, although you bear the semblance of one, forbear, lest the thunderbolt of Heaven's wrath should descend upon your guilty head, and crush you in the midst of your iniquity. Oh, are you destitute of every feeling of pity and of shame ? But you have told me, dreadful experience tells me that you are. Still I warn you to abandon your monstrous, your atrocious designs, and to leave me, lest that retribution I have invoked should overtake you."

"I am sorry, sweet Lady Celestia," returned that inhuman ruffian, with a sarcastic and triumphant smile, " to be compelled to refuse any request you may make, but really in this one instance I must most positively decline. Your charms are so transcendent, and have obtained such an irresistible influence over me, weak and susceptible individual as I am, that I should perish, languish, out of your sight. Again I must repeat my ardent vows of love, and, even though it be in anger, listen to the melodious music of your voice. Why turn so coolly and disdainfully away from me? Am I not all that the most virtuous mind and the most tender heart can desire? 'Tis true that a few more years have passed over my head than Lord Malensbury's, but is he for a moment to be compared with me in personal charms? He has wealth! granted. But I have not only wealth but power also, which I believe that you and others, especially the members of your own noble family, have experienced. Then what can possibly be your objections? Oh, no; it is only maiden bashfulness and timidity, which make you act thus towards me, and for which I can make every allowance. You will, you must consent to become mine, for mark me, once more I tell you that you cannot help yourself. Here I have you secure, far away from your home, and with no one at hand to assist you. I defy detection, for no one but my own myrmidons are aware of the place of my retreat. All resistance, all obduracy, therefore, is completely futile, and will only compel me to violence. You must, you shall, I say again, be mine; you are my chosen mistress, or rather the slave of my wishes, and, therefore, submission to that fate which you cannot avoid is your best policy. However, to show you that I am not urgenerous or impetuous, I will yet give you three more days to reflect upon what I have said, and if at the expiration of that period you still remain obstinate, by every power I swear that I will no longer delay the execution of that purpose upon which I have fixed my soul."

As the villain thus spoke, he arose to his feet, and all the ferocious and guilty passions of his mind were strongly expressed in his countenance. Celestia averted her gaze from him with horror, and dreadful and overpowering was the feeling which came over her. For a few moments she was entirely bereft of speech, but at length she gasped forth in accents which were sufficient to make an impression upon the most insensible and obdurate heart—

" Great God of Heaven, look down upon me, and save me, for in you is now my only hope. Oh, all-merciful creator, as I have never wilfully offended your laws, oh, save me now from the hideous designs of this cruel man. Spirit of my murdered mother, once more I appeal to you, and devoutly trust that my prayers may not be in vain."

At this moment the villain caught the poor trembling girl in his arms. The power of the ruffian was too much for the weak and fragile young girl to contend with for any very great length of time. In her struggle to preserve that purity which was dearer to her than life, she lost the knife, which might in more energetic hands have been a means of defence; and at the same time that she lost the weapon, she lost consciousness and became completely at the will of the man whose ruling passions were vice and revenge. He raised her in his arms, and while he still gazed upon her pale but beauteous countenance, he was tempted to pollute her lips with his unlawful kisses, when at that moment, was it his imagination, or could it be reality? a hollow groan saluted his ear, and standing before him, he beheld or fancied he beheld a shadowy form, clad in long flowing garments of white, with its sunken, glass-like eyes fixed upon him, and in whose ghastly features he recognised those of his murdered victim, the Marchioness D'Aunville, the mother of that poor girl whom he held in his arms. It could be no imagination! There the shade of the murdered woman stood before him, with her long, bony, fleshless hand directed towards him in a menacing manner, and her filmy eyes fixed upon him with an expression which chilled his very soul. He could have sworn that he heard her hollow voice exclaim—

"Forbear, murderer, forbear! or the most awful curses of offended Heaven shall light upon thine head, and plunge thee at once to that eternal sea of burning torment, to which thine atro-cious crimes have render ttyhyiled gu soul forfeit!"

Whether or not it was the delusion of the villain's guilty conscience, he stood appalled. A sensation of horror came over him, which completely enervated him, and as his frightened

imagination depicted to him the ghastly phantom of that unfortunate and inno-cent being whom he had consigned to an early, an untimely grave, every limb trembled, and uttering a cry of horror, he relinquished his hold of the poor girl he held in his arms, and hastily placing her on the sofa, he covered his face with his hands and retreated from the room. On the stairs he met Mrs. Baldwin, who, sur-prised at the wildness and agitation of his demeanour, inquired what had happened.

"By hell! he exclaimed, "she is there! She gazed just now upon me with her fearful eyes, and warned me from my purpose."

"She?" repeated the old woman, secretly pleased at the violence of his emotions, and exulting in his terror; "have you turned coward? or are you mad? Whom do you mean?"

"No, no," said Bonville, slightly recovering himself; "I am not mad, but something has occurred to agitate me; send Lady Elvina to the chamber of Celestia, and then return to me, I wish to consult you."

The old woman muttered something which he did not hear, and then obeyed his commands, and Bonville, with a feeling of the most inexpressible horror, rushed into his apartment and threw himself panting with emotion and terror into a chair, and almost feared to raise his eyes and look around him, lest they should again encounter that ghastly form which his imagination had conjured up, and which had appalled his very soul. How true indeed the observation of the immortal barb, that

'Conscience doth make cowards of us all;'

and it was never more fully exemplified than on this occasion in the case of Bonville. He trembled in every limb, and the least sound that was stirring in the house increased his agitation. That wretch who had perpetrated so many awful crimes and who had hitherto scoffed at the superstitious terrors of the vulgar and the ignorant, was now himself appalled and rendered as imbecile as an infant, by the power of his own guilty conscience, and the horrors that his excited imagination had conjured up.

"I could not have been deceived," he at length said in a tremulous voice, and looking fearfully around him; "no, it was the ghastly shade of her I sacrificed in my vengeance. Her filmy eyes were fixed upon me with all the horrors—Ah! who is there?"

The terrified imagination of the guilty man pictured to himself all kinds of frightful sounds and hideous phantoms, and his limbs were convulsed with emotion, whilst large drops of perspiration stood upon his forehead.

When he had a little recovered he felt so sorely chagrined at what had happened that he vented his spleen upon his accomplice, the old woman Baldwin, who retorted in more offensive tones than he had ever experienced from her. She left him, and was in two hours far from the abode of vice in which she had taken so conspicuous a part, vowing to be revenged on the villain Bonville. When he found that she had left him, he became furious and sent his band of desperadoes in search of her; but their chief did not return, and the remainder brought him intelligence that she was nowhere to be found. As time rolled on and neither the old woman nor his captain returned, he began to imagine that matters wore a gloomy aspect. But for fear of the results of treachery being close at hand, he resolved to accomplish the ruin of Celestia, and for that purpose had caused a powerful drug to be administered to her, so that he should the more easily accomplish his base purpose. He was on his way to her apartment when one of his band overtook him at the door, and told him that the place was besieged by more than fifty armed men, and that Earl Bathurst and Lord Malensbury were among the number. He turned pale with fear, and was unresolved what to do, when the proximity of his foes told him that it was time to fly.

"Quick, quick," said his companion, "to the subterranean passage; it is the only mode of escape now."

Bonville saw that such was really the case, and preceded his villanous dependant: they had not proceeded far when the report of a musket caused Bonville to turn round, and there he saw his follower a corpse.

There was a door in the passage, very massive, with strong bolts on the outer side; he knew that if he could reach there he should be safe for a time. He continued to pass from pillar to pillar till at last he reached the desired point, and succeeded in fastening the door in the face of his pursuers; after which he had the hardihood to stop and breathe maledictions on the heads of his enemies, and to threaten them all with his vengeance. He completely escaped.

CHAPTER XXXIV.

THE MEETING OF CELESTIA AND LADY ELVINA WITH THEIR FRIENDS, AND OTHER MATTERS EQUALLY INTERESTING TO THE READER.

IT was nearly two hours after the attack upon the house and the flight of Bonville, before our heroine recovered from the effects of the powerful drug of which she had partaken; and she could scarcely believe her senses when she beheld Mabel Henderson and Mrs. Baldwin standing by the side of the bed on which she was reclining, and watching her recovery with the most anxious solicitude. For a moment or two she was quite bewildered, and scarcely could she believe the evidence of her eyes; but she was quickly convinced that it was no dream, and raising herself up in the bed, she ejaculated—

"What is the meaning of all this? What is the cause of your being here, and where is my cruel persecutor?"

"The meaning of it is simply this, Lady Celestia," replied Mabel, "that you are released from the power of the villain Bonville, who has taken to flight, and that you will shortly be restored to those friends from whom you have been so cruelly separated. There is not time for further explanation at present; and I beg of you to collect yourself, for I trust now your troubles are at an end."

With feelings such as it would be a most arduous task adequately to portray, our heroine started from the bed, and sinking upon her knees, clasped her hands vehemently together, and raised her eyes towards Heaven as she fervently ejaculated—

"All-merciful God, for this I thank Thee! Thou hast indeed heard my prayers, and I am fully repaid for all the severe trials I have experienced. But," she added, turning anxiously towards Mabel Henderson and Mrs. Baldwin, "where are my dear friends and relations? Where is the unfortunate and deeply wronged Lady Elvina?"

"Lord Elverton was persuaded to remain at Sungrove Abbey," said Mabel, "where he is anxiously awaiting your restoration. Your noble cousin, Lord Malensbury, his father, and Sir Roderick Ainslie, are in the house, and with them Lady Elvina."

"Oh! let me hasten to meet them," said Celestia, preparing to leave the room. "I must not delay a moment."

"Compose yourself, Miss Celestia," said Mrs. Baldwin, "and we will conduct you to them."

Celestia made no reply, but eagerly and with a palpitating heart followed Mabel and Mrs. Baldwin out of the room, and quickly gained the door of that apartment in which those dear friends, from whom she had been so long separated, and whom she never expected to behold again, were assembled. Here they left her, and with an exclamation of the most rapturous joy she rushed into the room, and was so overpowered by her feelings that she almost fainted. It would be a fruitless task to attempt to describe the meeting. It was some time ere they could gain the least composure, and then they all gave expression to their feelings of gratitude to the Most High in the most fervent manner. How can we do justice to the emotions of Lord Malensbury, as he gazed upon the beauteous countenance of that beloved being whom he feared was lost to them for ever, and thought upon the bitter sufferings she must have undergone? And the emotions and sentiments of our heroine towards him were of a similar and not less fervent description. Lady Elvina, too, how great was her agitation; how thankful was she to Providence for its merciful interposition! and terrible as had been her sufferings for so many years, in the joy of the present moment, and the sanguine anticipations of the future, she began to look upon the dismal past as merely a frightful dream.

"But, my dear grandpapa," said Celestia, "oh, how is he? What must have been the anguish he has endured?"

"He has certainly suffered much, my dear Celestia," replied Lord Bathurst; "upon the whole, however, he has supported this severe trial with much more fortitude than might have been expected. I need not tell you how great was the transport of his feelings when he received the joyful intelligence from Mabel Henderson that she had discovered the place where you and Lady Elvina were confined, and that she and her companions, this woman Baldwin, and an old man, her father, whom she had not seen for many years, and whom she accidentally met while wandering in this part of the country, were resolved to release you. You may imagine his feelings, but I cannot properly describe them. It was with the greatest difficulty we could dissuade him from accompanying us hither, so great was his impatience once more to clasp to his bosom his gentle Celestia, and that unfortunate wife from whom fate had so cruelly separated him for so many years."

"Much injured husband!" sighed Lady Elvina, while tears of mingled joy and sorrow started to her eyes, "and are we indeed destined to meet again, and shall I hear your lips pronounce my forgiveness? God grant that the few remaining years we may have to live may be those of tranquillity and peace!"

Fervently all those present responded to her wish, and a few minutes elapsed in silence, during which they indulged in the various thoughts which rushed upon their minds under the joyful and exciting circumstances.

"But it is now long past midnight," observed Lord Bathurst, "and you, Celestia and Lady Elvina, will require some rest before we commence our journey in the morning; we had better, therefore, separate for an hour or two."

To the necessity of this every one agreed; but Lord Bathurst and his friends, not feeling inclined for rest, resolved to sit up and keep watch till it was time to depart, in case of any attempt at treachery. On reaching their chamber, Lady Elvina and our heroine again embraced, and gave vent to the powerful feelings of joy and gratitude in a copious flood of tears. They then knelt down and mentally poured forth their thanks to that Supreme Being through whose merciful interposition they were rescued from a fate too dreadful even to think upon. The event had been so sudden and so unex-

pected that it scarcely seemed to be a reality; and the joy which was in store for them was so great it was almost overwhelming.

"Oh, my Celestia," said Lady Elvina, "and can it be possible that, after the lapse of so many years, I am about to be restored to that deeply injured husband from whom I ought never to have been separated, had it not been for my blind infatuation and folly? How can I meet him upon whom I have been the cause of inflicting so many sufferings and calamities? Anxious as I am to behold him, I yet tremble at the thought of doing so."

"Do not, my beloved relative," replied Celestia, "distress yourself by those gloomy thoughts. Have you not, by the unparalleled sufferings you have endured with such exemplary patience and fortitude, made ample atonement for the one error with which you so bitterly reproach yourself?—Oh, yes; and I trust to God that you will now live many years to experience uninterrupted happiness, and that you may be able to bury the unfortunate past in oblivion."

Lady Elvina shook her head and sighed deeply.

"Alas!" she ejaculated, "I feel that that is impossible, though I will endeavour to be tranquil and resigned to my fate, whatever it may be, and contribute to the happiness of my beloved lord. But what do we not owe to Mabel Henderson, who has been the cause of our deliverance and the defeat of the villain Bonville?"

"Heaven will reward her," said Celestia, "for we can never sufficiently do so. But Bonville escaped uninjured—did he not?"

"He did," answered Lady Elvina, "although he did so with difficulty."

"It is unfortunate that he is at large," remarked our heroine, "for we may still have danger to apprehend from him."

"After having met with so complete a defeat, and being deserted by his associates in villany, I am inclined to imagine that he will deem it prudent to abandon his atrocious designs, and seek safety by making his escape to some other country where he is not known."

"I fear he is too desperate a man,"

replied Celestia. "to relinquish his monstrous schemes of vengeance so easily, and this disappointment will but urge him on to some more determined plan. May Heaven protect us, and avert any future calamity with which we may be threatened."

"Do not alarm yourself with such apprehensions, my dear Celestia," said Lady Elvina, "for I sincerely hope that they will prove entirely groundless, and that we may neither see nor hear any more of Bonville. But come, my love, let us retire to rest, for it will soon be daylight, and we shall commence our journey at an early hour in the morning. Thank Heaven, this is the last night we shall pass in this dreary place!"

Celestia yielded to the importunities of Lady Elvina, and with lighter hearts than they had experienced for many a day, they sought their couch and were soon wrapped in a refreshing sleep, from which they did not awake until after the sun had arisen some time. They now arose, and having dressed themselves and made every preparation for the journey, they quitted the chamber and made their way to the room in which the gentlemen had assembled. The meeting was as joyful as it had been on the previous night, and their friends were delighted to perceive the favourable change which only two or three hours' rest had wrought in the appearance of Celestia and Lady Elvina. Breakfast had been prepared by Mrs. Baldwin, of which they all partook, and the repast was no sooner over than the necessary travelling vehicle which had been sent for from the nearest town drove up to the door, and the moment of departure had arrived. At that moment the feelings of Celestia and Lady Elvina, particularly the latter, may be imagined. In a few hours she would be restored to the arms of that affectionate husband whom she had abandoned so many years before, and the joy of that thought was so great that she could scarcely contain herself; but yet it was mingled with some feelings of sorrow, fear, and regret. All the preparations being made, the gentlemen conducted Celestia and her noble relative to the carriages, into one of which Lord Bathurst and his son assisted them and then followed

themselves. The other gentlemen disposed of themselves in like manner, and they drove away from that house in which Lady Elvina and Celestia had been so long confined, and from which they had entertained such little hope of being able to escape. Mabel Henderson and Mrs. Baldwin remained behind for the present, but they were desired to make their appearance at some future time at Sungrove Abbey, in order that some arrangement might be made as to their future settlement, and to reward them for the services they had rendered them; and the house which had been so recently the secure retreat of the villain Bonville was taken possession of by the authorities, and every prudent means which might lead to the apprehension of that desperate and guilty man were promptly adopted. We forgot to mention that a messenger had been despatched to Sungrove Abbey on the previous night to inform the anxious Lord Elverton of the success they had met with, and that they would lose no time in returning to the abbey. The morning was fine, and as the travellers proceeded, and they got farther and farther from the late residence of Bonville, their spirits became more exhilarated, and they conversed freely, and Lord Bathurst informed our heroine of all that had taken place since her abduction from the abbey.

"But after the lapse of so many weeks," he continued, "and all our efforts to discover you were fruitless, and we had received two or three communications from Mabel Henderson, which informed us that she had hitherto met with no better success, we began to despair entirely, and to give you up for lost; for what could we expect but that the most dreadful fate would befall you, being as you were in the power of such a cruel and revengeful man as Bonville? Lord Elverton was completely distracted, and for some time he would not listen to the voice of consolation; while we were all so agitated and bewildered that we knew not what course to adopt. But at length, how great was our joy when we received a letter from the faithful and indefatigable Mabel, in which she informed us that she had become acquainted with the place in which you and Lady Elvina were confined, and that if we would meet her and her companions at a certain place, not far from here, your rescue would be certain. I need not tell you how promptly we hastened to comply with this request; and most grateful should we be to Omnipotence who has caused the result· to be as favourable as we could wish. It was by the contrivances of the man Desmond and Mrs. Baldwin that we were admitted secretly to the house at the very moment you were placed in such imminent danger, and most of the ruffians whom we found there, seeing our numbers and determination, offered little or no resistance, so that our wishes were accomplished without one of us receiving the least injury."

"But how did Mabel become acquainted with the place of our confinement?" asked Lady Elvina.

"There has been a special Providence throughout the whole affair," replied Lord Bathurst; "it was pure accident that guided Mabel to the neighbourhood where Bonville resided, and it being night, and as she felt tired and footsore, she felt anxious to meet with some inn or cottage where she might procure shelter for the night. Travelling on she came in sight of the house we have just quitted, and she was half resolved to test the hospitality of the person who kept it, but something made her hesitate, and after gazing at the house for a few minutes she walked on."

"That must have been the very night when we first saw her," said Celestia.

"No doubt of it," coincided Lady Elvina; "but proceed, my lord."

"Mabel then made her way to the nearest town or village," continued his lordship, "where she put up at a small tavern for the night. She was partaking off some refreshment previous to retiring to rest, when another person entered the room, and advanced towards a table opposite to the one at which she was seated, and no sooner did their eyes meet than they uttered an exclamation of astonishment and joy, at which you will not feel surprised when I inform you that Mabel recognized in the features of the old man her own father, and whom she had not seen for many years and knew not whether he

was living or dead. I need not tell you what was the joy of this meeting, which was not a little increased when the old man informed her that he had discovered the place of Bonville's concealment, which was the very house Mabel had seen, and that you were confined there. He added that it had been his determination to make his way to Sungrove Abbey, to make your friends acquainted with all he knew, so that, you see, if even he had not encountered his daughter, your deliverance would have been equally certain, though it might not have been obtained without more difficulty and danger."

"Oh, how fortunate has everything turned out, and at the very moment when we had almost abandoned ourselves entirely to despair," said our heroine. "But how was it that Mabel and her father met Desmond and Mrs. Baldwin?"

"That was purely accidental," replied Lord Bathurst; "and it was fortunate that they did so, for without their co-operation, they might not have been able to accomplish their designs so easily. They now thought it would be prudent for them to remain concealed in the neighbourhood, so that they might mature their plans; and in the meantime Mabel despatched her important communications to us to Sungrove Abbey; the rest you know; and thank Heaven you are now once more secure under the protection of your friends, and I sincerely trust that nothing will ever again occur to interrupt your happiness. I regret that guilty wretch Bonville contrived to make his escape, but I do hope that he will soon be apprehended and brought to that punishment his monstrous crimes deserve. At any rate, I do not think it is likely that he will again venture to make any attempt against your peace, for he will be sure that we shall use the utmost precaution to frustrate any future designs he may have in contemplation, and likewise to bring him to justice."

"I fervently hope that your ideas will be realized, my lord," said Lady Elvina; "but Bonville is a most determined and daring man, and while he is at large, I think it is not unlikely that he may still cherish his deadly feelings of revenge. Alas! how fearfully have I experienced the terrible extremes to which his cruelty will go."

"Your ladyship must indeed have suffered greatly," remarked Lord Bathurst; "and perhaps if the task is not too painful to you at present you will relate to us the particulars of what you have undergone during your long and cruel separation from your friends."

"Not now, my lord," returned Lady Elvina; "I do not feel myself competent to the task; but on arrival at the abbey, in the presence of my injured husband, I will explain everything; and then you will see, that though I have greatly erred, I have been severely punished for it."

"Alas!" said Lord Bathurst, compassionately, "I fear you have indeed; but indeed you reproach yourself too severely for that which was an error of youth and inexperience, and placing too great a reliance upon the arguments of a wicked and designing man. It is Bonville who is the cruel author of all the misfortunes that have befallen you and your family, and most assuredly he will be punished severely for it, both in this world and the next. But let us drop this melancholy subject, and look forward to the future with feelings of hope and confidence."

"Yes," said Lady Elvina, "I will strive to do so, and endeavour to show to my husband how sincerely I repent the misery I have caused him, and how anxious I am to make all the atonement in my power."

Lord Bathurst now changed the topic of conversation, and endeavoured to divert the thoughts of Lady Elvina and our heroine, by pointing out to them any particular beauty in the scenery through which they were travelling. This had the desired effect, and the further they left the place of their late captivity behind them, the more tranquil and cheerful became their spirits. Arriving at a respectable inn, they now stopped to change horses and to partake of some refreshment, but the feelings of both Celestia and Lady Elvina were too much excited to suffer them to eat only sparingly; and they were most impatient to resume their journey, for every minute appeared an age to them until they

should arrive at the place of their destination; and yet Lady Elvina almost dreaded to meet her husband, and there were moments when strange and melancholy misgivings beset her mind. The horses having been put to, they again proceeded on their way, but the road they had now to travel along was a very bad one for several miles, and they could only proceed at a very slow pace, which, added to the suspense and impatience of our heroine and Lady Elvina, and particularly as the day was now advancing, it did not seem at all unlikely that they would not be able to complete the journey until the following morning.

"Have we many miles further to go?" asked her ladyship, eagerly.

Lord Bathurst shook his head, and said that they had, and that he was afraid that they would not be able to complete the journey that day, for there was not a town where they could procure a relay of horses for several miles, and it would not be prudent for them to travel at night. Lady Elvina and her fair companion felt vexed and disappointed, but there was no help for it, and, therefore, they had nothing to do but to resign themselves to it.

"Besides," continued his lordship, after a pause, "you will require rest, and the delay of a few hours cannot make much difference."

"But Lord Elverton will be in a terrible state of apprehension and suspense," said Lady Elvina, "lest anything should have happened to us on the road."

"He cannot entertain any such fears while we are with you, and he is now aware that you are at liberty, and that a few hours only can elapse before you are restored to each other. Make your mind easy, for the moment of your happiness is at hand."

Lady Elvina said no more; and the carriages drew their slow length along, the horses, who were also nearly jaded, being able to proceed at scarcely more than a walking pace. The shadows of evening began to fall fast around, and it was quite dark when they had reached the extremity of this road and entered upon a gloomy lane, the cheerless aspect of which increased the sadness of their feelings. When they had got some distance up the lane, some doubts entered the mind of Lord Bathurst, and he desired the postilion to stop, and inquired whether he was certain that he had not mistaken the road. The man was evidently confused at this question, and it was not until his lordship had repeated it in a more impatient and peremptory manner than before, that he answered—

"I beg your lordship's pardon a thousand times; I—I am very sorry, my lord; I don't know how I came to make the mistake, but I'm afraid I have made a bit of a blunder. I recollect now I ought to have turned off a little to the left when we came to the finger-post, but it is too far to go back now, besides this lane will only lead us about a couple of miles out of the way."

"How unfortunate is this!" said his lordship, in a tone of vexation, "where does this lane terminate?"

"At the entrance to the town of Dashton, my lord," replied the postilion, "where I have no doubt your lordship and your friends will be able to obtain accommodation for the night, for there is a very good inn there, and——"

"Drive on, then, as quick as you can," interrupted Lord Bathurst.

The man obeyed; but the horses now were almost worn-out, and they could only proceed at a very slow pace indeed; but Lord Bathurst and his son endeavoured to console their companions, and they at length partly succeeded.

"We will resume our journey by daylight in the morning," he remarked, "and we shall soon be able to accomplish the remainder of it."

This lane seemed interminable, and Lord Bathurst frequently demanded of the postilion how much further they had to go; but at last they did come to the end of it, and they then beheld the town of which the man had spoken, and in two or three minutes more they stopped at the door of the inn, and were immediately ushered into a comfortable apartment, where they seated themselves, and tried to make themselves as contented as they could. Having partaken of a slight repast, and made arrangements with the landlord for their departure at an early hour in the morning, after a short conversation they separated for the night, and Lady Elvina and Celestia were conducted to their chamber. They sat for some time after they had retired, conversing; but at length, being really fatigued with their journey, they sought their pillow and were soon wrapped in repose. At an early hour in the morning the servant aroused them according to instructions, and they arose more cheerful in spirits, and were soon in readiness to join their fellow travellers. The horses had been put to, and they were soon fairly on the road again, and now that they had resumed their journey, they felt satisfied, and they looked forward to the happiness which was in store for them with the most sanguine anticipations. The farther they proceeded, and the face of the country became more familiar, their emotions increased, and the heart of Lady Elvina beat so violently against her side, that it seemed as if it would burst its tenement, and she could scarcely contain herself. Nor was the agitation of our heroine less than hers, and she looked forward to her restoration to Lord Elverton and her aunt, Lady Eugenia, with the utmost impatience. And there was another individual whom Celestia was most anxious to meet again. That was the beauteous and amiable Lady Eglantine, whom she looked upon with the warm affection of a sister, and who, she was certain, felt the same attachment towards her. They had now arrived at within five miles of the abbey, and a servant was sent foward to announce their approach, and to prepare the earl and the others to meet them. The emotion of Lady Elvina now became truly painful and insupportable, and her heart sank within her as though something terrible was about to happen. Her fellow travellers endeavoured to inspire her with confidence; but when the abbey burst upon their view, a deadly faintness came over her, tears gushed to her eyes, and she covered her face with her hands. Celestia also was in a pitiable state, but she conquered her feelings as well as she could, and endeavoured to soothe her noble and unfortunate relative as much as possible.

"Oh, God!" ejaculated Lady Elvina, "give me fortitude to support this trial.

their reason and full force, but he found himself placed in a dilemma from which he could not conveniently extricate himself and he became more and more bewildered and distracted, and was completely at a loss what course to pursue for the best, or what plan to hit upon for the better security of himself and his unfortunate prisoners. The longer he reflected, the greater his uneasiness became; and all kinds of terrors, by turns, beset his mind. He listened attentively to catch the slightest sound that might be stirring in the house,

but all was perfectly silent, and he chided himself for his fears, knowing that it was impossible for any stranger or strangers to gain admittance to the house without his knowledge, and that he must be immediately apprized of any attack that might be attempted. It was now nearly midnight, and Bonville having once more examined all the doors to ascertain that they were secure, retired to his chamber; but previously to doing so, he could not avoid the temptation of cautiously stealing to the door of the apartment in which Celestia and the Lady Elvina were confined, and listening attentively but not a sound, nor a breath met his ear, and satisfied that they had retired to rest, he moved on to his own chamber. His mind, however, was too much disturbed to suffer him to think of retiring to rest, and he threw himself in a chair, and gave himself up to reflecton. The thought of the old man in the morning, and the appearance of Mabel Henderson, filled his bosom with the greatest dread, and he in vain attempted to treat it with the indifference he had affected before Mrs. Baldwin. It was evident that the old man was acquainted with all his secrets, and while he was still at liberty, he was entirely at his mercy, and it could not be expected after the hatred he had expressed towards him that he would show him any forbearance. If such was the case he was not safe a moment, and all his nefarious plans might be at once defeated, and himself brought to shame and an ignominous fate. By what accursed chance had the old man discovered him?—And by what means had he acquired the knowledge he evidently possessed? Who was he?—and why was his hatred excited so strongly against him? These were questions he found it impossible to solve, and he therefore racked his brain to no purpose. And then the unexpected appearance of Mabel Henderson so near to the house added to his alarm, and increased his perplexity.

"Can she have seen the old man?" he muttered to himself, "and is she aware that I reside there, and that Celestia and the lady Elvina are in my power? It is not unlikely that it is so. Why did she not perish years ago? Had I managed this business with my usual skill, she would not have been here now to annoy me; but let me not alarm myself unnecessarily; something may yet occur to rid me of both these enemies, and to prevent them from putting their designs into execution. I will not give way to despair."

With these thoughts he endeavoured to become more calm, but it was a fruitless task, and he continued in the same restless state, without being able to make up his mind to retire to bed. A fine night had succeeded the tempest of the day, and the moon was at that moment shining brilliantly in at the window, whilst myriads of stars twinkled in the heavens. The beauty of the night, however, was entirely lost upon Bonville, whose mind was fully occupied by his own dark thoughts, and he gazed vacantly at the objects before him. But suddenly his attention was arrested by a shadow on the wall which surrounded the house, and he started up hastily and gazed eagerly towards the spot. He could not perceive anything, however, and the next moment the shadow seemed to move, and in another moment it was gone.

"Strange," said Bonville; "who can it be wandering about the house at this time of the night? My eyes could not deceive me; I am certain it was the shadow of a human form, and yet I could not perceive any one. I must fathom this mystery, if possible, for some danger may threaten me, which it will be necessary to guard against in time."

As he spoke he took down a pistol which was placed over the mantel-piece, and taking the lamp in his hand, he cautiously quitted the chamber and descended the stairs. On reaching the door of the room in which the ruffians whom he employed usually sat, he was glad to find by their talking that they had not yet separated, and he, therefore, instantly opened the door, and presented himself before them. He hastily inquired whether any of them had left the house lately, and being answered in the negative, he informed them of what had taken place, and desired two of them to attend him to search the grounds to ascertain whether any one was lurking there or not. They obeyed, and every part of the grounds were strictly searched but not the least traces of a human being could be seen, and having opened the gates, and looked out, as far as their eyes could penetrate through the darkness, the coast was entirely clear.

"This is most extraordinary and bewildering," remarked Bonville, "and yet I am positive that some one must have been here, or how could I have seen the shadow on the wall?"

"Are you quite sure that you were not mistaken?" asked one of the men."

"Oh, it is impossible that my eyes

could deceive me," said Bonville, " it was on this part of the wall that I saw the shadow as plainly as I see you now. I do not half like this occurrence, and I fear that there is some treachery at work."

" But how could any one get into the grounds without scaling the wall ?" said the other man, " for the gates were secure."

" It is a mystery I cannot solve," said Bonville, " but that some person has been here I am quite confident ; and if there have, it could have been for no good purpose. We must be upon our guard, for we may have enemies nearer than we imagine."

"And if we have," said one of the ruffians, " they may find a much warmer reception than they anticipate."

They now re-entered the house.

" This adventure," observed Bonville, " has excited my doubts and suspicions, it will be advisable for you to keep watch during the night, and you will find me ready to join you at a moment's notice, should anything occur to alarm you."

The men promised to obey his orders, and Bonville once more returned to his chamber, and resumed his seat at the window, less than ever inclined for sleep, after this adventure. He tried to persuade himself that he had suffered his imagination to deceive him, but it was all to no purpose, and the longer he reflected upon the subject the more uneasy and suspicious he became. But how could the individual, whoever it was, have gained admission into the grounds ? The gates were fast, and the wall was so high that it would have been impossible for any one to scale it without the help of a ladder; and by what means could they so quickly have effected their escape. He was lost in amazement and perplexity. Some danger certainly threatened him, he reflected, and how it might be best avoided he was at a loss to imagine. But the night passed away without anything more occurring, and morning found Bonville still seated by the window, he never having for a moment attempted to compose his mind to sleep.

———

CHAPTER XXXIII.

THE CONTINUED PERSECUTION OF CELESTIA AND ELVINA.

BONVILLE cautiously made every inquiry in the neighbourhood, with the hope of discovering the old man or Mable Henderson ; but his efforts were not attended with any success, and when three days had elapsed without his hearing anything more of them, or anything occurring to alarm him, he became more confident, endeavoured to treat the circumstance with indifference, and devoted his whole thoughts to Celestia, and to the completion of his diabolical plans. His patience was now quite exhausted, and as his devoted victim continued to get better, he determined that only two or three days should elapse before he would have another interview with her, and at once convince her that it was useless her offering any longer an obstinate resistance to his desires. He cursed the accident that had so long retarted his hopes, but he was resolved in spite of whatever consequences might follow that he would not delay the gratification of them much longer. Our herione was now indeed perfectly convalescent, but when she reflected on her wretched situation and that of her noble relative, and remembered the threats of the villain Bonville, her agitation and alarm may be easily imagined ; she could not but firmly believe he would put his nefarious and monstrous designs into effect, and if so she was most unquestionably lost for ever ; she shuddered with horror at the bare thought, and all the efforts of Lady Elvina failed to quiet her apprehensions. Every day she expected he would obtrude himself upon her, and she shrunk from the idea of meeting him with the same feeling of dread as if he had been something superhuman. How could she help herself ? how resist the miscreant Bonville's frightful and disgusting designs ? To have entertained the thought of being able to do so, would have been preposterous, and she therefore almost gave herself up entirely to despair. Then she was in constant fear lest her persecutor should seperate her from the Lady Elvina, and once more consign that unfortunate lady to the dungeon in which she had for so many months been incarcerated, and should he do so, she would not have a hope remaining, and the speedy fate of the hapless Lady Elvina would be certain. These thoughts were sufficient to distract her, and it was no wonder that her unfortunate companion found it impossible to console her, for under all the circumstances she could not but entertain the same apprehensions herself, although she endeavoured to conceal her real thoughts and feelings from Celestia. How constantly and fervently she prayed to Heaven to interpose to save her, and to defeat the plans of their cruel oppressor; but alas! no ray of hope could be admitted to her bosom. Whichever way she directed her attention the greatest and most imminent danger evidently beset them; and there was not the least shadow of probability of their being able to effect their escape. Bonville had taken so many precautions to prevent that, and they were entirely at his mercy, unless Providence should interfere and r escue them. It was not likely that he would delay much longer to put his diabolical threats into execution, and she looked forward to each succeeding day with the greatest feelings of dread. Celestia could not but penetrate her thoughts, and that increased her own fears and misery. The agony which lord Elverton and her other friends were doubtless enduring also occupied her mind, and added to her mental torture, and many were the tears she shed when she reflected on the painful probability that she would never behold them again, or if she did that it would be under such circumstances that her heart sickened to think upon.

"Better, far better, that I should die," she ejaculated, "than that such a dreadful, such a revolting fate should befal me. Oh, my beloved Lady Elvina, what will become of me, if the ruffian Bonville should persist in his cruel designs? and unfeeling and determined as he is, how can I hope that he will relent, and act with any forbearance towards me?"

"Do not give way entirely to despair, my love," replied Lady Elvina, "for, however determined the villain Bonville may be, Providence is good, and will, I feel certain, never suffer you to become the victim of his violence.

Depend upon it, that something will occur to rescue you, and to restore you to those who are so dear to you.'

Celestia shook her head with a melancholy expression of countenance, as she observed,—

"I would fain think as you say, my dear madam, but alas! when I reflect upon all the circumstances of my hard case, I find it utterly impossible to do so. The dark hints, also, threw out by Mrs. Baldwin, all but confirm my worst fears; has she not intimated that I may prepare myself to meet Bonville in a day or two, and what his intentions are on that occasion, I have too much reason to know, and to apprehend."

"Be firm, my sweet Celestia;" said Lady Elvina, "and depend upon it, however gloomy and threatening your prospects may at present appear to be, something will occur to save you. It would be monstrous to suppose that the Almighty would suffer the miscreant Bonville to triumph in his iniquitous intentions. Keep up your spirits, and hope for the best."

"But should he separate us, and once more immure you in that frightful dungeon;" sighed our heroine, "how horrible will be your fate, and what will then become of me?"

"Do not give way to such sad thoughts, dear Celestia," returned Lady Elvina, "for I do trust that they are not destined to be realized. Be firm, and, notwithstanding, Bonville now holds you in his power and at his mercy, I am confident that you will yet triumph over him; that a terrible retribution will overtake him, for the hideous crimes he has already perpetrated, and that you will again be restored to happiness, and the arms of your afflicted relations."

"You are sanguine, my dear Lady Elvina;" sighed Celestia, "but God grant that your predictions may be verified, and that the time may not be far distant when I shall see you restored to the arms of that noble and deeply persecuted husband, from whom you have been so many years separated. May All-Merciful Heaven give him strength to support and survive the numerous and unparalelled troubles with which he is afflicted."

Ardently Lady Elvina responded to this prayer, although she could not really entertain the hopes which our heroine had expressed, and feared that her fate at any rate was sealed, and that her and her injured husband were never destined to meet again. In fact, she almost dreaded such a meeting, for notwithstanding the assurance which she felt that the earl would forgive her past errors, and freely and fondly take her back to his bosom again, she could not forgive herself, and knew not how she should have the courage to stand in his presence again, and to notice the melancholy change which so many years of trouble and anxiety must have wrought in his person: trouble and anxiety of which she had been the principal, if not the sole cause. It must be admitted that the hapless lady reproached herself too severely, for surely she had been sufficiently punished; but she could not help it, and that greatly added to the anguish of her mind. Had Celestia and Lady Elvina been aware of the circumstances which had occurred within the last few days to Bonville, and the threats which the mysterious old man whom he had encountered had held out to him; their hopes of deliverance would indeed, have been excited, and they would have been enabled to bear the persecution of Bonville with more firmness and patience. Three days passed away in this manner, and Bonville did not visit them nor could they ascertain from the old woman when he intended to do so; and their hopes revived at the delay, for in the meantime something might occur, they reflected, to render the plans of the villain abortive, and to rescue them from their present melancholy and perilous situation.

"I do not understand the meaning of his delay," remarked Celestia; "oh, should he have relented! but alas, there is no hope of that. He is not the man to be moved from the execution of anything upon which he has fixed his mind, especially when he has his victims so completely in his power. The cause of his delay is probably to give me time to recover, fearful as he may be that if he was to appear too suddenly before me I might suffer a relapse, and then his guilty wishes might be entirely frustrated."

This was precisely the opinion which Lady Elvina entertained, but still she concealed it as well as she could, and endeavoured to quiet the apprehensions of Celestia, and to raise in her bosom a feeling of hope. On the third evening Lady Elviva and Celestia were seated at the window which commanded a view of the most cheerful part of the country. It was a very fine evening, the moon shone brightly over the earth, and rendered objects perfectly distinct at a considerable distance. All was perfectly tranquil, and the beauty and serenity of the night had a beneficial effect upon the spirits of our heroine and the Lady Elvina, and they continued to converse more freely, and with greater composure and confidence than they had been able to do for some time before. While they were thus occupied, their attention was suddenly arrested by observing a person emerge from behind a thick set hedge at a short distance, and approach towards the house with slow and measured steps. Celestia knew not how it was, but the sight of this individual created a more than usual degree of interest in her breast, and Lady Evina felt her curiosity greatly excited, although, why the sight of this solitary traveller should thus agitate her she could not imagine. The form was that of a woman, and as well as the light of the moon would permit her to observe, it struck her as being familiar to Celestia. The woman at last arrived to within a few yards of the wall which surrounded the house, and there she suddenly paused, and folding her arms, she raised her eyes, and seemed to be taking a minute survey of the building. And now the moon shed its broad beams full upon her person and features, and rendered them perfectly distinct to our heroine and her companion.

"Gracious Heaven!" exclaimed the former, as she gazed eagerly towards her, "do you not recognise her, my dear madam? Has the lapse of so many years so changed her features that you do not know her? See, see, it is Mabel Henderson!"

"Ah!" cried Lady Elvina, "I know her now, though time has, indeed, so greatly altered her; it is, it is Mabel Henderson. What can have brought her to this neighbourhood?" And see how earnestly she contemplates the house, can she have any suspicion that it is the residence of the villain Bonville, and that here we are confined ? If she has there is every hope for us, for depend upon it our deliverance is speedily at hand."

"Oh, would to Heaven that we could make ourselves heard by her;" said our heroine, "or attract her attention towards us. This suspense is most torturing. Can we not raise the window, and by some signal which she could not misunderstand make ourselves known to her."

"Alas!" replied Lady Elvina, "the window is too well secured, and we have no means of opening it, and if we could she is too far off to observe us. See, she still continues to gaze earnestly towards the house, and it evidently arrests her whole attention. She must certainly have some suspicion that it is the retreat of the heartless miscreant who holds us in his power. Courage, my dear Celestia, and hope for the best."

"Alas! alas! she cannot, she will not perceive us," said Celestia, "and she will, therefore, still remain in ignorance of the place of our confinement. And yet she must surely have obtained some important information, or what has brought her to this neighbourhood?"

Lady Elvina returned no answer, but remained with her eyes fixed stedfastly upon the form of Mabel Henderson, and in a state of the greatest suspense; and the anxiety of Celestia increased to such a degree that she could scarcely contain herself. For a few moments Mabel remained fixed in the same attitude, and never once removed her eyes from the house. But, at length, she moved a few paces nearer, and then suddenly paused again, and seemed to deliberate with herself what it was best for her to do. She evidently changed her mind, for she suddenly turned round and retraced her steps towards the spot from which she had come, much to the disappointment of Celestia and Lady Elvina, and was soon lost to the view in the distance.

"Oh, how torturing is this," ejaculated Celestia, "alas! the hopes that had arisen in my mind on her appearance are now annihilated, and this disappointment only leaves me in greater agony and suspense than ever."

"Wait patiently, my love," observed Lady Elvina, "and from this adventure the utmost good may result. I cannot still help thinking that the suspicions of Mabel Henderson are aroused, and if so, she will lose no time in adopting some means for our rescue; but it is indispensibly necessary that she should act with the utmost caution, for the slightest act of imprudence might frustrate all the plans she may have in contemplation."

"But how can she have obtained her information?" said our heroine.

"That, of course, I cannot say;" replied Lady Elvina: "but you remember what she told you, and no doubt she hos been most indefatigable in tracing out the retreat of Bonville, and will put her threats into execution, if possible, and at all hazards. She has ample reasons to hate Bonville, and to pursue him to destruction."

"Oh, that your hopes may be realized;" ejaculated Celestia, "but I confess that I am not so sanguine on the subject as you seem to be, my dear Lady Elvina."

"I think, Celestia," said Lady Elvina, "that, at any rate we have very good cause for hope. You many depend upon it that it is not accident alone which has brought Mabel to this neighbourhood, and if her suspicions are aroused, she will no doubt watch secretly and vigilantly near the house until they are corroborated."

"You say that there is not another house near this place for several miles," observed Celestia.

"There is not."

"And Bonville is unknown to any of the inhabitants of this town or village?"

"I believe he is," answered Lady Elvina. "Then of course Mabel could not obtain any information there?"

"But Bonville, of course, sometimes leaves the house," said Lady Elvina, "and Mabel may then observe him, and watching him to his residence, at once have her doubts satisfied."

"Could I but think so," said Celestia, "I should indeed be inspired with hope, for I feel the greatest confidence in the sincerity of Mabel."

"You may well do so, my love, for as I before observed, Mabel has the greatest cause to detest the inhuman Bonville, since he was the author of her ruin. She was ever my most faithful friend and confidant, and I know well, from what she has said to you that there is no sacrifice that she would hesitate to make to serve me or any of my unfortunate family. I cannot help thinking that she is yet destined to be the means of delivering us from the power of Bonville, and bringing him to that punishment his enormous crimes so justly merit."

They now withdrew from the window, for the moon had disappeared, and all was buried in profound darkness; but they still continued to converse upon the remarkable and exciting event of the night, and to indulge in m ingled hopes and apprehensions. At length, having first on their knees earnestly supplicated the protection of Omnipotence, they retired to rest, but their thoughts were so busy that it was some time before they could compose themselves to sleep. They awoke in the morning, however, more cheerful, and much refreshed, and hope once more began to animate the breast of our heroine; which Lady Elvina being delighted to see, encouraged her all that she possibly could in it. The conversation again turned upon Mabel Henderson, and Lady Elvina at last succeeded in persuading Celestia to believe that the suspicions of the former were excited, and that if they were so, they might quickly anticipate some interposition in their favour, and look forward to their deliverance as almost certain. But although our heroine did begin to hope, she could not be so sanguine as Lady Elvina; for the idea was too gratifying and delightful to be wholly encouraged until something else took place.

"Oh, we could never be sufficiently grateful to the Almighty,' said Celestia; "if these hopes should be realized. What future happiness would be ours, if we should again be restored to those so dear to us, and whose sufferings at the present time must be dreadful to think upon."

"Father of mercy!" fervently ejaculated Lady Elvina, "oh, grant that in that respect our wishes may not be doomed to be disappointed. Not for my sake do I thus supplicate thee, but for that of this poor girl and that beloved husband from whom I have been separated for so many years. Grant me this, I humbly beseech you, and then I shall

be amply repaid for all the sorrows of the past, and, if it be thy will, I can die in peace."

Most devoutly did Celestia respond to this prayer; they remained silent for a few minutes, and gave themselves up entirely to their own reflections. They were interrupted by hearing the bolts of the room door being withdrawn, and at first a cold, trembling sensation came over Celestia, for she feared it was the villain Bonville. Her apprehensions were, however, quickly dissipated, for the room door was thrown open, and the old woman Baldwin entered, bringing them a fresh supply of provisions. There was a disagreeable expression of exultation upon her repulsive features, and Celestia and Lady Elvina immediately perceived that she had something to communicate. Having placed the provisions on the table, she stood and gazed at our heroine and her Ladyship alternately, and at length she said, addressing herself to Celestia:

"I am very glad to see you looking so well, young lady, and I have no doubt that Mr. Bonville will also be very glad to hear it; especially as he bade me inform you that it is his intention to do himself the pleasure of visiting you to-morrow."

"To-morrow!" exclaimed Celestia, clasping her hands in agony.

"Yes, Miss;" replied Baldwin, "to-morrow; he does not think proper to defer that pleasure any longer; and I think he has acted with great patience and forbearance to delay it till now; so you had better prepare yourself to meet him."

"Oh, Heaven forbid!" cried the distracted damsel; "I cannot endure the presence of that brutal man, or listen to the revolting language with which he will shock my ears."

"But I am much deceived if you do not find that you must;" returned the old woman.

"Bonville surely cannot be so cruel and so head-strong;" remarked Lady Elvina; "tell him to remember what were the consequences of his conduct before, and to spare this poor girl for the present, at any rate."

"I am not going to be the deliverer of any message you may think proper to send to Mr. Bonville," said Mrs.

Baldwin, "since you will have an opportunity of seeing him yourself. But if you will only take my advice, Lady Elverton, you will not interfere, lest you should exasperate him, and I suppose you can form a pretty shrewd guess what the consequences of that would be."

"Alas! alas!" sighed Lady Elvina, and Celestia threw herself sobbing and weeping on her bosom. Baldwin fixed upon them another malignant look of triumph, and quitted the room.

Our heroine was so completely absorbed by the violence of her grief that it was sometime ere she had the power to give utterance to a syllable, and Lady Elvina sought in vain to console her, for she stood much in need of consolation herself.

"Oh, my dear Lady Elvina," at length sobbed the poor girl; "how can I express the horror and disgust of my feelings at the intimation I have received? To-morrow!—so soon! Oh, how can I ever endure the presence of that odious man? What resistance can I offer to his guilty importunities? No supplications, no tears, no prayers can, I am convinced, move his hardened heart to pity, and I am, therefore, lost, lost entirely—there is not the shadow of a hope for me. My God! what have I done that I should be subjected to such a cruel fate as this?"

"My poor child, my innocent Celestia," replied Lady Elvina, "exert yourself to meet with firmness and determination this bad man, for it is only by that you can hope to defeat him, and ultimately to escape from his power. Put your trust in the infinite mercy of the most high, who never fails to watch over and protect the good and innocent. Bonville may at present appear to triumph, but it will not be for long he will be crushed in the very midst of his integrity, and you will yet be restored to peace and happiness, and learn to look back upon the painful past only as a frightful dream."

Celestia shook her head mournfully, and tears of anguish again chased each other down her cheeks.

"Heaven help me!" she sighed, "for I fear the crisis of my fate is approaching. How can I help shuddering with nutterable horror, when I remember the dreadful threats which that inhuman miscreant has held out to me? Alas! he never yet failed to fulfil his promises, as we know, too well, to our sorrow."

"Be calm, be calm, Celestia," said Lady Elvina, "and do not give way to these terrible thoughts, which I cannot, I do not believe are destined to be realized. Remember, that I shall be by your side while Bonville is present, and that surely will check him in the violence of his conduct."

"Ah! my dear madam," ejaculated Celestia; "what resistance could you offer to that desperate and cruel man? Are you not also his prisoner, and does he not like to torture you? Your agony will but add to the gratification of his vengeance. Besides, do you suppose that he will permit you to be present during the dreaded interview?"

"Oh, he surely will not separate me from you, Celestia;" said Lady Elvina with a shudder, as the probability of Bonville doing so arose vividly to her mind. "But if he should, let me entreat you to be firm, and you may thus prevent him from going to extremities, and in the meantime something may occur to rescue us both from his power, and to frustrate his monstrous designs."

"Alas!" sighed our heroine, "how difficult is the task you would impose on me, and how, oh, how can I hope to accomplish it? Bonville will only mock my suffering; he will scorn my resistance, and laugh at my supplications. Oh, God! what a wretched and unfortunate being I am!"

She again threw herself sobbing on the bosom of Lady Elvina, and became completely inconsolable. The agony of her ladyship was equal to her own, and she knew not what to say that might impart the least ray of comfort to her.

CHAPTER XXXIV.

THE INTERVIEW.— THE VILLAIN'S IM-
PORTUNITIES. — CELESTIA'S DETER-
MINED RESISTANCE.

DISMALLY the day passed away, and poor Celestia looked forward to the approaching morrow with a feeling of horror which may be well imagined. But

Have I become a child again?—Psha! Bonville, arouse yourself, and meet the worst which can befall you with fortitude. I must be put upon my trial, and some fortunate accident may yet release me from that fate which I so much dread."

But in spite of all his efforts, the villain could not acquire the fortitude he wished, and he awaited the hour of his trial in a state of the most trembling fear and anxiety. The day of the trial came, and the evidence of his various monstrous crimes was so strong

against him, that the reader will not require to be told he was convicted and sentenced to death. Falcon and Snareswell were transported, and Mrs. Falcon was sentenced to a lengthened term of imprisonment; thus at last punishment overtook those who had been guilty of so many abominable crimes. The trial over, the excitement of Bonville increased, and he sunk into absolute despair now that every chance of his escaping from the ignominious fate he so richly merited was at an end. He paced the condemned cell with disordered steps, and many were the bitter curses to which he gave utterance on his hard destiny, for such he could not help considering it.

"Are there no means of escape?" he soliloquised; "is there no hope?—Must I die the death of a dog?—Shall they triumph altogether?—No, they shall not. I will yet devise some plan to put a period to my own existence."

Again the poor, guilty, despairing wretch paced his gloomy cell, at times giving utterance to the most horrible imprecations on his hard destiny, and the ignominious fate which had at last overtaken him, and at others bemoaning it with all the weakness of a child. The daring, reckless spirit of the monster Bonville was at last subdued, and he presented a fearful example of defeated guilt and abject cowardice. Then he would utter the most dreadful maledictions against those whom he had sought to destroy, and who, he doubted not, were now exulting in his downfall and the shameful death that awaited him.

"May lightnings blast them!" he cried, fiercely; "may every earthly misery be their lot—may poverty, in its most wretched character, overtake them, and hurl them from their present proud station to the lowest depths of degradation. May the offspring of Malensbury and the scornful Celestia, should they have any, bring shame and misery upon their heads, and wring their hearts to bursting. Oh, that I had them now before me, methinks I could dart upon them like a tiger upon his prey, and pressing my fingers in their throats, gloat upon their dying agony. Had I but succeeded in completing my revenge, I could meet my fate without a murmur; but to perish thus, and to leave those whom I so mortally hate to triumph—oh, it goads my very soul to madness. Why did I delay the execution of my designs against the girl, when I had so many opportunities of accomplishing them? Why did I suffer myself to be restrained by her pretended anguish? And why suffer the proud stripling Malensbury to live a day, when I had him so securely in my power? Oh, I have acted as a consum-

mate fool throughout, and now, when it is too late, I can see my folly. Had I acted with my usual promptitude and daring, they could not have escaped, and I might still have been at liberty to exult in my triumph, and to work fresh misery till the cup of my vengeance was full to the brim. Despair! despair!—my guilty course is run, and ere many hours shall have elapsed, my ghastly corpse will be swinging in the air, the subject for execration of all who gaze upon it."

He threw himself on a seat, and smote his breast and tore his hair, in the very agony of his feelings. It was vain for him to look for hope—hope to a wretch like him?—No, all was darkness and horror. Night came (though it was always night in that gloomy dungeon), and with it accumulated terrors to the wretched culprit. Conscience was fearfully awakened—fiendish voices seemed to laugh and murmur in his ears, and to remind him of the future and everlasting tortures that awaited him. And then arose to his tortured imagination the ghastly forms of those unfortunate beings who had perished by his hands. The beauteous mother of Celestia, whom by his diabolical artifices he consigned to the scaffold—the ill-fated Lord Coningsby, who had never injured him by word or deed—and then the grisly shades of other victims passed in fearful array before his eyes, and shouted their curses in his ears. He started up, he was unable to endure this horrible state of agony any longer, and in a loud hoarse voice, which made the dreary place re-echo again, he shouted—

"Fiends of hell! I defy ye all! Cease then your tortures, for they are useless. I did the deeds, and glory in them, and only regret being prevented from accomplishing the whole of my designs, then could I have mounted the scaffold without a murmur. But no, I will escape yet—the hangman shall never perform his revolting office on me, for thus do I prevent it!"

As the miserable man gave utterance to those words, he dashed his head violently against the stone wall of his dungeon, and dropped insensible, but not seriously injured, upon the floor. In this condition one of the turnkeys found him a short time afterwards, and giving the alarm, proper means were resorted to to restore him to his senses, and at length with success. Staring wildly around him, he exclaimed in accents of the deepest despair—

"Ah! have I then failed, and am I still alive? Oh, curses, bitter curses light upon ye all, for having restored me to existence merely that you may have the gratification of hanging me like a dog. But no, I will not shrink! The murderer Bonville defies ye all, and mocks at the future! Where is the hangman?—Let him do his bloody work; I am ready to meet my fate! You shall not see me flinch, though you were to tear the flesh from my bones with red-hot pincers. Ha! ha! ha! —What care I for death!—Ha! ha! ha! ha!"

Exhausted completely by the vehemence with which he had given utterance to these terrible words, the poor wretch sunk back in his seat, and became speechless. His features were frightfully distorted, and the livid hue of death was upon his countenance, and his eyes glared in their sockets with an unearthly fire. Those who were in attendance upon him turned away with horror from the terrible spectacle, albeit such scenes were perfectly familiar to them. From that time to the hour when the unfortunate criminal was led forth to meet that dreadful fate which was so justly due to his monstrous crimes, he was never left alone, so that all opportunity for destroying himself was at an end. Although at times he endeavoured to assume an air of recklessness and bravado, and to laugh at his approaching fate, it was quite evident to all that the tortures of his guilty mind were most excruciating, and that he shrunk appalled from the approach of death with all those coward fears which villains ever feel when their career is at end, and they know that there is no hope for them. Sometimes, indeed, his despair was so intense, that he was totally unable to conceal it, and then his melancholy ravings were quite pitiable to listen to. Yes, there was pity even for such a blood-stained miscreant as he. At length the awful morning of the execution arrived, and at an early hour vast crowds of persons, from all parts of the country, assembled in front of the gaol, anxious to feast their eyes on the ghastly spectacle. Desperate ruffians there were in numbers, whose time was not yet come, but for whom a similar fate was in store. Women, too (if such scandals to their sex are worthy of the name), were among the most anxious of the spectators. Any stranger to the country would have imagined that it was an occasion of some festivity, instead of a public strangulation of a human being. The lewd jest was bandied about immediately beneath the gallows, and many there were who at the very time were engaged in picking pockets and other acts of depredation. Such is the moral lesson taught from the gallows! The poor guilty wretch had passed a fearful night, madness had seized upon his brain, and his fierce ravings were quite horrible to listen to. But as the fatal hour approached, he was quite exhausted, and reduced to such a pitiable condition, that the spark of life seemed all but extinguished within him. The priest exhorted him to repentance, but he seemed not to hear him, or if he did, not to heed him, his guilty soul was pressed down by the overwhelming weight of despair. From that time to the moment when he was led out to execution, he never rallied, and death might almost be said to already have performed his office. He could not walk, and was, therefore, obliged to be carried to the place of execution. His appearance upon the scaffold was the signal for one universal and frightful burst of execration, which rent the very air. Once, and once only, he turned his glassy eyes upon the vast assemblage, and the expression of his countenance was appalling to behold. His lips quivered, but he uttered no sound— the power of speech had left him. The executioner performed his awful task promptly, and in a few minutes the corpse of the guilty Bonville swung in the air.

*　　*　　*　　*

Turn we now from this frightful scene to one more congenial to the feelings, to the happiness of our friends at Sungrove Abbey. Their troubles were at an end, their bitter enemy was no more, and the prospect now before them was one of tranquillity and peace. Due time having been suffered to elapse after these stirring events, Lord Malensbury and his beauteous Celestia were united, and on the same day Collingwood Aubrey led the amiable Lady Eglantine to the altar. The marriages were celebrated in the most magnificent manner, and the neighbourhood was one continued scene of festivity for many days afterwards. We have but little more to say in conclusion; the happiness of all parties was complete, and they received an ample reward for the many severe trials it had been their lot to experience, but which they had born with such virtuous fortitude and resignation. Lord and Lady Elverton lived for many years afterwards, and in the present happiness that surrounded them, learnt to forget the heavy sorrows of the past, which had, by a chain of unforeseen and almost unavoidable circumstances, thrown such a veil of gloom over their youthful days.

THE END.